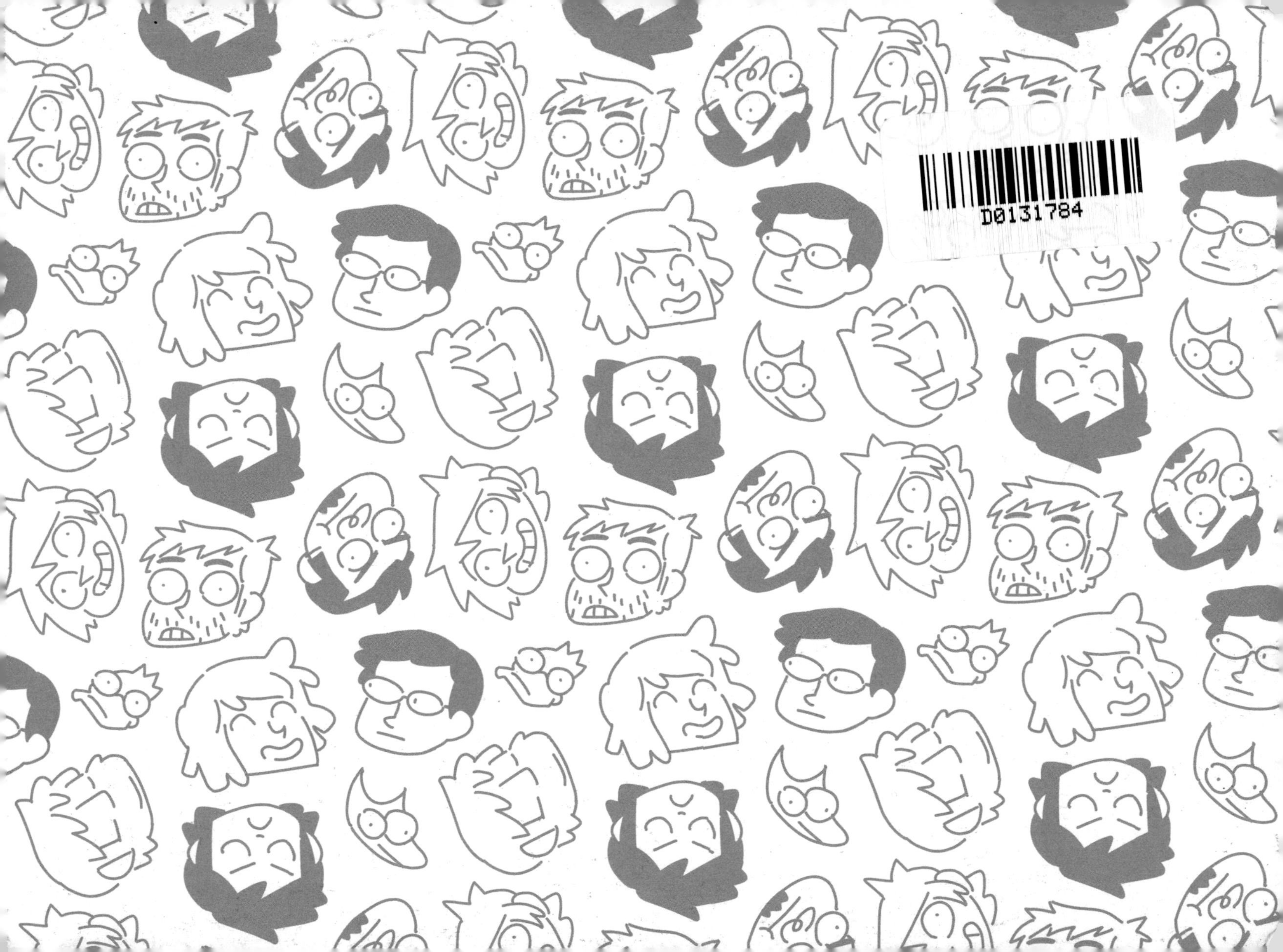

octopus pie
volume 1

by Meredith Gran

IMAGE COMICS, INC.
Robert Kirkman – Chief Operating Officer
Erik Larsen – Chief Financial Officer
Todd McFarlane – President
Marc Silvestri – Chief Executive Officer
Jim Valentino – Vice-President

Eric Stephenson – Publisher
Corey Murphy – Director of Sales
Jeff Boison – Director of Publishing Planning & Book Trade Sales
Jeremy Sullivan – Director of Digital Sales
Kat Salazar – Director of PR & Marketing
Emily Miller – Director of Operations
Branwyn Bigglestone – Senior Accounts Manager
Sarah Mello – Accounts Manager
Drew Gill – Art Director
Jonathan Chan – Production Manager
Meredith Wallace – Print Manager
Briah Skelly – Publicity Assistant
Randy Okamura – Marketing Production Designer
David Brothers – Branding Manager
Ally Power – Content Manager
Addison Duke – Production Artist
Vincent Kukua – Production Artist
Sasha Head – Production Artist
Tricia Ramos – Production Artist
Jeff Stang – Direct Market Sales Representative
Emilio Bautista – Digital Sales Associate
Chloe Ramos-Peterson – Administrative Assistant
IMAGECOMICS.COM

OCTOPUS PIE, VOL 1 First printing. February 2016. Copyright © 2016 Meredith Gran. All rights reserved.

Published by Image Comics, Inc. Office of publication:
2001 Center Street, Sixth Floor, Berkeley, CA 94704.

Originally published by Villard Books as Octopus Pie: There Are No Stars in Brooklyn.

"Octopus Pie," its logos, and the likenesses of all characters herein are trademarks of Meredith Gran, unless otherwise noted. "Image" and the Image Comics logos are registered trademarks of Image Comics, Inc. No part of this publication may be reproduced or transmitted, in any form or by any means (except for short excerpts for journalistic or review purposes), without the express written permission of Meredith Gran or Image Comics, Inc. All names, characters, events, and locales in this publication are entirely fictional. Any resemblance to actual persons (living or dead), events, or places, without satiric intent, is coincidental.

Printed in the USA. For information regarding the CPSIA on this printed material call: 203-595-3636 and provide reference #RICH–662378.

For international rights, contact: foreignlicensing@imagecomics.com.

ISBN: 978-1-63215-632-7

www.octopuspie.com

Interior designed by Meredith Gran and Kou Chen.
Cover art colors by Valeria Halla.

For Jackie & Joe, who never let me take this stuff too seriously.

Thanks to R. Stevens for encouraging and designing the original self-published books. Thank you to Judy Hansen, who's been talking me up for years. And a big thanks to Vera Brosgol, Raina Telgemeier, Hope Larson, Jeffrey Rowland, Jon Rosenberg, David McGuire, and countless friends in the comics community who held my hand when this project was small.

Thanks always to Mike Holmes for his tireless input, and for loving me.

Contents

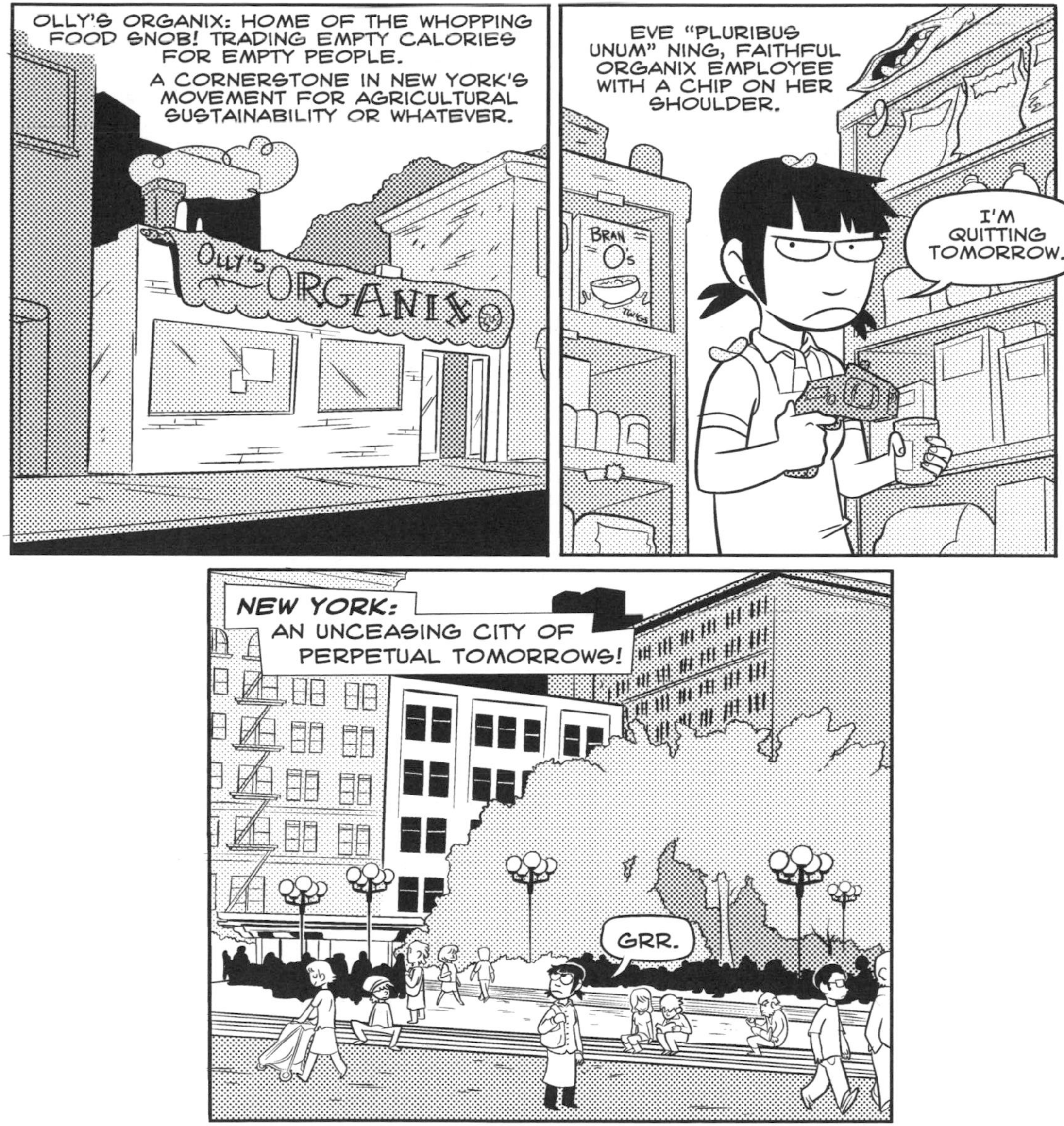
OLLY'S ORGANIX: HOME OF THE WHOPPING FOOD SNOB! TRADING EMPTY CALORIES FOR EMPTY PEOPLE.
A CORNERSTONE IN NEW YORK'S MOVEMENT FOR AGRICULTURAL SUSTAINABILITY OR WHATEVER.
OLLY'S ORGANIX
EVE "PLURIBUS UNUM" NING, FAITHFUL ORGANIX EMPLOYEE WITH A CHIP ON HER SHOULDER.
BRAN O's
I'M QUITTING TOMORROW.
NEW YORK:
AN UNCEASING CITY OF PERPETUAL TOMORROWS!
GRR.

In 2007, I was fresh out of school, working freelance and sorely hungering for an outlet. I wanted to do a simple, personal work: stories that began and ended with tidiness and a clear status quo. I wanted to build and connect with an audience consistently, one page at a time. I feared a creative ball and chain — a commitment that would greedily occupy my time and soul, and my goal was to avoid that.

One soul and my entire twenties later, I'm grateful for that foundation. I think my cautiousness informed the sitcom appeal of this first volume. It's an approachable concept: Eve and Hanna are forced together as roommates, and their clashes and hard-won friendship make for most of the plot. This was a safe and fun template to grow in, and as the strip developed I let it fall away.

The one consistent thing I've managed to do with *Octopus Pie* is dig up (and sort through) the fresh nuggets of my own consciousness. In turn, the series has changed a lot. Within this volume alone, the seams are more than visible. The warring digital and traditional media, the subject matter, the vantage points...

much of this book feels completely outside of me. At twenty-two, I had a lot to say about feminist theory, post-9/11 paranoia, time-honored literature, the state of indie rock, how funny weed is, and the quest for a parentally-unguided existence. Eve shares my cynicism for just about anything she's yet to experience. Hanna tries to mold reality around her own insatiable desires. The facade of pop culture, fear of missing out, and the newfound limitations of adult life are their greatest foes.

It's impossible to return to that point of view — the years have given me a new, unrecognizable set of hard & fast rules. In the beginning, I may have regarded Eve and her friends as secret grownups. Their logic is mathematical, they're impossibly clever, and their ability to fend for themselves runs on the rails of the story. The episodes are tight, dense with gags, rarely meandering. There is a sense of reason and rhyme in every moment, every motivation.

Still, the confusion and longing in these early chapters comes through. My routine was one of constant, obsessive work, precious few social moments, and

little sleep. Going through the motions of stability was not enough. I was looking for the love and amusement and chaos that Eve gradually accepts in her life.

When I reread this book, I got a kick out of revisiting the "Dumbo" chapter. It really has it all: changing neighborhoods, nods to the collapsing economy and in-progress Freedom Tower, fantastical beings, time-sensitive pop references, flamboyant shoutouts to the classics, and my youthful indulgence in song lyrics. Truly a story and a Meredith of its time.

All that said, this book is where *Octopus Pie* was born, and it couldn't have come about any other way. These years were a playground to study the craft of comics and piece together a voice. There's a lot I'm proud of in these pages. A few of them make me cringe. But they're a real-time capsule of what felt most urgent, then. They hold truth and meaning in the right context. And if I concentrate hard enough, I can remember the powerful catharsis of drawing each one.

-Meredith Gran,
December 2015

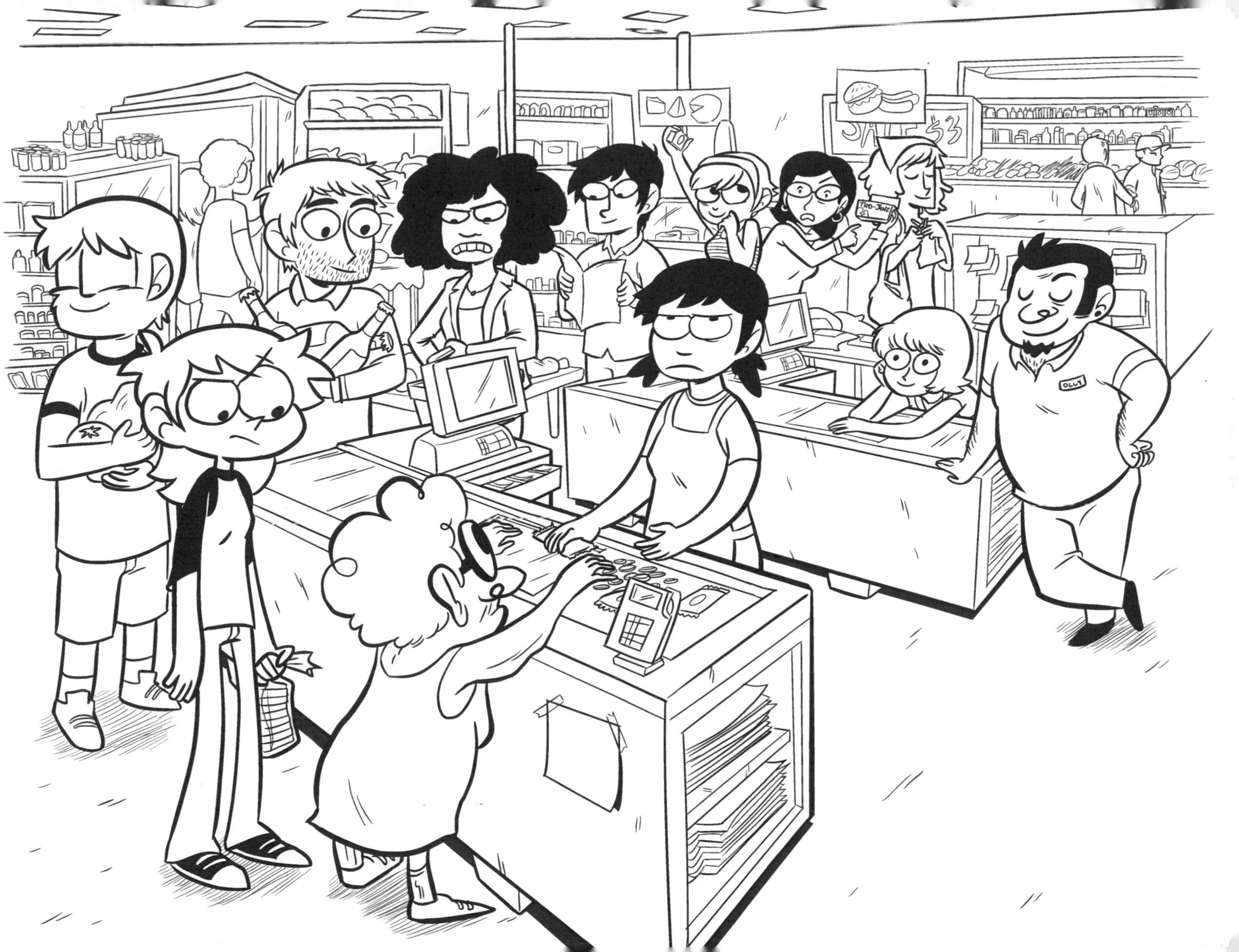
$3
TRO-JENZ
OLLY

UNCOMFORTABLE, OVERCROWDED, OVER-PRICED, OVER-MARKETED.
OLLY'S ORGANIX
PUSHY, OBNOXIOUS, INCOMPETENT PEOPLE RUSHING AROUND IN CRAMPED TIN CANS.
TRASH. NEW YORK IS UTTER *TRASH.*
WELL, WHY DO YOU LIVE HERE, THEN?
ARE YOU KIDDING?
HAVE YOU SEEN THE *REST* OF THE COUNTRY?

octopus pie

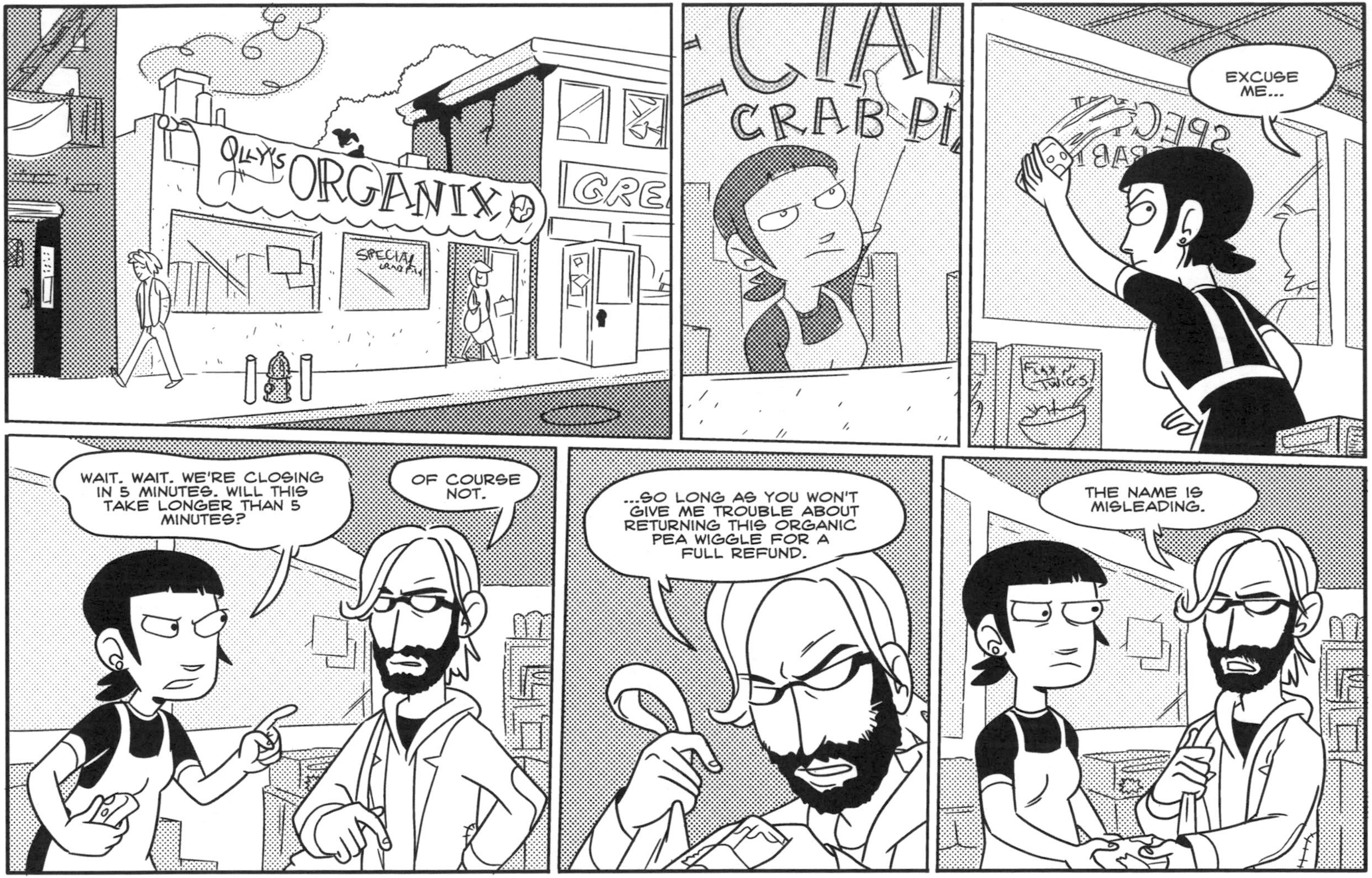
OLLY'S ORGANIX
EXCUSE ME...
WAIT. WAIT. WE'RE CLOSING IN 5 MINUTES. WILL THIS TAKE LONGER THAN 5 MINUTES?
OF COURSE NOT.
...SO LONG AS YOU WON'T GIVE ME TROUBLE ABOUT RETURNING THIS ORGANIC PEA WIGGLE FOR A FULL REFUND.
THE NAME IS MISLEADING.

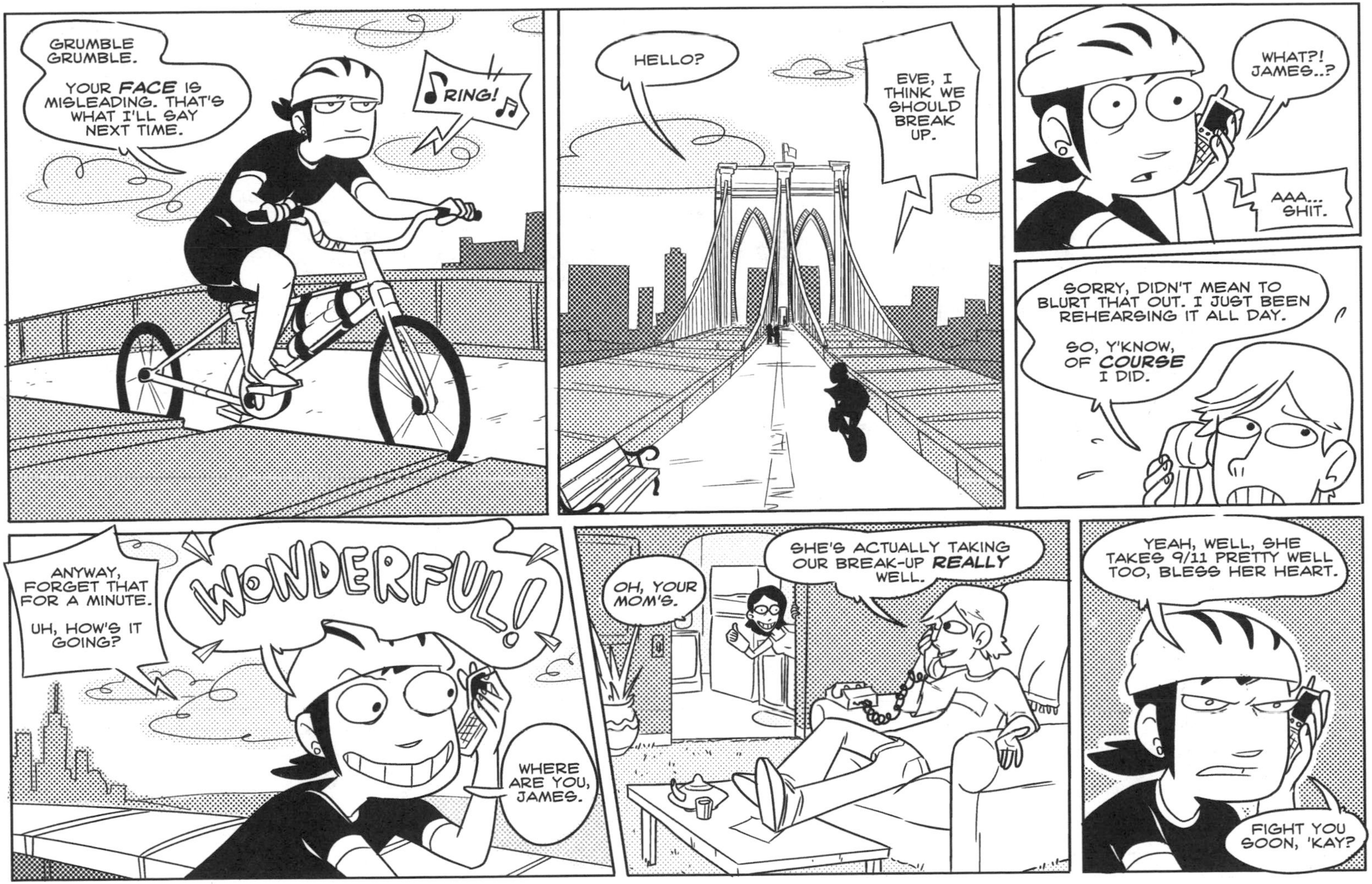
GRUMBLE GRUMBLE.
YOUR FACE IS MISLEADING. THAT'S WHAT I'LL SAY NEXT TIME.
RING!
HELLO?
EVE, I THINK WE SHOULD BREAK UP.
WHAT?! JAMES..?
AAA... SHIT.
SORRY, DIDN'T MEAN TO BLURT THAT OUT. I JUST BEEN REHEARSING IT ALL DAY.
SO, Y'KNOW, OF COURSE I DID.
ANYWAY, FORGET THAT FOR A MINUTE.
UH, HOW'S IT GOING?
WONDERFUL!
WHERE ARE YOU, JAMES.
OH, YOUR MOM'S.
SHE'S ACTUALLY TAKING OUR BREAK-UP REALLY WELL.
YEAH, WELL, SHE TAKES 9/11 PRETTY WELL TOO, BLESS HER HEART.
FIGHT YOU SOON, 'KAY?

AND I MEAN, THE FACT IS THAT BILLIONS OF UNIVERSES EXIST WHERE EVE AND I *AREN'T* DATING. WE MAINLY EXIST TO BE BROKEN UP FOREVER, Y'KNOW?

AND LIKE, YOU CAN TOTALLY APPLY THAT TO LIFE AND DEATH. EVERYTHING'S JUST A BLIP ON THE RADAR. SOMETIMES I'LL JUST SIT FOR HOURS WONDERING IF ANYTHING I DO MAKES ANY DIFFERENCE AT ALL.

MAN, LIKE GUYS ARGU... NTERNET FORUMS? Y SCRABBLE OR 6 OU'RE JUST THROW UMAN-DERIVED VOC G ONE MOTHERFU TELL ME I WAS LA SEE THE REALITY O COULD GO ON AND TERALLY FOR DAYS

MEAN THIS TEA IS OUS BUT IT'S ALMO WORTH NOTING, S A BIG MUG OF WAT HINGS WE CAN HA MORE THAN DUST ENSE UNIVERSE W DED BY. WHO'S TO S EXISTS BEYO IGHT HAV

ALL RIGHT, STEVEN SCHPIELBERG. OUT WE GO.

BUT I'M NOT DONE SCHPIELING!

DON'T BE SILLY. YOU'VE ALREADY SHOWN ME THE LIGHT!

I HAVE? REALLY?

HELL YES. *NO MORE EXISTENTIAL BOYFRIENDS!!*

SLAM!

NOT EVEN IN THE MULTIVERSE?

NEVER!

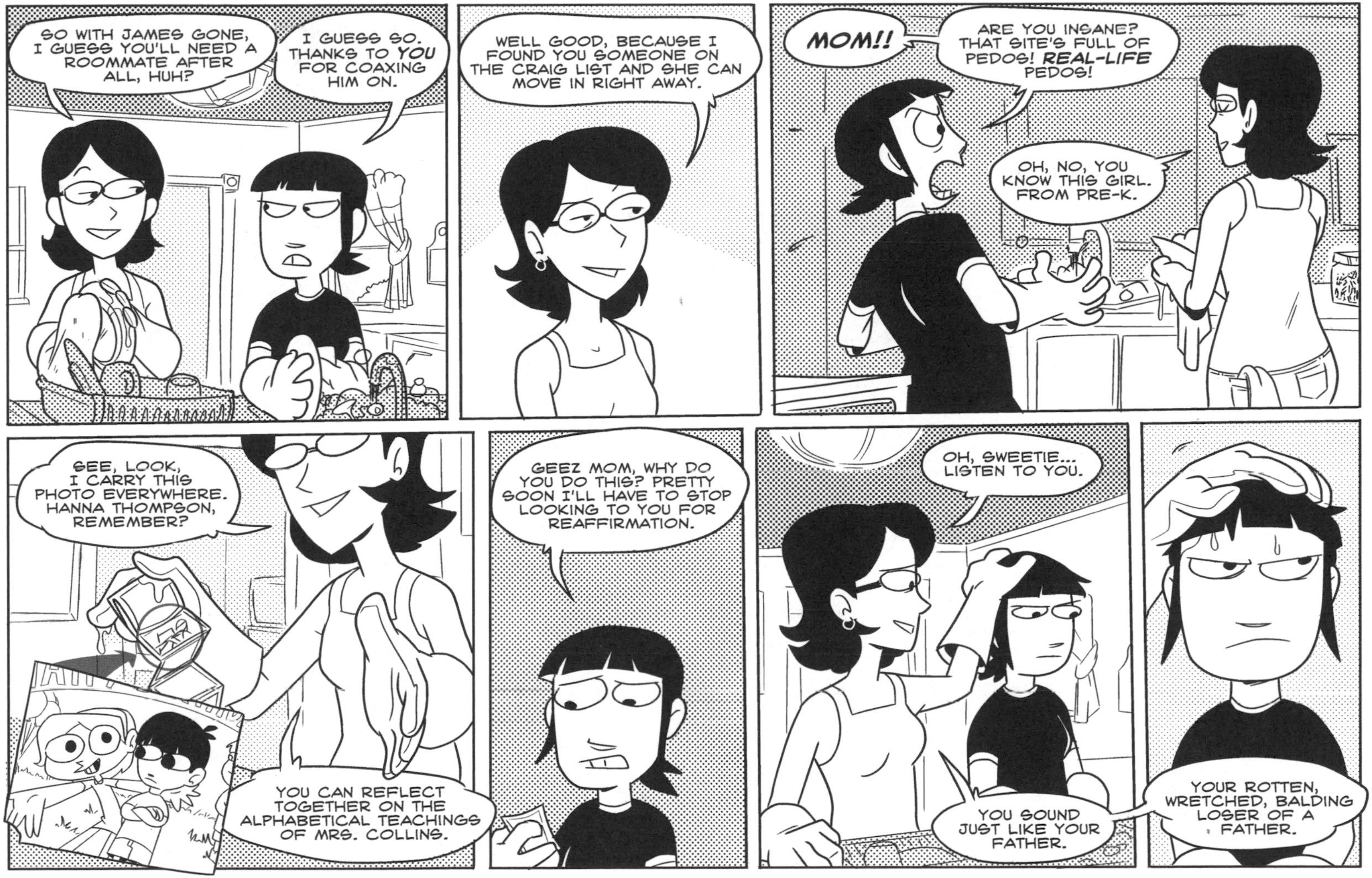
SO WITH JAMES GONE, I GUESS YOU'LL NEED A ROOMMATE AFTER ALL, HUH?
I GUESS SO. THANKS TO *YOU* FOR COAXING HIM ON.
WELL GOOD, BECAUSE I FOUND YOU SOMEONE ON THE CRAIG LIST AND SHE CAN MOVE IN RIGHT AWAY.
MOM!!
ARE YOU INSANE? THAT SITE'S FULL OF PEDOS! *REAL-LIFE* PEDOS!
OH, NO, YOU KNOW THIS GIRL. FROM PRE-K.
SEE, LOOK, I CARRY THIS PHOTO EVERYWHERE. HANNA THOMPSON, REMEMBER?
YOU CAN REFLECT TOGETHER ON THE ALPHABETICAL TEACHINGS OF MRS. COLLINS.
GEEZ MOM, WHY DO YOU DO THIS? PRETTY SOON I'LL HAVE TO STOP LOOKING TO YOU FOR REAFFIRMATION.
OH, SWEETIE... LISTEN TO YOU.
YOU SOUND JUST LIKE YOUR FATHER.
YOUR ROTTEN, WRETCHED, BALDING LOSER OF A FATHER.

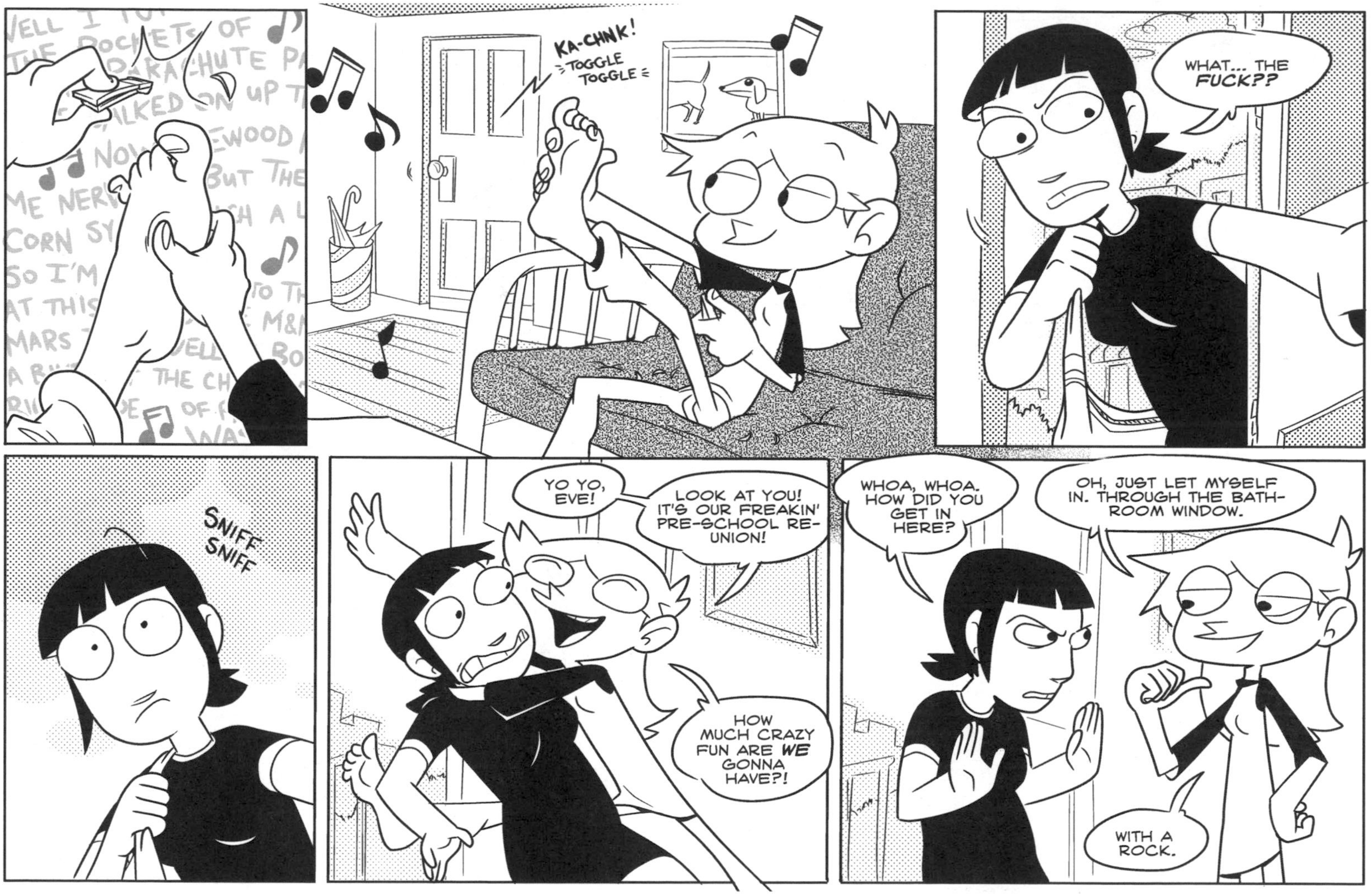
KA-CHINK!
TOGGLE TOGGLE
WHAT... THE FUCK??
SNIFF SNIFF
YO YO, EVE!
LOOK AT YOU! IT'S OUR FREAKIN' PRE-SCHOOL RE-UNION!
HOW MUCH CRAZY FUN ARE WE GONNA HAVE?!
WHOA, WHOA. HOW DID YOU GET IN HERE?
OH, JUST LET MYSELF IN. THROUGH THE BATH-ROOM WINDOW.
WITH A ROCK.

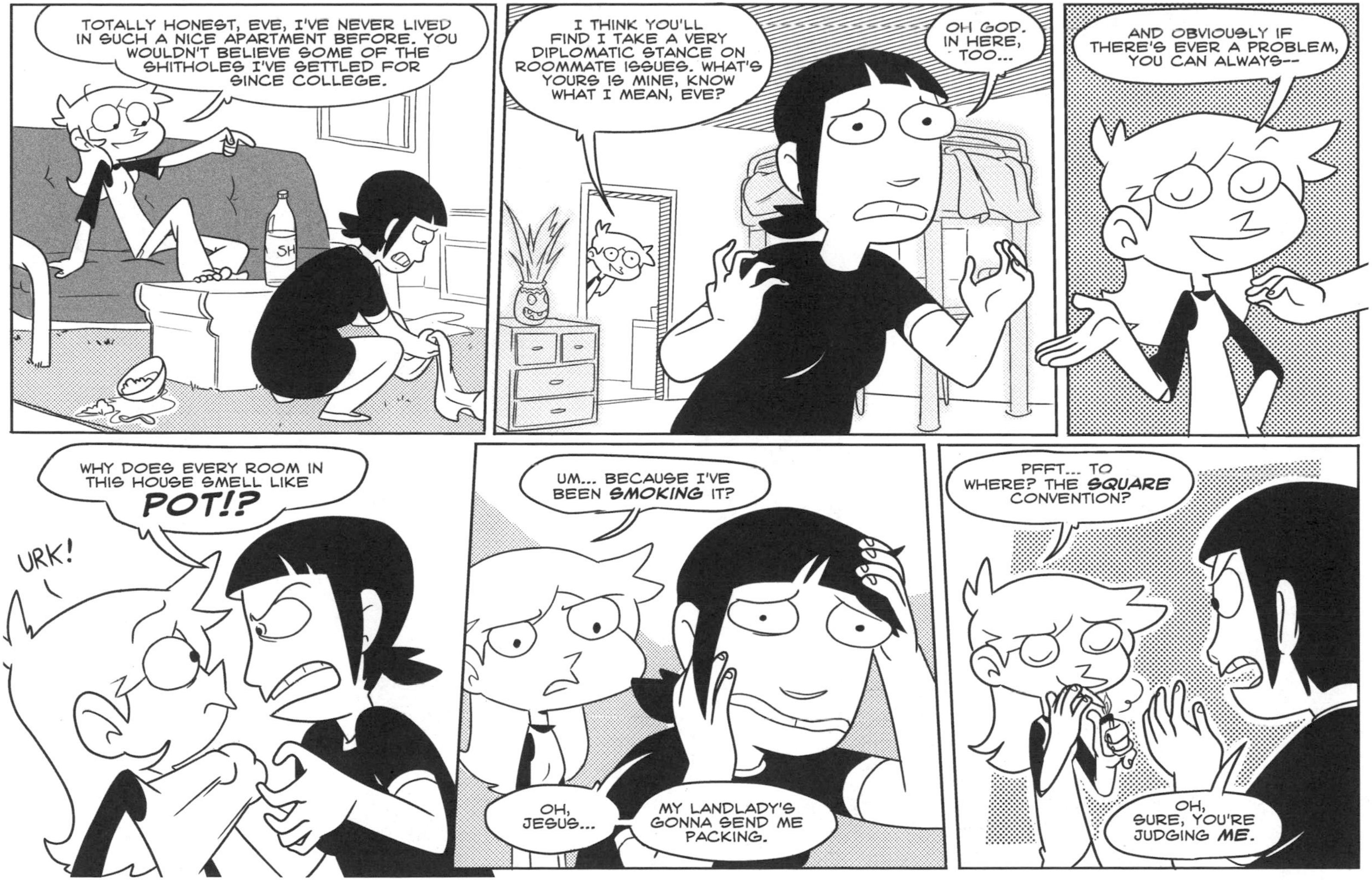
TOTALLY HONEST, EVE, I'VE NEVER LIVED IN SUCH A NICE APARTMENT BEFORE. YOU WOULDN'T BELIEVE SOME OF THE SHITHOLES I'VE SETTLED FOR SINCE COLLEGE.
I THINK YOU'LL FIND I TAKE A VERY DIPLOMATIC STANCE ON ROOMMATE ISSUES. WHAT'S YOURS IS MINE, KNOW WHAT I MEAN, EVE?
OH GOD. IN HERE, TOO...
AND OBVIOUSLY IF THERE'S EVER A PROBLEM, YOU CAN ALWAYS--
WHY DOES EVERY ROOM IN THIS HOUSE SMELL LIKE **POT!?**
URK!
UM... BECAUSE I'VE BEEN **SMOKING** IT?
OH, JESUS...
MY LANDLADY'S GONNA SEND ME PACKING.
PFFT... TO WHERE? THE **SQUARE** CONVENTION?
OH, SURE, YOU'RE JUDGING **ME**.

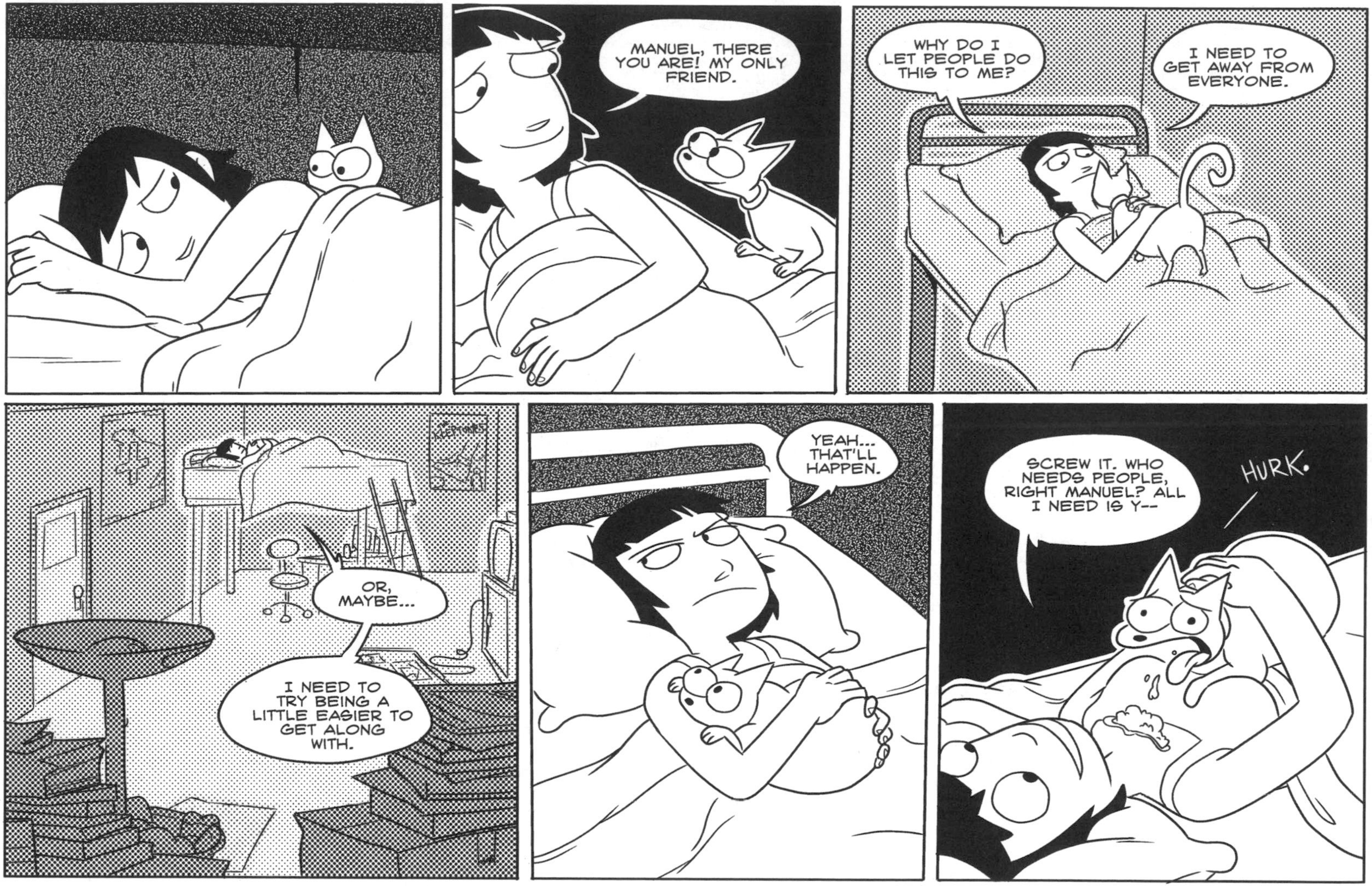
MANUEL, THERE YOU ARE! MY ONLY FRIEND.
WHY DO I LET PEOPLE DO THIS TO ME?
I NEED TO GET AWAY FROM EVERYONE.
OR, MAYBE...
I NEED TO TRY BEING A LITTLE EASIER TO GET ALONG WITH.
YEAH... THAT'LL HAPPEN.
SCREW IT. WHO NEEDS PEOPLE, RIGHT MANUEL? ALL I NEED IS Y--
HURK.

2

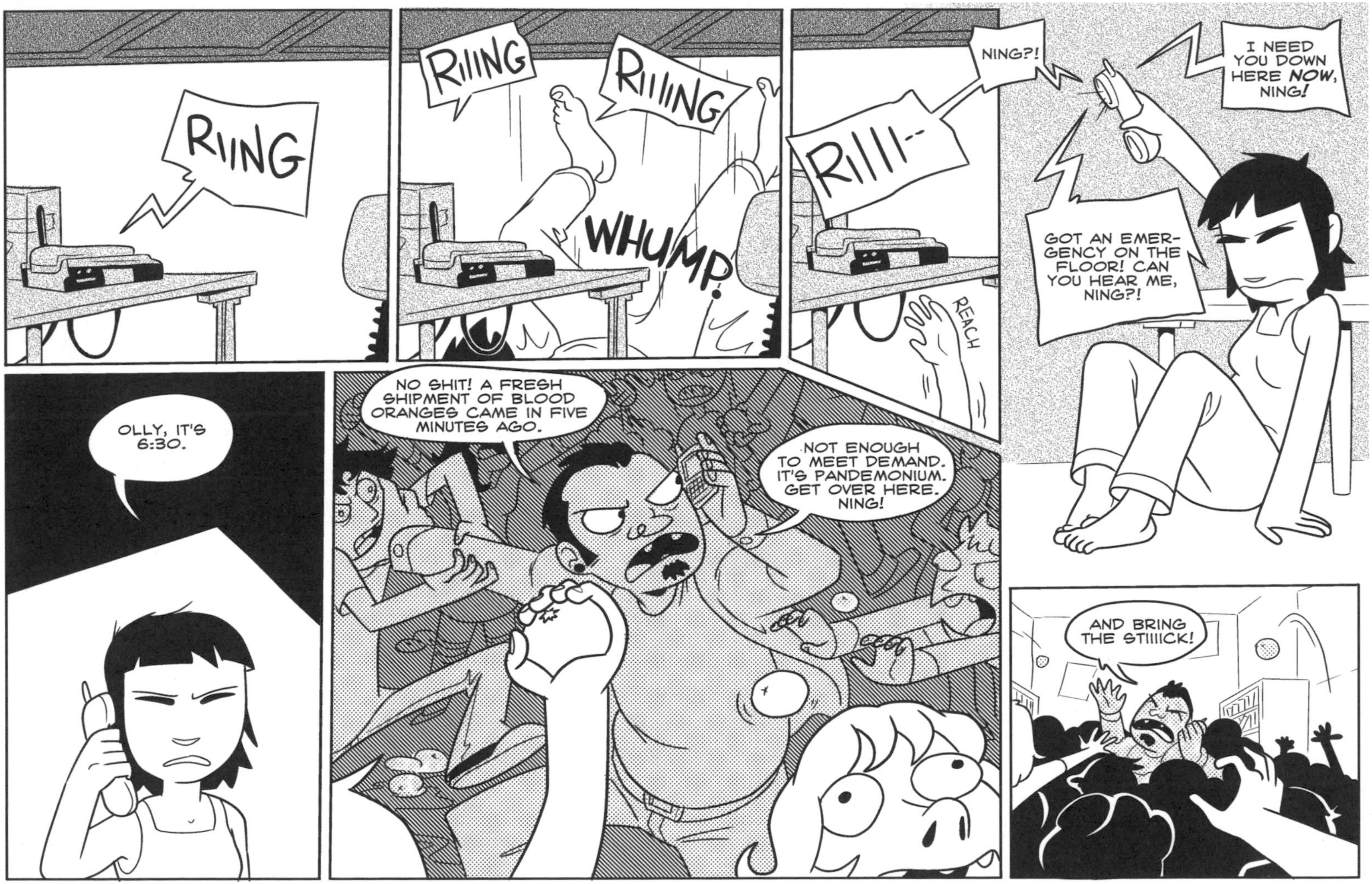
RIIING
RIIING
RIIIING
WHUMP
RIIII--
REACH
NING?!
I NEED YOU DOWN HERE NOW, NING!
GOT AN EMERGENCY ON THE FLOOR! CAN YOU HEAR ME, NING?!
OLLY, IT'S 6:30.
NO SHIT! A FRESH SHIPMENT OF BLOOD ORANGES CAME IN FIVE MINUTES AGO.
NOT ENOUGH TO MEET DEMAND. IT'S PANDEMONIUM. GET OVER HERE. NING!
AND BRING THE STIIIICK!

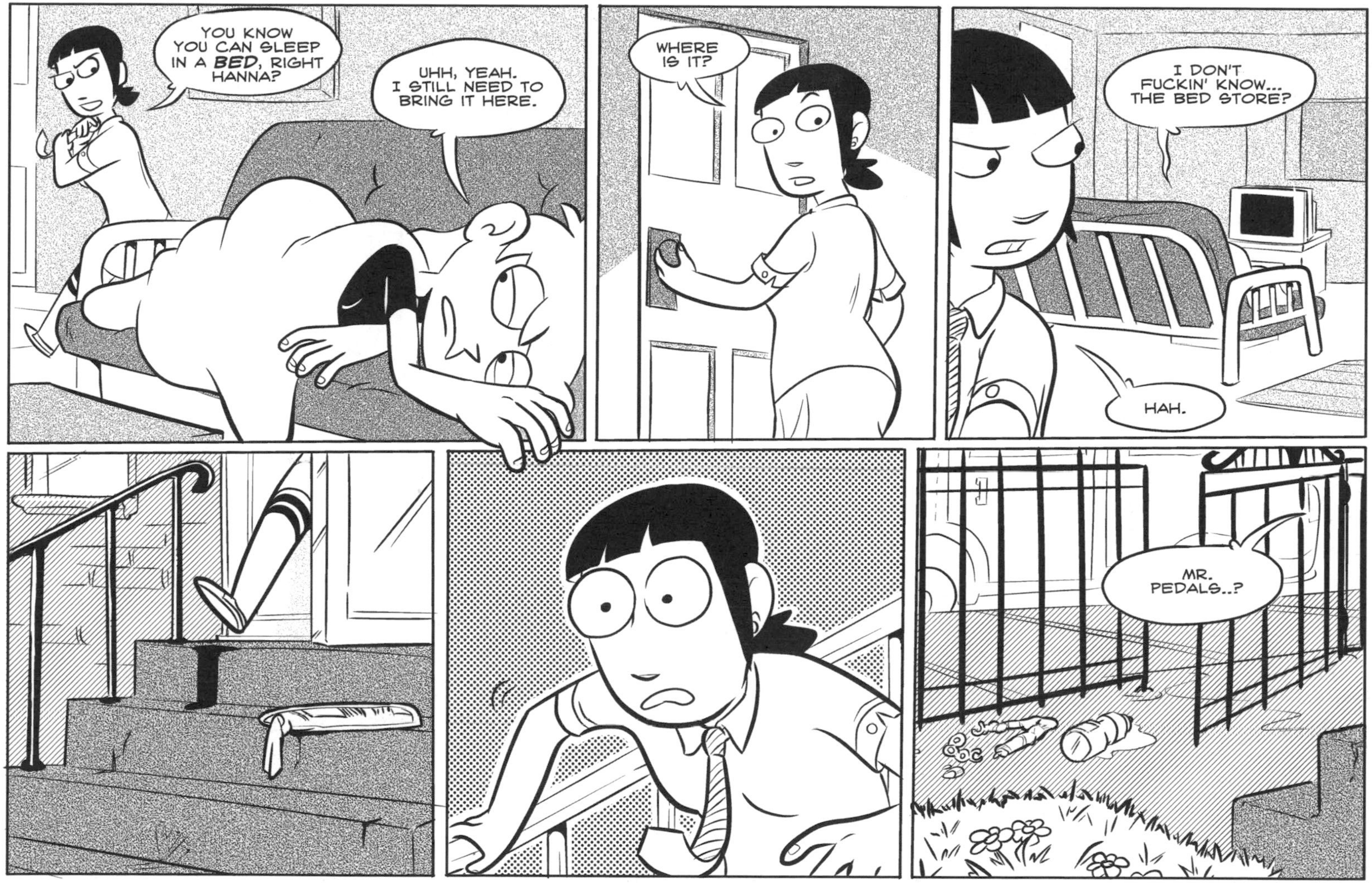
YOU KNOW YOU CAN SLEEP IN A BED, RIGHT HANNA?
UHH, YEAH. I STILL NEED TO BRING IT HERE.
WHERE IS IT?
I DON'T FUCKIN' KNOW... THE BED STORE?
HAH.
MR. PEDALS..?

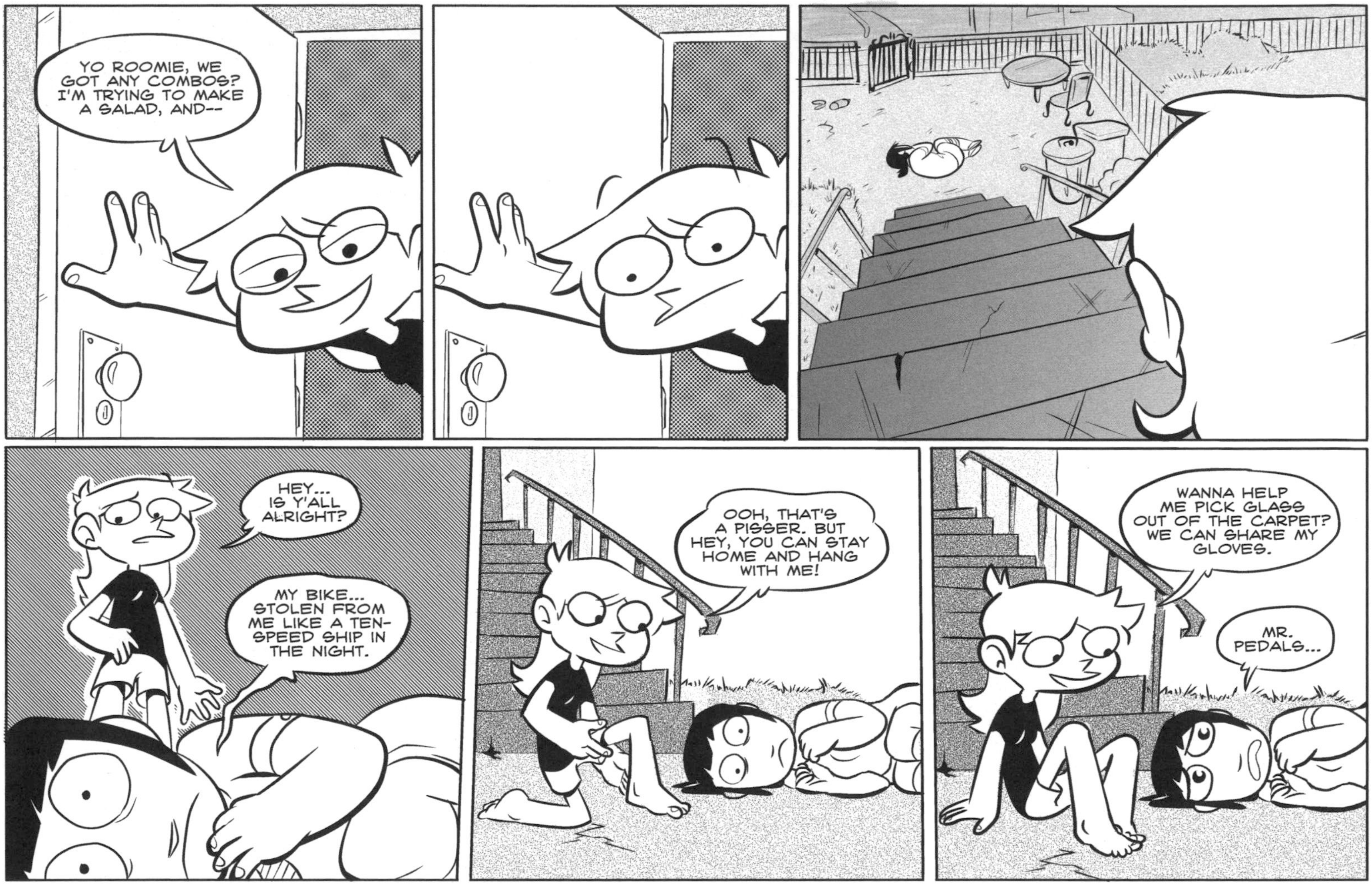
YO ROOMIE, WE GOT ANY COMBOS? I'M TRYING TO MAKE A SALAD, AND--
HEY... IS Y'ALL ALRIGHT?
MY BIKE... STOLEN FROM ME LIKE A TEN-SPEED SHIP IN THE NIGHT.
OOH, THAT'S A PISSER. BUT HEY, YOU CAN STAY HOME AND HANG WITH ME!
WANNA HELP ME PICK GLASS OUT OF THE CARPET? WE CAN SHARE MY GLOVES.
MR. PEDALS...

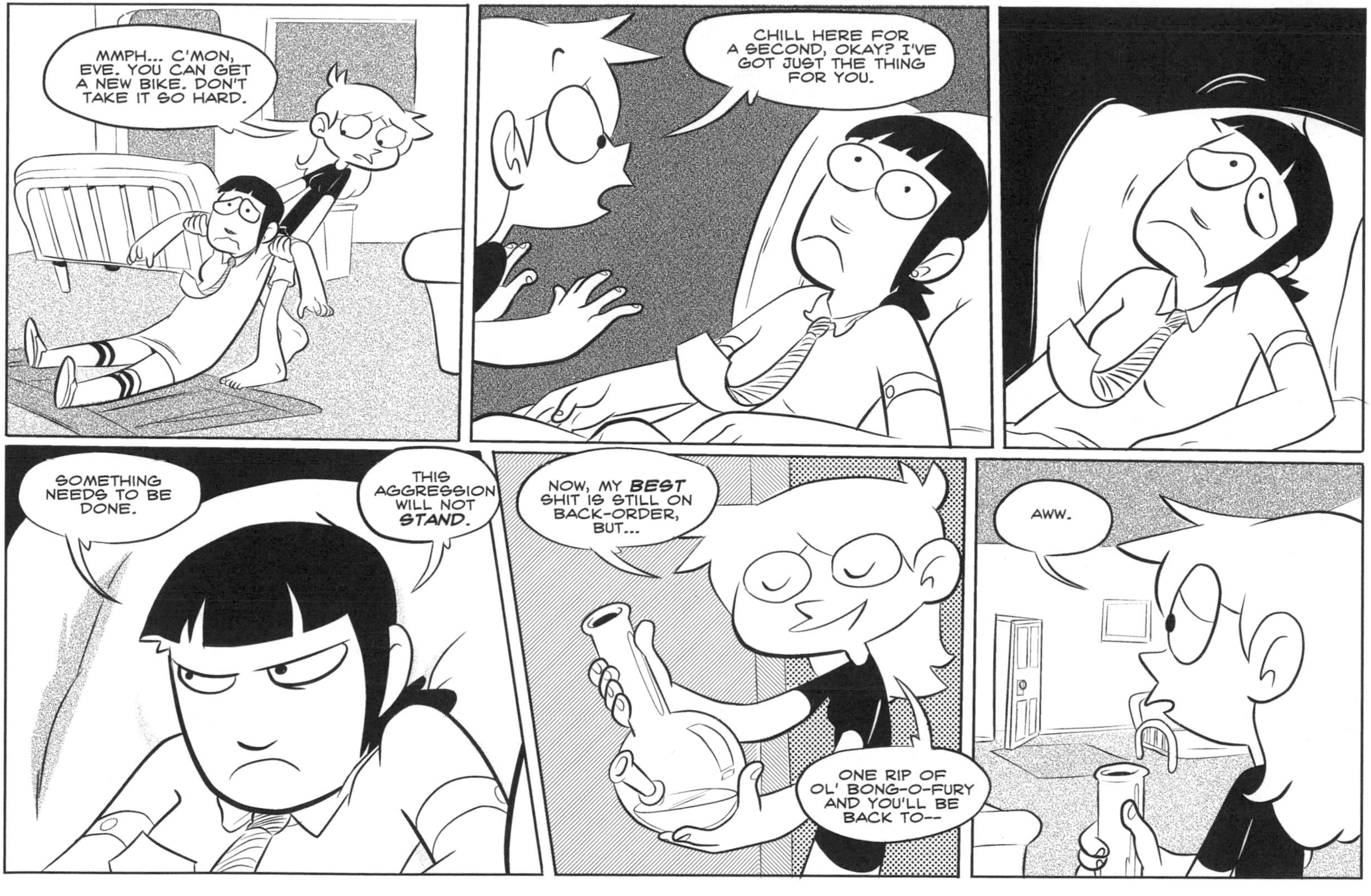
MMPH... C'MON, EVE. YOU CAN GET A NEW BIKE. DON'T TAKE IT SO HARD.
CHILL HERE FOR A SECOND, OKAY? I'VE GOT JUST THE THING FOR YOU.
SOMETHING NEEDS TO BE DONE.
THIS AGGRESSION WILL NOT STAND.
NOW, MY BEST SHIT IS STILL ON BACK-ORDER, BUT...
ONE RIP OF OL' BONG-O-FURY AND YOU'LL BE BACK TO--
AWW.

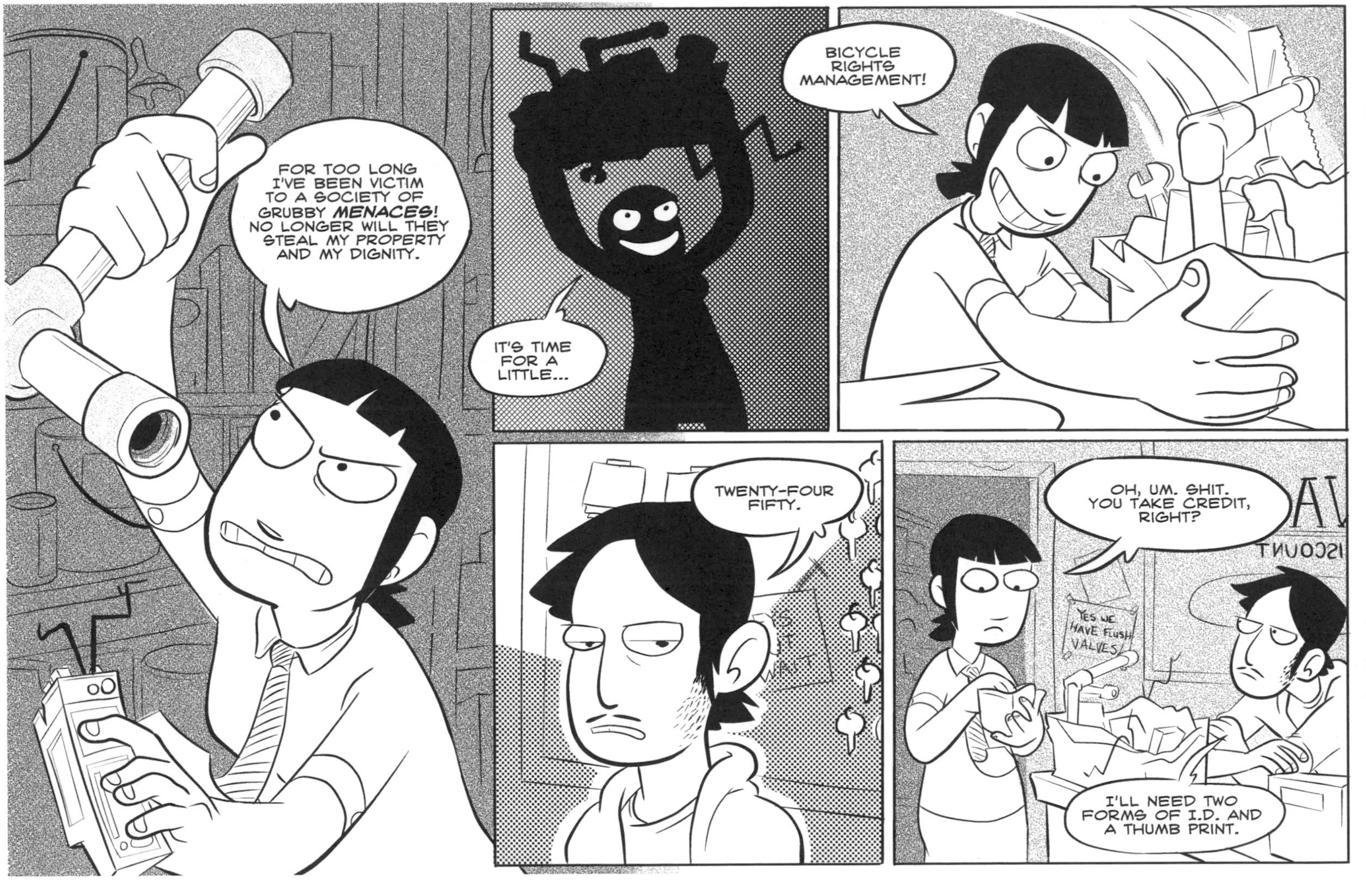
FOR TOO LONG I'VE BEEN VICTIM TO A SOCIETY OF GRUBBY MENACES! NO LONGER WILL THEY STEAL MY PROPERTY AND MY DIGNITY.
IT'S TIME FOR A LITTLE...
BICYCLE RIGHTS MANAGEMENT!
TWENTY-FOUR FIFTY.
OH, UM. SHIT. YOU TAKE CREDIT, RIGHT?
YES WE HAVE FLUSH VALVES
I'LL NEED TWO FORMS OF I.D. AND A THUMB PRINT.

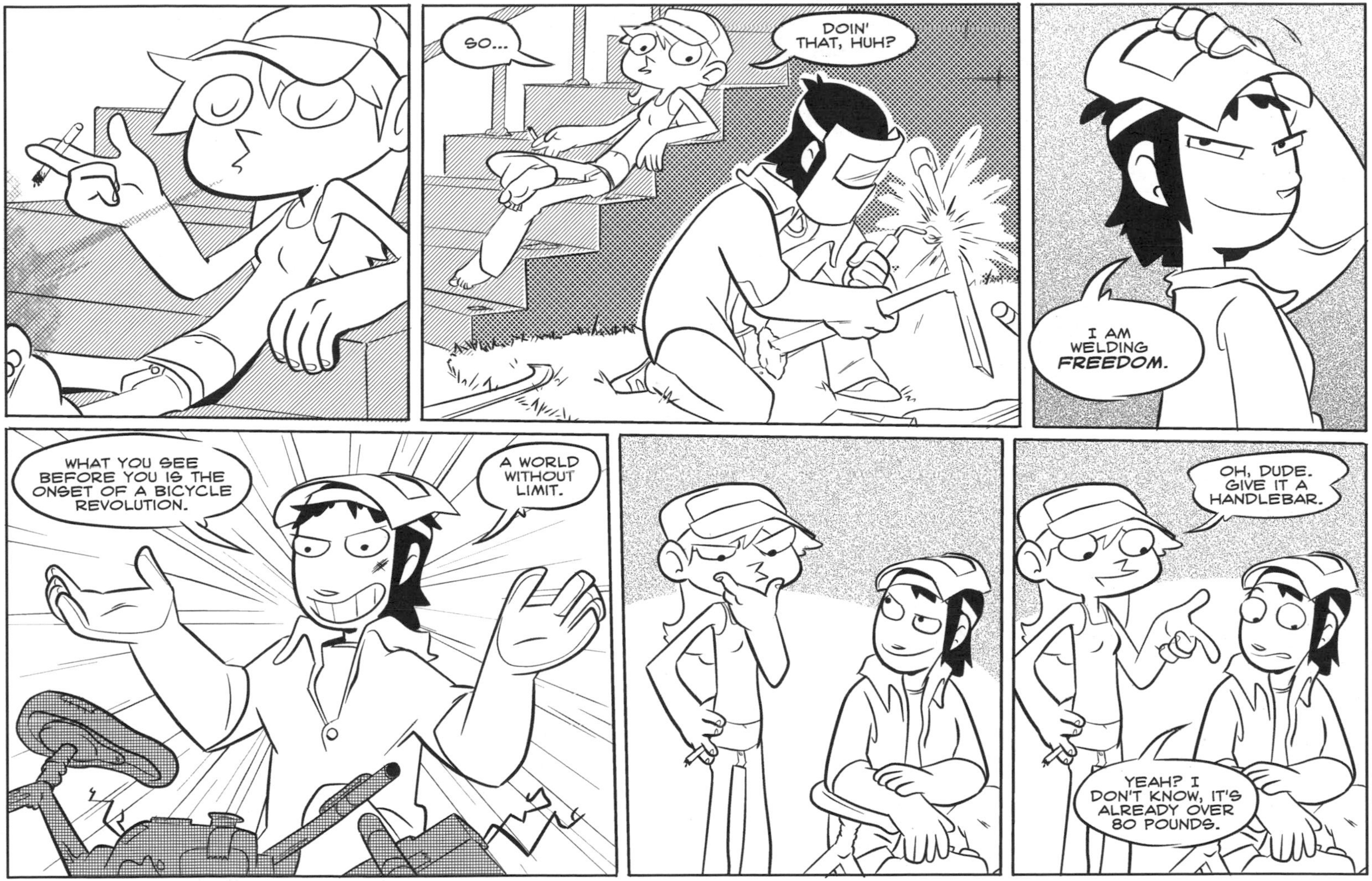
SO...
DOIN' THAT, HUH?
I AM WELDING *FREEDOM.*
WHAT YOU SEE BEFORE YOU IS THE ONSET OF A BICYCLE REVOLUTION.
A WORLD WITHOUT LIMIT.
OH, DUDE. GIVE IT A HANDLEBAR.
YEAH? I DON'T KNOW, IT'S ALREADY OVER 80 POUNDS.

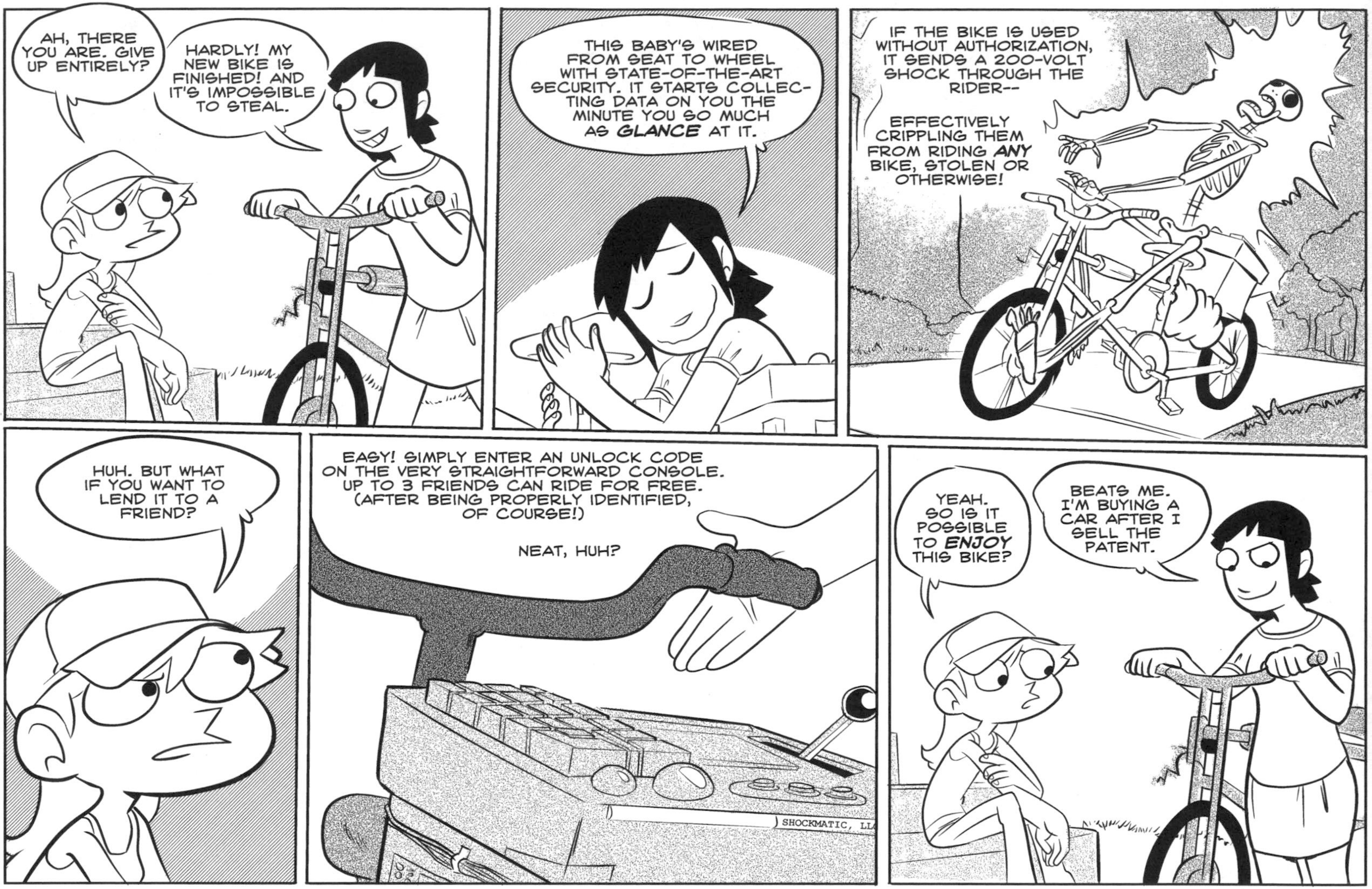
AH, THERE YOU ARE. GIVE UP ENTIRELY?
HARDLY! MY NEW BIKE IS FINISHED! AND IT'S IMPOSSIBLE TO STEAL.
THIS BABY'S WIRED FROM SEAT TO WHEEL WITH STATE-OF-THE-ART SECURITY. IT STARTS COLLECTING DATA ON YOU THE MINUTE YOU SO MUCH AS GLANCE AT IT.
IF THE BIKE IS USED WITHOUT AUTHORIZATION, IT SENDS A 200-VOLT SHOCK THROUGH THE RIDER--
EFFECTIVELY CRIPPLING THEM FROM RIDING ANY BIKE, STOLEN OR OTHERWISE!
HUH. BUT WHAT IF YOU WANT TO LEND IT TO A FRIEND?
EASY! SIMPLY ENTER AN UNLOCK CODE ON THE VERY STRAIGHTFORWARD CONSOLE. UP TO 3 FRIENDS CAN RIDE FOR FREE. (AFTER BEING PROPERLY IDENTIFIED, OF COURSE!)
NEAT, HUH?
SHOCKMATIC, LL
YEAH. SO IS IT POSSIBLE TO ENJOY THIS BIKE?
BEATS ME. I'M BUYING A CAR AFTER I SELL THE PATENT.

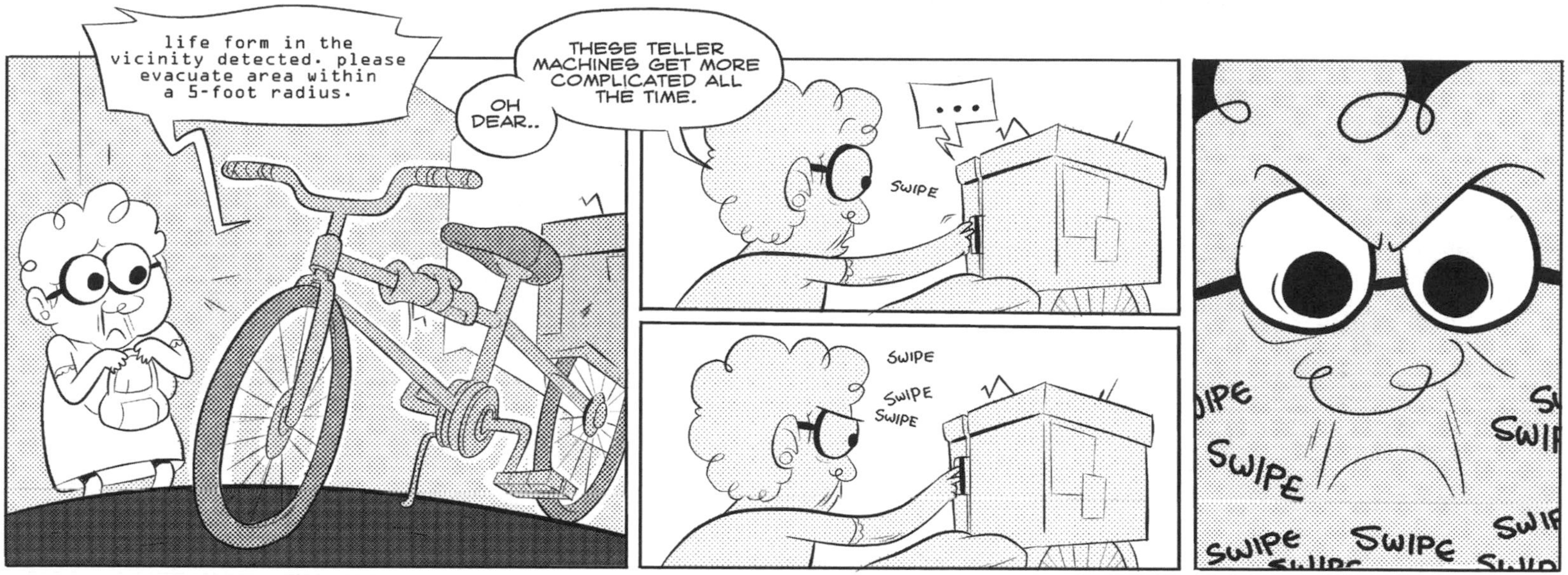
life form in the vicinity detected. please evacuate area within a 5-foot radius.
OH DEAR..
THESE TELLER MACHINES GET MORE COMPLICATED ALL THE TIME.
...
SWIPE
SWIPE
SWIPE
SWIPE
SWIPE
SWIPE
SWIPE

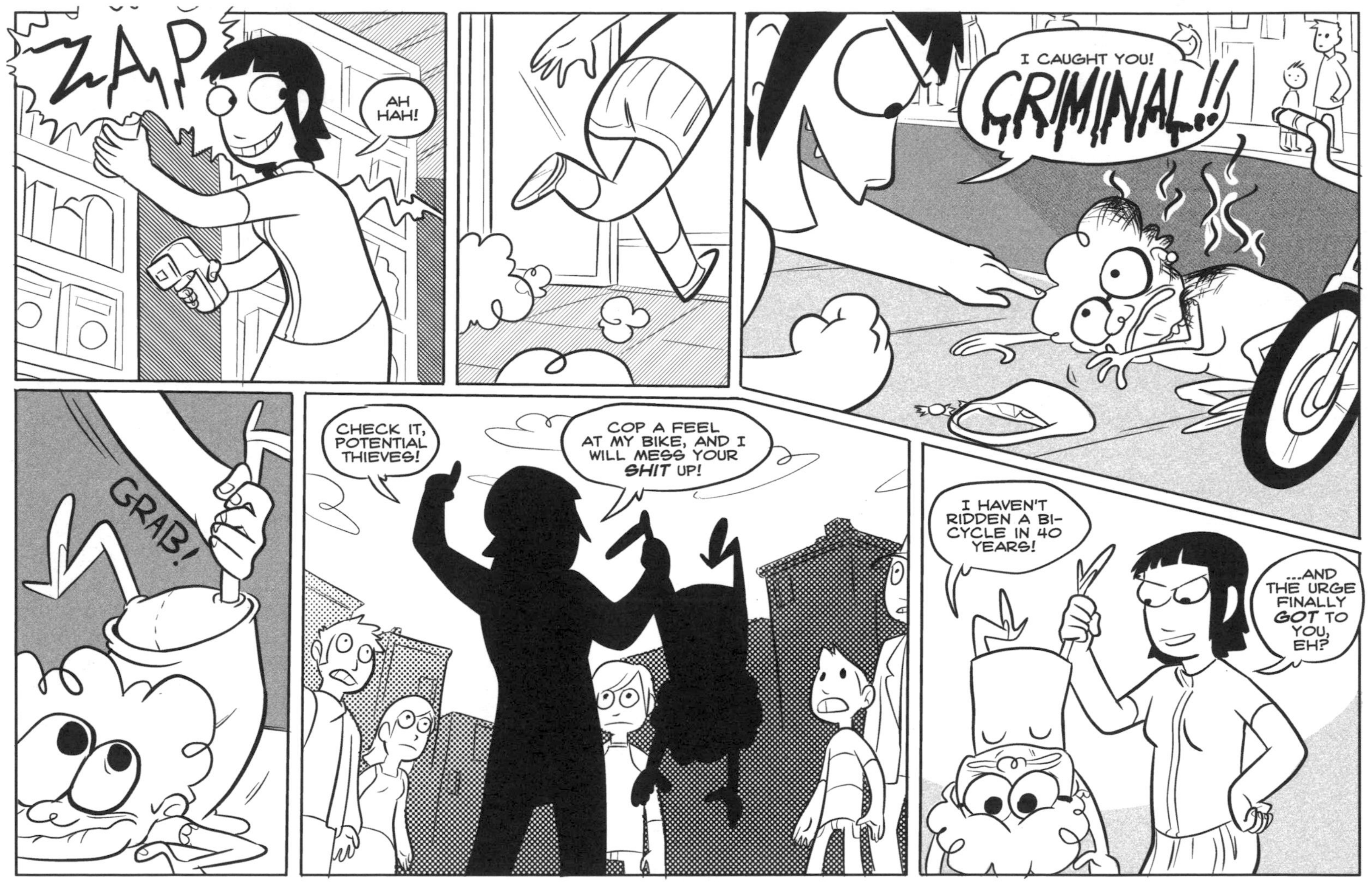
ZAP
AH HAH!
I CAUGHT YOU! CRIMINAL!!
GRAB!
CHECK IT, POTENTIAL THIEVES!
COP A FEEL AT MY BIKE, AND I WILL MESS YOUR SHIT UP!
I HAVEN'T RIDDEN A BI-CYCLE IN 40 YEARS!
...AND THE URGE FINALLY GOT TO YOU, EH?

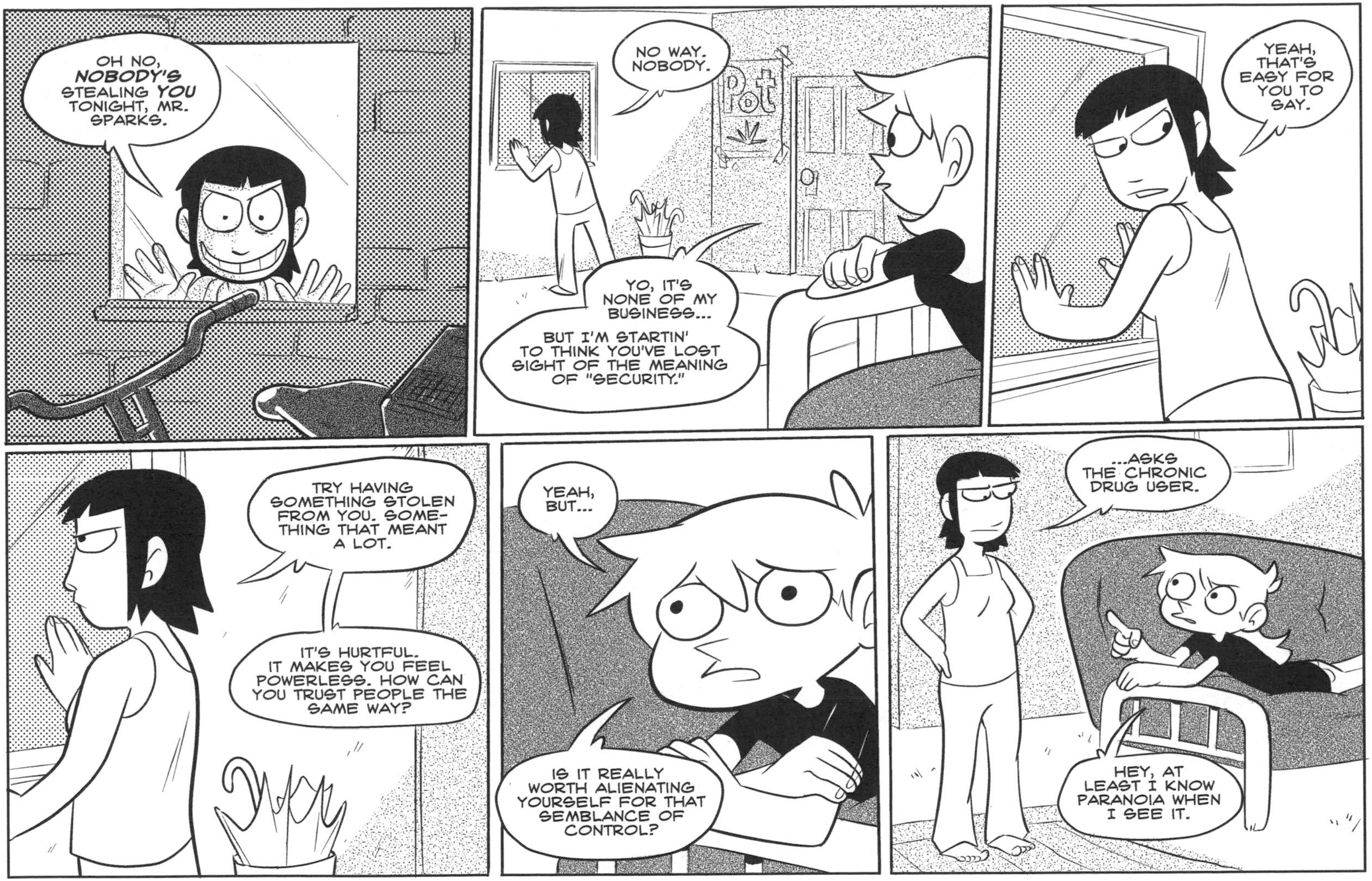

OH NO, ***NOBODY'S*** STEALING ***YOU*** TONIGHT, MR. SPARKS.
NO WAY. NOBODY.
YO, IT'S NONE OF MY BUSINESS...
BUT I'M STARTIN' TO THINK YOU'VE LOST SIGHT OF THE MEANING OF "SECURITY."
YEAH, THAT'S EASY FOR YOU TO SAY.
TRY HAVING SOMETHING STOLEN FROM YOU. SOMETHING THAT MEANT A LOT.
IT'S HURTFUL. IT MAKES YOU FEEL POWERLESS. HOW CAN YOU TRUST PEOPLE THE SAME WAY?
YEAH, BUT...
IS IT REALLY WORTH ALIENATING YOURSELF FOR THAT SEMBLANCE OF CONTROL?
...ASKS THE CHRONIC DRUG USER.
HEY, AT LEAST I KNOW PARANOIA WHEN I SEE IT.

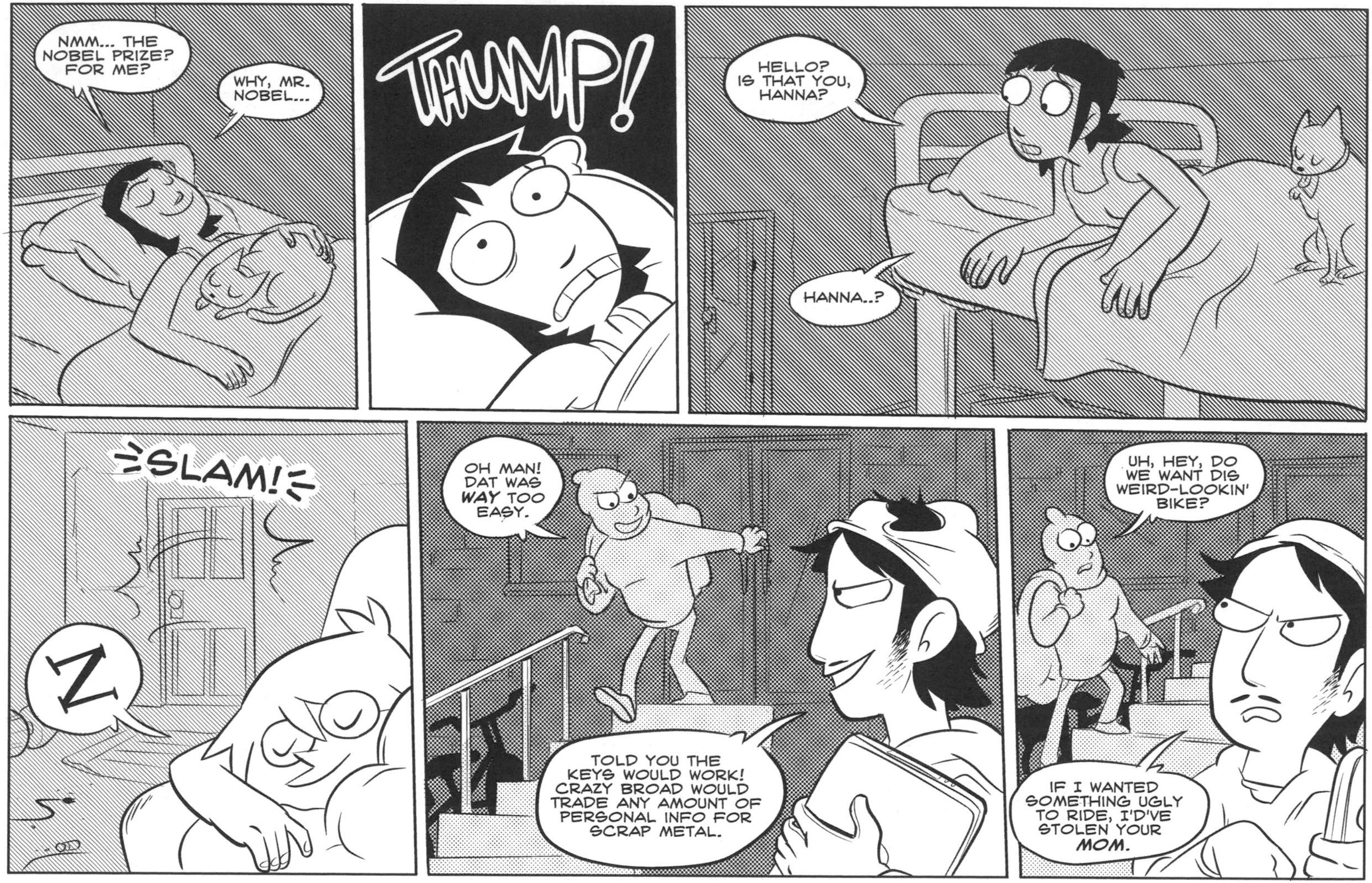

NMM... THE NOBEL PRIZE? FOR ME?
WHY, MR. NOBEL...
THUMP!
HELLO? IS THAT YOU, HANNA?
HANNA..?
SLAM!
N
OH MAN! DAT WAS **WAY** TOO EASY.
TOLD YOU THE KEYS WOULD WORK! CRAZY BROAD WOULD TRADE ANY AMOUNT OF PERSONAL INFO FOR SCRAP METAL.
UH, HEY, DO WE WANT DIS WEIRD-LOOKIN' BIKE?
IF I WANTED SOMETHING UGLY TO RIDE, I'D'VE STOLEN YOUR **MOM**.

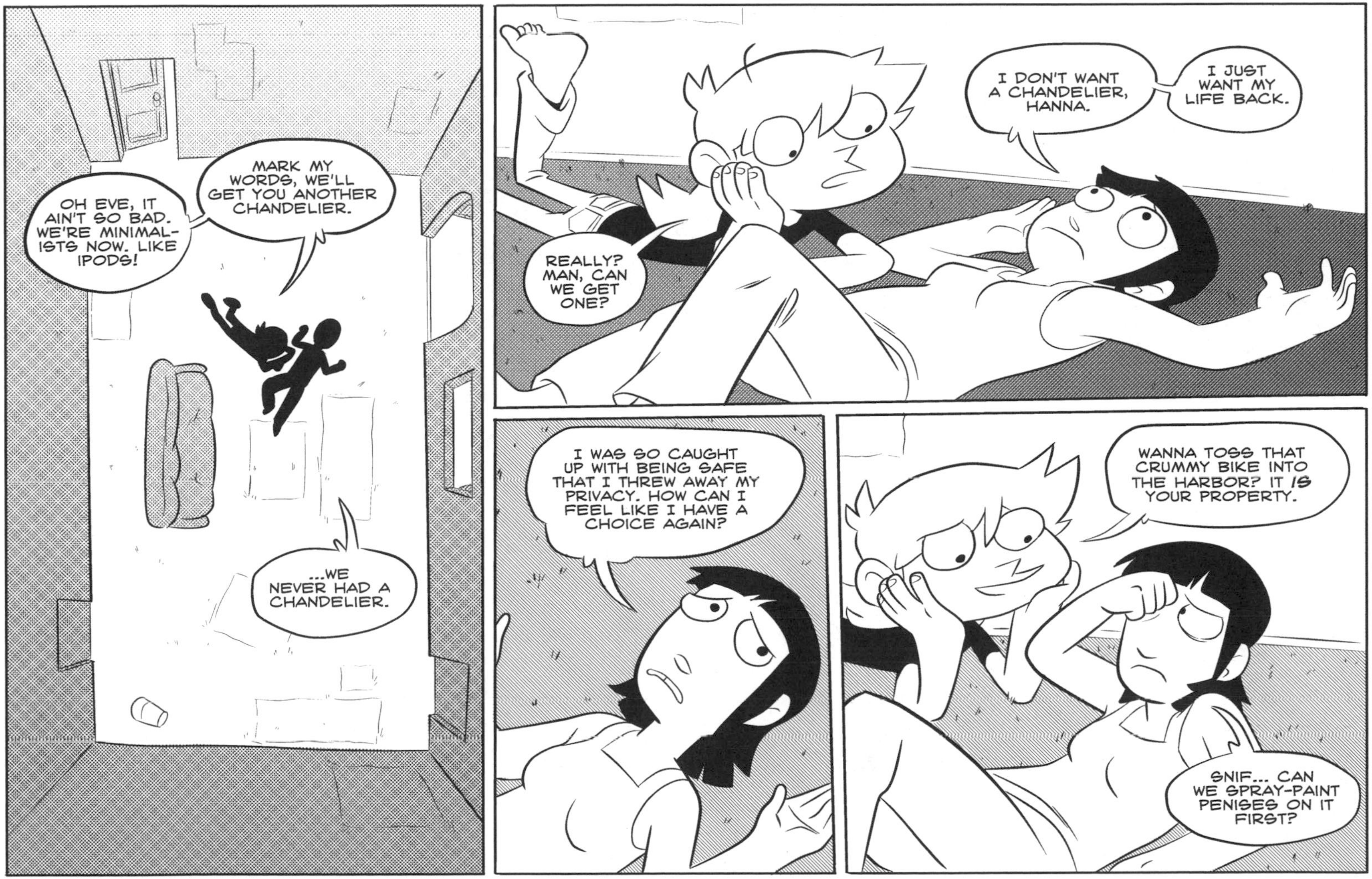
OH EVE, IT AIN'T SO BAD. WE'RE MINIMAL-ISTS NOW. LIKE IPODS!
MARK MY WORDS, WE'LL GET YOU ANOTHER CHANDELIER.
...WE NEVER HAD A CHANDELIER.
REALLY? MAN, CAN WE GET ONE?
I DON'T WANT A CHANDELIER, HANNA.
I JUST WANT MY LIFE BACK.
I WAS SO CAUGHT UP WITH BEING SAFE THAT I THREW AWAY MY PRIVACY. HOW CAN I FEEL LIKE I HAVE A CHOICE AGAIN?
WANNA TOSS THAT CRUMMY BIKE INTO THE HARBOR? IT *IS* YOUR PROPERTY.
SNIF... CAN WE SPRAY-PAINT PENISES ON IT FIRST?

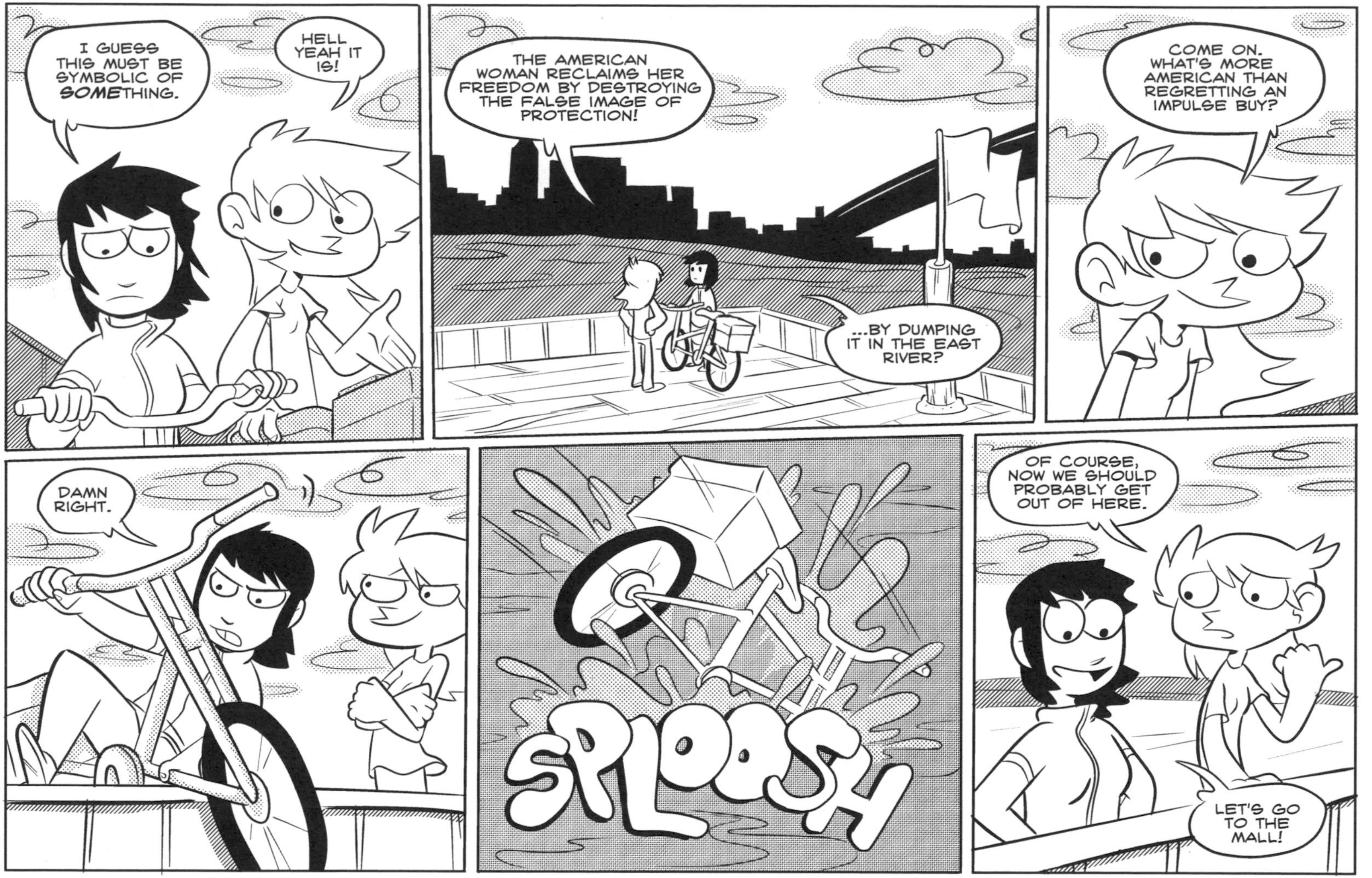

I GUESS THIS MUST BE SYMBOLIC OF *SOME*THING.
HELL YEAH IT IS!
THE AMERICAN WOMAN RECLAIMS HER FREEDOM BY DESTROYING THE FALSE IMAGE OF PROTECTION!
...BY DUMPING IT IN THE EAST RIVER?
COME ON. WHAT'S MORE AMERICAN THAN REGRETTING AN IMPULSE BUY?
DAMN RIGHT.
SPLOOSH
OF COURSE, NOW WE SHOULD PROBABLY GET OUT OF HERE.
LET'S GO TO THE MALL!

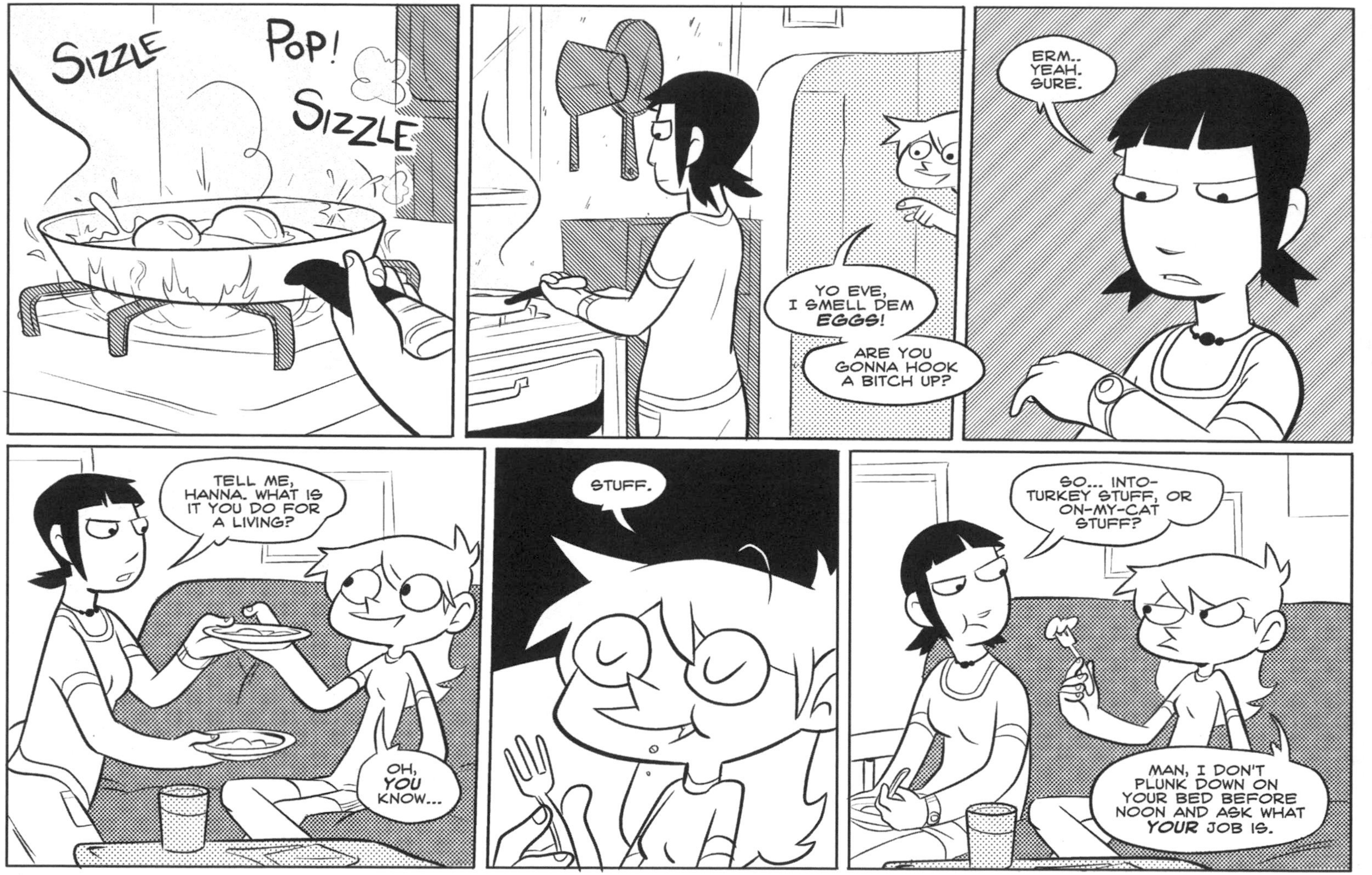
SIZZLE
POP!
SIZZLE
YO EVE, I SMELL DEM EGGS!
ARE YOU GONNA HOOK A BITCH UP?
ERM.. YEAH. SURE.
TELL ME, HANNA. WHAT IS IT YOU DO FOR A LIVING?
OH, YOU KNOW...
STUFF.
SO... INTO-TURKEY STUFF, OR ON-MY-CAT STUFF?
MAN, I DON'T PLUNK DOWN ON YOUR BED BEFORE NOON AND ASK WHAT YOUR JOB IS.

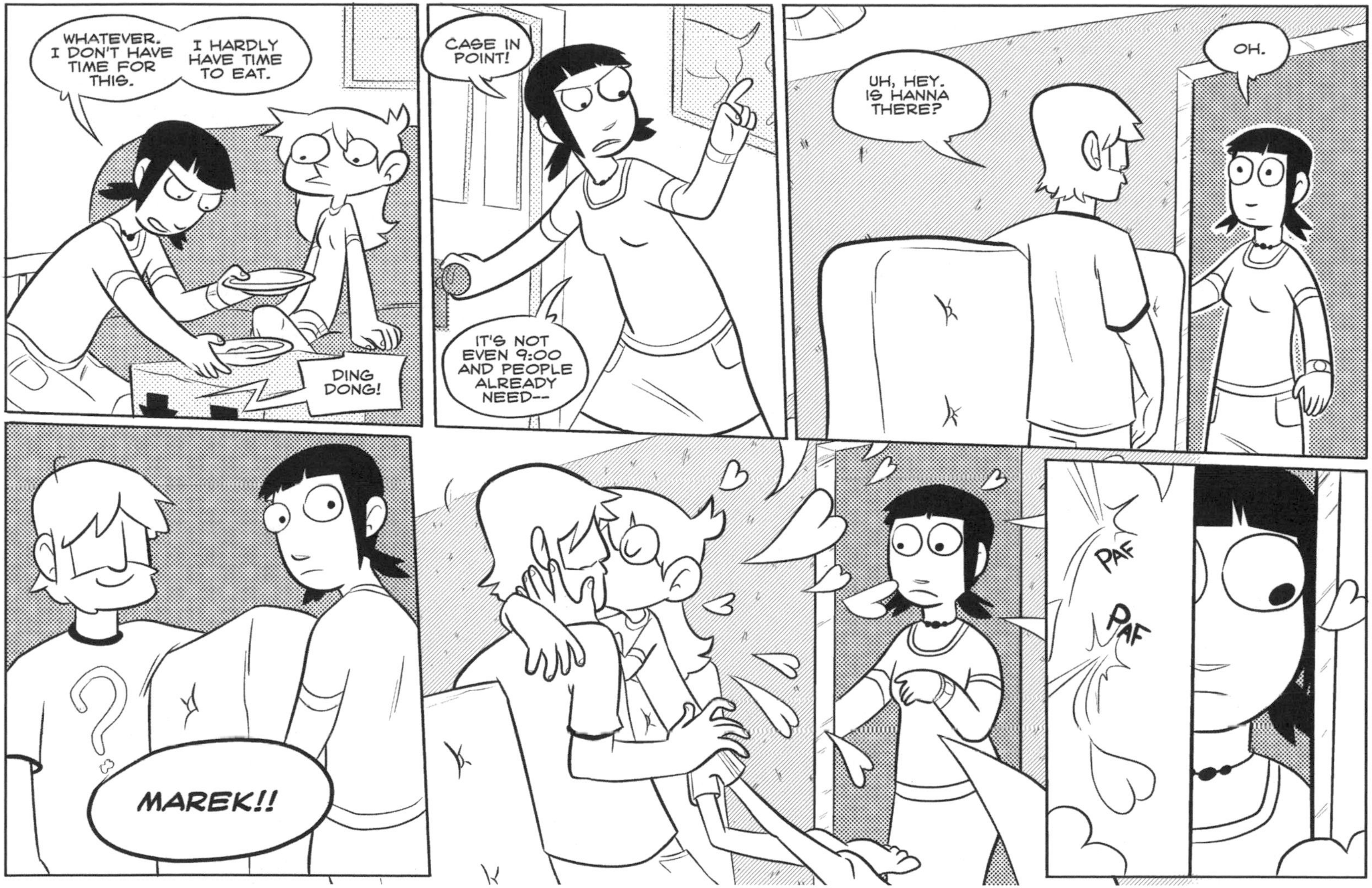
WHATEVER. I DON'T HAVE TIME FOR THIS.
I HARDLY HAVE TIME TO EAT.
DING DONG!
CASE IN POINT!
IT'S NOT EVEN 9:00 AND PEOPLE ALREADY NEED--
UH, HEY. IS HANNA THERE?
OH.
MAREK!!
PAF
PAF

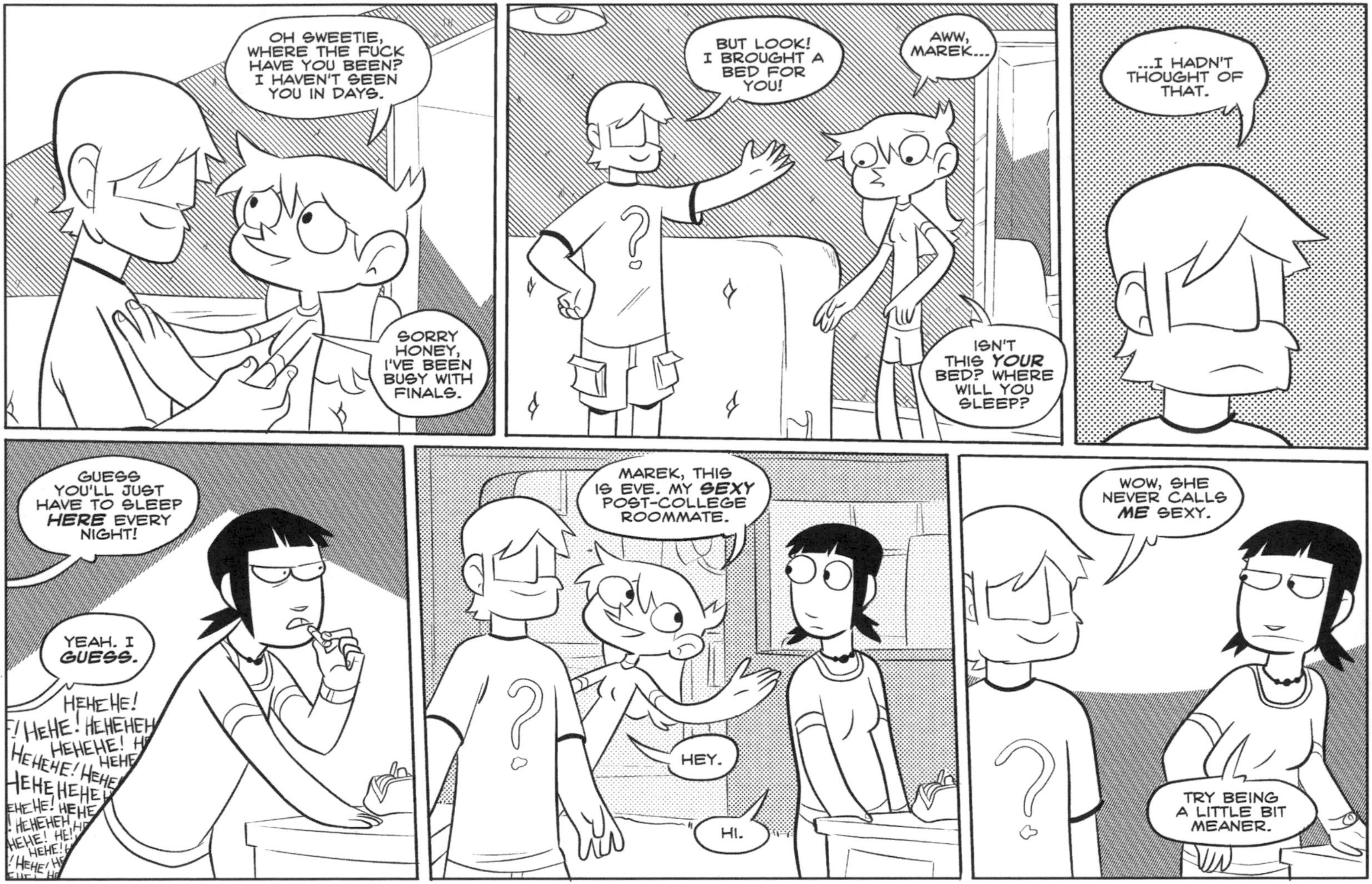
OH SWEETIE, WHERE THE FUCK HAVE YOU BEEN? I HAVEN'T SEEN YOU IN DAYS.
SORRY HONEY, I'VE BEEN BUSY WITH FINALS.
BUT LOOK! I BROUGHT A BED FOR YOU!
AWW, MAREK...
ISN'T THIS YOUR BED? WHERE WILL YOU SLEEP?
...I HADN'T THOUGHT OF THAT.
GUESS YOU'LL JUST HAVE TO SLEEP HERE EVERY NIGHT!
YEAH. I GUESS.
HEHEHE! HEHE! HEHEHEHE HEHEHE! HEHEHE!
MAREK, THIS IS EVE. MY SEXY POST-COLLEGE ROOMMATE.
HEY.
HI.
WOW, SHE NEVER CALLS ME SEXY.
TRY BEING A LITTLE BIT MEANER.

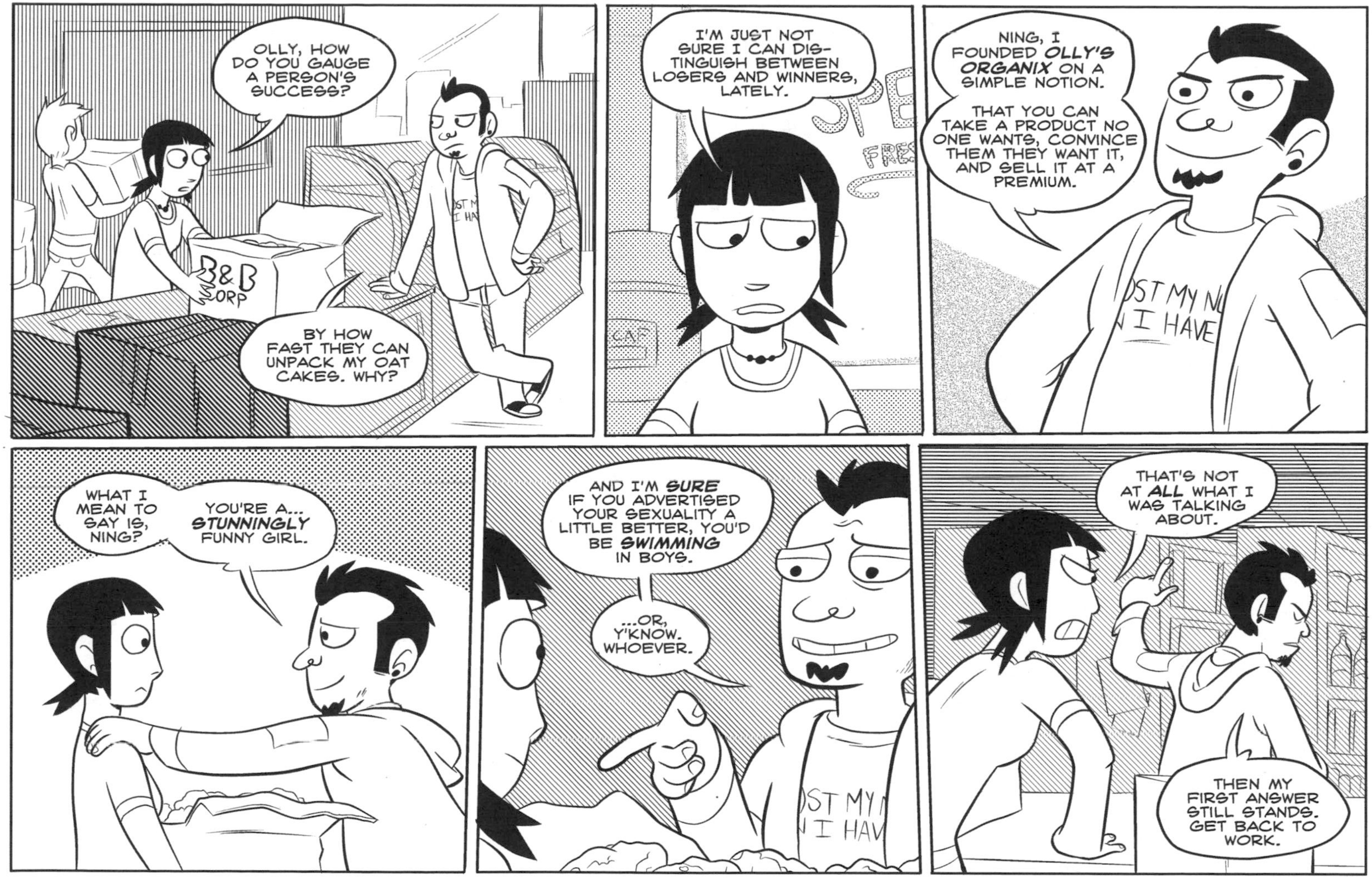
OLLY, HOW DO YOU GAUGE A PERSON'S SUCCESS?
B&B CORP
BY HOW FAST THEY CAN UNPACK MY OAT CAKES. WHY?
I'M JUST NOT SURE I CAN DIS-TINGUISH BETWEEN LOSERS AND WINNERS, LATELY.
NING, I FOUNDED OLLY'S ORGANIX ON A SIMPLE NOTION.
THAT YOU CAN TAKE A PRODUCT NO ONE WANTS, CONVINCE THEM THEY WANT IT, AND SELL IT AT A PREMIUM.
WHAT I MEAN TO SAY IS, NING?
YOU'RE A... STUNNINGLY FUNNY GIRL.
AND I'M SURE IF YOU ADVERTISED YOUR SEXUALITY A LITTLE BETTER, YOU'D BE SWIMMING IN BOYS.
...OR, Y'KNOW. WHOEVER.
THAT'S NOT AT ALL WHAT I WAS TALKING ABOUT.
THEN MY FIRST ANSWER STILL STANDS. GET BACK TO WORK.

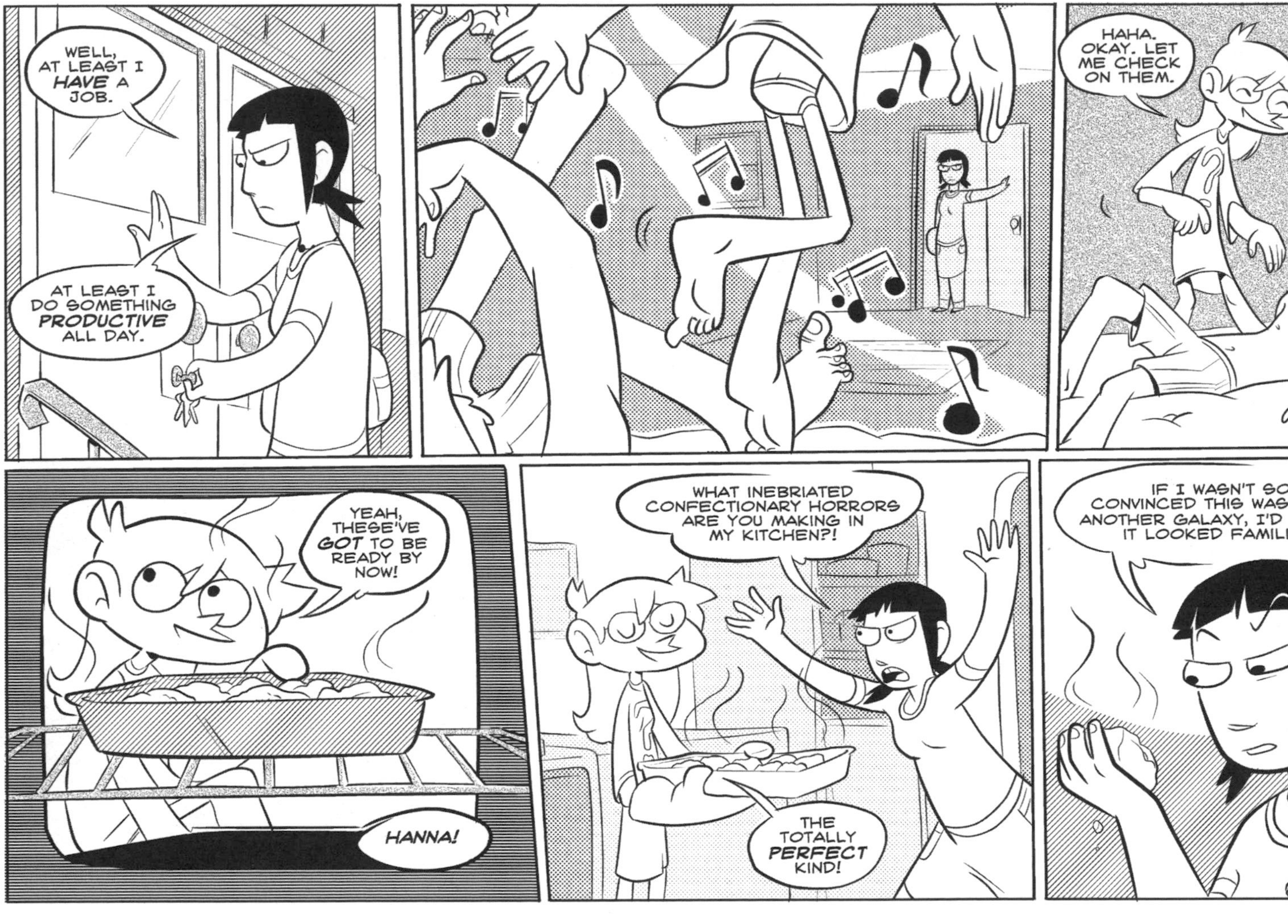
WELL, AT LEAST I HAVE A JOB.
AT LEAST I DO SOMETHING PRODUCTIVE ALL DAY.
HAHA. OKAY. LET ME CHECK ON THEM.
YEAH, THESE'VE GOT TO BE READY BY NOW!
HANNA!
WHAT INEBRIATED CONFECTIONARY HORRORS ARE YOU MAKING IN MY KITCHEN?!
THE TOTALLY PERFECT KIND!
IF I WASN'T SO CONVINCED THIS WAS FROM ANOTHER GALAXY, I'D SWEAR IT LOOKED FAMILIAR.

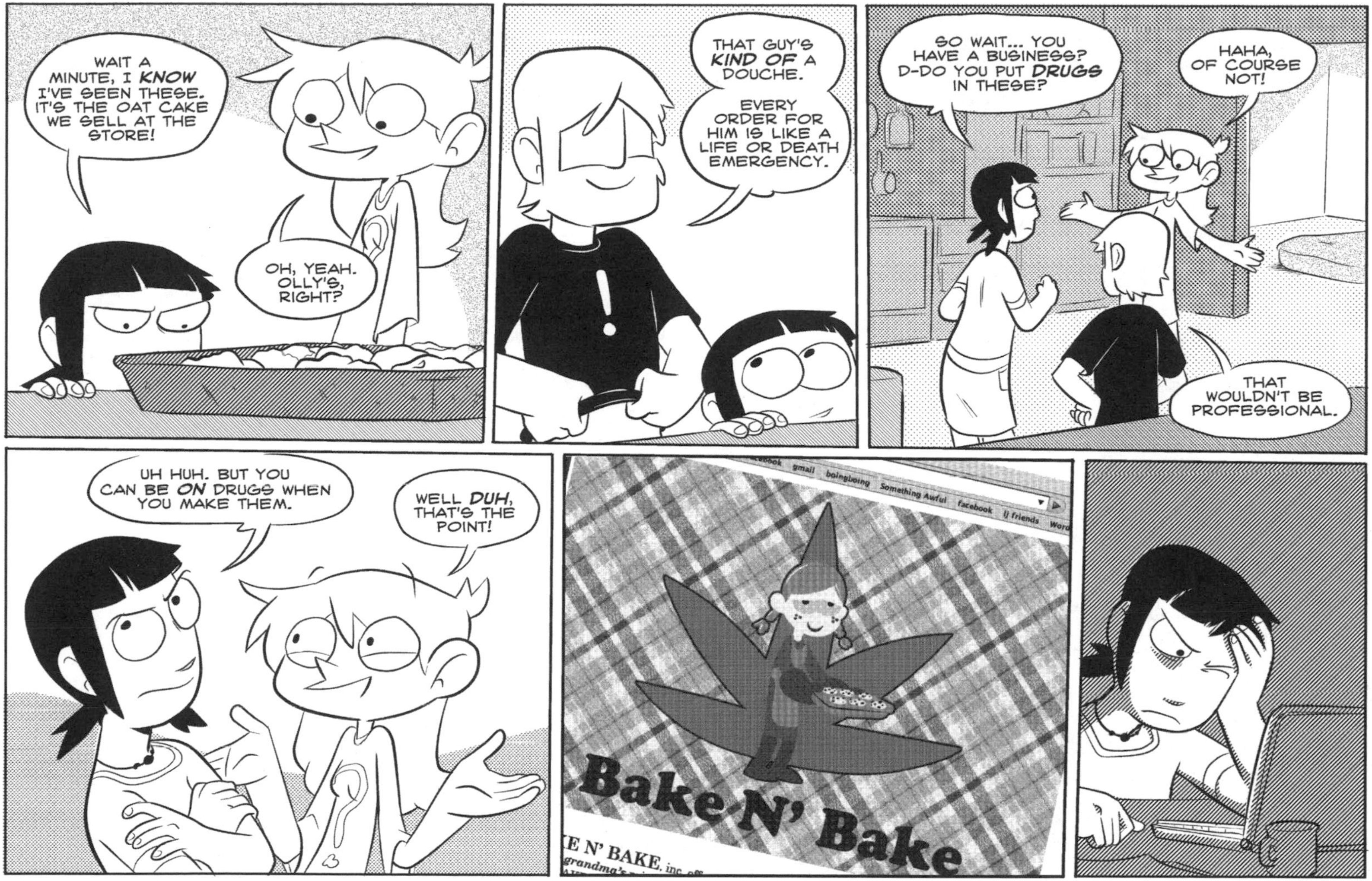
WAIT A MINUTE, I KNOW I'VE SEEN THESE. IT'S THE OAT CAKE WE SELL AT THE STORE!
OH, YEAH. OLLY'S, RIGHT?
THAT GUY'S KIND OF A DOUCHE.
EVERY ORDER FOR HIM IS LIKE A LIFE OR DEATH EMERGENCY.
SO WAIT... YOU HAVE A BUSINESS? D-DO YOU PUT DRUGS IN THESE?
HAHA, OF COURSE NOT!
THAT WOULDN'T BE PROFESSIONAL.
UH HUH. BUT YOU CAN BE ON DRUGS WHEN YOU MAKE THEM.
WELL DUH, THAT'S THE POINT!
gmail
boingboing
Something Awful
facebook
lj friends
Bake N' Bake

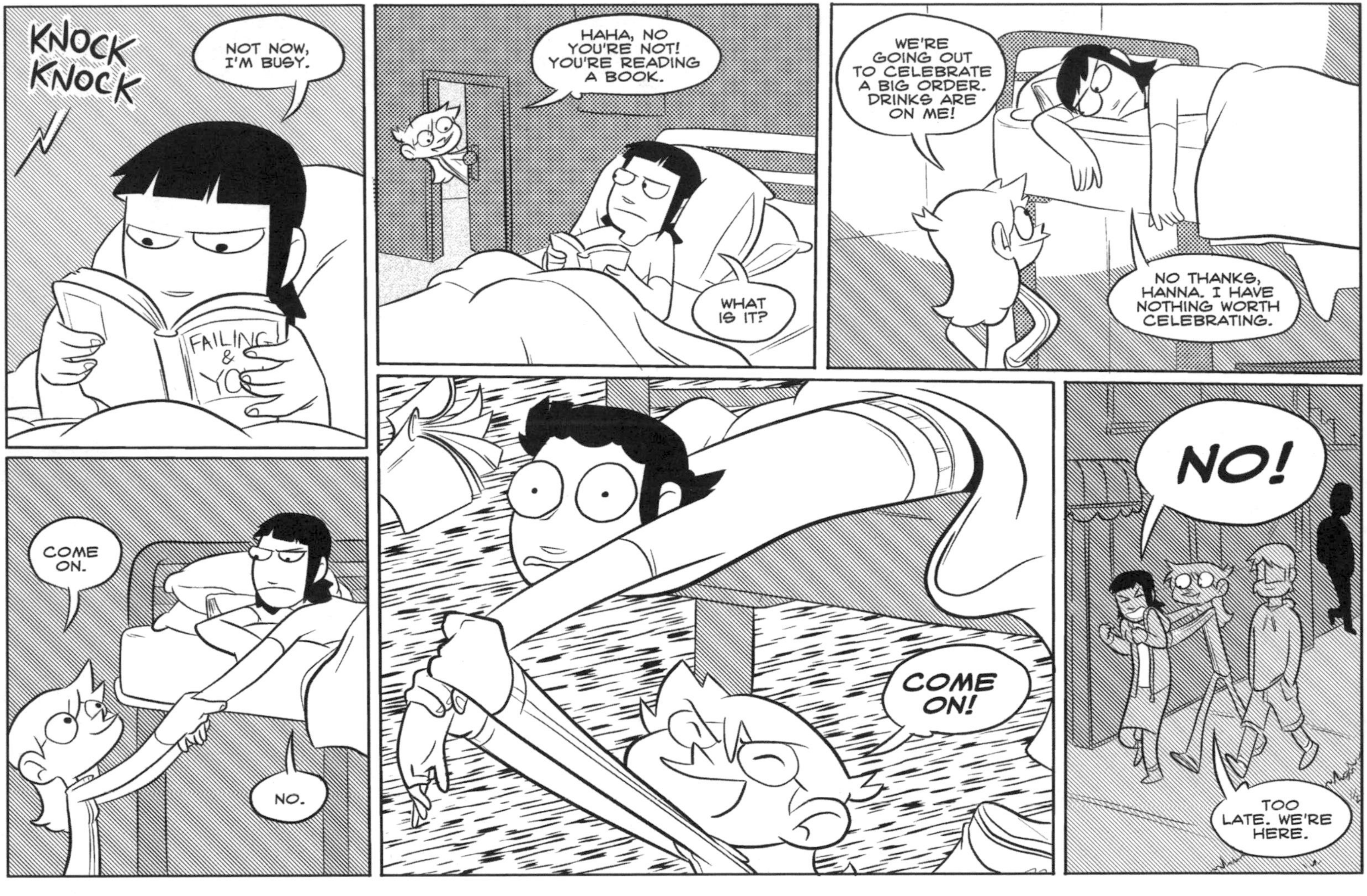
KNOCK KNOCK
NOT NOW, I'M BUSY.
FAILING & YOU
HAHA, NO YOU'RE NOT! YOU'RE READING A BOOK.
WHAT IS IT?
WE'RE GOING OUT TO CELEBRATE A BIG ORDER. DRINKS ARE ON ME!
NO THANKS, HANNA. I HAVE NOTHING WORTH CELEBRATING.
COME ON.
NO.
COME ON!
NO!
TOO LATE. WE'RE HERE.

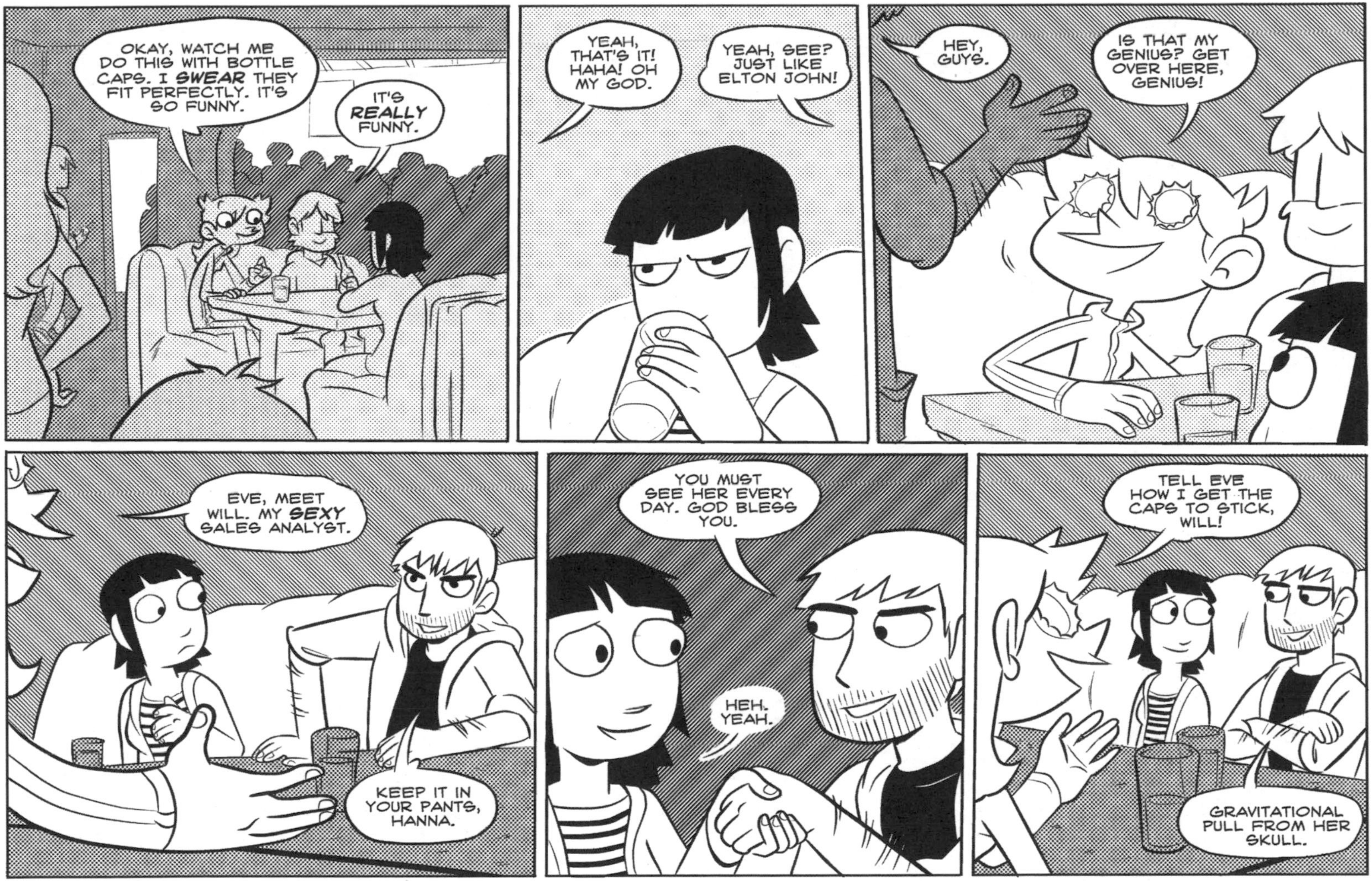
OKAY, WATCH ME DO THIS WITH BOTTLE CAPS. I **SWEAR** THEY FIT PERFECTLY. IT'S SO FUNNY.
IT'S **REALLY** FUNNY.
YEAH, THAT'S IT! HAHA! OH MY GOD.
YEAH, SEE? JUST LIKE ELTON JOHN!
HEY, GUYS.
IS THAT MY GENIUS? GET OVER HERE, GENIUS!
EVE, MEET WILL. MY **SEXY** SALES ANALYST.
KEEP IT IN YOUR PANTS, HANNA.
YOU MUST SEE HER EVERY DAY. GOD BLESS YOU.
HEH. YEAH.
TELL EVE HOW I GET THE CAPS TO STICK, WILL!
GRAVITATIONAL PULL FROM HER SKULL.

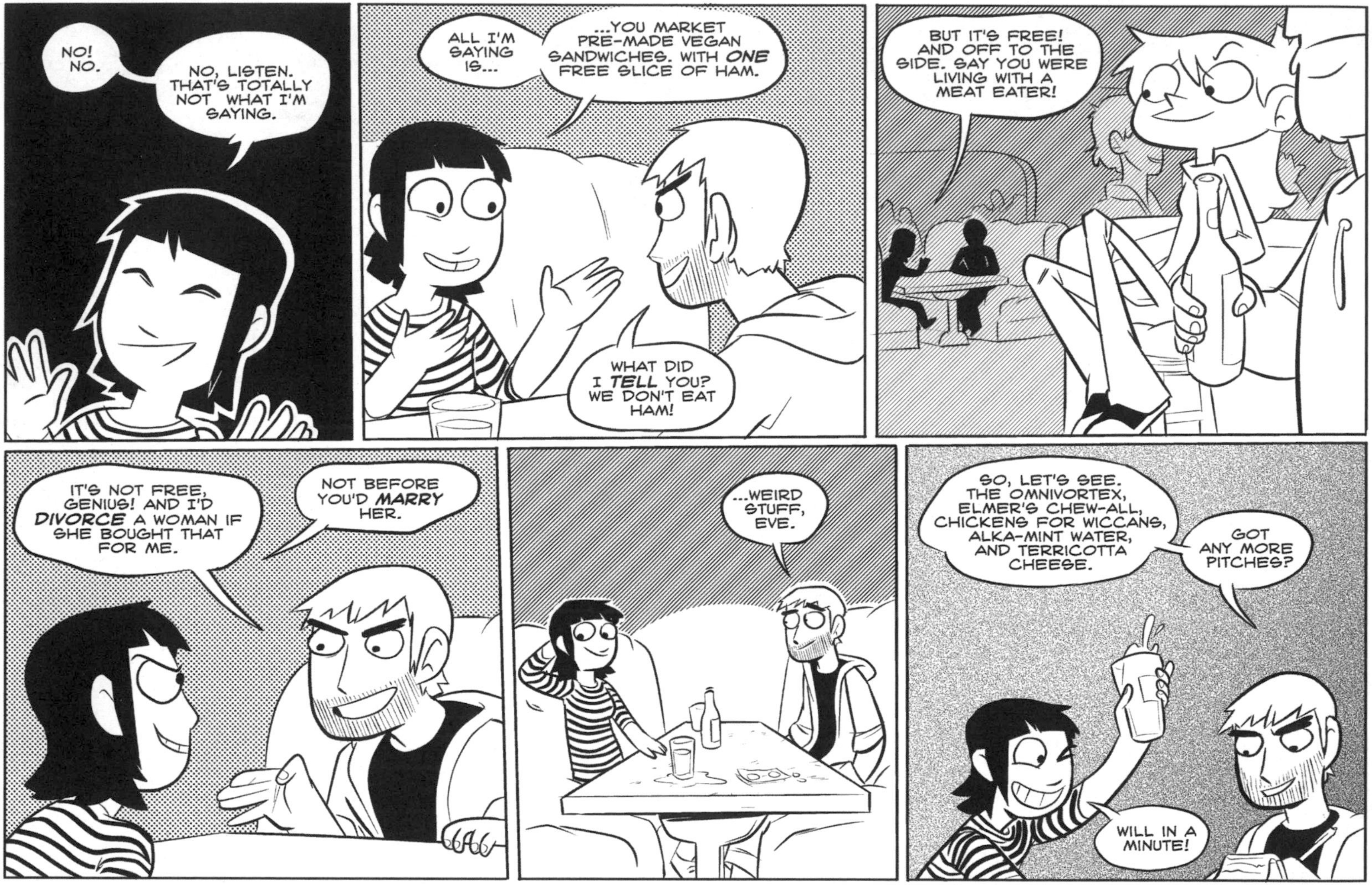

NO! NO.
NO, LISTEN. THAT'S TOTALLY NOT WHAT I'M SAYING.
ALL I'M SAYING IS...
...YOU MARKET PRE-MADE VEGAN SANDWICHES. WITH *ONE* FREE SLICE OF HAM.
WHAT DID I *TELL* YOU? WE DON'T EAT HAM!
BUT IT'S FREE! AND OFF TO THE SIDE. SAY YOU WERE LIVING WITH A MEAT EATER!
IT'S NOT FREE, GENIUS! AND I'D *DIVORCE* A WOMAN IF SHE BOUGHT THAT FOR ME.
NOT BEFORE YOU'D *MARRY* HER.
...WEIRD STUFF, EVE.
SO, LET'S SEE. THE OMNIVORTEX, ELMER'S CHEW-ALL, CHICKENS FOR WICCANS, ALKA-MINT WATER, AND TERRICOTTA CHEESE.
GOT ANY MORE PITCHES?
WILL IN A MINUTE!

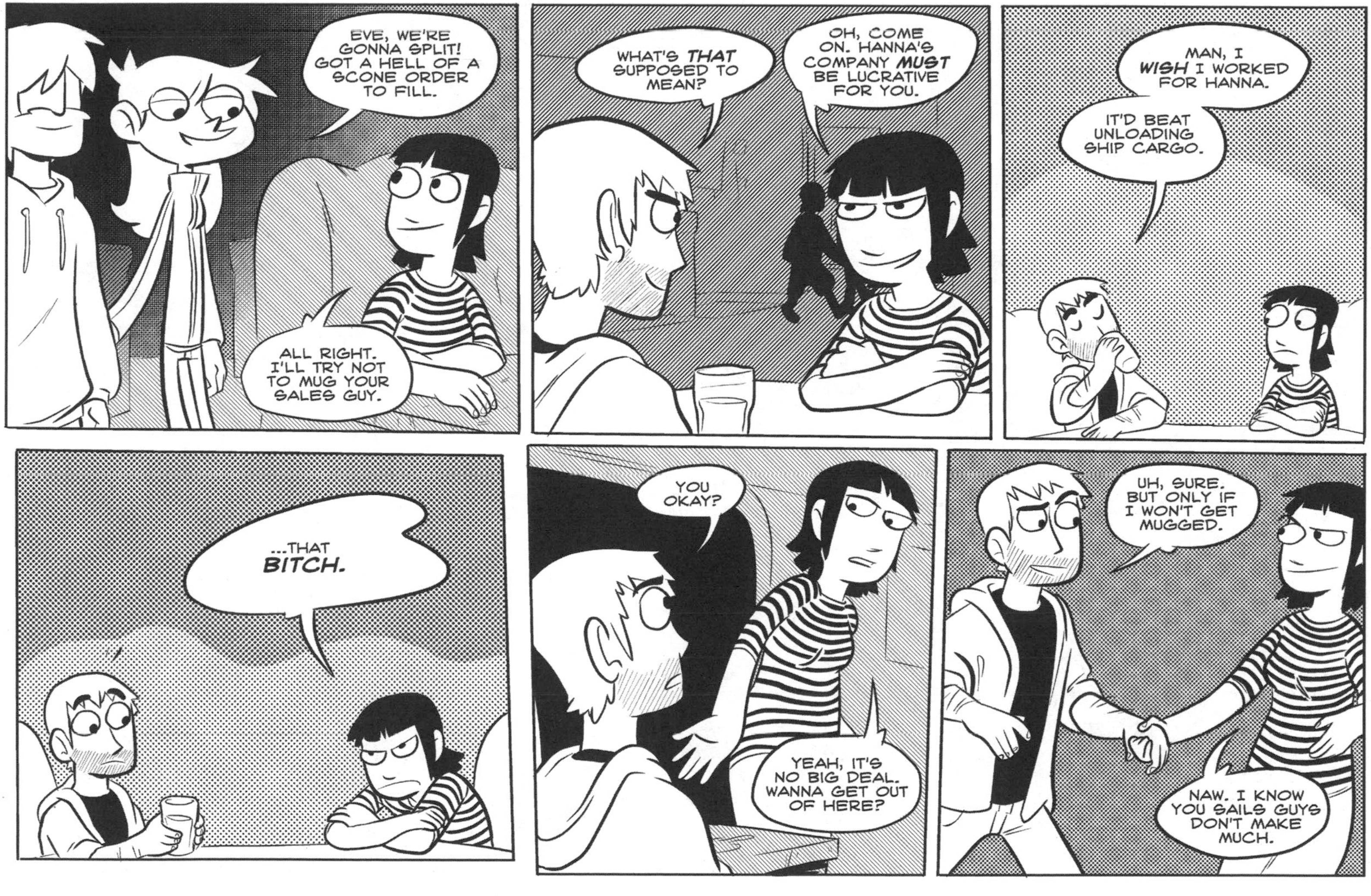
EVE, WE'RE GONNA SPLIT! GOT A HELL OF A SCONE ORDER TO FILL.
ALL RIGHT. I'LL TRY NOT TO MUG YOUR SALES GUY.
WHAT'S THAT SUPPOSED TO MEAN?
OH, COME ON. HANNA'S COMPANY MUST BE LUCRATIVE FOR YOU.
MAN, I WISH I WORKED FOR HANNA.
IT'D BEAT UNLOADING SHIP CARGO.
...THAT BITCH.
YOU OKAY?
YEAH, IT'S NO BIG DEAL. WANNA GET OUT OF HERE?
UH, SURE. BUT ONLY IF I WON'T GET MUGGED.
NAW. I KNOW YOU SAILS GUYS DON'T MAKE MUCH.

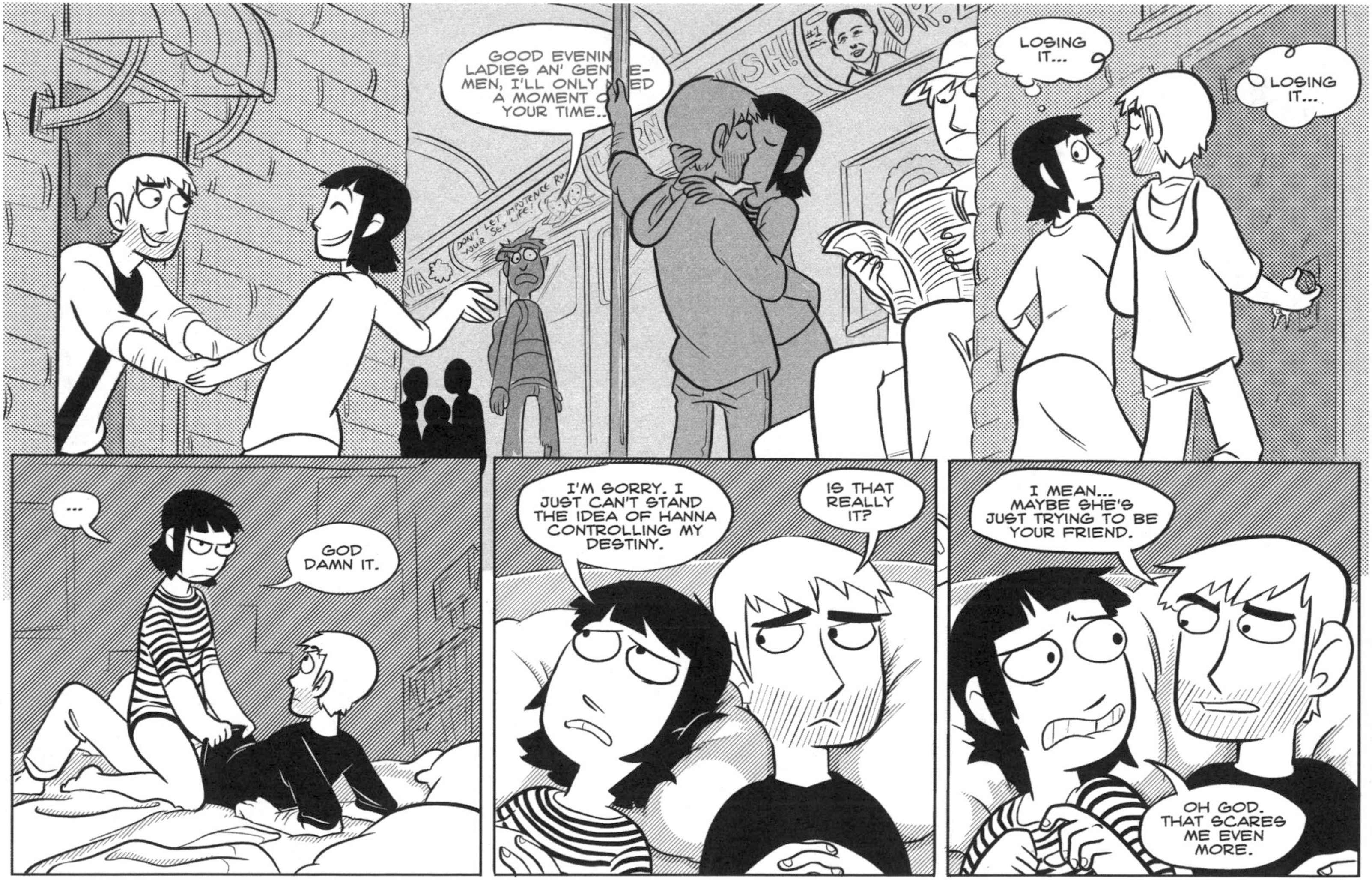
GOOD EVENIN' LADIES AN' GENTLEMEN, I'LL ONLY NEED A MOMENT OF YOUR TIME...
DON'T LET IMPOTENCE RUIN YOUR SEX LIFE!
LOSING IT...
LOSING IT...
...
GOD DAMN IT.
I'M SORRY. I JUST CAN'T STAND THE IDEA OF HANNA CONTROLLING MY DESTINY.
IS THAT REALLY IT?
I MEAN... MAYBE SHE'S JUST TRYING TO BE YOUR FRIEND.
OH GOD. THAT SCARES ME EVEN MORE.

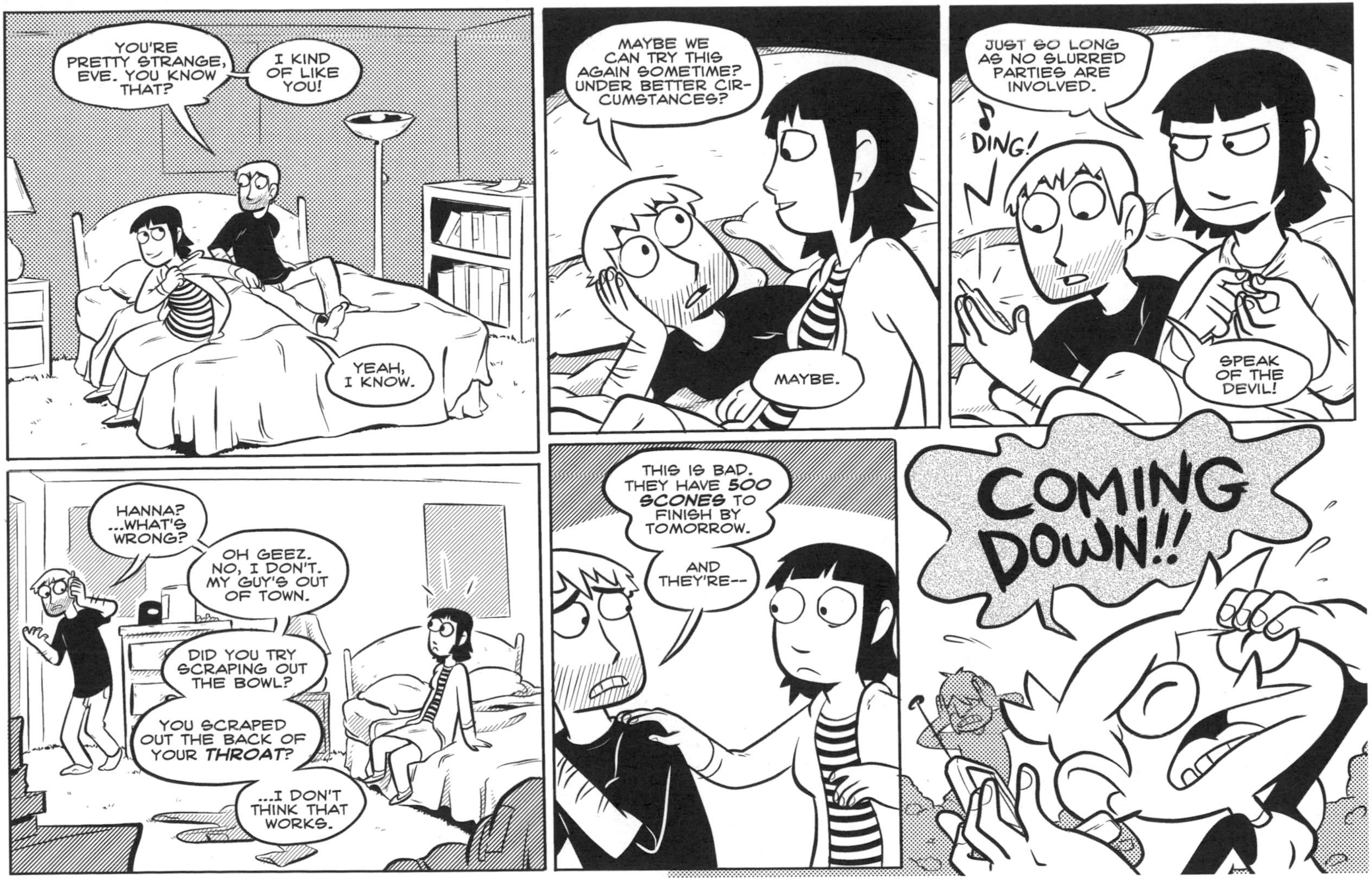

YOU'RE PRETTY STRANGE, EVE. YOU KNOW THAT?
I KIND OF LIKE YOU!
YEAH, I KNOW.
MAYBE WE CAN TRY THIS AGAIN SOMETIME? UNDER BETTER CIR-CUMSTANCES?
MAYBE.
JUST SO LONG AS NO SLURRED PARTIES ARE INVOLVED.
DING!
SPEAK OF THE DEVIL!
HANNA? ...WHAT'S WRONG?
OH GEEZ. NO, I DON'T. MY GUY'S OUT OF TOWN.
DID YOU TRY SCRAPING OUT THE BOWL?
YOU SCRAPED OUT THE BACK OF YOUR THROAT?
...I DON'T THINK THAT WORKS.
THIS IS BAD. THEY HAVE 500 SCONES TO FINISH BY TOMORROW.
AND THEY'RE--
COMING DOWN!!

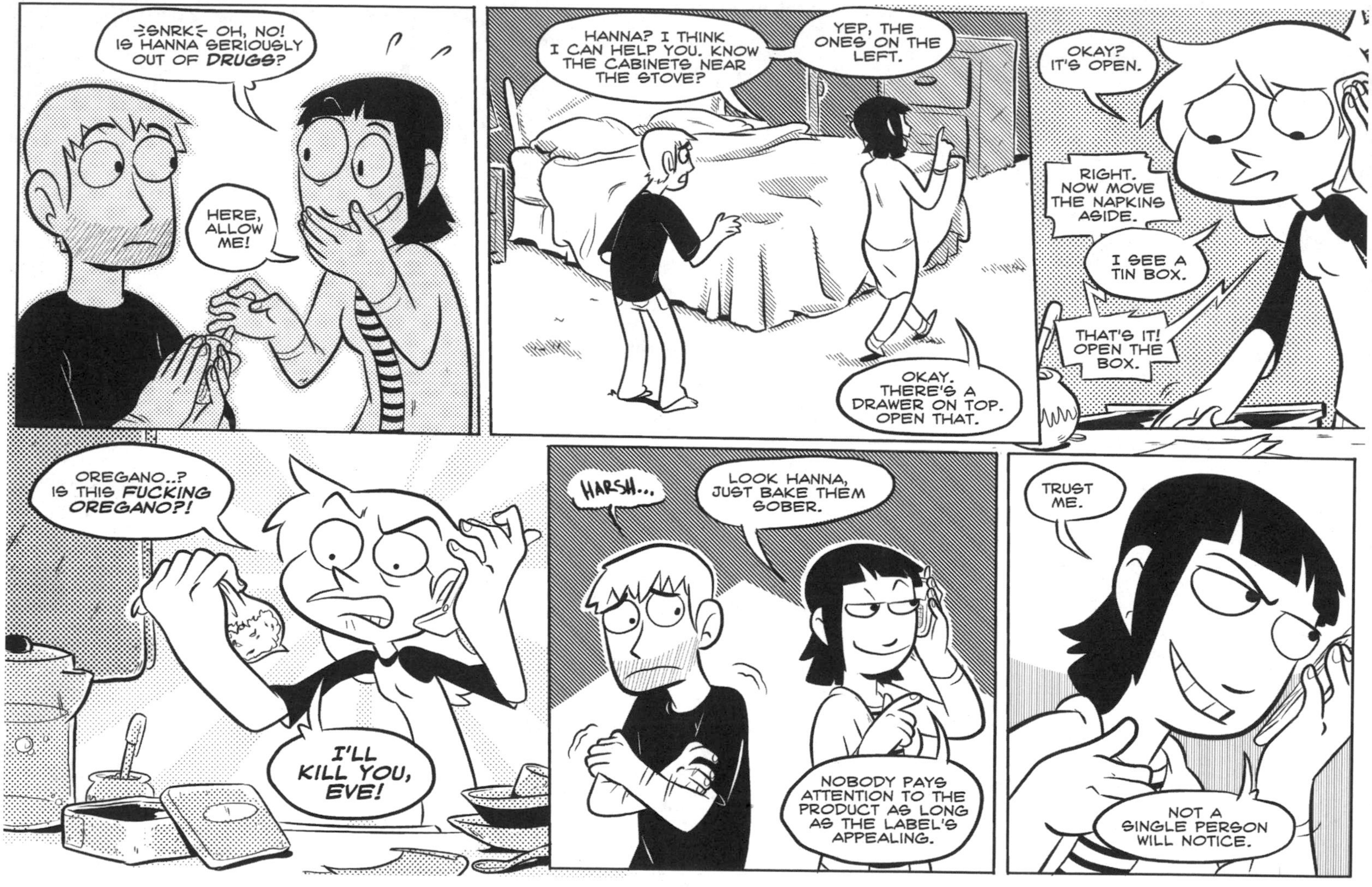

=SNRK= OH, NO! IS HANNA SERIOUSLY OUT OF DRUGS?
HERE, ALLOW ME!
HANNA? I THINK I CAN HELP YOU. KNOW THE CABINETS NEAR THE STOVE?
YEP, THE ONES ON THE LEFT.
OKAY. THERE'S A DRAWER ON TOP. OPEN THAT.
OKAY? IT'S OPEN.
RIGHT. NOW MOVE THE NAPKINS ASIDE.
I SEE A TIN BOX.
THAT'S IT! OPEN THE BOX.
OREGANO..? IS THIS FUCKING OREGANO?!
I'LL KILL YOU, EVE!
HARSH...
LOOK HANNA, JUST BAKE THEM SOBER.
NOBODY PAYS ATTENTION TO THE PRODUCT AS LONG AS THE LABEL'S APPEALING.
TRUST ME.
NOT A SINGLE PERSON WILL NOTICE.

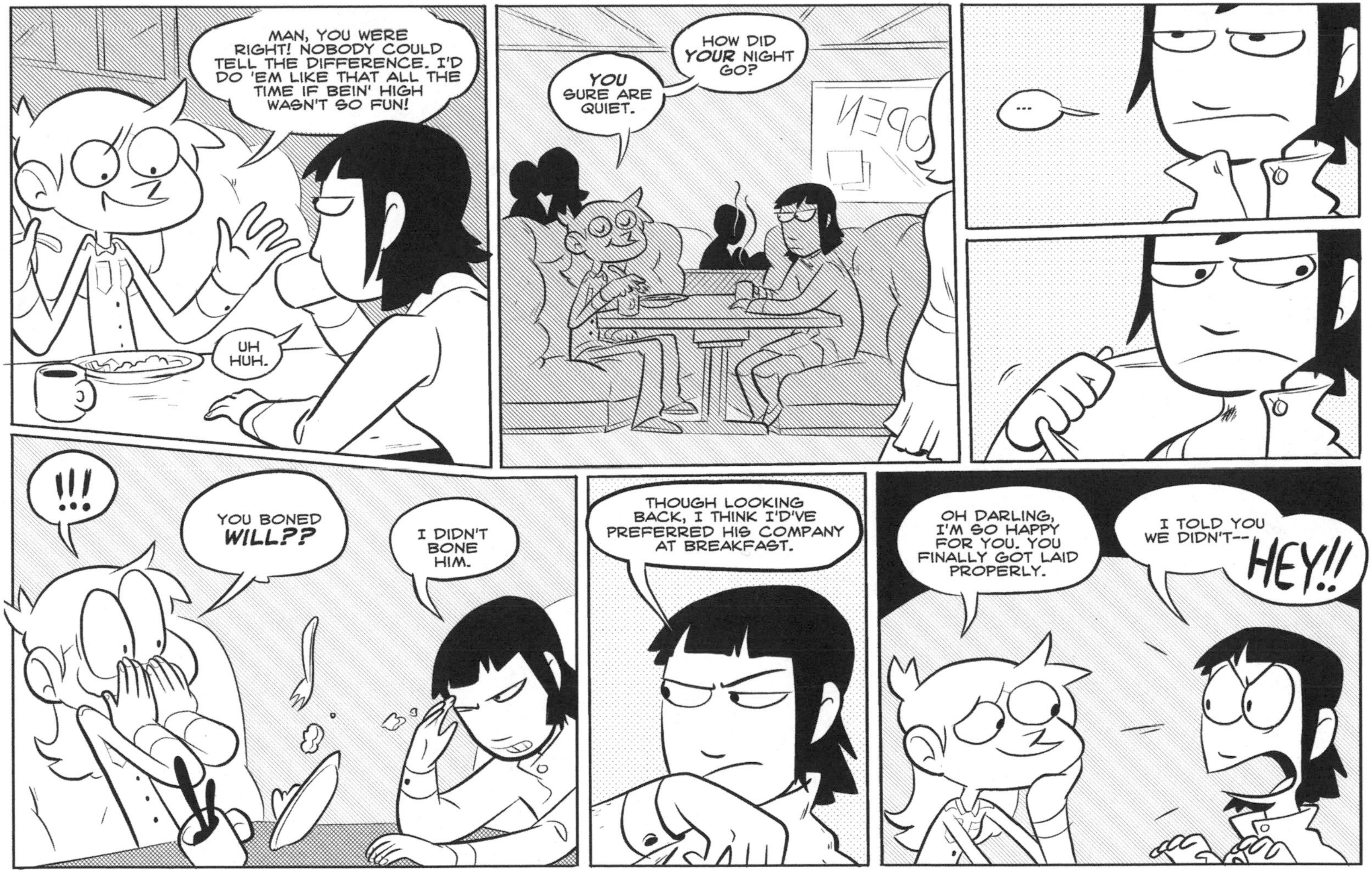
MAN, YOU WERE RIGHT! NOBODY COULD TELL THE DIFFERENCE. I'D DO 'EM LIKE THAT ALL THE TIME IF BEIN' HIGH WASN'T SO FUN!
UH HUH.
YOU SURE ARE QUIET.
HOW DID YOUR NIGHT GO?
OPEN
...
!!!
YOU BONED WILL??
I DIDN'T BONE HIM.
THOUGH LOOKING BACK, I THINK I'D'VE PREFERRED HIS COMPANY AT BREAKFAST.
OH DARLING, I'M SO HAPPY FOR YOU. YOU FINALLY GOT LAID PROPERLY.
I TOLD YOU WE DIDN'T--
HEY!!

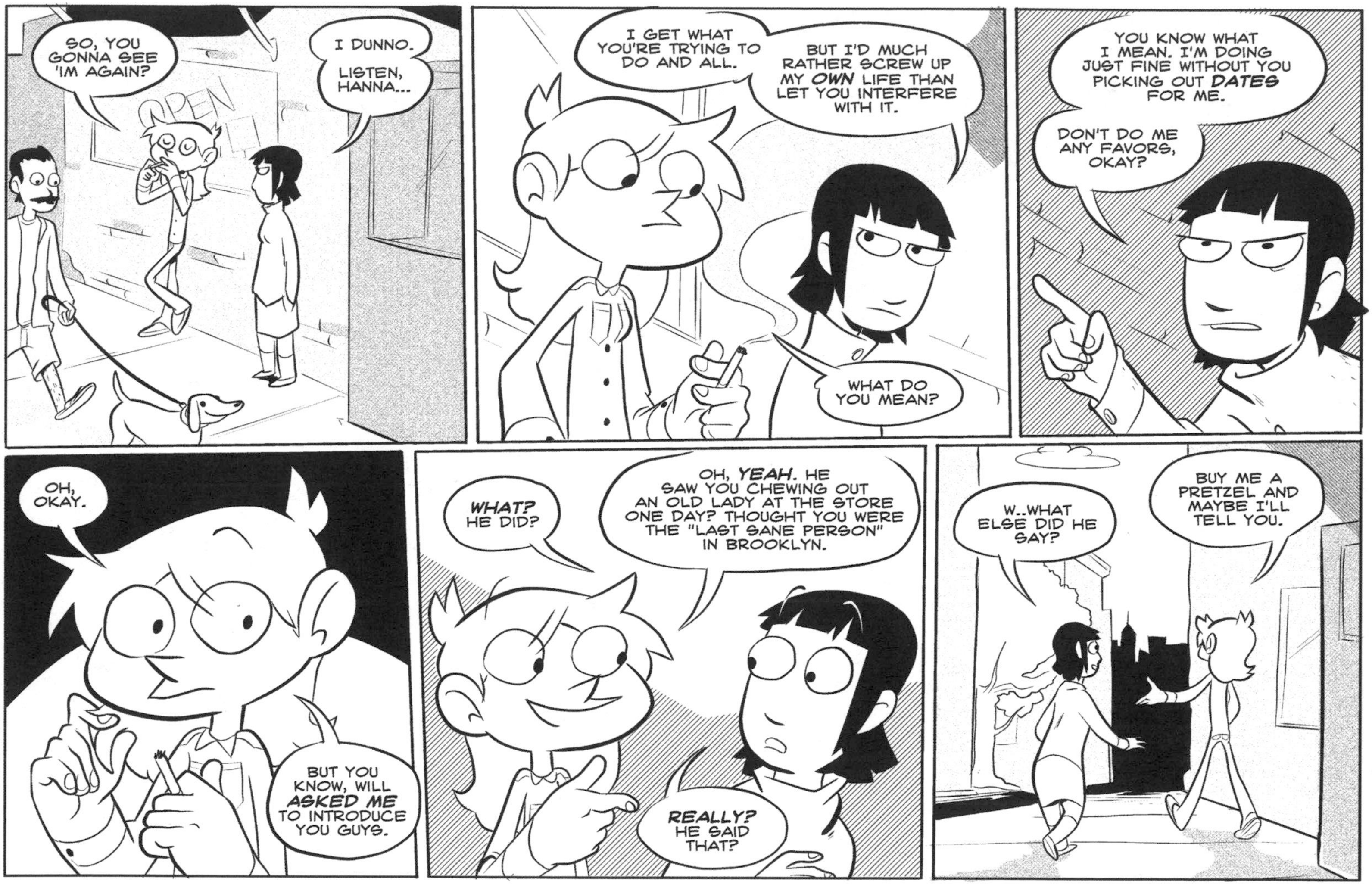
SO, YOU GONNA SEE 'IM AGAIN?
I DUNNO.
LISTEN, HANNA...
OPEN
I GET WHAT YOU'RE TRYING TO DO AND ALL.
BUT I'D MUCH RATHER SCREW UP MY *OWN* LIFE THAN LET YOU INTERFERE WITH IT.
WHAT DO YOU MEAN?
YOU KNOW WHAT I MEAN. I'M DOING JUST FINE WITHOUT YOU PICKING OUT *DATES* FOR ME.
DON'T DO ME ANY FAVORS, OKAY?
OH, OKAY.
BUT YOU KNOW, WILL *ASKED ME* TO INTRODUCE YOU GUYS.
WHAT? HE DID?
OH, *YEAH*. HE SAW YOU CHEWING OUT AN OLD LADY AT THE STORE ONE DAY? THOUGHT YOU WERE THE "LAST SANE PERSON" IN BROOKLYN.
REALLY? HE SAID THAT?
W..WHAT ELSE DID HE SAY?
BUY ME A PRETZEL AND MAYBE I'LL TELL YOU.

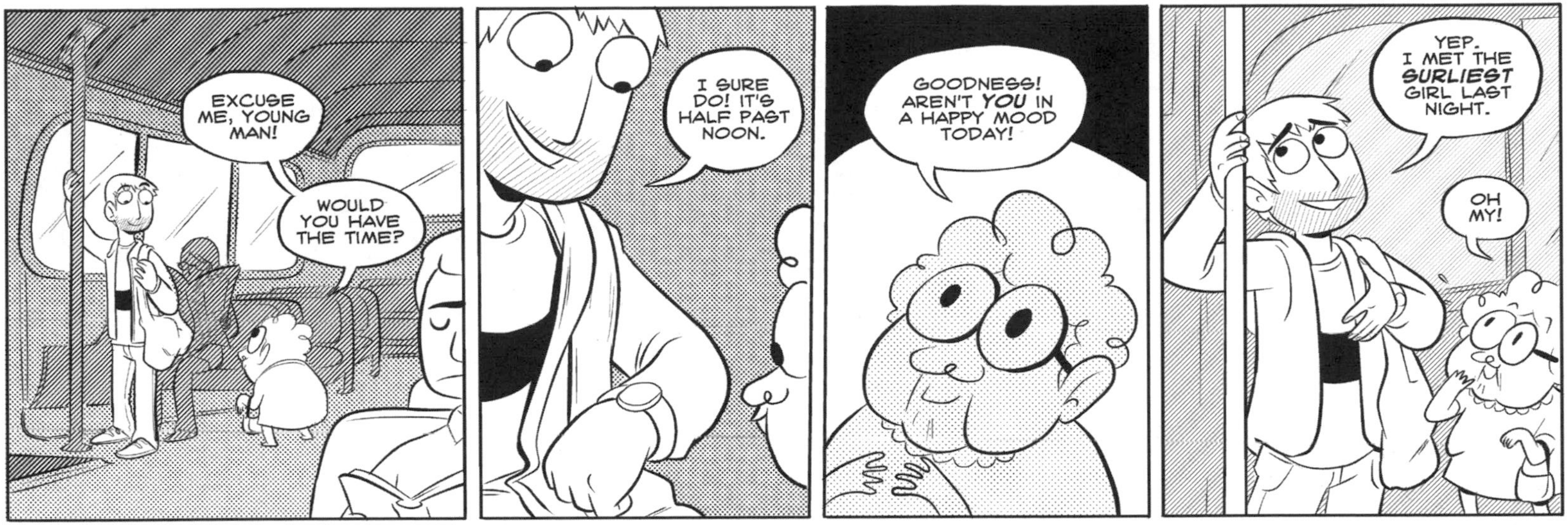
EXCUSE ME, YOUNG MAN!
WOULD YOU HAVE THE TIME?
I SURE DO! IT'S HALF PAST NOON.
GOODNESS! AREN'T **YOU** IN A HAPPY MOOD TODAY!
YEP. I MET THE **SURLIEST** GIRL LAST NIGHT.
OH MY!

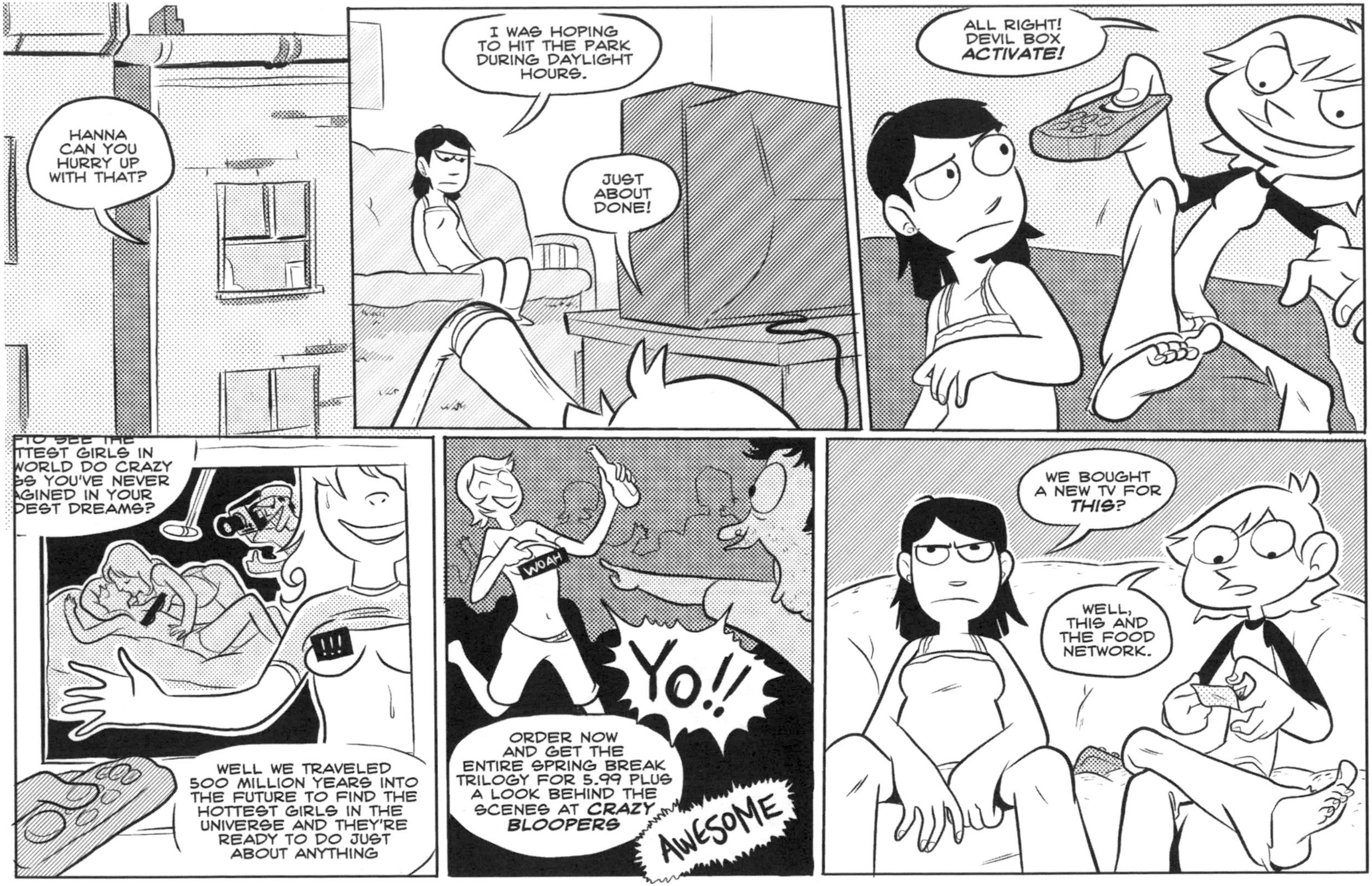
HANNA CAN YOU HURRY UP WITH THAT?
I WAS HOPING TO HIT THE PARK DURING DAYLIGHT HOURS.
JUST ABOUT DONE!
ALL RIGHT! DEVIL BOX ACTIVATE!
TTEST GIRLS IN WORLD DO CRAZY GS YOU'VE NEVER AGINED IN YOUR DEST DREAMS?
!!!
WELL WE TRAVELED 500 MILLION YEARS INTO THE FUTURE TO FIND THE HOTTEST GIRLS IN THE UNIVERSE AND THEY'RE READY TO DO JUST ABOUT ANYTHING
WOAH
YO!!
ORDER NOW AND GET THE ENTIRE SPRING BREAK TRILOGY FOR 5.99 PLUS A LOOK BEHIND THE SCENES AT CRAZY BLOOPERS
AWESOME
WE BOUGHT A NEW TV FOR THIS?
WELL, THIS AND THE FOOD NETWORK.

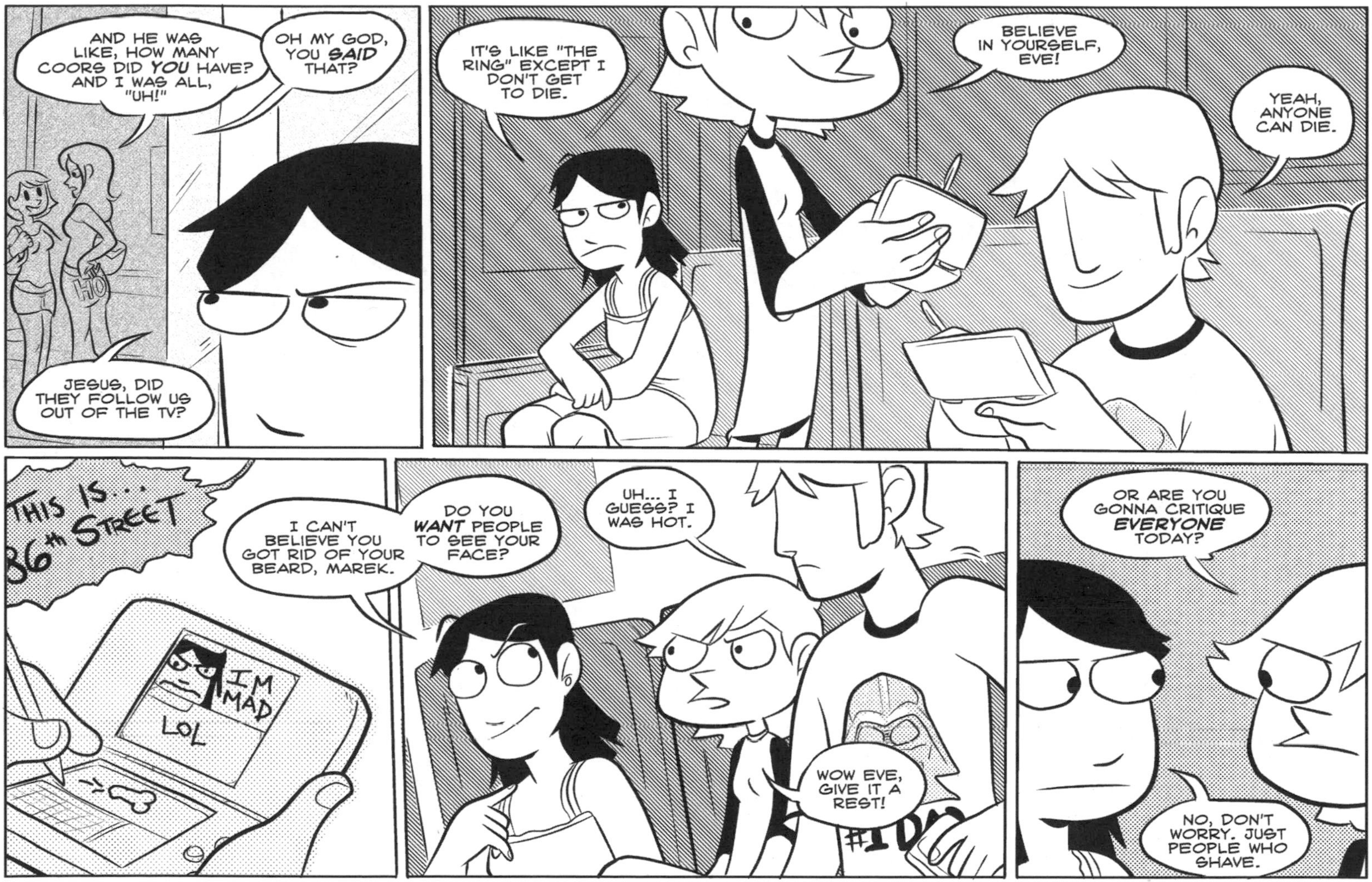
AND HE WAS LIKE, HOW MANY COORS DID YOU HAVE? AND I WAS ALL, "UH!"
OH MY GOD, YOU SAID THAT?
JESUS, DID THEY FOLLOW US OUT OF THE TV?
HO
IT'S LIKE "THE RING" EXCEPT I DON'T GET TO DIE.
BELIEVE IN YOURSELF, EVE!
YEAH, ANYONE CAN DIE.
THIS IS... 86th STREET
IM MAD
LOL
I CAN'T BELIEVE YOU GOT RID OF YOUR BEARD, MAREK.
DO YOU WANT PEOPLE TO SEE YOUR FACE?
UH... I GUESS? I WAS HOT.
WOW EVE, GIVE IT A REST!
OR ARE YOU GONNA CRITIQUE EVERYONE TODAY?
NO, DON'T WORRY. JUST PEOPLE WHO SHAVE.

WELCOME TO MY SUPAH MARKET! CASH ONLY.
IS YOUR BREAD GLUTEN FREE? I HAVE A DISEASE, MISS.
JEREMY. WHERE DID YOU HEAR THAT TRASH?!
THE MAN IN THE STORE.
GOD DAMN IT!
I SWEAR I'M GOING TO CLOCK THE NEXT GRANOLA FACED, TREE-FUCKING HIPPIE I SEE.

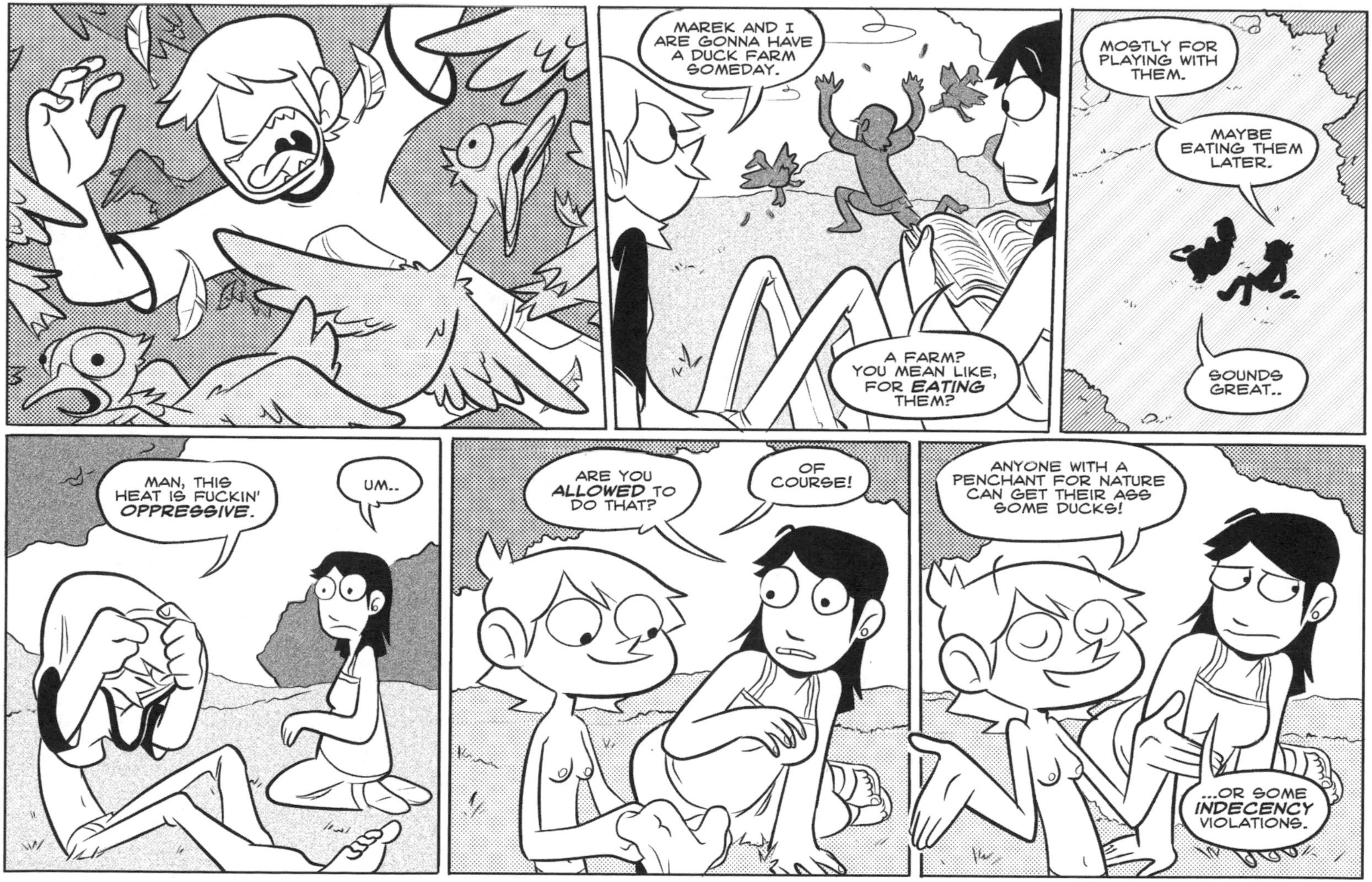
MAREK AND I ARE GONNA HAVE A DUCK FARM SOMEDAY.
A FARM? YOU MEAN LIKE, FOR EATING THEM?
MOSTLY FOR PLAYING WITH THEM.
MAYBE EATING THEM LATER.
SOUNDS GREAT..
MAN, THIS HEAT IS FUCKIN' OPPRESSIVE.
UM..
ARE YOU ALLOWED TO DO THAT?
OF COURSE!
ANYONE WITH A PENCHANT FOR NATURE CAN GET THEIR ASS SOME DUCKS!
...OR SOME INDECENCY VIOLATIONS.

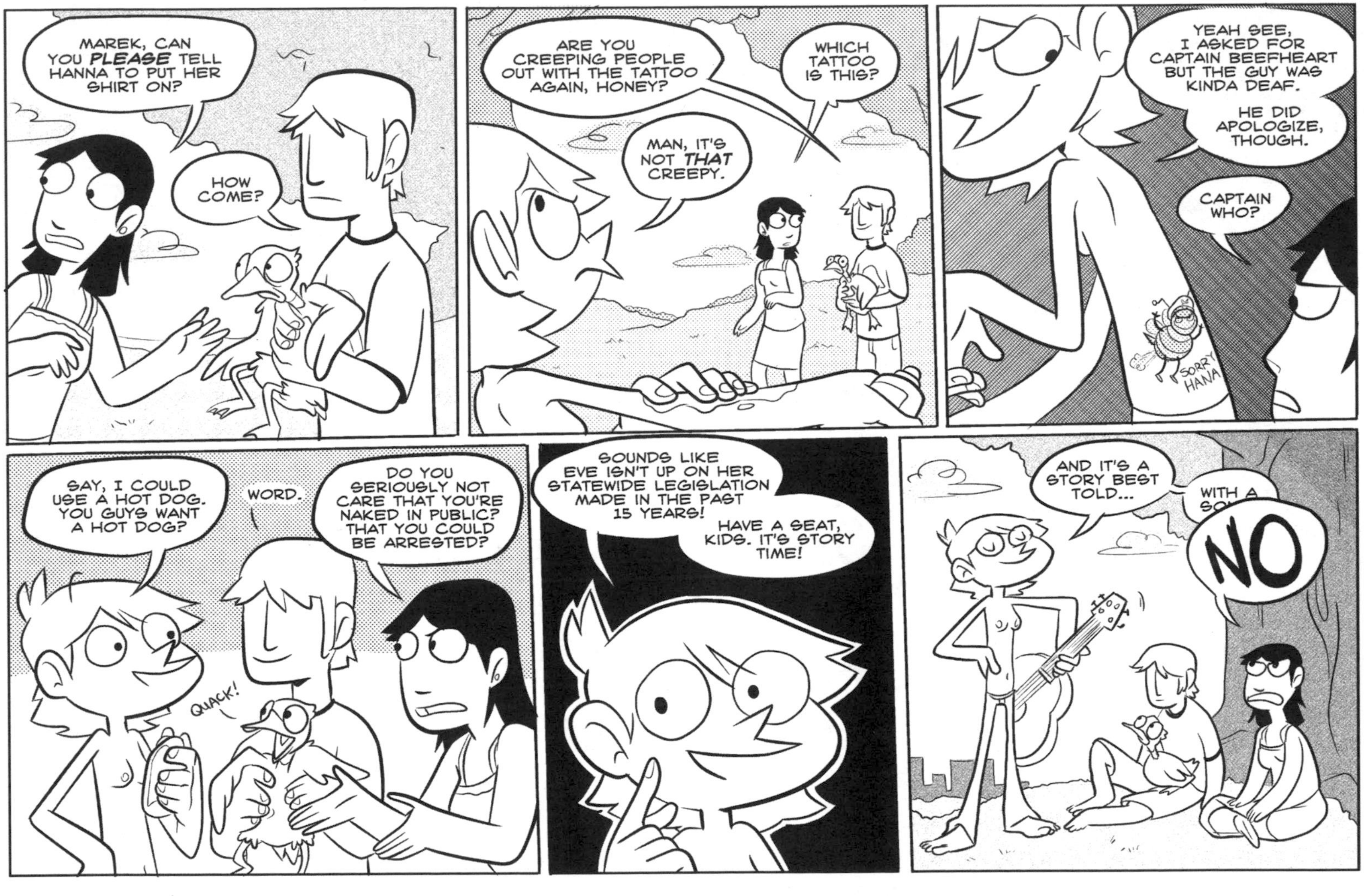
MAREK, CAN YOU *PLEASE* TELL HANNA TO PUT HER SHIRT ON?
HOW COME?
ARE YOU CREEPING PEOPLE OUT WITH THE TATTOO AGAIN, HONEY?
WHICH TATTOO IS THIS?
MAN, IT'S NOT *THAT* CREEPY.
YEAH SEE, I ASKED FOR CAPTAIN BEEFHEART BUT THE GUY WAS KINDA DEAF.
HE DID APOLOGIZE, THOUGH.
CAPTAIN WHO?
SORRY HANA
SAY, I COULD USE A HOT DOG. YOU GUYS WANT A HOT DOG?
WORD.
DO YOU SERIOUSLY NOT CARE THAT YOU'RE NAKED IN PUBLIC? THAT YOU COULD BE ARRESTED?
QUACK!
SOUNDS LIKE EVE ISN'T UP ON HER STATEWIDE LEGISLATION MADE IN THE PAST 15 YEARS!
HAVE A SEAT, KIDS. IT'S STORY TIME!
AND IT'S A STORY BEST TOLD...
WITH A
NO

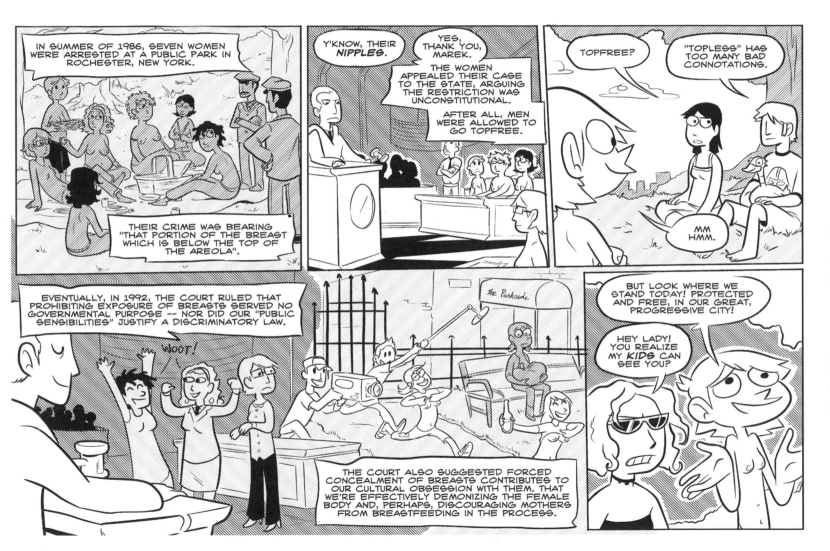

IN SUMMER OF 1986, SEVEN WOMEN WERE ARRESTED AT A PUBLIC PARK IN ROCHESTER, NEW YORK.

THEIR CRIME WAS BEARING "THAT PORTION OF THE BREAST WHICH IS BELOW THE TOP OF THE AREOLA".

Y'KNOW, THEIR *NIPPLES.*

YES, THANK YOU, MAREK.

THE WOMEN APPEALED THEIR CASE TO THE STATE, ARGUING THE RESTRICTION WAS UNCONSTITUTIONAL.

AFTER ALL, MEN WERE ALLOWED TO GO TOPFREE.

TOPFREE?

"TOPLESS" HAS TOO MANY BAD CONNOTATIONS.

MM HMM.

EVENTUALLY, IN 1992, THE COURT RULED THAT PROHIBITING EXPOSURE OF BREASTS SERVED NO GOVERNMENTAL PURPOSE -- NOR DID OUR "PUBLIC SENSIBILITIES" JUSTIFY A DISCRIMINATORY LAW.

WOOT!

the Parkside

THE COURT ALSO SUGGESTED FORCED CONCEALMENT OF BREASTS CONTRIBUTES TO OUR CULTURAL OBSESSION WITH THEM. THAT WE'RE EFFECTIVELY DEMONIZING THE FEMALE BODY AND, PERHAPS, DISCOURAGING MOTHERS FROM BREASTFEEDING IN THE PROCESS.

BUT LOOK WHERE WE STAND TODAY! PROTECTED AND FREE, IN OUR GREAT, PROGRESSIVE CITY!

HEY LADY! YOU REALIZE MY *KIDS* CAN SEE YOU?

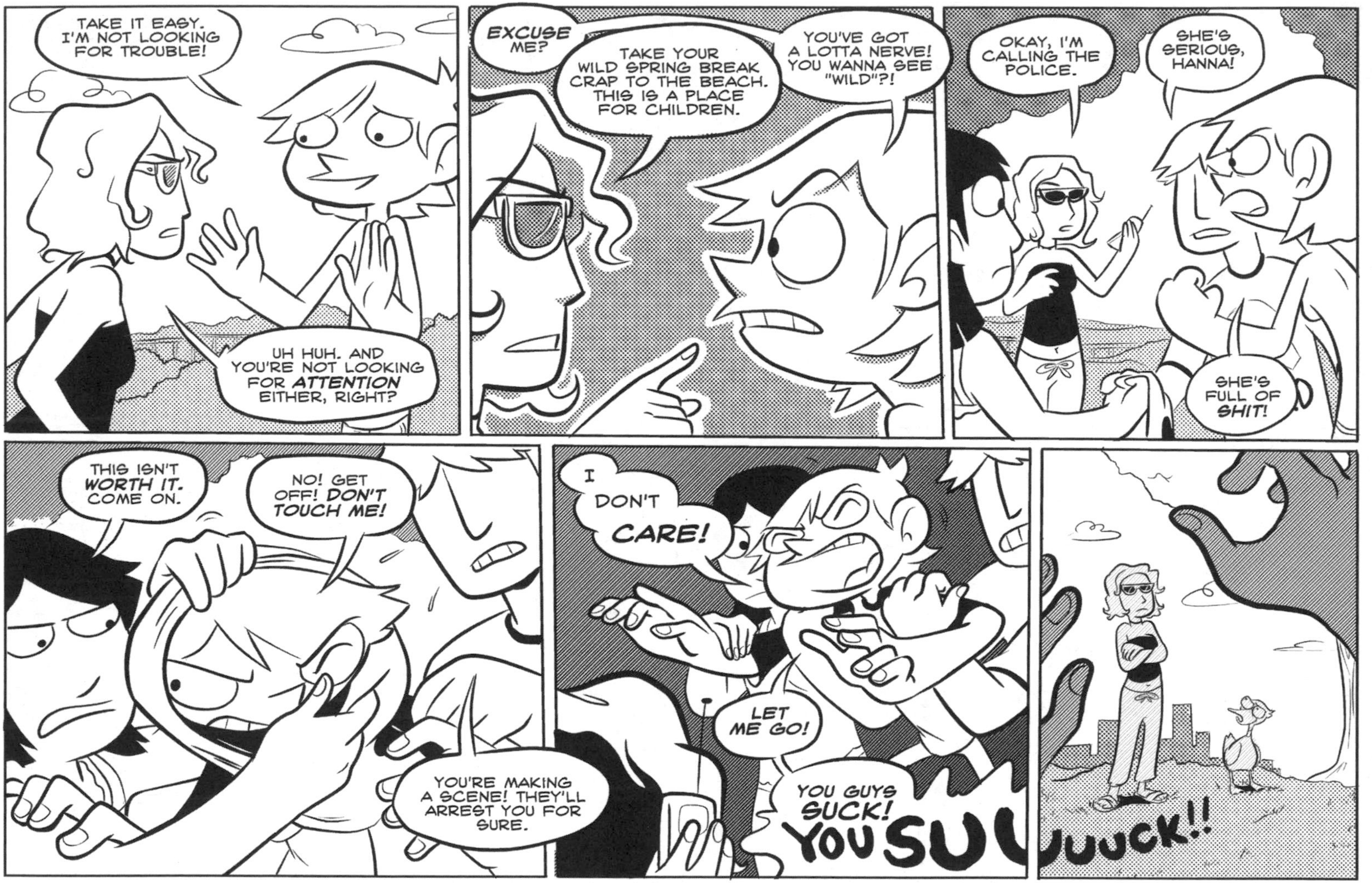
TAKE IT EASY. I'M NOT LOOKING FOR TROUBLE!
UH HUH. AND YOU'RE NOT LOOKING FOR ATTENTION EITHER, RIGHT?
EXCUSE ME?
TAKE YOUR WILD SPRING BREAK CRAP TO THE BEACH. THIS IS A PLACE FOR CHILDREN.
YOU'VE GOT A LOTTA NERVE! YOU WANNA SEE "WILD"?!
OKAY, I'M CALLING THE POLICE.
SHE'S SERIOUS, HANNA!
SHE'S FULL OF SHIT!
THIS ISN'T WORTH IT. COME ON.
NO! GET OFF! DON'T TOUCH ME!
YOU'RE MAKING A SCENE! THEY'LL ARREST YOU FOR SURE.
I DON'T CARE!
LET ME GO!
YOU GUYS SUCK!
YOU SUUUUUCK!!

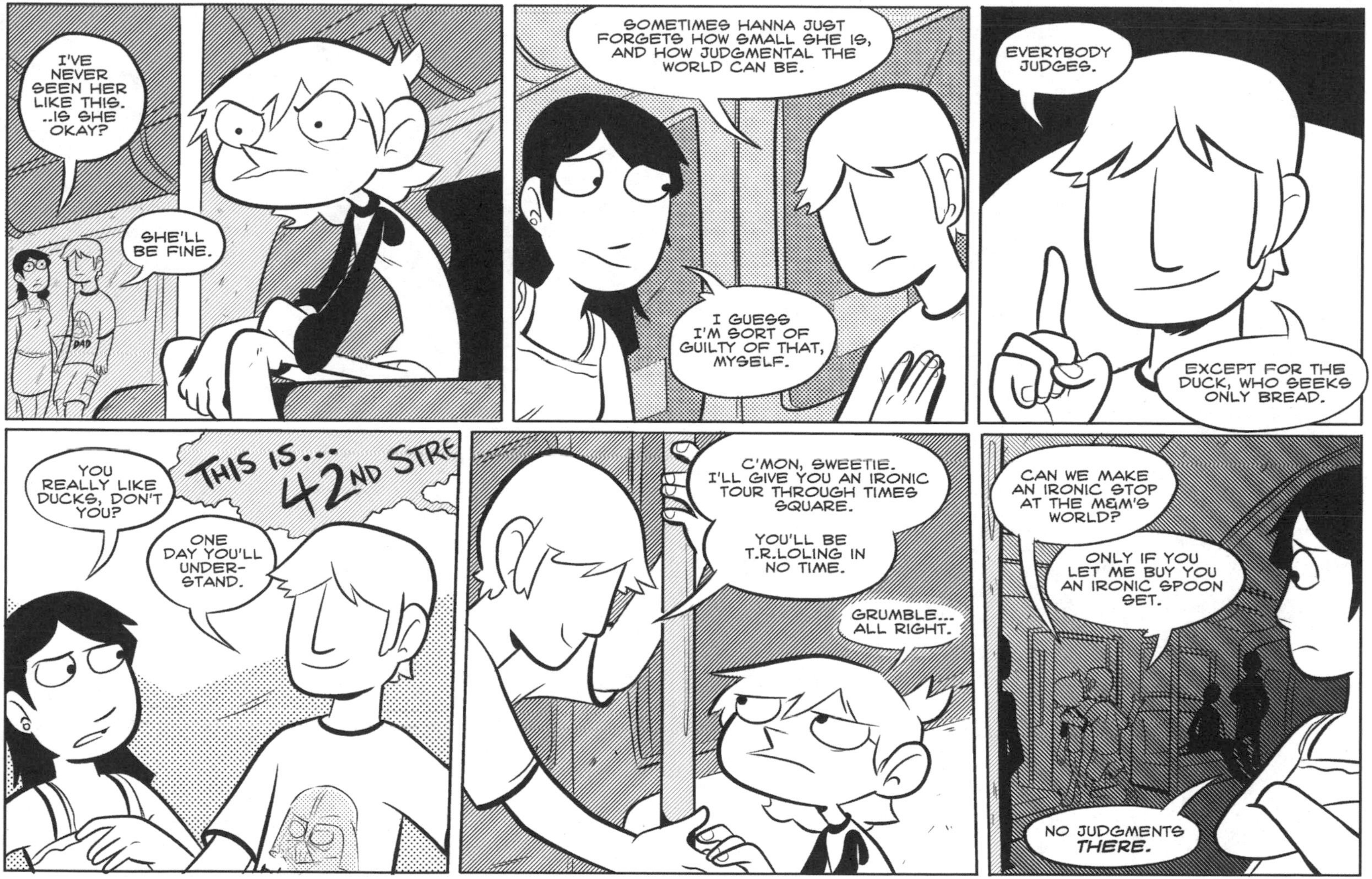
I'VE NEVER SEEN HER LIKE THIS. ..IS SHE OKAY?
SHE'LL BE FINE.
DAD
SOMETIMES HANNA JUST FORGETS HOW SMALL SHE IS, AND HOW JUDGMENTAL THE WORLD CAN BE.
I GUESS I'M SORT OF GUILTY OF THAT, MYSELF.
EVERYBODY JUDGES.
EXCEPT FOR THE DUCK, WHO SEEKS ONLY BREAD.
YOU REALLY LIKE DUCKS, DON'T YOU?
THIS IS... 42ND STRE
ONE DAY YOU'LL UNDER-STAND.
C'MON, SWEETIE. I'LL GIVE YOU AN IRONIC TOUR THROUGH TIMES SQUARE.
YOU'LL BE T.R.LOLING IN NO TIME.
GRUMBLE... ALL RIGHT.
CAN WE MAKE AN IRONIC STOP AT THE M&M'S WORLD?
ONLY IF YOU LET ME BUY YOU AN IRONIC SPOON SET.
NO JUDGMENTS THERE.

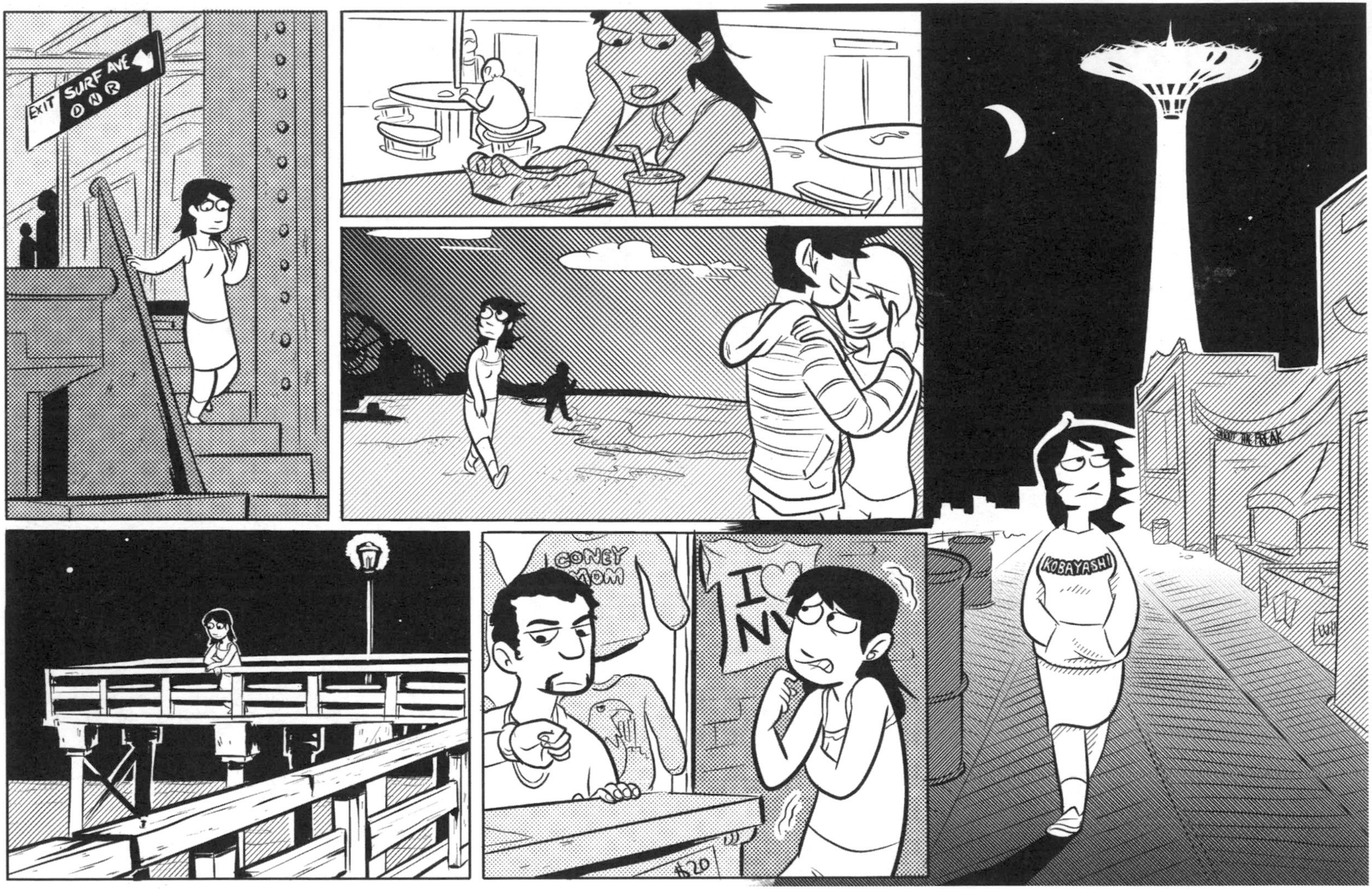
EXIT
SURF AVE
D N R
CONEY MOM
I ♥ NY
$20
SHOOT THE FREAK
KOBAYASHI

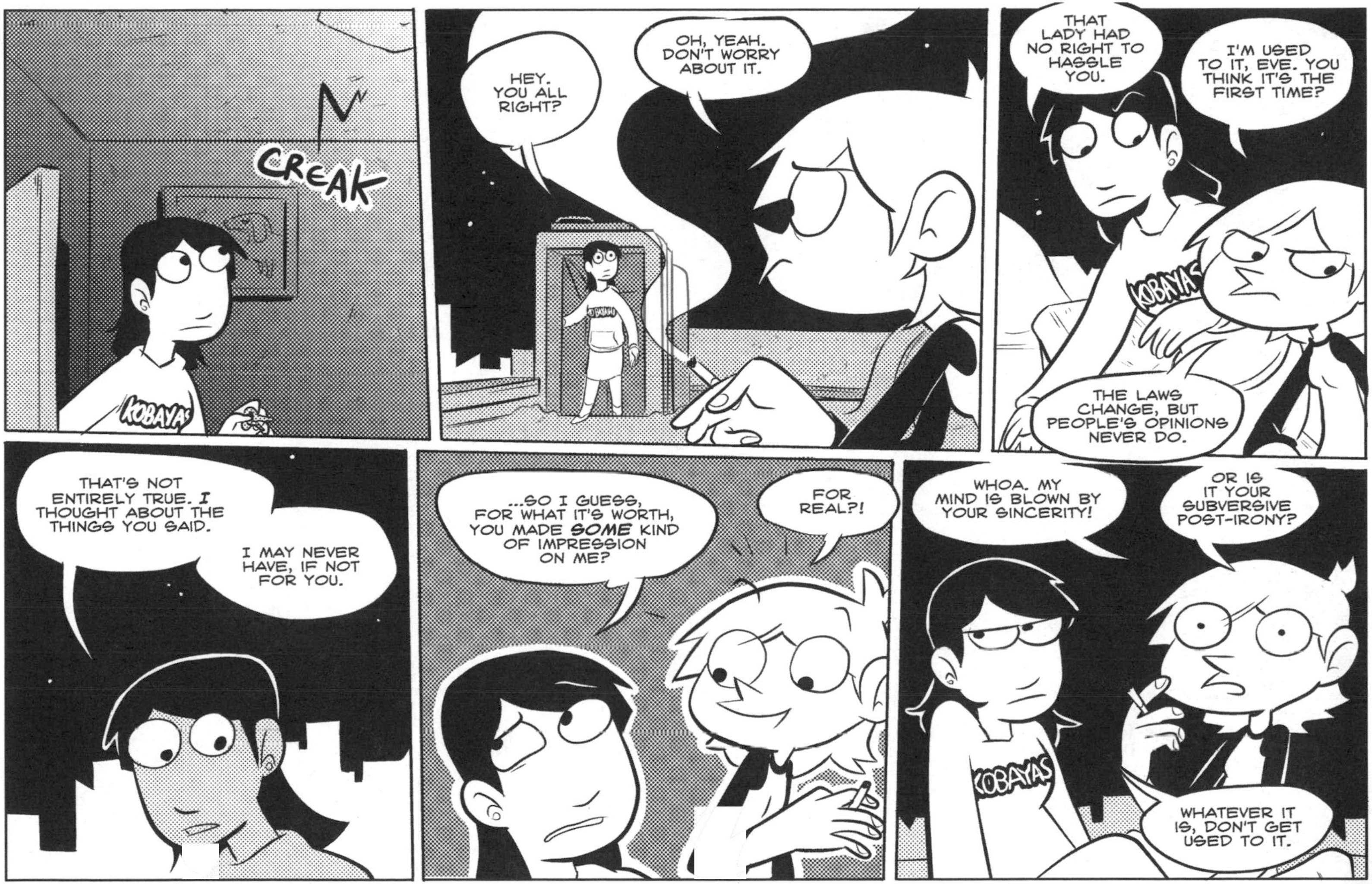
CREAK
HEY. YOU ALL RIGHT?
OH, YEAH. DON'T WORRY ABOUT IT.
THAT LADY HAD NO RIGHT TO HASSLE YOU.
I'M USED TO IT, EVE. YOU THINK IT'S THE FIRST TIME?
THE LAWS CHANGE, BUT PEOPLE'S OPINIONS NEVER DO.
THAT'S NOT ENTIRELY TRUE. *I* THOUGHT ABOUT THE THINGS YOU SAID.
I MAY NEVER HAVE, IF NOT FOR YOU.
...SO I GUESS, FOR WHAT IT'S WORTH, YOU MADE **SOME** KIND OF IMPRESSION ON ME?
FOR REAL?!
WHOA. MY MIND IS BLOWN BY YOUR SINCERITY!
OR IS IT YOUR SUBVERSIVE POST-IRONY?
WHATEVER IT IS, DON'T GET USED TO IT.

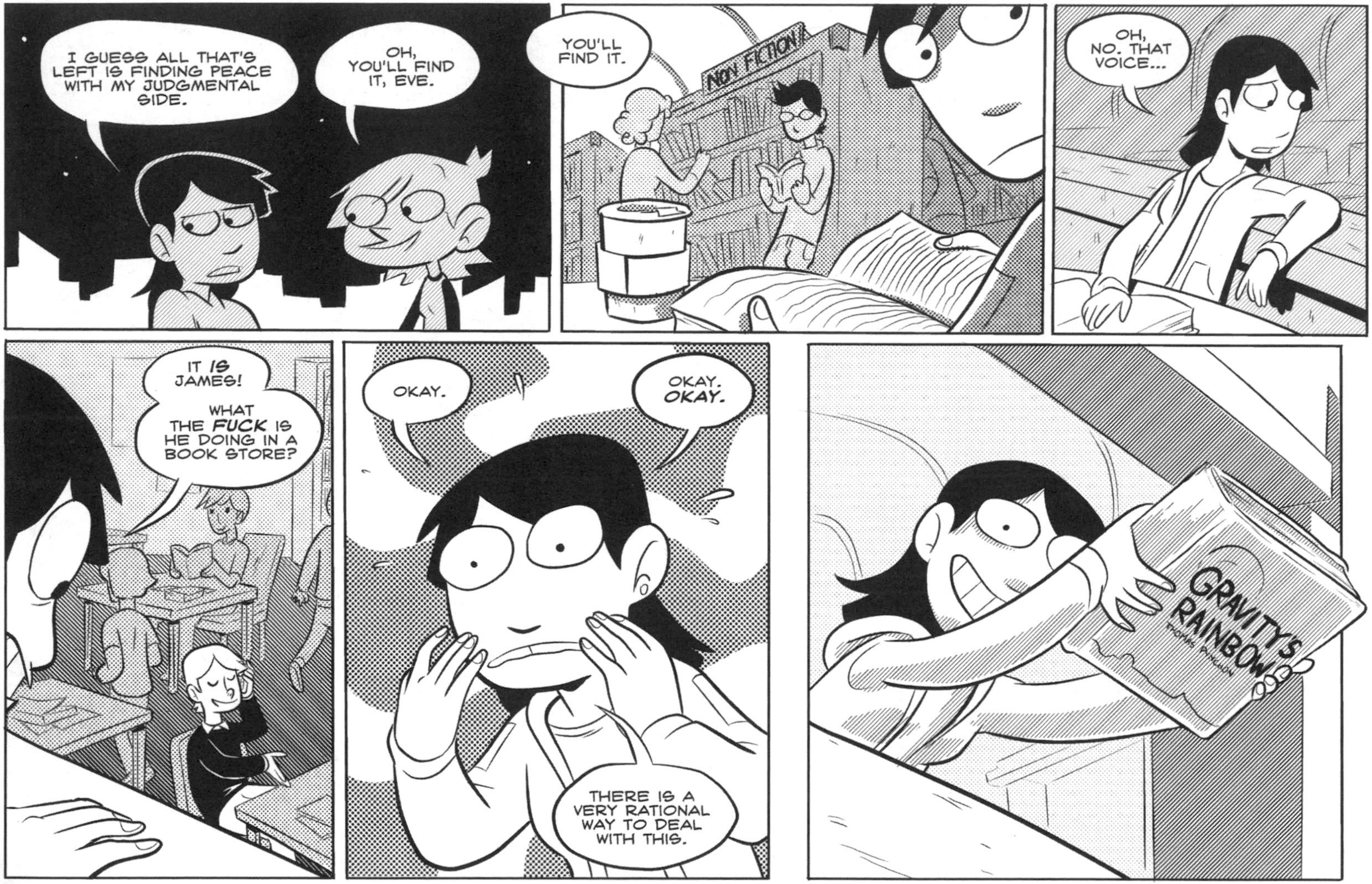
I GUESS ALL THAT'S LEFT IS FINDING PEACE WITH MY JUDGMENTAL SIDE.
OH, YOU'LL FIND IT, EVE.
YOU'LL FIND IT.
NON FICTION
OH, NO. THAT VOICE...
IT *IS* JAMES!
WHAT THE ***FUCK*** IS HE DOING IN A BOOK STORE?
OKAY.
OKAY. ***OKAY.***
THERE IS A VERY RATIONAL WAY TO DEAL WITH THIS.
GRAVITY'S RAINBOW
THOMAS PYNCHON

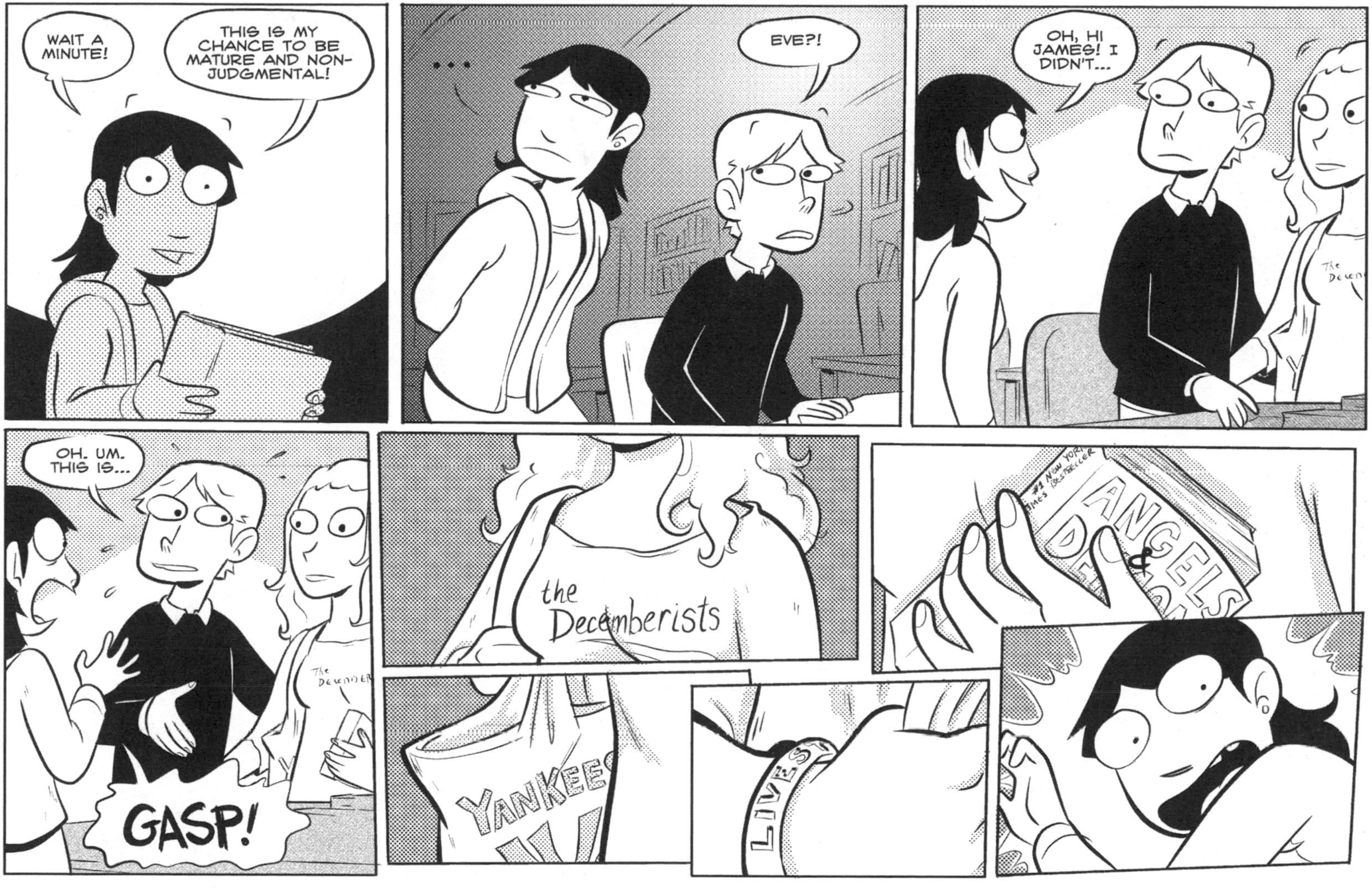
WAIT A MINUTE!
THIS IS MY CHANCE TO BE MATURE AND NON-JUDGMENTAL!
...
EVE?!
OH, HI JAMES! I DIDN'T...
OH. UM. THIS IS...
GASP!
the Decemberists
#1 NEW YORK TIMES BESTSELLER
ANGELS
YANKEES
LIVES

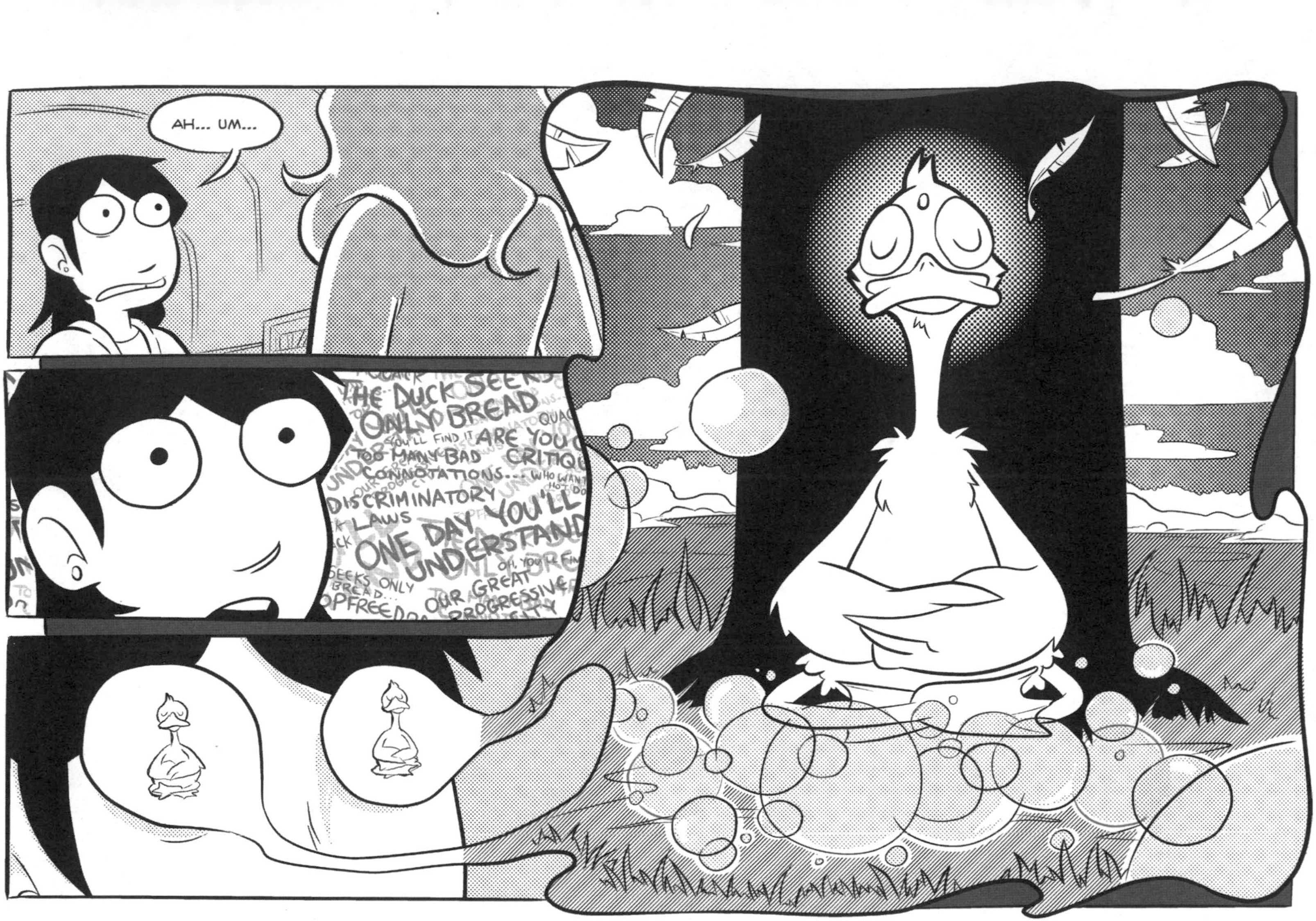
AH... UM...
THE DUCK SEEKS ONLY BREAD
YOU'LL FIND IT
ARE YOU
TOO MANY BAD CONNOTATIONS...
WHO WANT
DISCRIMINATORY LAWS
ONE DAY YOU'LL UNDERSTAND
OH, YOU'LL FIN
SEEKS ONLY BREAD...
OUR GREAT PROGRESSIVE

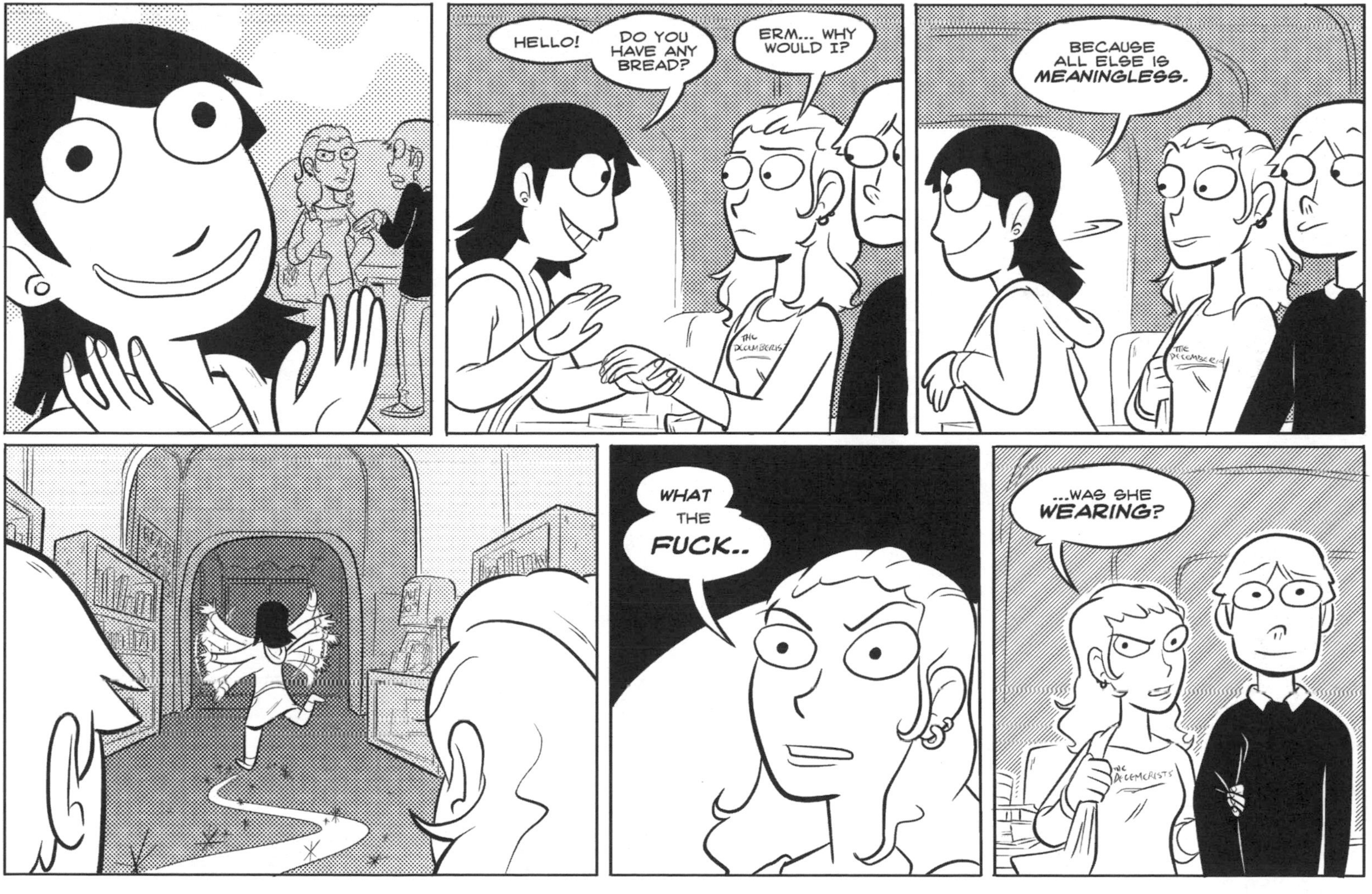
HELLO!
DO YOU HAVE ANY BREAD?
ERM... WHY WOULD I?
BECAUSE ALL ELSE IS *MEANINGLESS.*
WHAT THE *FUCK..*
...WAS SHE *WEARING?*

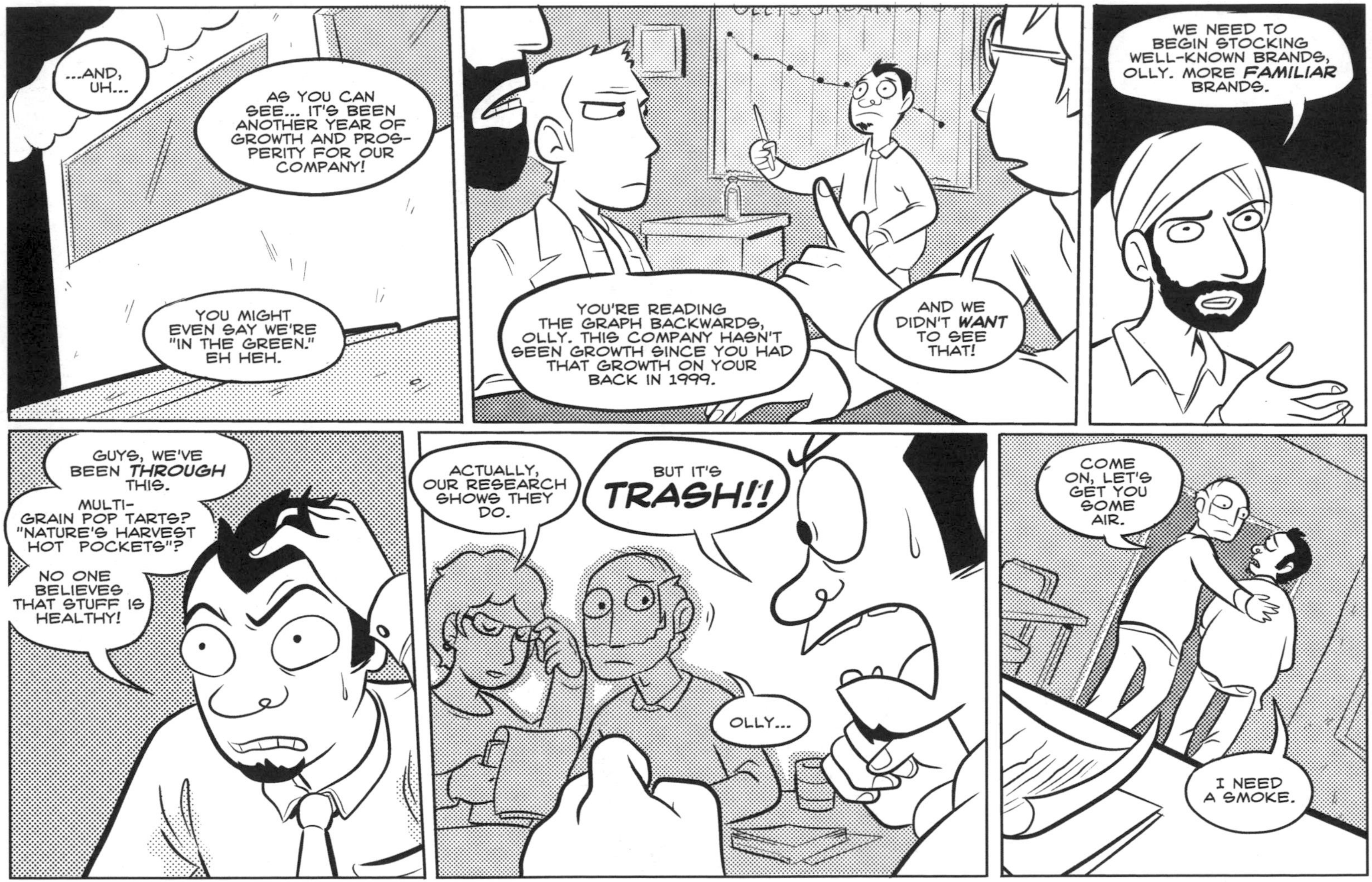
...AND, UH...
AS YOU CAN SEE... IT'S BEEN ANOTHER YEAR OF GROWTH AND PROS-PERITY FOR OUR COMPANY!
YOU MIGHT EVEN SAY WE'RE "IN THE GREEN." EH HEH.
YOU'RE READING THE GRAPH BACKWARDS, OLLY. THIS COMPANY HASN'T SEEN GROWTH SINCE YOU HAD THAT GROWTH ON YOUR BACK IN 1999.
AND WE DIDN'T *WANT* TO SEE THAT!
WE NEED TO BEGIN STOCKING WELL-KNOWN BRANDS, OLLY. MORE *FAMILIAR* BRANDS.
GUYS, WE'VE BEEN *THROUGH* THIS.
MULTI-GRAIN POP TARTS? "NATURE'S HARVEST HOT POCKETS"?
NO ONE BELIEVES THAT STUFF IS HEALTHY!
ACTUALLY, OUR RESEARCH SHOWS THEY DO.
BUT IT'S *TRASH!!*
OLLY...
COME ON, LET'S GET YOU SOME AIR.
I NEED A SMOKE.

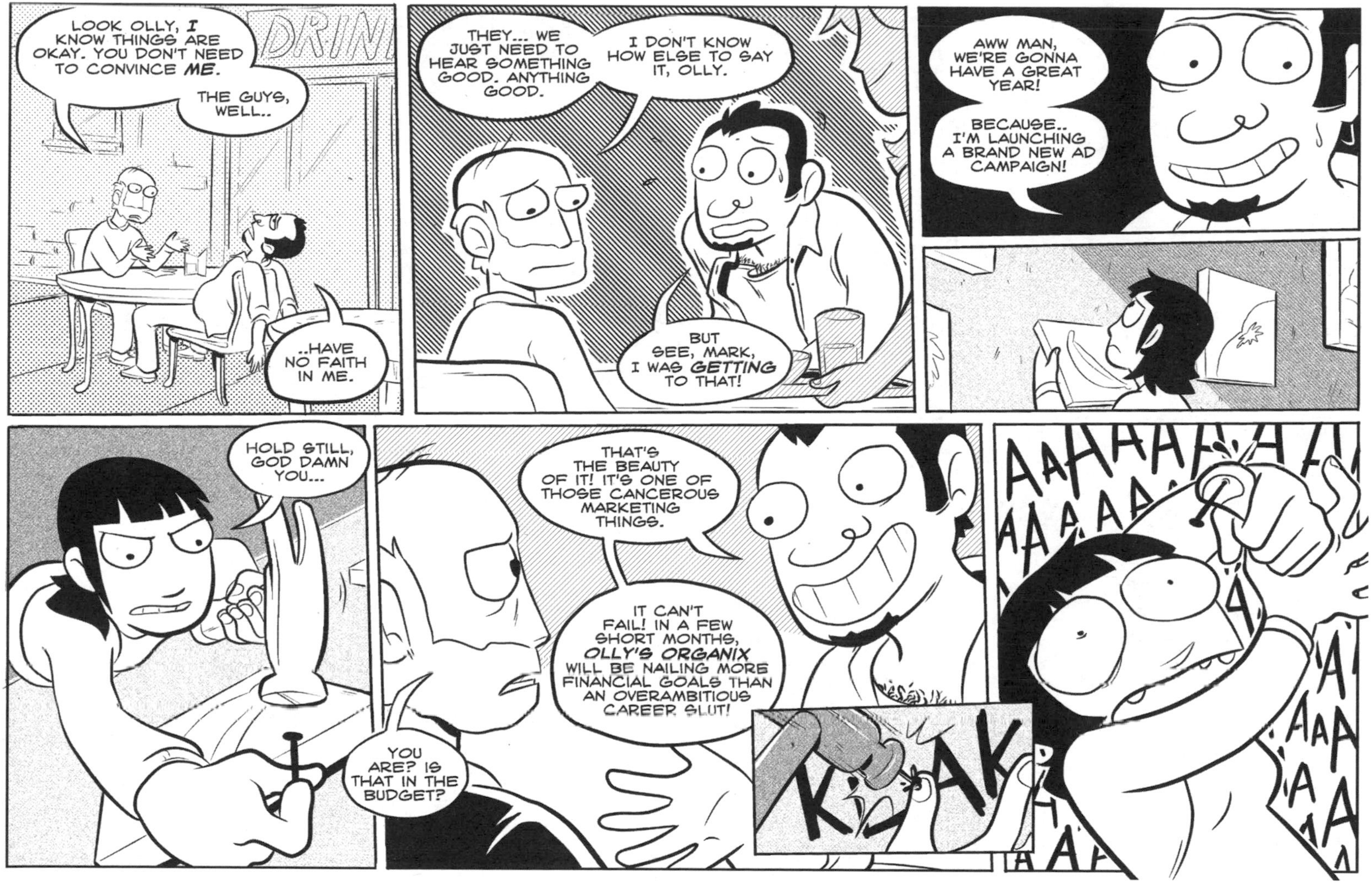
LOOK OLLY, I KNOW THINGS ARE OKAY. YOU DON'T NEED TO CONVINCE ME.
THE GUYS, WELL..
..HAVE NO FAITH IN ME.
DRIN
THEY... WE JUST NEED TO HEAR SOMETHING GOOD. ANYTHING GOOD.
I DON'T KNOW HOW ELSE TO SAY IT, OLLY.
BUT SEE, MARK, I WAS GETTING TO THAT!
AWW MAN, WE'RE GONNA HAVE A GREAT YEAR!
BECAUSE.. I'M LAUNCHING A BRAND NEW AD CAMPAIGN!
HOLD STILL, GOD DAMN YOU...
THAT'S THE BEAUTY OF IT! IT'S ONE OF THOSE CANCEROUS MARKETING THINGS.
IT CAN'T FAIL! IN A FEW SHORT MONTHS, OLLY'S ORGANIX WILL BE NAILING MORE FINANCIAL GOALS THAN AN OVERAMBITIOUS CAREER SLUT!
YOU ARE? IS THAT IN THE BUDGET?
KI-AK
AAAAAAAAAAA

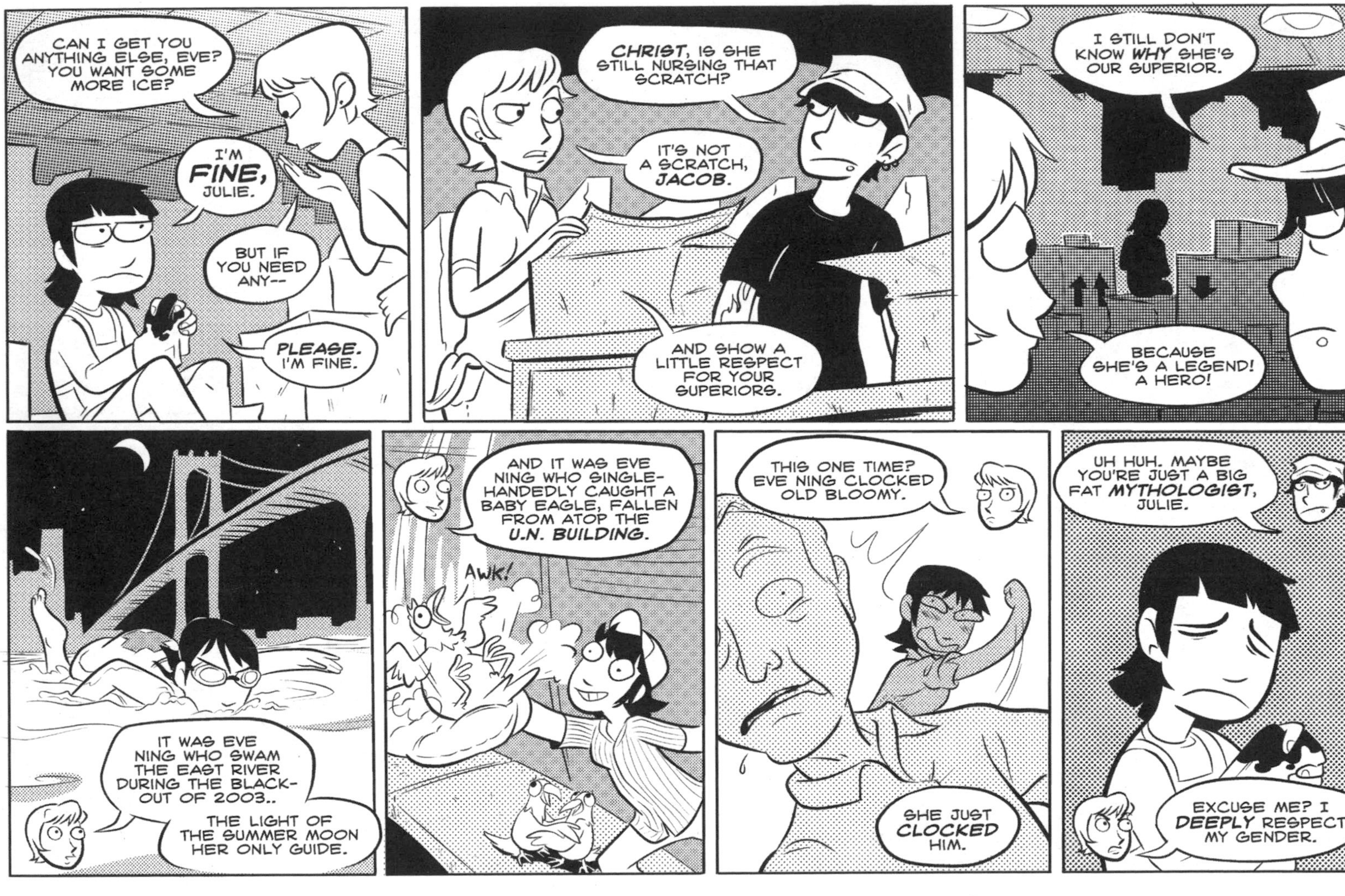
CAN I GET YOU ANYTHING ELSE, EVE? YOU WANT SOME MORE ICE?
I'M FINE, JULIE.
BUT IF YOU NEED ANY--
PLEASE. I'M FINE.
CHRIST, IS SHE STILL NURSING THAT SCRATCH?
IT'S NOT A SCRATCH, JACOB.
AND SHOW A LITTLE RESPECT FOR YOUR SUPERIORS.
I STILL DON'T KNOW WHY SHE'S OUR SUPERIOR.
BECAUSE SHE'S A LEGEND! A HERO!
IT WAS EVE NING WHO SWAM THE EAST RIVER DURING THE BLACK-OUT OF 2003..
THE LIGHT OF THE SUMMER MOON HER ONLY GUIDE.
AND IT WAS EVE NING WHO SINGLE-HANDEDLY CAUGHT A BABY EAGLE, FALLEN FROM ATOP THE U.N. BUILDING.
AWK!
THIS ONE TIME? EVE NING CLOCKED OLD BLOOMY.
SHE JUST CLOCKED HIM.
UH HUH. MAYBE YOU'RE JUST A BIG FAT MYTHOLOGIST, JULIE.
EXCUSE ME? I DEEPLY RESPECT MY GENDER.

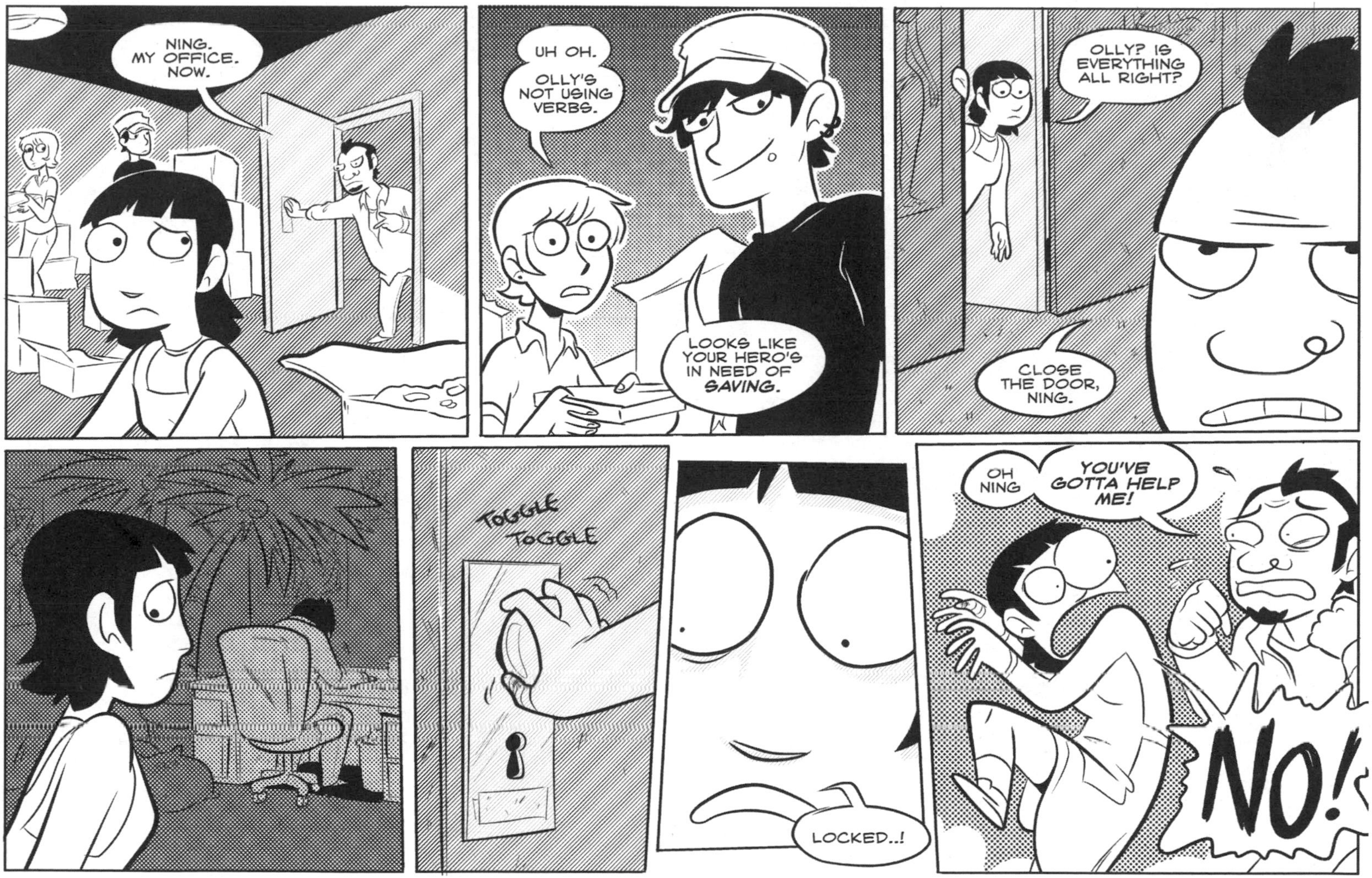
NING. MY OFFICE. NOW.
UH OH.
OLLY'S NOT USING VERBS.
LOOKS LIKE YOUR HERO'S IN NEED OF SAVING.
OLLY? IS EVERYTHING ALL RIGHT?
CLOSE THE DOOR, NING.
TOGGLE TOGGLE
LOCKED..!
OH NING
YOU'VE GOTTA HELP ME!
NO!

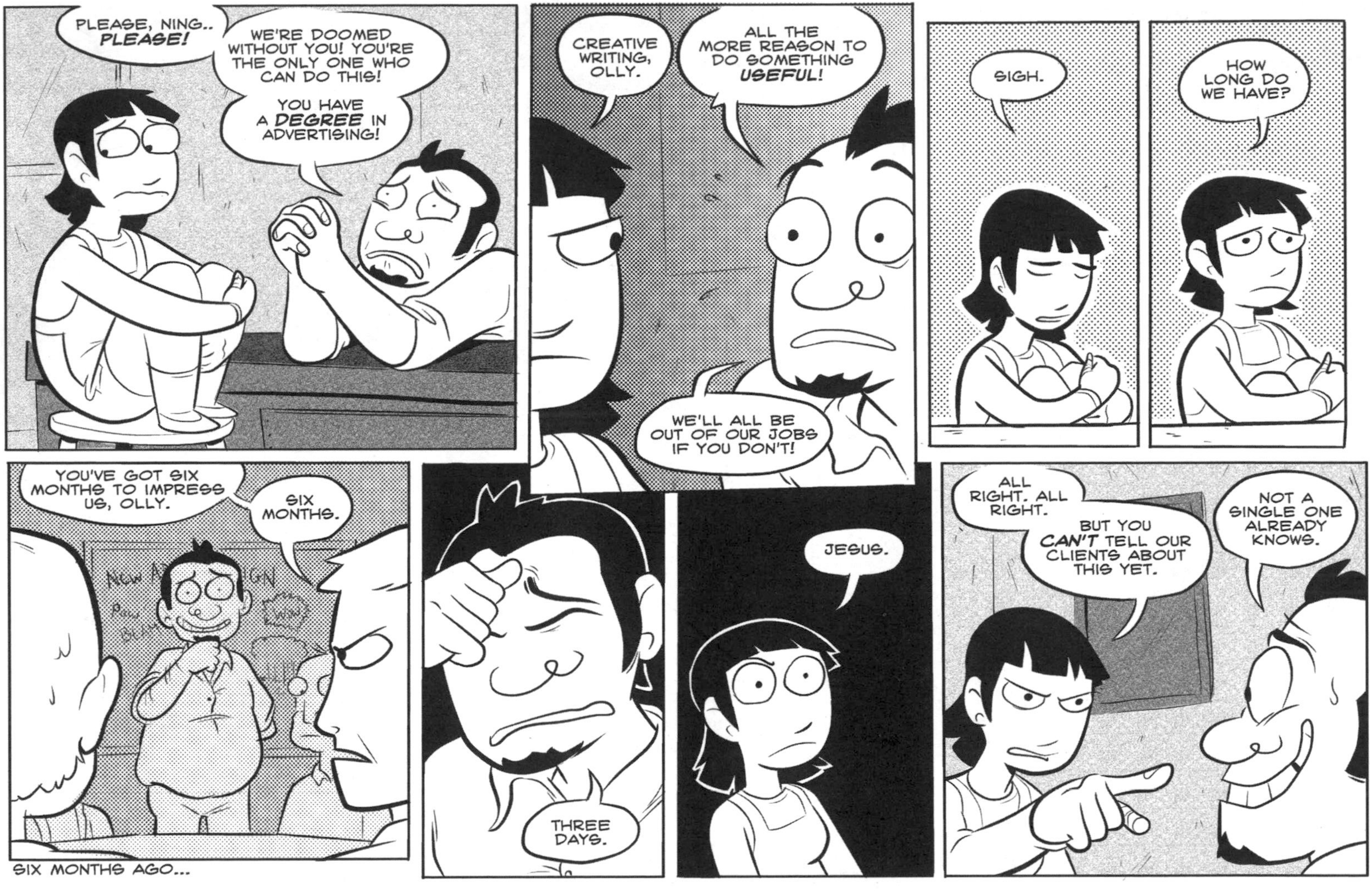
PLEASE, NING.. *PLEASE!*
WE'RE DOOMED WITHOUT YOU! YOU'RE THE ONLY ONE WHO CAN DO THIS!
YOU HAVE A *DEGREE* IN ADVERTISING!
CREATIVE WRITING, OLLY.
ALL THE MORE REASON TO DO SOMETHING *USEFUL!*
WE'LL ALL BE OUT OF OUR JOBS IF YOU DON'T!
SIGH.
HOW LONG DO WE HAVE?
YOU'VE GOT SIX MONTHS TO IMPRESS US, OLLY.
SIX MONTHS.
SIX MONTHS AGO...
THREE DAYS.
JESUS.
ALL RIGHT. ALL RIGHT.
BUT YOU *CAN'T* TELL OUR CLIENTS ABOUT THIS YET.
NOT A SINGLE ONE ALREADY KNOWS.

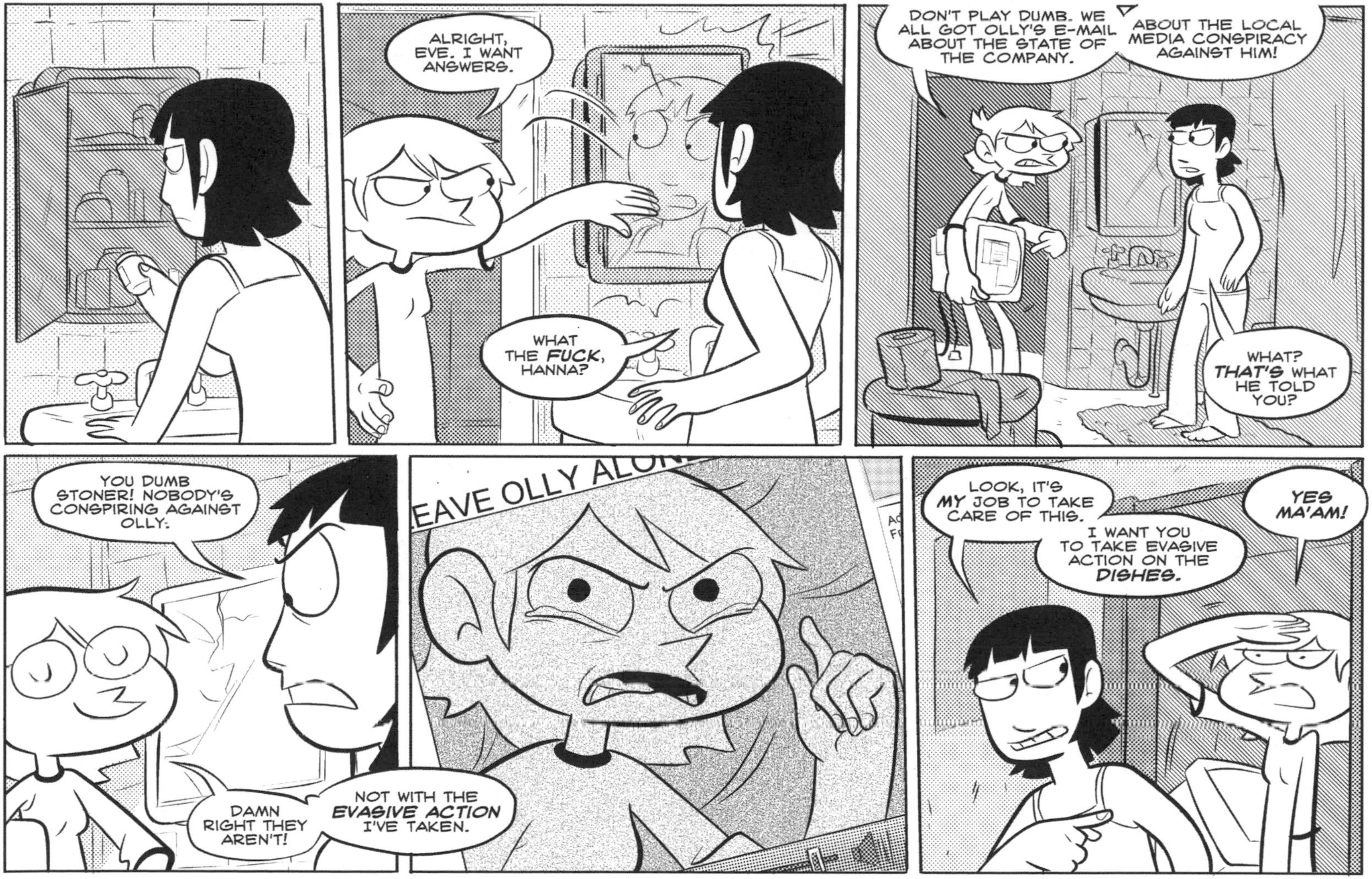
ALRIGHT, EVE. I WANT ANSWERS.
WHAT THE FUCK, HANNA?
DON'T PLAY DUMB. WE ALL GOT OLLY'S E-MAIL ABOUT THE STATE OF THE COMPANY.
ABOUT THE LOCAL MEDIA CONSPIRACY AGAINST HIM!
WHAT? THAT'S WHAT HE TOLD YOU?
YOU DUMB STONER! NOBODY'S CONSPIRING AGAINST OLLY.
DAMN RIGHT THEY AREN'T!
NOT WITH THE EVASIVE ACTION I'VE TAKEN.
EAVE OLLY ALON
LOOK, IT'S MY JOB TO TAKE CARE OF THIS.
I WANT YOU TO TAKE EVASIVE ACTION ON THE DISHES.
YES MA'AM!

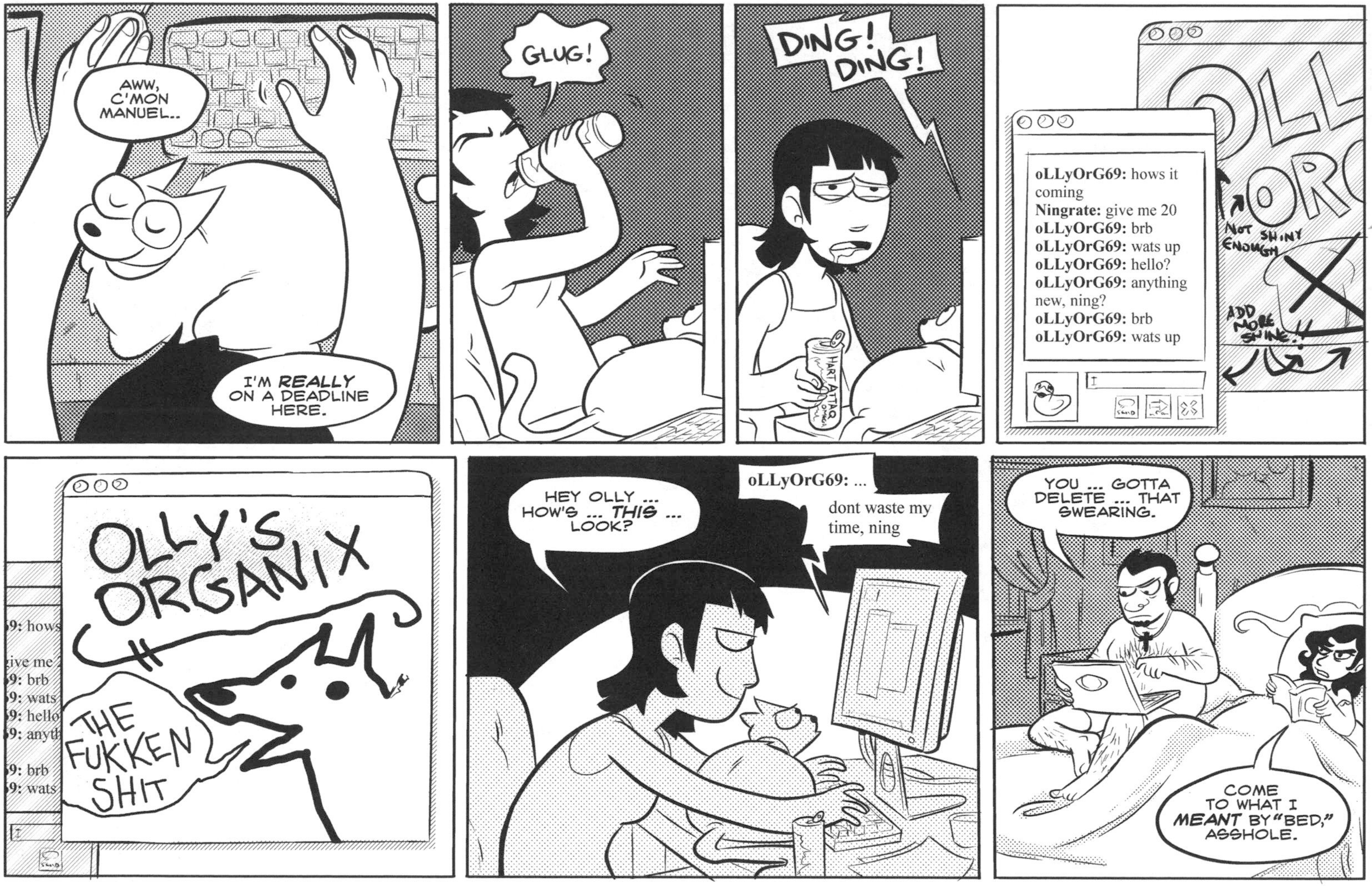
AWW, C'MON MANUEL..
I'M REALLY ON A DEADLINE HERE.
GLUG!
DING! DING!
HART ATTAQ
oLLyOrG69: hows it coming
Ningrate: give me 20
oLLyOrG69: brb
oLLyOrG69: wats up
oLLyOrG69: hello?
oLLyOrG69: anything new, ning?
oLLyOrG69: brb
oLLyOrG69: wats up
NOT SHINY ENOUGH
ADD MORE SHINE!!
OLLY'S ORGANIX
THE FUKKEN SHIT
HEY OLLY ... HOW'S ... THIS ... LOOK?
oLLyOrG69: ...
dont waste my time, ning
YOU ... GOTTA DELETE ... THAT SWEARING.
COME TO WHAT I MEANT BY "BED," ASSHOLE.

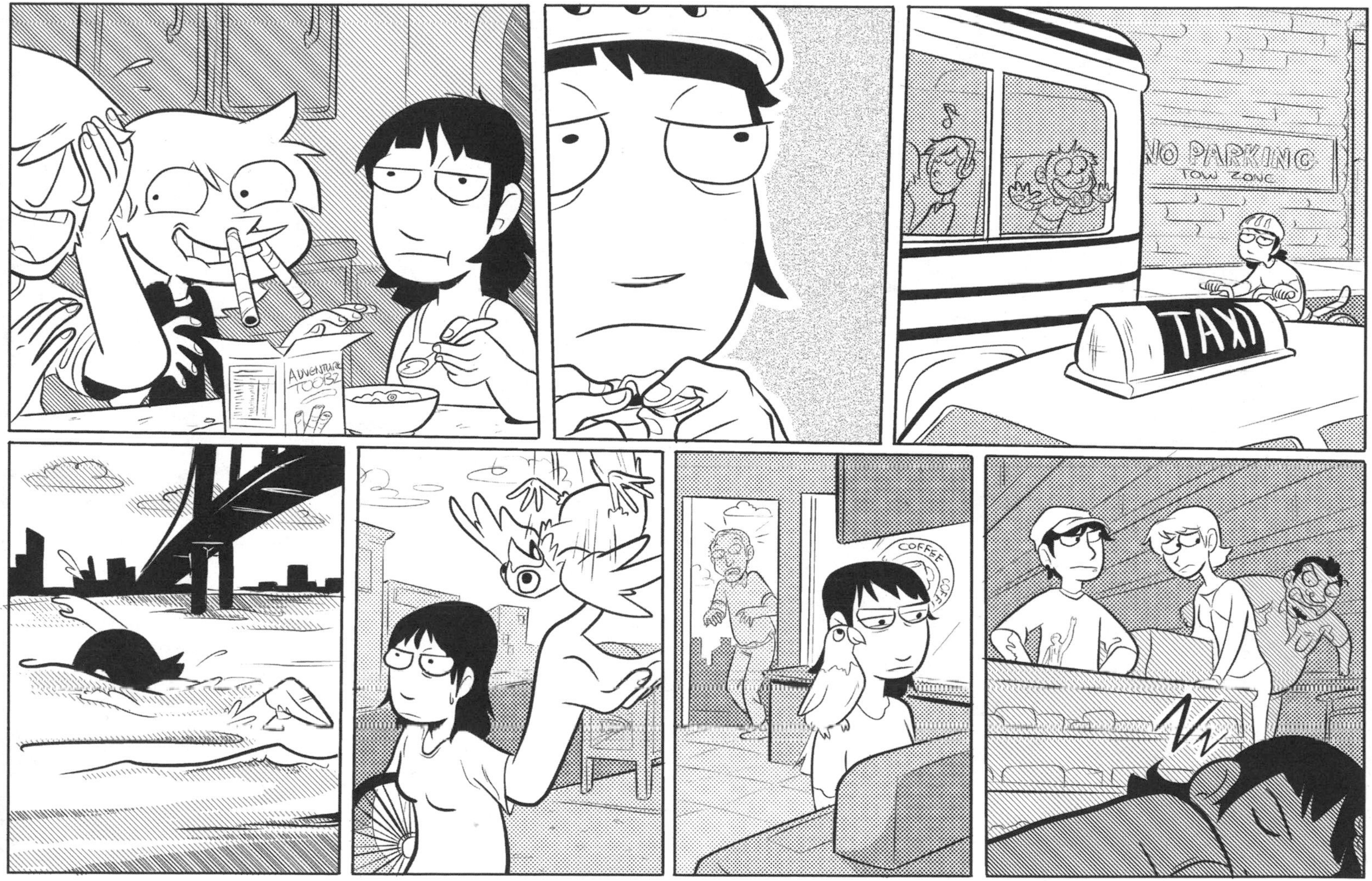
ADVENTURE TOOBZ
NO PARKING
TOW ZONE
TAXI
COFFEE

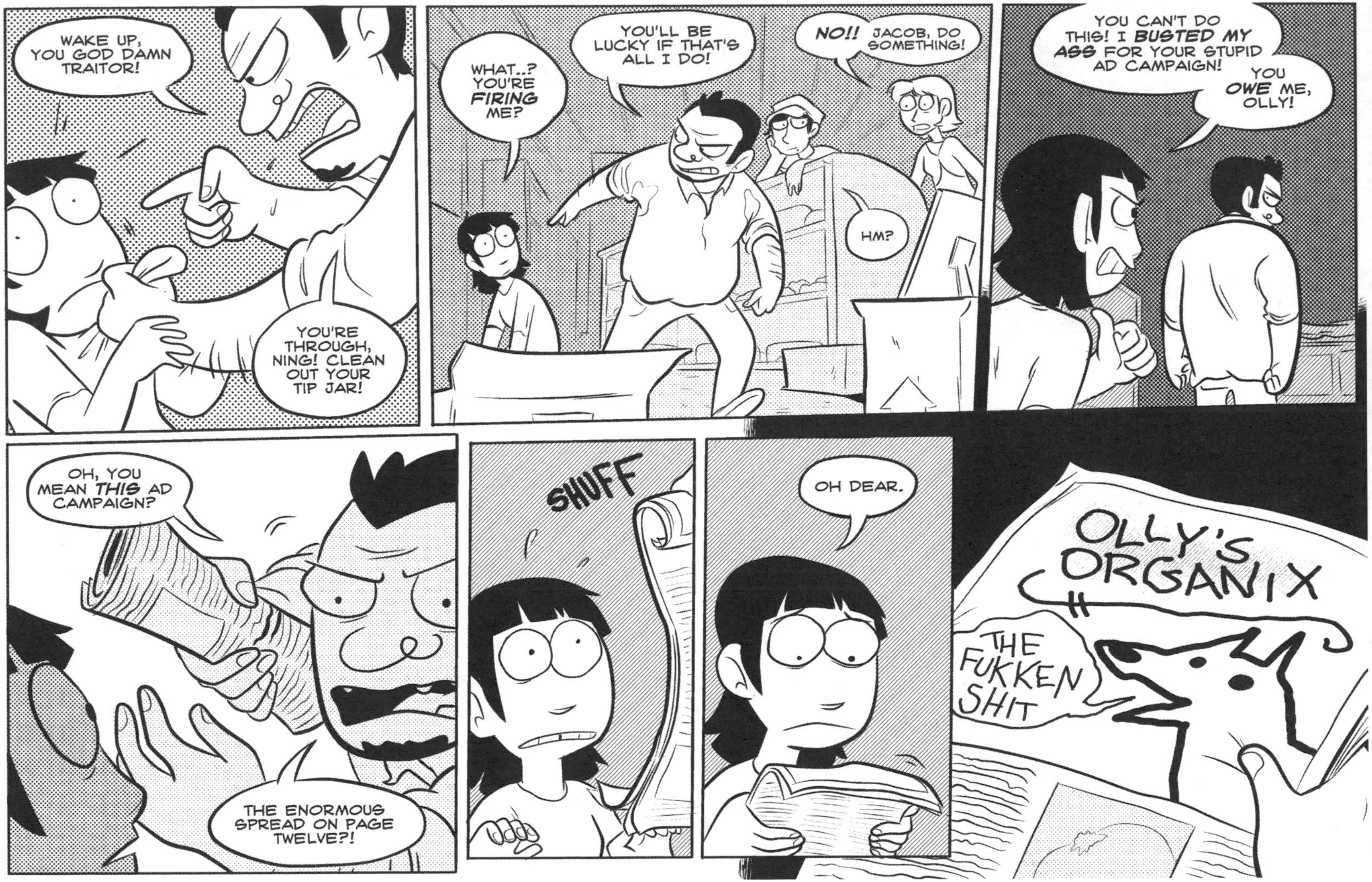
WAKE UP, YOU GOD DAMN TRAITOR!
YOU'RE THROUGH, NING! CLEAN OUT YOUR TIP JAR!
WHAT..? YOU'RE FIRING ME?
YOU'LL BE LUCKY IF THAT'S ALL I DO!
NO!! JACOB, DO SOMETHING!
HM?
YOU CAN'T DO THIS! I BUSTED MY ASS FOR YOUR STUPID AD CAMPAIGN!
YOU OWE ME, OLLY!
OH, YOU MEAN THIS AD CAMPAIGN?
THE ENORMOUS SPREAD ON PAGE TWELVE?!
SHUFF
OH DEAR.
OLLY'S ORGANIX
THE FUKKEN SHIT

I AM CRAWLING. OUT OF MY **SKIN.**

I WARNED YOU ABOUT THAT SKITTLE CAKE, HANNA.

NOT THAT. IT'S EVE, ALL UP IN MY SHIT!

I CAN'T FOCUS WHEN SHE'S AROUND! I CAN'T GET ANY **WORK** DONE!

HMM.

WANT ME TO SEND HER ON A PEPTO BISMOL RUN?

NAH... THEY'LL DRAMATICALLY RE-HIRE HER AS SOON AS THIS THING GOES VIRAL.

...I ALWAYS SAY, GOD HELP US ALL.

OLLY'S ORGANI...

THE ████ SHIT

BREAKING NEWS

THE NEWS NEWS 10:30

AND IN CITY NEWS, A VULGAR MISPRINT HAS WRAPPED LOCAL GROCERY "OLLY'S ORGANIX" IN A GLUTEN-FREE PITA OF TROUBLE.

THEY ALSO REASSURED THE PUBLIC THAT ALL PARTIES RESPONSIBLE FOR THE CAMPAIGN HAVE BEEN RELIEVED OF THEIR DUTIES.

AT A PRESS CONFERENCE TUESDAY, COMPANY REPS CALLED THE ADS -- WHICH FEATURE AN ENTHUSIASTIC BUT FOUL-MOUTHED SPOKESDOG -- A REGRETTABLE OVERSIGHT.

'BYE, OLLY.

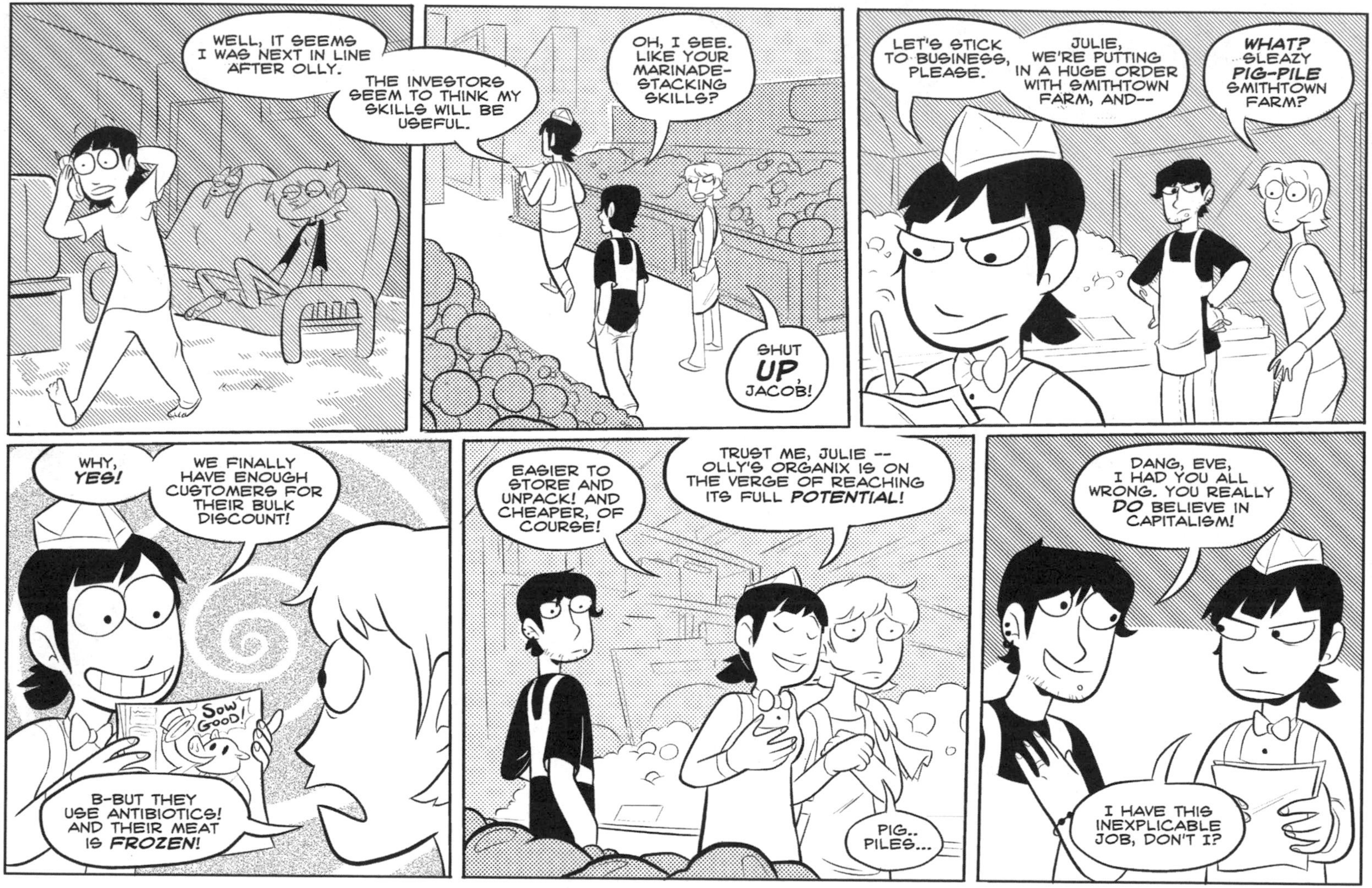
WELL, IT SEEMS I WAS NEXT IN LINE AFTER OLLY.
THE INVESTORS SEEM TO THINK MY SKILLS WILL BE USEFUL.
OH, I SEE. LIKE YOUR MARINADE-STACKING SKILLS?
SHUT *UP*, JACOB!
LET'S STICK TO BUSINESS, PLEASE.
JULIE, WE'RE PUTTING IN A HUGE ORDER WITH SMITHTOWN FARM, AND--
WHAT? SLEAZY *PIG-PILE* SMITHTOWN FARM?
WHY, *YES!*
WE FINALLY HAVE ENOUGH CUSTOMERS FOR THEIR BULK DISCOUNT!
SOW GOOD!
B-BUT THEY USE ANTIBIOTICS! AND THEIR MEAT IS *FROZEN!*
EASIER TO STORE AND UNPACK! AND CHEAPER, OF COURSE!
TRUST ME, JULIE -- OLLY'S ORGANIX IS ON THE VERGE OF REACHING ITS FULL *POTENTIAL!*
PIG.. PILES...
DANG, EVE, I HAD YOU ALL WRONG. YOU REALLY *DO* BELIEVE IN CAPITALISM!
I HAVE THIS INEXPLICABLE JOB, DON'T I?

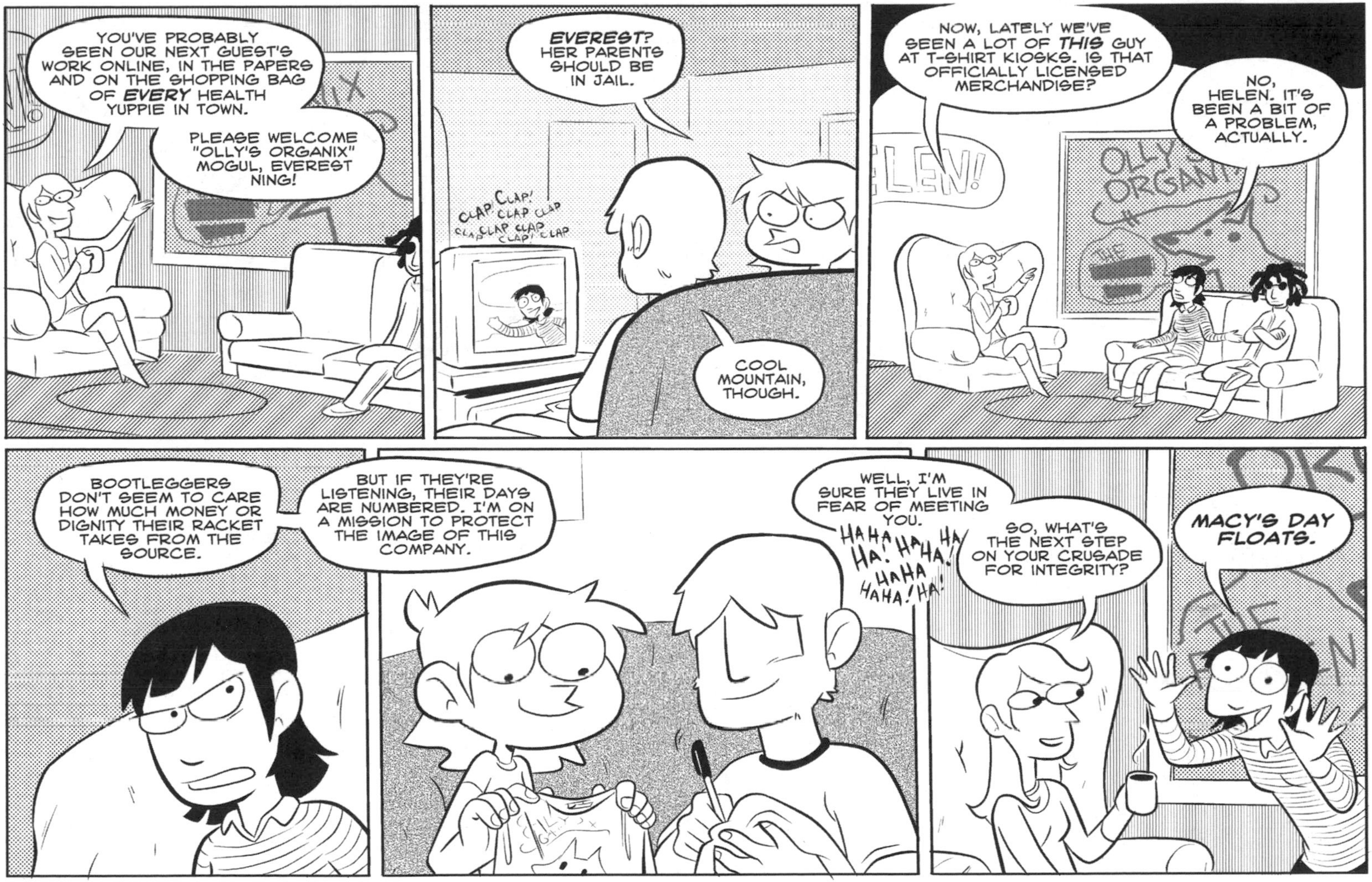

YOU'VE PROBABLY SEEN OUR NEXT GUEST'S WORK ONLINE, IN THE PAPERS AND ON THE SHOPPING BAG OF EVERY HEALTH YUPPIE IN TOWN.
PLEASE WELCOME "OLLY'S ORGANIX" MOGUL, EVEREST NING!
CLAP! CLAP! CLAP CLAP CLAP CLAP CLAP CLAP CLAP! CLAP
EVEREST? HER PARENTS SHOULD BE IN JAIL.
COOL MOUNTAIN, THOUGH.
NOW, LATELY WE'VE SEEN A LOT OF THIS GUY AT T-SHIRT KIOSKS. IS THAT OFFICIALLY LICENSED MERCHANDISE?
NO, HELEN. IT'S BEEN A BIT OF A PROBLEM, ACTUALLY.
BOOTLEGGERS DON'T SEEM TO CARE HOW MUCH MONEY OR DIGNITY THEIR RACKET TAKES FROM THE SOURCE.
BUT IF THEY'RE LISTENING, THEIR DAYS ARE NUMBERED. I'M ON A MISSION TO PROTECT THE IMAGE OF THIS COMPANY.
WELL, I'M SURE THEY LIVE IN FEAR OF MEETING YOU.
HAHA HA HA! HA HA! HAHA HAHA! HA!
SO, WHAT'S THE NEXT STEP ON YOUR CRUSADE FOR INTEGRITY?
MACY'S DAY FLOATS.

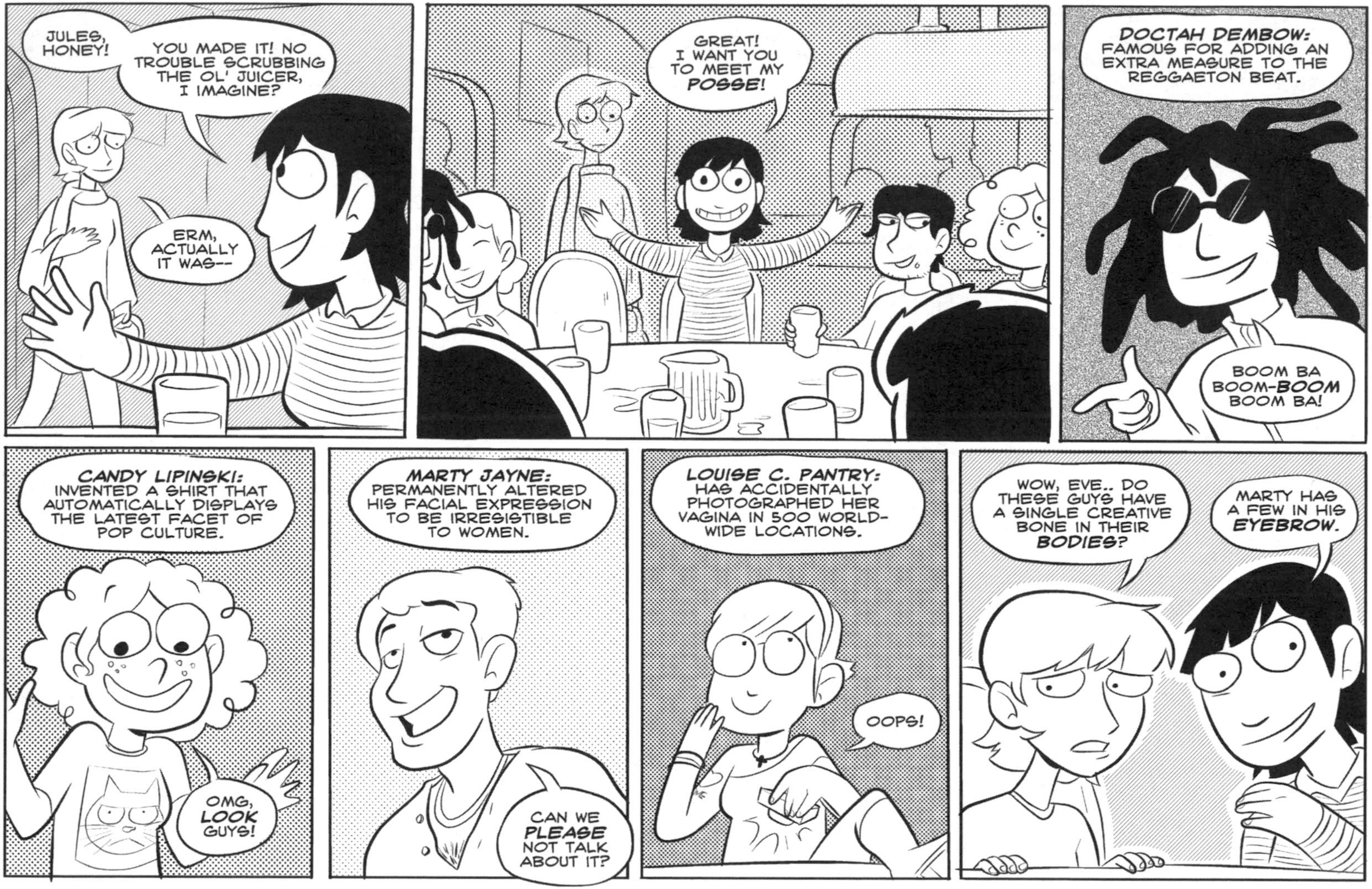
JULES, HONEY!
YOU MADE IT! NO TROUBLE SCRUBBING THE OL' JUICER, I IMAGINE?
ERM, ACTUALLY IT WAS--
GREAT! I WANT YOU TO MEET MY *POSSE*!
DOCTAH DEMBOW: FAMOUS FOR ADDING AN EXTRA MEASURE TO THE REGGAETON BEAT.
BOOM BA BOOM-*BOOM* BOOM BA!
CANDY LIPINSKI: INVENTED A SHIRT THAT AUTOMATICALLY DISPLAYS THE LATEST FACET OF POP CULTURE.
OMG, *LOOK* GUYS!
MARTY JAYNE: PERMANENTLY ALTERED HIS FACIAL EXPRESSION TO BE IRRESISTIBLE TO WOMEN.
CAN WE *PLEASE* NOT TALK ABOUT IT?
LOUISE C. PANTRY: HAS ACCIDENTALLY PHOTOGRAPHED HER VAGINA IN 500 WORLD-WIDE LOCATIONS.
OOPS!
WOW, EVE.. DO THESE GUYS HAVE A SINGLE CREATIVE BONE IN THEIR *BODIES*?
MARTY HAS A FEW IN HIS *EYEBROW*.

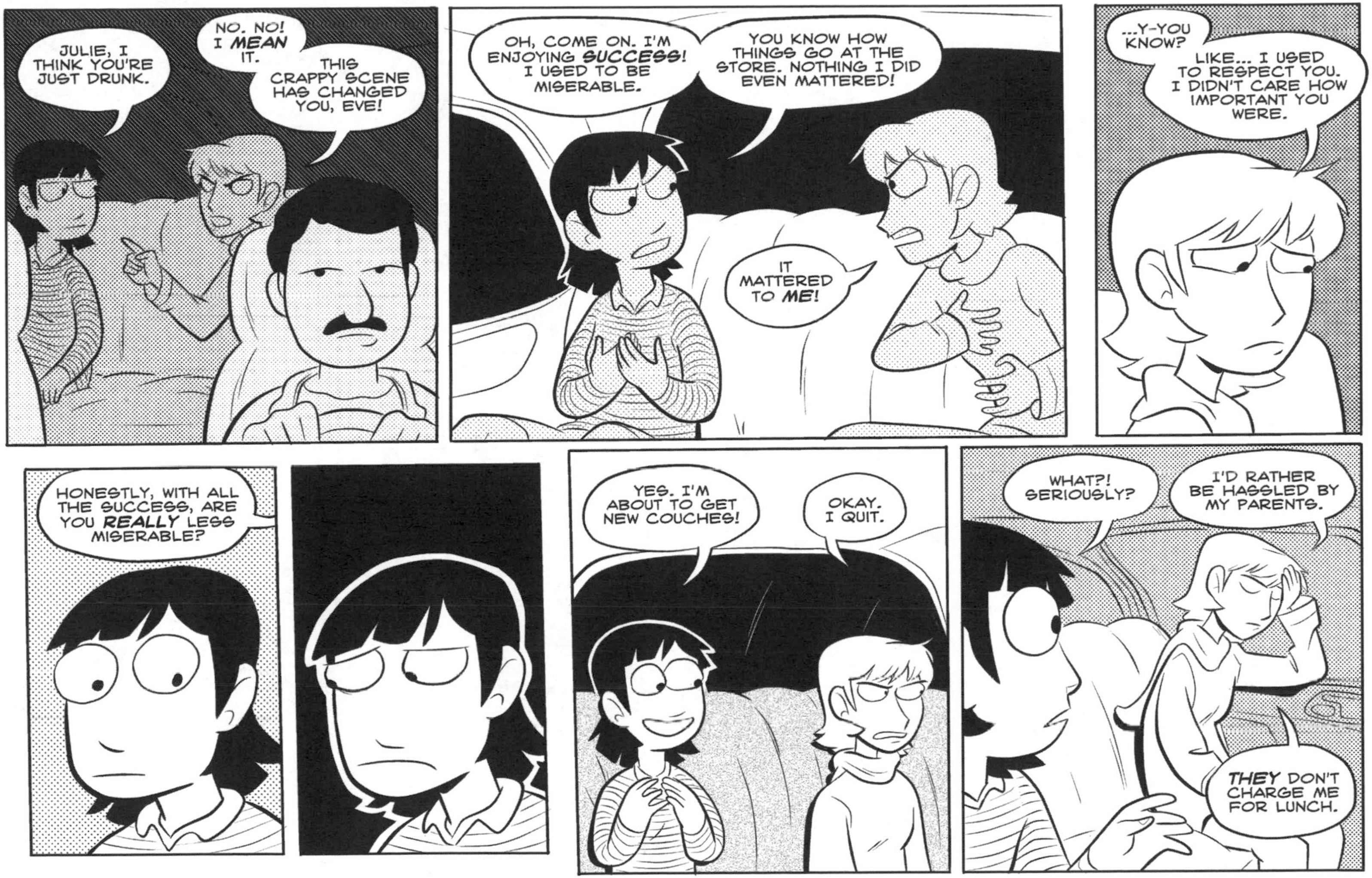
JULIE, I THINK YOU'RE JUST DRUNK.
NO. NO! I MEAN IT.
THIS CRAPPY SCENE HAS CHANGED YOU, EVE!
OH, COME ON. I'M ENJOYING SUCCESS! I USED TO BE MISERABLE.
YOU KNOW HOW THINGS GO AT THE STORE. NOTHING I DID EVEN MATTERED!
IT MATTERED TO ME!
...Y-YOU KNOW?
LIKE... I USED TO RESPECT YOU. I DIDN'T CARE HOW IMPORTANT YOU WERE.
HONESTLY, WITH ALL THE SUCCESS, ARE YOU REALLY LESS MISERABLE?
YES. I'M ABOUT TO GET NEW COUCHES!
OKAY. I QUIT.
WHAT?! SERIOUSLY?
I'D RATHER BE HASSLED BY MY PARENTS.
THEY DON'T CHARGE ME FOR LUNCH.

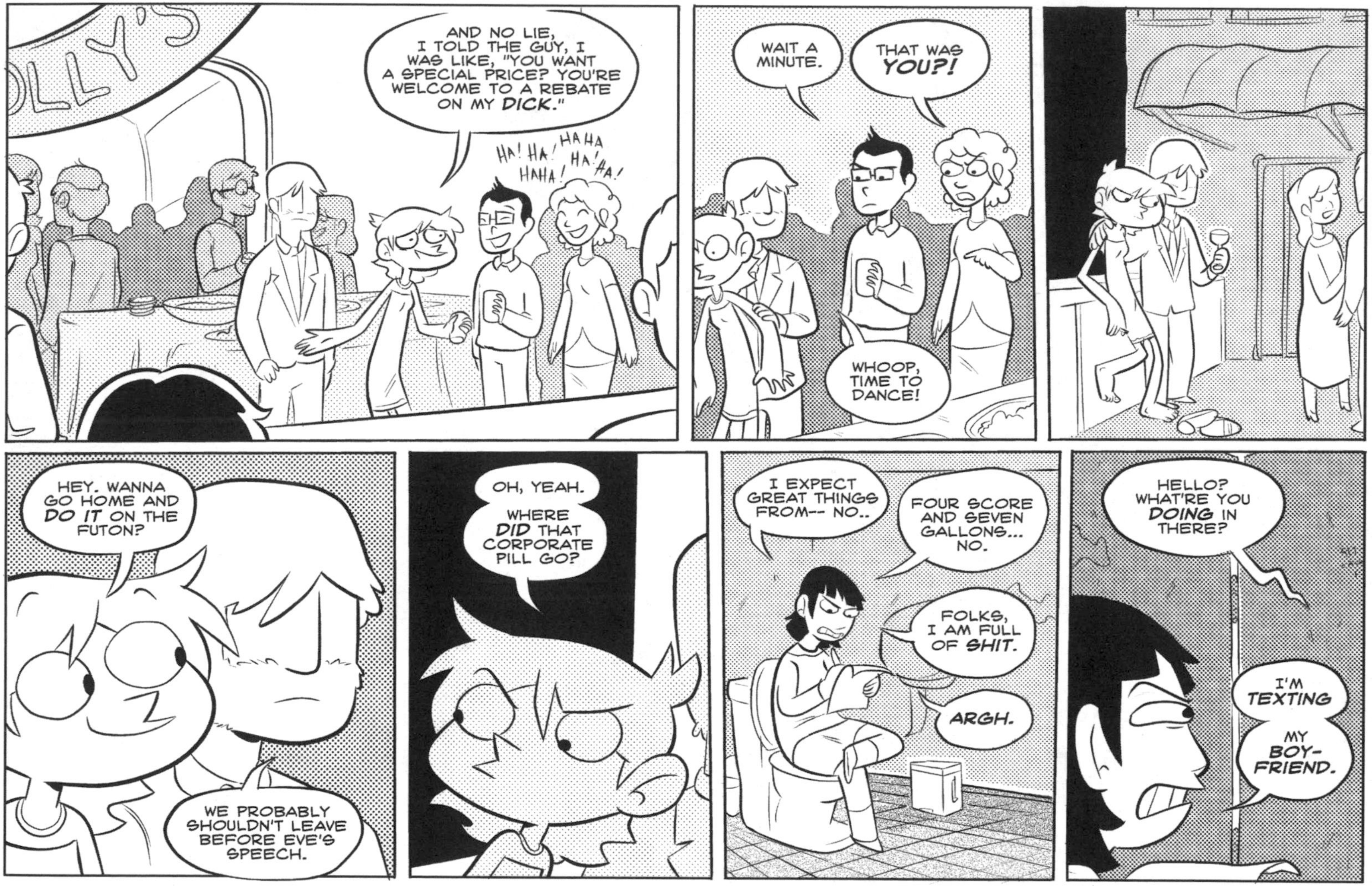
OLLY'S
AND NO LIE, I TOLD THE GUY, I WAS LIKE, "YOU WANT A SPECIAL PRICE? YOU'RE WELCOME TO A REBATE ON MY DICK."
HA! HA! HAHA HA! HAHA! HA!
WAIT A MINUTE.
THAT WAS YOU?!
WHOOP, TIME TO DANCE!
HEY. WANNA GO HOME AND DO IT ON THE FUTON?
WE PROBABLY SHOULDN'T LEAVE BEFORE EVE'S SPEECH.
OH, YEAH.
WHERE DID THAT CORPORATE PILL GO?
I EXPECT GREAT THINGS FROM-- NO..
FOUR SCORE AND SEVEN GALLONS... NO.
FOLKS, I AM FULL OF SHIT.
ARGH.
HELLO? WHAT'RE YOU DOING IN THERE?
I'M TEXTING
MY BOY-FRIEND.

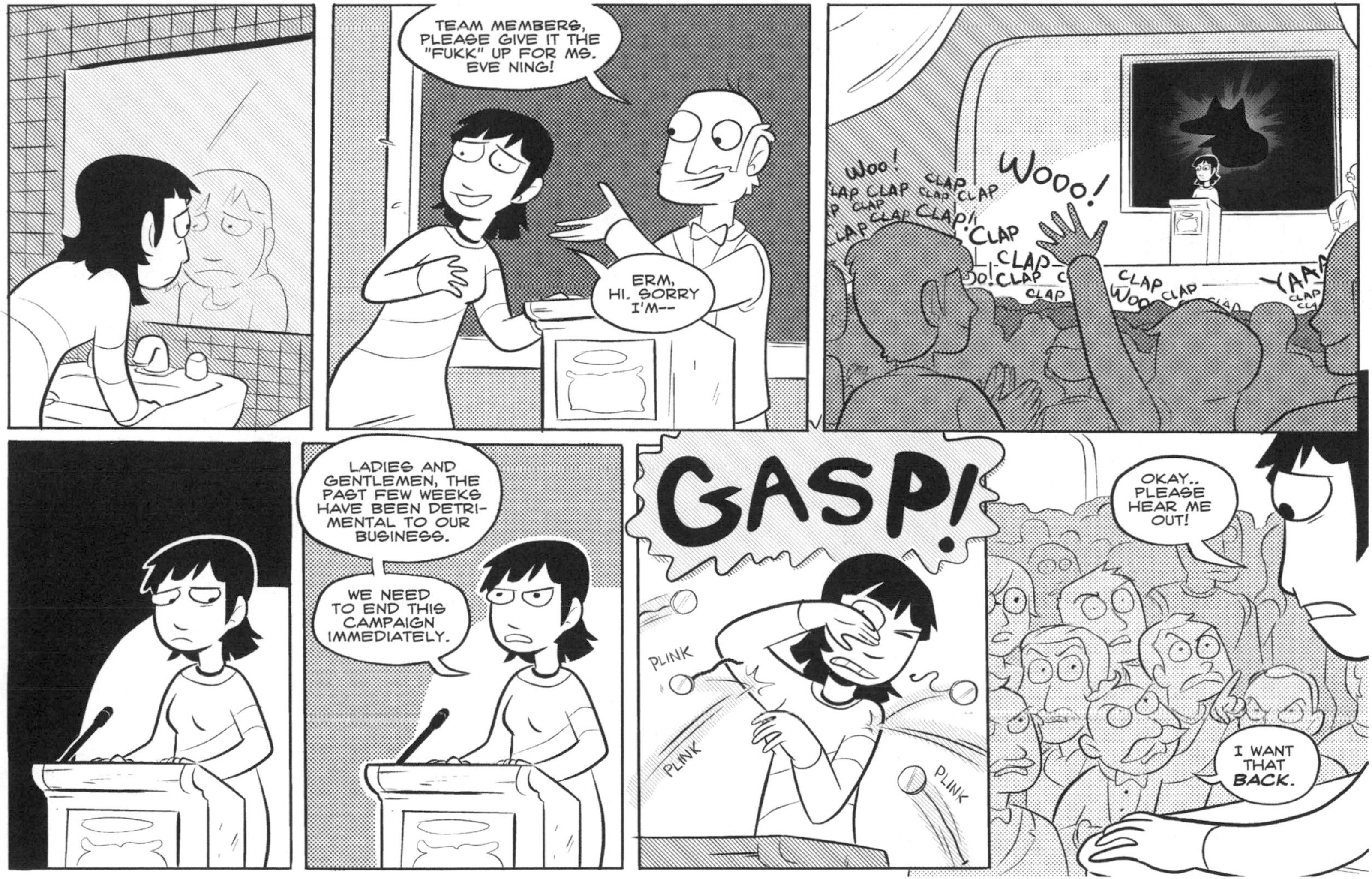
TEAM MEMBERS, PLEASE GIVE IT THE "FUKK" UP FOR MS. EVE NING!
ERM, HI. SORRY I'M--
WOO!
CLAP CLAP CLAP CLAP CLAP
WOOO!
CLAP CLAP CLAP!
CLAP
CLAP
CLAP
CLAP
LADIES AND GENTLEMEN, THE PAST FEW WEEKS HAVE BEEN DETRIMENTAL TO OUR BUSINESS.
WE NEED TO END THIS CAMPAIGN IMMEDIATELY.
GASP!
PLINK
PLINK
PLINK
OKAY.. PLEASE HEAR ME OUT!
I WANT THAT BACK.

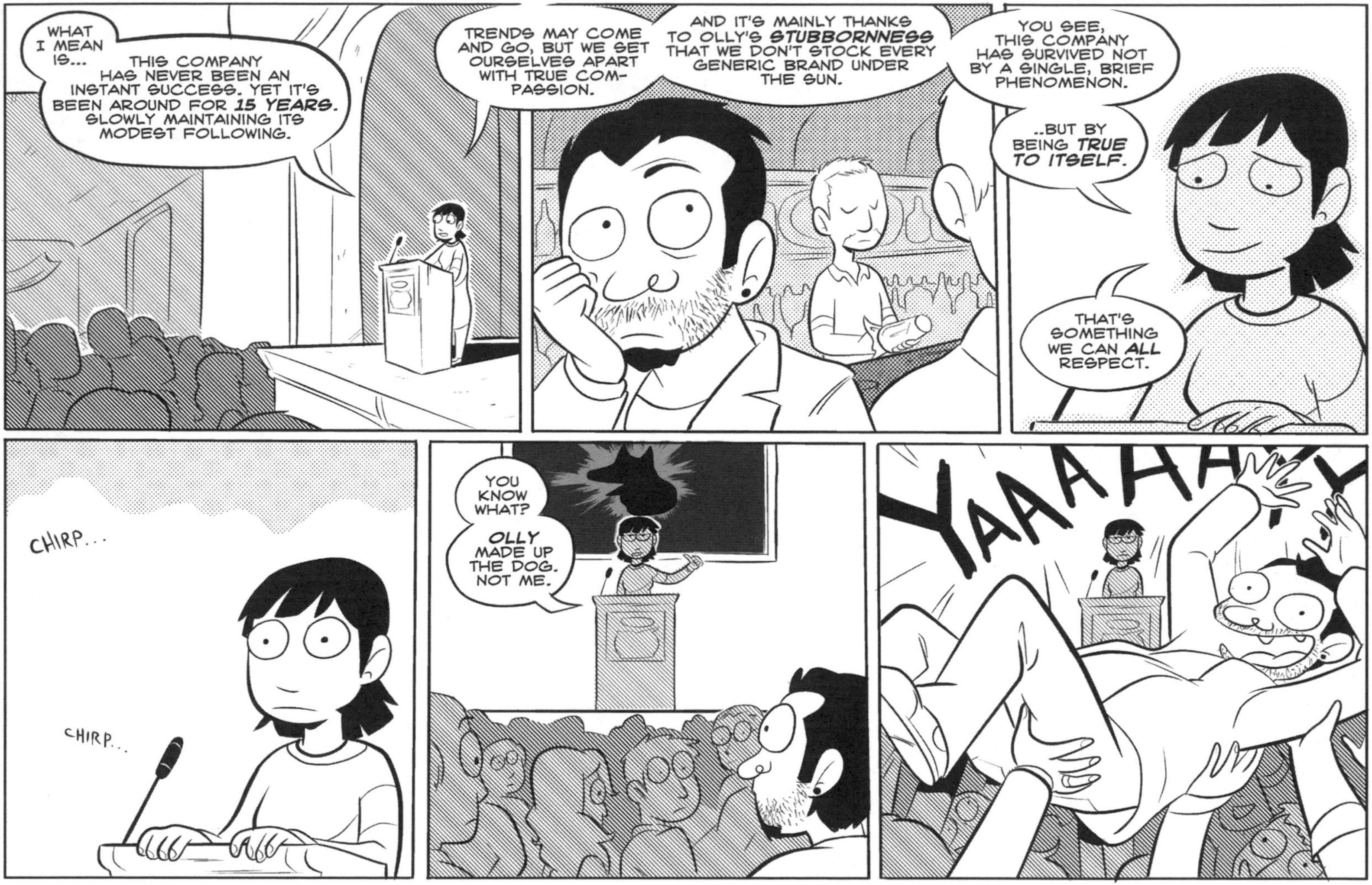
WHAT I MEAN IS...
THIS COMPANY HAS NEVER BEEN AN INSTANT SUCCESS. YET IT'S BEEN AROUND FOR 15 YEARS. SLOWLY MAINTAINING ITS MODEST FOLLOWING.
TRENDS MAY COME AND GO, BUT WE SET OURSELVES APART WITH TRUE COMPASSION.
AND IT'S MAINLY THANKS TO OLLY'S STUBBORNNESS THAT WE DON'T STOCK EVERY GENERIC BRAND UNDER THE SUN.
YOU SEE, THIS COMPANY HAS SURVIVED NOT BY A SINGLE, BRIEF PHENOMENON.
..BUT BY BEING TRUE TO ITSELF.
THAT'S SOMETHING WE CAN ALL RESPECT.
CHIRP...
CHIRP...
YOU KNOW WHAT?
OLLY MADE UP THE DOG. NOT ME.
YAAAAAY

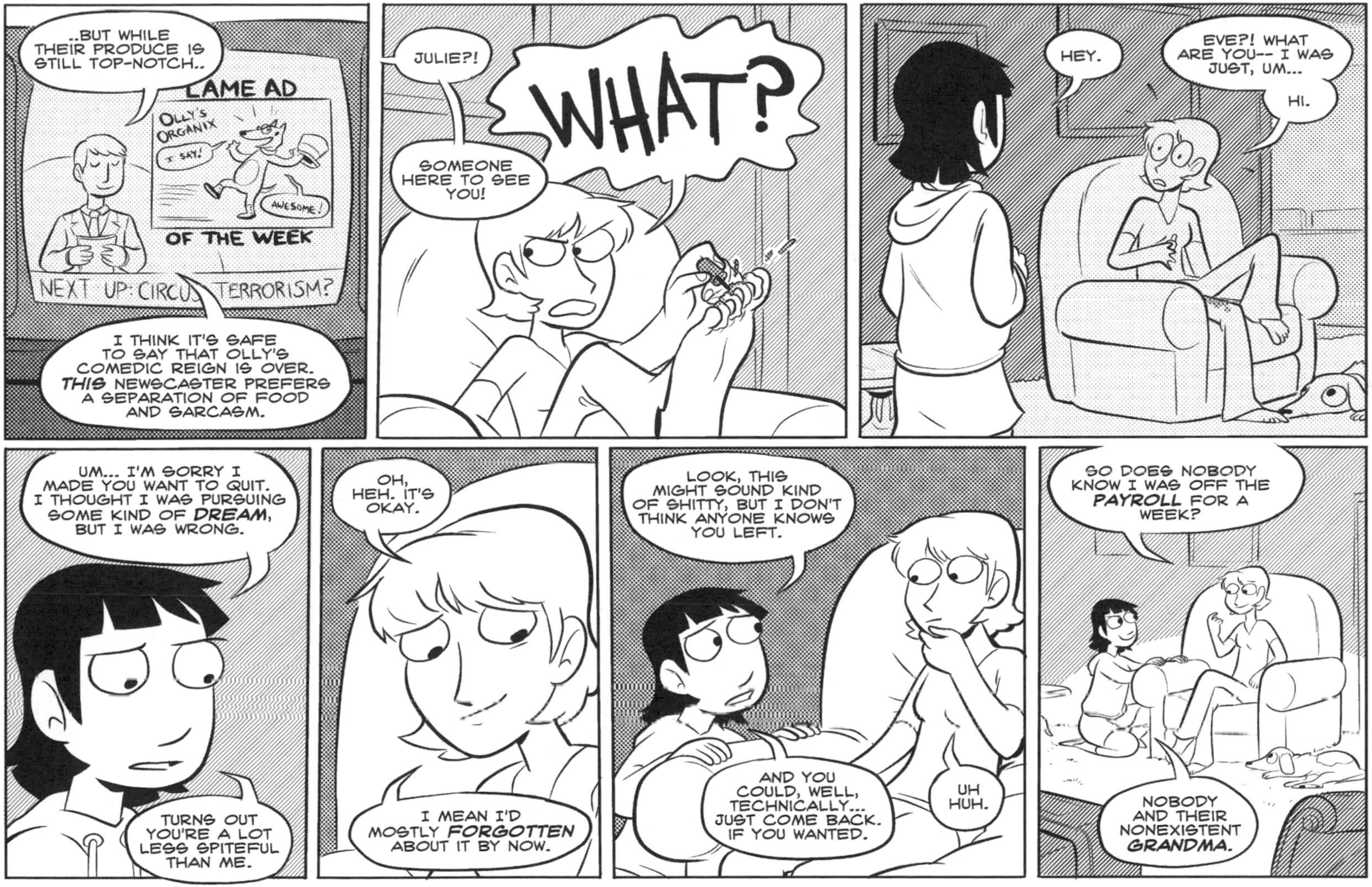
..BUT WHILE THEIR PRODUCE IS STILL TOP-NOTCH..
LAME AD
OLLY'S ORGANIX
I SAY!
AWESOME!
OF THE WEEK
NEXT UP: CIRCUS TERRORISM?
I THINK IT'S SAFE TO SAY THAT OLLY'S COMEDIC REIGN IS OVER. THIS NEWSCASTER PREFERS A SEPARATION OF FOOD AND SARCASM.
JULIE?!
WHAT?
SOMEONE HERE TO SEE YOU!
HEY.
EVE?! WHAT ARE YOU-- I WAS JUST, UM...
HI.
UM... I'M SORRY I MADE YOU WANT TO QUIT. I THOUGHT I WAS PURSUING SOME KIND OF DREAM, BUT I WAS WRONG.
TURNS OUT YOU'RE A LOT LESS SPITEFUL THAN ME.
OH, HEH. IT'S OKAY.
I MEAN I'D MOSTLY FORGOTTEN ABOUT IT BY NOW.
LOOK, THIS MIGHT SOUND KIND OF SHITTY, BUT I DON'T THINK ANYONE KNOWS YOU LEFT.
AND YOU COULD, WELL, TECHNICALLY... JUST COME BACK. IF YOU WANTED.
UH HUH.
SO DOES NOBODY KNOW I WAS OFF THE PAYROLL FOR A WEEK?
NOBODY AND THEIR NONEXISTENT GRANDMA.

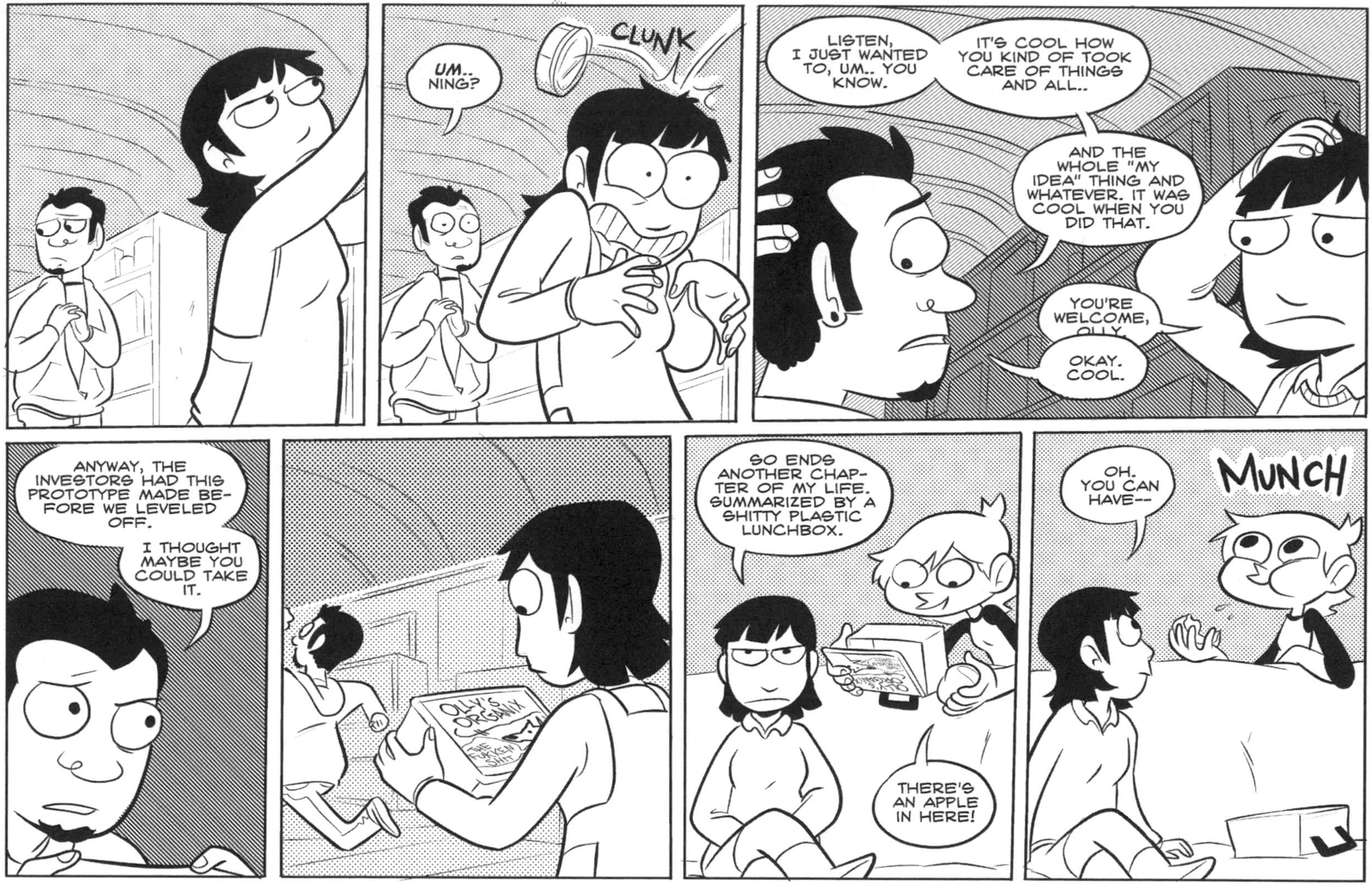
UM..
NING?
CLUNK
LISTEN, I JUST WANTED TO, UM.. YOU KNOW.
IT'S COOL HOW YOU KIND OF TOOK CARE OF THINGS AND ALL..
AND THE WHOLE "MY IDEA" THING AND WHATEVER. IT WAS COOL WHEN YOU DID THAT.
YOU'RE WELCOME, OLLY.
OKAY. COOL.
ANYWAY, THE INVESTORS HAD THIS PROTOTYPE MADE BEFORE WE LEVELED OFF.
I THOUGHT MAYBE YOU COULD TAKE IT.
OLLY'S ORGANIX
SO ENDS ANOTHER CHAPTER OF MY LIFE. SUMMARIZED BY A SHITTY PLASTIC LUNCHBOX.
THERE'S AN APPLE IN HERE!
OH. YOU CAN HAVE--
MUNCH

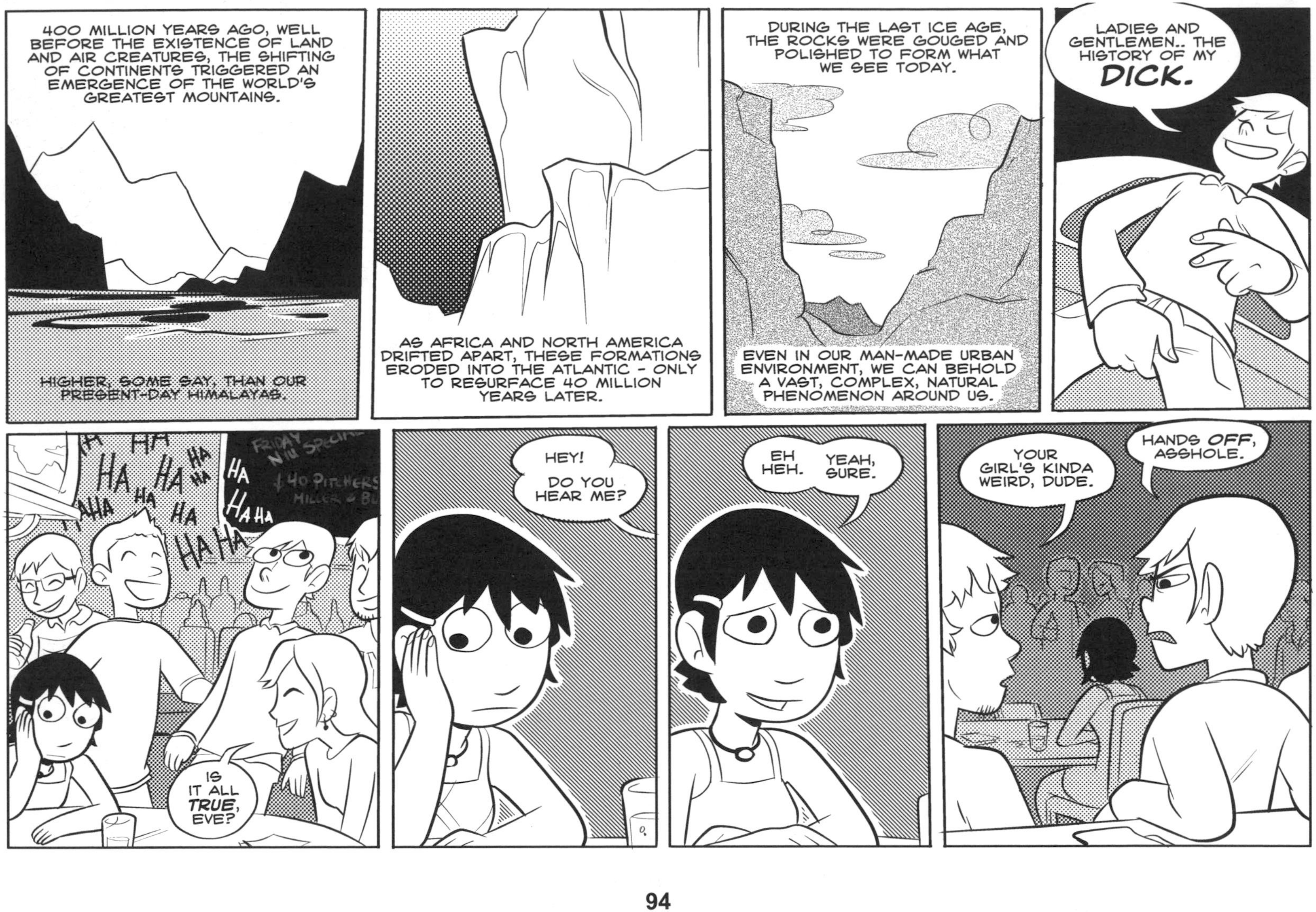
400 MILLION YEARS AGO, WELL BEFORE THE EXISTENCE OF LAND AND AIR CREATURES, THE SHIFTING OF CONTINENTS TRIGGERED AN EMERGENCE OF THE WORLD'S GREATEST MOUNTAINS.
HIGHER, SOME SAY, THAN OUR PRESENT-DAY HIMALAYAS.
AS AFRICA AND NORTH AMERICA DRIFTED APART, THESE FORMATIONS ERODED INTO THE ATLANTIC - ONLY TO RESURFACE 40 MILLION YEARS LATER.
DURING THE LAST ICE AGE, THE ROCKS WERE GOUGED AND POLISHED TO FORM WHAT WE SEE TODAY.
EVEN IN OUR MAN-MADE URBAN ENVIRONMENT, WE CAN BEHOLD A VAST, COMPLEX, NATURAL PHENOMENON AROUND US.
LADIES AND GENTLEMEN.. THE HISTORY OF MY DICK.
HA HA HA HA HA HA HA HA HA HA HAHA HA HA
IS IT ALL TRUE, EVE?
HEY!
DO YOU HEAR ME?
EH HEH.
YEAH, SURE.
YOUR GIRL'S KINDA WEIRD, DUDE.
HANDS OFF, ASSHOLE.

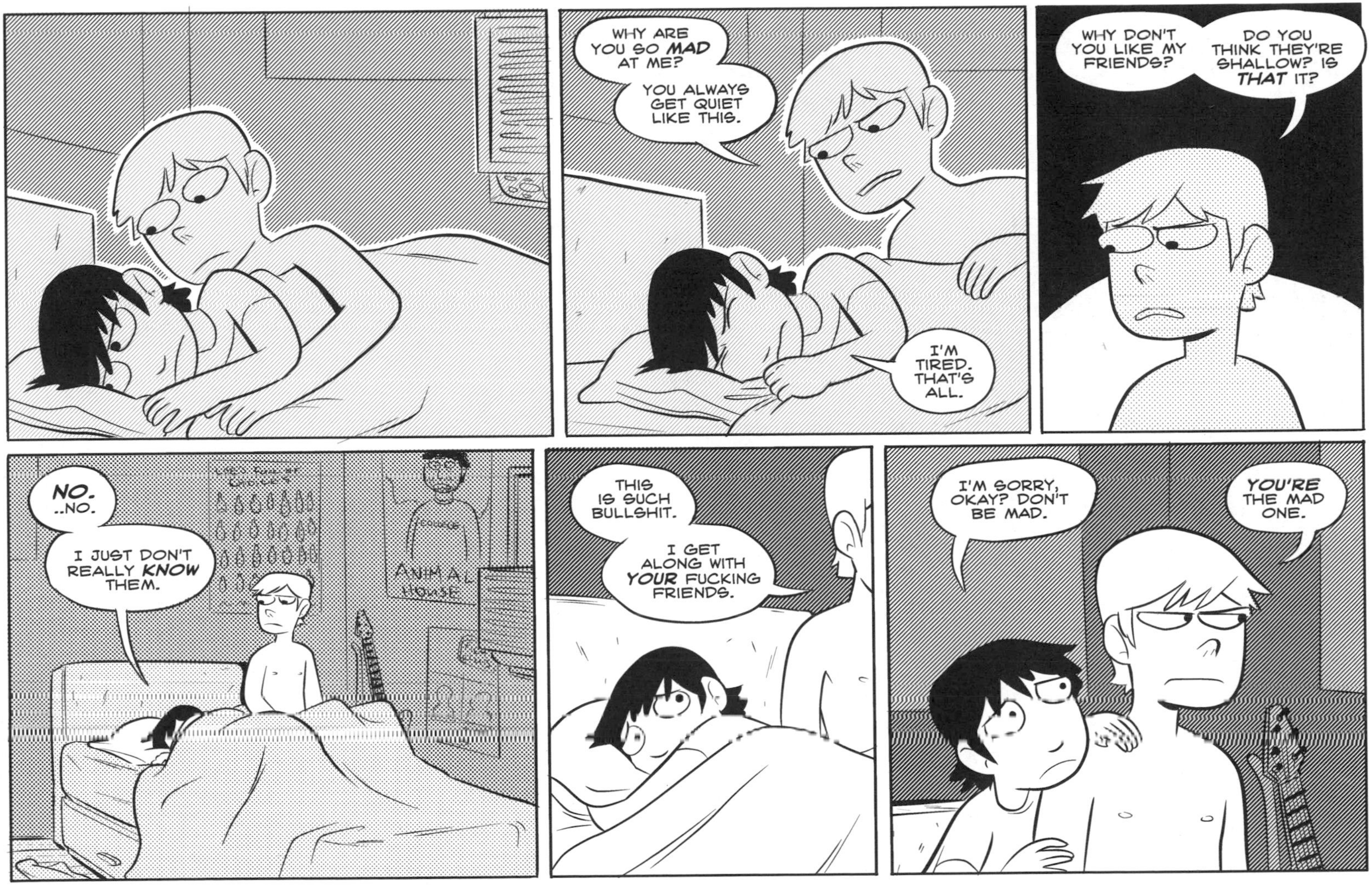
WHY ARE YOU SO MAD AT ME?
YOU ALWAYS GET QUIET LIKE THIS.
I'M TIRED. THAT'S ALL.
WHY DON'T YOU LIKE MY FRIENDS?
DO YOU THINK THEY'RE SHALLOW? IS THAT IT?
NO. ..NO.
I JUST DON'T REALLY KNOW THEM.
ANIMAL HOUSE
THIS IS SUCH BULLSHIT.
I GET ALONG WITH YOUR FUCKING FRIENDS.
I'M SORRY, OKAY? DON'T BE MAD.
YOU'RE THE MAD ONE.

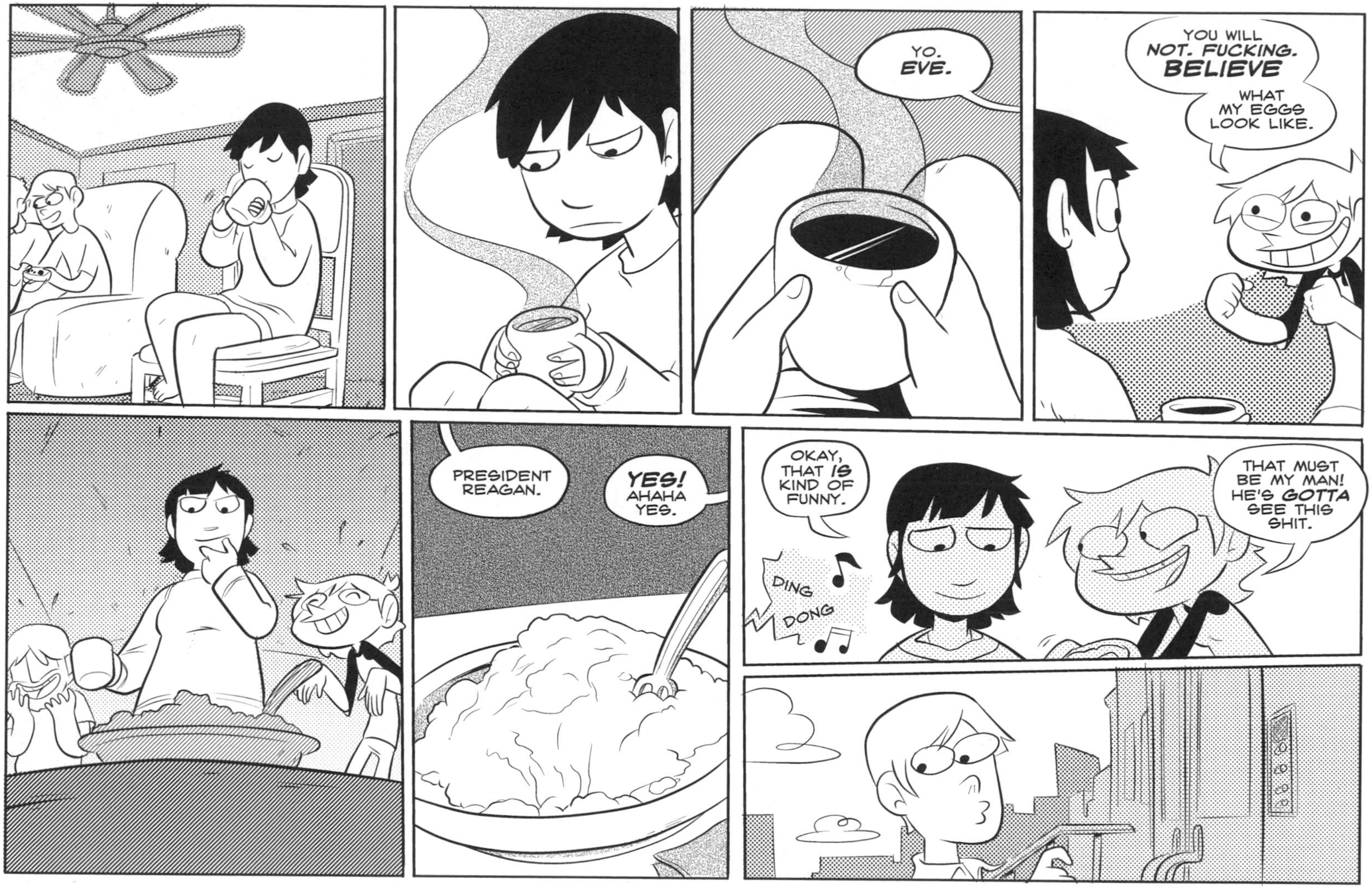
YO. EVE.
YOU WILL NOT. FUCKING. BELIEVE
WHAT MY EGGS LOOK LIKE.
PRESIDENT REAGAN.
YES! AHAHA YES.
OKAY, THAT IS KIND OF FUNNY.
DING DONG
THAT MUST BE MY MAN! HE'S GOTTA SEE THIS SHIT.

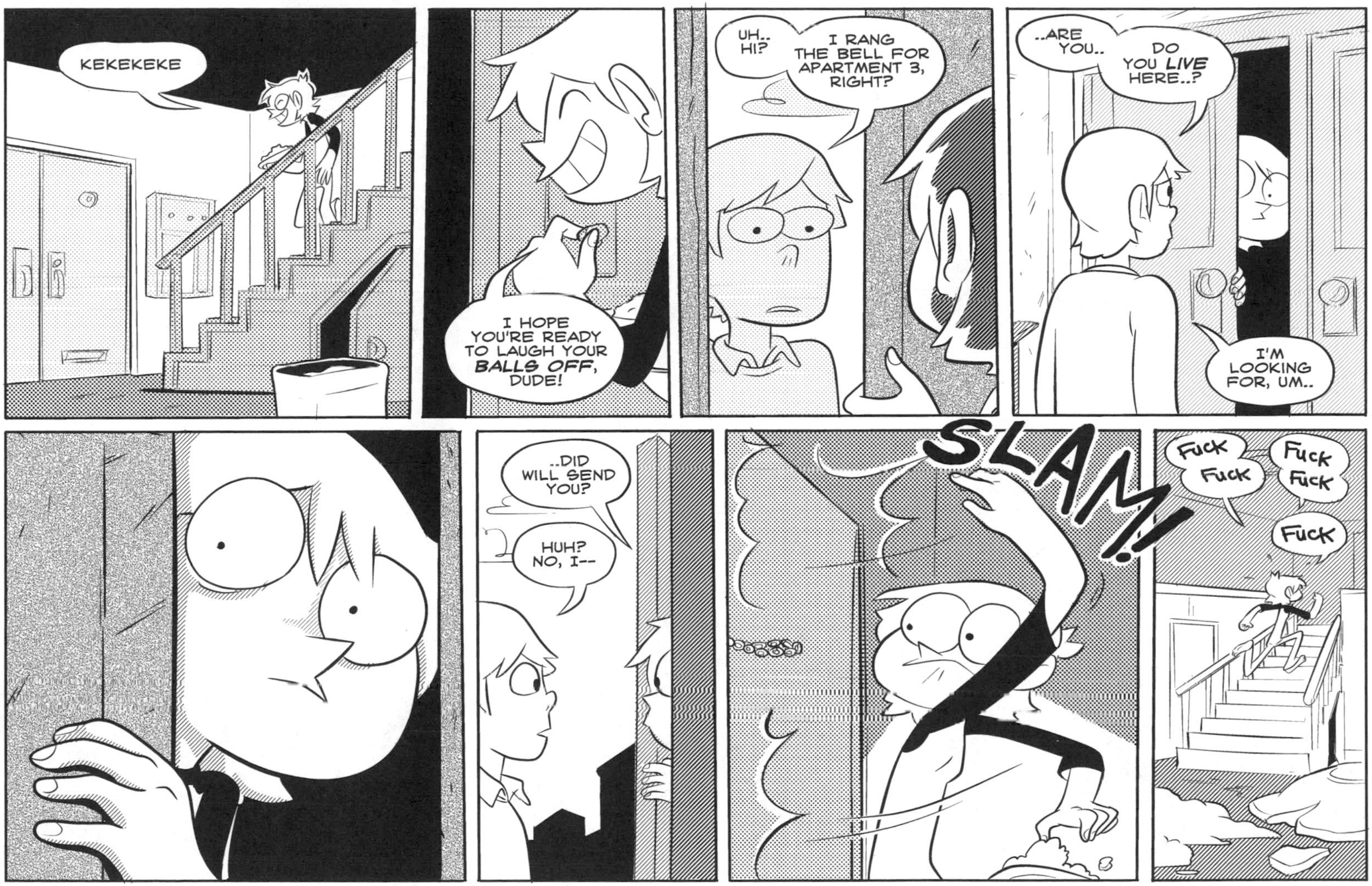
KEKEKEKE
I HOPE YOU'RE READY TO LAUGH YOUR BALLS OFF, DUDE!
UH.. HI?
I RANG THE BELL FOR APARTMENT 3, RIGHT?
..ARE YOU..
DO YOU LIVE HERE..?
I'M LOOKING FOR, UM..
..DID WILL SEND YOU?
HUH? NO, I--
SLAM!!
FUCK FUCK
FUCK FUCK
FUCK

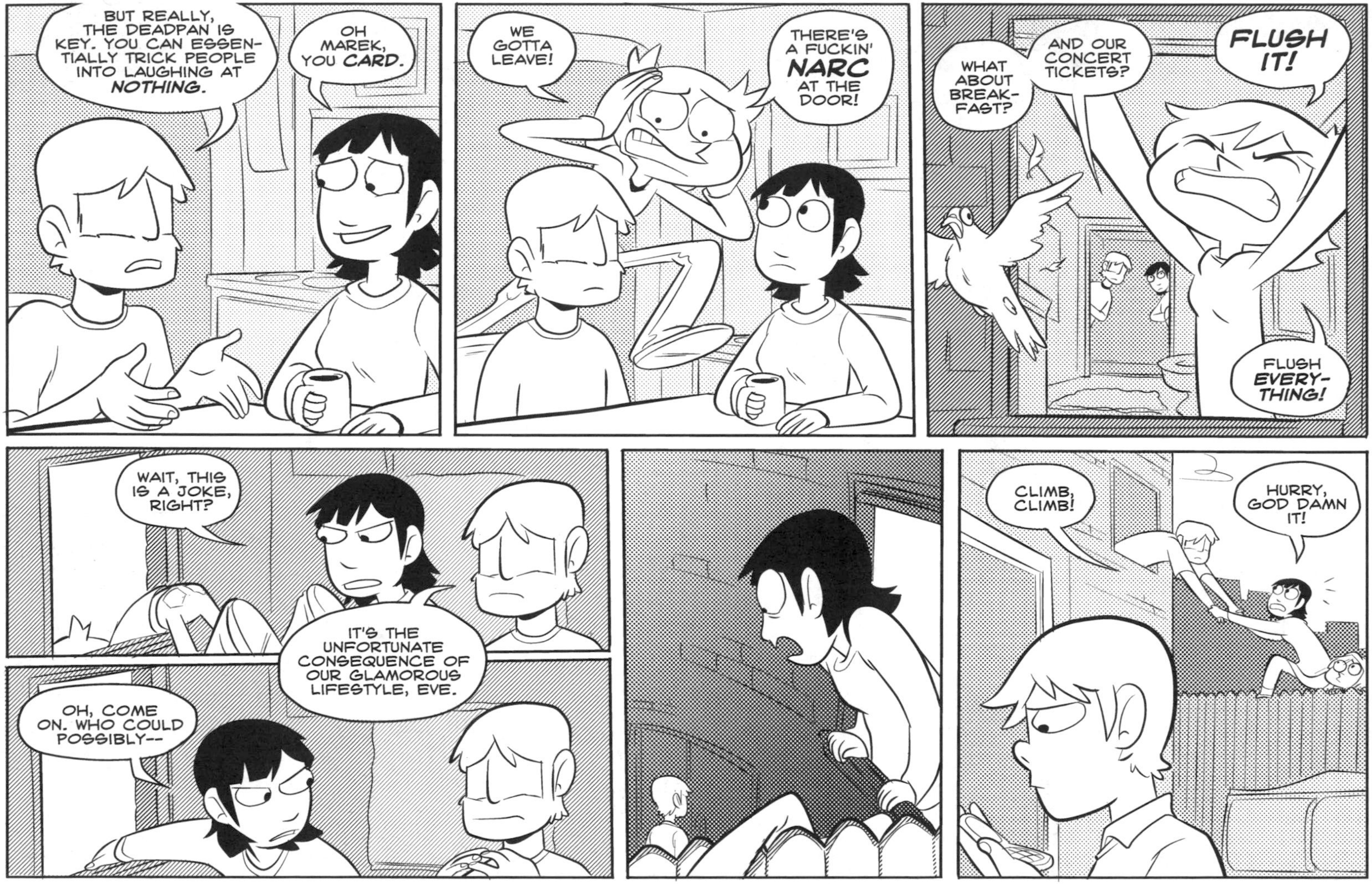
BUT REALLY, THE DEADPAN IS KEY. YOU CAN ESSEN-TIALLY TRICK PEOPLE INTO LAUGHING AT NOTHING.
OH MAREK, YOU CARD.
WE GOTTA LEAVE!
THERE'S A FUCKIN' NARC AT THE DOOR!
WHAT ABOUT BREAK-FAST?
AND OUR CONCERT TICKETS?
FLUSH IT!
FLUSH EVERY-THING!
WAIT, THIS IS A JOKE, RIGHT?
IT'S THE UNFORTUNATE CONSEQUENCE OF OUR GLAMOROUS LIFESTYLE, EVE.
OH, COME ON. WHO COULD POSSIBLY--
CLIMB, CLIMB!
HURRY, GOD DAMN IT!

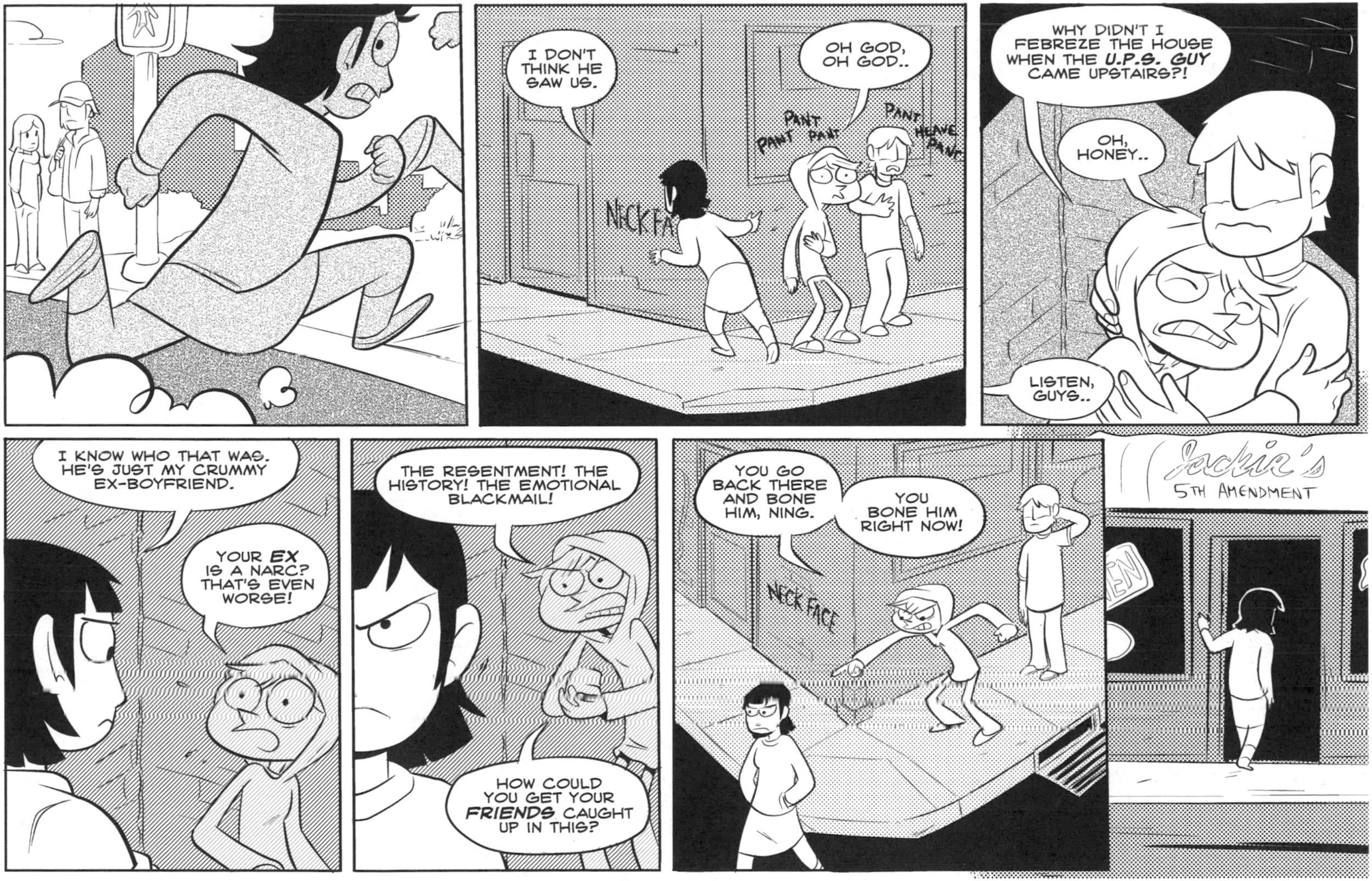

I DON'T THINK HE SAW US.
OH GOD, OH GOD..
PANT PANT PANT
PANT HEAVE PANT
NECK FA
WHY DIDN'T I FEBREZE THE HOUSE WHEN THE U.P.S. GUY CAME UPSTAIRS?!
OH, HONEY..
LISTEN, GUYS..
I KNOW WHO THAT WAS. HE'S JUST MY CRUMMY EX-BOYFRIEND.
YOUR EX IS A NARC? THAT'S EVEN WORSE!
THE RESENTMENT! THE HISTORY! THE EMOTIONAL BLACKMAIL!
HOW COULD YOU GET YOUR FRIENDS CAUGHT UP IN THIS?
YOU GO BACK THERE AND BONE HIM, NING.
YOU BONE HIM RIGHT NOW!
NECK FACE
Jackie's
5TH AMENDMENT

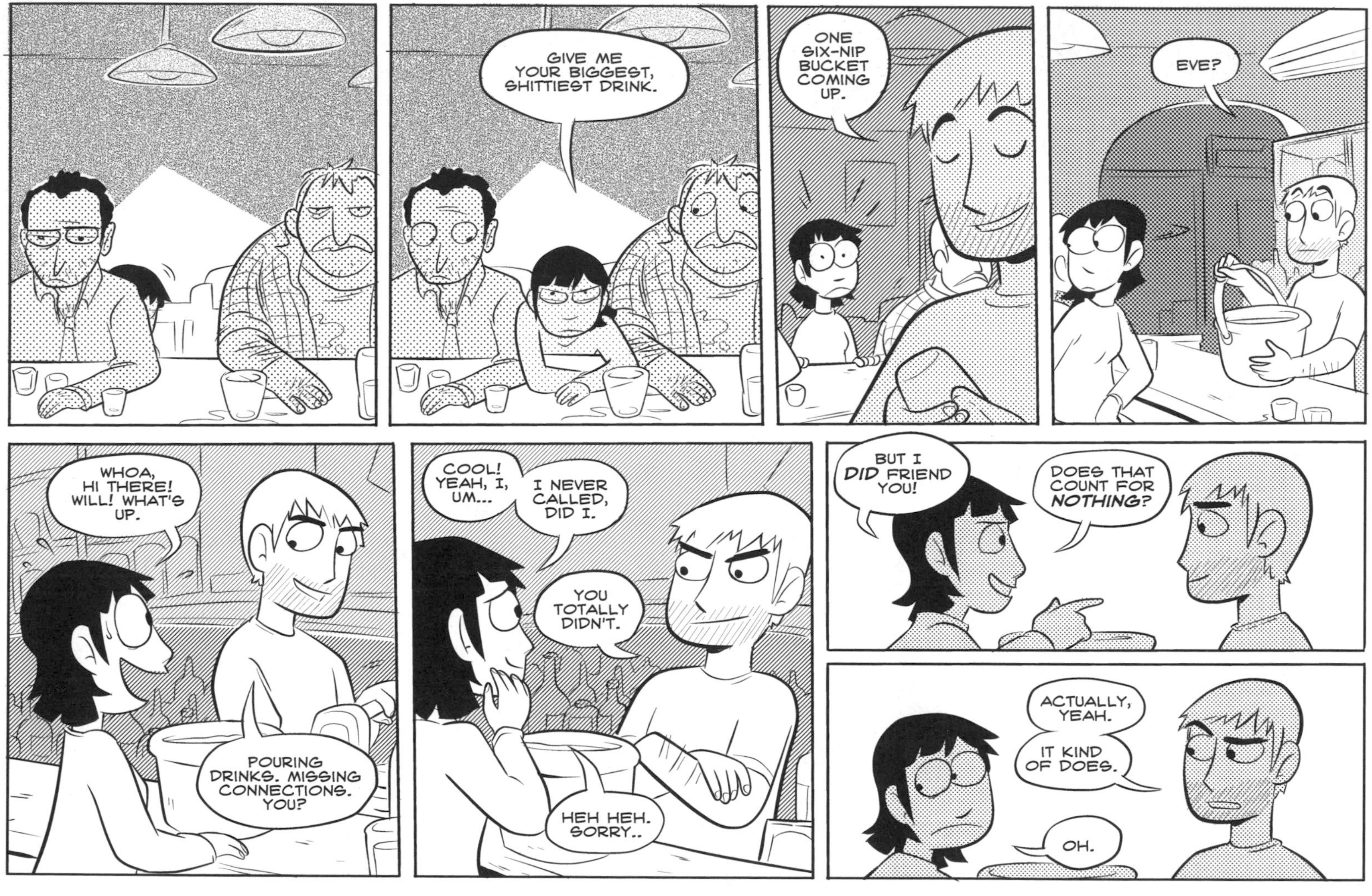
GIVE ME YOUR BIGGEST, SHITTIEST DRINK.
ONE SIX-NIP BUCKET COMING UP.
EVE?
WHOA, HI THERE! WILL! WHAT'S UP.
POURING DRINKS. MISSING CONNECTIONS. YOU?
COOL! YEAH, I, UM...
I NEVER CALLED, DID I.
YOU TOTALLY DIDN'T.
HEH HEH. SORRY..
BUT I *DID* FRIEND YOU!
DOES THAT COUNT FOR *NOTHING*?
ACTUALLY, YEAH.
IT KIND OF DOES.
OH.

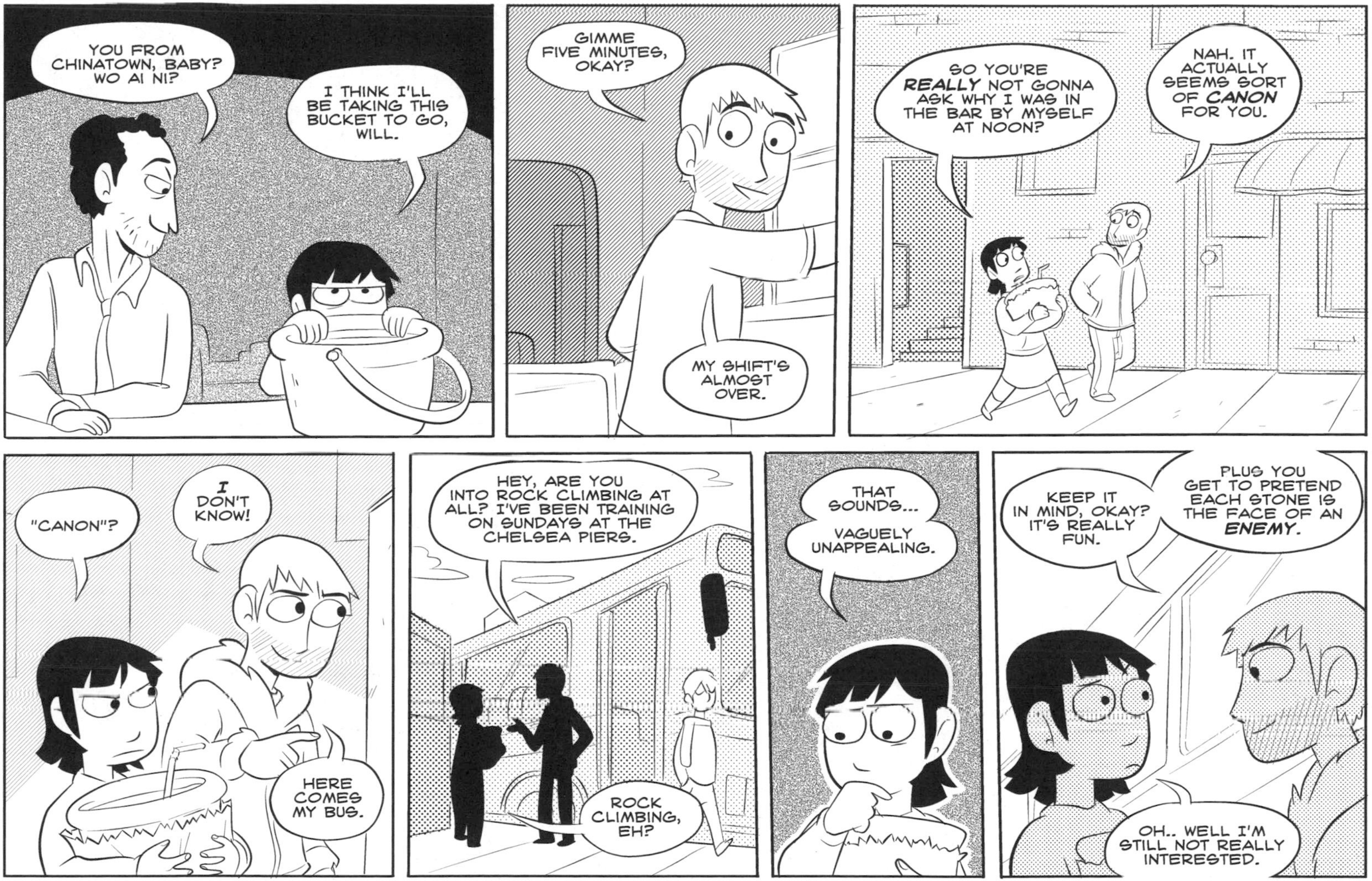
YOU FROM CHINATOWN, BABY? WO AI NI?
I THINK I'LL BE TAKING THIS BUCKET TO GO, WILL.
GIMME FIVE MINUTES, OKAY?
MY SHIFT'S ALMOST OVER.
SO YOU'RE **REALLY** NOT GONNA ASK WHY I WAS IN THE BAR BY MYSELF AT NOON?
NAH. IT ACTUALLY SEEMS SORT OF **CANON** FOR YOU.
"CANON"?
I DON'T KNOW!
HERE COMES MY BUS.
HEY, ARE YOU INTO ROCK CLIMBING AT ALL? I'VE BEEN TRAINING ON SUNDAYS AT THE CHELSEA PIERS.
ROCK CLIMBING, EH?
THAT SOUNDS...
VAGUELY UNAPPEALING.
KEEP IT IN MIND, OKAY? IT'S REALLY FUN.
PLUS YOU GET TO PRETEND EACH STONE IS THE FACE OF AN **ENEMY**.
OH.. WELL I'M STILL NOT REALLY INTERESTED.

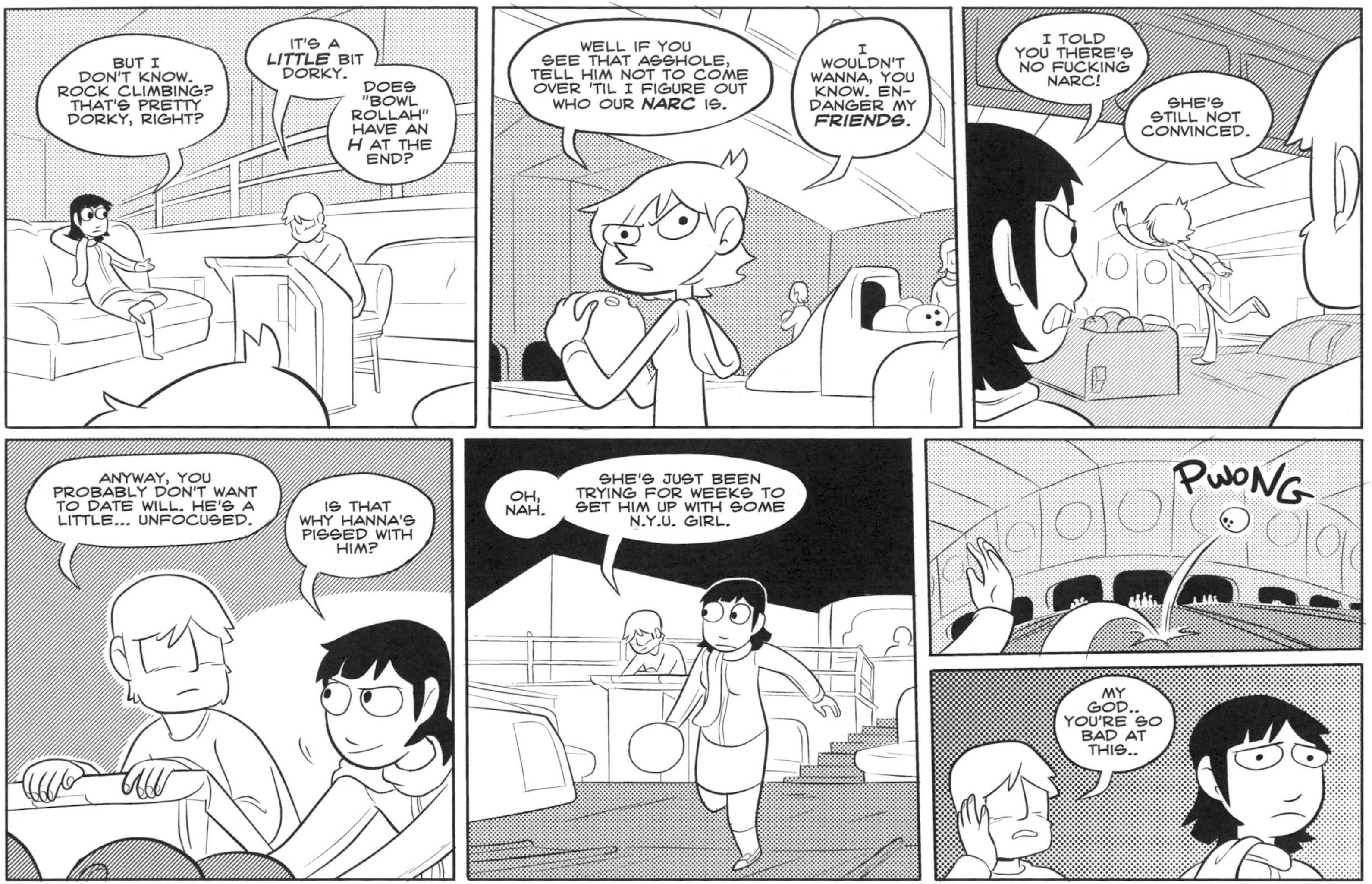
BUT I DON'T KNOW. ROCK CLIMBING? THAT'S PRETTY DORKY, RIGHT?
IT'S A *LITTLE* BIT DORKY.
DOES "BOWL ROLLAH" HAVE AN *H* AT THE END?
WELL IF YOU SEE THAT ASSHOLE, TELL HIM NOT TO COME OVER 'TIL I FIGURE OUT WHO OUR *NARC* IS.
I WOULDN'T WANNA, YOU KNOW. EN-DANGER MY *FRIENDS*.
I TOLD YOU THERE'S NO FUCKING NARC!
SHE'S STILL NOT CONVINCED.
ANYWAY, YOU PROBABLY DON'T WANT TO DATE WILL. HE'S A LITTLE... UNFOCUSED.
IS THAT WHY HANNA'S PISSED WITH HIM?
OH, NAH.
SHE'S JUST BEEN TRYING FOR WEEKS TO SET HIM UP WITH SOME N.Y.U. GIRL.
PWONG
MY GOD.. YOU'RE SO BAD AT THIS..

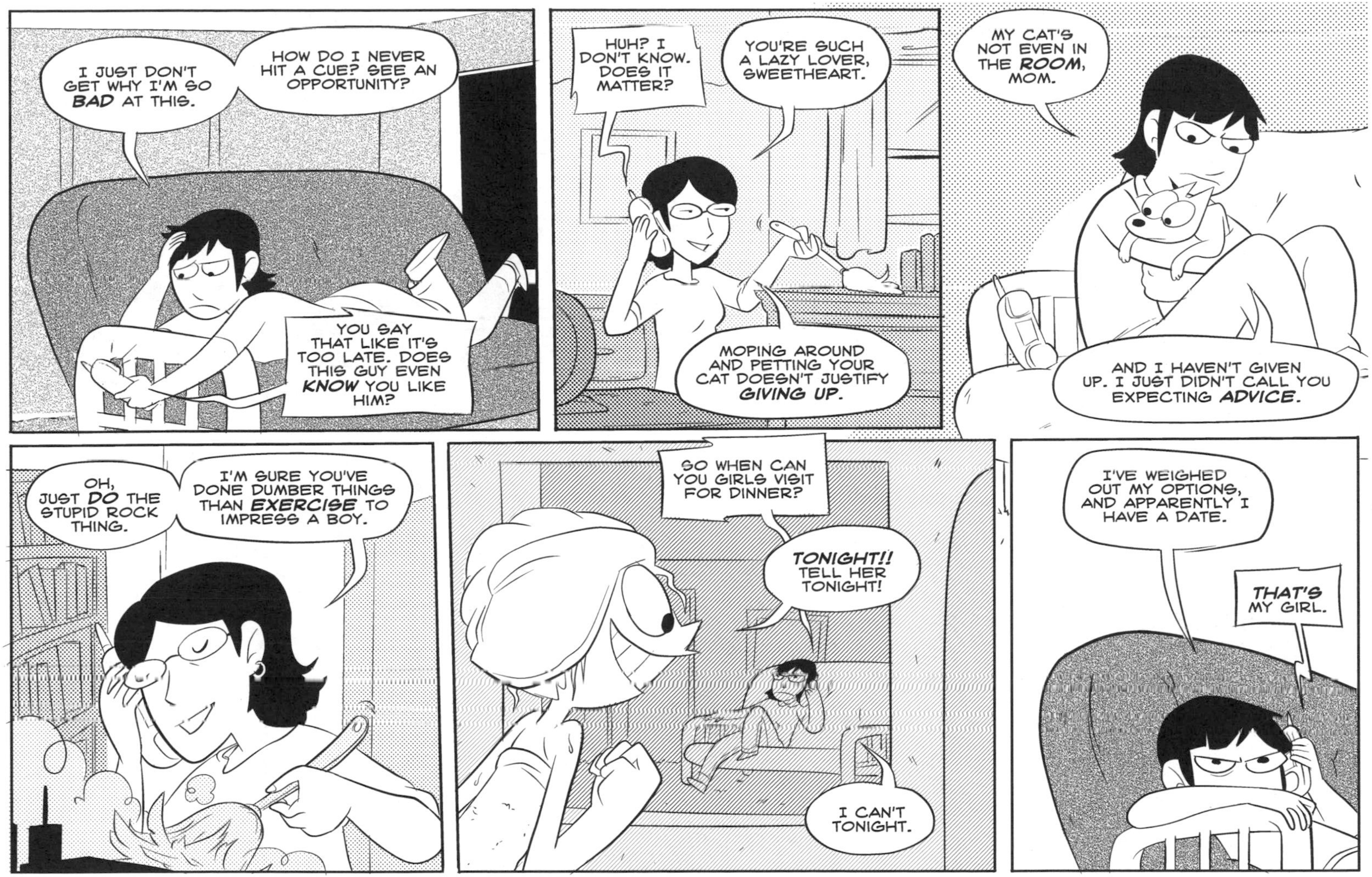
I JUST DON'T GET WHY I'M SO *BAD* AT THIS.
HOW DO I NEVER HIT A CUE? SEE AN OPPORTUNITY?
YOU SAY THAT LIKE IT'S TOO LATE. DOES THIS GUY EVEN *KNOW* YOU LIKE HIM?
HUH? I DON'T KNOW. DOES IT MATTER?
YOU'RE SUCH A LAZY LOVER, SWEETHEART.
MOPING AROUND AND PETTING YOUR CAT DOESN'T JUSTIFY *GIVING UP*.
MY CAT'S NOT EVEN IN THE *ROOM*, MOM.
AND I HAVEN'T GIVEN UP. I JUST DIDN'T CALL YOU EXPECTING *ADVICE*.
OH, JUST *DO* THE STUPID ROCK THING.
I'M SURE YOU'VE DONE DUMBER THINGS THAN *EXERCISE* TO IMPRESS A BOY.
SO WHEN CAN YOU GIRLS VISIT FOR DINNER?
TONIGHT!! TELL HER TONIGHT!
I CAN'T TONIGHT.
I'VE WEIGHED OUT MY OPTIONS, AND APPARENTLY I HAVE A DATE.
THAT'S MY GIRL.

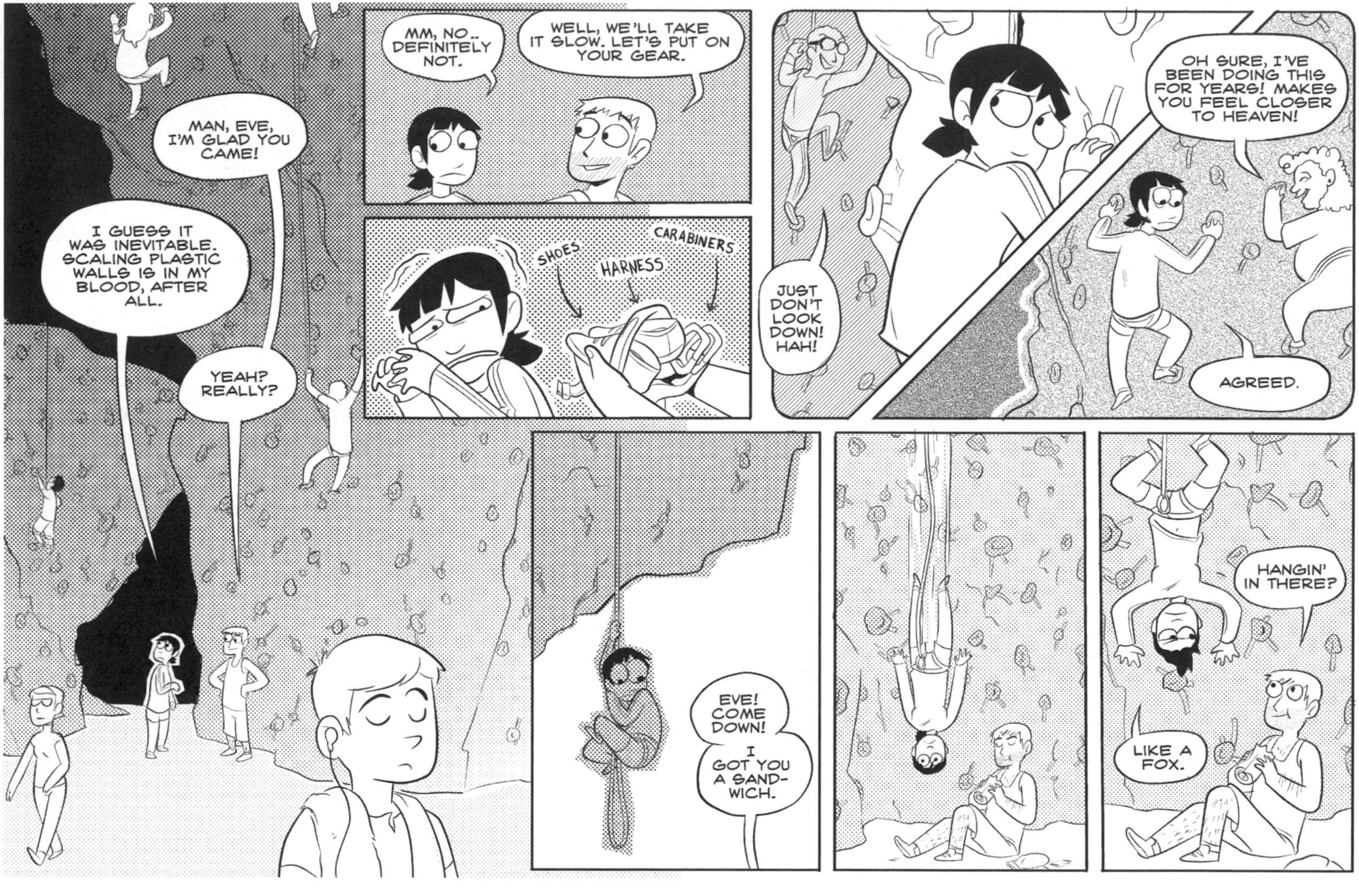
MAN, EVE, I'M GLAD YOU CAME!
I GUESS IT WAS INEVITABLE. SCALING PLASTIC WALLS IS IN MY BLOOD, AFTER ALL.
YEAH? REALLY?
MM, NO.. DEFINITELY NOT.
WELL, WE'LL TAKE IT SLOW. LET'S PUT ON YOUR GEAR.
SHOES
HARNESS
CARABINERS
JUST DON'T LOOK DOWN! HAH!
OH SURE, I'VE BEEN DOING THIS FOR YEARS! MAKES YOU FEEL CLOSER TO HEAVEN!
AGREED.
EVE! COME DOWN!
I GOT YOU A SAND-WICH.
HANGIN' IN THERE?
LIKE A FOX.

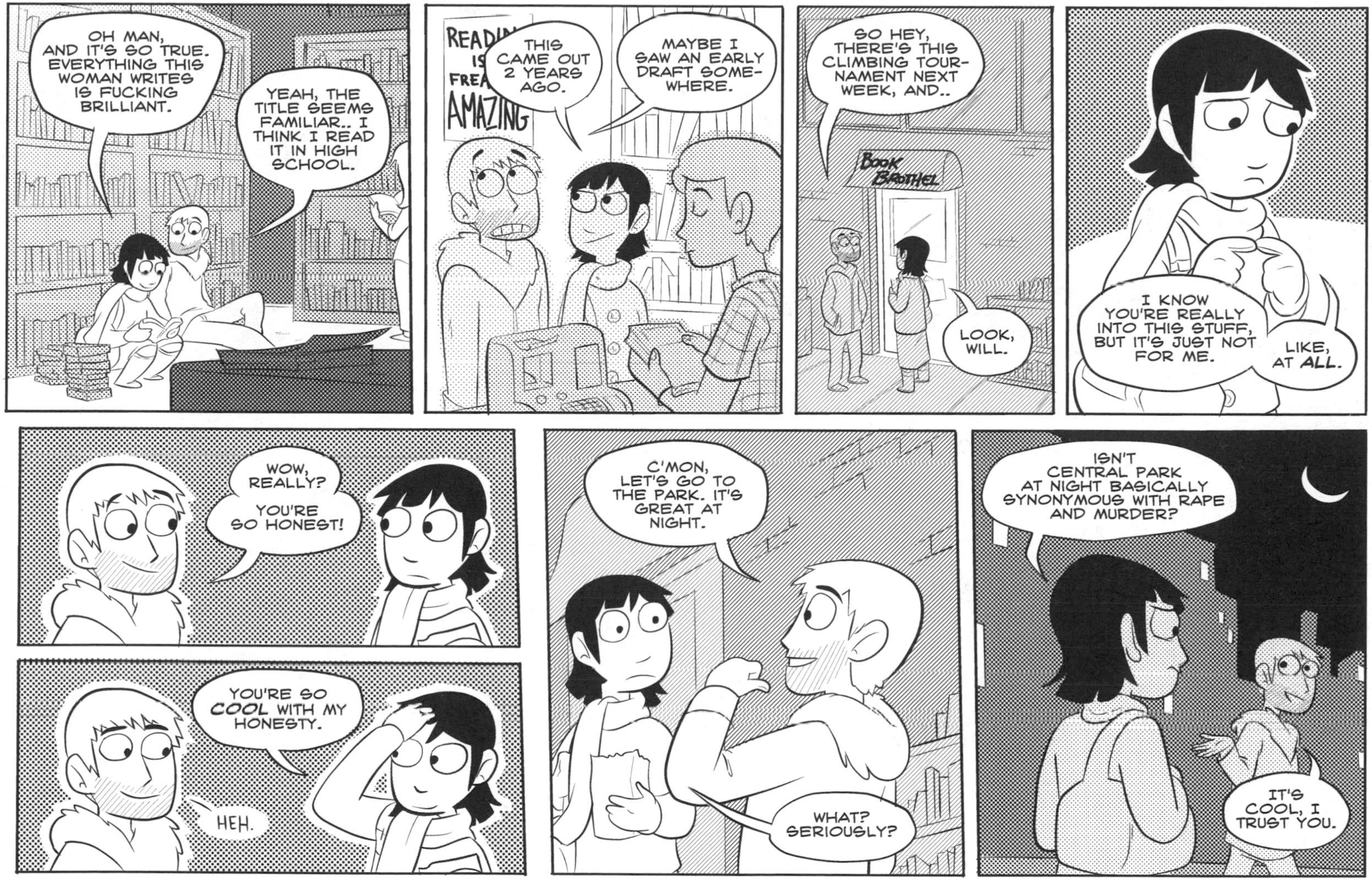
OH MAN, AND IT'S SO TRUE. EVERYTHING THIS WOMAN WRITES IS FUCKING BRILLIANT.
YEAH, THE TITLE SEEMS FAMILIAR.. I THINK I READ IT IN HIGH SCHOOL.
AMAZING
THIS CAME OUT 2 YEARS AGO.
MAYBE I SAW AN EARLY DRAFT SOME-WHERE.
SO HEY, THERE'S THIS CLIMBING TOUR-NAMENT NEXT WEEK, AND..
BOOK BROTHEL
LOOK, WILL.
I KNOW YOU'RE REALLY INTO THIS STUFF, BUT IT'S JUST NOT FOR ME.
LIKE, AT ALL.
WOW, REALLY?
YOU'RE SO HONEST!
YOU'RE SO COOL WITH MY HONESTY.
HEH.
C'MON, LET'S GO TO THE PARK. IT'S GREAT AT NIGHT.
WHAT? SERIOUSLY?
ISN'T CENTRAL PARK AT NIGHT BASICALLY SYNONYMOUS WITH RAPE AND MURDER?
IT'S COOL, I TRUST YOU.

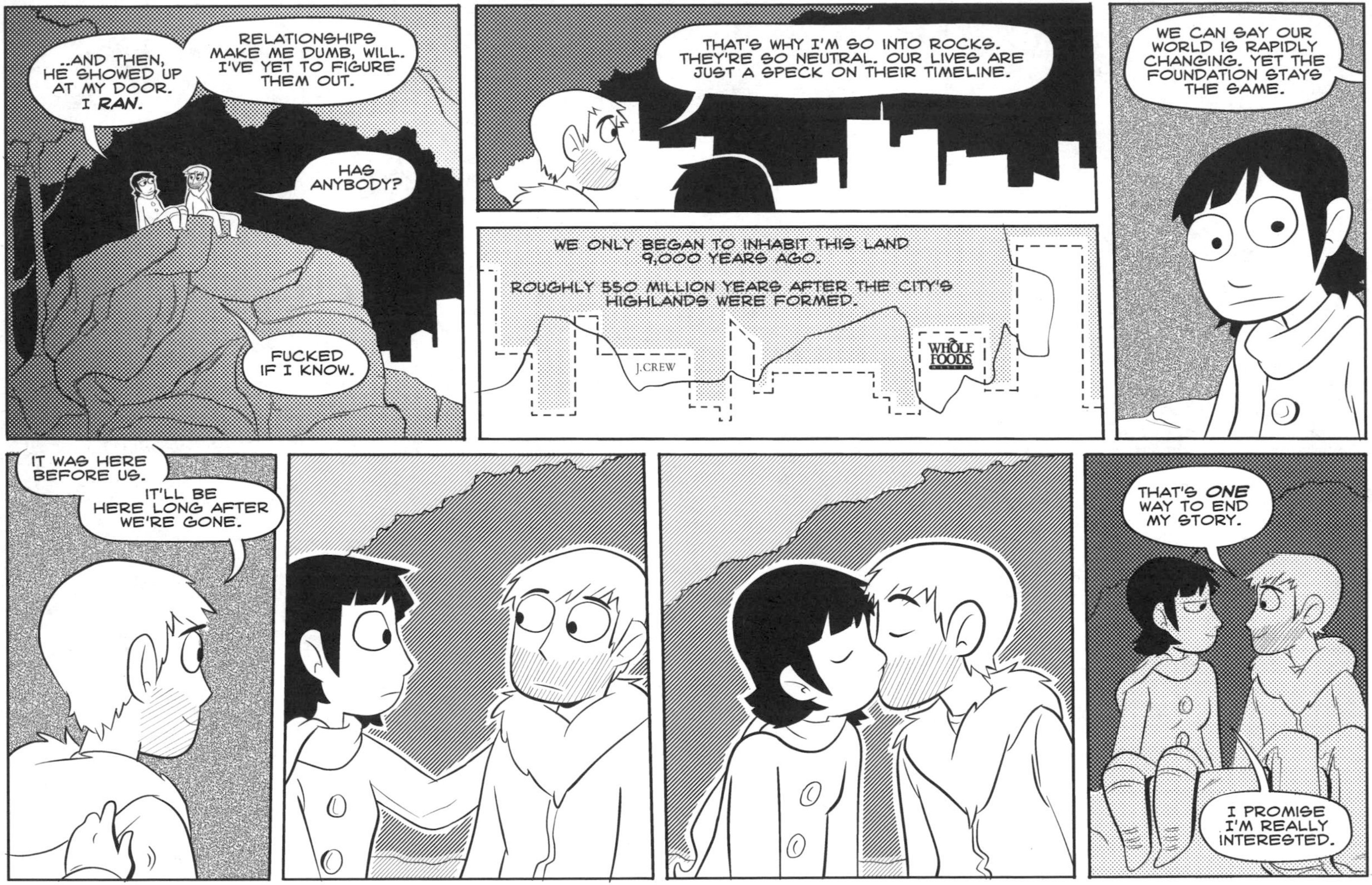
...AND THEN, HE SHOWED UP AT MY DOOR. I RAN.
RELATIONSHIPS MAKE ME DUMB, WILL. I'VE YET TO FIGURE THEM OUT.
HAS ANYBODY?
FUCKED IF I KNOW.
THAT'S WHY I'M SO INTO ROCKS. THEY'RE SO NEUTRAL. OUR LIVES ARE JUST A SPECK ON THEIR TIMELINE.
WE ONLY BEGAN TO INHABIT THIS LAND 9,000 YEARS AGO.
ROUGHLY 550 MILLION YEARS AFTER THE CITY'S HIGHLANDS WERE FORMED.
J.CREW
WHOLE FOODS
WE CAN SAY OUR WORLD IS RAPIDLY CHANGING. YET THE FOUNDATION STAYS THE SAME.
IT WAS HERE BEFORE US.
IT'LL BE HERE LONG AFTER WE'RE GONE.
THAT'S ONE WAY TO END MY STORY.
I PROMISE I'M REALLY INTERESTED.

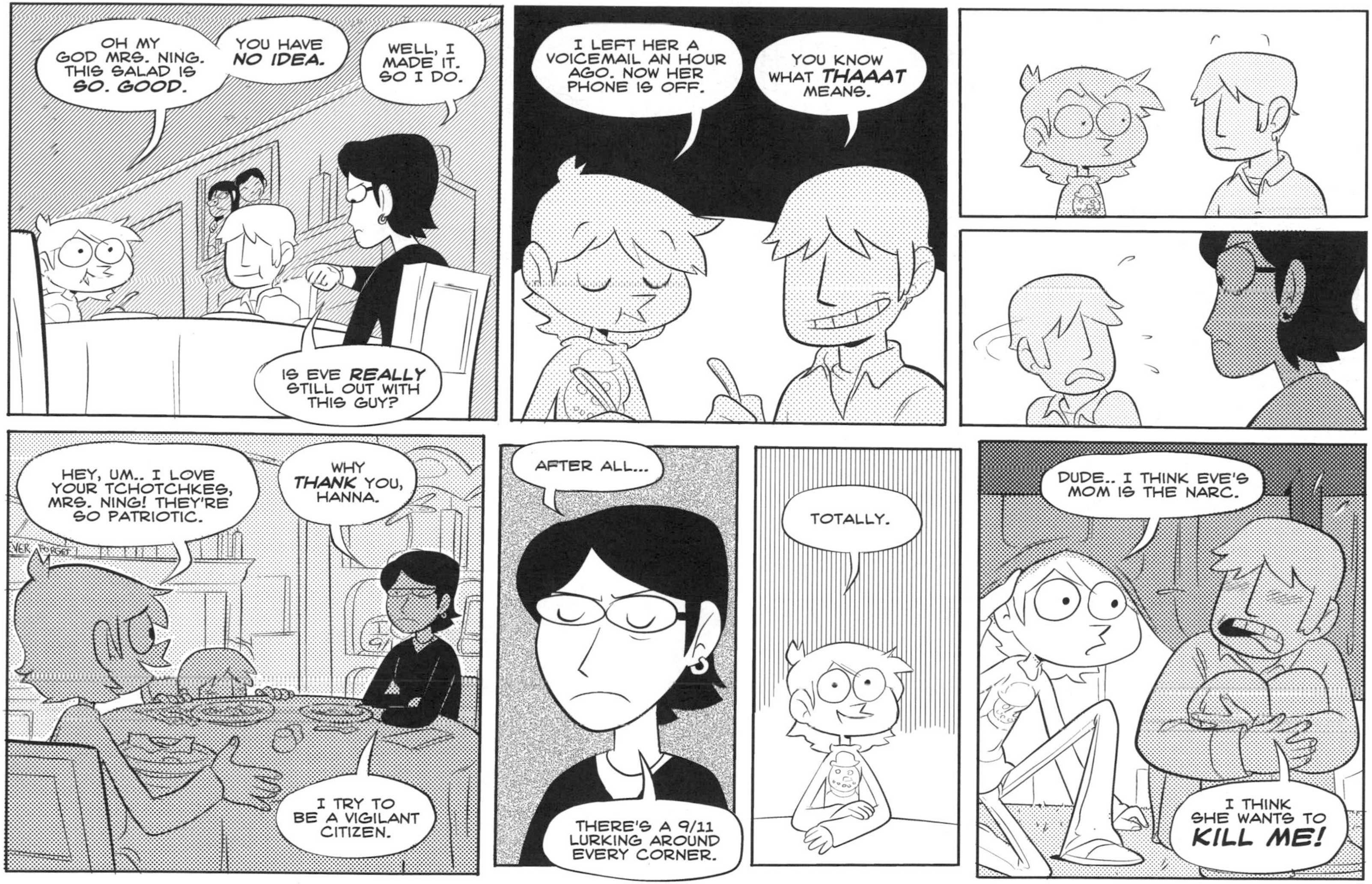
OH MY GOD MRS. NING. THIS SALAD IS SO. GOOD.
YOU HAVE NO IDEA.
WELL, I MADE IT. SO I DO.
IS EVE REALLY STILL OUT WITH THIS GUY?
I LEFT HER A VOICEMAIL AN HOUR AGO. NOW HER PHONE IS OFF.
YOU KNOW WHAT THAAAT MEANS.
HEY, UM.. I LOVE YOUR TCHOTCHKES, MRS. NING! THEY'RE SO PATRIOTIC.
WHY THANK YOU, HANNA.
I TRY TO BE A VIGILANT CITIZEN.
AFTER ALL...
THERE'S A 9/11 LURKING AROUND EVERY CORNER.
TOTALLY.
DUDE.. I THINK EVE'S MOM IS THE NARC.
I THINK SHE WANTS TO KILL ME!

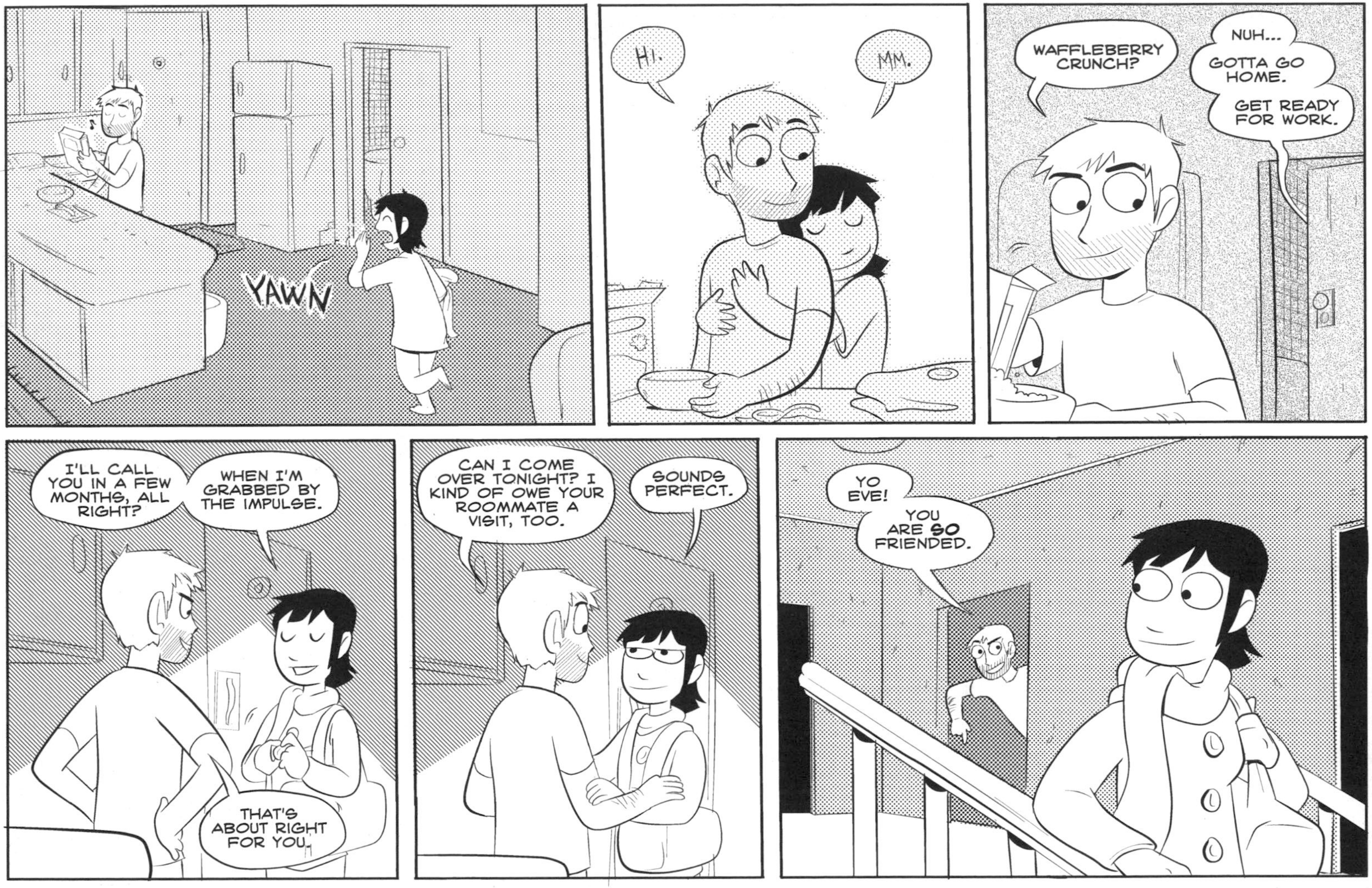
YAWN
HI.
MM.
WAFFLEBERRY CRUNCH?
NUH...
GOTTA GO HOME.
GET READY FOR WORK.
I'LL CALL YOU IN A FEW MONTHS, ALL RIGHT?
WHEN I'M GRABBED BY THE IMPULSE.
THAT'S ABOUT RIGHT FOR YOU.
CAN I COME OVER TONIGHT? I KIND OF OWE YOUR ROOMMATE A VISIT, TOO.
SOUNDS PERFECT.
YO EVE!
YOU ARE **SO** FRIENDED.

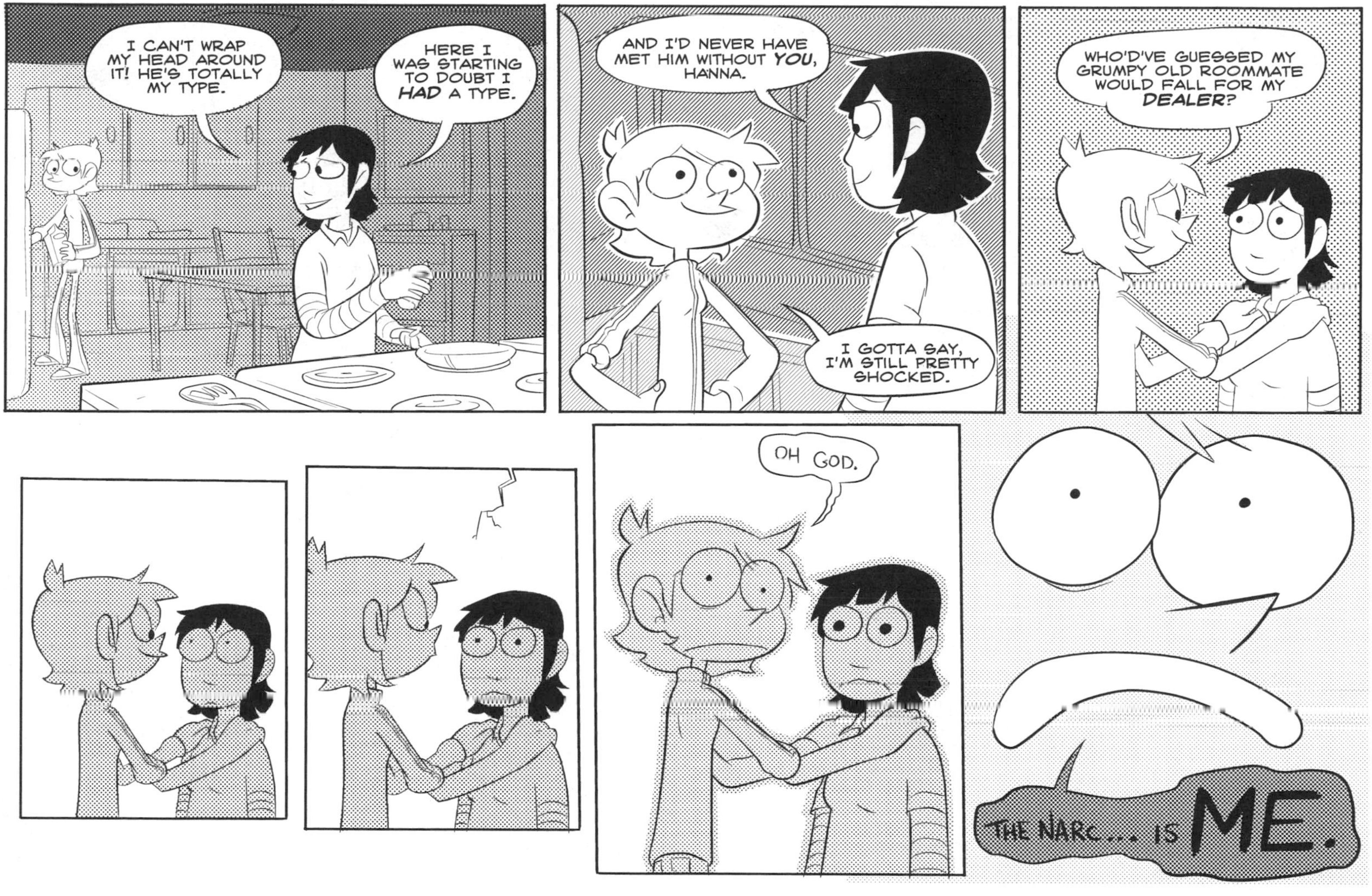
I CAN'T WRAP MY HEAD AROUND IT! HE'S TOTALLY MY TYPE.
HERE I WAS STARTING TO DOUBT I HAD A TYPE.
AND I'D NEVER HAVE MET HIM WITHOUT YOU, HANNA.
I GOTTA SAY, I'M STILL PRETTY SHOCKED.
WHO'D'VE GUESSED MY GRUMPY OLD ROOMMATE WOULD FALL FOR MY DEALER?
OH GOD.
THE NARC... IS ME.

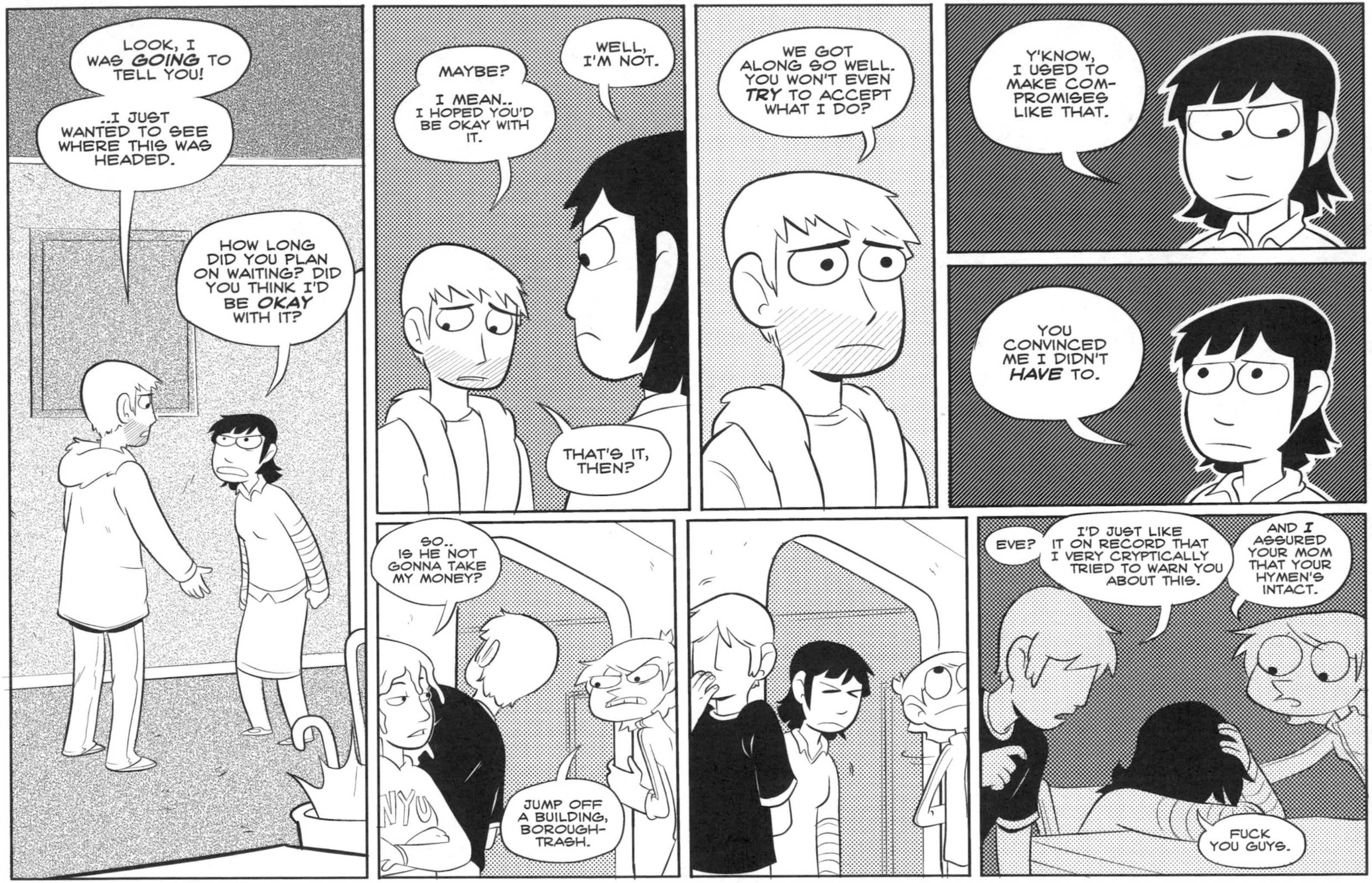
LOOK, I WAS GOING TO TELL YOU!
..I JUST WANTED TO SEE WHERE THIS WAS HEADED.
HOW LONG DID YOU PLAN ON WAITING? DID YOU THINK I'D BE OKAY WITH IT?
MAYBE?
I MEAN.. I HOPED YOU'D BE OKAY WITH IT.
WELL, I'M NOT.
THAT'S IT, THEN?
WE GOT ALONG SO WELL. YOU WON'T EVEN TRY TO ACCEPT WHAT I DO?
Y'KNOW, I USED TO MAKE COM-PROMISES LIKE THAT.
YOU CONVINCED ME I DIDN'T HAVE TO.
SO.. IS HE NOT GONNA TAKE MY MONEY?
NYU
JUMP OFF A BUILDING, BOROUGH-TRASH.
EVE?
I'D JUST LIKE IT ON RECORD THAT I VERY CRYPTICALLY TRIED TO WARN YOU ABOUT THIS.
AND I ASSURED YOUR MOM THAT YOUR HYMEN'S INTACT.
FUCK YOU GUYS.

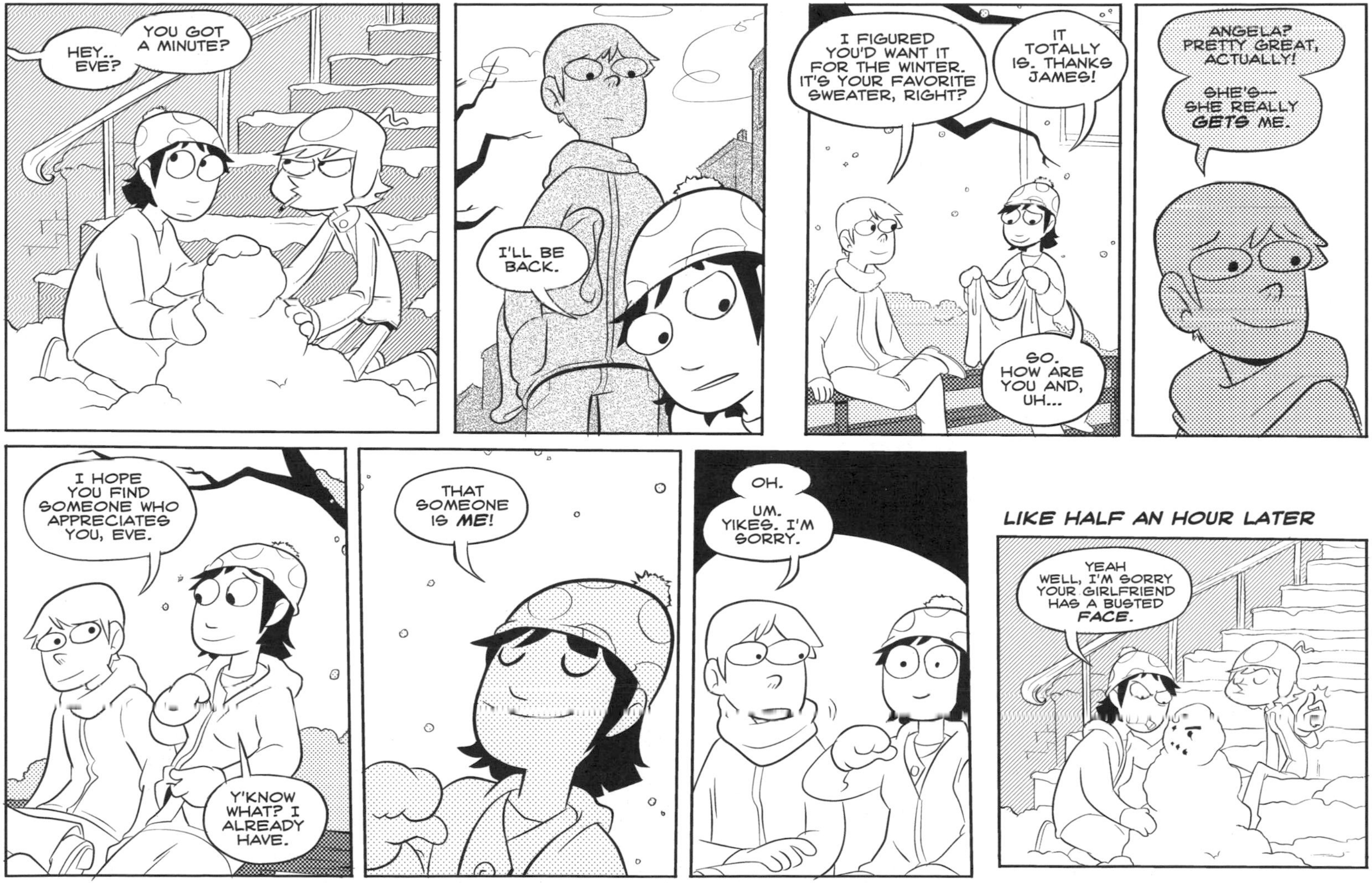
HEY.. EVE?
YOU GOT A MINUTE?
I'LL BE BACK.
I FIGURED YOU'D WANT IT FOR THE WINTER. IT'S YOUR FAVORITE SWEATER, RIGHT?
IT TOTALLY IS. THANKS JAMES!
SO. HOW ARE YOU AND, UH...
ANGELA? PRETTY GREAT, ACTUALLY!
SHE'S-- SHE REALLY GETS ME.
I HOPE YOU FIND SOMEONE WHO APPRECIATES YOU, EVE.
Y'KNOW WHAT? I ALREADY HAVE.
THAT SOMEONE IS ME!
OH.
UM. YIKES. I'M SORRY.
LIKE HALF AN HOUR LATER
YEAH WELL, I'M SORRY YOUR GIRLFRIEND HAS A BUSTED FACE.

7

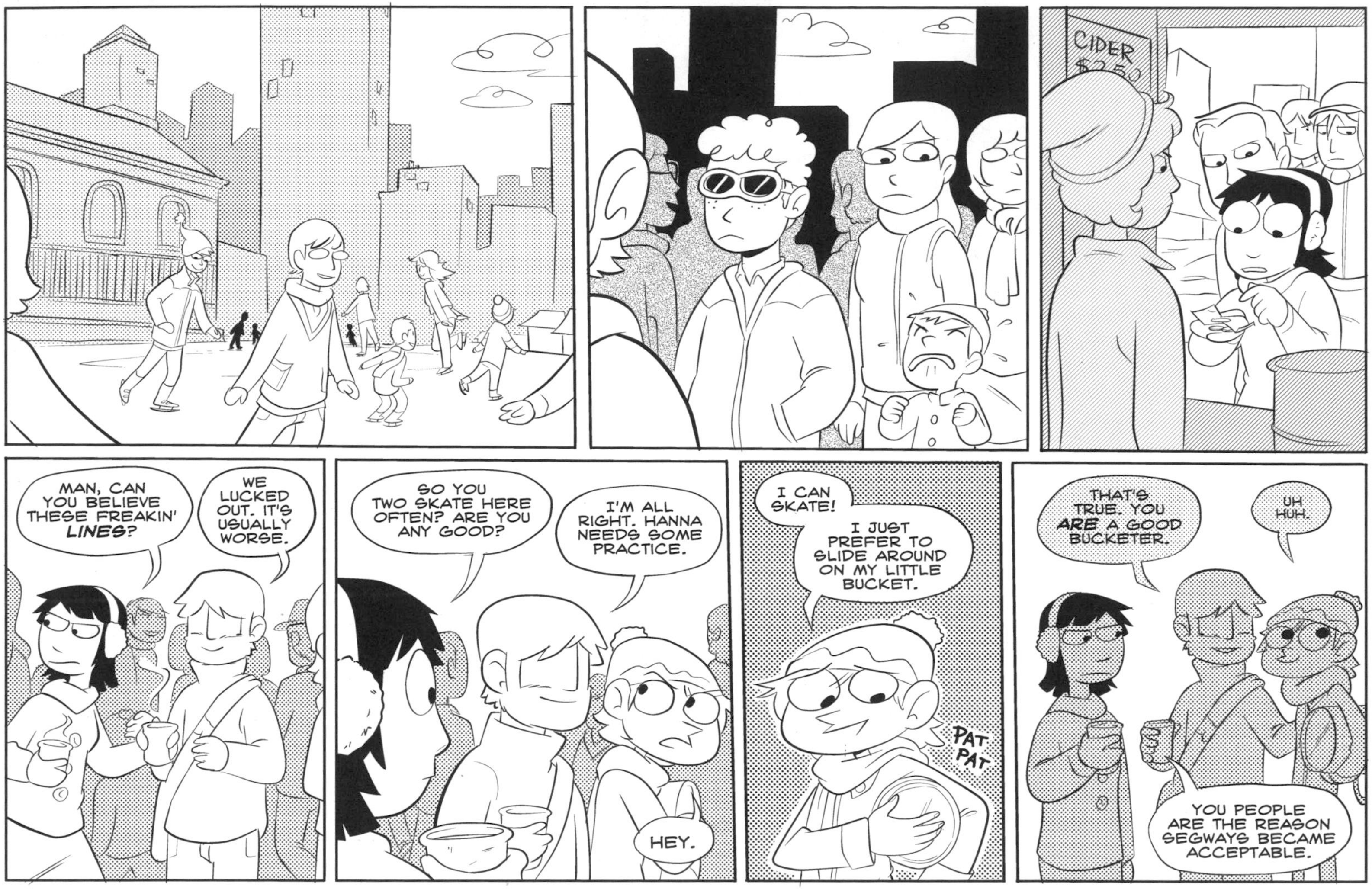
CIDER $2.50
MAN, CAN YOU BELIEVE THESE FREAKIN' *LINES*?
WE LUCKED OUT. IT'S USUALLY WORSE.
SO YOU TWO SKATE HERE OFTEN? ARE YOU ANY GOOD?
I'M ALL RIGHT. HANNA NEEDS SOME PRACTICE.
HEY.
I CAN SKATE!
I JUST PREFER TO SLIDE AROUND ON MY LITTLE BUCKET.
PAT PAT
THAT'S TRUE. YOU *ARE* A GOOD BUCKETER.
UH HUH.
YOU PEOPLE ARE THE REASON SEGWAYS BECAME ACCEPTABLE.

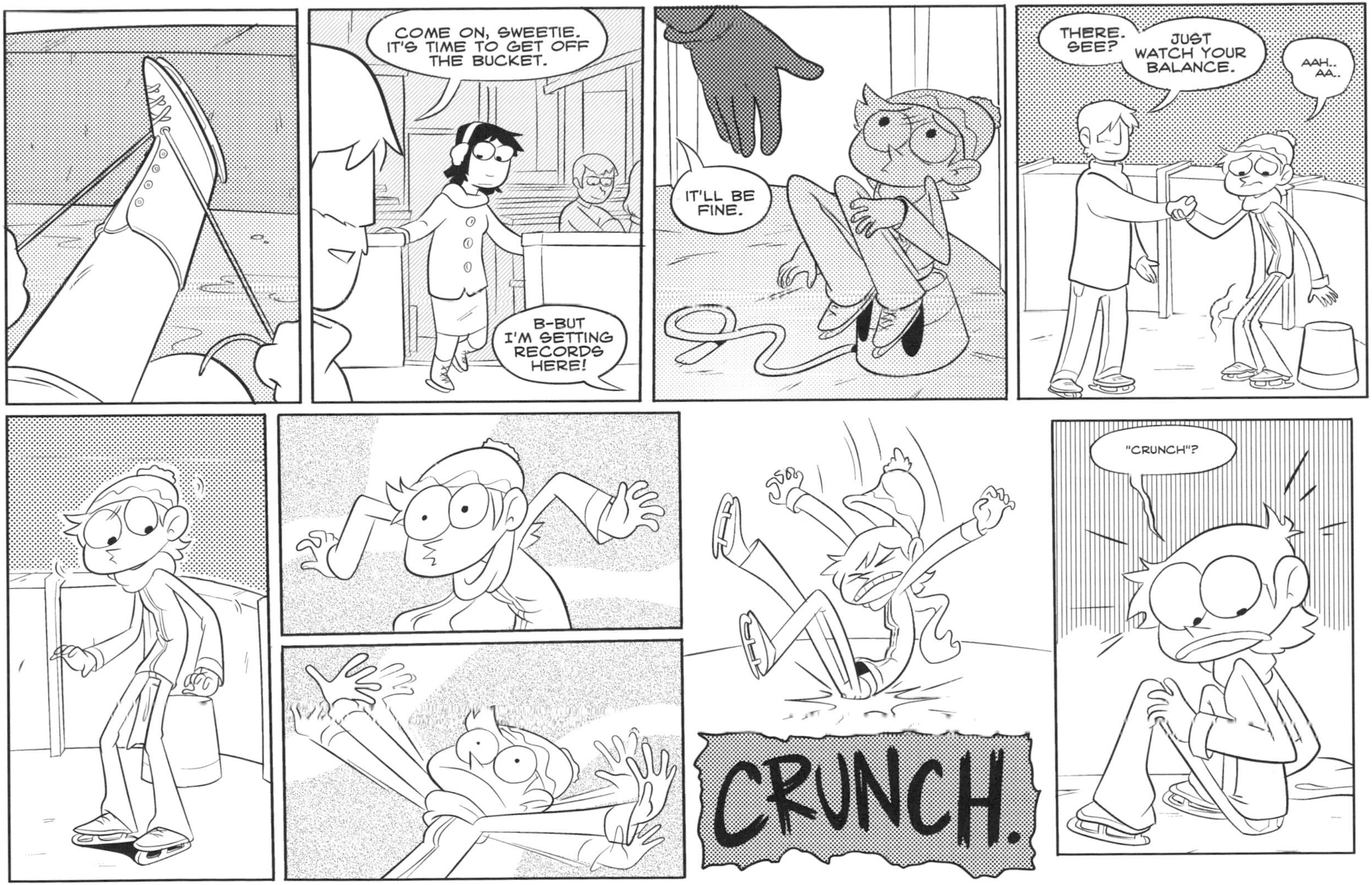
COME ON, SWEETIE. IT'S TIME TO GET OFF THE BUCKET.
B-BUT I'M SETTING RECORDS HERE!
IT'LL BE FINE.
THERE. SEE?
JUST WATCH YOUR BALANCE.
AAH.. AA..
CRUNCH.
"CRUNCH"?

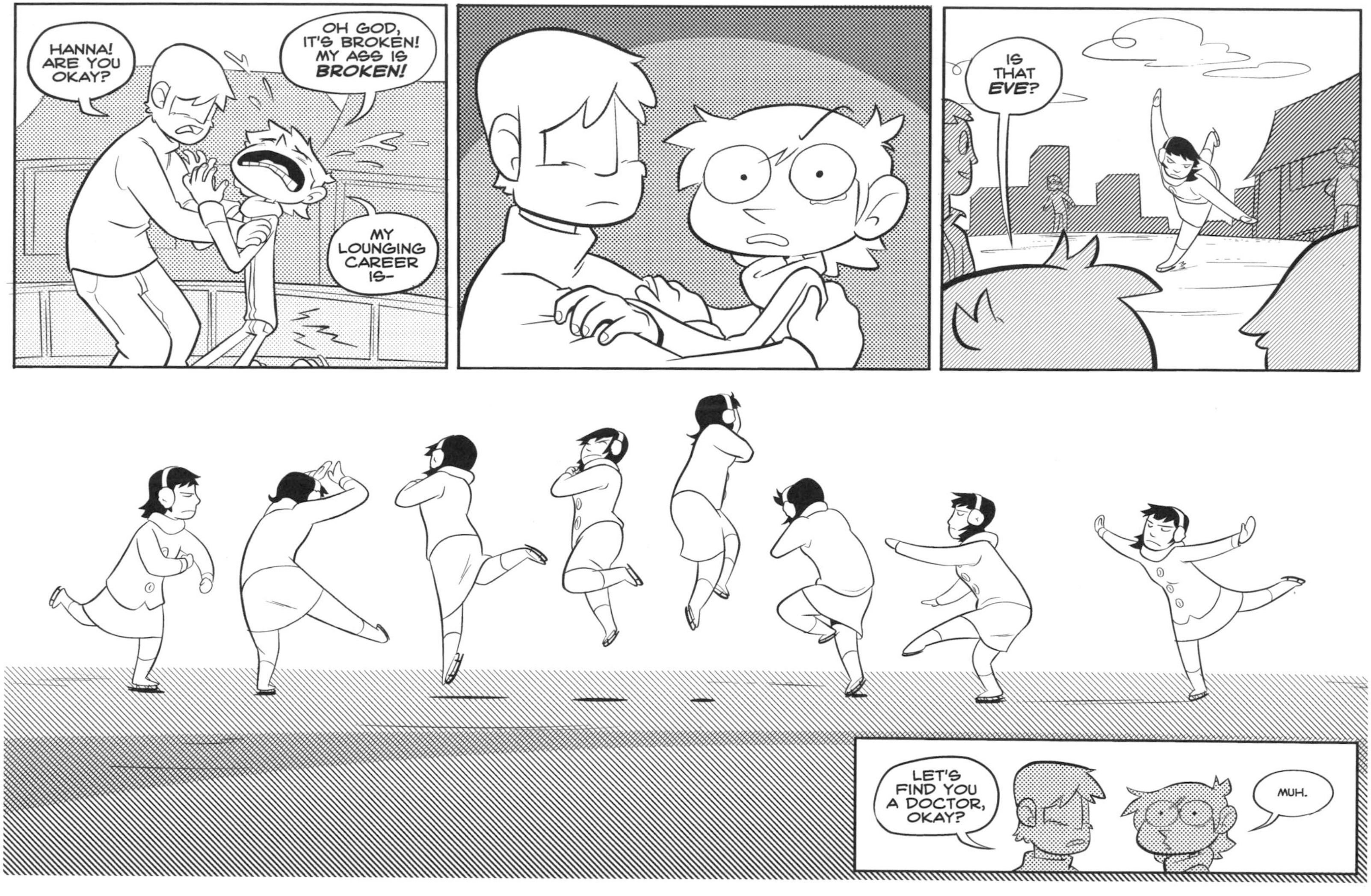
HANNA! ARE YOU OKAY?
OH GOD, IT'S BROKEN! MY ASS IS BROKEN!
MY LOUNGING CAREER IS-
IS THAT EVE?
LET'S FIND YOU A DOCTOR, OKAY?
MUH.

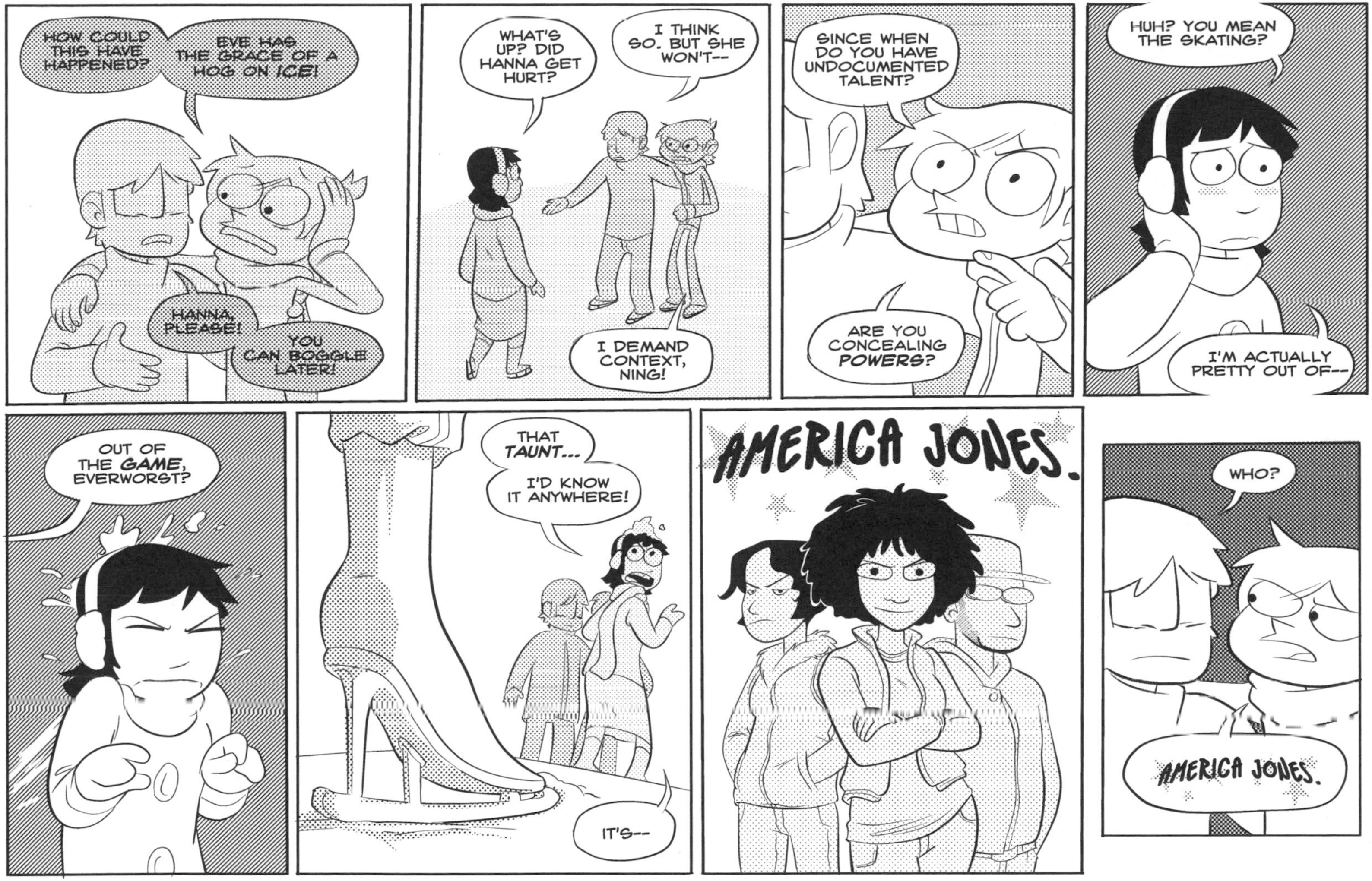
HOW COULD THIS HAVE HAPPENED?
EVE HAS THE GRACE OF A HOG ON *ICE*!
HANNA, PLEASE!
YOU CAN BOGGLE LATER!
WHAT'S UP? DID HANNA GET HURT?
I THINK SO. BUT SHE WON'T--
I DEMAND CONTEXT, NING!
SINCE WHEN DO YOU HAVE UNDOCUMENTED TALENT?
ARE YOU CONCEALING *POWERS*?
HUH? YOU MEAN THE SKATING?
I'M ACTUALLY PRETTY OUT OF--
OUT OF THE *GAME*, EVERWORST?
THAT *TAUNT*...
I'D KNOW IT ANYWHERE!
IT'S--
AMERICA JONES.
WHO?
AMERICA JONES.

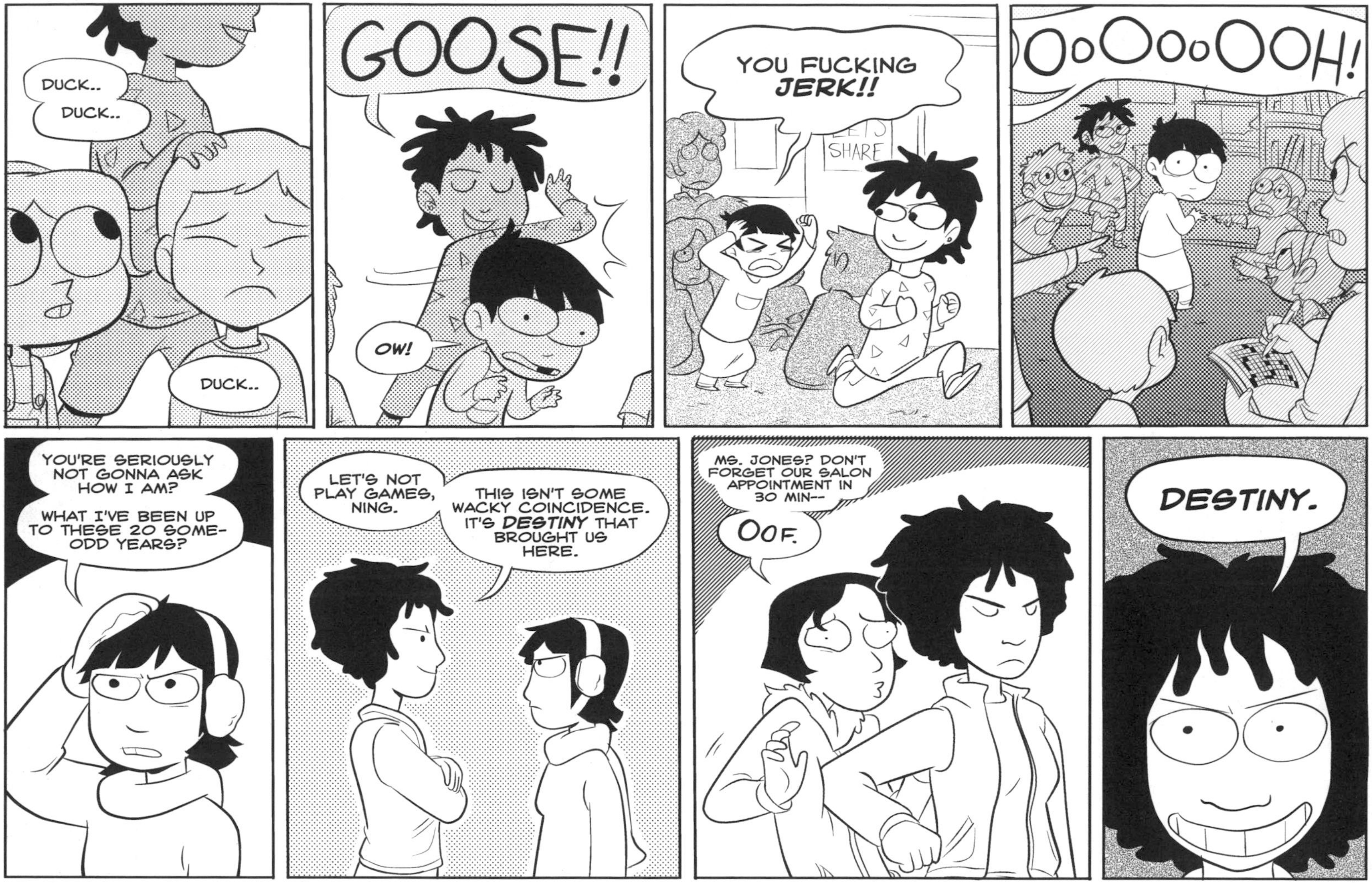
DUCK..
DUCK..
DUCK..
GOOSE!!
OW!
YOU FUCKING JERK!!
LET'S SHARE
OOoOOoOOH!
YOU'RE SERIOUSLY NOT GONNA ASK HOW I AM?
WHAT I'VE BEEN UP TO THESE 20 SOME-ODD YEARS?
LET'S NOT PLAY GAMES, NING.
THIS ISN'T SOME WACKY COINCIDENCE. IT'S DESTINY THAT BROUGHT US HERE.
MS. JONES? DON'T FORGET OUR SALON APPOINTMENT IN 30 MIN--
OOF.
DESTINY.

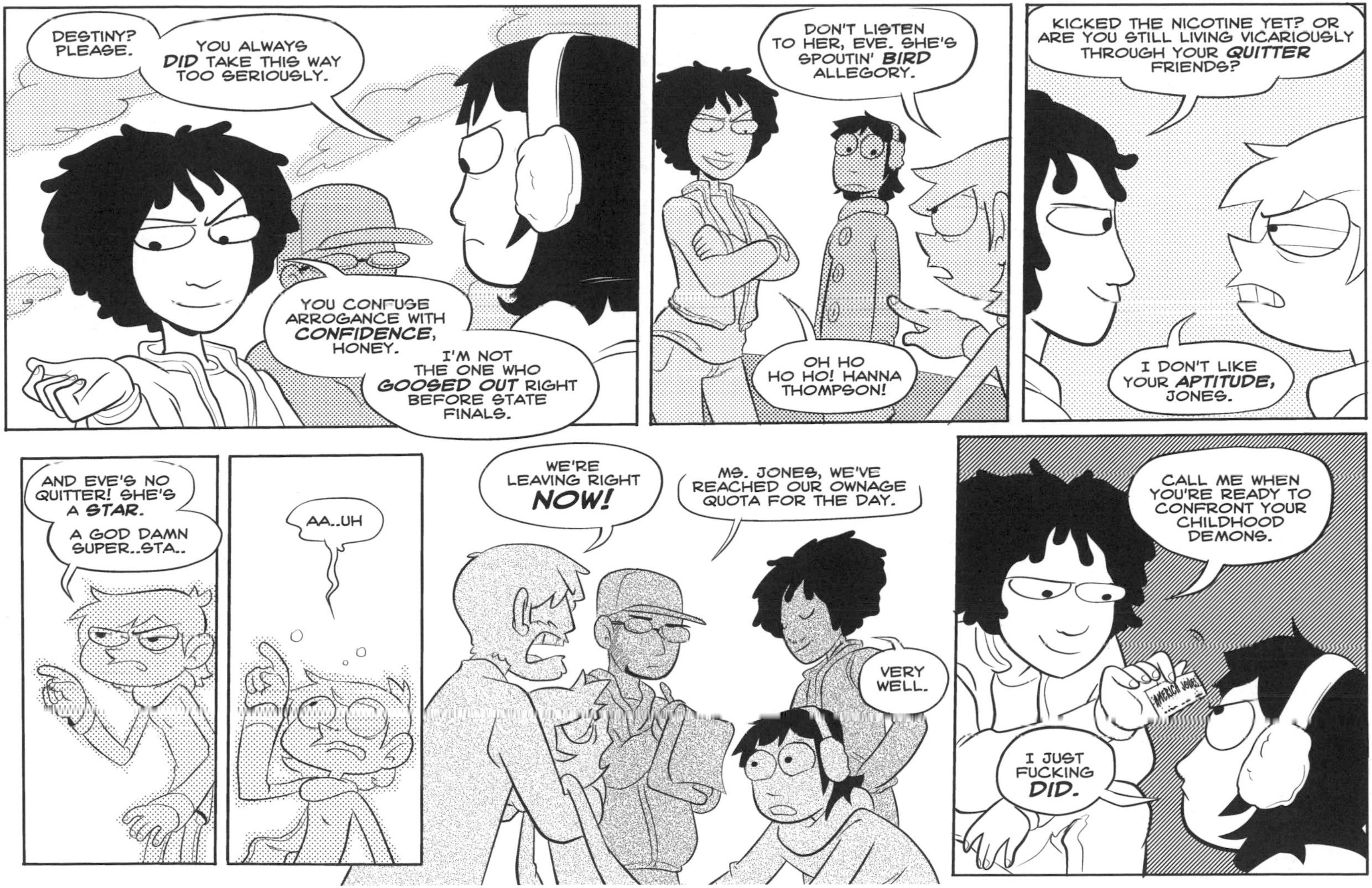
DESTINY? PLEASE.
YOU ALWAYS DID TAKE THIS WAY TOO SERIOUSLY.
YOU CONFUSE ARROGANCE WITH CONFIDENCE, HONEY.
I'M NOT THE ONE WHO GOOSED OUT RIGHT BEFORE STATE FINALS.
DON'T LISTEN TO HER, EVE. SHE'S SPOUTIN' BIRD ALLEGORY.
OH HO HO HO! HANNA THOMPSON!
KICKED THE NICOTINE YET? OR ARE YOU STILL LIVING VICARIOUSLY THROUGH YOUR QUITTER FRIENDS?
I DON'T LIKE YOUR APTITUDE, JONES.
AND EVE'S NO QUITTER! SHE'S A STAR.
A GOD DAMN SUPER..STA..
AA..UH
WE'RE LEAVING RIGHT NOW!
MS. JONES, WE'VE REACHED OUR OWNAGE QUOTA FOR THE DAY.
VERY WELL.
CALL ME WHEN YOU'RE READY TO CONFRONT YOUR CHILDHOOD DEMONS.
I JUST FUCKING DID.

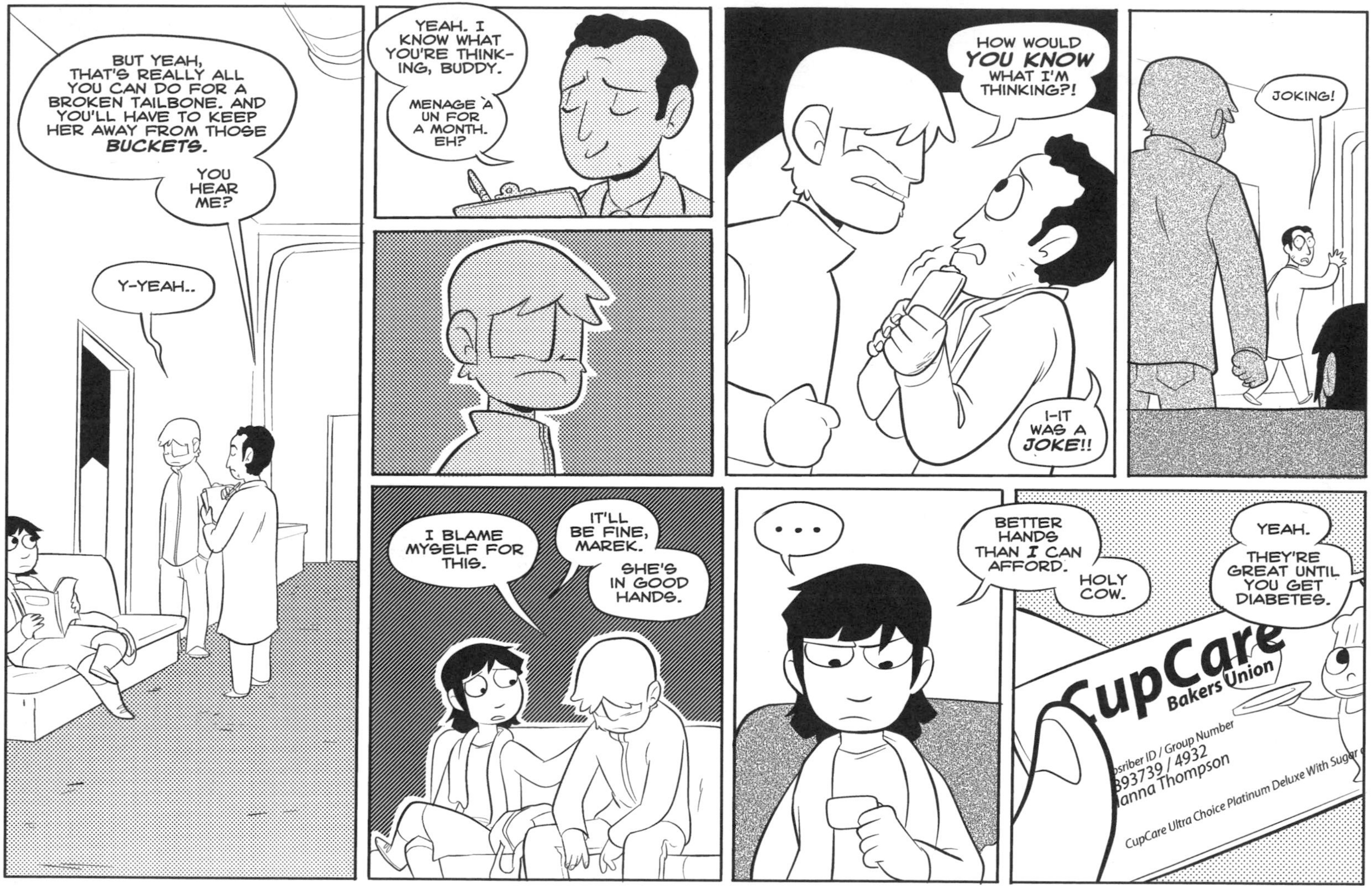
BUT YEAH, THAT'S REALLY ALL YOU CAN DO FOR A BROKEN TAILBONE. AND YOU'LL HAVE TO KEEP HER AWAY FROM THOSE **BUCKETS**.
YOU HEAR ME?
Y-YEAH..
YEAH. I KNOW WHAT YOU'RE THINKING, BUDDY.
MENAGE À UN FOR A MONTH. EH?
HOW WOULD ***YOU KNOW*** WHAT I'M THINKING?!
I-IT WAS A ***JOKE***!!
JOKING!
I BLAME MYSELF FOR THIS.
IT'LL BE FINE, MAREK.
SHE'S IN GOOD HANDS.
. . .
BETTER HANDS THAN ***I*** CAN AFFORD.
HOLY COW.
YEAH.
THEY'RE GREAT UNTIL YOU GET DIABETES.
CupCare
Bakers Union
Group Number
4932
Thompson
CupCare Ultra Choice Platinum Deluxe With Sugar

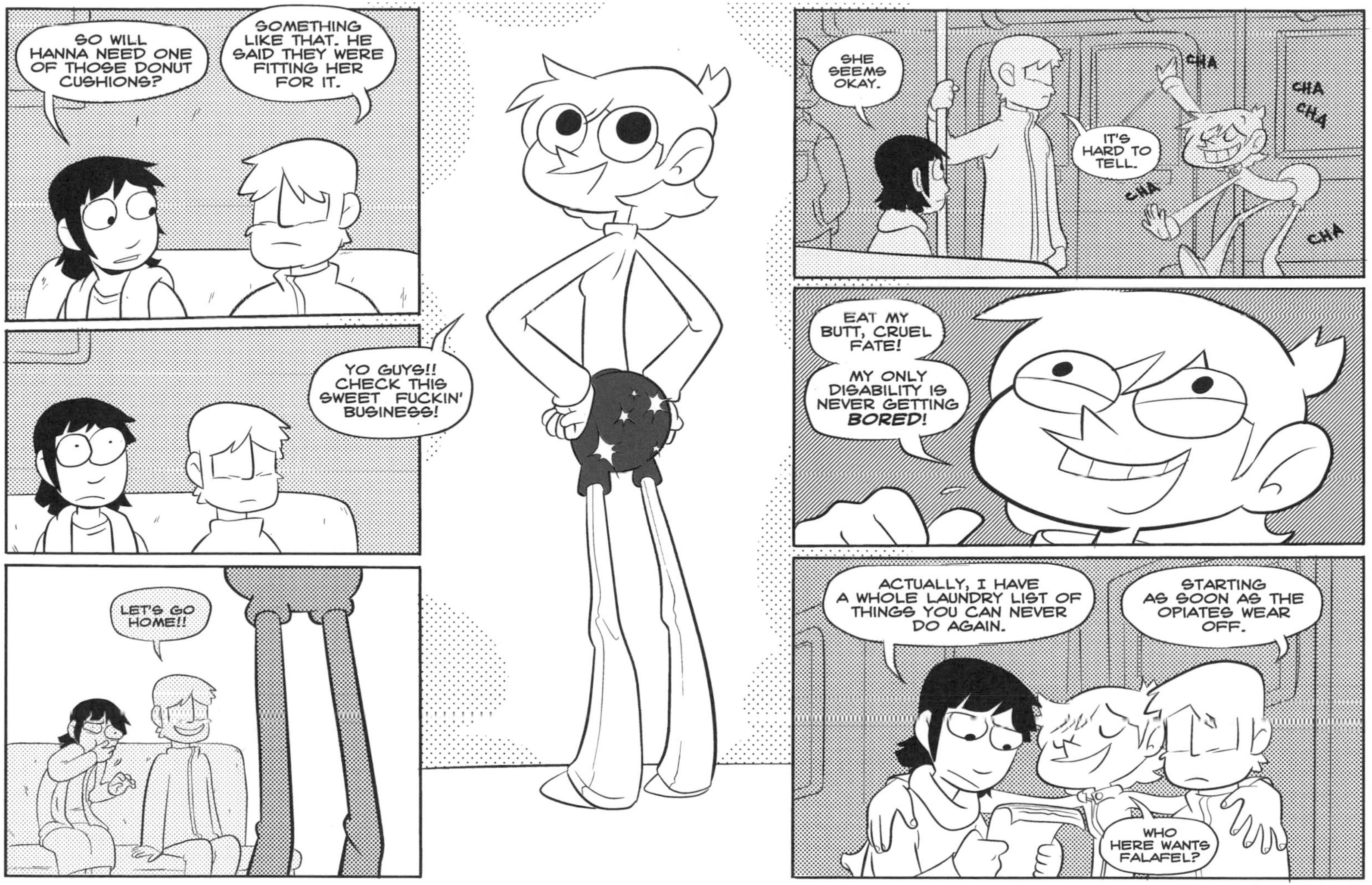
SO WILL HANNA NEED ONE OF THOSE DONUT CUSHIONS?
SOMETHING LIKE THAT. HE SAID THEY WERE FITTING HER FOR IT.
YO GUYS!! CHECK THIS SWEET FUCKIN' BUSINESS!
LET'S GO HOME!!
SHE SEEMS OKAY.
IT'S HARD TO TELL.
CHA
CHA
CHA
CHA
CHA
EAT MY BUTT, CRUEL FATE!
MY ONLY DISABILITY IS NEVER GETTING *BORED!*
ACTUALLY, I HAVE A WHOLE LAUNDRY LIST OF THINGS YOU CAN NEVER DO AGAIN.
STARTING AS SOON AS THE OPIATES WEAR OFF.
WHO HERE WANTS FALAFEL?

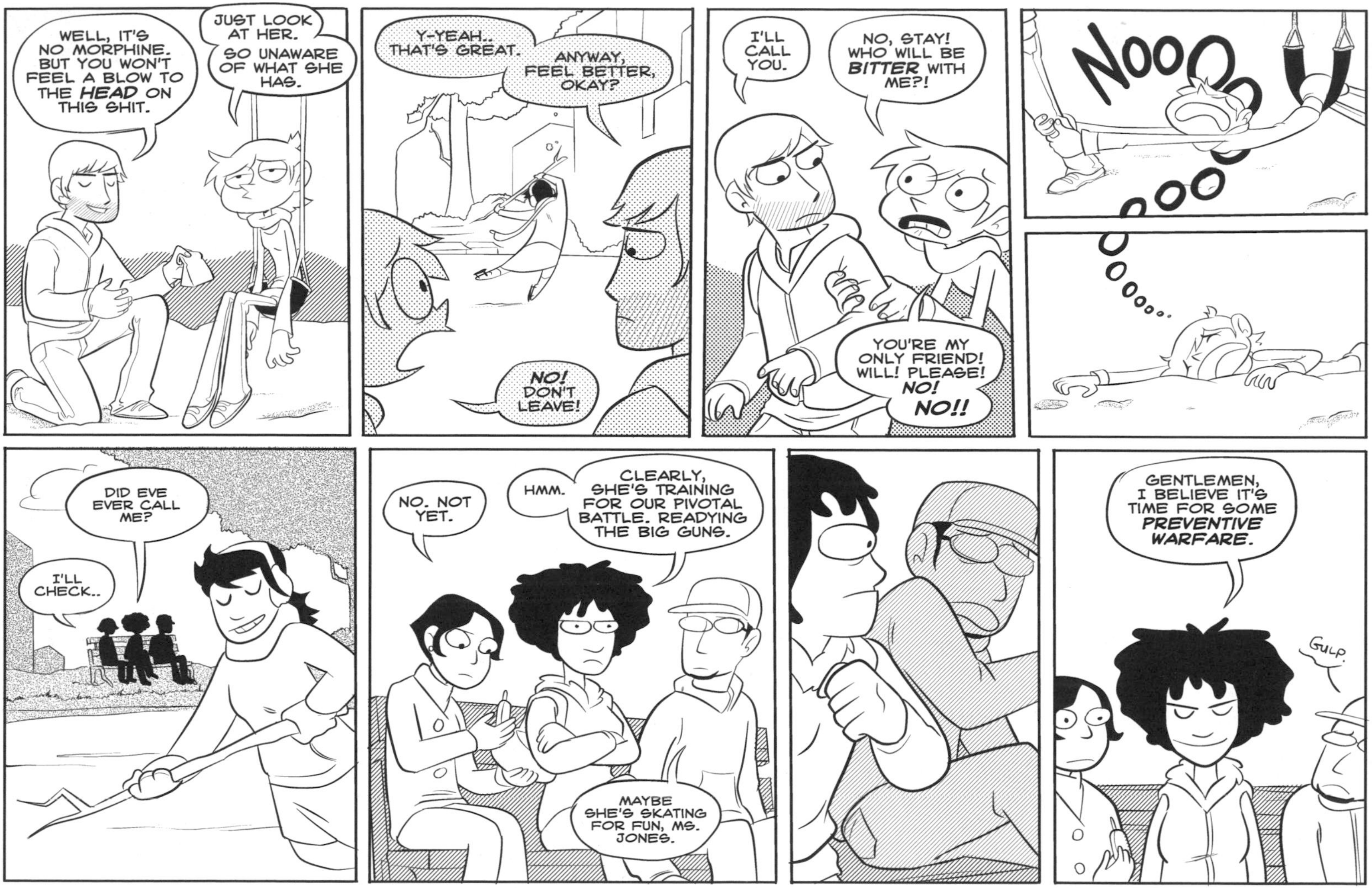
WELL, IT'S NO MORPHINE. BUT YOU WON'T FEEL A BLOW TO THE HEAD ON THIS SHIT.
JUST LOOK AT HER.
SO UNAWARE OF WHAT SHE HAS.
Y-YEAH.. THAT'S GREAT.
ANYWAY, FEEL BETTER, OKAY?
NO! DON'T LEAVE!
I'LL CALL YOU.
NO, STAY! WHO WILL BE BITTER WITH ME?!
YOU'RE MY ONLY FRIEND! WILL! PLEASE! NO! NO!!
NOOOOOOOOOOOOOoooo..
DID EVE EVER CALL ME?
I'LL CHECK..
NO. NOT YET.
HMM.
CLEARLY, SHE'S TRAINING FOR OUR PIVOTAL BATTLE. READYING THE BIG GUNS.
MAYBE SHE'S SKATING FOR FUN, MS. JONES.
GENTLEMEN, I BELIEVE IT'S TIME FOR SOME PREVENTIVE WARFARE.
GULP.

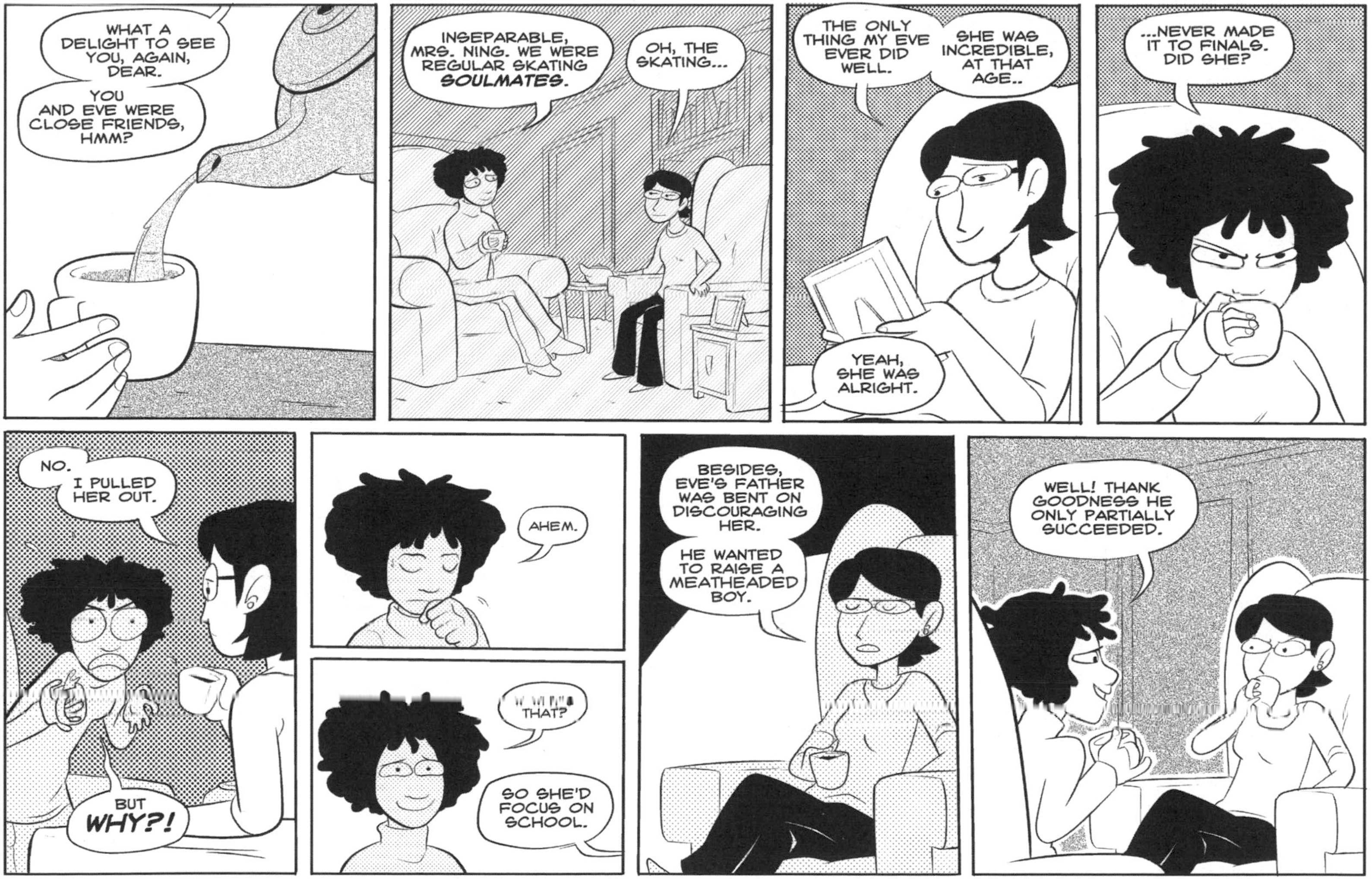
WHAT A DELIGHT TO SEE YOU, AGAIN, DEAR.
YOU AND EVE WERE CLOSE FRIENDS, HMM?
INSEPARABLE, MRS. NING. WE WERE REGULAR SKATING SOULMATES.
OH, THE SKATING...
THE ONLY THING MY EVE EVER DID WELL.
SHE WAS INCREDIBLE, AT THAT AGE..
YEAH, SHE WAS ALRIGHT.
...NEVER MADE IT TO FINALS. DID SHE?
NO. I PULLED HER OUT.
BUT WHY?!
AHEM.
THAT?
SO SHE'D FOCUS ON SCHOOL.
BESIDES, EVE'S FATHER WAS BENT ON DISCOURAGING HER.
HE WANTED TO RAISE A MEATHEADED BOY.
WELL! THANK GOODNESS HE ONLY PARTIALLY SUCCEEDED.

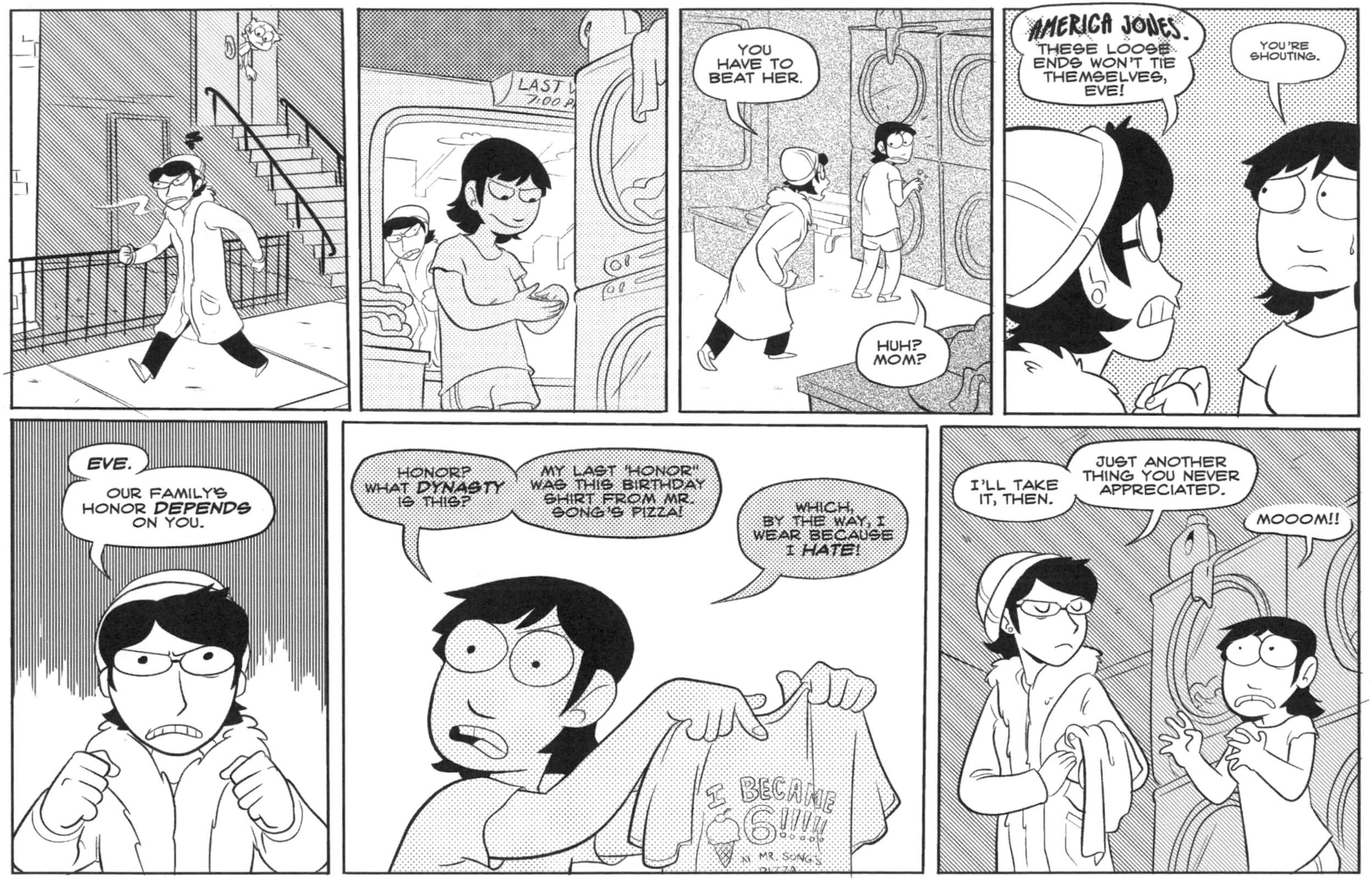
LAST
7:00 P
YOU HAVE TO BEAT HER.
HUH? MOM?
AMERICA JONES. THESE LOOSE ENDS WON'T TIE THEMSELVES, EVE!
YOU'RE SHOUTING.
EVE. OUR FAMILY'S HONOR DEPENDS ON YOU.
HONOR? WHAT DYNASTY IS THIS?
MY LAST "HONOR" WAS THIS BIRTHDAY SHIRT FROM MR. SONG'S PIZZA!
WHICH, BY THE WAY, I WEAR BECAUSE I HATE!
I BECAME 6!!!!!
I'LL TAKE IT, THEN.
JUST ANOTHER THING YOU NEVER APPRECIATED.
MOOOM!!

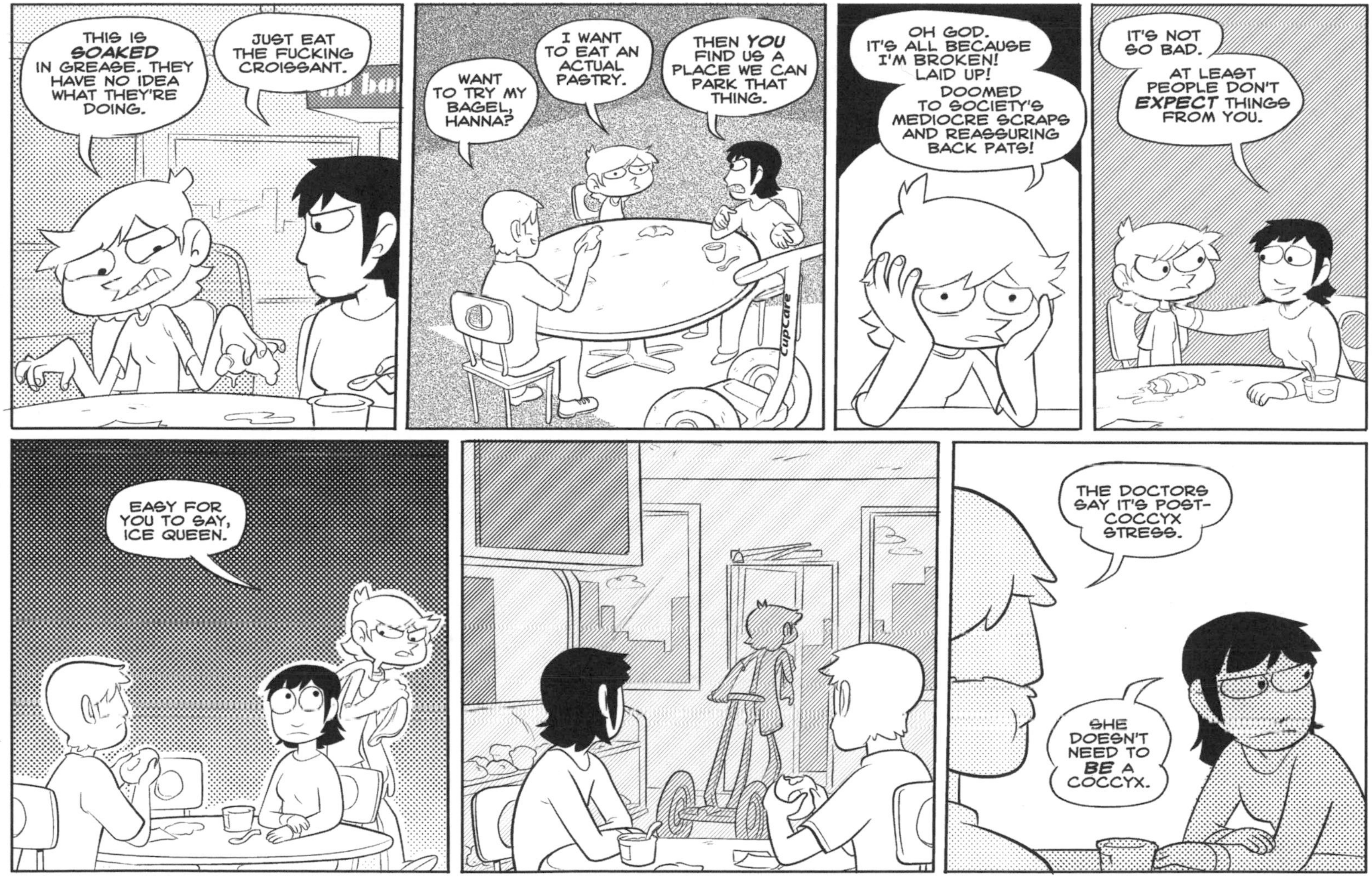
THIS IS SOAKED IN GREASE. THEY HAVE NO IDEA WHAT THEY'RE DOING.
JUST EAT THE FUCKING CROISSANT.
WANT TO TRY MY BAGEL, HANNA?
I WANT TO EAT AN ACTUAL PASTRY.
THEN YOU FIND US A PLACE WE CAN PARK THAT THING.
CupCare
OH GOD. IT'S ALL BECAUSE I'M BROKEN! LAID UP!
DOOMED TO SOCIETY'S MEDIOCRE SCRAPS AND REASSURING BACK PATS!
IT'S NOT SO BAD.
AT LEAST PEOPLE DON'T EXPECT THINGS FROM YOU.
EASY FOR YOU TO SAY, ICE QUEEN.
THE DOCTORS SAY IT'S POST-COCCYX STRESS.
SHE DOESN'T NEED TO BE A COCCYX.

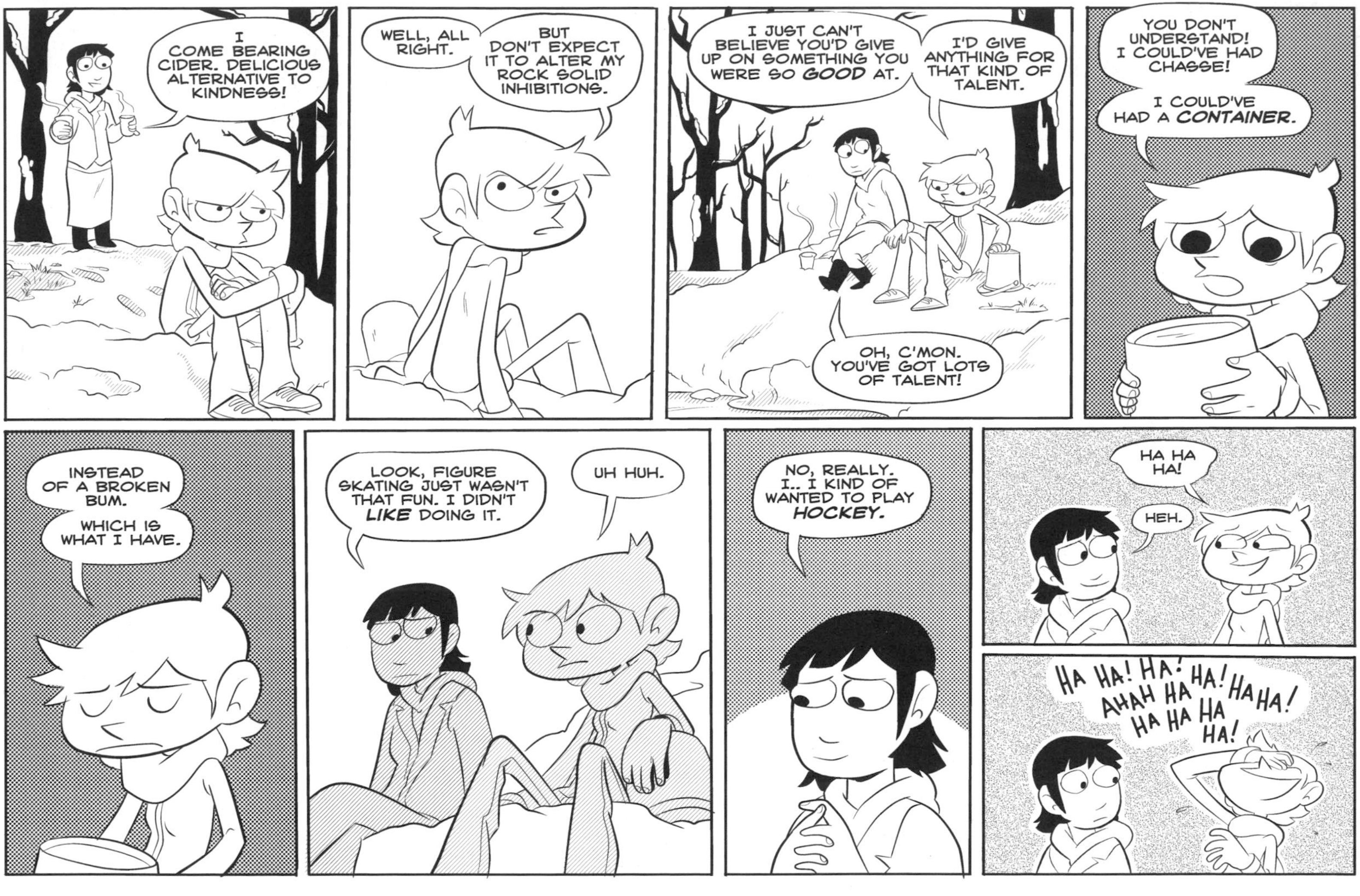
I COME BEARING CIDER. DELICIOUS ALTERNATIVE TO KINDNESS!
WELL, ALL RIGHT.
BUT DON'T EXPECT IT TO ALTER MY ROCK SOLID INHIBITIONS.
I JUST CAN'T BELIEVE YOU'D GIVE UP ON SOMETHING YOU WERE SO *GOOD* AT.
I'D GIVE ANYTHING FOR THAT KIND OF TALENT.
OH, C'MON. YOU'VE GOT LOTS OF TALENT!
YOU DON'T UNDERSTAND! I COULD'VE HAD CHASSE!
I COULD'VE HAD A *CONTAINER.*
INSTEAD OF A BROKEN BUM.
WHICH IS WHAT I HAVE.
LOOK, FIGURE SKATING JUST WASN'T THAT FUN. I DIDN'T *LIKE* DOING IT.
UH HUH.
NO, REALLY. I.. I KIND OF WANTED TO PLAY *HOCKEY.*
HA HA HA!
HEH.
HA HA! HA! HA! HA HA! AHAH HA HA HA HA HA!

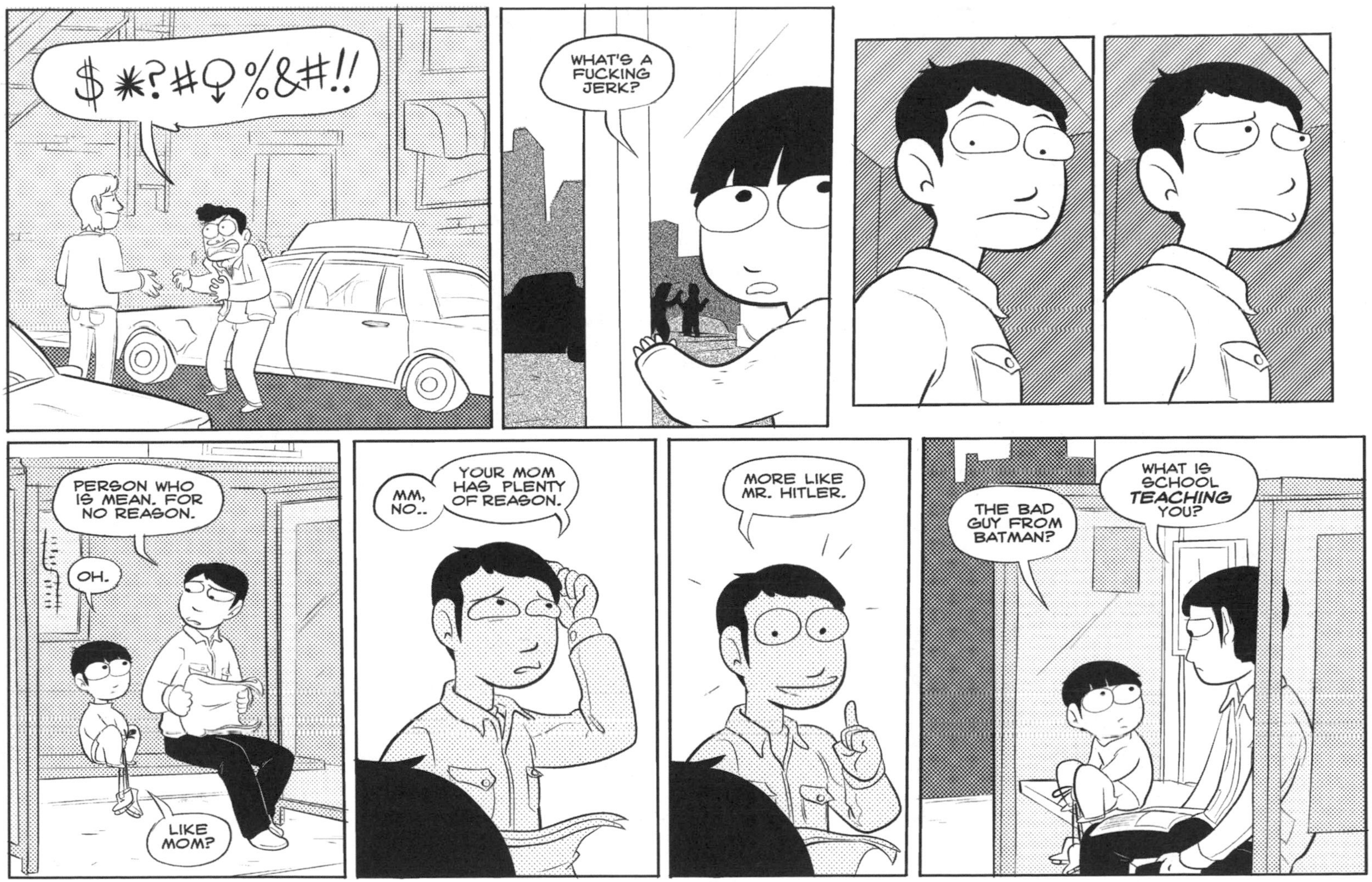
$*?#♀%&#!!
WHAT'S A FUCKING JERK?
PERSON WHO IS MEAN. FOR NO REASON.
OH.
LIKE MOM?
MM, NO..
YOUR MOM HAS PLENTY OF REASON.
MORE LIKE MR. HITLER.
THE BAD GUY FROM BATMAN?
WHAT IS SCHOOL TEACHING YOU?

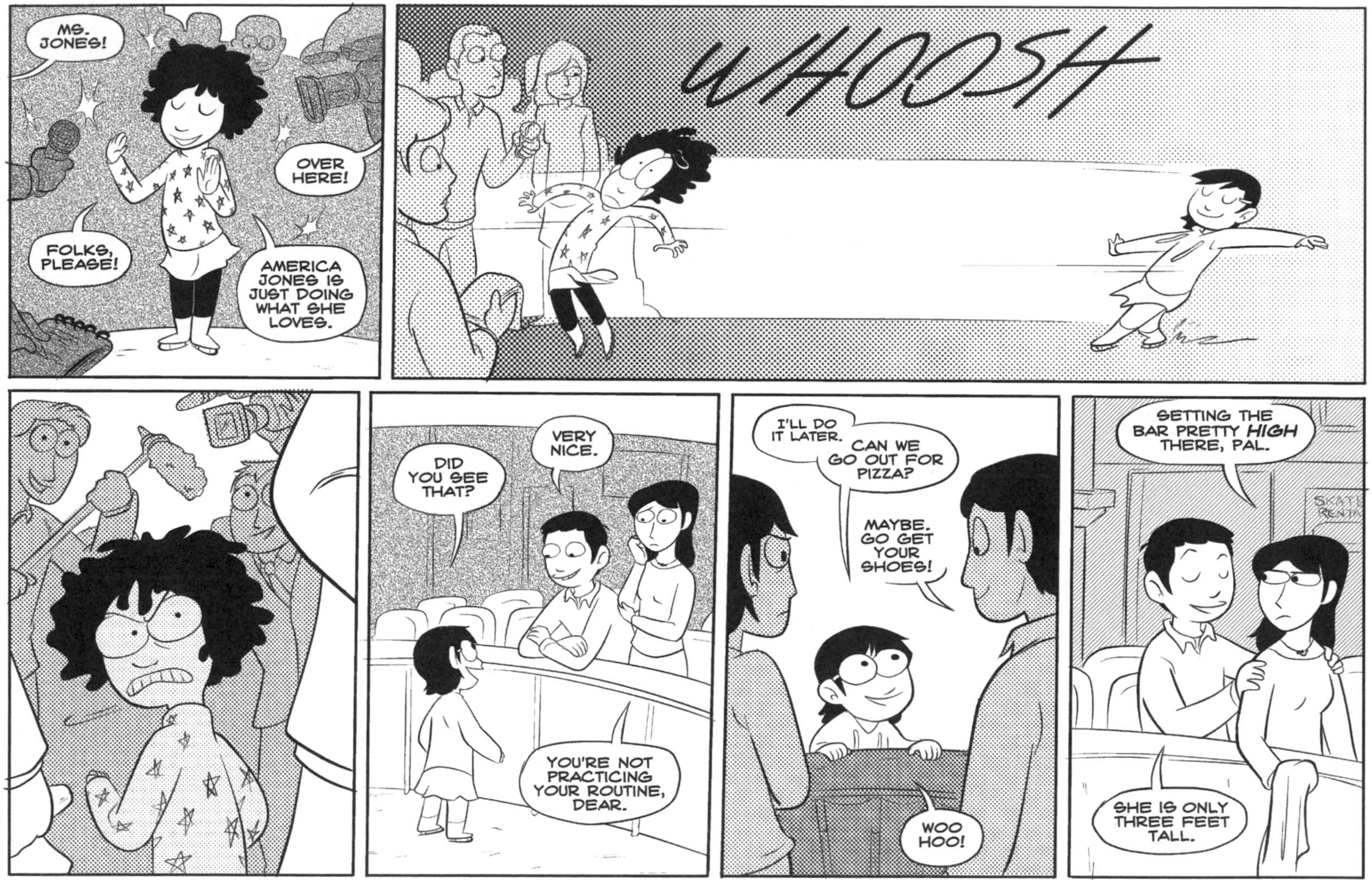
MS. JONES!
OVER HERE!
FOLKS, PLEASE!
AMERICA JONES IS JUST DOING WHAT SHE LOVES.
WHOOSH
DID YOU SEE THAT?
VERY NICE.
YOU'RE NOT PRACTICING YOUR ROUTINE, DEAR.
I'LL DO IT LATER.
CAN WE GO OUT FOR PIZZA?
MAYBE. GO GET YOUR SHOES!
WOO HOO!
SETTING THE BAR PRETTY HIGH THERE, PAL.
SKATE RENTA
SHE IS ONLY THREE FEET TALL.

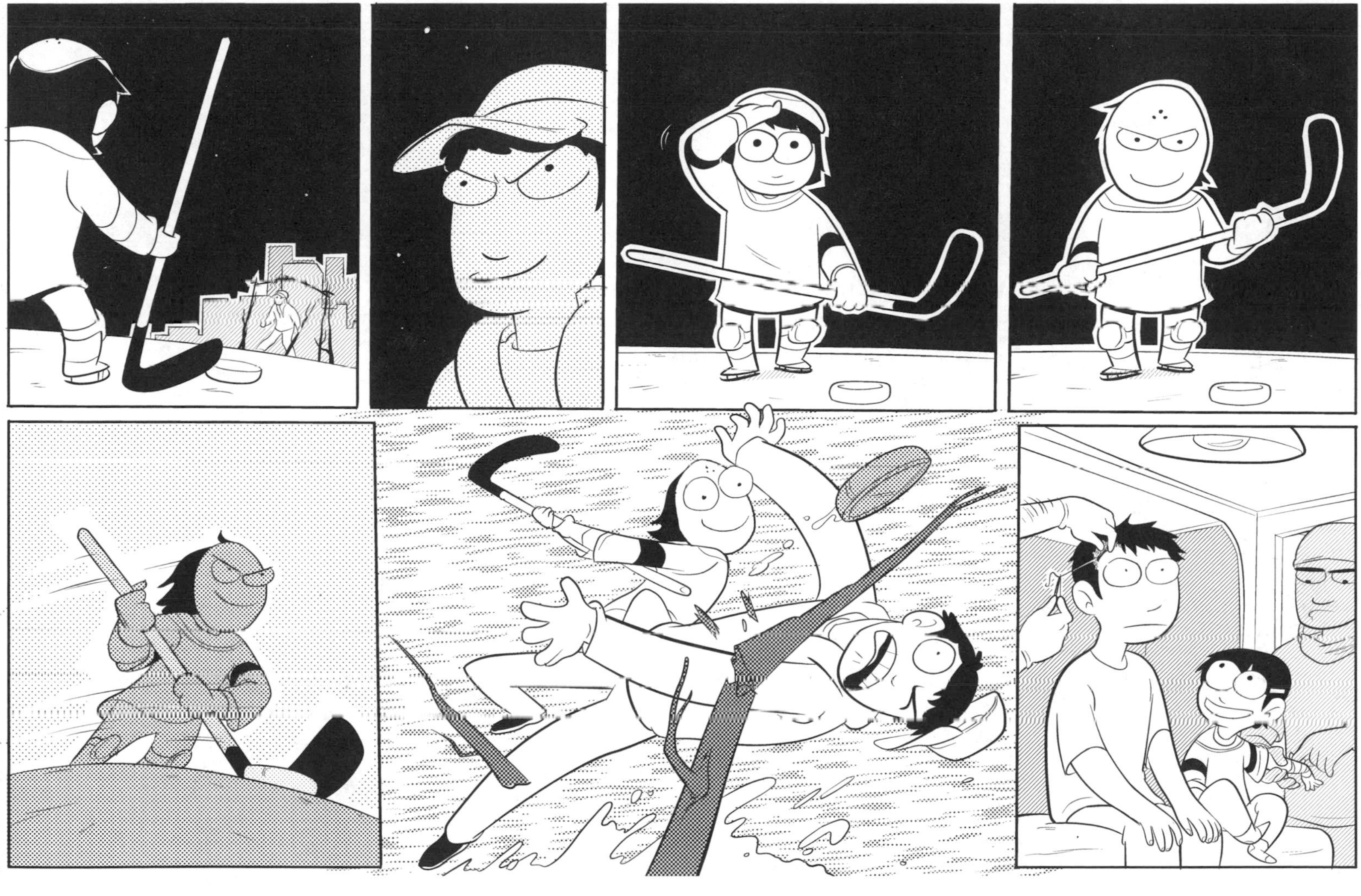

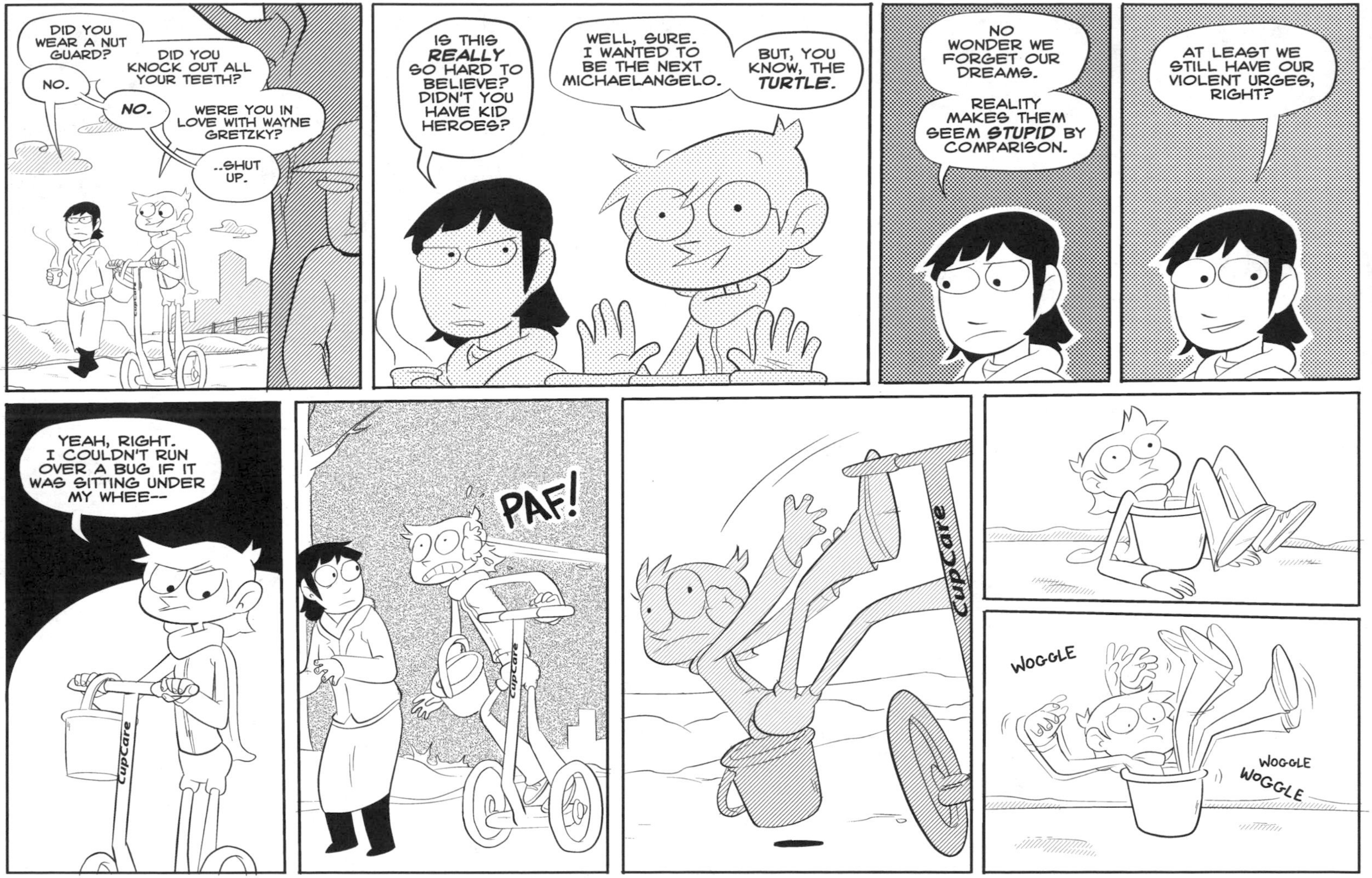
DID YOU WEAR A NUT GUARD?
NO.
DID YOU KNOCK OUT ALL YOUR TEETH?
NO.
WERE YOU IN LOVE WITH WAYNE GRETZKY?
..SHUT UP.
IS THIS REALLY SO HARD TO BELIEVE? DIDN'T YOU HAVE KID HEROES?
WELL, SURE. I WANTED TO BE THE NEXT MICHAELANGELO.
BUT, YOU KNOW, THE TURTLE.
NO WONDER WE FORGET OUR DREAMS.
REALITY MAKES THEM SEEM STUPID BY COMPARISON.
AT LEAST WE STILL HAVE OUR VIOLENT URGES, RIGHT?
YEAH, RIGHT. I COULDN'T RUN OVER A BUG IF IT WAS SITTING UNDER MY WHEE--
PAF!
CupCare
WOGGLE
WOGGLE
WOGGLE

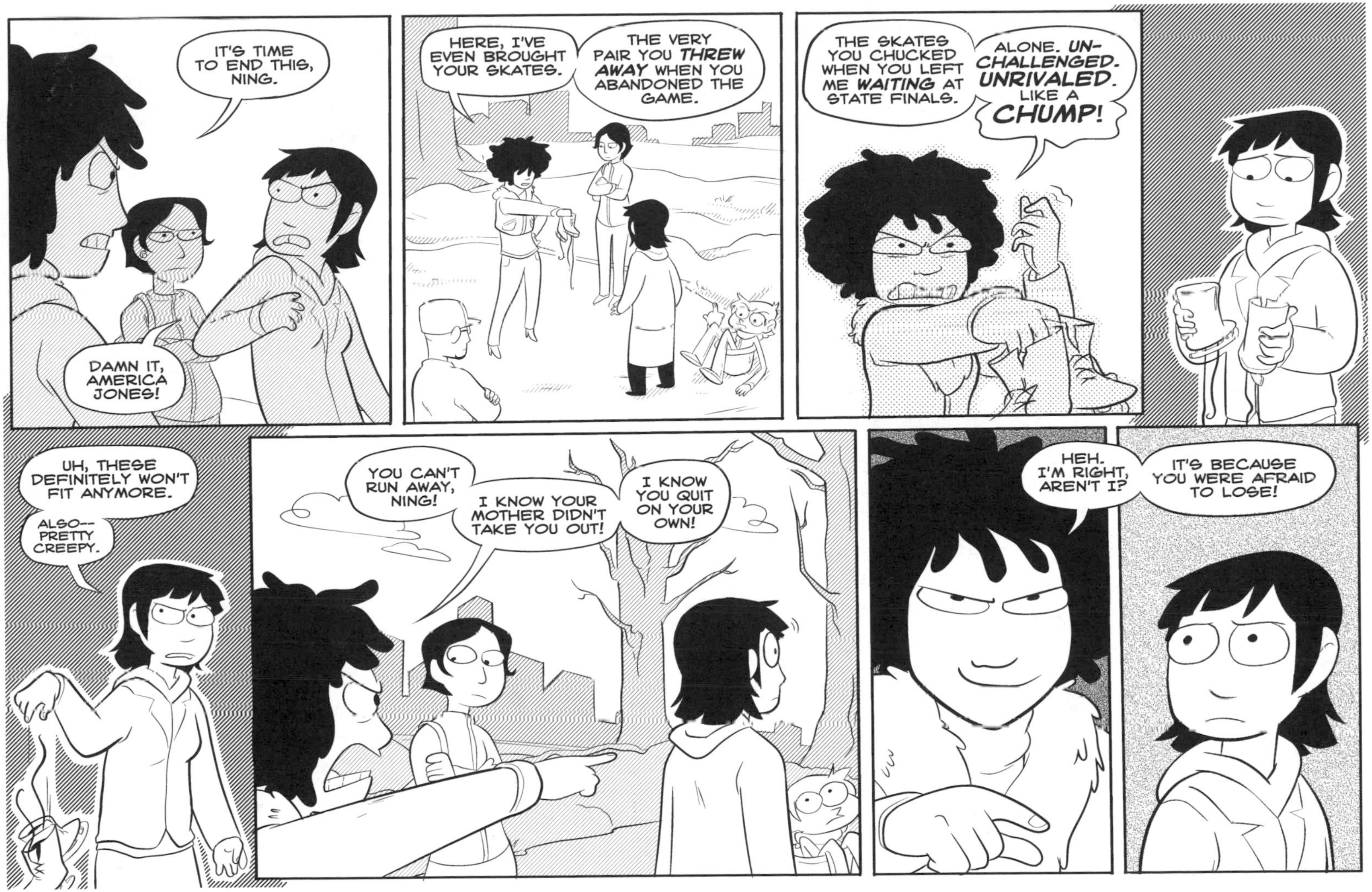
IT'S TIME TO END THIS, NING.
DAMN IT, AMERICA JONES!
HERE, I'VE EVEN BROUGHT YOUR SKATES.
THE VERY PAIR YOU **THREW AWAY** WHEN YOU ABANDONED THE GAME.
THE SKATES YOU CHUCKED WHEN YOU LEFT ME **WAITING** AT STATE FINALS.
ALONE. **UN-CHALLENGED. UNRIVALED.** LIKE A **CHUMP!**
UH, THESE DEFINITELY WON'T FIT ANYMORE.
ALSO-- PRETTY CREEPY.
YOU CAN'T RUN AWAY, NING!
I KNOW YOUR MOTHER DIDN'T TAKE YOU OUT!
I KNOW YOU QUIT ON YOUR OWN!
HEH. I'M RIGHT, AREN'T I?
IT'S BECAUSE YOU WERE AFRAID TO LOSE!

THIS IS

STUPID!!

YOU NEED TO KNOW WHY, AMERICA? YOU NEED TO KNOW WHY I **FUCKING QUIT?!**

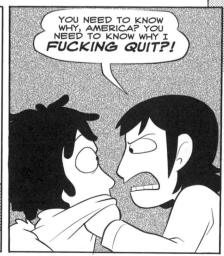

I-IT WAS REALLY MORE OF A FLEETING CURIOSITY.

THAN ANYTHING.

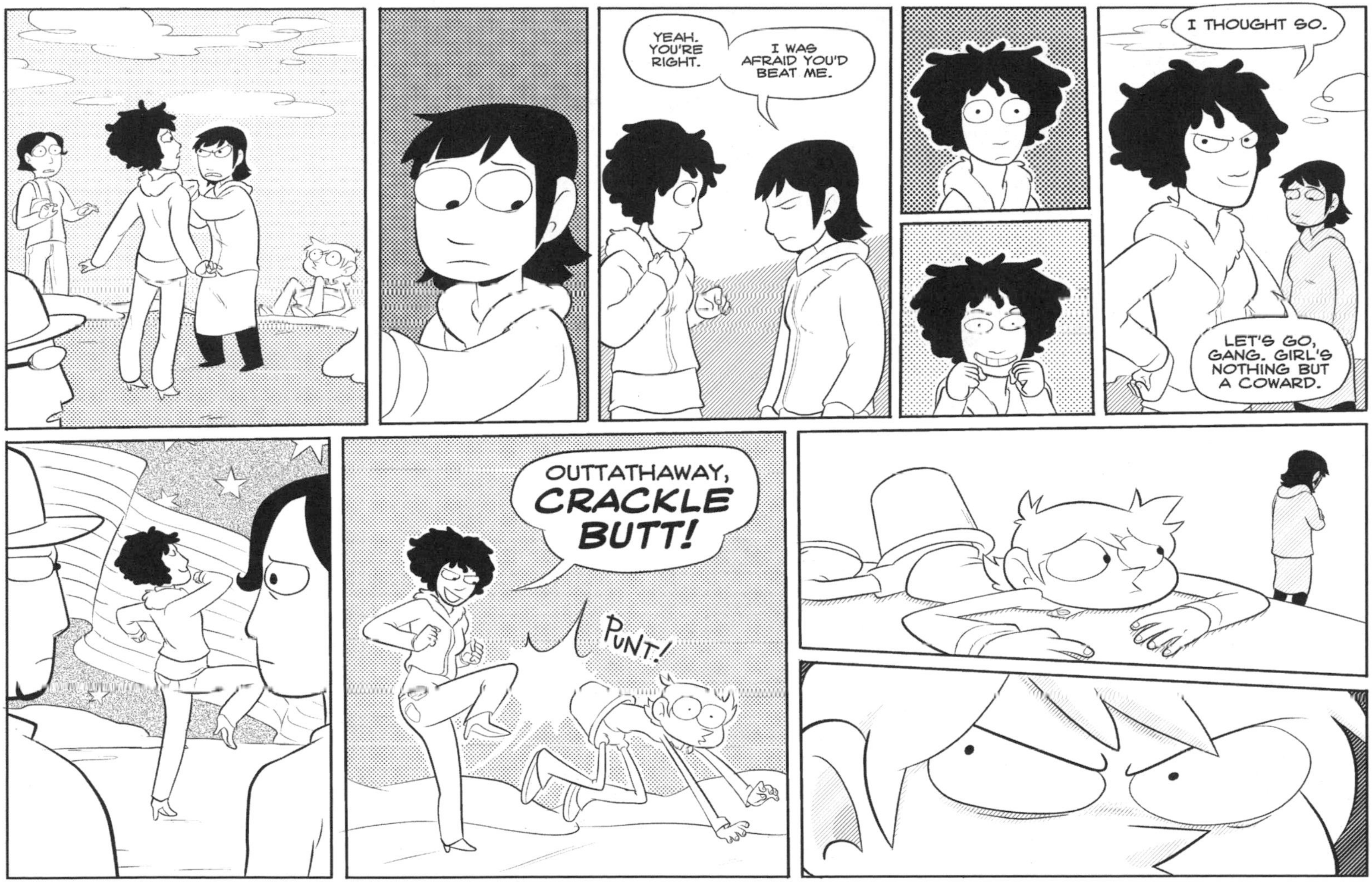
YEAH. YOU'RE RIGHT.
I WAS AFRAID YOU'D BEAT ME.
I THOUGHT SO.
LET'S GO, GANG. GIRL'S NOTHING BUT A COWARD.
OUTTATHAWAY, CRACKLE BUTT!
PUNT!

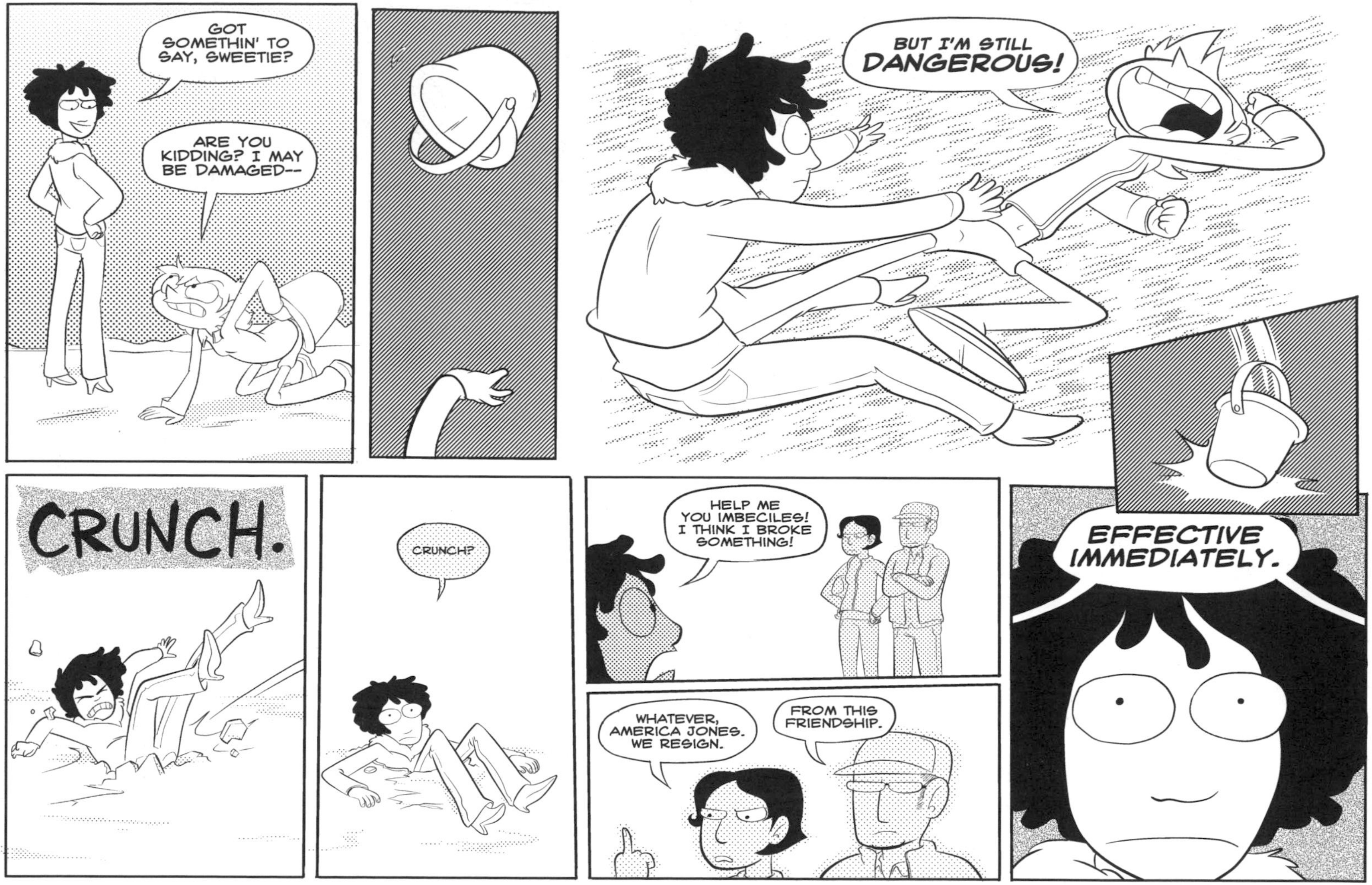

GOT SOMETHIN' TO SAY, SWEETIE?
ARE YOU KIDDING? I MAY BE DAMAGED--
BUT I'M STILL DANGEROUS!
CRUNCH.
CRUNCH?
HELP ME YOU IMBECILES! I THINK I BROKE SOMETHING!
WHATEVER, AMERICA JONES. WE RESIGN.
FROM THIS FRIENDSHIP.
EFFECTIVE IMMEDIATELY.

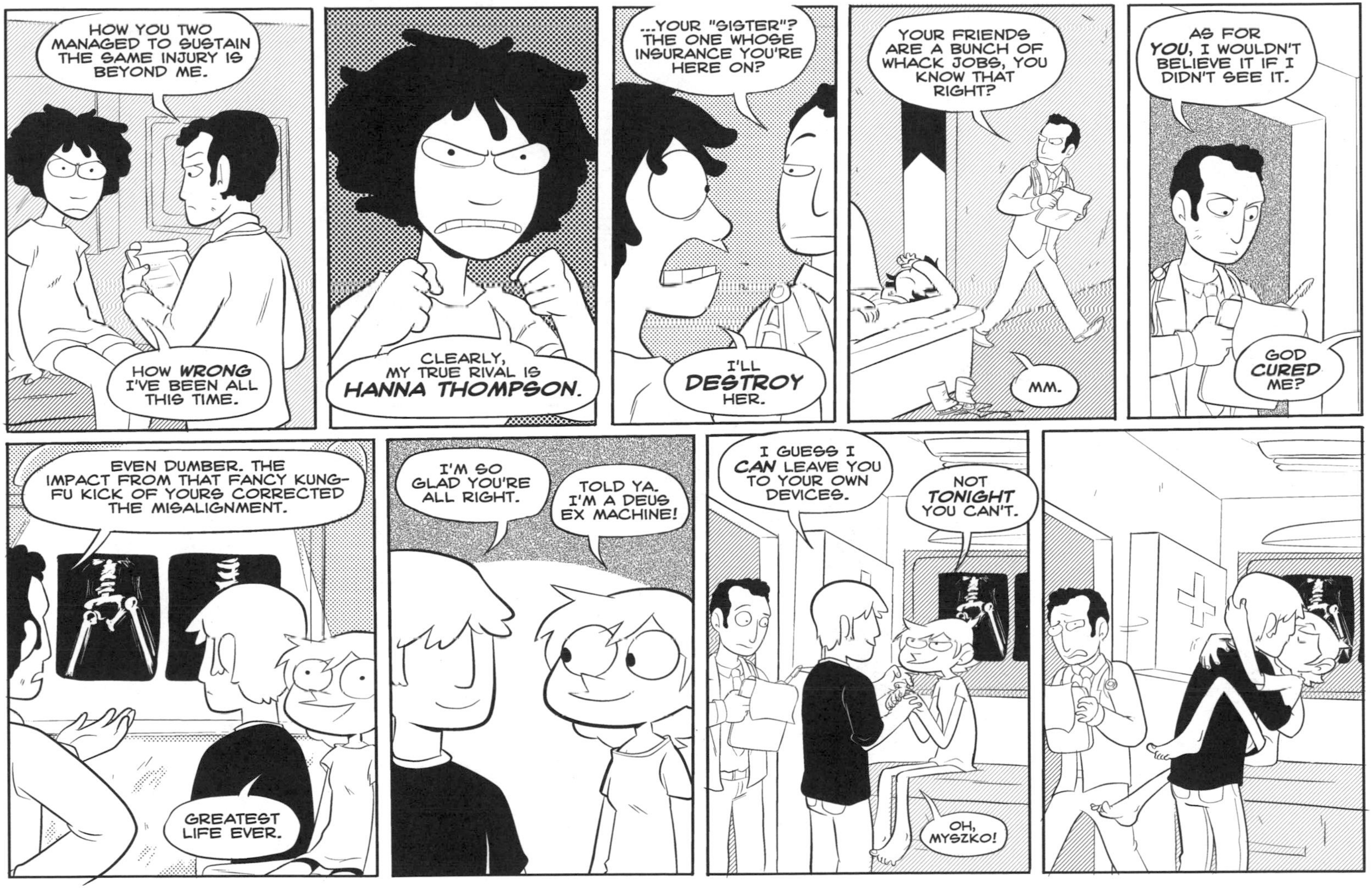

HOW YOU TWO MANAGED TO SUSTAIN THE SAME INJURY IS BEYOND ME.
HOW **WRONG** I'VE BEEN ALL THIS TIME.
CLEARLY, MY TRUE RIVAL IS ***HANNA THOMPSON.***
...YOUR "SISTER"? THE ONE WHOSE INSURANCE YOU'RE HERE ON?
I'LL **DESTROY** HER.
YOUR FRIENDS ARE A BUNCH OF WHACK JOBS, YOU KNOW THAT RIGHT?
MM.
AS FOR ***YOU***, I WOULDN'T BELIEVE IT IF I DIDN'T SEE IT.
GOD ***CURED*** ME?
EVEN DUMBER. THE IMPACT FROM THAT FANCY KUNG-FU KICK OF YOURS CORRECTED THE MISALIGNMENT.
GREATEST LIFE EVER.
I'M SO GLAD YOU'RE ALL RIGHT.
TOLD YA. I'M A DEUS EX MACHINE!
I GUESS I ***CAN*** LEAVE YOU TO YOUR OWN DEVICES.
NOT ***TONIGHT*** YOU CAN'T.
OH, MYSZKO!

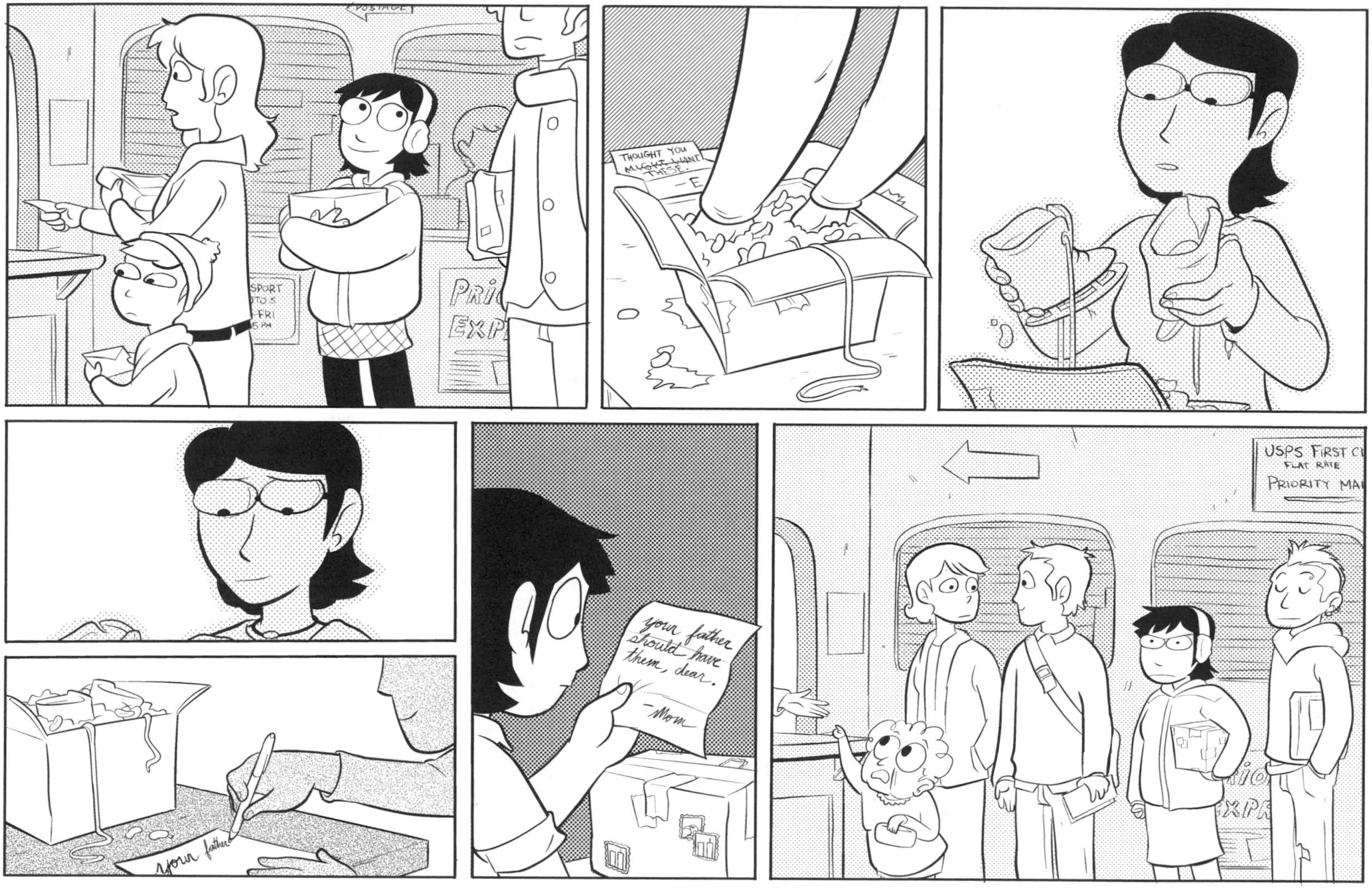
POSTAGE
THOUGHT YOU MIGHT WANT THESE.
—E
your father
your father should have them, dear.
—Mom
FLAT RATE

8

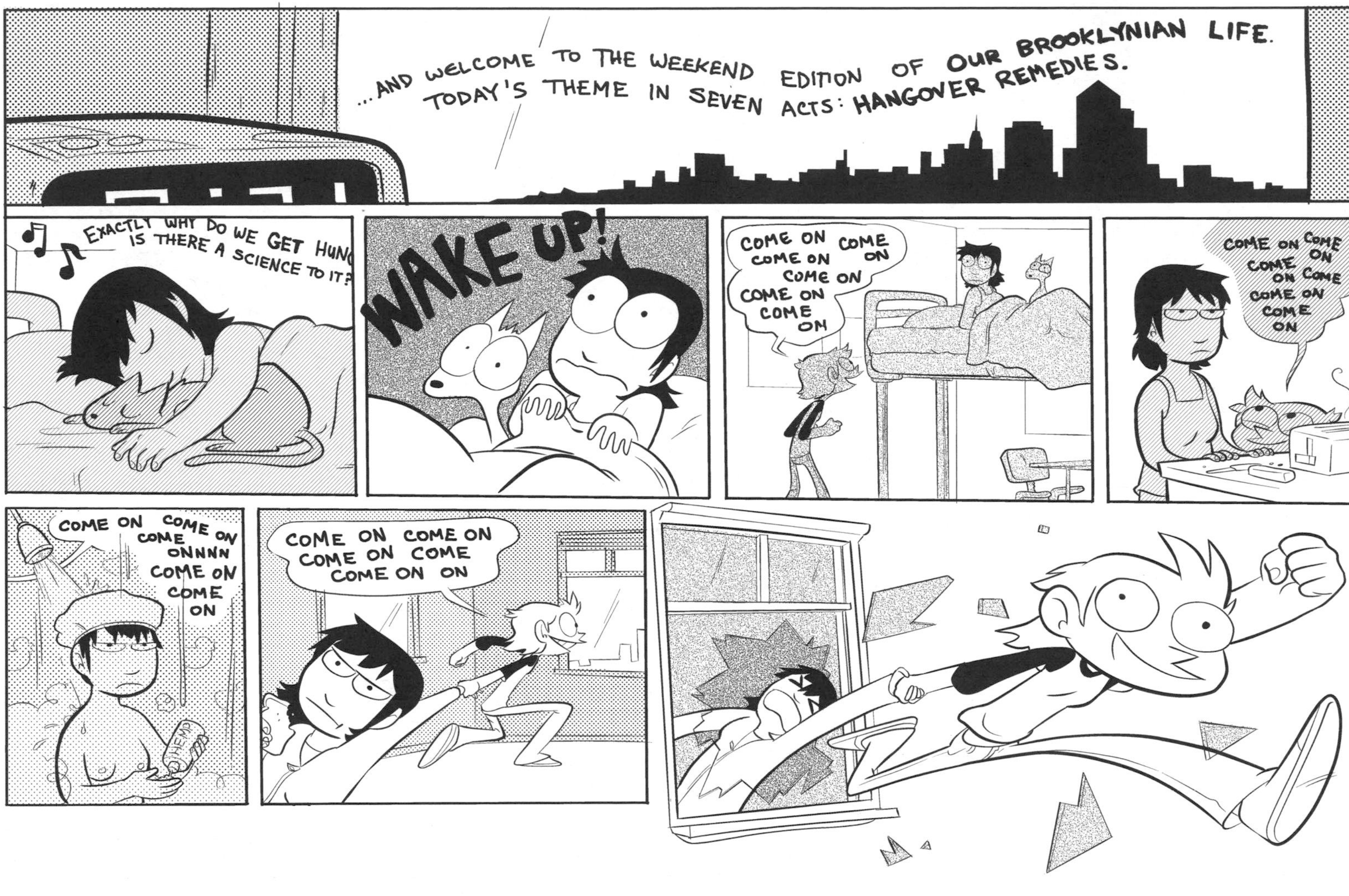
...AND WELCOME TO THE WEEKEND EDITION OF OUR BROOKLYNIAN LIFE.
TODAY'S THEME IN SEVEN ACTS: HANGOVER REMEDIES.
EXACTLY WHY DO WE GET HUNG IS THERE A SCIENCE TO IT?
WAKE UP!
COME ON COME ON COME ON COME ON COME ON COME ON COME ON
COME ON COME ON COME ON ON COME COME ON COME ON
COME ON COME ON COME ONNNN COME ON COME ON
COME ON COME ON COME ON COME COME ON ON

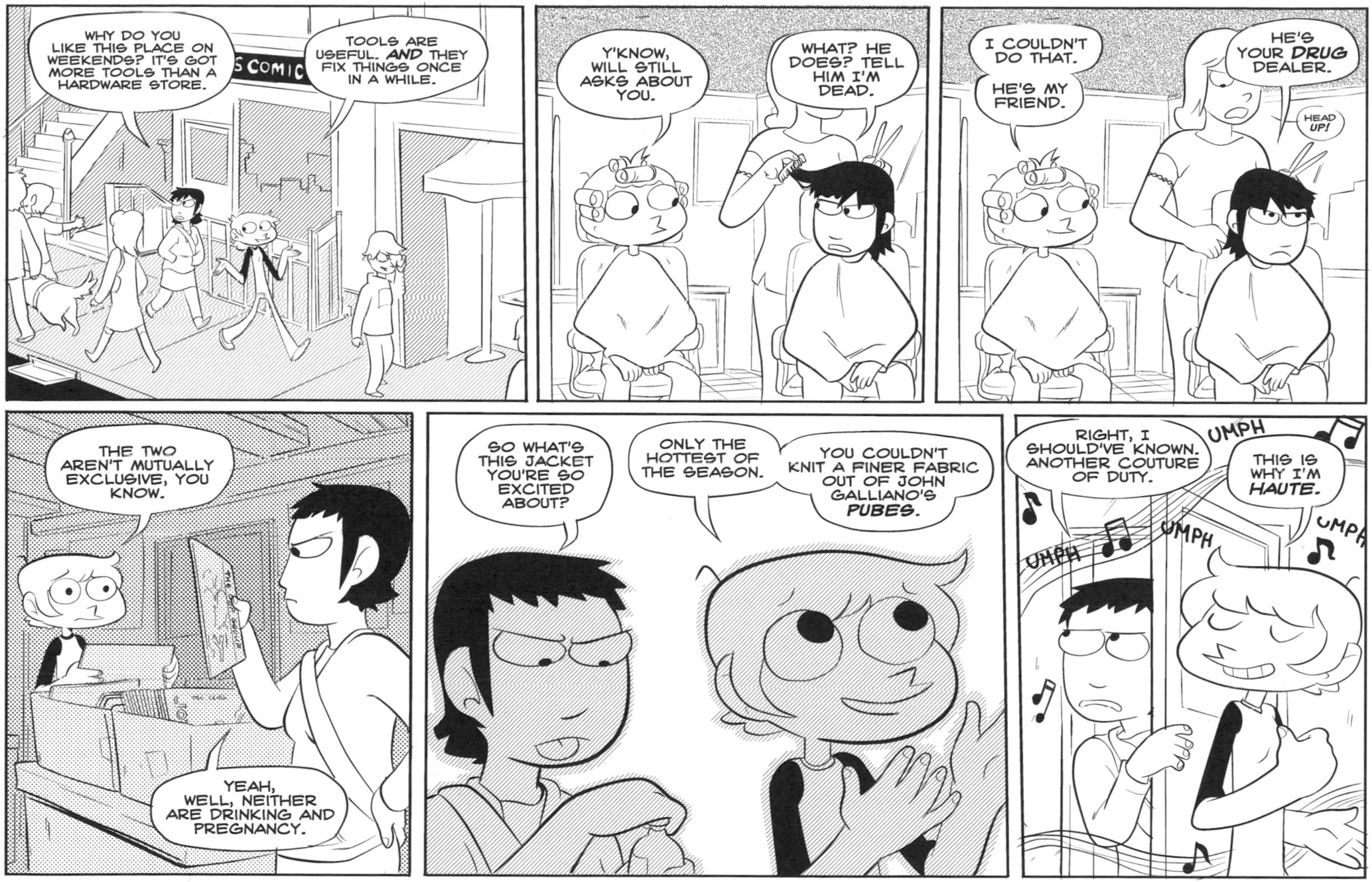
WHY DO YOU LIKE THIS PLACE ON WEEKENDS? IT'S GOT MORE TOOLS THAN A HARDWARE STORE.
S COMIC
TOOLS ARE USEFUL. AND THEY FIX THINGS ONCE IN A WHILE.
Y'KNOW, WILL STILL ASKS ABOUT YOU.
WHAT? HE DOES? TELL HIM I'M DEAD.
I COULDN'T DO THAT.
HE'S MY FRIEND.
HE'S YOUR DRUG DEALER.
HEAD UP!
THE TWO AREN'T MUTUALLY EXCLUSIVE, YOU KNOW.
YEAH, WELL, NEITHER ARE DRINKING AND PREGNANCY.
SO WHAT'S THIS JACKET YOU'RE SO EXCITED ABOUT?
ONLY THE HOTTEST OF THE SEASON.
YOU COULDN'T KNIT A FINER FABRIC OUT OF JOHN GALLIANO'S PUBES.
RIGHT, I SHOULD'VE KNOWN. ANOTHER COUTURE OF DUTY.
UMPH
THIS IS WHY I'M HAUTE.
UMPH
UMPH
UMPH

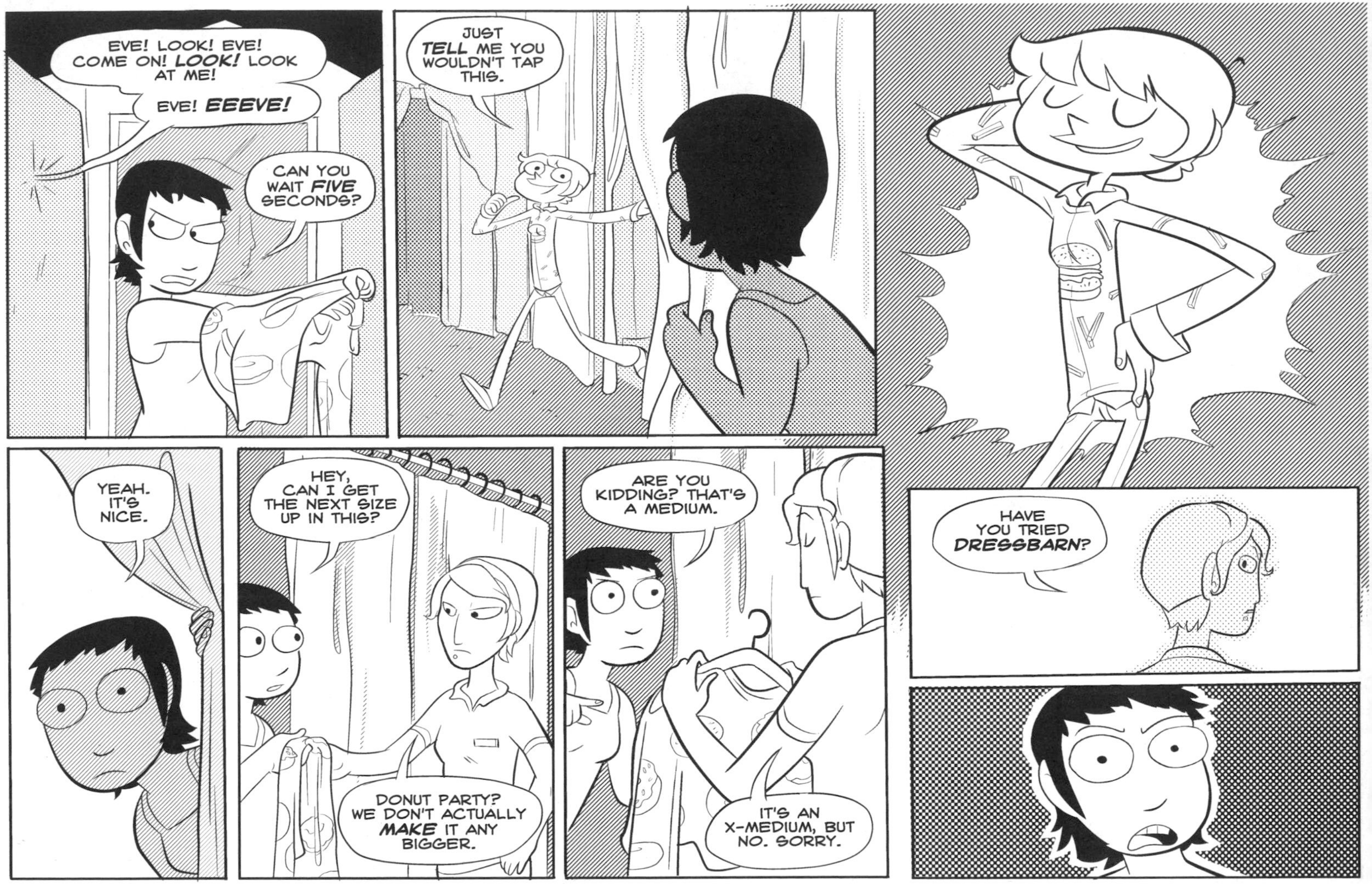
EVE! LOOK! EVE! COME ON! LOOK! LOOK AT ME!
EVE! EEEVE!
CAN YOU WAIT FIVE SECONDS?
JUST TELL ME YOU WOULDN'T TAP THIS.
YEAH. IT'S NICE.
HEY, CAN I GET THE NEXT SIZE UP IN THIS?
DONUT PARTY? WE DON'T ACTUALLY MAKE IT ANY BIGGER.
ARE YOU KIDDING? THAT'S A MEDIUM.
IT'S AN X-MEDIUM, BUT NO. SORRY.
HAVE YOU TRIED DRESSBARN?

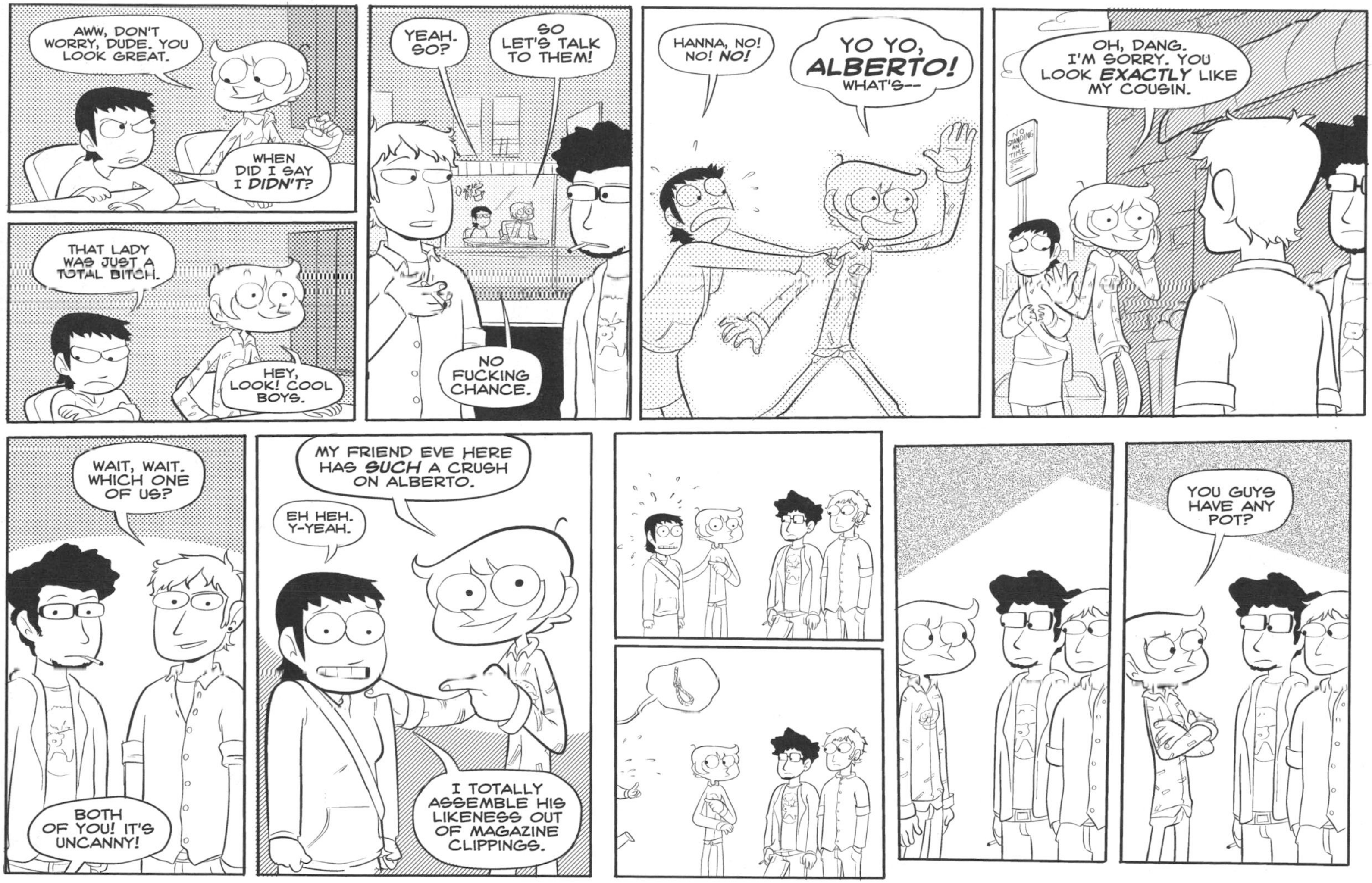
AWW, DON'T WORRY, DUDE. YOU LOOK GREAT.
WHEN DID I SAY I *DIDN'T*?
THAT LADY WAS JUST A TOTAL BITCH.
HEY, LOOK! COOL BOYS.
YEAH. SO?
SO LET'S TALK TO THEM!
NO FUCKING CHANCE.
HANNA, NO! NO! *NO!*
YO YO, *ALBERTO!* WHAT'S--
NO STANDING ANY TIME
OH, DANG. I'M SORRY. YOU LOOK *EXACTLY* LIKE MY COUSIN.
WAIT, WAIT. WHICH ONE OF US?
BOTH OF YOU! IT'S UNCANNY!
MY FRIEND EVE HERE HAS *SUCH* A CRUSH ON ALBERTO.
EH HEH. Y-YEAH.
I TOTALLY ASSEMBLE HIS LIKENESS OUT OF MAGAZINE CLIPPINGS.
YOU GUYS HAVE ANY POT?

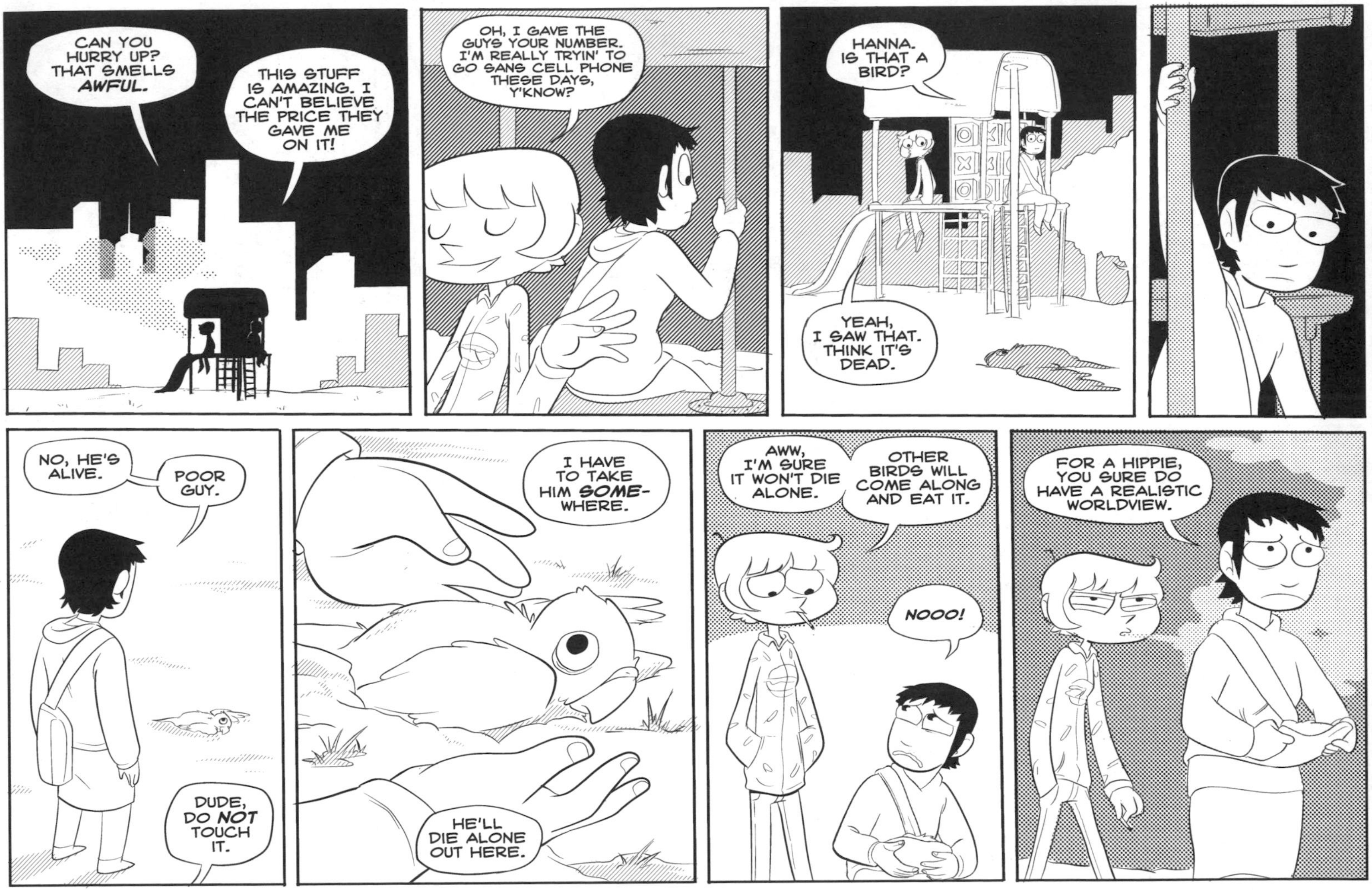
CAN YOU HURRY UP? THAT SMELLS AWFUL.
THIS STUFF IS AMAZING. I CAN'T BELIEVE THE PRICE THEY GAVE ME ON IT!
OH, I GAVE THE GUYS YOUR NUMBER. I'M REALLY TRYIN' TO GO SANS CELL PHONE THESE DAYS, Y'KNOW?
HANNA. IS THAT A BIRD?
YEAH, I SAW THAT. THINK IT'S DEAD.
NO, HE'S ALIVE.
POOR GUY.
DUDE, DO NOT TOUCH IT.
I HAVE TO TAKE HIM SOME-WHERE.
HE'LL DIE ALONE OUT HERE.
AWW, I'M SURE IT WON'T DIE ALONE.
OTHER BIRDS WILL COME ALONG AND EAT IT.
NOOO!
FOR A HIPPIE, YOU SURE DO HAVE A REALISTIC WORLDVIEW.

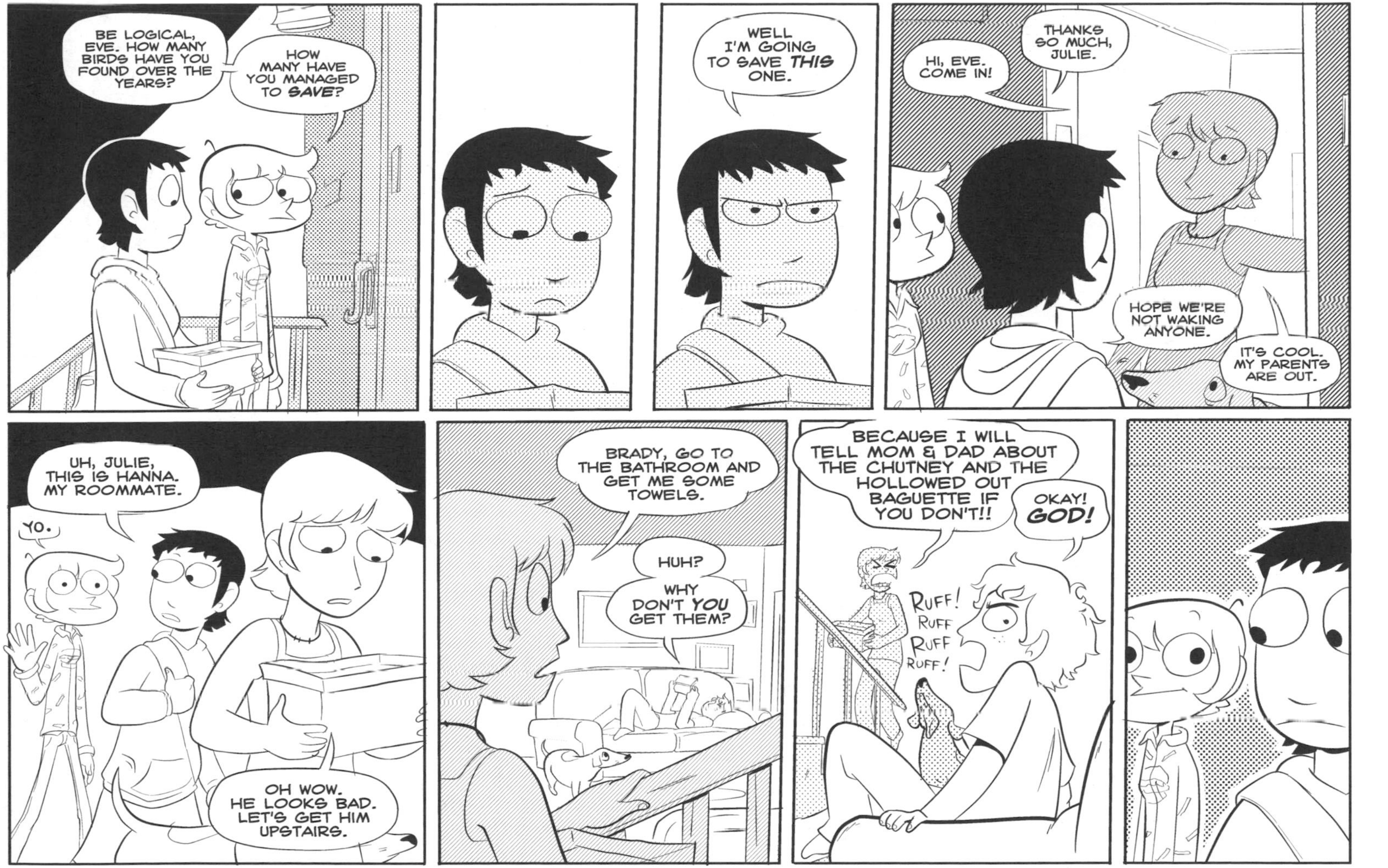
BE LOGICAL, EVE. HOW MANY BIRDS HAVE YOU FOUND OVER THE YEARS?
HOW MANY HAVE YOU MANAGED TO SAVE?
WELL I'M GOING TO SAVE THIS ONE.
HI, EVE. COME IN!
THANKS SO MUCH, JULIE.
HOPE WE'RE NOT WAKING ANYONE.
IT'S COOL. MY PARENTS ARE OUT.
UH, JULIE, THIS IS HANNA. MY ROOMMATE.
YO.
OH WOW. HE LOOKS BAD. LET'S GET HIM UPSTAIRS.
BRADY, GO TO THE BATHROOM AND GET ME SOME TOWELS.
HUH?
WHY DON'T YOU GET THEM?
BECAUSE I WILL TELL MOM & DAD ABOUT THE CHUTNEY AND THE HOLLOWED OUT BAGUETTE IF YOU DON'T!!
OKAY! GOD!
RUFF! RUFF RUFF RUFF!

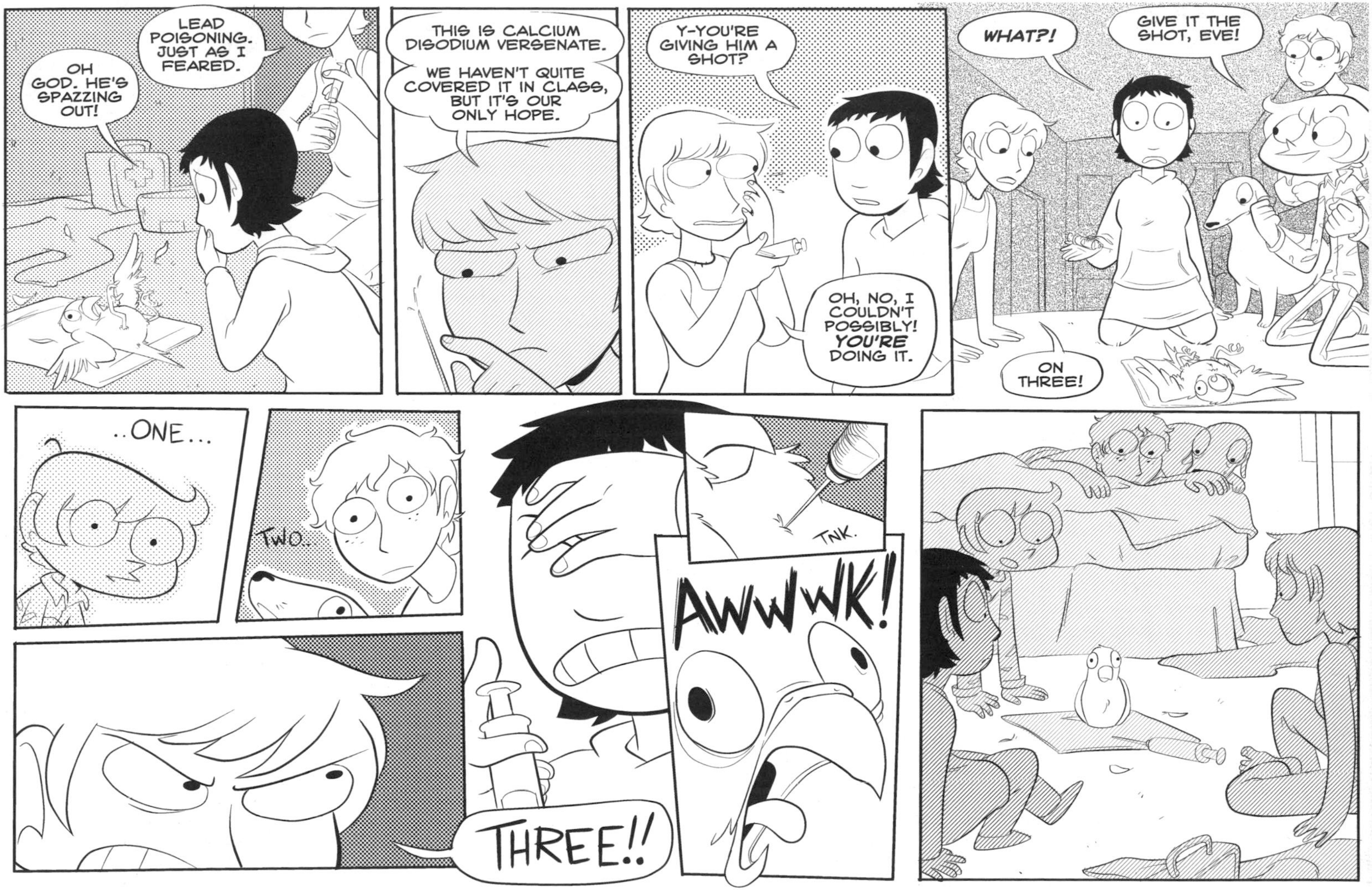

OH GOD. HE'S SPAZZING OUT!
LEAD POISONING. JUST AS I FEARED.
THIS IS CALCIUM DISODIUM VERSENATE.
WE HAVEN'T QUITE COVERED IT IN CLASS, BUT IT'S OUR ONLY HOPE.
Y-YOU'RE GIVING HIM A SHOT?
OH, NO, I COULDN'T POSSIBLY! YOU'RE DOING IT.
WHAT?!
GIVE IT THE SHOT, EVE!
ON THREE!
..ONE...
TWO..
THREE!!
TNK.
AWWWK!

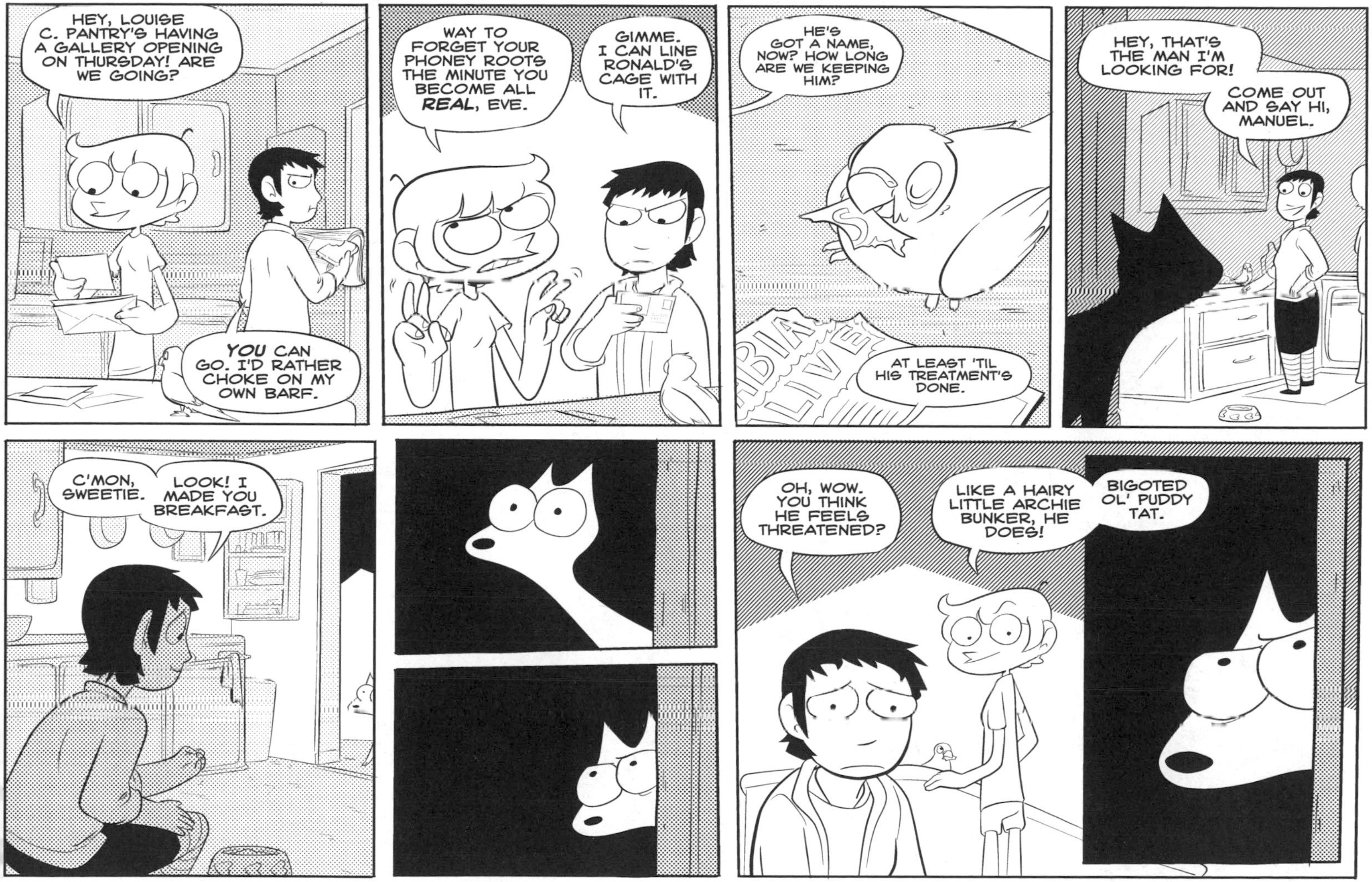
HEY, LOUISE C. PANTRY'S HAVING A GALLERY OPENING ON THURSDAY! ARE WE GOING?
YOU CAN GO. I'D RATHER CHOKE ON MY OWN BARF.
WAY TO FORGET YOUR PHONEY ROOTS THE MINUTE YOU BECOME ALL REAL, EVE.
GIMME. I CAN LINE RONALD'S CAGE WITH IT.
HE'S GOT A NAME, NOW? HOW LONG ARE WE KEEPING HIM?
AT LEAST 'TIL HIS TREATMENT'S DONE.
HEY, THAT'S THE MAN I'M LOOKING FOR!
COME OUT AND SAY HI, MANUEL.
C'MON, SWEETIE.
LOOK! I MADE YOU BREAKFAST.
OH, WOW. YOU THINK HE FEELS THREATENED?
LIKE A HAIRY LITTLE ARCHIE BUNKER, HE DOES!
BIGOTED OL' PUDDY TAT.

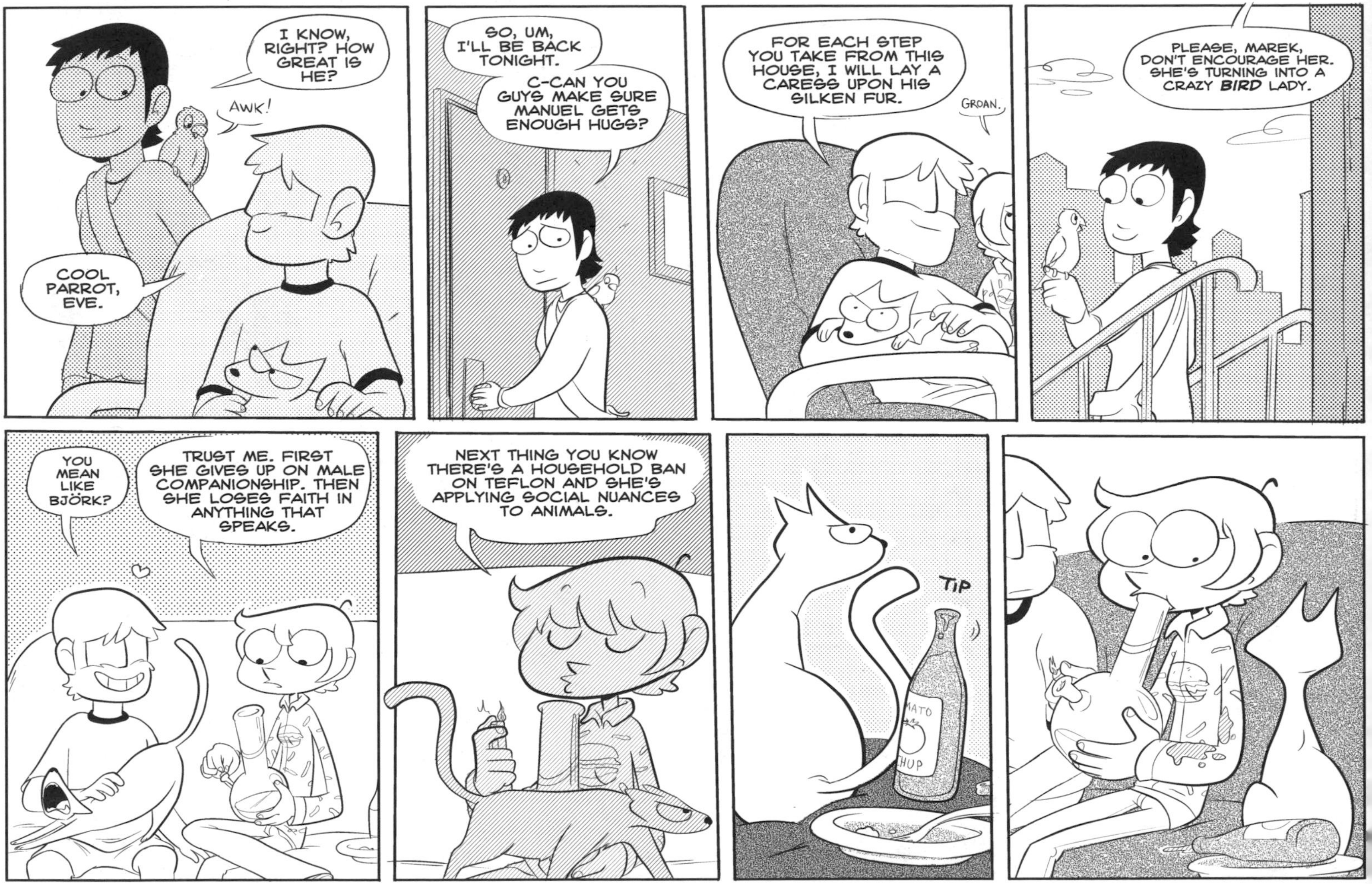
I KNOW, RIGHT? HOW GREAT IS HE?
AWK!
COOL PARROT, EVE.
SO, UM, I'LL BE BACK TONIGHT.
C-CAN YOU GUYS MAKE SURE MANUEL GETS ENOUGH HUGS?
FOR EACH STEP YOU TAKE FROM THIS HOUSE, I WILL LAY A CARESS UPON HIS SILKEN FUR.
GROAN.
PLEASE, MAREK, DON'T ENCOURAGE HER. SHE'S TURNING INTO A CRAZY BIRD LADY.
YOU MEAN LIKE BJÖRK?
TRUST ME. FIRST SHE GIVES UP ON MALE COMPANIONSHIP. THEN SHE LOSES FAITH IN ANYTHING THAT SPEAKS.
NEXT THING YOU KNOW THERE'S A HOUSEHOLD BAN ON TEFLON AND SHE'S APPLYING SOCIAL NUANCES TO ANIMALS.
TIP

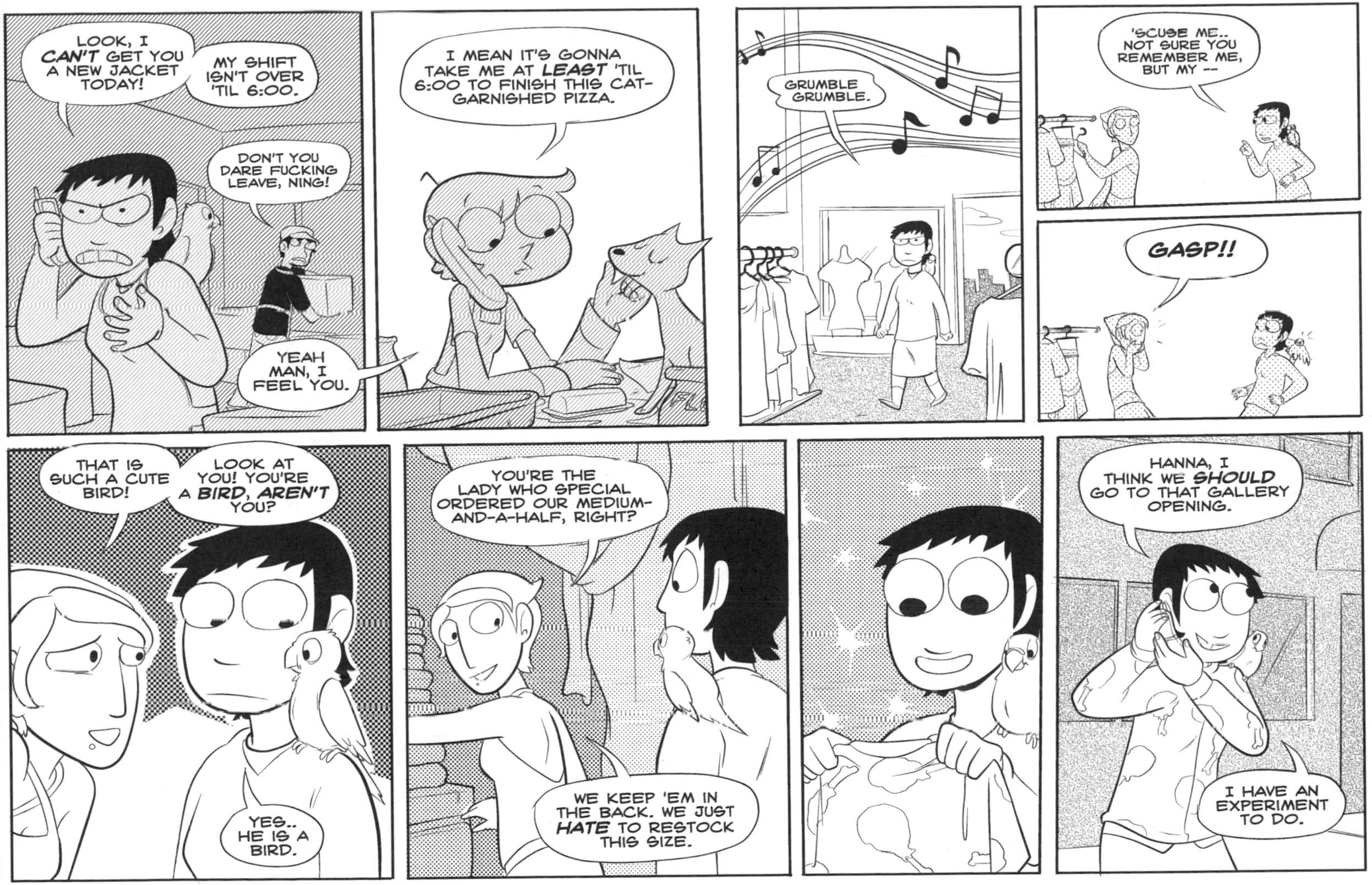
LOOK, I CAN'T GET YOU A NEW JACKET TODAY!
MY SHIFT ISN'T OVER 'TIL 6:00.
DON'T YOU DARE FUCKING LEAVE, NING!
YEAH MAN, I FEEL YOU.
I MEAN IT'S GONNA TAKE ME AT LEAST 'TIL 6:00 TO FINISH THIS CAT-GARNISHED PIZZA.
GRUMBLE GRUMBLE.
'SCUSE ME.. NOT SURE YOU REMEMBER ME, BUT MY --
GASP!!
THAT IS SUCH A CUTE BIRD!
LOOK AT YOU! YOU'RE A BIRD, AREN'T YOU?
YES.. HE IS A BIRD.
YOU'RE THE LADY WHO SPECIAL ORDERED OUR MEDIUM-AND-A-HALF, RIGHT?
WE KEEP 'EM IN THE BACK. WE JUST HATE TO RESTOCK THIS SIZE.
HANNA, I THINK WE SHOULD GO TO THAT GALLERY OPENING.
I HAVE AN EXPERIMENT TO DO.

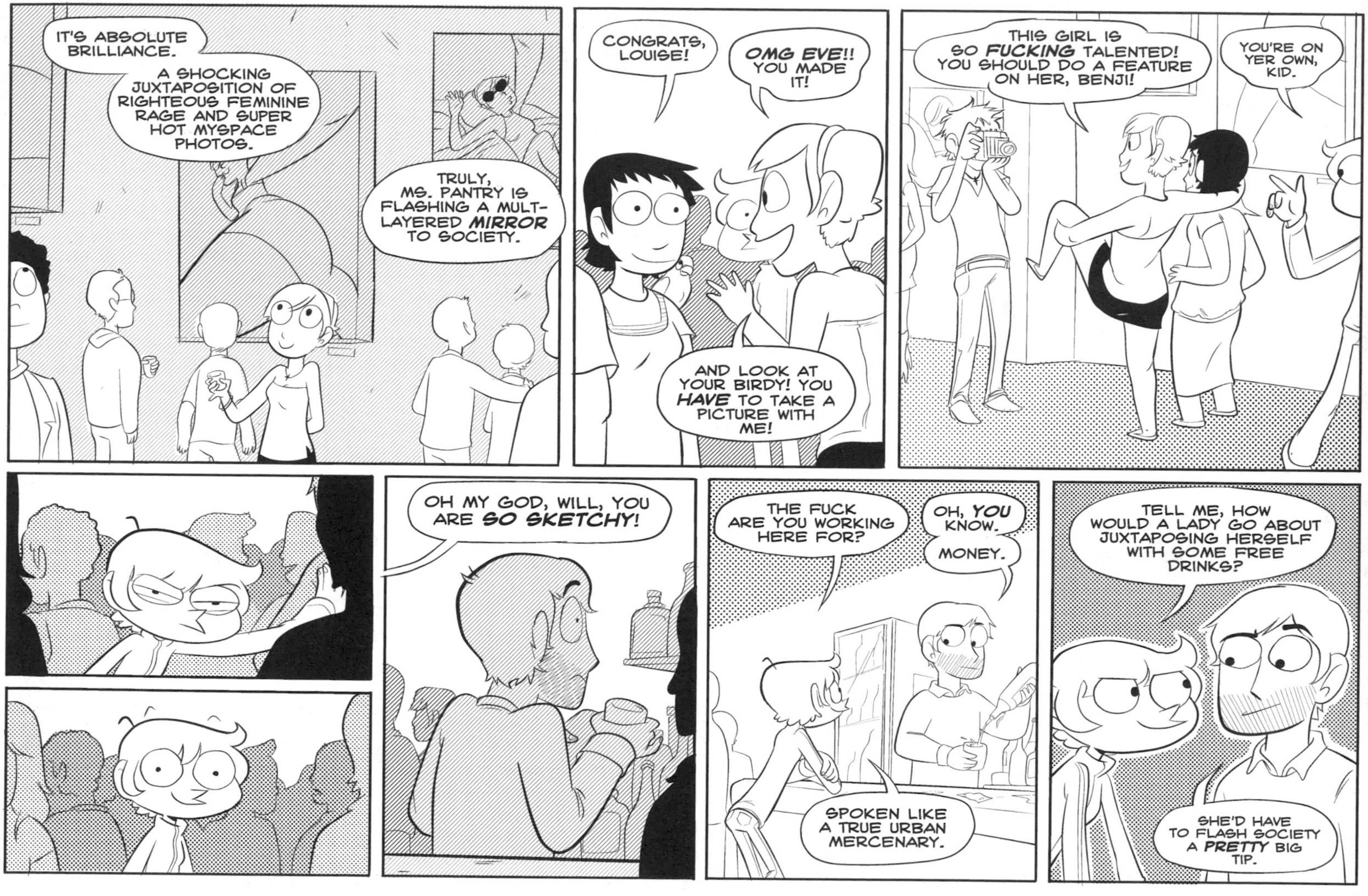
IT'S ABSOLUTE BRILLIANCE.
A SHOCKING JUXTAPOSITION OF RIGHTEOUS FEMININE RAGE AND SUPER HOT MYSPACE PHOTOS.
TRULY, MS. PANTRY IS FLASHING A MULT-LAYERED **MIRROR** TO SOCIETY.
CONGRATS, LOUISE!
OMG EVE!! YOU MADE IT!
AND LOOK AT YOUR BIRDY! YOU **HAVE** TO TAKE A PICTURE WITH ME!
THIS GIRL IS SO **FUCKING** TALENTED! YOU SHOULD DO A FEATURE ON HER, BENJI!
YOU'RE ON YER OWN, KID.
OH MY GOD, WILL, YOU ARE **SO SKETCHY**!
THE FUCK ARE YOU WORKING HERE FOR?
OH, **YOU** KNOW.
MONEY.
SPOKEN LIKE A TRUE URBAN MERCENARY.
TELL ME, HOW WOULD A LADY GO ABOUT JUXTAPOSING HERSELF WITH SOME FREE DRINKS?
SHE'D HAVE TO FLASH SOCIETY A **PRETTY** BIG TIP.

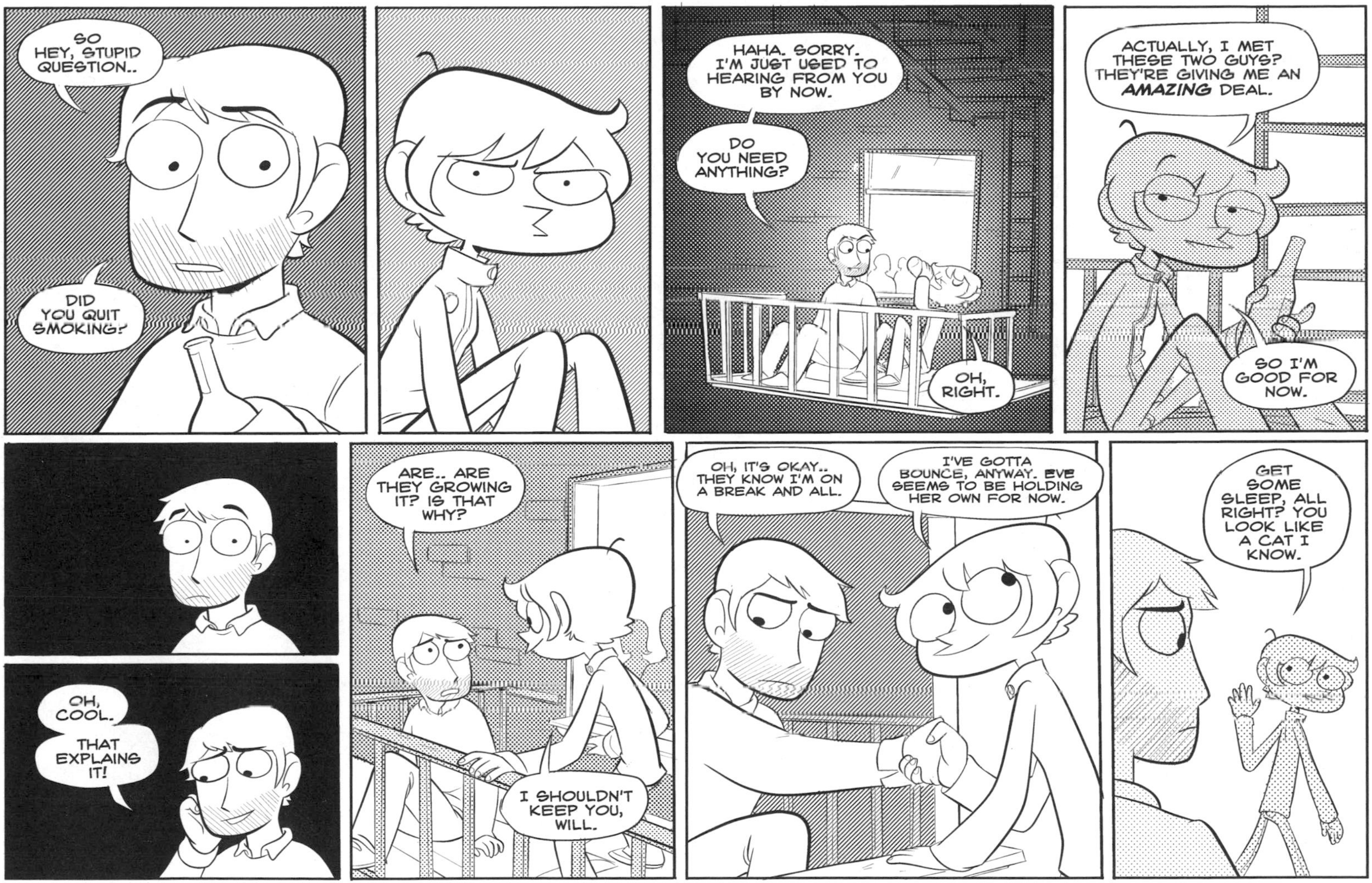
SO HEY, STUPID QUESTION..
DID YOU QUIT SMOKING?
HAHA. SORRY. I'M JUST USED TO HEARING FROM YOU BY NOW.
DO YOU NEED ANYTHING?
OH, RIGHT.
ACTUALLY, I MET THESE TWO GUYS? THEY'RE GIVING ME AN **AMAZING** DEAL.
SO I'M GOOD FOR NOW.
OH, COOL.
THAT EXPLAINS IT!
ARE.. ARE THEY GROWING IT? IS THAT WHY?
I SHOULDN'T KEEP YOU, WILL.
OH, IT'S OKAY.. THEY KNOW I'M ON A BREAK AND ALL.
I'VE GOTTA BOUNCE, ANYWAY. EVE SEEMS TO BE HOLDING HER OWN FOR NOW.
GET SOME SLEEP, ALL RIGHT? YOU LOOK LIKE A CAT I KNOW.

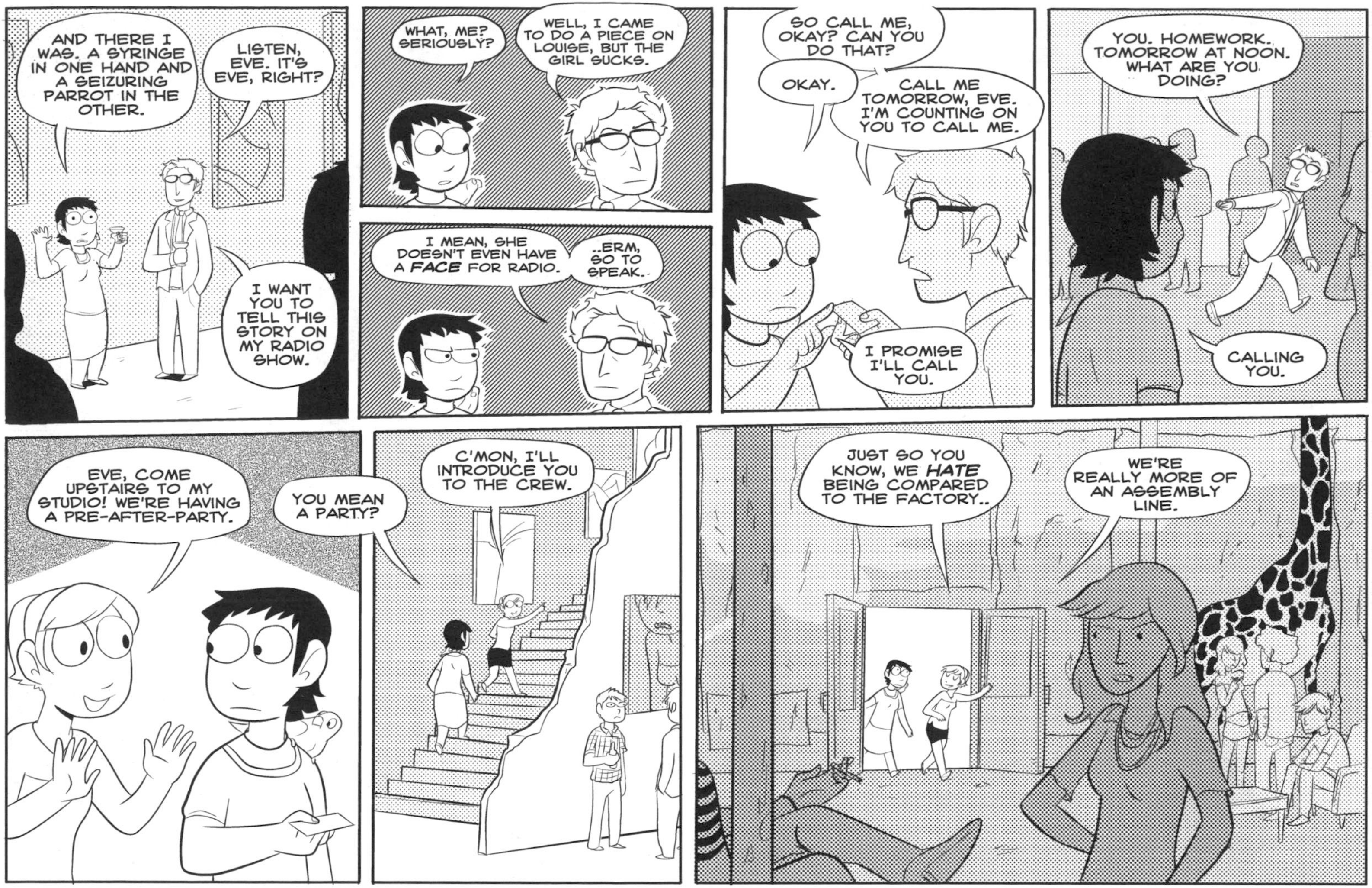
AND THERE I WAS. A SYRINGE IN ONE HAND AND A SEIZURING PARROT IN THE OTHER.
LISTEN, EVE. IT'S EVE, RIGHT?
I WANT YOU TO TELL THIS STORY ON MY RADIO SHOW.
WHAT, ME? SERIOUSLY?
WELL, I CAME TO DO A PIECE ON LOUISE, BUT THE GIRL SUCKS.
I MEAN, SHE DOESN'T EVEN HAVE A *FACE* FOR RADIO.
..ERM, SO TO SPEAK..
SO CALL ME, OKAY? CAN YOU DO THAT?
OKAY.
CALL ME TOMORROW, EVE. I'M COUNTING ON YOU TO CALL ME.
I PROMISE I'LL CALL YOU.
YOU. HOMEWORK. TOMORROW AT NOON. WHAT ARE YOU DOING?
CALLING YOU.
EVE, COME UPSTAIRS TO MY STUDIO! WE'RE HAVING A PRE-AFTER-PARTY.
YOU MEAN A PARTY?
C'MON, I'LL INTRODUCE YOU TO THE CREW.
JUST SO YOU KNOW, WE *HATE* BEING COMPARED TO THE FACTORY..
WE'RE REALLY MORE OF AN ASSEMBLY LINE.

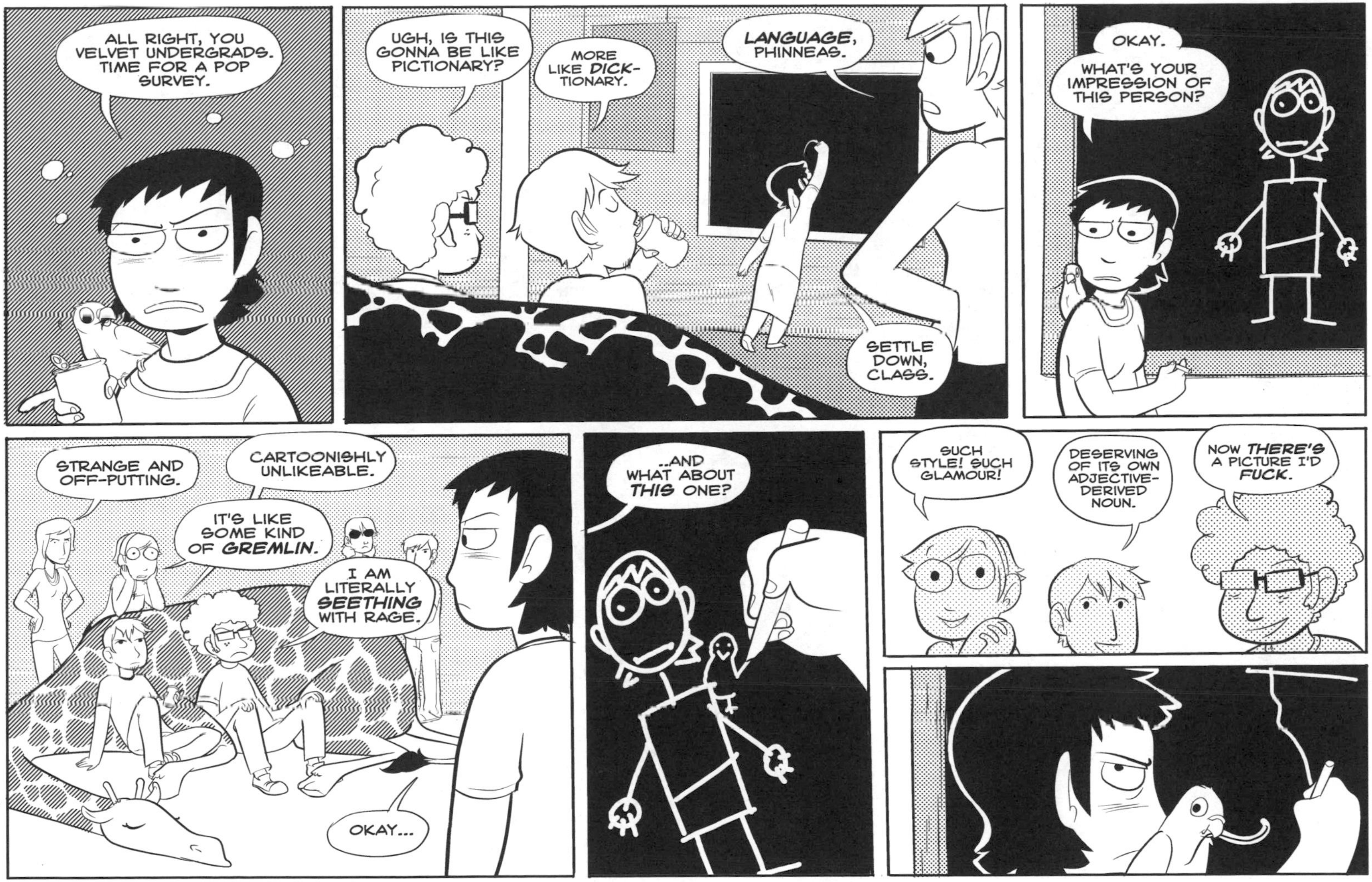

ALL RIGHT, YOU VELVET UNDERGRADS. TIME FOR A POP SURVEY.
UGH, IS THIS GONNA BE LIKE PICTIONARY?
MORE LIKE DICK-TIONARY.
LANGUAGE, PHINNEAS.
SETTLE DOWN, CLASS.
OKAY.
WHAT'S YOUR IMPRESSION OF THIS PERSON?
STRANGE AND OFF-PUTTING.
CARTOONISHLY UNLIKEABLE.
IT'S LIKE SOME KIND OF GREMLIN.
I AM LITERALLY SEETHING WITH RAGE.
OKAY...
..AND WHAT ABOUT THIS ONE?
SUCH STYLE! SUCH GLAMOUR!
DESERVING OF ITS OWN ADJECTIVE-DERIVED NOUN.
NOW THERE'S A PICTURE I'D FUCK.

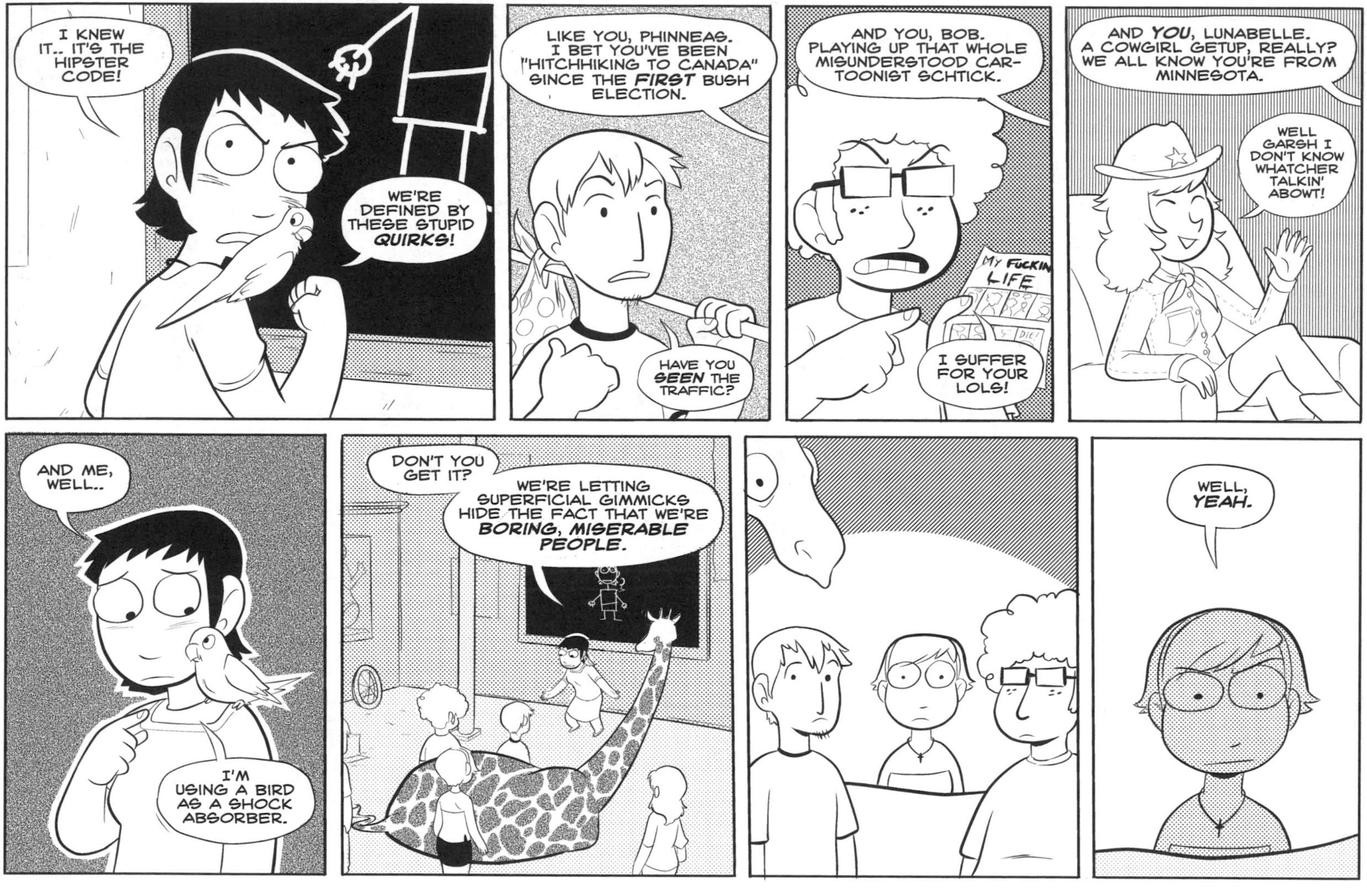
I KNEW IT.. IT'S THE HIPSTER CODE!
WE'RE DEFINED BY THESE STUPID QUIRKS!
LIKE YOU, PHINNEAS. I BET YOU'VE BEEN "HITCHHIKING TO CANADA" SINCE THE FIRST BUSH ELECTION.
HAVE YOU SEEN THE TRAFFIC?
AND YOU, BOB. PLAYING UP THAT WHOLE MISUNDERSTOOD CAR-TOONIST SCHTICK.
MY FUCKIN LIFE
I SUFFER FOR YOUR LOLS!
AND YOU, LUNABELLE. A COWGIRL GETUP, REALLY? WE ALL KNOW YOU'RE FROM MINNESOTA.
WELL GARSH I DON'T KNOW WHATCHER TALKIN' ABOWT!
AND ME, WELL..
I'M USING A BIRD AS A SHOCK ABSORBER.
DON'T YOU GET IT?
WE'RE LETTING SUPERFICIAL GIMMICKS HIDE THE FACT THAT WE'RE BORING, MISERABLE PEOPLE.
WELL, YEAH.

DID YOU MISS THE *MEMO*, EVE? NO ONE IS UNIQUE. NO ONE IS SPECIAL.

LOUISE..?

THIS WORLD WAS MADE TO FORGET WE WERE EVEN *HERE*.

BUT THAT'S THE *BEAUTY* OF POP CULTURE.

WE CAN *ALL* BE FAMOUS FOR A LITTLE WHILE!

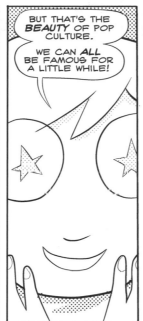

INCLUDING YOU, EVE!

AAA!

STAY BACK! *BACK!*

OR I'LL INSPIRE EVERY GOD DAMNED *ONE* OF YOU!

HA!

HAH HA!

SHE'S BLUFFING!

DON'T PATRONIZE US, EVE.

WE'VE READ THE *CLIFF NOTES!*

AAAA!

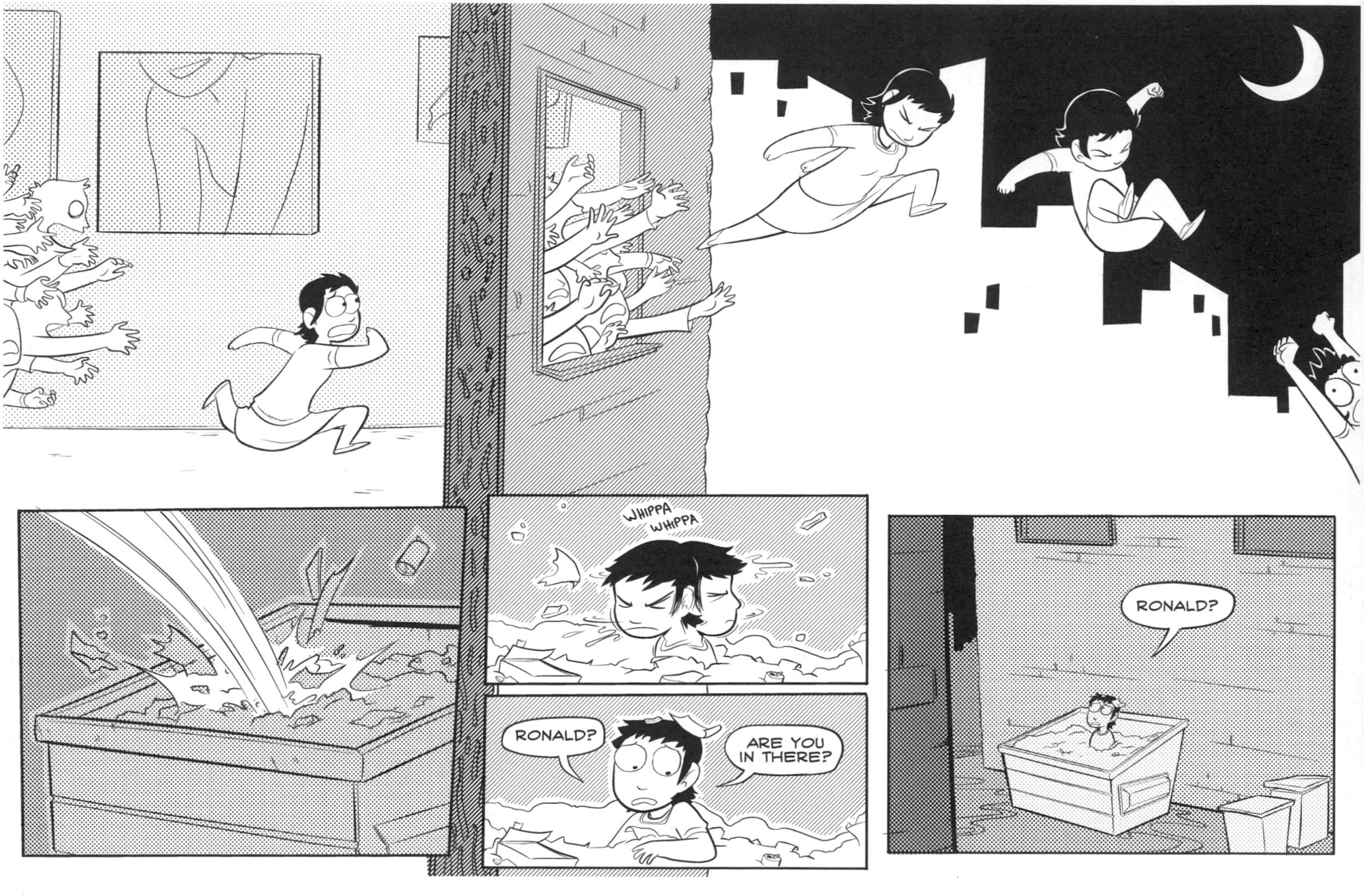
WHIPPA WHIPPA
RONALD?
ARE YOU IN THERE?
RONALD?

RONALD, WHERE ARE YOU?

I PROMISE THE CULTURE SHOCK IS OVER!

RONALD..?

SKITTER SKITTER

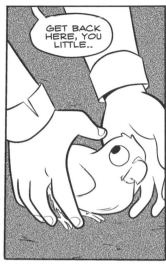

GET BACK HERE, YOU LITTLE..

IS THIS YOUR...

HI.

..HI.

IS THIS YOUR BIRD?

SORRY, WHAT?

UM..

OH, YOU FOUND...

THIS IS YOUR BIRD, RIGHT..?

YEAH.

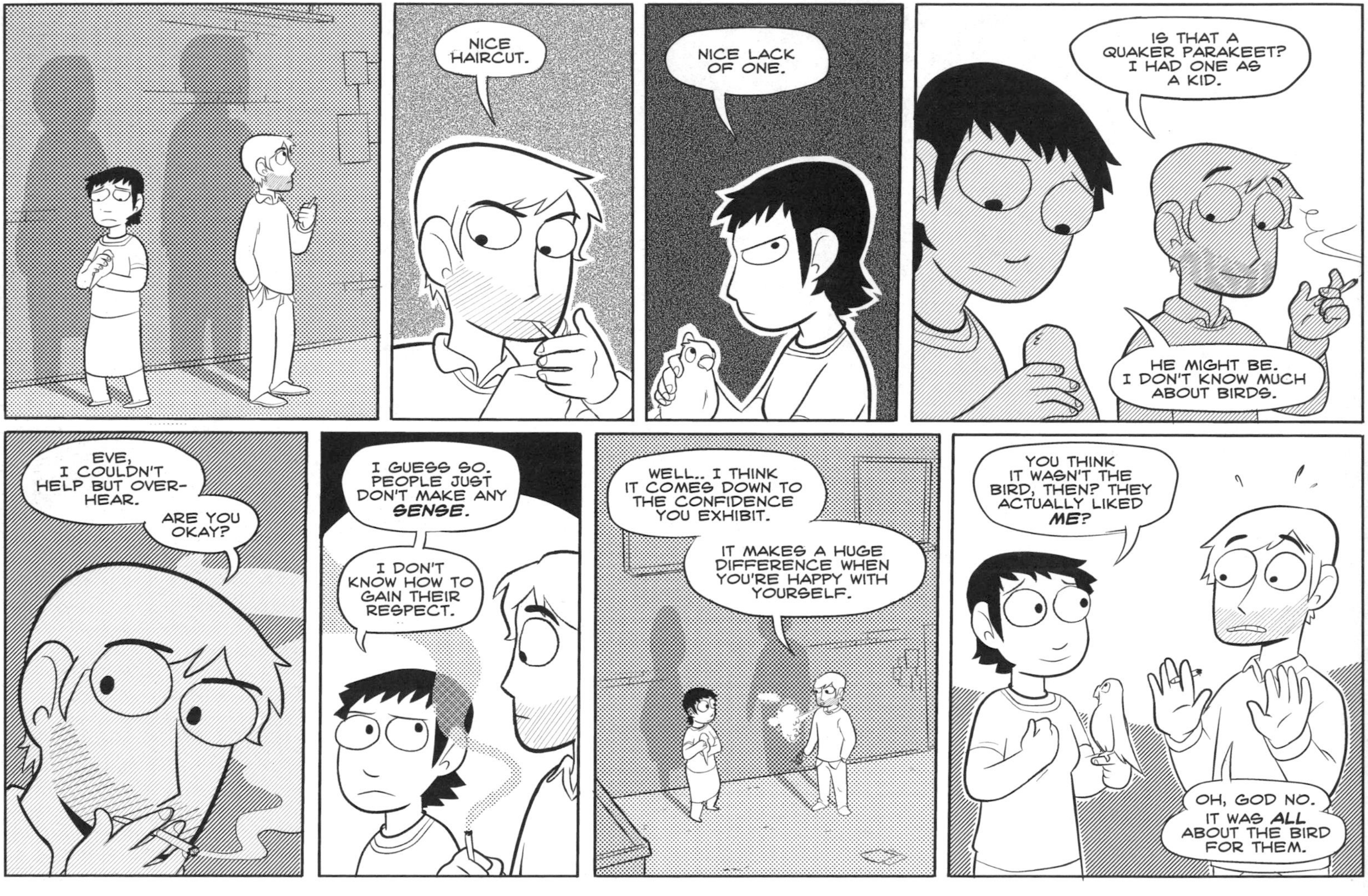
NICE HAIRCUT.
NICE LACK OF ONE.
IS THAT A QUAKER PARAKEET? I HAD ONE AS A KID.
HE MIGHT BE. I DON'T KNOW MUCH ABOUT BIRDS.
EVE, I COULDN'T HELP BUT OVER-HEAR.
ARE YOU OKAY?
I GUESS SO. PEOPLE JUST DON'T MAKE ANY SENSE.
I DON'T KNOW HOW TO GAIN THEIR RESPECT.
WELL.. I THINK IT COMES DOWN TO THE CONFIDENCE YOU EXHIBIT.
IT MAKES A HUGE DIFFERENCE WHEN YOU'RE HAPPY WITH YOURSELF.
YOU THINK IT WASN'T THE BIRD, THEN? THEY ACTUALLY LIKED ME?
OH, GOD NO. IT WAS ALL ABOUT THE BIRD FOR THEM.

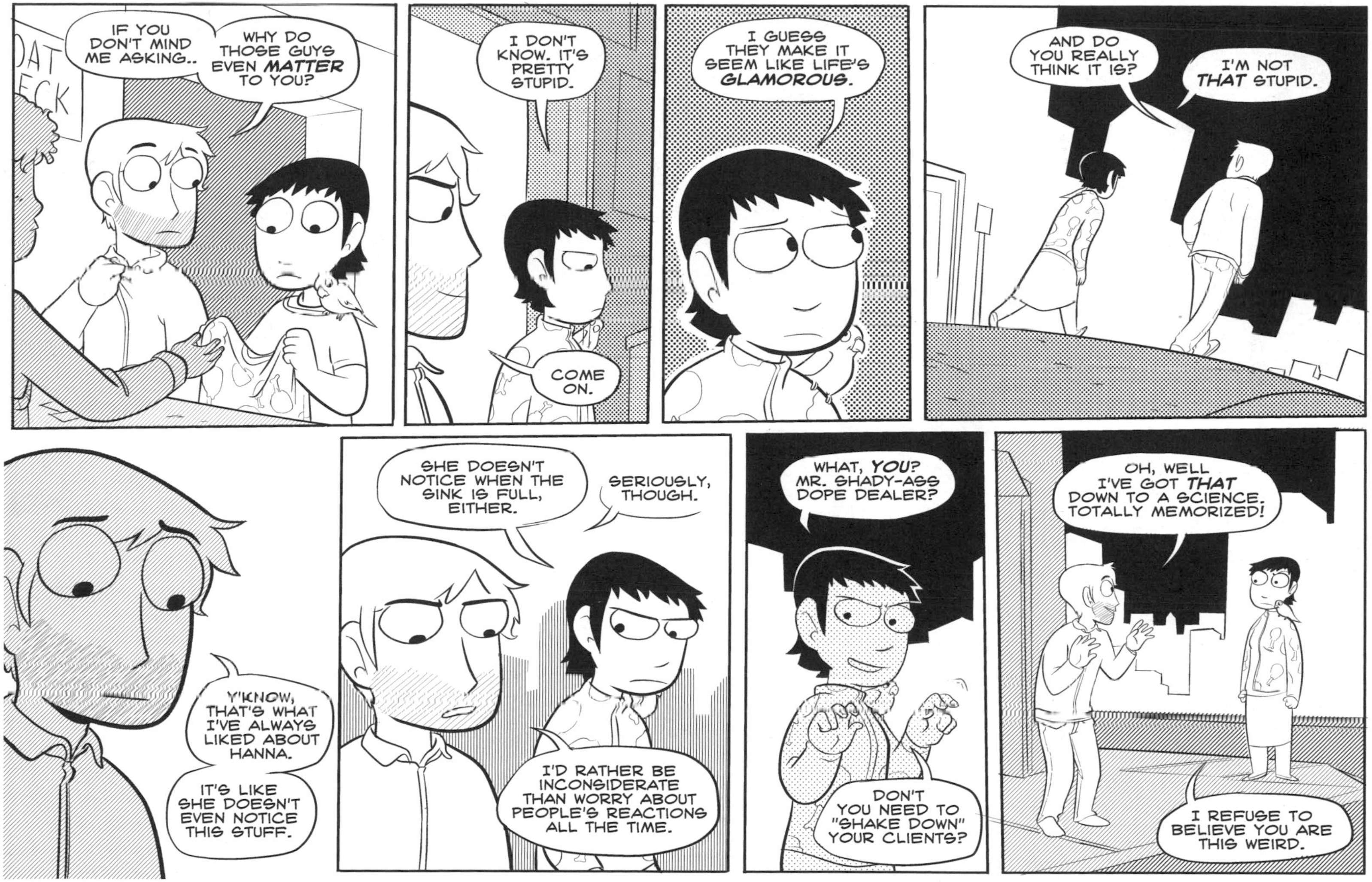
OAT
ECK
IF YOU DON'T MIND ME ASKING..
WHY DO THOSE GUYS EVEN *MATTER* TO YOU?
I DON'T KNOW. IT'S PRETTY STUPID.
COME ON.
I GUESS THEY MAKE IT SEEM LIKE LIFE'S *GLAMOROUS*.
AND DO YOU REALLY THINK IT IS?
I'M NOT *THAT* STUPID.
Y'KNOW, THAT'S WHAT I'VE ALWAYS LIKED ABOUT HANNA.
IT'S LIKE SHE DOESN'T EVEN NOTICE THIS STUFF.
SHE DOESN'T NOTICE WHEN THE SINK IS FULL, EITHER.
SERIOUSLY, THOUGH.
I'D RATHER BE INCONSIDERATE THAN WORRY ABOUT PEOPLE'S REACTIONS ALL THE TIME.
WHAT, *YOU*? MR. SHADY-ASS DOPE DEALER?
DON'T YOU NEED TO "SHAKE DOWN" YOUR CLIENTS?
OH, WELL I'VE GOT *THAT* DOWN TO A SCIENCE. TOTALLY MEMORIZED!
I REFUSE TO BELIEVE YOU ARE THIS WEIRD.

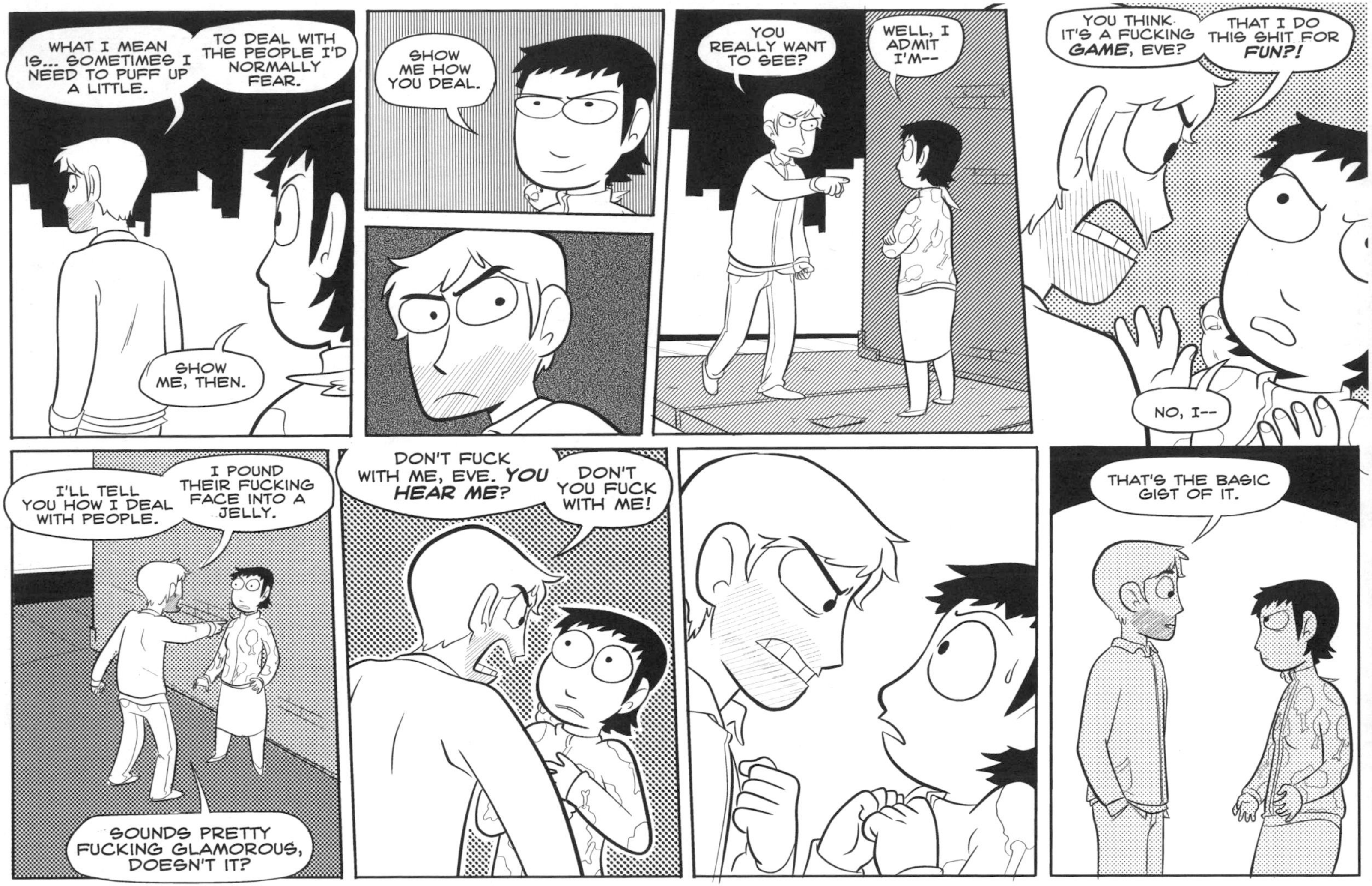
WHAT I MEAN IS... SOMETIMES I NEED TO PUFF UP A LITTLE.
TO DEAL WITH THE PEOPLE I'D NORMALLY FEAR.
SHOW ME, THEN.
SHOW ME HOW YOU DEAL.
YOU REALLY WANT TO SEE?
WELL, I ADMIT I'M--
YOU THINK IT'S A FUCKING GAME, EVE?
THAT I DO THIS SHIT FOR FUN?!
NO, I--
I'LL TELL YOU HOW I DEAL WITH PEOPLE.
I POUND THEIR FUCKING FACE INTO A JELLY.
SOUNDS PRETTY FUCKING GLAMOROUS, DOESN'T IT?
DON'T FUCK WITH ME, EVE. YOU HEAR ME?
DON'T YOU FUCK WITH ME!
THAT'S THE BASIC GIST OF IT.

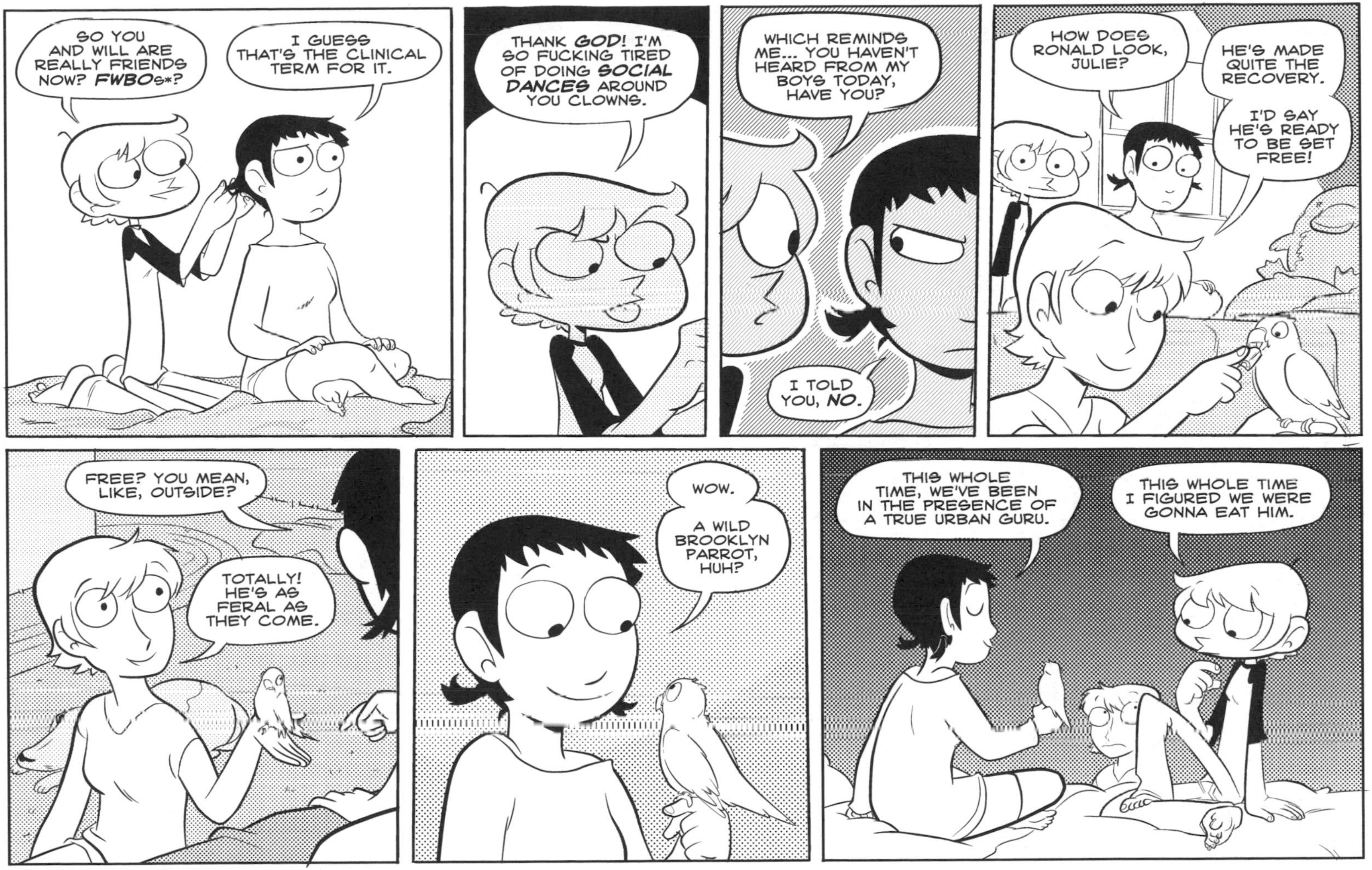

SO YOU AND WILL ARE REALLY FRIENDS NOW? **FWBO**s*?
I GUESS THAT'S THE CLINICAL TERM FOR IT.
THANK **GOD**! I'M SO FUCKING TIRED OF DOING **SOCIAL DANCES** AROUND YOU CLOWNS.
WHICH REMINDS ME... YOU HAVEN'T HEARD FROM MY BOYS TODAY, HAVE YOU?
I TOLD YOU, **NO**.
HOW DOES RONALD LOOK, JULIE?
HE'S MADE QUITE THE RECOVERY.
I'D SAY HE'S READY TO BE SET FREE!
FREE? YOU MEAN, LIKE, OUTSIDE?
TOTALLY! HE'S AS FERAL AS THEY COME.
WOW.
A WILD BROOKLYN PARROT, HUH?
THIS WHOLE TIME, WE'VE BEEN IN THE PRESENCE OF A TRUE URBAN GURU.
THIS WHOLE TIME I FIGURED WE WERE GONNA EAT HIM.

*ED - FRIENDS WHO BONED ONCE

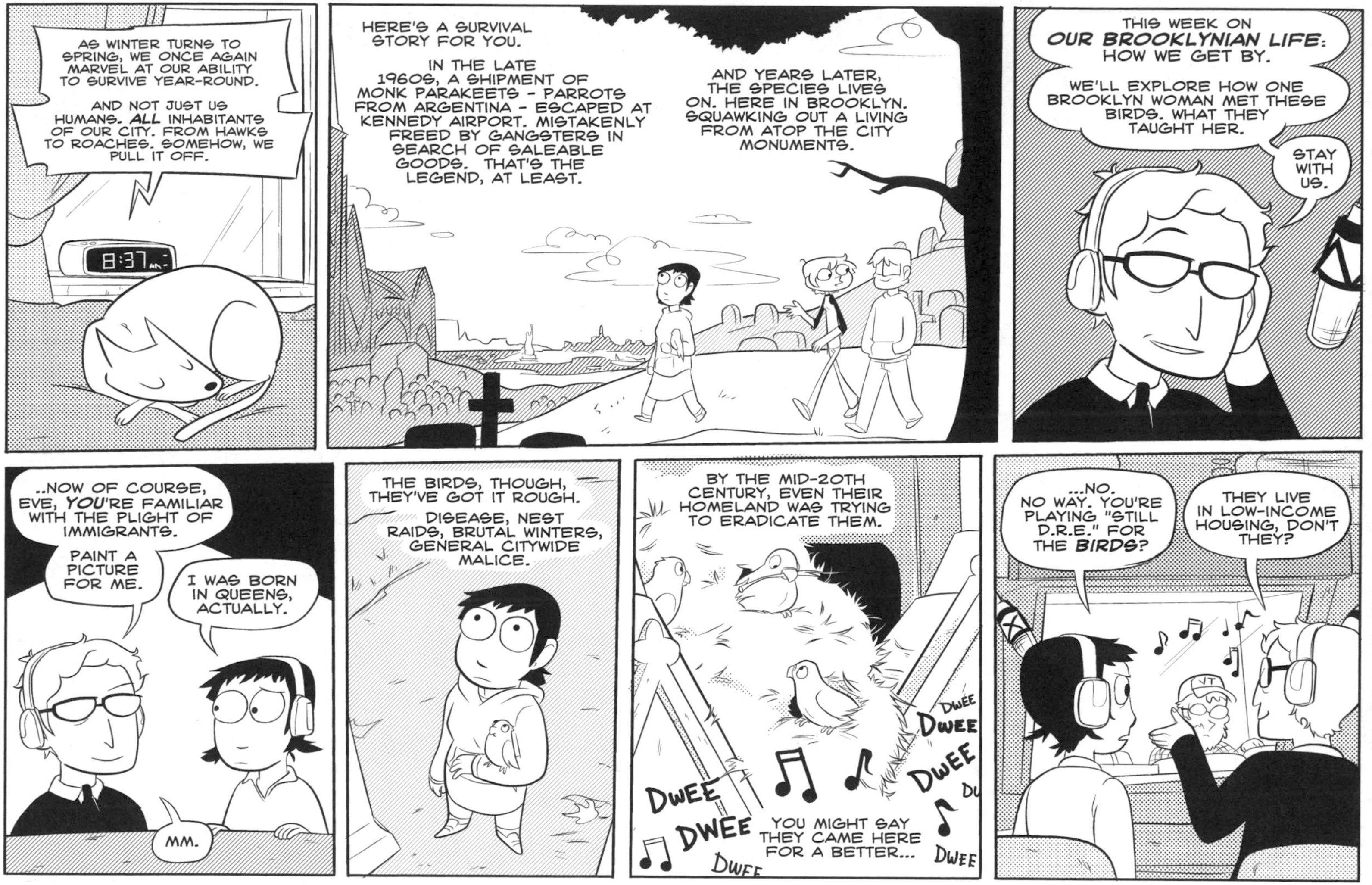
AS WINTER TURNS TO SPRING, WE ONCE AGAIN MARVEL AT OUR ABILITY TO SURVIVE YEAR-ROUND.
AND NOT JUST US HUMANS. ALL INHABITANTS OF OUR CITY. FROM HAWKS TO ROACHES. SOMEHOW, WE PULL IT OFF.
HERE'S A SURVIVAL STORY FOR YOU.
IN THE LATE 1960S, A SHIPMENT OF MONK PARAKEETS - PARROTS FROM ARGENTINA - ESCAPED AT KENNEDY AIRPORT. MISTAKENLY FREED BY GANGSTERS IN SEARCH OF SALEABLE GOODS. THAT'S THE LEGEND, AT LEAST.
AND YEARS LATER, THE SPECIES LIVES ON. HERE IN BROOKLYN. SQUAWKING OUT A LIVING FROM ATOP THE CITY MONUMENTS.
THIS WEEK ON OUR BROOKLYNIAN LIFE: HOW WE GET BY.
WE'LL EXPLORE HOW ONE BROOKLYN WOMAN MET THESE BIRDS. WHAT THEY TAUGHT HER.
STAY WITH US.
..NOW OF COURSE, EVE, YOU'RE FAMILIAR WITH THE PLIGHT OF IMMIGRANTS.
PAINT A PICTURE FOR ME.
I WAS BORN IN QUEENS, ACTUALLY.
MM.
THE BIRDS, THOUGH, THEY'VE GOT IT ROUGH.
DISEASE, NEST RAIDS, BRUTAL WINTERS, GENERAL CITYWIDE MALICE.
BY THE MID-20TH CENTURY, EVEN THEIR HOMELAND WAS TRYING TO ERADICATE THEM.
DWEE DWEE DWEE DU DWEE DWEE DWEE DWEE
YOU MIGHT SAY THEY CAME HERE FOR A BETTER...
...NO. NO WAY. YOU'RE PLAYING "STILL D.R.E." FOR THE BIRDS?
THEY LIVE IN LOW-INCOME HOUSING, DON'T THEY?

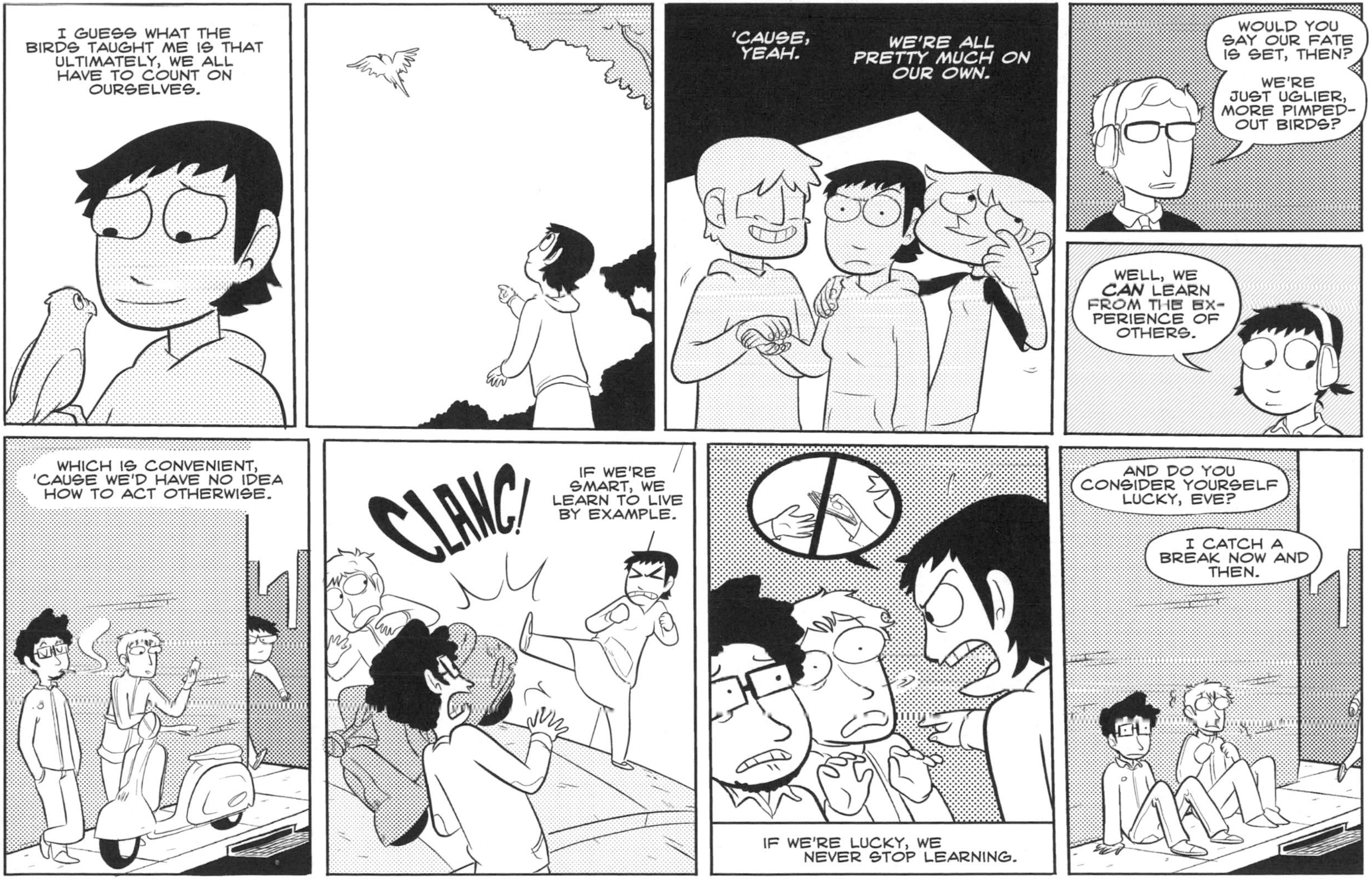
I GUESS WHAT THE BIRDS TAUGHT ME IS THAT ULTIMATELY, WE ALL HAVE TO COUNT ON OURSELVES.
'CAUSE, YEAH.
WE'RE ALL PRETTY MUCH ON OUR OWN.
WOULD YOU SAY OUR FATE IS SET, THEN?
WE'RE JUST UGLIER, MORE PIMPED-OUT BIRDS?
WELL, WE *CAN* LEARN FROM THE EXPERIENCE OF OTHERS.
WHICH IS CONVENIENT, 'CAUSE WE'D HAVE NO IDEA HOW TO ACT OTHERWISE.
CLANG!
IF WE'RE SMART, WE LEARN TO LIVE BY EXAMPLE.
IF WE'RE LUCKY, WE NEVER STOP LEARNING.
AND DO YOU CONSIDER YOURSELF LUCKY, EVE?
I CATCH A BREAK NOW AND THEN.

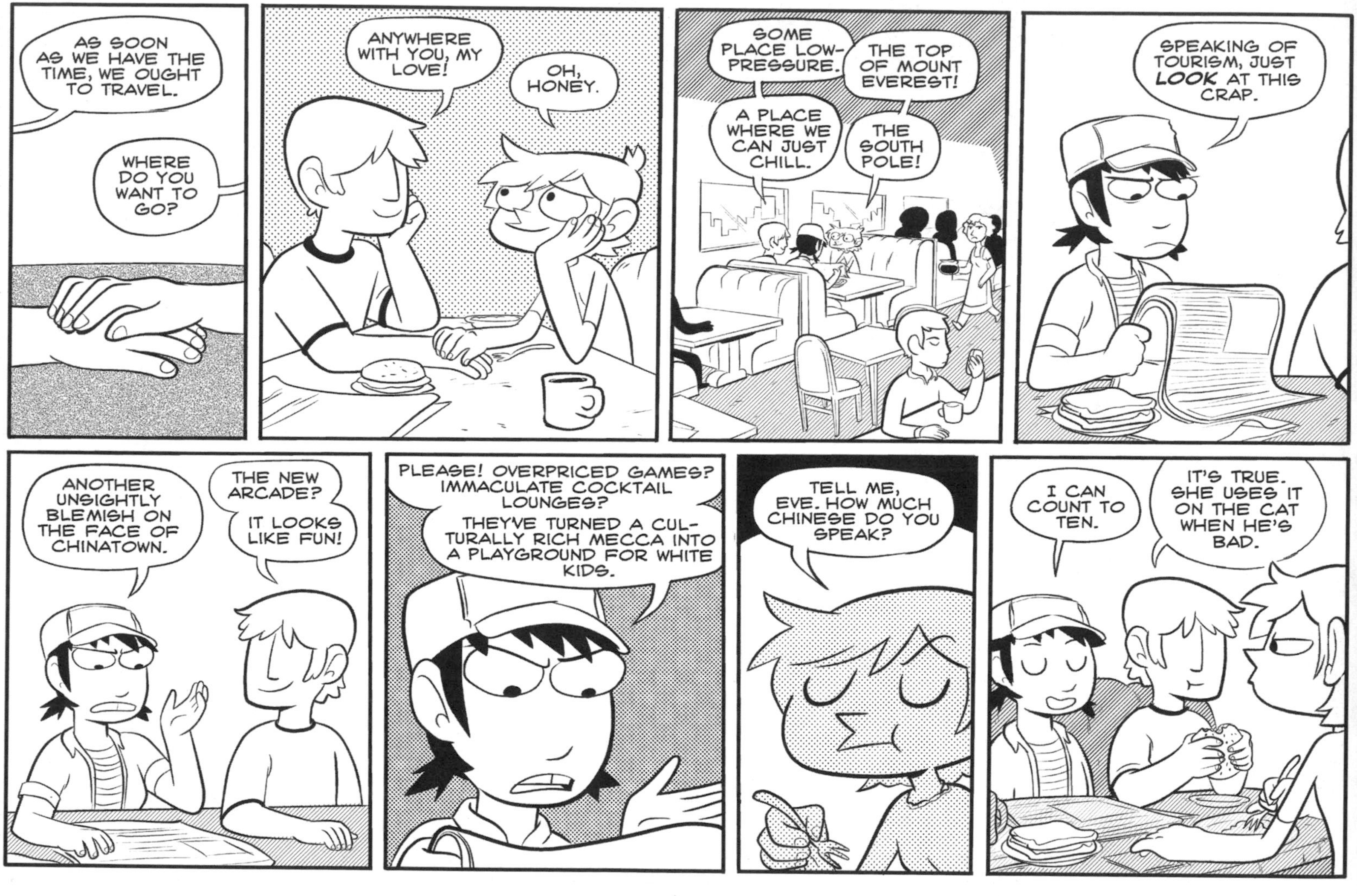
AS SOON AS WE HAVE THE TIME, WE OUGHT TO TRAVEL.
WHERE DO YOU WANT TO GO?
ANYWHERE WITH YOU, MY LOVE!
OH, HONEY.
SOME PLACE LOW-PRESSURE.
THE TOP OF MOUNT EVEREST!
A PLACE WHERE WE CAN JUST CHILL.
THE SOUTH POLE!
SPEAKING OF TOURISM, JUST LOOK AT THIS CRAP.
ANOTHER UNSIGHTLY BLEMISH ON THE FACE OF CHINATOWN.
THE NEW ARCADE?
IT LOOKS LIKE FUN!
PLEASE! OVERPRICED GAMES? IMMACULATE COCKTAIL LOUNGES?
THEY'VE TURNED A CUL-TURALLY RICH MECCA INTO A PLAYGROUND FOR WHITE KIDS.
TELL ME, EVE. HOW MUCH CHINESE DO YOU SPEAK?
I CAN COUNT TO TEN.
IT'S TRUE. SHE USES IT ON THE CAT WHEN HE'S BAD.

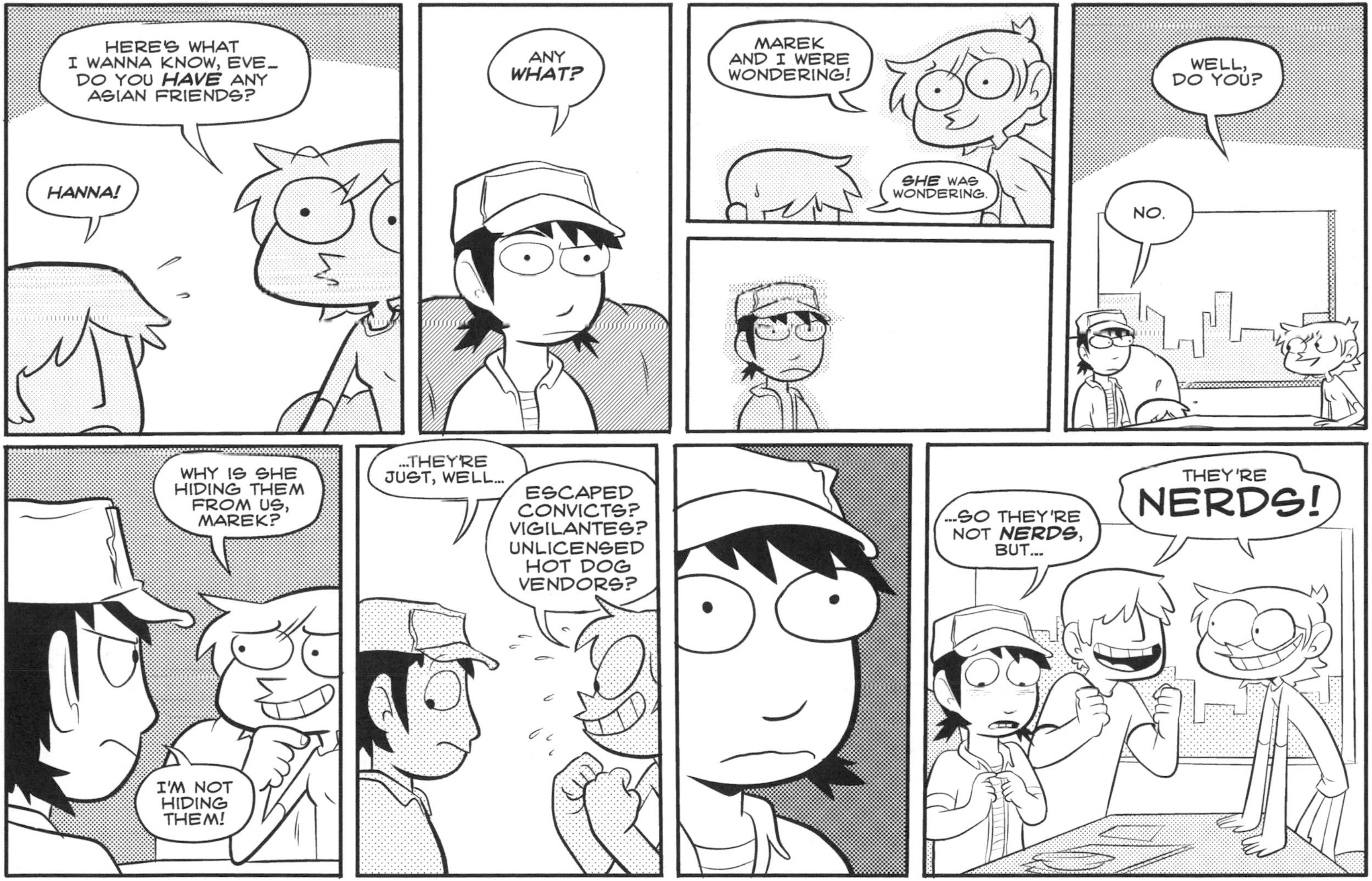
HERE'S WHAT I WANNA KNOW, EVE... DO YOU *HAVE* ANY ASIAN FRIENDS?
HANNA!
ANY *WHAT?*
MAREK AND I WERE WONDERING!
SHE WAS WONDERING.
WELL, DO YOU?
NO.
WHY IS SHE HIDING THEM FROM US, MAREK?
I'M NOT HIDING THEM!
...THEY'RE JUST, WELL...
ESCAPED CONVICTS? VIGILANTES? UNLICENSED HOT DOG VENDORS?
...SO THEY'RE NOT *NERDS*, BUT...
THEY'RE **NERDS!**

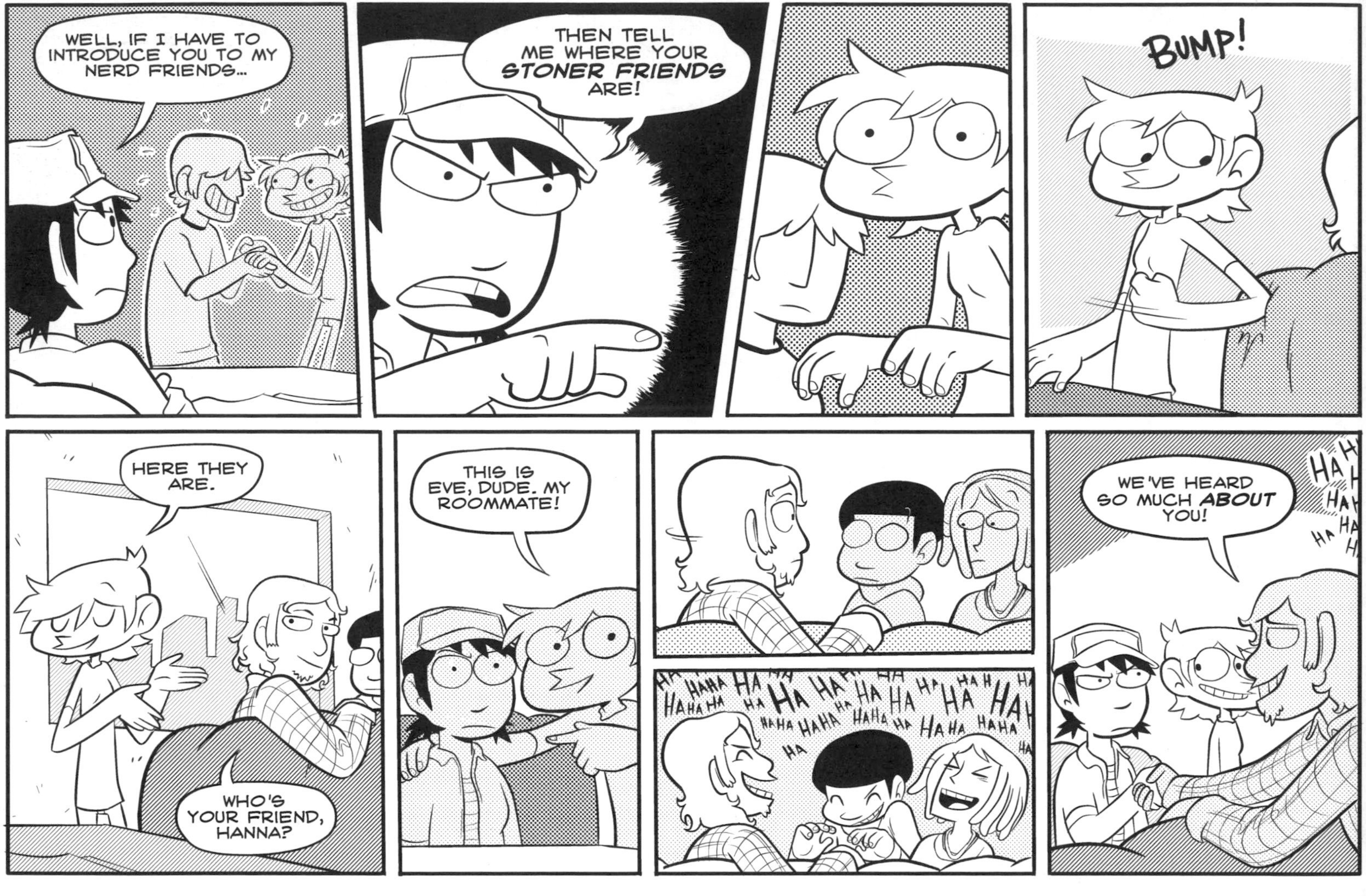
WELL, IF I HAVE TO INTRODUCE YOU TO MY NERD FRIENDS...
THEN TELL ME WHERE YOUR STONER FRIENDS ARE!
BUMP!
HERE THEY ARE.
WHO'S YOUR FRIEND, HANNA?
THIS IS EVE, DUDE. MY ROOMMATE!
HAHA HAHAHA HA HA HA HA HA HA HA HA HA HA HA HAHA HAHA HAHA HAHA HA HAHA HAHA HA
WE'VE HEARD SO MUCH ABOUT YOU!
HA HA HA HA HA HA

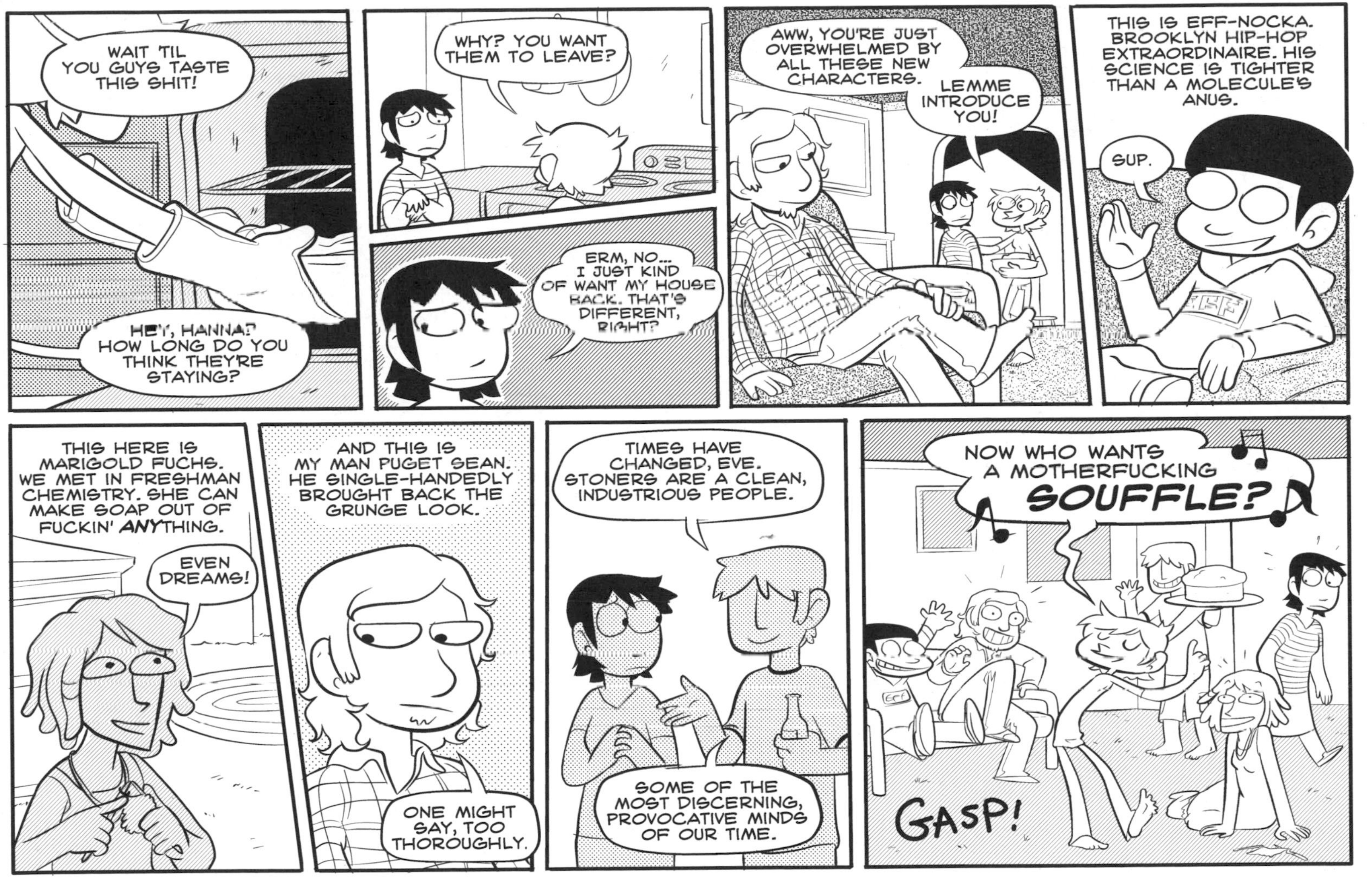
WAIT 'TIL YOU GUYS TASTE THIS SHIT!
HEY, HANNA? HOW LONG DO YOU THINK THEY'RE STAYING?
WHY? YOU WANT THEM TO LEAVE?
ERM, NO... I JUST KIND OF WANT MY HOUSE BACK. THAT'S DIFFERENT, RIGHT?
AWW, YOU'RE JUST OVERWHELMED BY ALL THESE NEW CHARACTERS.
LEMME INTRODUCE YOU!
THIS IS EFF-NOCKA. BROOKLYN HIP-HOP EXTRAORDINAIRE. HIS SCIENCE IS TIGHTER THAN A MOLECULE'S ANUS.
SUP.
THIS HERE IS MARIGOLD FUCHS. WE MET IN FRESHMAN CHEMISTRY. SHE CAN MAKE SOAP OUT OF FUCKIN' ***ANY***THING.
EVEN DREAMS!
AND THIS IS MY MAN PUGET SEAN. HE SINGLE-HANDEDLY BROUGHT BACK THE GRUNGE LOOK.
ONE MIGHT SAY, TOO THOROUGHLY.
TIMES HAVE CHANGED, EVE. STONERS ARE A CLEAN, INDUSTRIOUS PEOPLE.
SOME OF THE MOST DISCERNING, PROVOCATIVE MINDS OF OUR TIME.
NOW WHO WANTS A MOTHERFUCKING ***SOUFFLE?***
GASP!

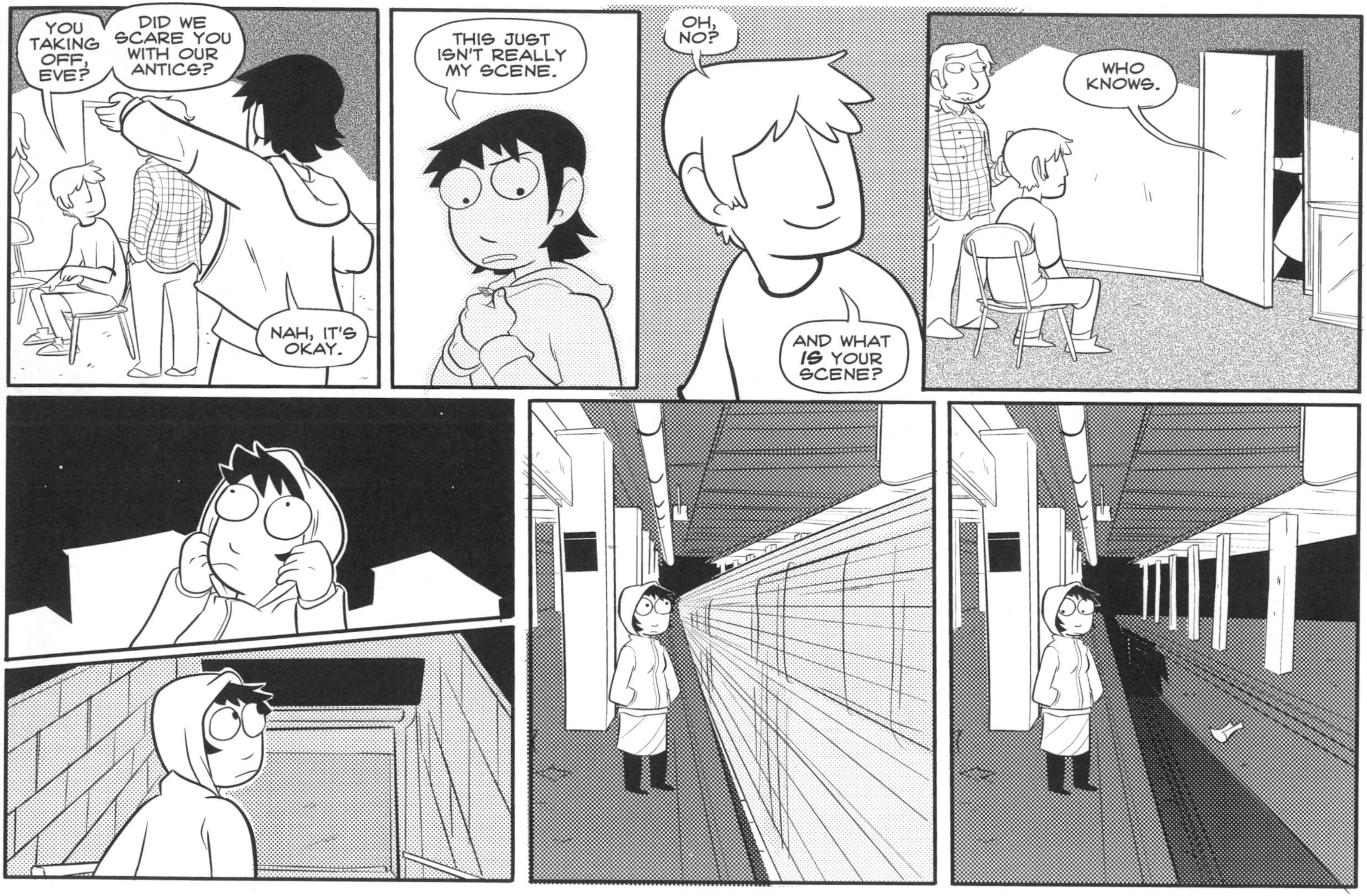
YOU TAKING OFF, EVE?
DID WE SCARE YOU WITH OUR ANTICS?
NAH, IT'S OKAY.
THIS JUST ISN'T REALLY MY SCENE.
OH, NO?
AND WHAT *IS* YOUR SCENE?
WHO KNOWS.

SIGH.

MR. SONG'S P

MING ON: ...TION LASER ...ME ARCADE

HEY, EVE!

WOAH! HEY GREG!

WHAT'S UP, STRANGER!

WELL, I'VE BEEN... YOU KNOW.

BUSY.

I SUCK! I'M SORRY!

ARE YOU GOING TO ICE CREAM FACTORY? CAN I COME?

I DON'T KNOW...

HAVEN'T YOU DONE ENOUGH DESSERTING LATELY?

OH BOY, THAT'S COLD.

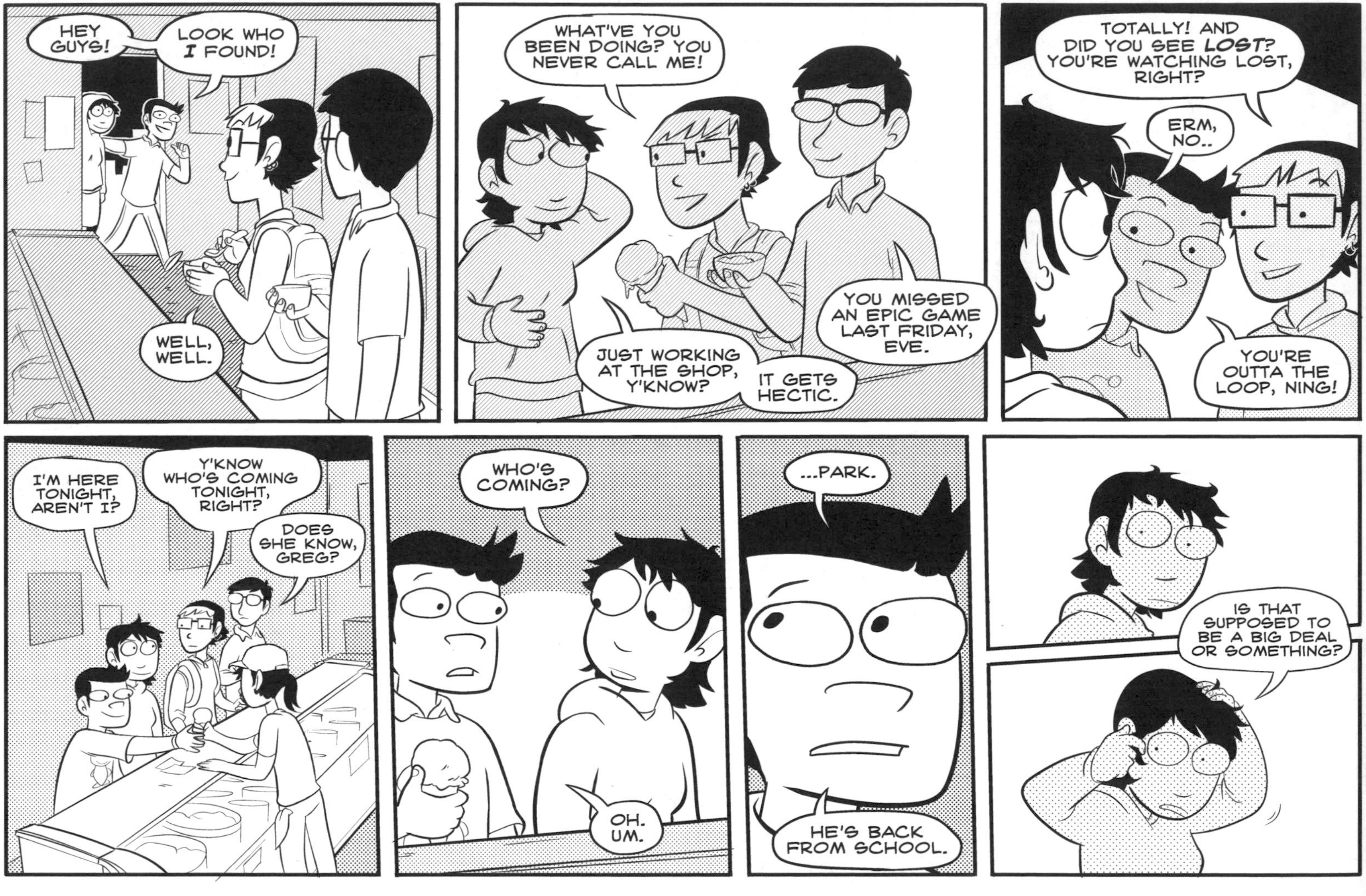
HEY GUYS!
LOOK WHO I FOUND!
WELL, WELL.
WHAT'VE YOU BEEN DOING? YOU NEVER CALL ME!
JUST WORKING AT THE SHOP, Y'KNOW?
IT GETS HECTIC.
YOU MISSED AN EPIC GAME LAST FRIDAY, EVE.
TOTALLY! AND DID YOU SEE LOST? YOU'RE WATCHING LOST, RIGHT?
ERM, NO..
YOU'RE OUTTA THE LOOP, NING!
I'M HERE TONIGHT, AREN'T I?
Y'KNOW WHO'S COMING TONIGHT, RIGHT?
DOES SHE KNOW, GREG?
WHO'S COMING?
OH. UM.
...PARK.
HE'S BACK FROM SCHOOL.
IS THAT SUPPOSED TO BE A BIG DEAL OR SOMETHING?

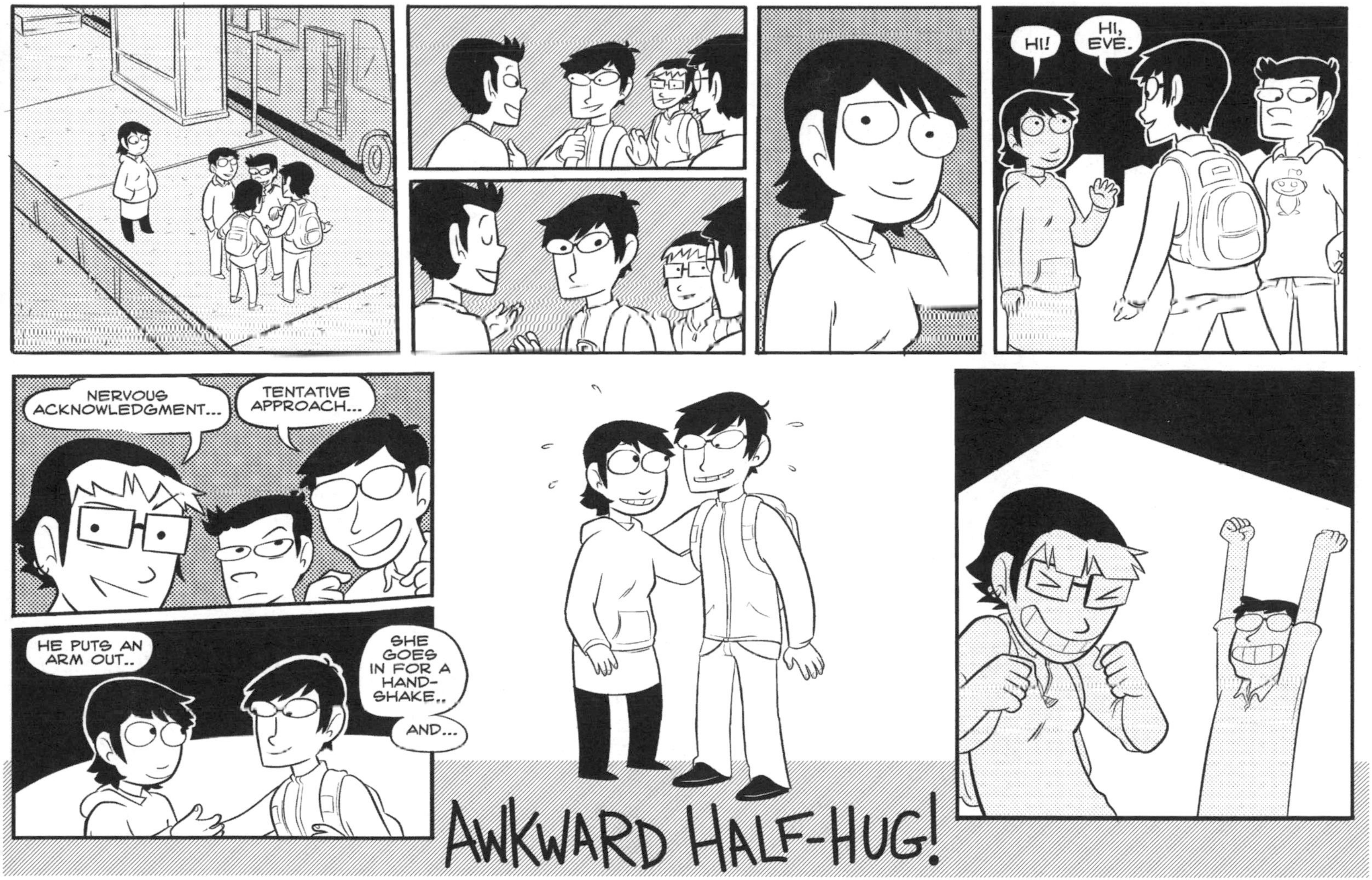
HI!
HI, EVE.
NERVOUS ACKNOWLEDGMENT...
TENTATIVE APPROACH...
HE PUTS AN ARM OUT..
SHE GOES IN FOR A HAND-SHAKE..
AND...
AWKWARD HALF-HUG!

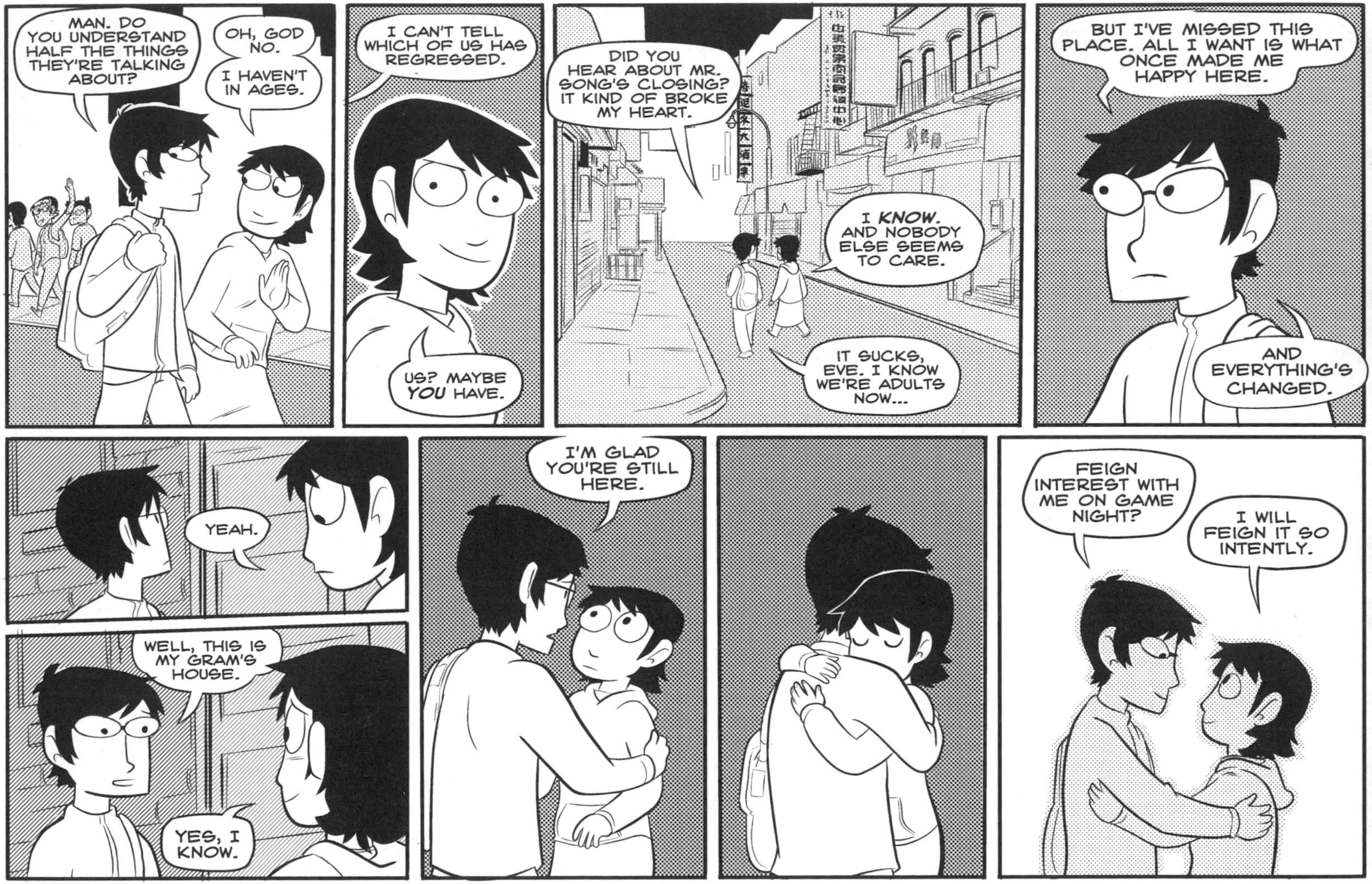
MAN. DO YOU UNDERSTAND HALF THE THINGS THEY'RE TALKING ABOUT?
OH, GOD NO.
I HAVEN'T IN AGES.
I CAN'T TELL WHICH OF US HAS REGRESSED.
US? MAYBE *YOU* HAVE.
DID YOU HEAR ABOUT MR. SONG'S CLOSING? IT KIND OF BROKE MY HEART.
I *KNOW*. AND NOBODY ELSE SEEMS TO CARE.
IT SUCKS, EVE. I KNOW WE'RE ADULTS NOW...
BUT I'VE MISSED THIS PLACE. ALL I WANT IS WHAT ONCE MADE ME HAPPY HERE.
AND EVERYTHING'S CHANGED.
YEAH.
WELL, THIS IS MY GRAM'S HOUSE.
YES, I KNOW.
I'M GLAD YOU'RE STILL HERE.
FEIGN INTEREST WITH ME ON GAME NIGHT?
I WILL FEIGN IT SO INTENTLY.

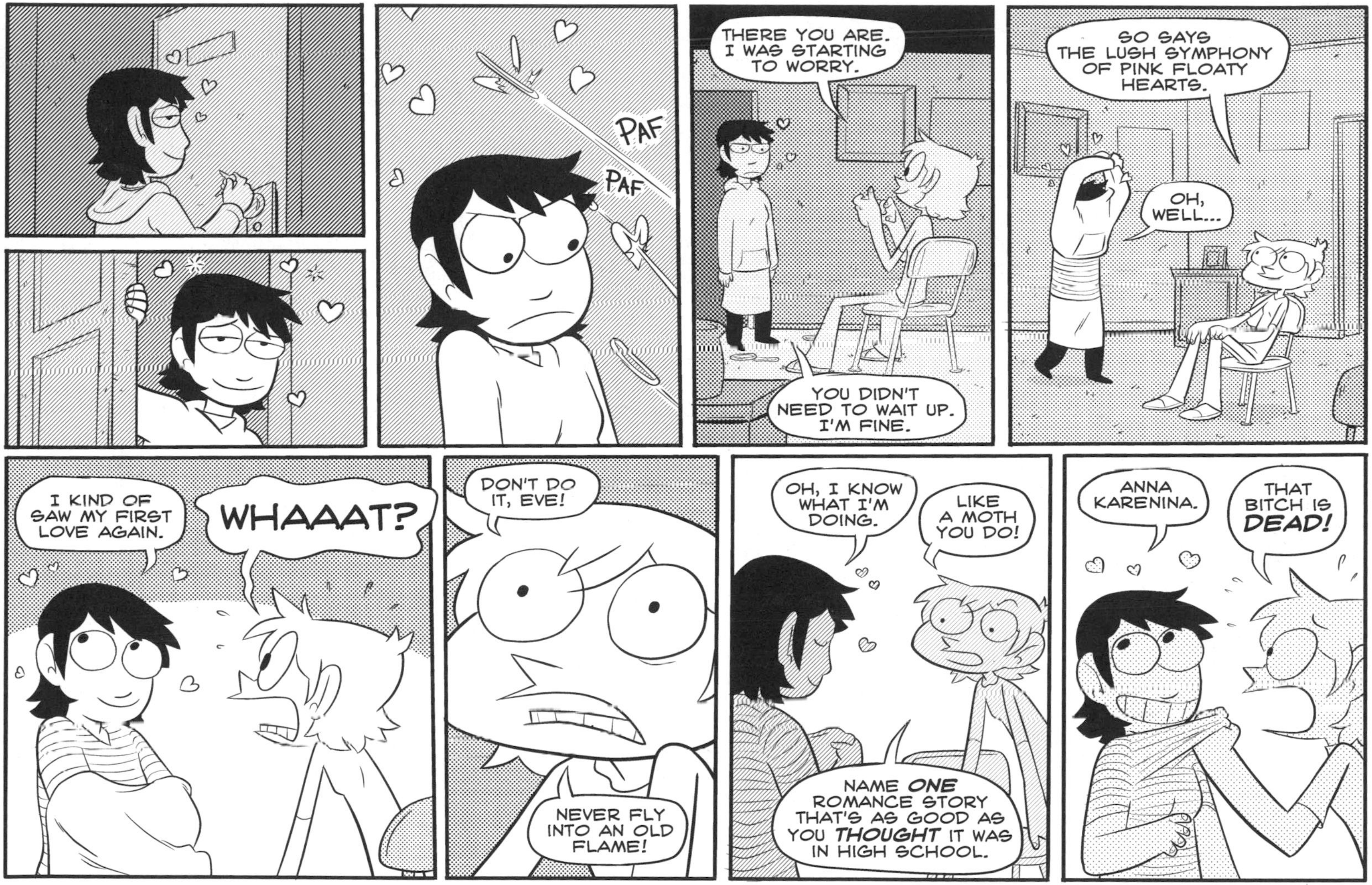
PAF
PAF
THERE YOU ARE. I WAS STARTING TO WORRY.
YOU DIDN'T NEED TO WAIT UP. I'M FINE.
SO SAYS THE LUSH SYMPHONY OF PINK FLOATY HEARTS.
OH, WELL...
I KIND OF SAW MY FIRST LOVE AGAIN.
WHAAAT?
DON'T DO IT, EVE!
NEVER FLY INTO AN OLD FLAME!
OH, I KNOW WHAT I'M DOING.
LIKE A MOTH YOU DO!
NAME ONE ROMANCE STORY THAT'S AS GOOD AS YOU THOUGHT IT WAS IN HIGH SCHOOL.
ANNA KARENINA.
THAT BITCH IS DEAD!

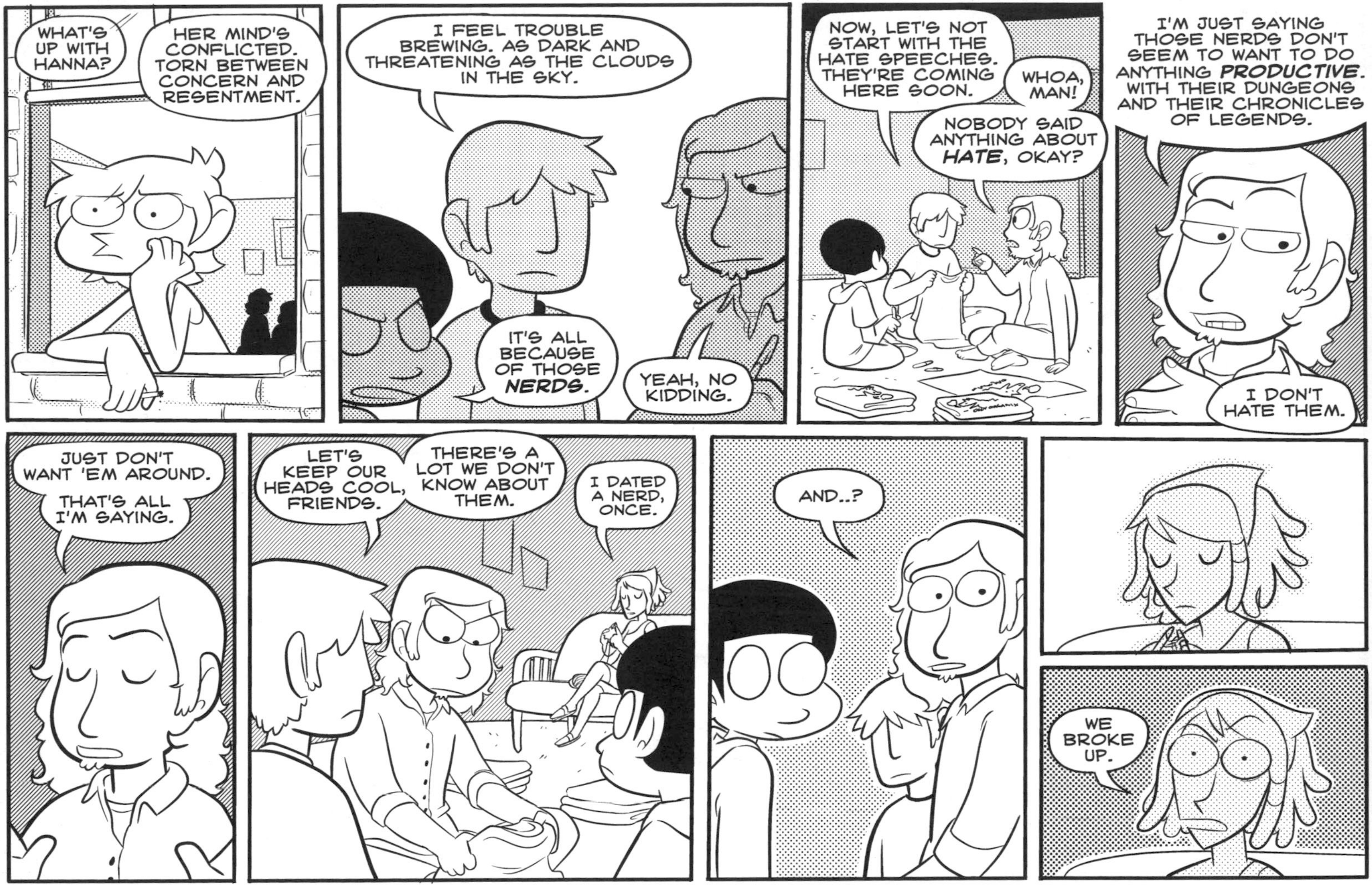
WHAT'S UP WITH HANNA?
HER MIND'S CONFLICTED. TORN BETWEEN CONCERN AND RESENTMENT.
I FEEL TROUBLE BREWING. AS DARK AND THREATENING AS THE CLOUDS IN THE SKY.
IT'S ALL BECAUSE OF THOSE NERDS.
YEAH, NO KIDDING.
NOW, LET'S NOT START WITH THE HATE SPEECHES. THEY'RE COMING HERE SOON.
WHOA, MAN!
NOBODY SAID ANYTHING ABOUT HATE, OKAY?
I'M JUST SAYING THOSE NERDS DON'T SEEM TO WANT TO DO ANYTHING PRODUCTIVE. WITH THEIR DUNGEONS AND THEIR CHRONICLES OF LEGENDS.
I DON'T HATE THEM.
JUST DON'T WANT 'EM AROUND.
THAT'S ALL I'M SAYING.
LET'S KEEP OUR HEADS COOL, FRIENDS.
THERE'S A LOT WE DON'T KNOW ABOUT THEM.
I DATED A NERD, ONCE.
AND..?
WE BROKE UP.

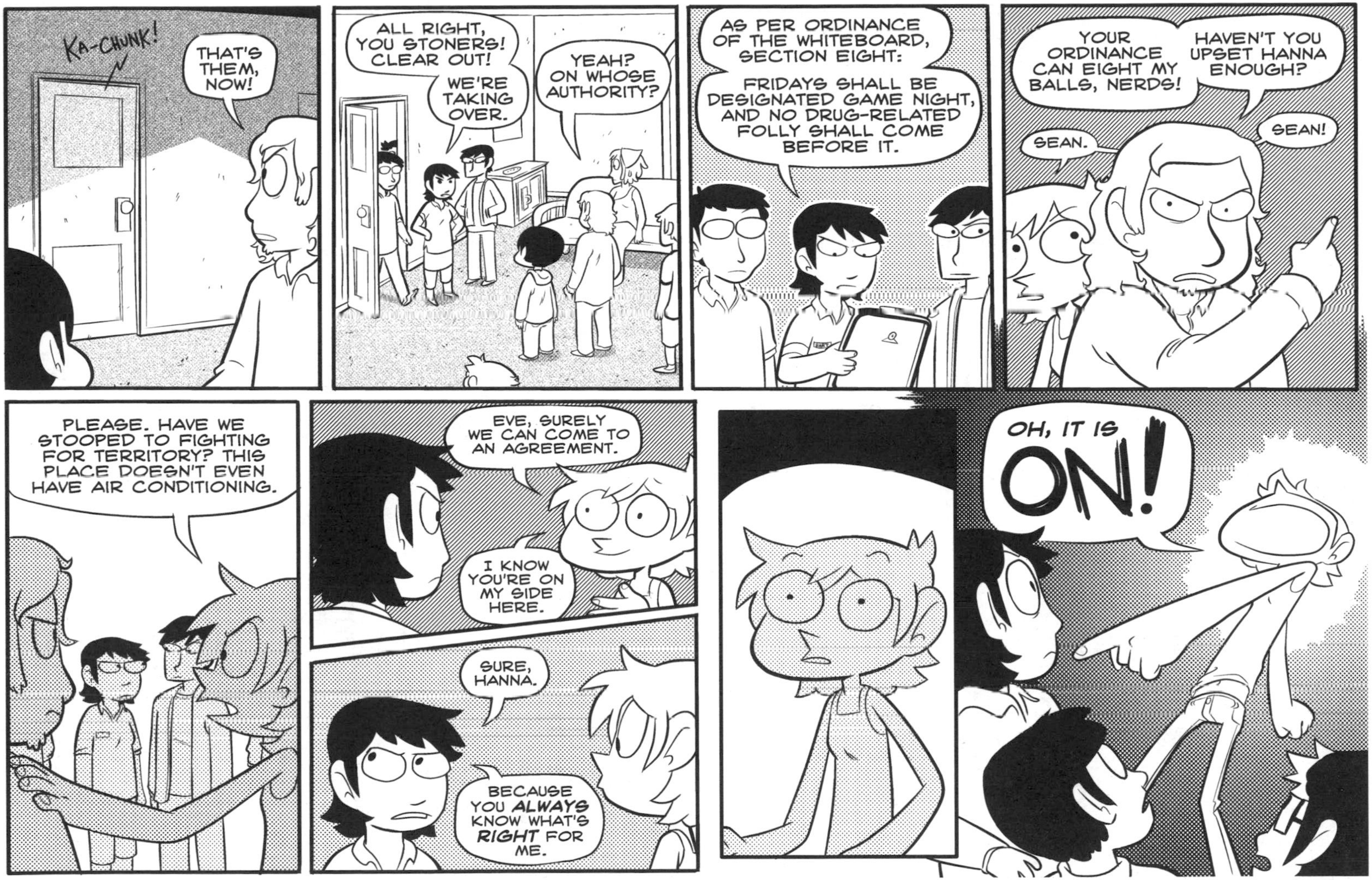
KA-CHUNK!
THAT'S THEM, NOW!
ALL RIGHT, YOU STONERS! CLEAR OUT!
WE'RE TAKING OVER.
YEAH? ON WHOSE AUTHORITY?
AS PER ORDINANCE OF THE WHITEBOARD, SECTION EIGHT:
FRIDAYS SHALL BE DESIGNATED GAME NIGHT, AND NO DRUG-RELATED FOLLY SHALL COME BEFORE IT.
YOUR ORDINANCE CAN EIGHT MY BALLS, NERDS!
HAVEN'T YOU UPSET HANNA ENOUGH?
SEAN.
SEAN!
PLEASE. HAVE WE STOOPED TO FIGHTING FOR TERRITORY? THIS PLACE DOESN'T EVEN HAVE AIR CONDITIONING.
EVE, SURELY WE CAN COME TO AN AGREEMENT.
I KNOW YOU'RE ON MY SIDE HERE.
SURE, HANNA.
BECAUSE YOU ALWAYS KNOW WHAT'S RIGHT FOR ME.
OH, IT IS ON!

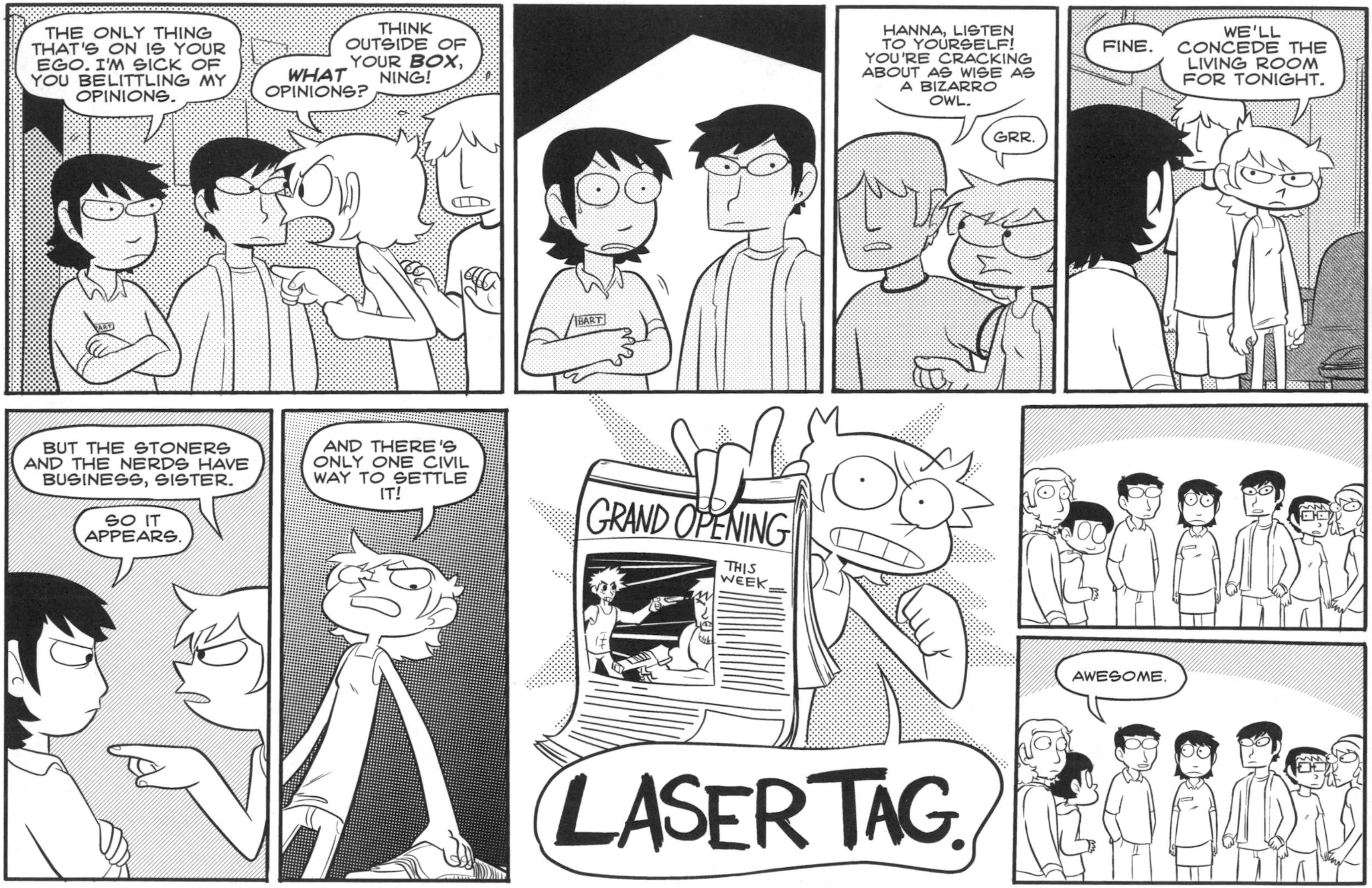
THE ONLY THING THAT'S ON IS YOUR EGO. I'M SICK OF YOU BELITTLING MY OPINIONS.
WHAT OPINIONS?
THINK OUTSIDE OF YOUR BOX, NING!
HANNA, LISTEN TO YOURSELF! YOU'RE CRACKING ABOUT AS WISE AS A BIZARRO OWL.
GRR.
FINE.
WE'LL CONCEDE THE LIVING ROOM FOR TONIGHT.
BUT THE STONERS AND THE NERDS HAVE BUSINESS, SISTER.
SO IT APPEARS.
AND THERE'S ONLY ONE CIVIL WAY TO SETTLE IT!
GRAND OPENING
THIS WEEK
LASER TAG.
AWESOME.

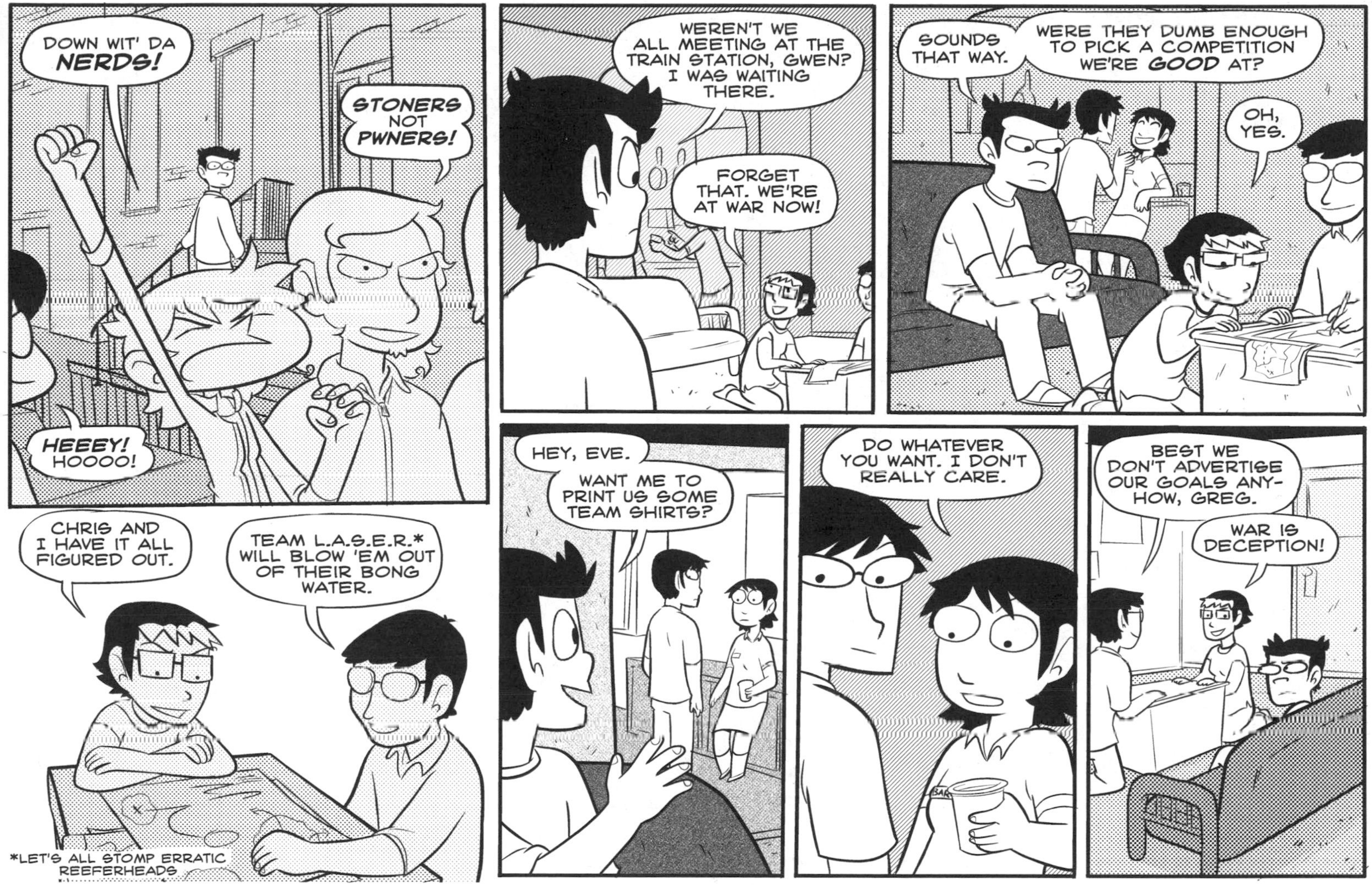
DOWN WIT' DA **NERDS!**
STONERS NOT **PWNERS!**
HEEEY! HOOOO!
CHRIS AND I HAVE IT ALL FIGURED OUT.
TEAM L.A.S.E.R.* WILL BLOW 'EM OUT OF THEIR BONG WATER.
*LET'S ALL STOMP ERRATIC REEFERHEADS
WEREN'T WE ALL MEETING AT THE TRAIN STATION, GWEN? I WAS WAITING THERE.
FORGET THAT. WE'RE AT WAR NOW!
SOUNDS THAT WAY.
WERE THEY DUMB ENOUGH TO PICK A COMPETITION WE'RE ***GOOD*** AT?
OH, YES.
HEY, EVE.
WANT ME TO PRINT US SOME TEAM SHIRTS?
DO WHATEVER YOU WANT. I DON'T REALLY CARE.
BEST WE DON'T ADVERTISE OUR GOALS ANYHOW, GREG.
WAR IS DECEPTION!

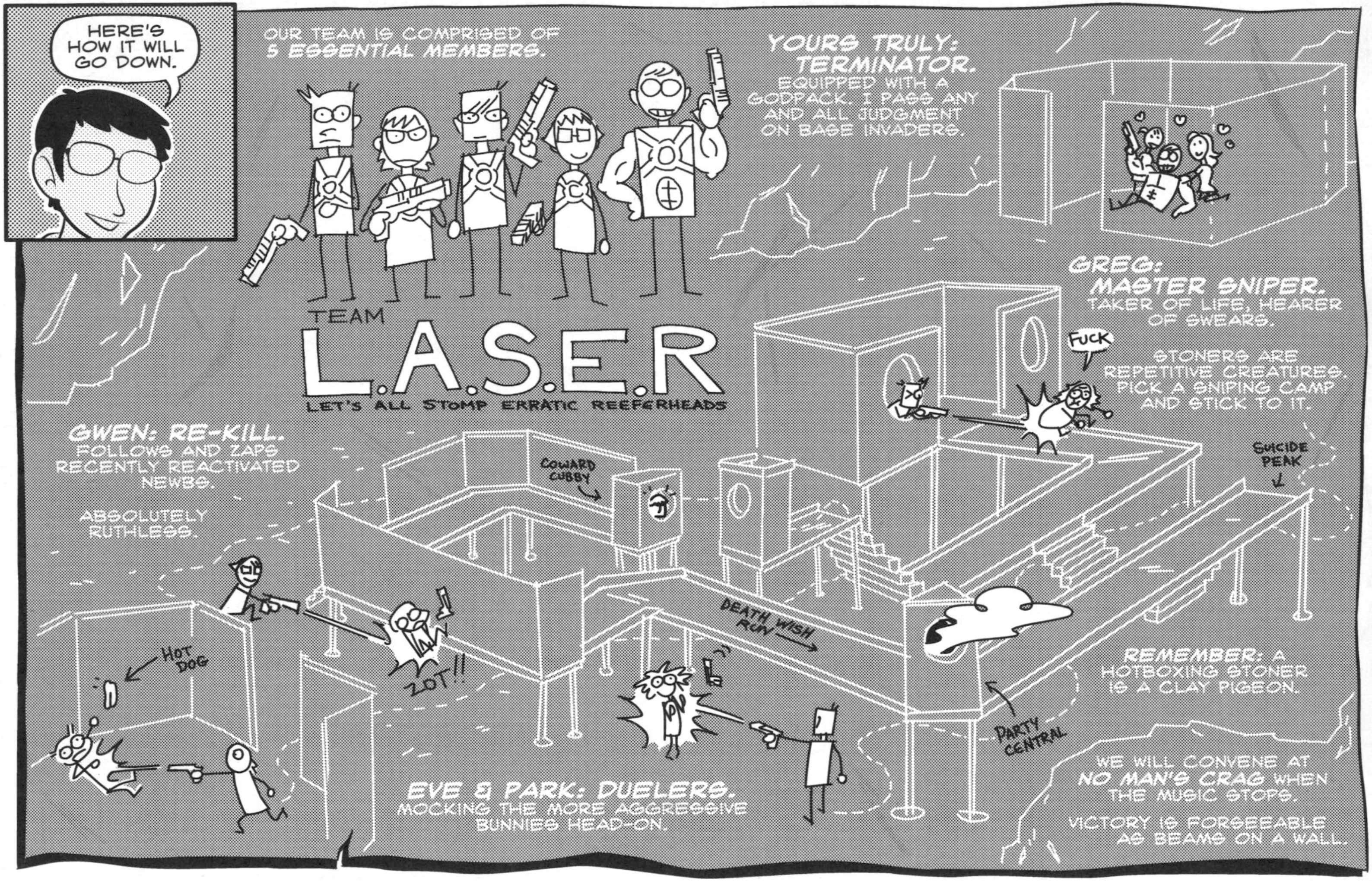
HERE'S HOW IT WILL GO DOWN.
OUR TEAM IS COMPRISED OF 5 ESSENTIAL MEMBERS.
TEAM L.A.S.E.R
LET'S ALL STOMP ERRATIC REEFERHEADS
YOURS TRULY: TERMINATOR.
EQUIPPED WITH A GODPACK. I PASS ANY AND ALL JUDGMENT ON BASE INVADERS.
GREG: MASTER SNIPER.
TAKER OF LIFE, HEARER OF SWEARS.
FUCK
STONERS ARE REPETITIVE CREATURES. PICK A SNIPING CAMP AND STICK TO IT.
GWEN: RE-KILL.
FOLLOWS AND ZAPS RECENTLY REACTIVATED NEWBS.
ABSOLUTELY RUTHLESS.
COWARD CUBBY
SUICIDE PEAK
DEATH WISH RUN
HOT DOG
ZOT!!
PARTY CENTRAL
REMEMBER: A HOTBOXING STONER IS A CLAY PIGEON.
EVE & PARK: DUELERS.
MOCKING THE MORE AGGRESSIVE BUNNIES HEAD-ON.
WE WILL CONVENE AT NO MAN'S CRAG WHEN THE MUSIC STOPS.
VICTORY IS FORSEEABLE AS BEAMS ON A WALL.

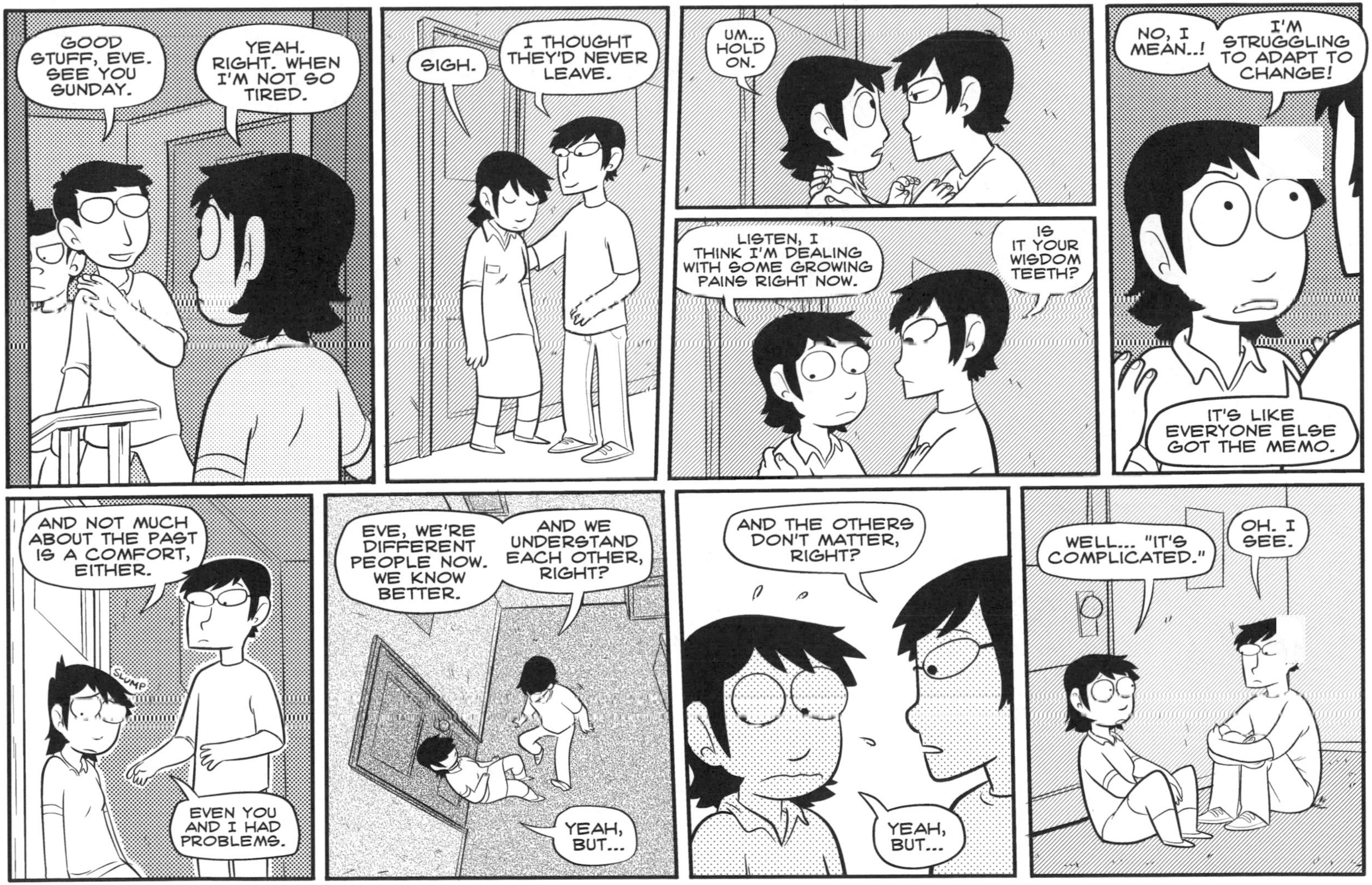
GOOD STUFF, EVE. SEE YOU SUNDAY.
YEAH. RIGHT. WHEN I'M NOT SO TIRED.
SIGH.
I THOUGHT THEY'D NEVER LEAVE.
UM... HOLD ON.
LISTEN, I THINK I'M DEALING WITH SOME GROWING PAINS RIGHT NOW.
IS IT YOUR WISDOM TEETH?
NO, I MEAN...!
I'M STRUGGLING TO ADAPT TO CHANGE!
IT'S LIKE EVERYONE ELSE GOT THE MEMO.
AND NOT MUCH ABOUT THE PAST IS A COMFORT, EITHER.
SLUMP
EVEN YOU AND I HAD PROBLEMS.
EVE, WE'RE DIFFERENT PEOPLE NOW. WE KNOW BETTER.
AND WE UNDERSTAND EACH OTHER, RIGHT?
YEAH, BUT...
AND THE OTHERS DON'T MATTER, RIGHT?
YEAH, BUT...
WELL... "IT'S COMPLICATED."
OH. I SEE.

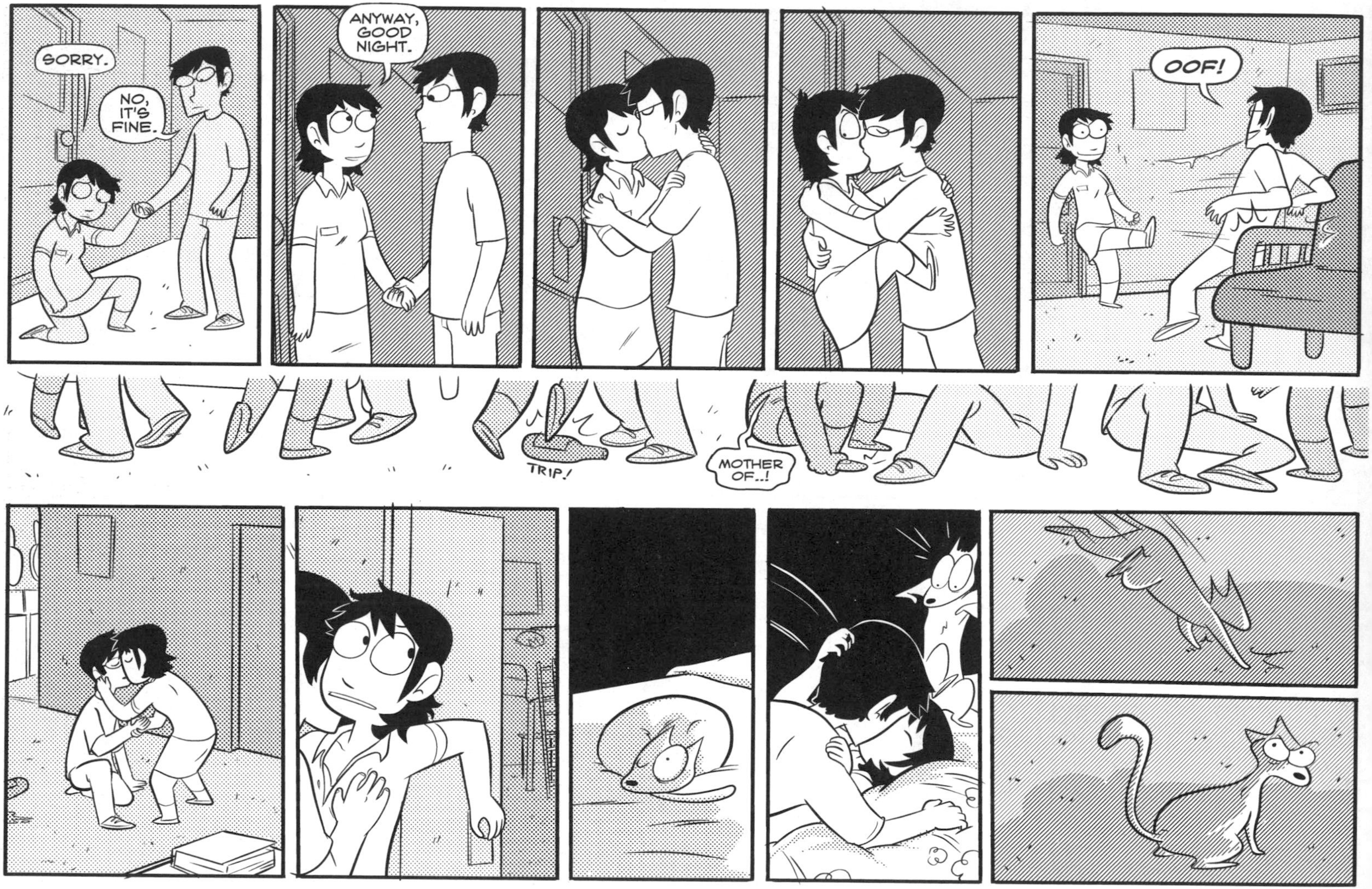
SORRY.
NO, IT'S FINE.
ANYWAY, GOOD NIGHT.
OOF!
TRIP!
MOTHER OF..!

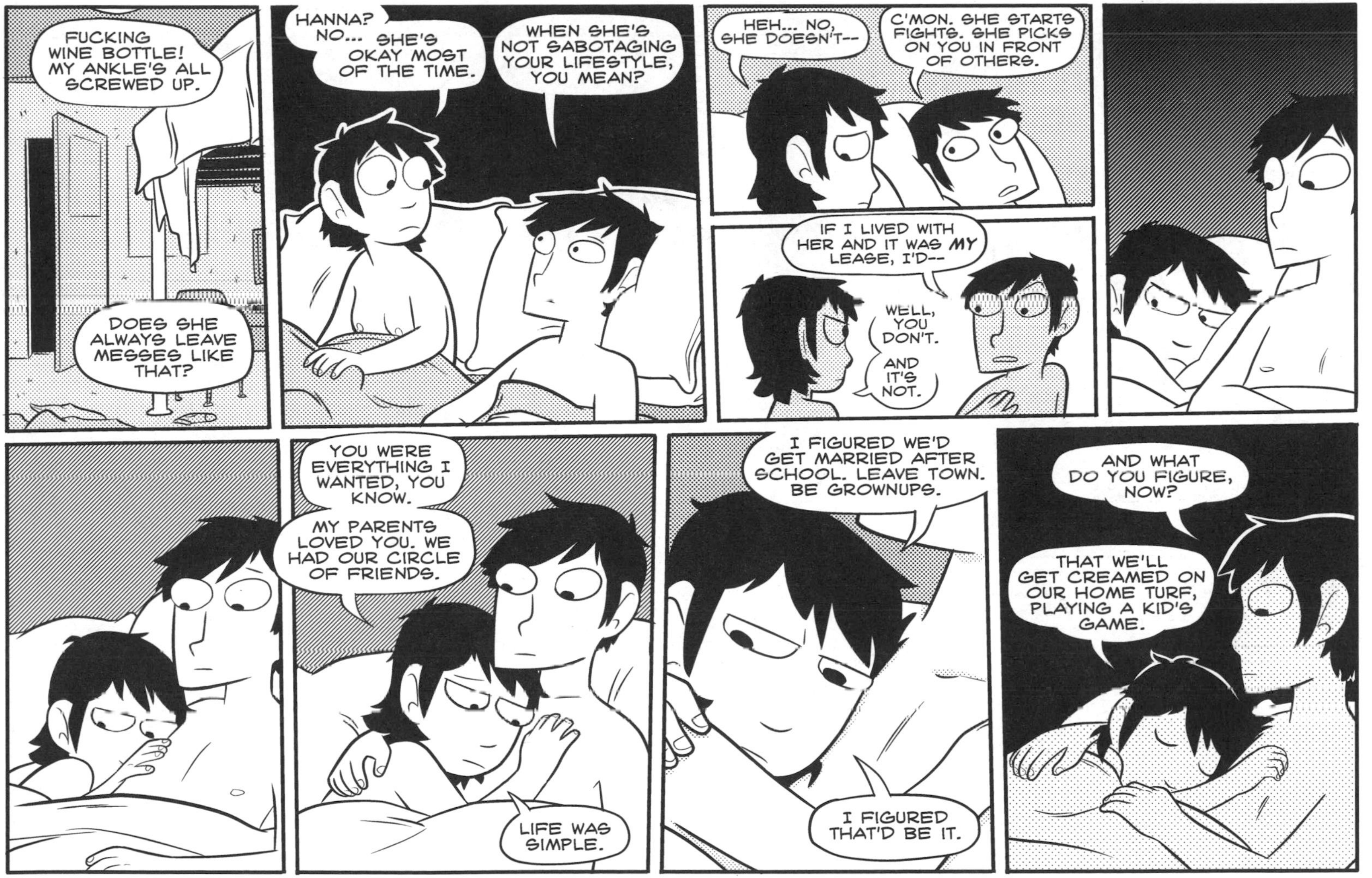
FUCKING WINE BOTTLE! MY ANKLE'S ALL SCREWED UP.
DOES SHE ALWAYS LEAVE MESSES LIKE THAT?
HANNA? NO... SHE'S OKAY MOST OF THE TIME.
WHEN SHE'S NOT SABOTAGING YOUR LIFESTYLE, YOU MEAN?
HEH... NO, SHE DOESN'T--
C'MON. SHE STARTS FIGHTS. SHE PICKS ON YOU IN FRONT OF OTHERS.
IF I LIVED WITH HER AND IT WAS MY LEASE, I'D--
WELL, YOU DON'T.
AND IT'S NOT.
YOU WERE EVERYTHING I WANTED, YOU KNOW.
MY PARENTS LOVED YOU. WE HAD OUR CIRCLE OF FRIENDS.
LIFE WAS SIMPLE.
I FIGURED WE'D GET MARRIED AFTER SCHOOL. LEAVE TOWN. BE GROWNUPS.
I FIGURED THAT'D BE IT.
AND WHAT DO YOU FIGURE, NOW?
THAT WE'LL GET CREAMED ON OUR HOME TURF, PLAYING A KID'S GAME.

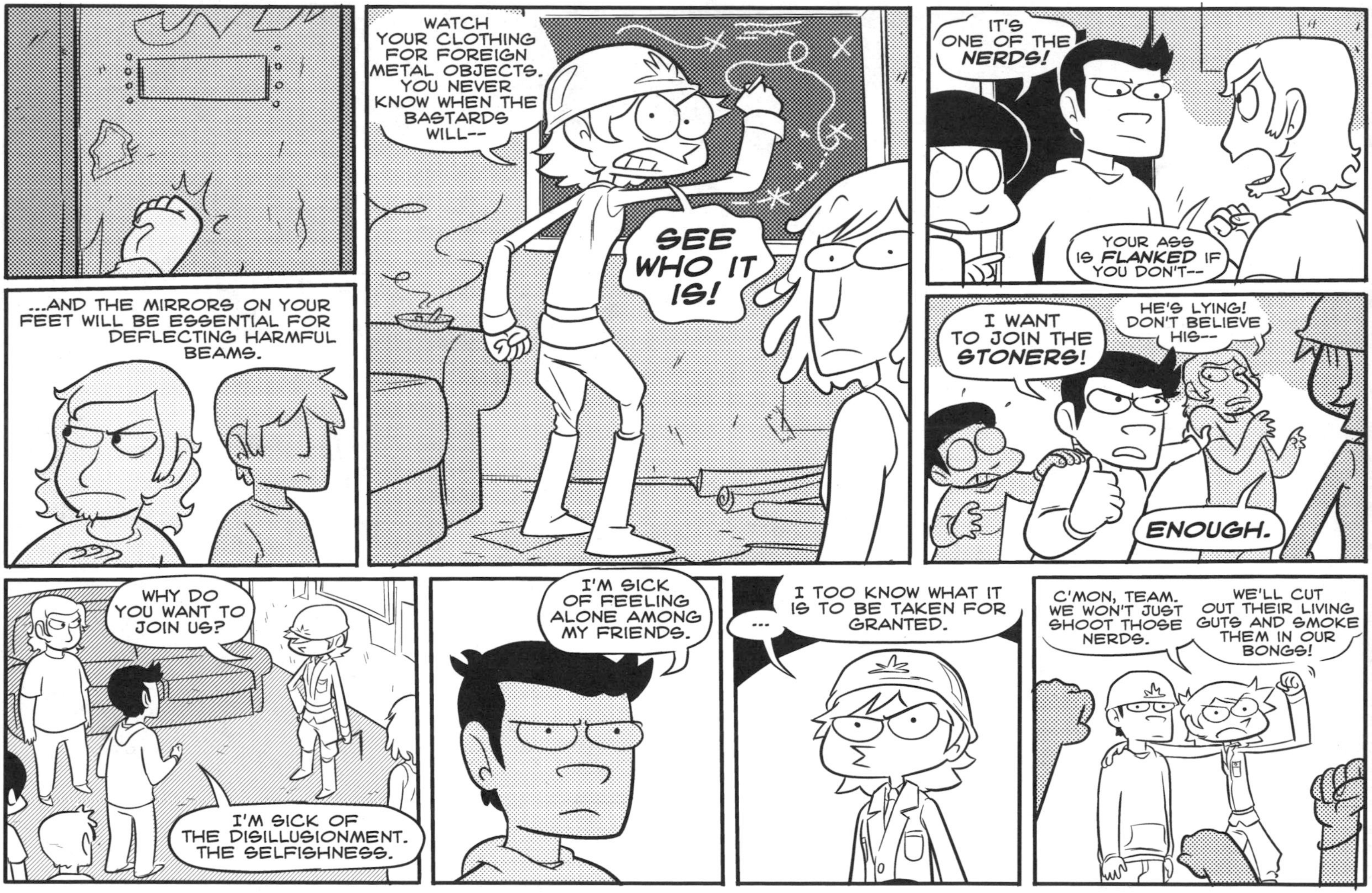

WATCH YOUR CLOTHING FOR FOREIGN METAL OBJECTS. YOU NEVER KNOW WHEN THE BASTARDS WILL--
SEE WHO IT IS!
IT'S ONE OF THE NERDS!
YOUR ASS IS FLANKED IF YOU DON'T--
...AND THE MIRRORS ON YOUR FEET WILL BE ESSENTIAL FOR DEFLECTING HARMFUL BEAMS.
I WANT TO JOIN THE STONERS!
HE'S LYING! DON'T BELIEVE HIS--
ENOUGH.
WHY DO YOU WANT TO JOIN US?
I'M SICK OF THE DISILLUSIONMENT. THE SELFISHNESS.
I'M SICK OF FEELING ALONE AMONG MY FRIENDS.
...
I TOO KNOW WHAT IT IS TO BE TAKEN FOR GRANTED.
C'MON, TEAM. WE WON'T JUST SHOOT THOSE NERDS.
WE'LL CUT OUT THEIR LIVING GUTS AND SMOKE THEM IN OUR BONGS!

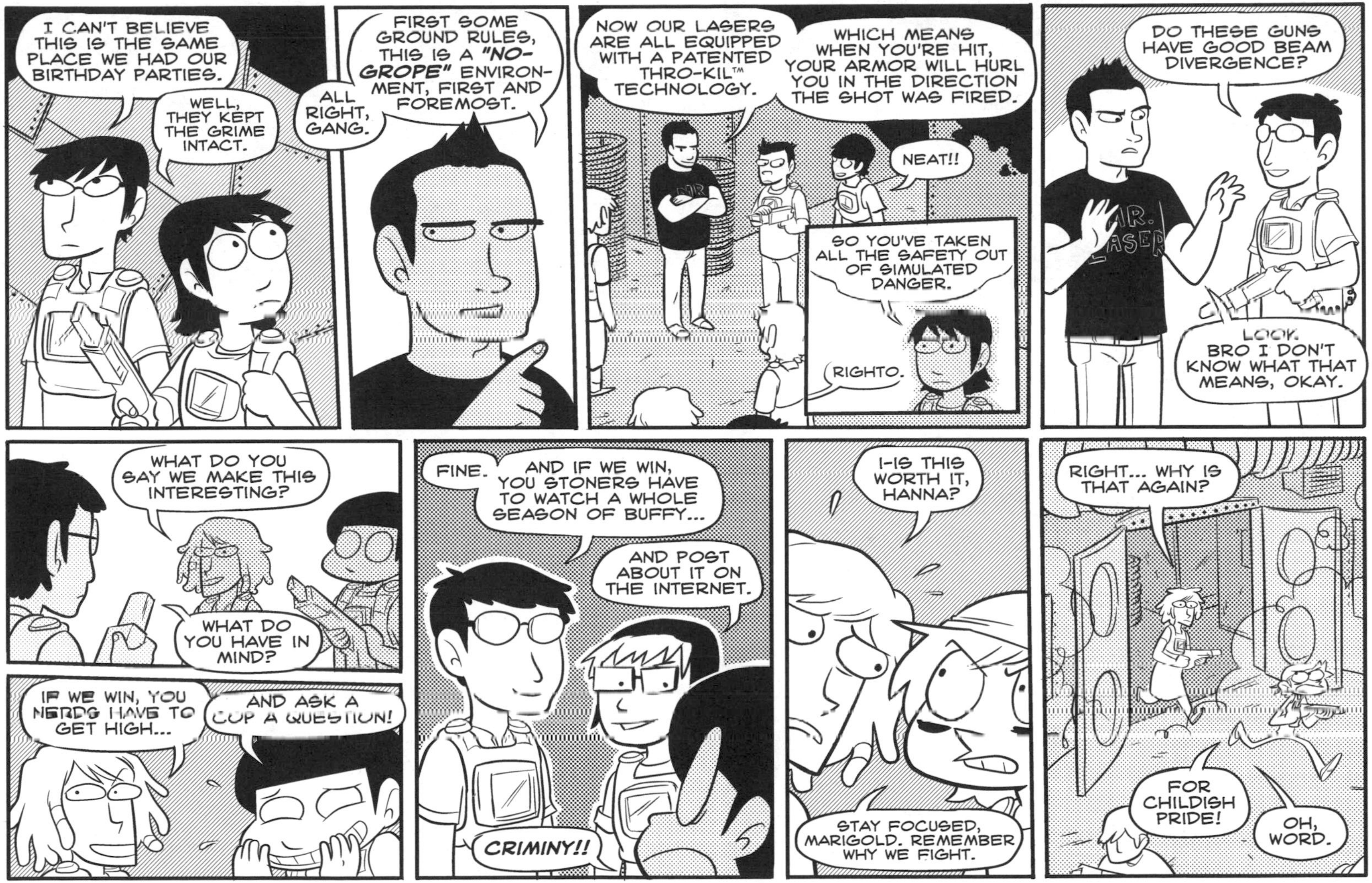
I CAN'T BELIEVE THIS IS THE SAME PLACE WE HAD OUR BIRTHDAY PARTIES.
WELL, THEY KEPT THE GRIME INTACT.
ALL RIGHT, GANG.
FIRST SOME GROUND RULES, THIS IS A "NO-GROPE" ENVIRONMENT, FIRST AND FOREMOST.
NOW OUR LASERS ARE ALL EQUIPPED WITH A PATENTED THRO-KIL™ TECHNOLOGY.
WHICH MEANS WHEN YOU'RE HIT, YOUR ARMOR WILL HURL YOU IN THE DIRECTION THE SHOT WAS FIRED.
NEAT!!
SO YOU'VE TAKEN ALL THE SAFETY OUT OF SIMULATED DANGER.
RIGHTO.
DO THESE GUNS HAVE GOOD BEAM DIVERGENCE?
LOOK. BRO I DON'T KNOW WHAT THAT MEANS, OKAY.
WHAT DO YOU SAY WE MAKE THIS INTERESTING?
WHAT DO YOU HAVE IN MIND?
IF WE WIN, YOU NERDS HAVE TO GET HIGH...
AND ASK A COP A QUESTION!
FINE.
AND IF WE WIN, YOU STONERS HAVE TO WATCH A WHOLE SEASON OF BUFFY...
AND POST ABOUT IT ON THE INTERNET.
CRIMINY!!
I-IS THIS WORTH IT, HANNA?
STAY FOCUSED, MARIGOLD. REMEMBER WHY WE FIGHT.
RIGHT... WHY IS THAT AGAIN?
FOR CHILDISH PRIDE!
OH, WORD.

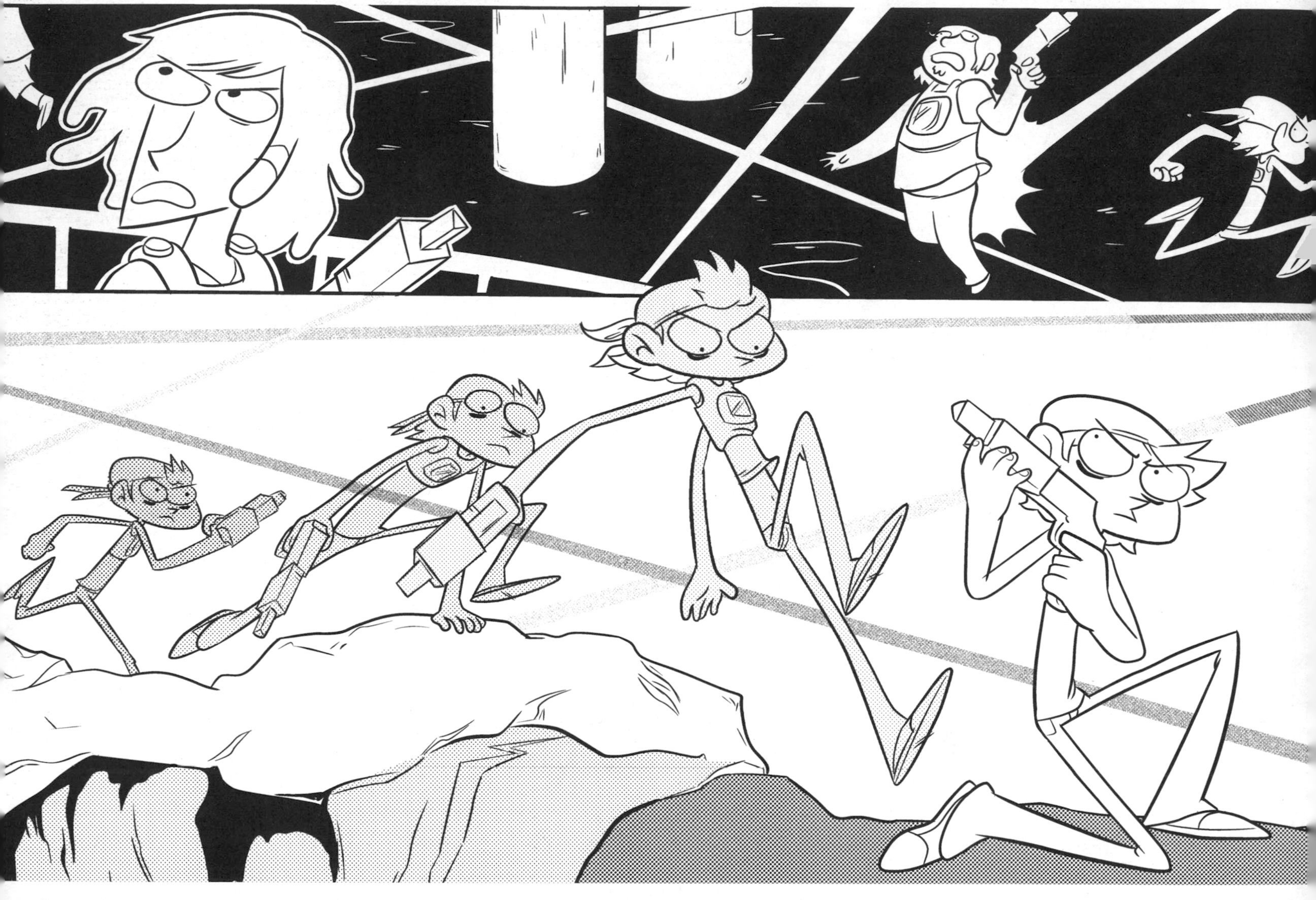

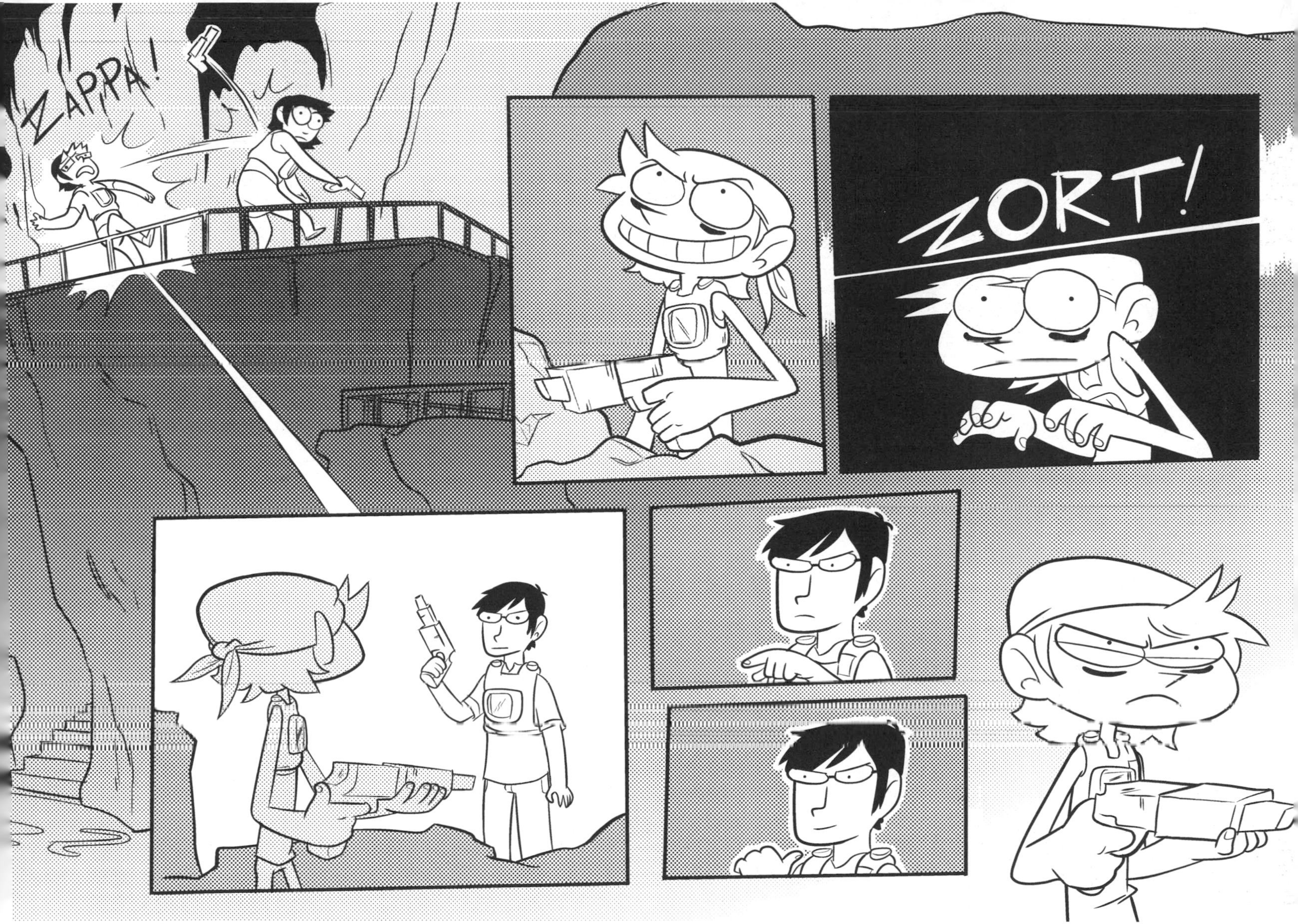
ZAPPA!
ZORT!

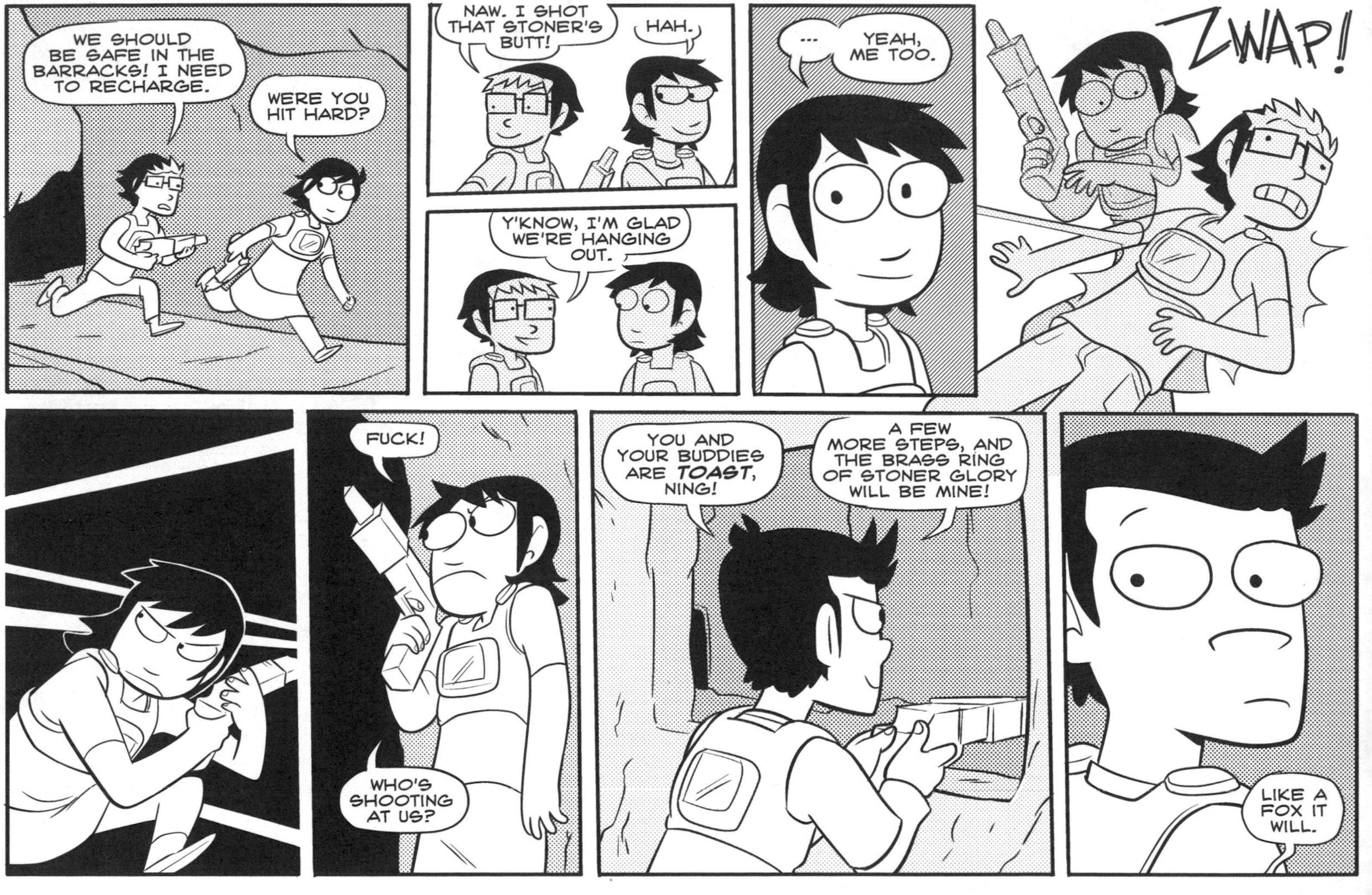
WE SHOULD BE SAFE IN THE BARRACKS! I NEED TO RECHARGE.
WERE YOU HIT HARD?
NAW. I SHOT THAT STONER'S BUTT!
HAH.
Y'KNOW, I'M GLAD WE'RE HANGING OUT.
...
YEAH, ME TOO.
ZWAP!
FUCK!
WHO'S SHOOTING AT US?
YOU AND YOUR BUDDIES ARE TOAST, NING!
A FEW MORE STEPS, AND THE BRASS RING OF STONER GLORY WILL BE MINE!
LIKE A FOX IT WILL.

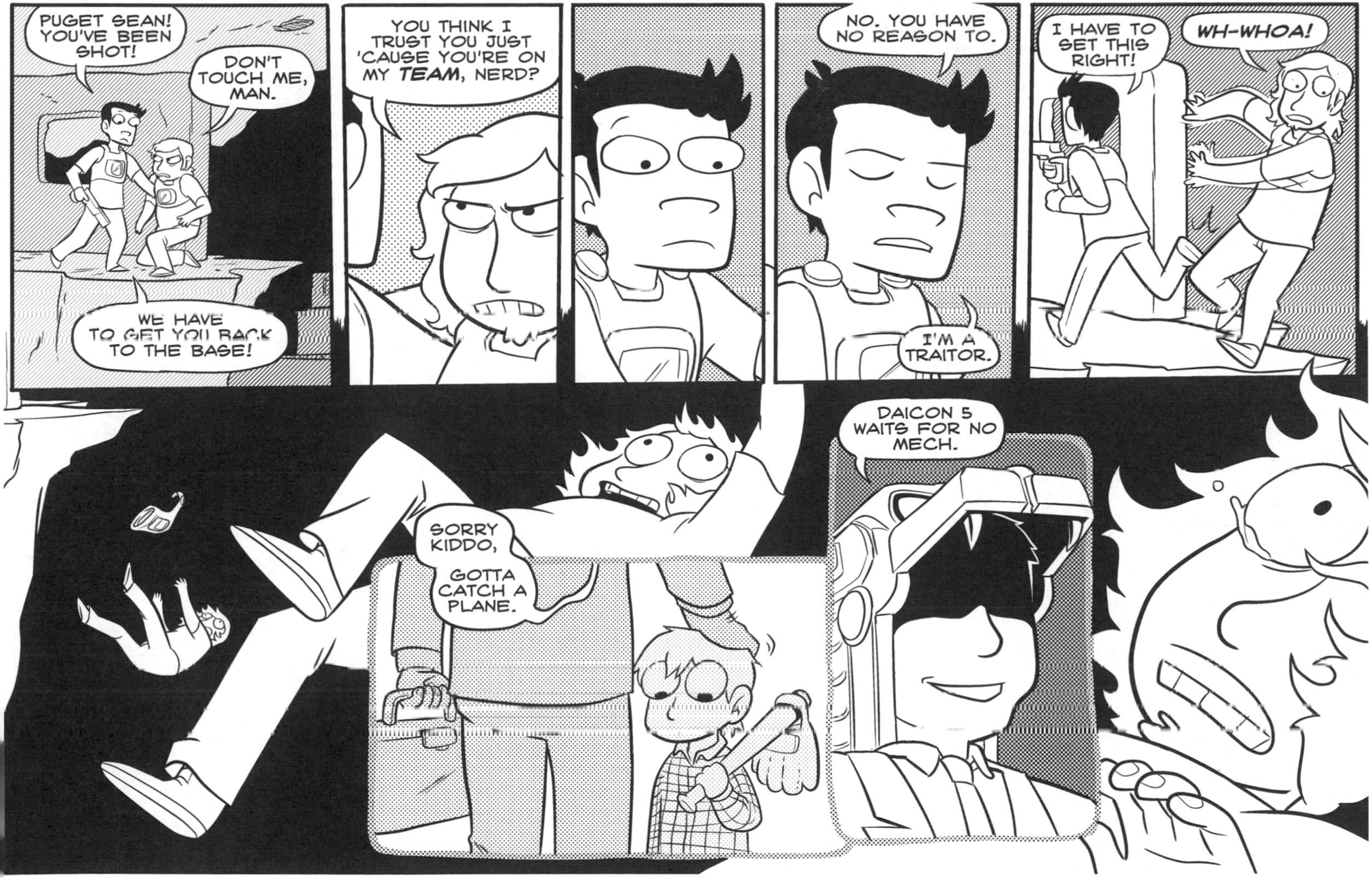
PUGET SEAN! YOU'VE BEEN SHOT!
DON'T TOUCH ME, MAN.
WE HAVE TO GET YOU BACK TO THE BASE!
YOU THINK I TRUST YOU JUST 'CAUSE YOU'RE ON MY *TEAM*, NERD?
NO. YOU HAVE NO REASON TO.
I'M A TRAITOR.
I HAVE TO SET THIS RIGHT!
WH-WHOA!
SORRY KIDDO,
GOTTA CATCH A PLANE.
DAICON 5 WAITS FOR NO MECH.

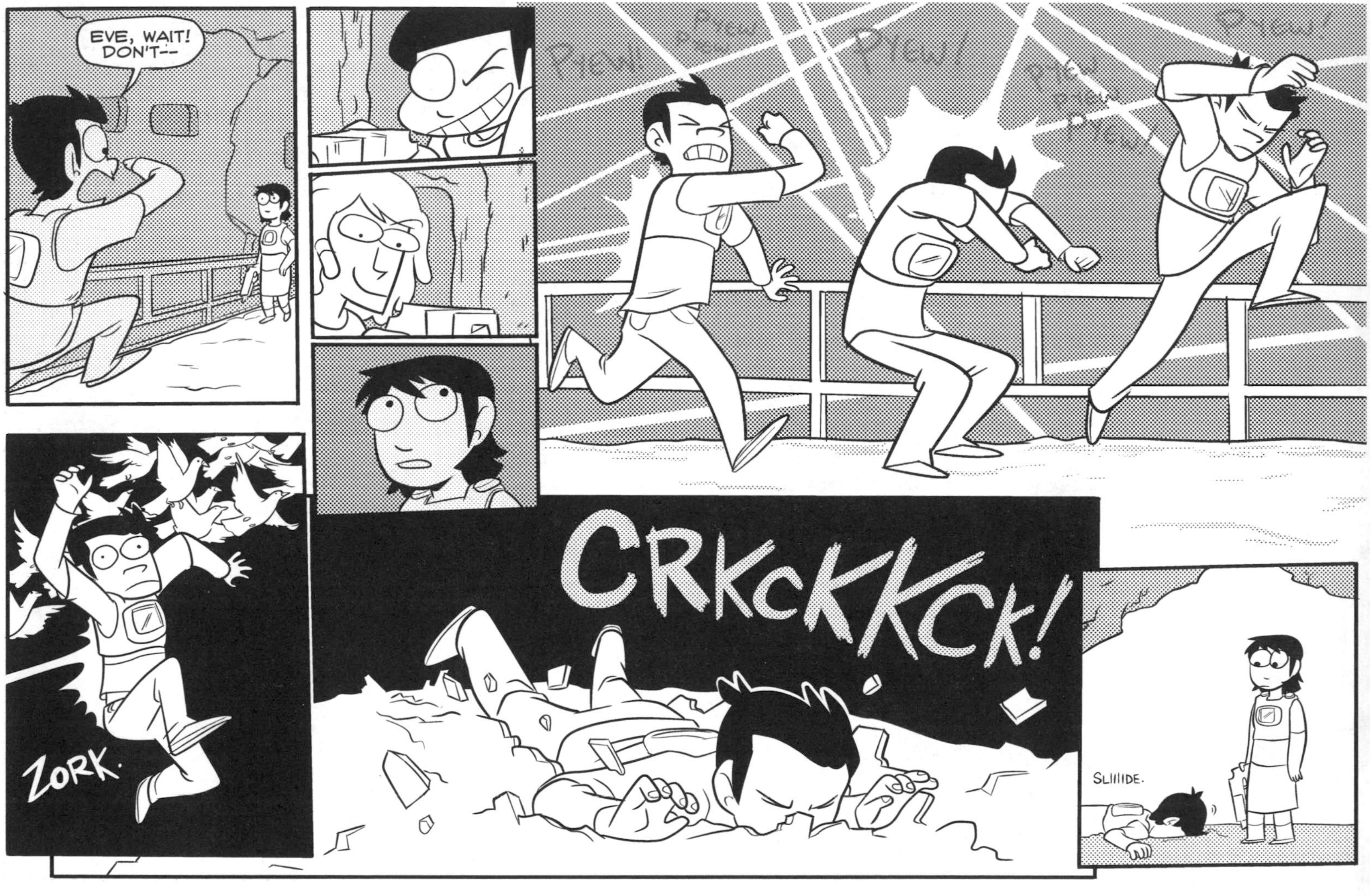
EVE, WAIT! DON'T--
PIEW!
PIEW!
ZORK.
CRKCKKCK!
SLIIIIDE.

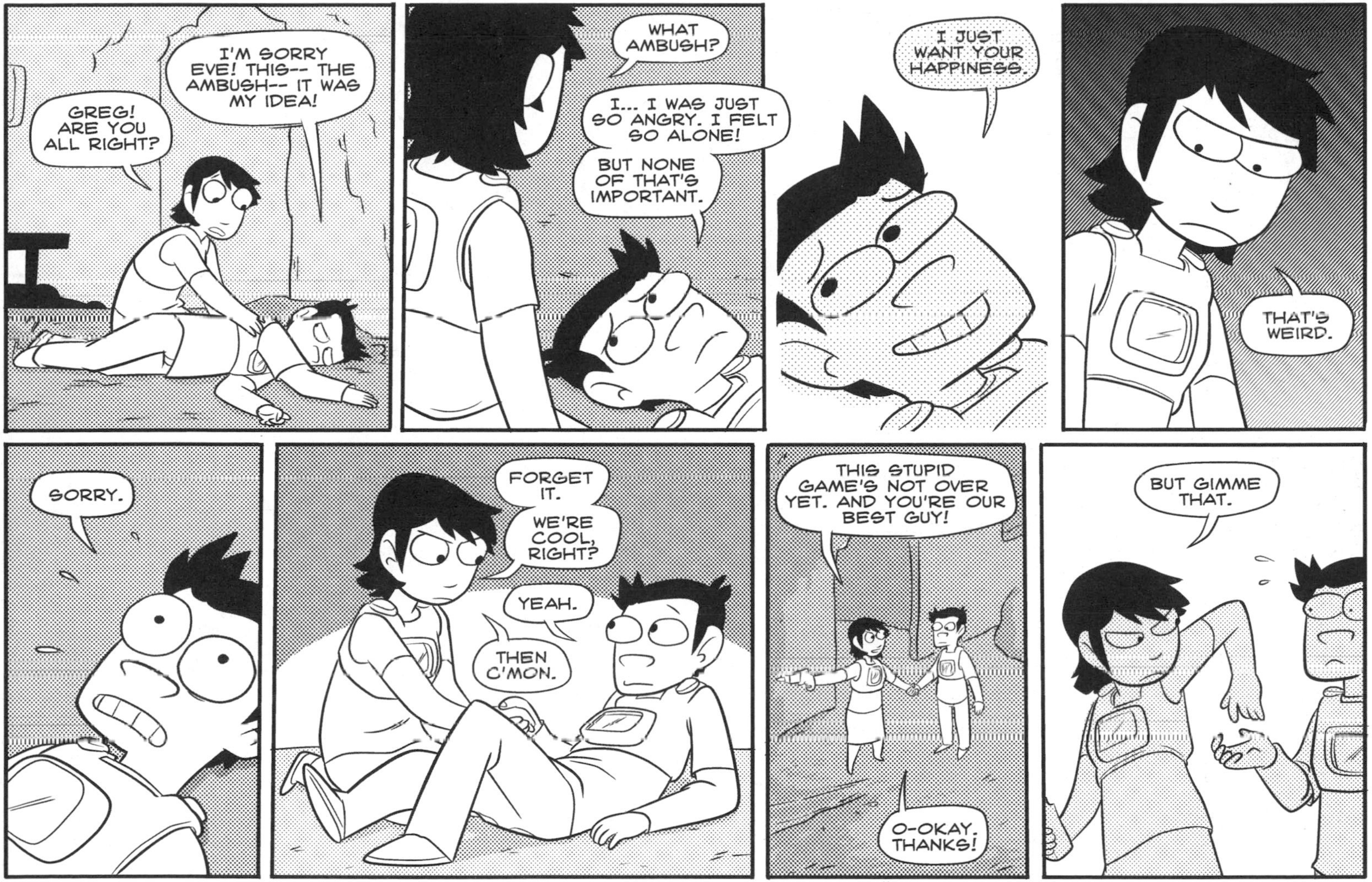
GREG! ARE YOU ALL RIGHT?
I'M SORRY EVE! THIS-- THE AMBUSH-- IT WAS MY IDEA!
WHAT AMBUSH?
I... I WAS JUST SO ANGRY. I FELT SO ALONE!
BUT NONE OF THAT'S IMPORTANT.
I JUST WANT YOUR HAPPINESS.
THAT'S WEIRD.
SORRY.
FORGET IT.
WE'RE COOL, RIGHT?
YEAH.
THEN C'MON.
THIS STUPID GAME'S NOT OVER YET. AND YOU'RE OUR BEST GUY!
O-OKAY. THANKS!
BUT GIMME THAT.

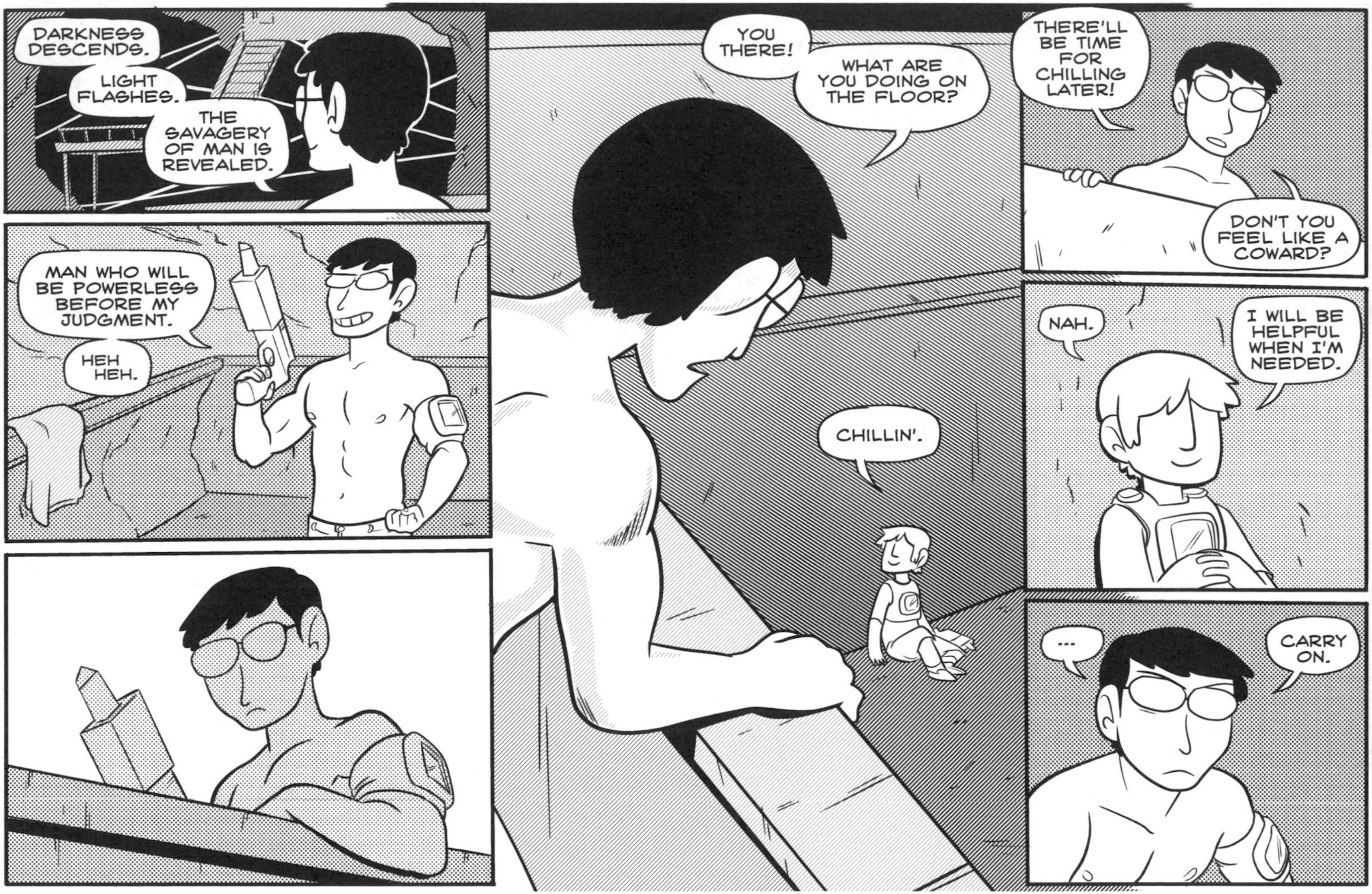
DARKNESS DESCENDS.
LIGHT FLASHES.
THE SAVAGERY OF MAN IS REVEALED.
MAN WHO WILL BE POWERLESS BEFORE MY JUDGMENT.
HEH HEH.
YOU THERE!
WHAT ARE YOU DOING ON THE FLOOR?
CHILLIN'.
THERE'LL BE TIME FOR CHILLING LATER!
DON'T YOU FEEL LIKE A COWARD?
NAH.
I WILL BE HELPFUL WHEN I'M NEEDED.
...
CARRY ON.

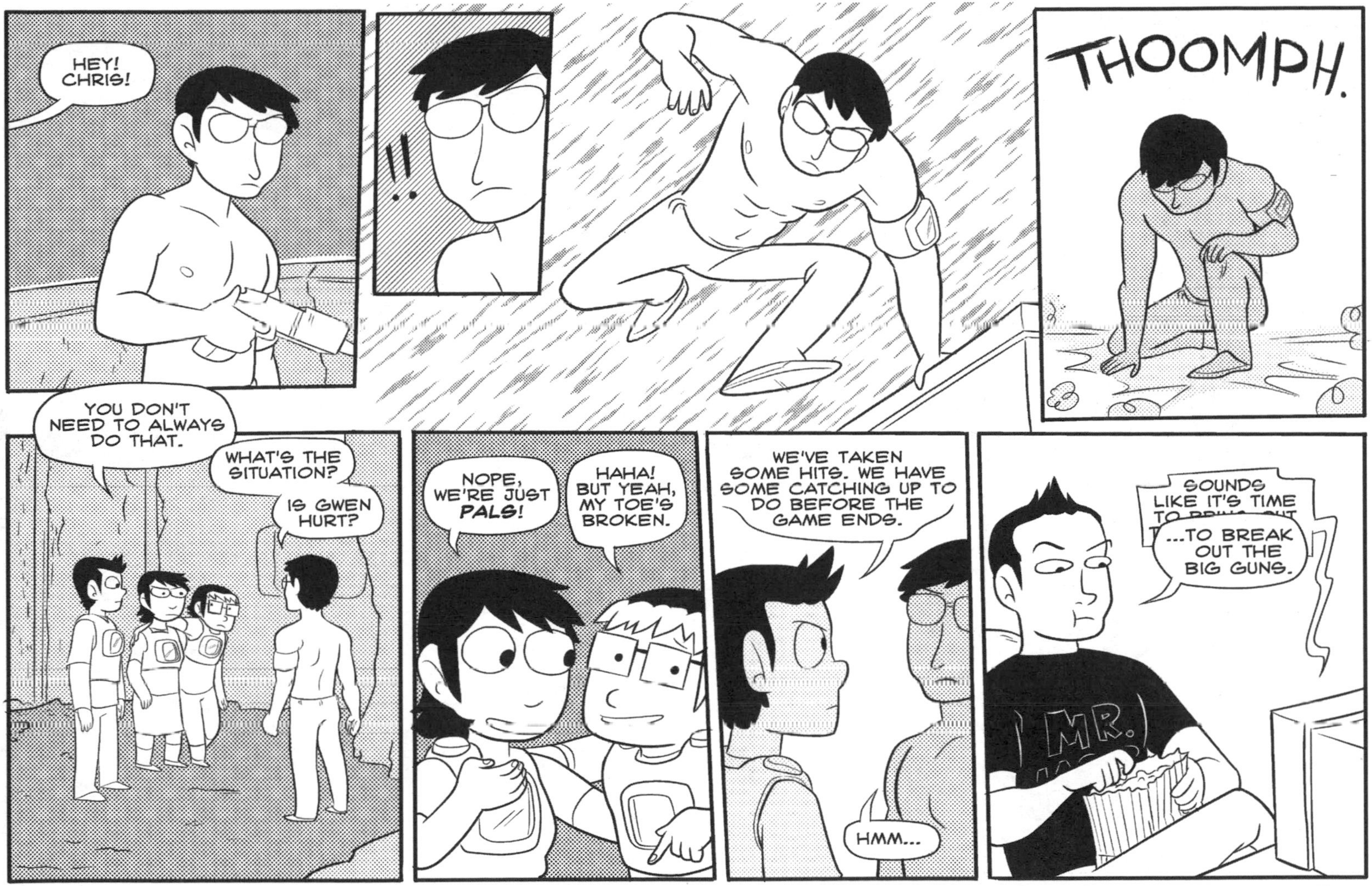
HEY! CHRIS!
!!
THOOMPH.
YOU DON'T NEED TO ALWAYS DO THAT.
WHAT'S THE SITUATION?
IS GWEN HURT?
NOPE, WE'RE JUST **PALS**!
HAHA! BUT YEAH, MY TOE'S BROKEN.
WE'VE TAKEN SOME HITS. WE HAVE SOME CATCHING UP TO DO BEFORE THE GAME ENDS.
HMM...
SOUNDS LIKE IT'S TIME
...TO BREAK OUT THE BIG GUNS.
MR.

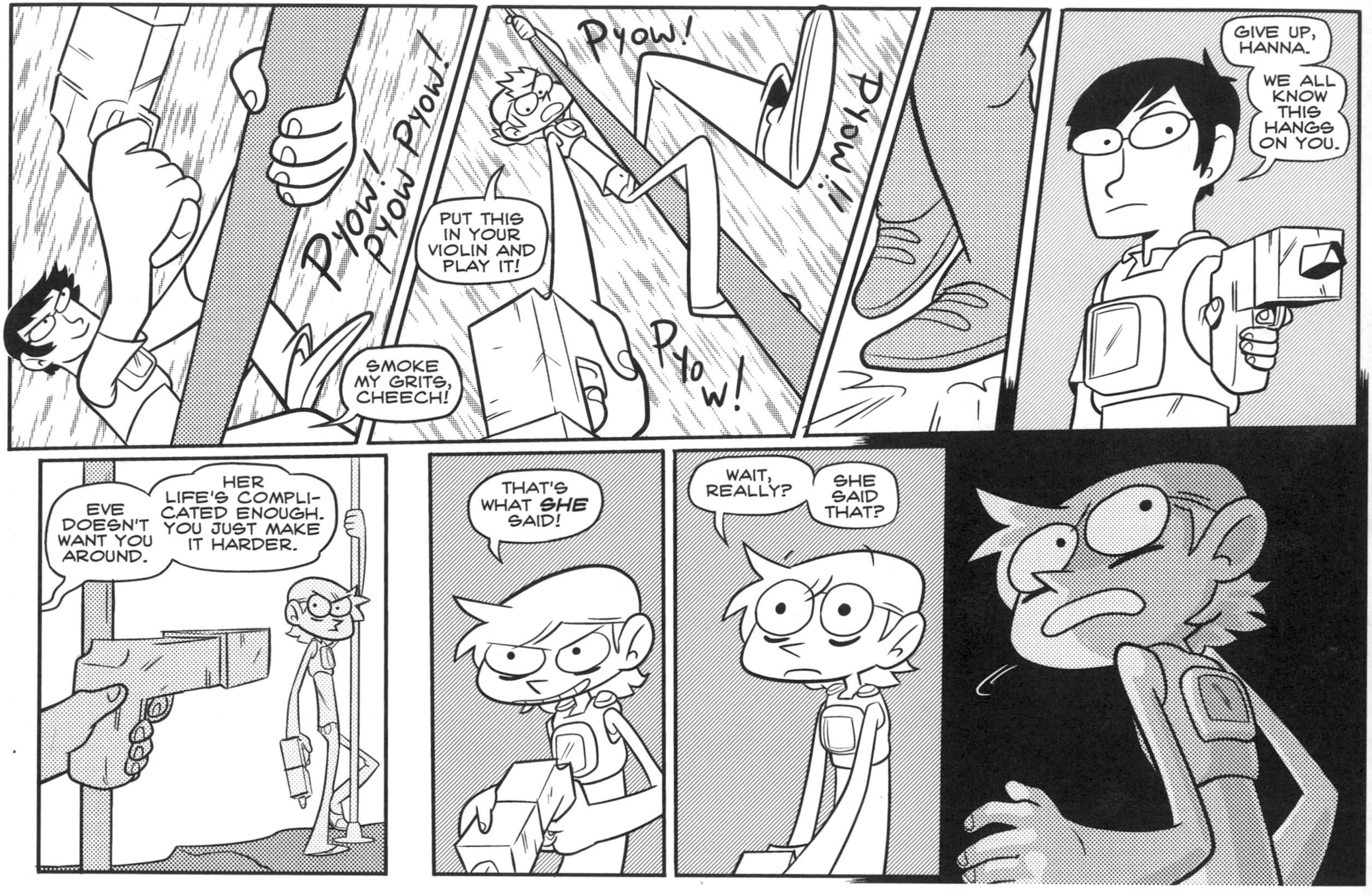
Pyow! Pyow Pyow! Pyow!
Smoke my grits, Cheech!
Pyow!
Put this in your violin and play it!
Pyow!!
Pyow!
Give up, Hanna.
We all know this hangs on you.
Eve doesn't want you around.
Her life's complicated enough. You just make it harder.
That's what *she* said!
Wait, really?
She said that?

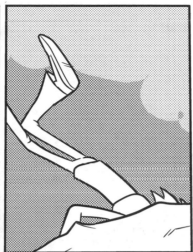

HI, HONEY.

DUDE, GET DOWN! NERDS BE PEEPIN' OUR ASSES THROUGH THE SMOKE!

THEY BE?

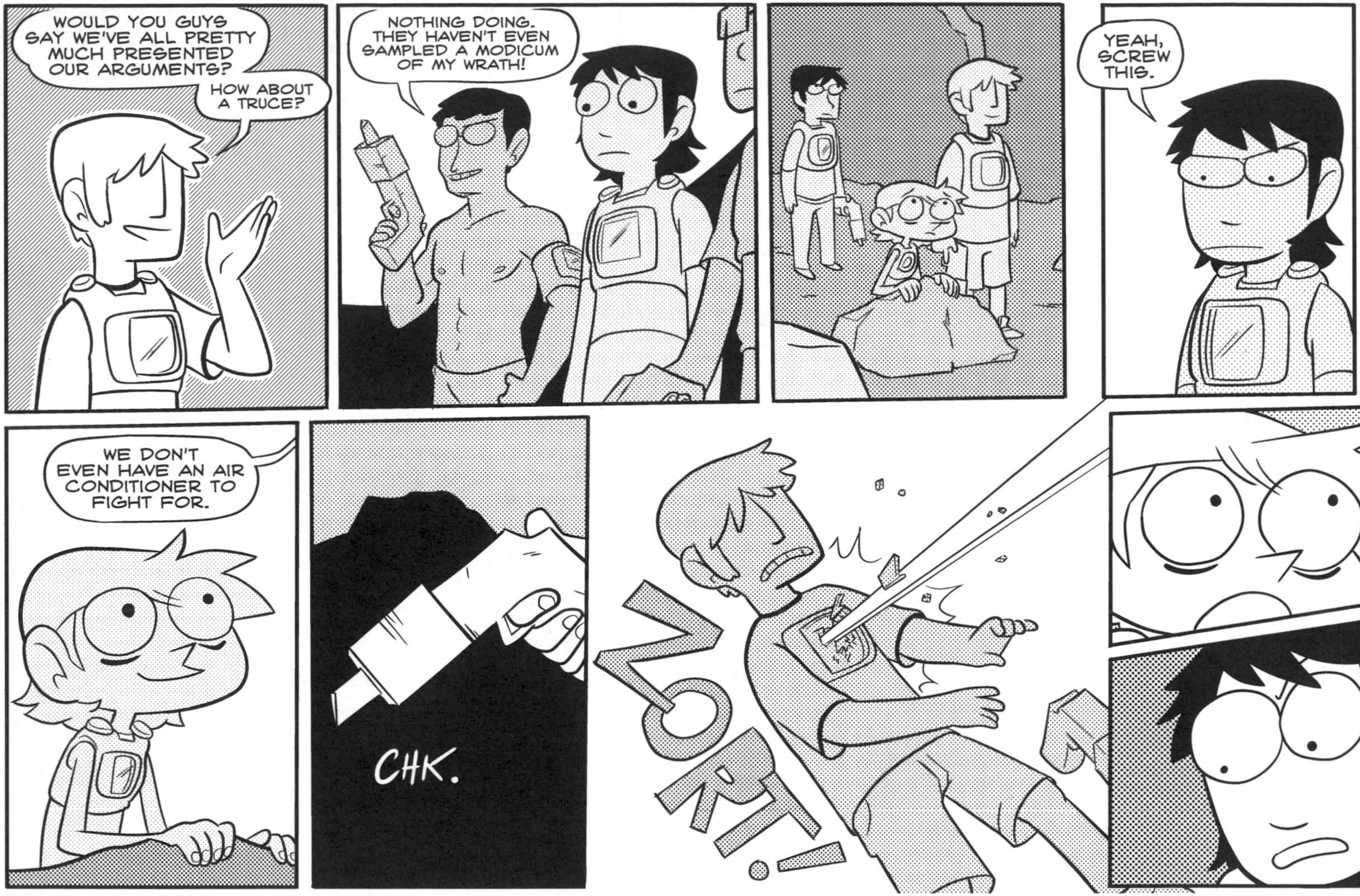
WOULD YOU GUYS SAY WE'VE ALL PRETTY MUCH PRESENTED OUR ARGUMENTS?
HOW ABOUT A TRUCE?
NOTHING DOING. THEY HAVEN'T EVEN SAMPLED A MODICUM OF MY WRATH!
YEAH, SCREW THIS.
WE DON'T EVEN HAVE AN AIR CONDITIONER TO FIGHT FOR.
CHK.
ZORT!

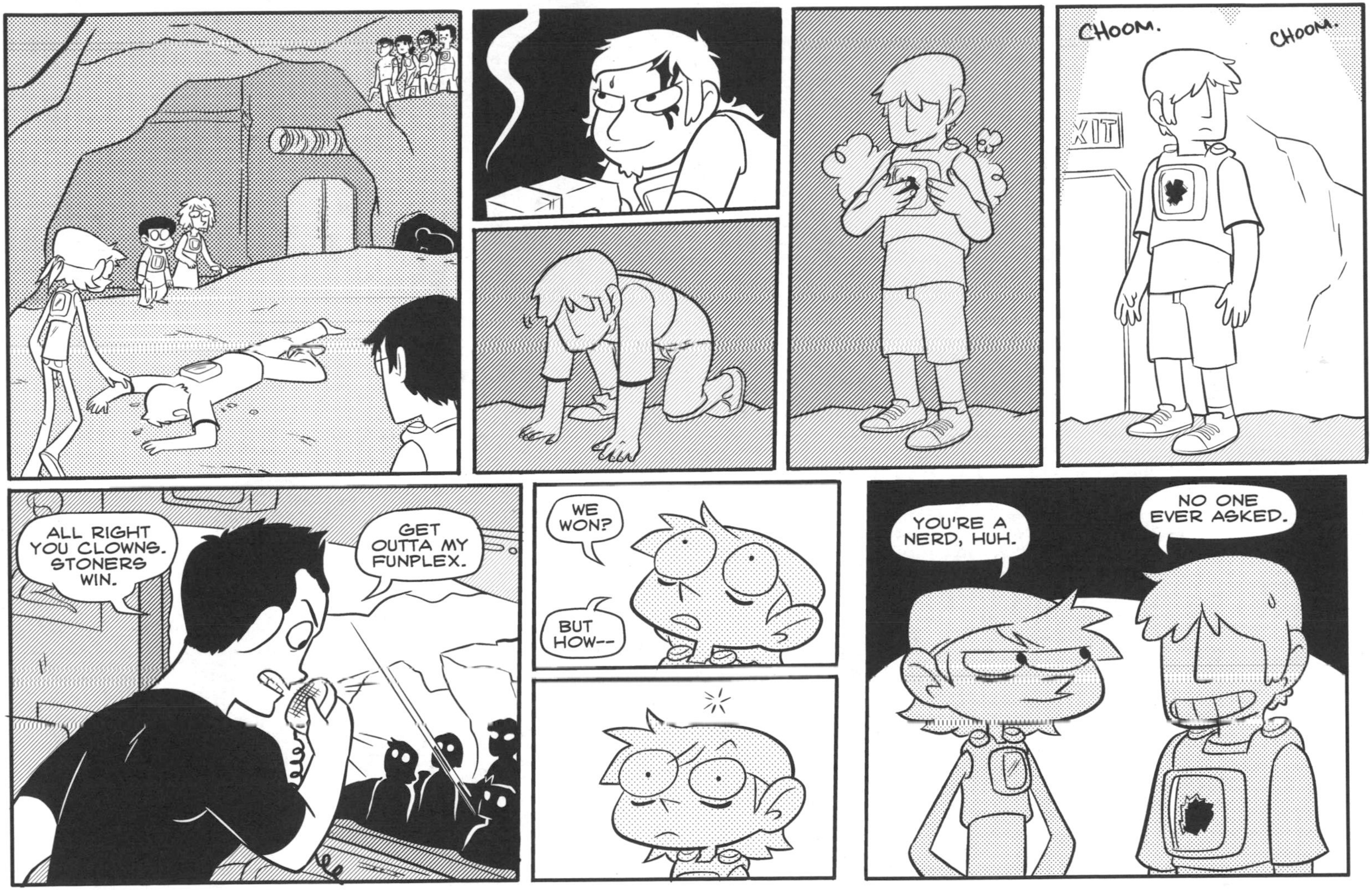
CHOOM.
CHOOM.
XIT
ALL RIGHT YOU CLOWNS. STONERS WIN.
GET OUTTA MY FUNPLEX.
WE WON?
BUT HOW--
YOU'RE A NERD, HUH.
NO ONE EVER ASKED.

AND THAT'S HOW I KNEW HE WAS WORKING AGAINST US! NOBODY ELSE KEEPS JACKSONIAN-ERA BIOGRAPHIES ON THEIR NIGHTSTAND!

MM HMM.

HERE, SEAN.

TO THE VICTOR BELONGS THE SPOILS.

HUH?

OH... OH WOW.

TH-THIS IS JUST...

=SNIFF!=

I LOVE YOU GUYS SO M

YOU NERDS FIGHT WITH HONOR AND CLASS.

PERHAPS WE ARE NOT SO DIFFERENT!

EH HEH! CHHH. HEH.

MAYBE THIS PLACE NEVER *WAS* THAT GOOD.

FRIDAY SPECIA

FUN AN

$15.9

R. SONG'S PIZZA

MAYBE I'M REMEMBERING IT FOR SOMETHING IT WASN'T.

I COULD'VE TOLD YOU THAT.

THE *PEOPLE* MADE IT SPECIAL, YOU KNOW? WE SHARED IT TOGETHER.

PARK, I DON'T WANT US TO BE GROUNDED IN NOSTALGIA.

IF WE LIVE BY THE PAST, THIS'LL NEVER WORK OUT.

OKAY, SO WE WON'T.

OKAY.

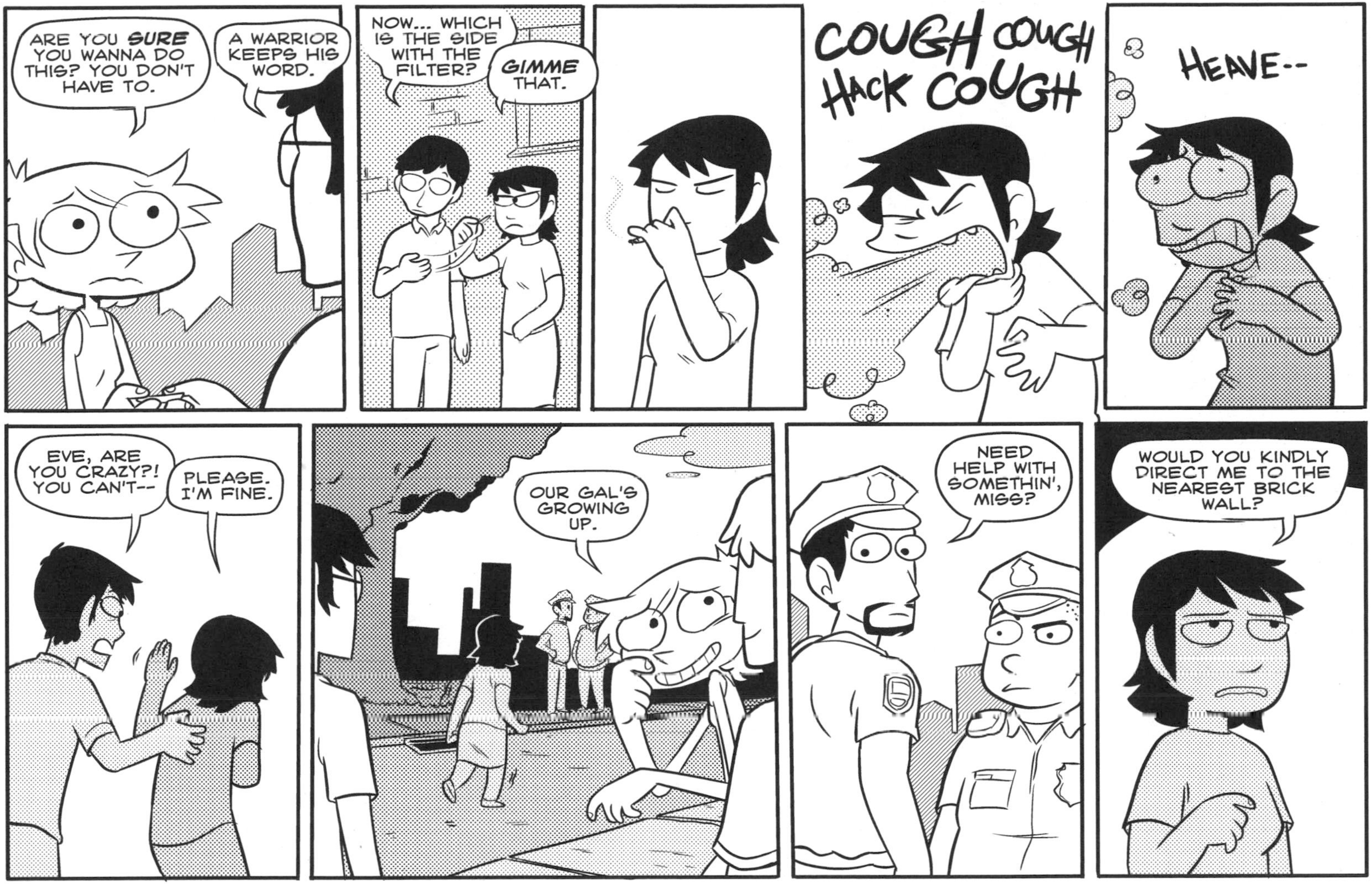
ARE YOU SURE YOU WANNA DO THIS? YOU DON'T HAVE TO.
A WARRIOR KEEPS HIS WORD.
NOW... WHICH IS THE SIDE WITH THE FILTER?
GIMME THAT.
COUGH COUGH
HACK COUGH
HEAVE--
EVE, ARE YOU CRAZY?! YOU CAN'T--
PLEASE. I'M FINE.
OUR GAL'S GROWING UP.
NEED HELP WITH SOMETHIN', MISS?
WOULD YOU KINDLY DIRECT ME TO THE NEAREST BRICK WALL?

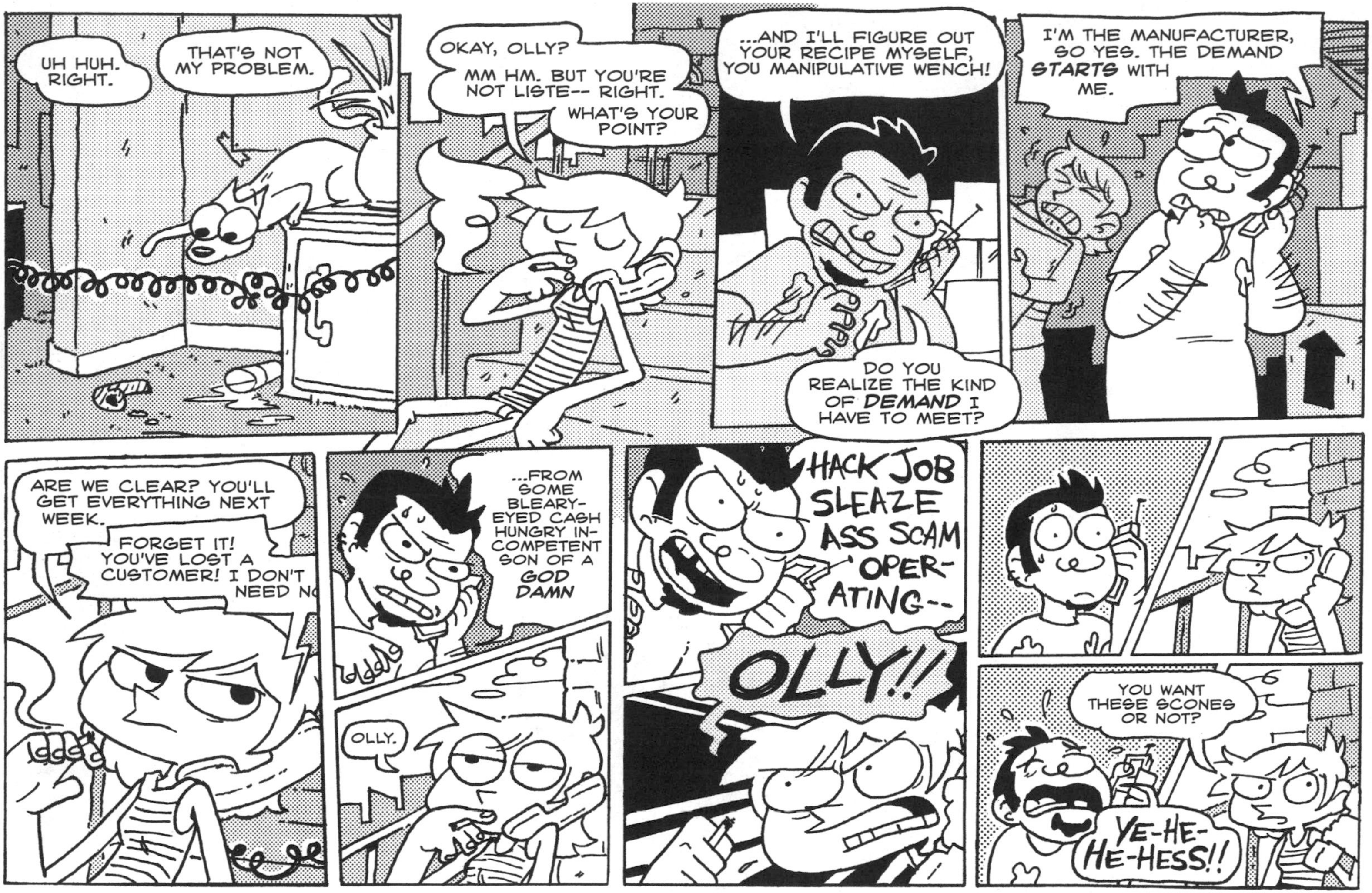
UH HUH. RIGHT.
THAT'S NOT MY PROBLEM.
OKAY, OLLY?
MM HM. BUT YOU'RE NOT LISTE-- RIGHT.
WHAT'S YOUR POINT?
...AND I'LL FIGURE OUT YOUR RECIPE MYSELF, YOU MANIPULATIVE WENCH!
DO YOU REALIZE THE KIND OF DEMAND I HAVE TO MEET?
I'M THE MANUFACTURER, SO YES. THE DEMAND STARTS WITH ME.
ARE WE CLEAR? YOU'LL GET EVERYTHING NEXT WEEK.
FORGET IT! YOU'VE LOST A CUSTOMER! I DON'T NEED N
...FROM SOME BLEARY-EYED CASH HUNGRY IN-COMPETENT SON OF A GOD DAMN
OLLY.
HACK JOB SLEAZE ASS SCAM OPER-ATING--
OLLY!!
YOU WANT THESE SCONES OR NOT?
YE-HE-HE-HESS!!

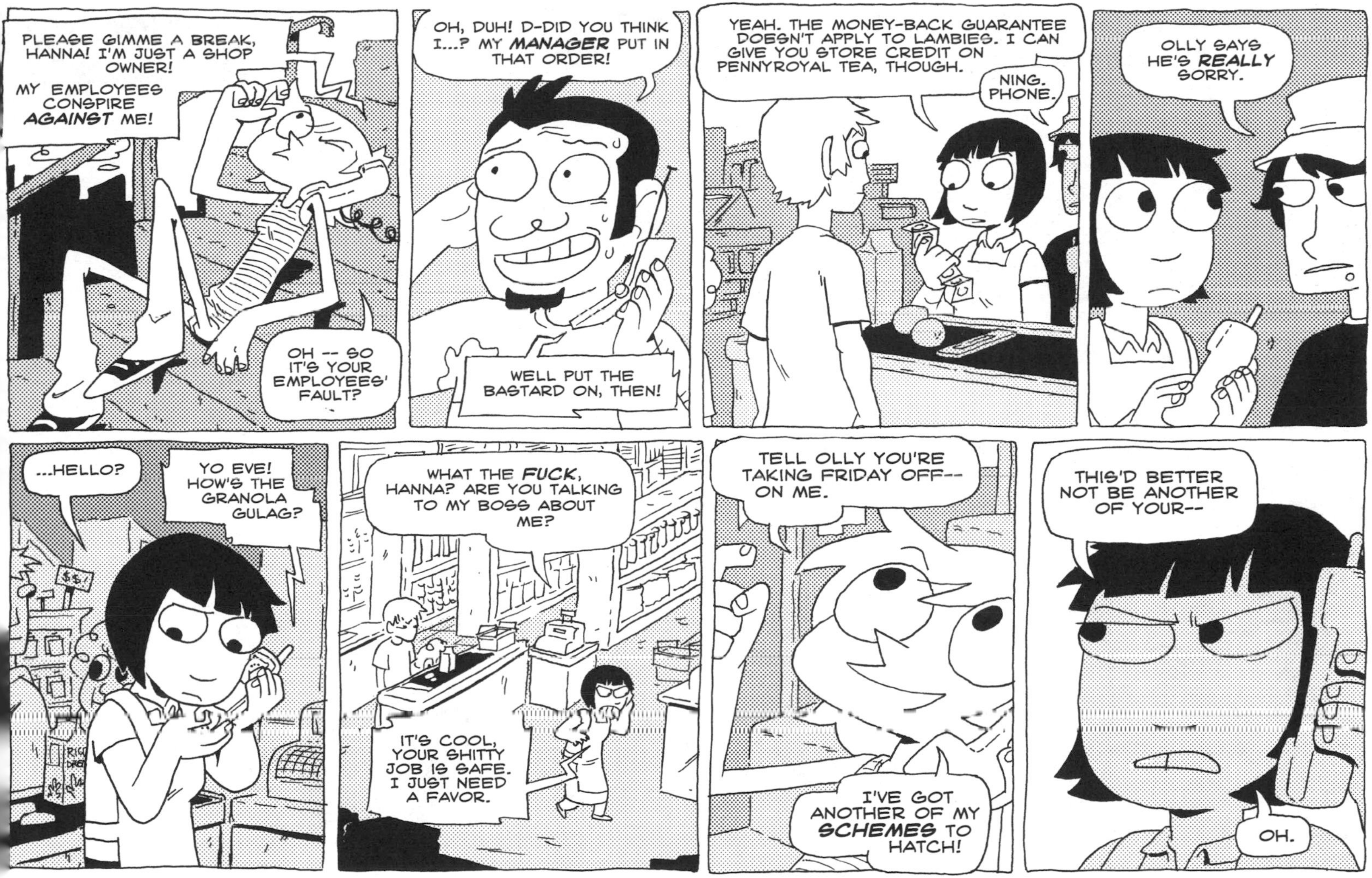
PLEASE GIMME A BREAK, HANNA! I'M JUST A SHOP OWNER!
MY EMPLOYEES CONSPIRE **AGAINST** ME!
OH -- SO IT'S YOUR EMPLOYEES' FAULT?
OH, DUH! D-DID YOU THINK I...? MY **MANAGER** PUT IN THAT ORDER!
WELL PUT THE BASTARD ON, THEN!
YEAH. THE MONEY-BACK GUARANTEE DOESN'T APPLY TO LAMBIES. I CAN GIVE YOU STORE CREDIT ON PENNYROYAL TEA, THOUGH.
NING. PHONE.
OLLY SAYS HE'S **REALLY** SORRY.
...HELLO?
YO EVE! HOW'S THE GRANOLA GULAG?
WHAT THE **FUCK**, HANNA? ARE YOU TALKING TO MY BOSS ABOUT ME?
IT'S COOL, YOUR SHITTY JOB IS SAFE. I JUST NEED A FAVOR.
TELL OLLY YOU'RE TAKING FRIDAY OFF-- ON ME.
I'VE GOT ANOTHER OF MY **SCHEMES** TO HATCH!
THIS'D BETTER NOT BE ANOTHER OF YOUR--
OH.

TELL HER TO MAKE ME A CAMBRIC SHIRT... ♪♫

MR. LEBLANC, THIS IS THE POLICE.

FUCK YOU. WHAT IS IT?

CALLING IN ONE OF MANY YOU-OWE-MES, DUDE.

HOW'S A WEEKEND OF SHILLING WARES IN THE MOUNTAINS SOUND?

WHAT *KIND* OF WARES?

LEGAL ONES, BRAINIAC.

I'VE HAD IT WITH THE GROCERY RACKET, WILL.

I NEED TO GET OUT. DISTRIBUTE MY SHIT DIRECTLY.

BEYOND THE REALM OF WESTCHESTER COUNTY, THERE LIES...

THE RIBALDRY CONTINUES!!

Winking Dragon

RENAISSANCE FESTIVAL

DULTS $10
REN $4
SS $15

AND WHAT BETTER SPECIALTY MARKET THAN A BUNCH OF GREASY, OBSESSIVE FETISHISTS WITH INCOME MELTING OUT OF THEIR *CORSETS*??

AND HEY, I BET WE'LL FIND YOU A GIRLFRIEND!

GREAT.

SO HERE'S HOW IT'LL GO DOWN.

SCRUFFY AND I RIDE THE RAIL UP TO THE SHOW WITH THE BARE ESSENTIALS.

THIS IS BARE? WHAT'S IN HERE?

OUR COSTUMES.

I HAD TO GET THE *AUTHENTIC* SHIT.

No STADIUM

RIGHT, SO EVE AND MAREK WILL TRANSPORT THE REST OF THE GOODS IN THE RENTAL.

PARTY CITY

SHOULD BE PRETTY DIRECT.

H-HEY! RENTAL?

YOU CAN *DRIVE*, EVE?

SUPER ANIMA

DON'T BE RIDICULOUS. I CAN'T--

HERE, DON'T FORGET THIS.

YOU LEFT IT ON THE KITCHEN COUNTER WHEN YOU SWORE TO STOP DRINKING FOREVER.

GOD DAMN IT.

YOU'RE THE MOST TALENTED PERSON I KNOW.

NEW YORK STATE

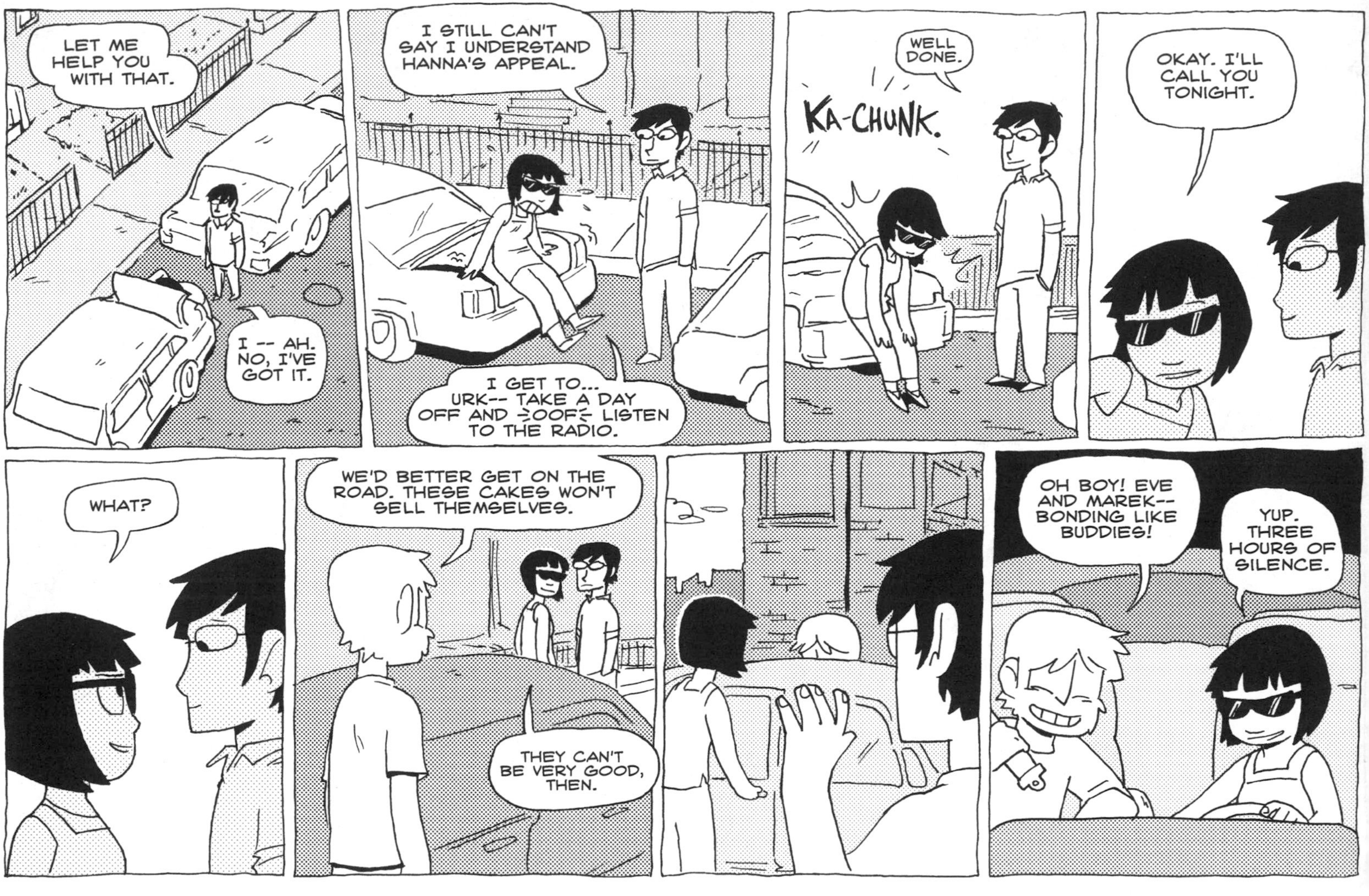
LET ME HELP YOU WITH THAT.
I -- AH. NO, I'VE GOT IT.
I STILL CAN'T SAY I UNDERSTAND HANNA'S APPEAL.
I GET TO... URK-- TAKE A DAY OFF AND OOF LISTEN TO THE RADIO.
KA-CHUNK.
WELL DONE.
OKAY. I'LL CALL YOU TONIGHT.
WHAT?
WE'D BETTER GET ON THE ROAD. THESE CAKES WON'T SELL THEMSELVES.
THEY CAN'T BE VERY GOOD, THEN.
OH BOY! EVE AND MAREK-- BONDING LIKE BUDDIES!
YUP. THREE HOURS OF SILENCE.

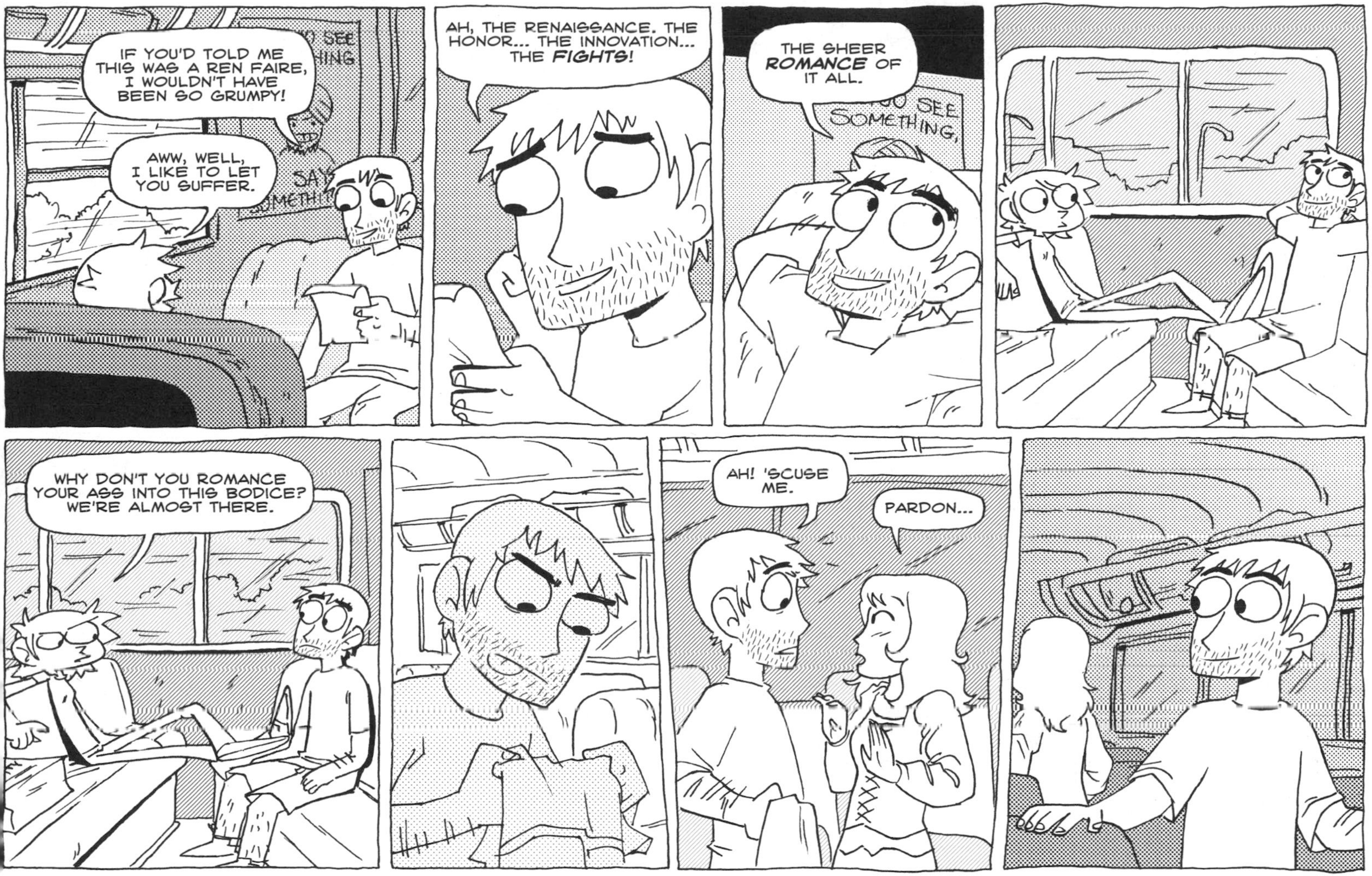
IF YOU'D TOLD ME THIS WAS A REN FAIRE, I WOULDN'T HAVE BEEN SO GRUMPY!
AWW, WELL, I LIKE TO LET YOU SUFFER.
AH, THE RENAISSANCE. THE HONOR... THE INNOVATION... THE *FIGHTS*!
THE SHEER *ROMANCE* OF IT ALL.
SOMETHING,
WHY DON'T YOU ROMANCE YOUR ASS INTO THIS BODICE? WE'RE ALMOST THERE.
AH! 'SCUSE ME.
PARDON...

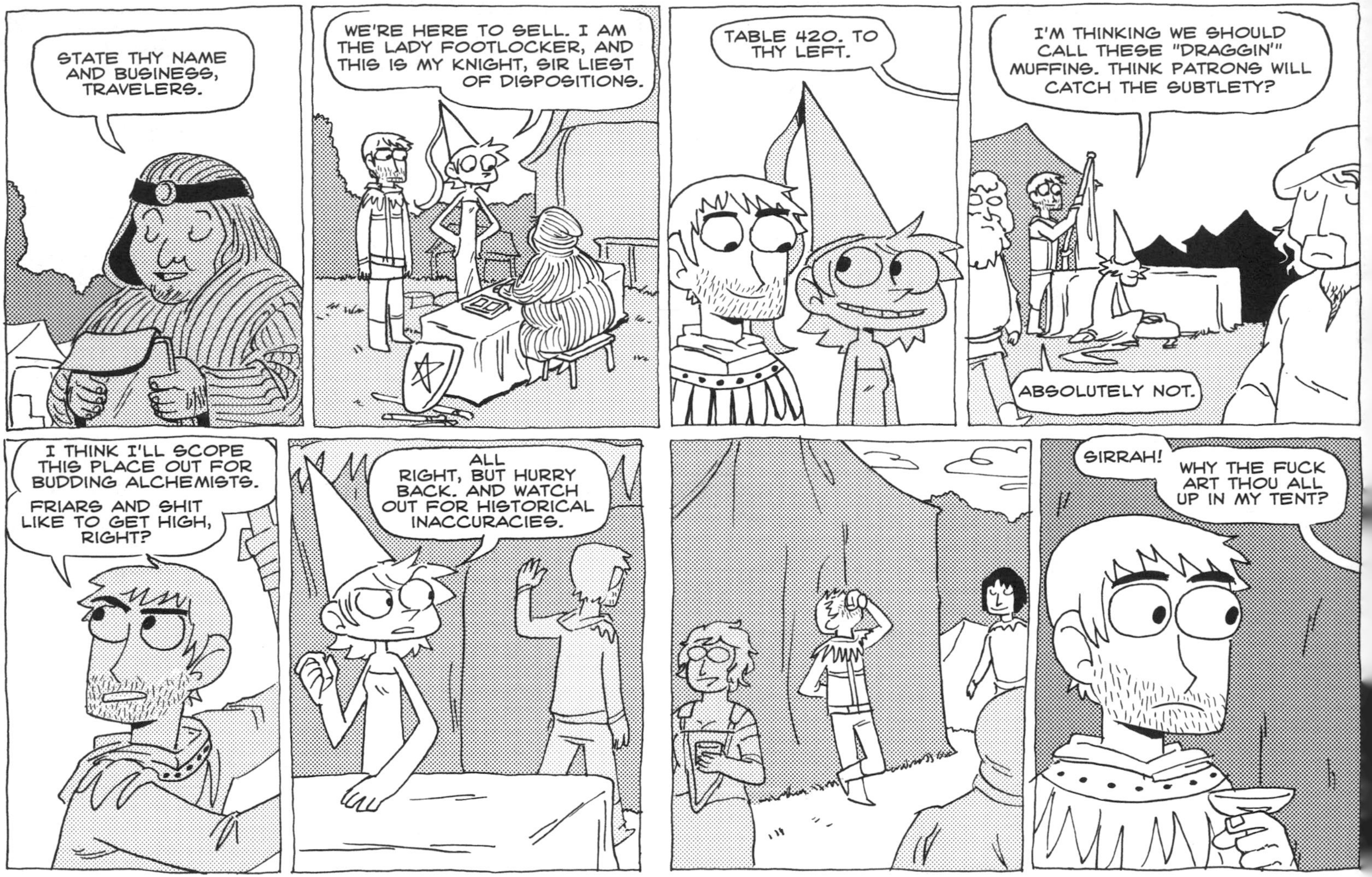
STATE THY NAME AND BUSINESS, TRAVELERS.
WE'RE HERE TO SELL. I AM THE LADY FOOTLOCKER, AND THIS IS MY KNIGHT, SIR LIEST OF DISPOSITIONS.
TABLE 420. TO THY LEFT.
I'M THINKING WE SHOULD CALL THESE "DRAGGIN'" MUFFINS. THINK PATRONS WILL CATCH THE SUBTLETY?
ABSOLUTELY NOT.
I THINK I'LL SCOPE THIS PLACE OUT FOR BUDDING ALCHEMISTS.
FRIARS AND SHIT LIKE TO GET HIGH, RIGHT?
ALL RIGHT, BUT HURRY BACK. AND WATCH OUT FOR HISTORICAL INACCURACIES.
SIRRAH!
WHY THE FUCK ART THOU ALL UP IN MY TENT?

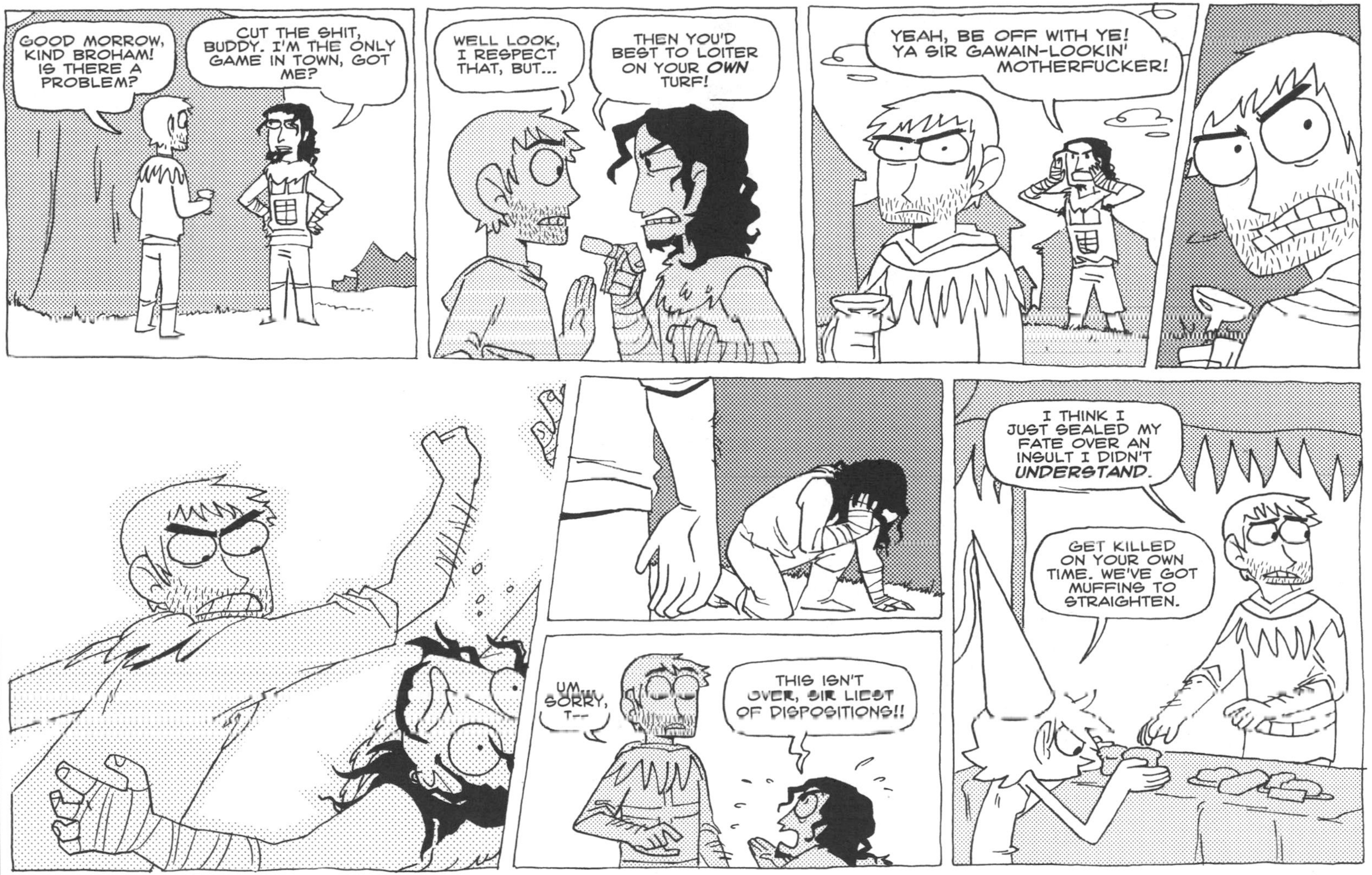
GOOD MORROW, KIND BROHAM! IS THERE A PROBLEM?
CUT THE SHIT, BUDDY. I'M THE ONLY GAME IN TOWN, GOT ME?
WELL LOOK, I RESPECT THAT, BUT...
THEN YOU'D BEST TO LOITER ON YOUR *OWN* TURF!
YEAH, BE OFF WITH YE! YA SIR GAWAIN-LOOKIN' MOTHERFUCKER!
UM... SORRY, I--
THIS ISN'T OVER, SIR LIEST OF DISPOSITIONS!!
I THINK I JUST SEALED MY FATE OVER AN INSULT I DIDN'T *UNDERSTAND*.
GET KILLED ON YOUR OWN TIME. WE'VE GOT MUFFINS TO STRAIGHTEN.

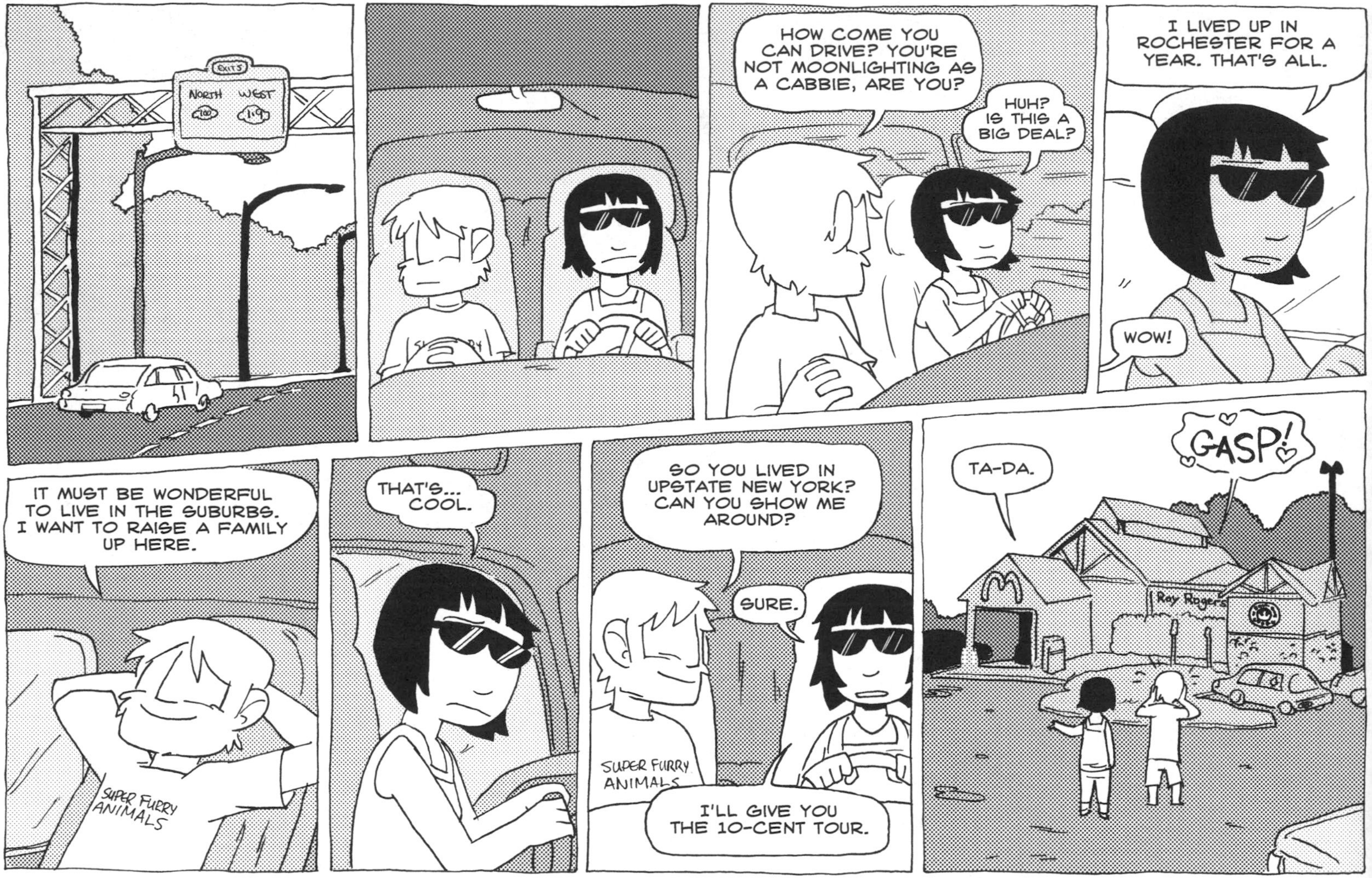
EXITS
NORTH
WEST
HOW COME YOU CAN DRIVE? YOU'RE NOT MOONLIGHTING AS A CABBIE, ARE YOU?
HUH? IS THIS A BIG DEAL?
I LIVED UP IN ROCHESTER FOR A YEAR. THAT'S ALL.
WOW!
IT MUST BE WONDERFUL TO LIVE IN THE SUBURBS. I WANT TO RAISE A FAMILY UP HERE.
SUPER FURRY ANIMALS
THAT'S... COOL.
SO YOU LIVED IN UPSTATE NEW YORK? CAN YOU SHOW ME AROUND?
SURE.
SUPER FURRY ANIMALS
I'LL GIVE YOU THE 10-CENT TOUR.
TA-DA.
GASP!
Roy Rogers

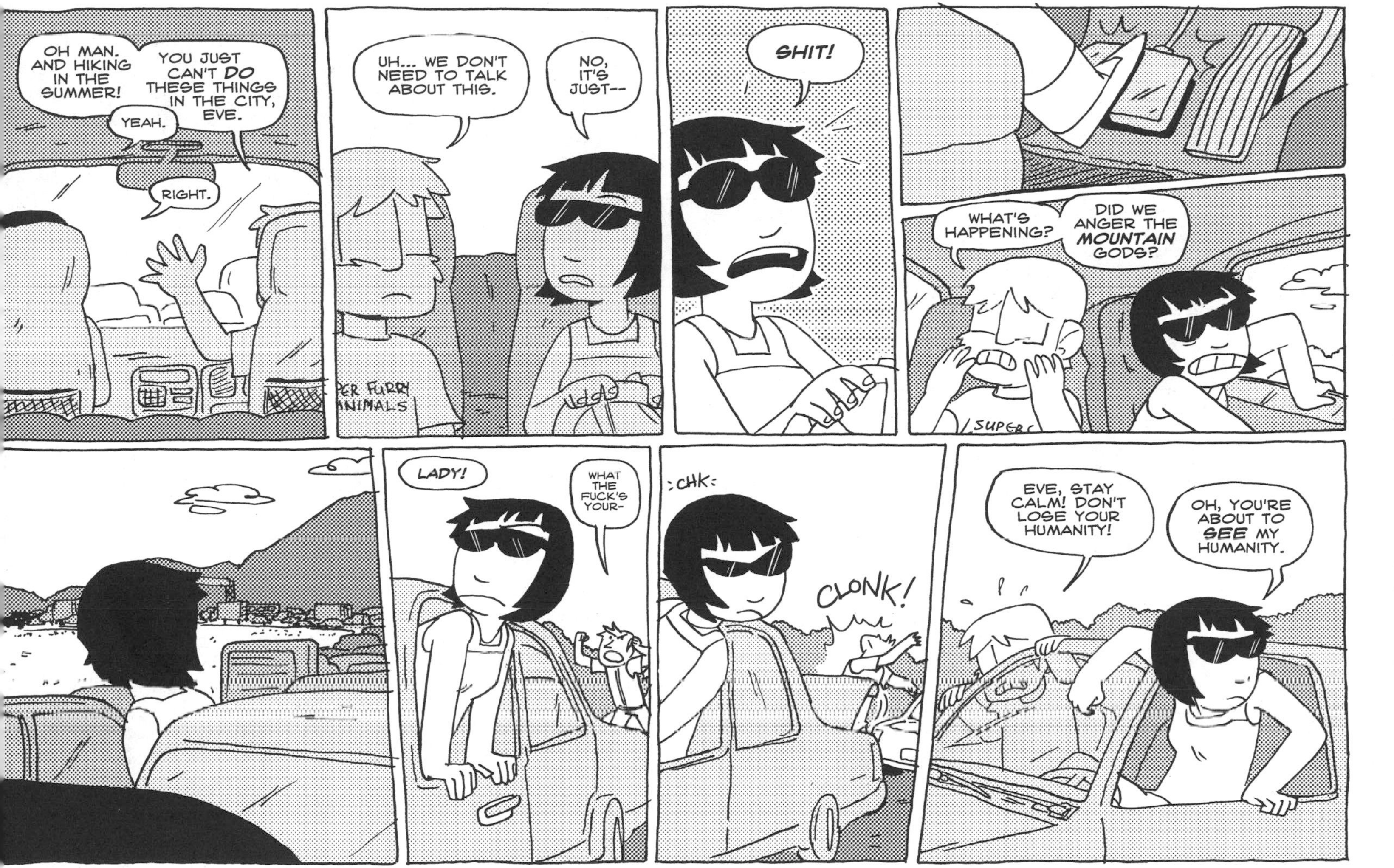
OH MAN. AND HIKING IN THE SUMMER!
YOU JUST CAN'T DO THESE THINGS IN THE CITY, EVE.
YEAH.
RIGHT.
UH... WE DON'T NEED TO TALK ABOUT THIS.
NO, IT'S JUST--
PER FURRY ANIMALS
SHIT!
WHAT'S HAPPENING?
DID WE ANGER THE MOUNTAIN GODS?
SUPER
LADY!
WHAT THE FUCK'S YOUR-
:CHK:
CLONK!
EVE, STAY CALM! DON'T LOSE YOUR HUMANITY!
OH, YOU'RE ABOUT TO SEE MY HUMANITY.

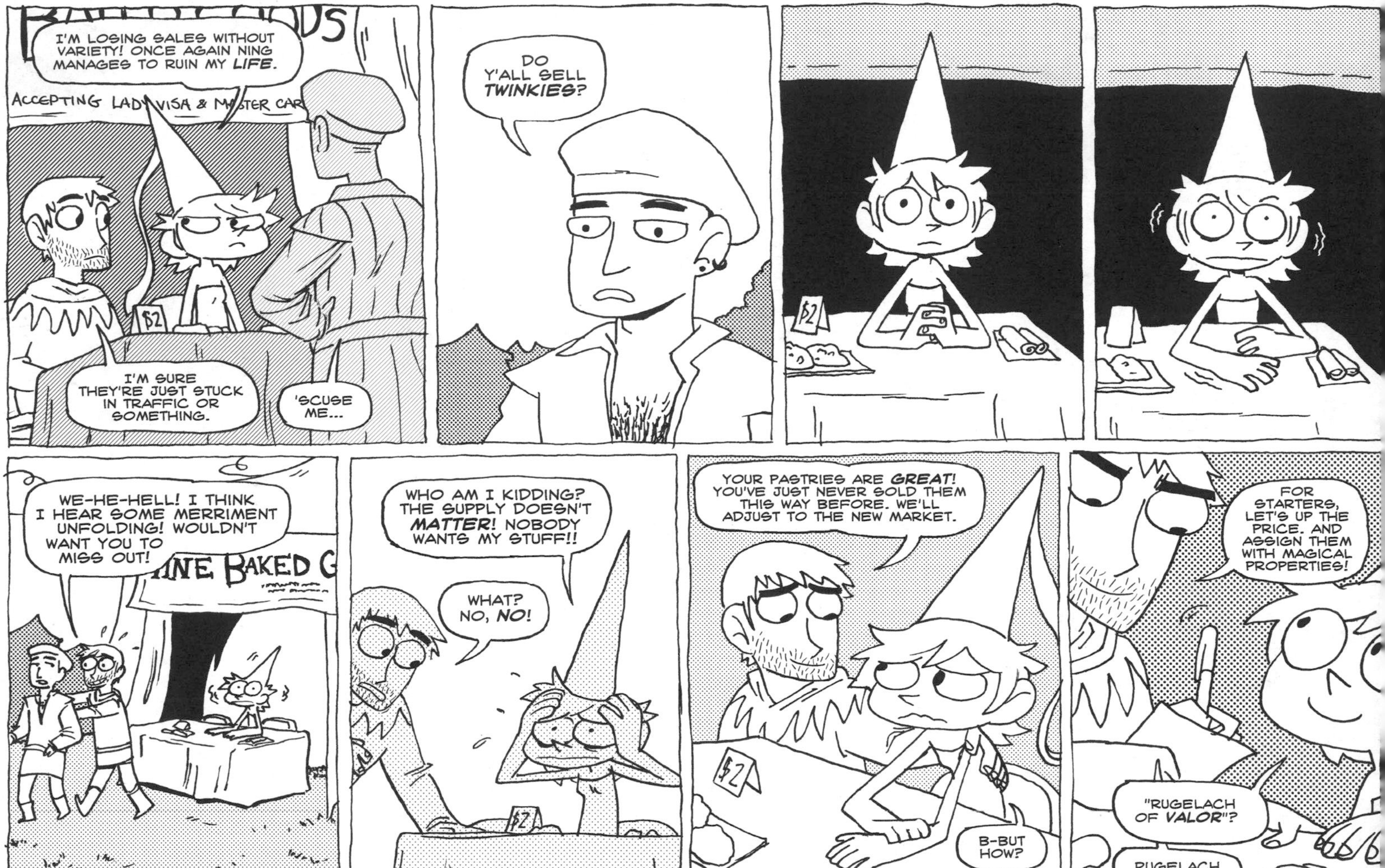
I'M LOSING SALES WITHOUT VARIETY! ONCE AGAIN NING MANAGES TO RUIN MY *LIFE*.
ACCEPTING LADY VISA & MASTER CAR
I'M SURE THEY'RE JUST STUCK IN TRAFFIC OR SOMETHING.
'SCUSE ME...
DO Y'ALL SELL *TWINKIES*?
$2
WE-HE-HELL! I THINK I HEAR SOME MERRIMENT UNFOLDING! WOULDN'T WANT YOU TO MISS OUT!
INE BAKED G
WHO AM I KIDDING? THE SUPPLY DOESN'T *MATTER*! NOBODY WANTS MY STUFF!!
WHAT? NO, *NO*!
YOUR PASTRIES ARE *GREAT*! YOU'VE JUST NEVER SOLD THEM THIS WAY BEFORE. WE'LL ADJUST TO THE NEW MARKET.
B-BUT HOW?
FOR STARTERS, LET'S UP THE PRICE. AND ASSIGN THEM WITH MAGICAL PROPERTIES!
"RUGELACH OF *VALOR*"?
RUGELACH OF VALOR.

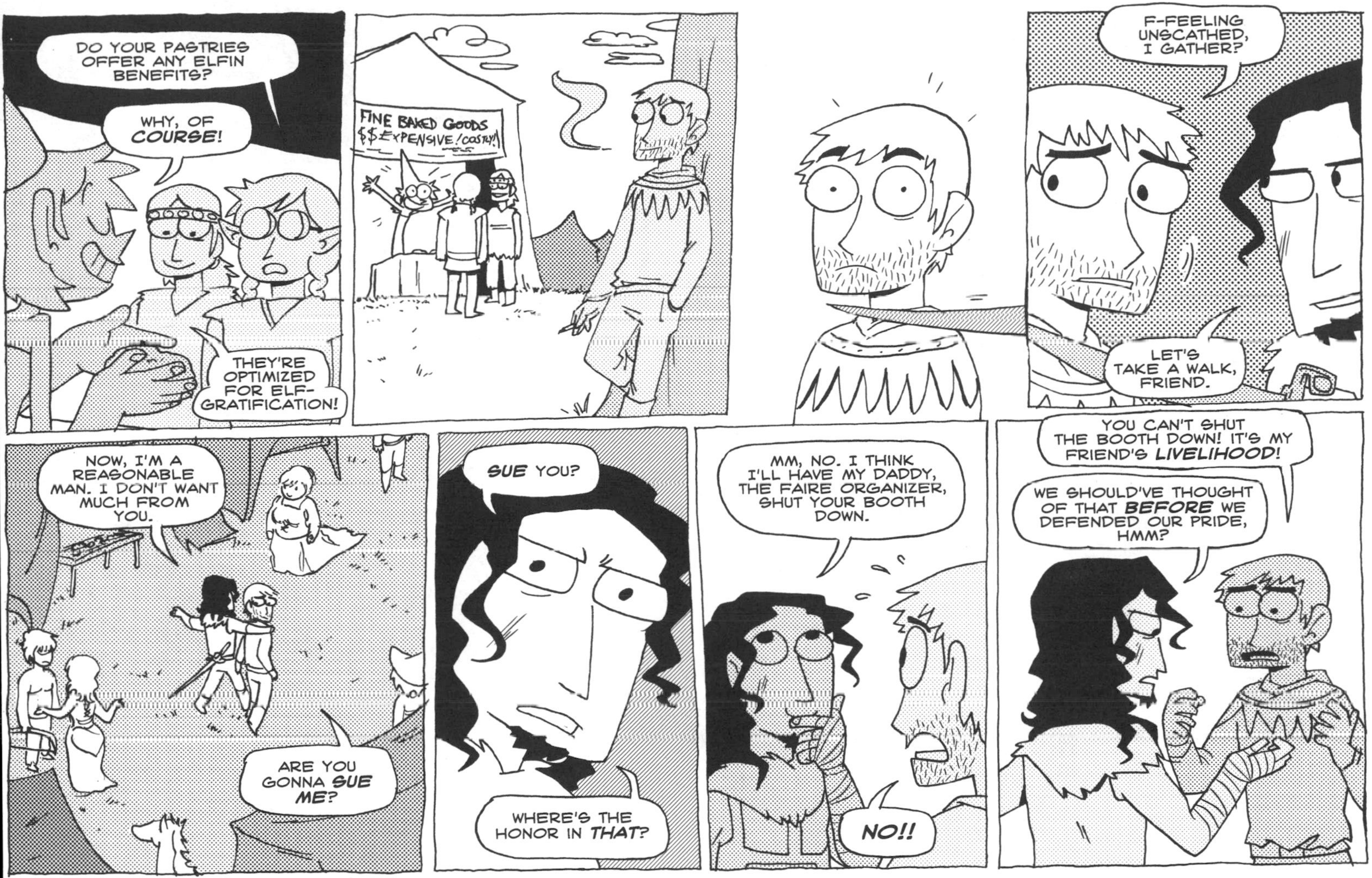
DO YOUR PASTRIES OFFER ANY ELFIN BENEFITS?
WHY, OF COURSE!
THEY'RE OPTIMIZED FOR ELF-GRATIFICATION!
FINE BAKED GOODS
$$EXPENSIVE! COSTLY!
F-FEELING UNSCATHED, I GATHER?
LET'S TAKE A WALK, FRIEND.
NOW, I'M A REASONABLE MAN. I DON'T WANT MUCH FROM YOU.
ARE YOU GONNA SUE ME?
SUE YOU?
WHERE'S THE HONOR IN THAT?
MM, NO. I THINK I'LL HAVE MY DADDY, THE FAIRE ORGANIZER, SHUT YOUR BOOTH DOWN.
NO!!
YOU CAN'T SHUT THE BOOTH DOWN! IT'S MY FRIEND'S LIVELIHOOD!
WE SHOULD'VE THOUGHT OF THAT BEFORE WE DEFENDED OUR PRIDE, HMM?

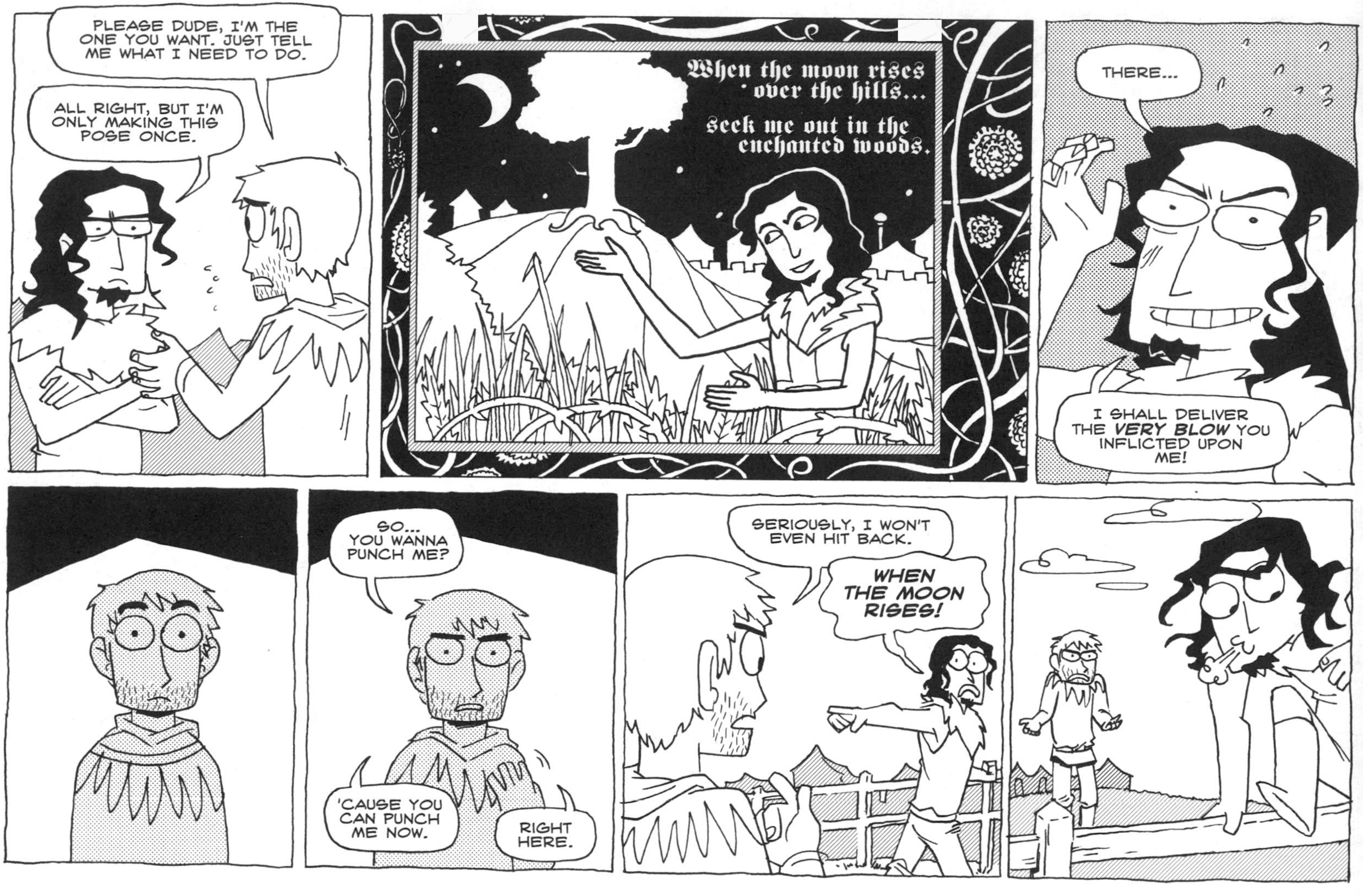

PLEASE DUDE, I'M THE ONE YOU WANT. JUST TELL ME WHAT I NEED TO DO.
ALL RIGHT, BUT I'M ONLY MAKING THIS POSE ONCE.
When the moon rises over the hills...
seek me out in the enchanted woods.
THERE...
I SHALL DELIVER THE VERY BLOW YOU INFLICTED UPON ME!
SO... YOU WANNA PUNCH ME?
'CAUSE YOU CAN PUNCH ME NOW.
RIGHT HERE.
SERIOUSLY, I WON'T EVEN HIT BACK.
WHEN THE MOON RISES!

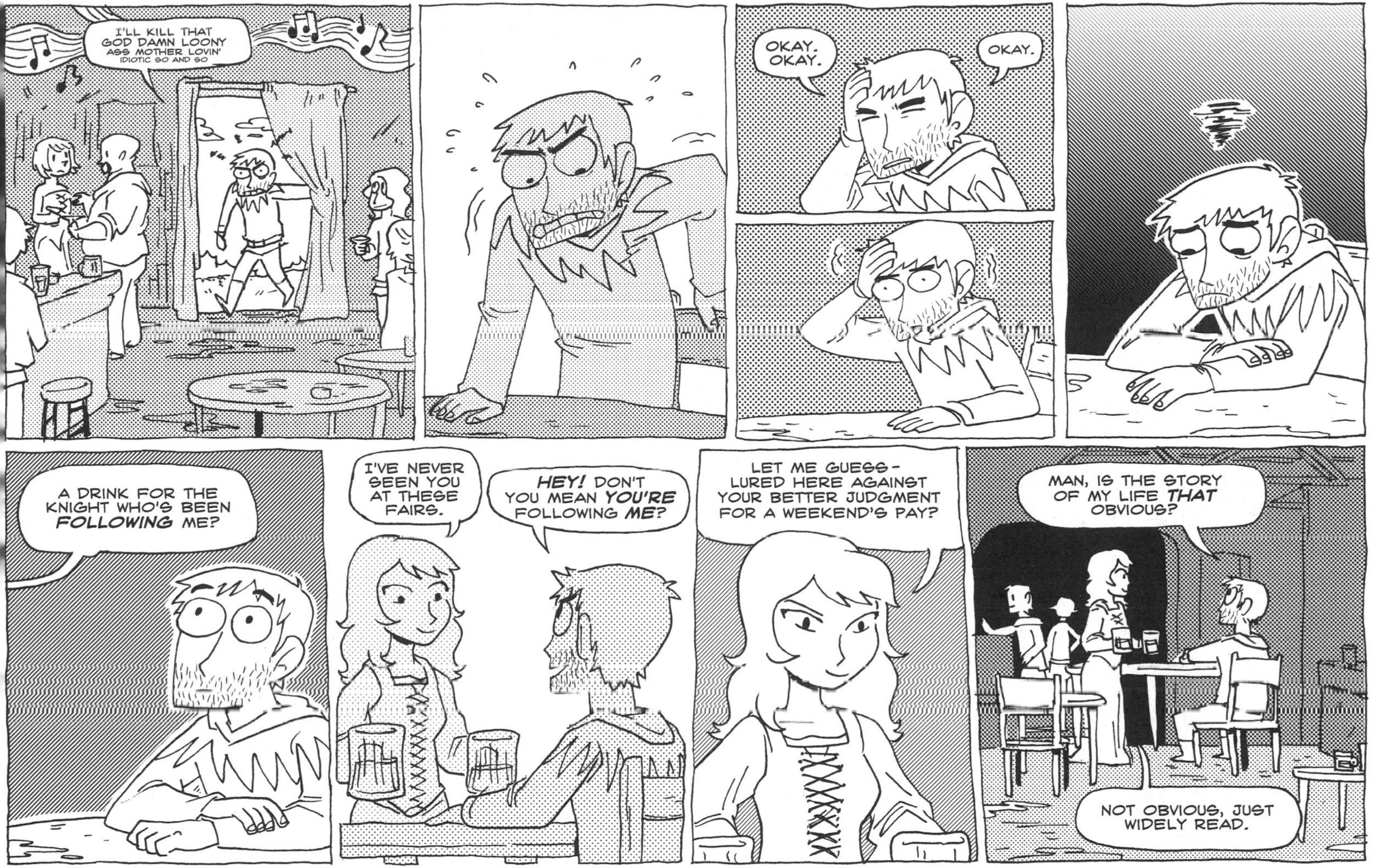

I'LL KILL THAT GOD DAMN LOONY ASS MOTHER LOVIN' IDIOTIC SO AND SO
OKAY. OKAY.
OKAY.
A DRINK FOR THE KNIGHT WHO'S BEEN ***FOLLOWING*** ME?
I'VE NEVER SEEN YOU AT THESE FAIRS.
HEY! DON'T YOU MEAN ***YOU'RE*** FOLLOWING ***ME***?
LET ME GUESS - LURED HERE AGAINST YOUR BETTER JUDGMENT FOR A WEEKEND'S PAY?
MAN, IS THE STORY OF MY LIFE ***THAT*** OBVIOUS?
NOT OBVIOUS, JUST WIDELY READ.

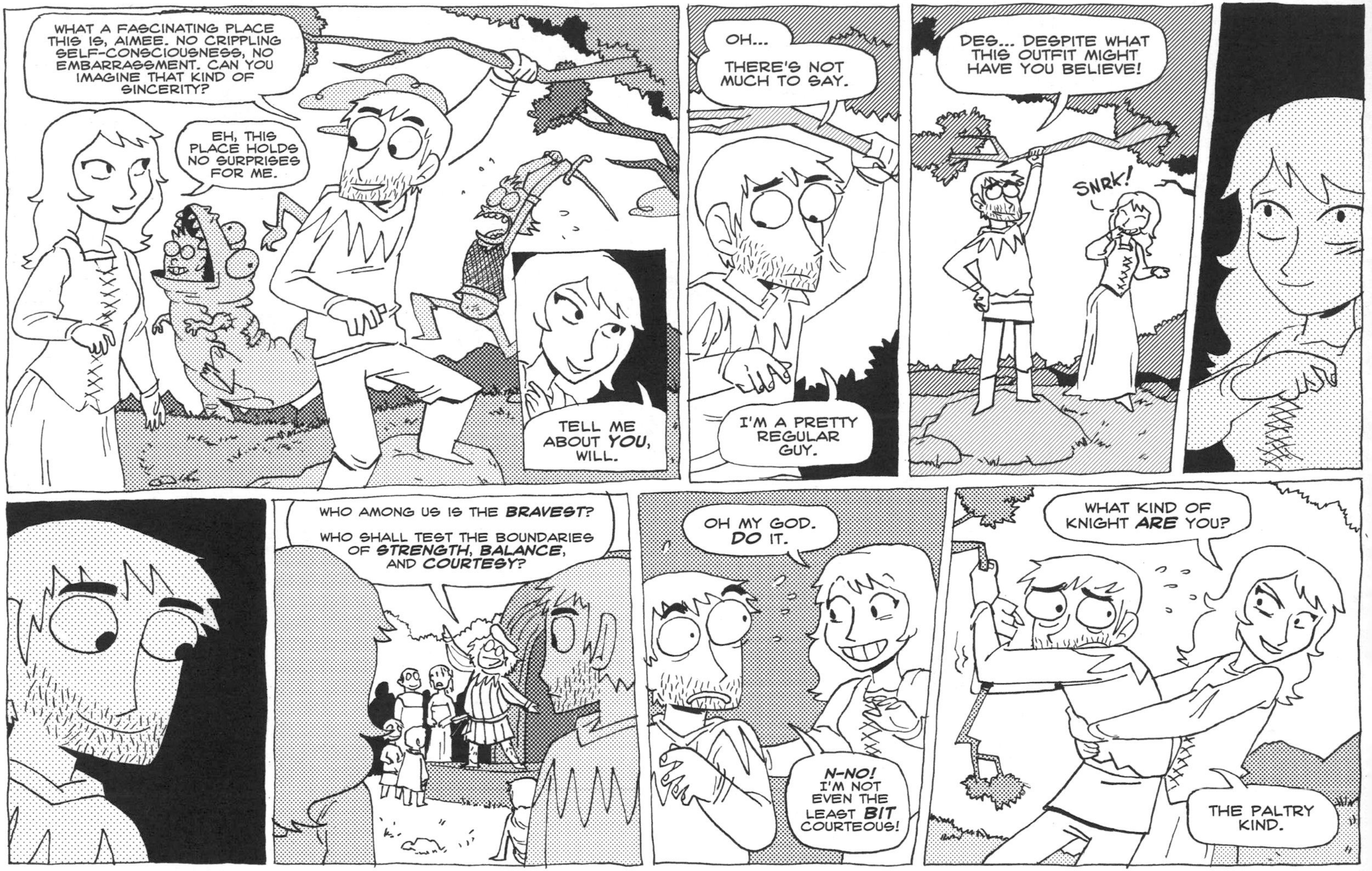
WHAT A FASCINATING PLACE THIS IS, AIMEE. NO CRIPPLING SELF-CONSCIOUSNESS, NO EMBARRASSMENT. CAN YOU IMAGINE THAT KIND OF SINCERITY?
EH, THIS PLACE HOLDS NO SURPRISES FOR ME.
TELL ME ABOUT *YOU*, WILL.
OH...
THERE'S NOT MUCH TO SAY.
I'M A PRETTY REGULAR GUY.
DES... DESPITE WHAT THIS OUTFIT MIGHT HAVE YOU BELIEVE!
SNRK!
WHO AMONG US IS THE *BRAVEST*?
WHO SHALL TEST THE BOUNDARIES OF *STRENGTH*, *BALANCE*, AND *COURTESY*?
OH MY GOD. *DO* IT.
N-NO! I'M NOT EVEN THE LEAST *BIT* COURTEOUS!
WHAT KIND OF KNIGHT *ARE* YOU?
THE PALTRY KIND.

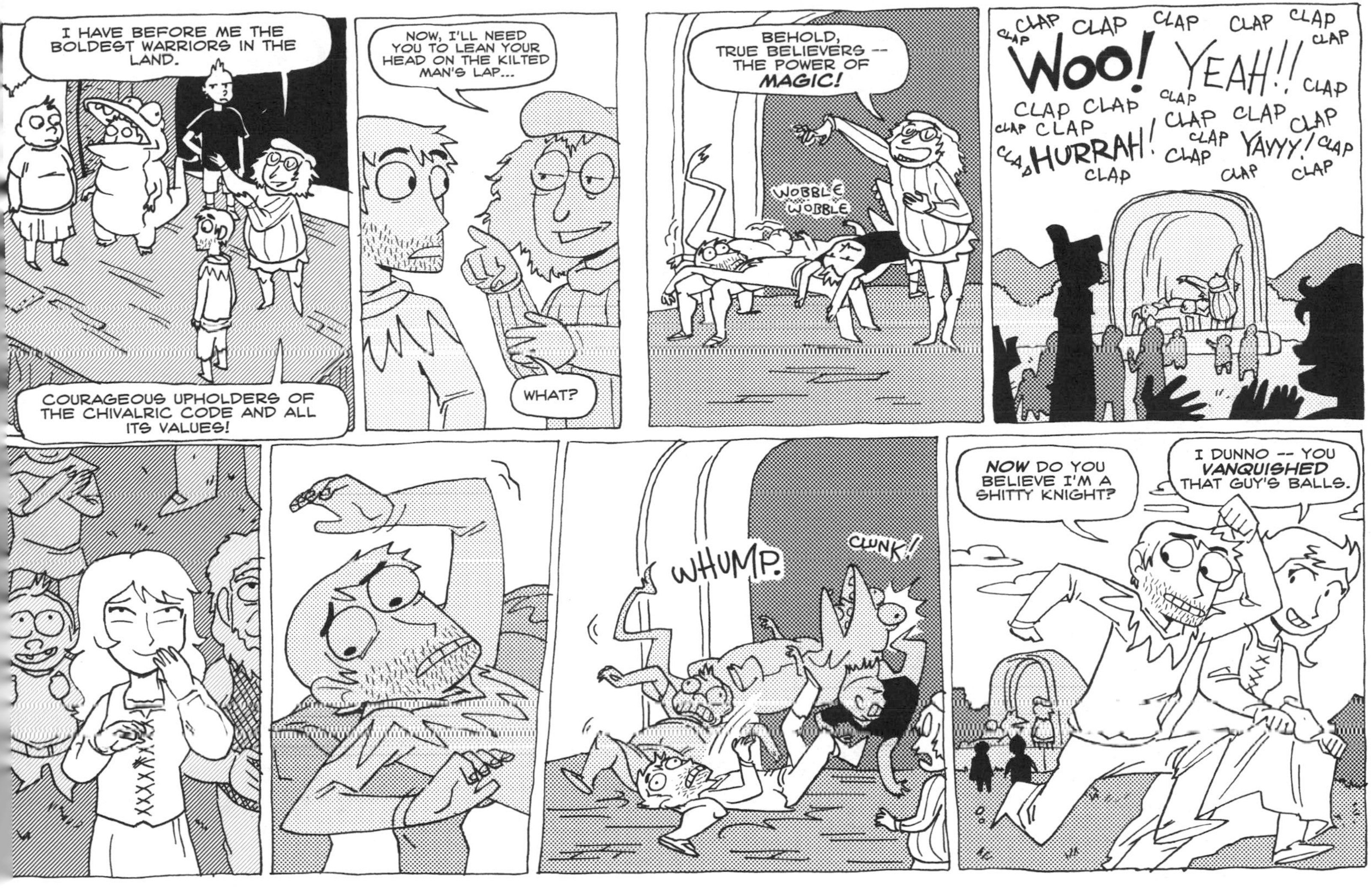

I HAVE BEFORE ME THE BOLDEST WARRIORS IN THE LAND.
COURAGEOUS UPHOLDERS OF THE CHIVALRIC CODE AND ALL ITS VALUES!
NOW, I'LL NEED YOU TO LEAN YOUR HEAD ON THE KILTED MAN'S LAP...
WHAT?
BEHOLD, TRUE BELIEVERS -- THE POWER OF MAGIC!
WOBBLE WOBBLE
CLAP CLAP CLAP CLAP CLAP CLAP CLAP
WOO! YEAH!!
CLAP
CLAP CLAP CLAP
CLAP CLAP CLAP CLAP CLAP
CLAP HURRAH! CLAP CLAP YAYYY! CLAP
CLAP CLAP CLAP
WHUMP.
CLUNK!
NOW DO YOU BELIEVE I'M A SHITTY KNIGHT?
I DUNNO -- YOU VANQUISHED THAT GUY'S BALLS.

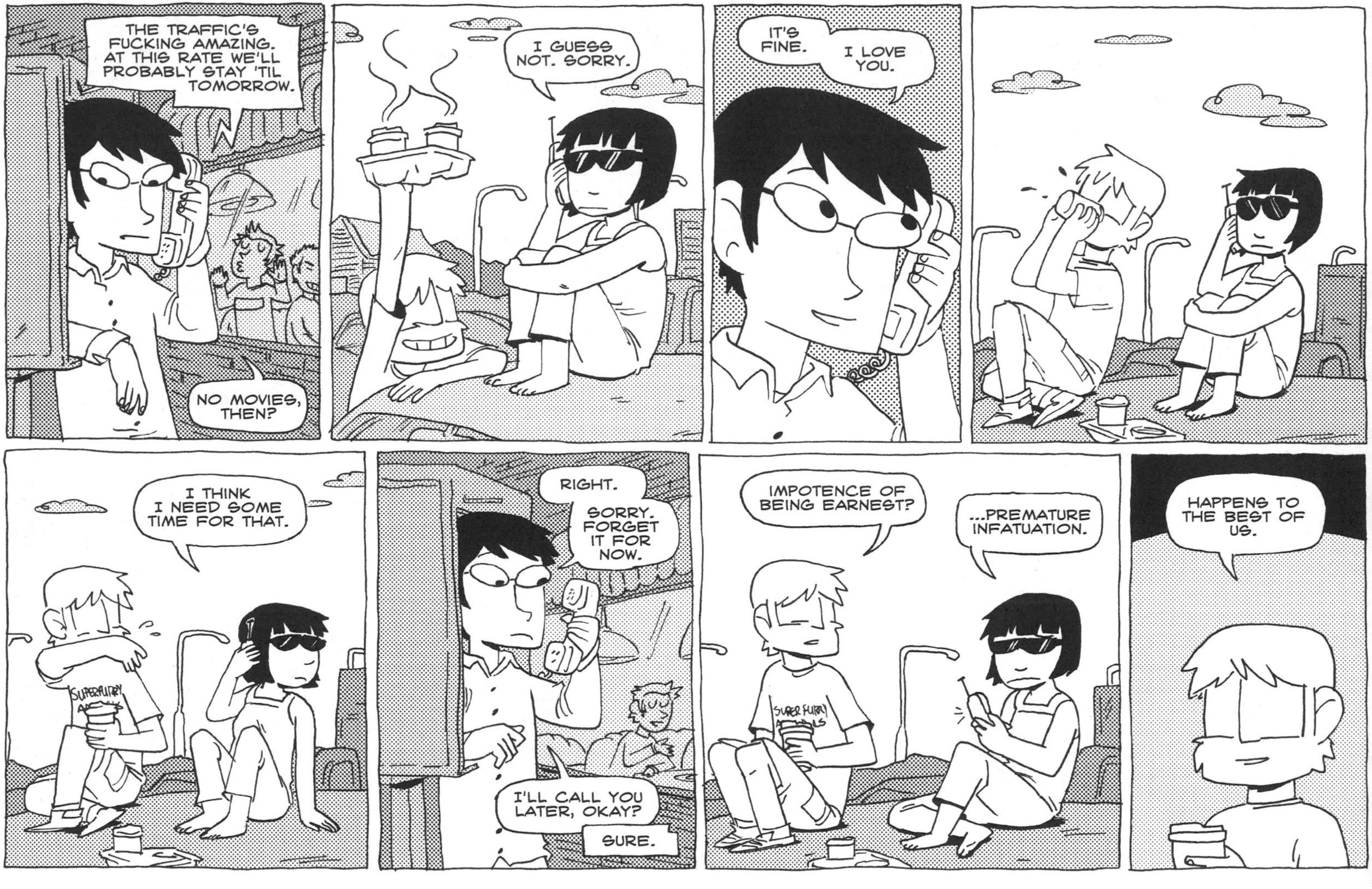
THE TRAFFIC'S FUCKING AMAZING. AT THIS RATE WE'LL PROBABLY STAY 'TIL TOMORROW.
NO MOVIES, THEN?
I GUESS NOT. SORRY.
IT'S FINE.
I LOVE YOU.
I THINK I NEED SOME TIME FOR THAT.
RIGHT.
SORRY. FORGET IT FOR NOW.
I'LL CALL YOU LATER, OKAY?
SURE.
IMPOTENCE OF BEING EARNEST?
...PREMATURE INFATUATION.
HAPPENS TO THE BEST OF US.

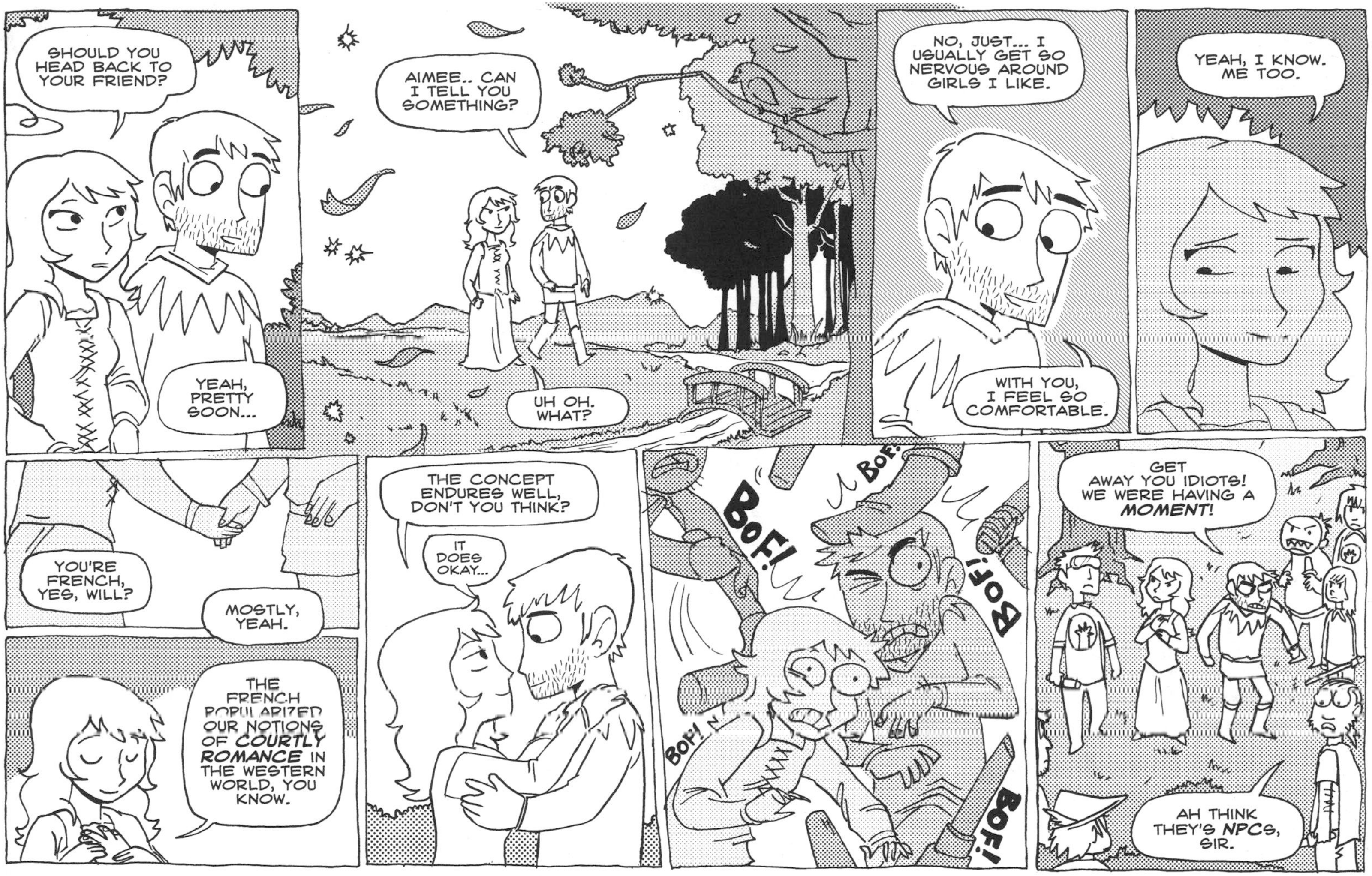
SHOULD YOU HEAD BACK TO YOUR FRIEND?
YEAH, PRETTY SOON...
AIMEE.. CAN I TELL YOU SOMETHING?
UH OH. WHAT?
NO, JUST... I USUALLY GET SO NERVOUS AROUND GIRLS I LIKE.
WITH YOU, I FEEL SO COMFORTABLE.
YEAH, I KNOW. ME TOO.
YOU'RE FRENCH, YES, WILL?
MOSTLY, YEAH.
THE FRENCH POPULARIZED OUR NOTIONS OF COURTLY ROMANCE IN THE WESTERN WORLD, YOU KNOW.
THE CONCEPT ENDURES WELL, DON'T YOU THINK?
IT DOES OKAY...
BOF!
BOF!
BOF!
BOF!
BOF!
BOF!
GET AWAY YOU IDIOTS! WE WERE HAVING A MOMENT!
AH THINK THEY'S NPCs, SIR.

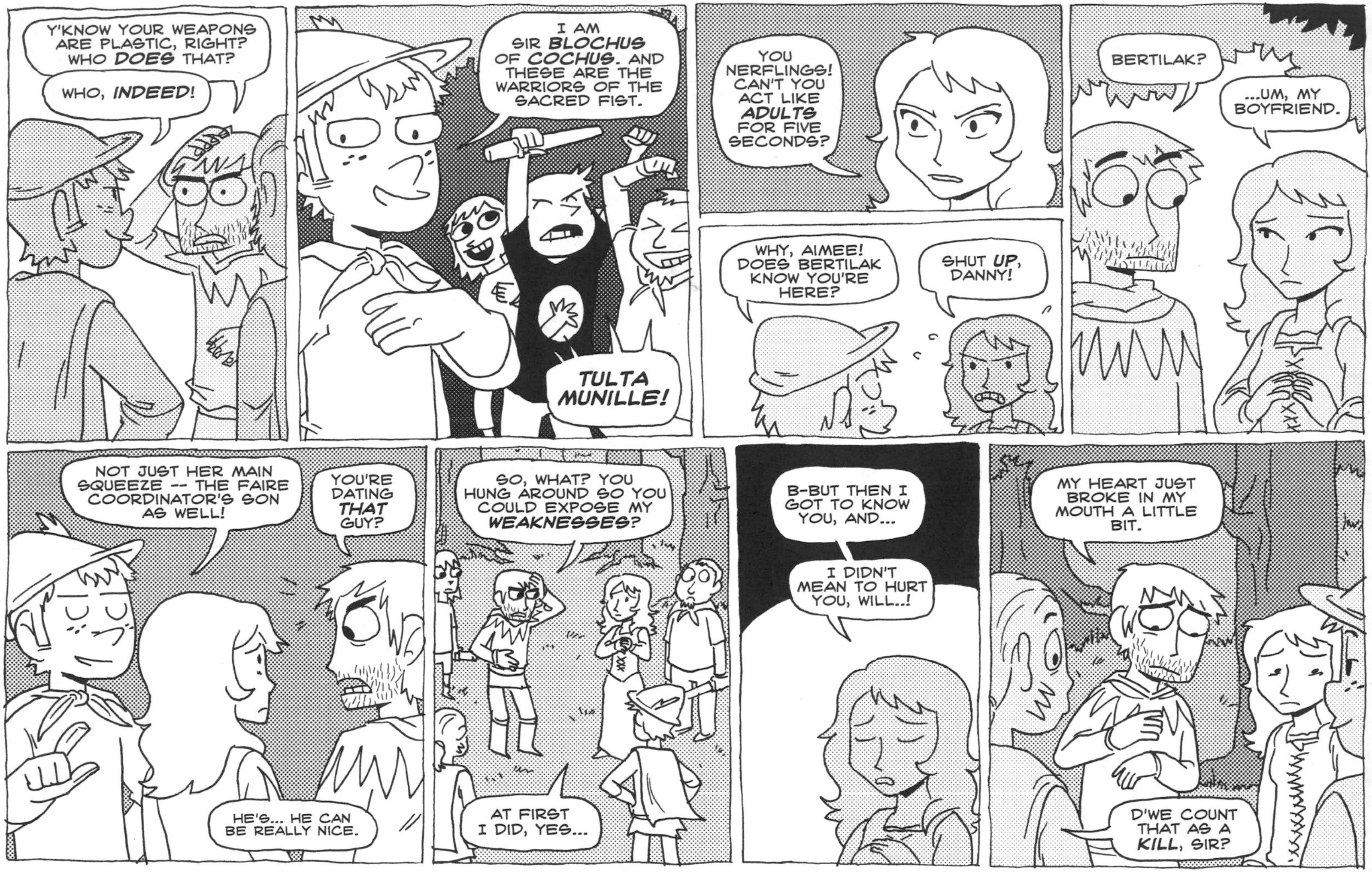

Y'KNOW YOUR WEAPONS ARE PLASTIC, RIGHT? WHO DOES THAT?
WHO, INDEED!
I AM SIR BLOCHUS OF COCHUS. AND THESE ARE THE WARRIORS OF THE SACRED FIST.
TULTA MUNILLE!
YOU NERFLINGS! CAN'T YOU ACT LIKE ADULTS FOR FIVE SECONDS?
WHY, AIMEE! DOES BERTILAK KNOW YOU'RE HERE?
SHUT UP, DANNY!
BERTILAK?
...UM, MY BOYFRIEND.
NOT JUST HER MAIN SQUEEZE -- THE FAIRE COORDINATOR'S SON AS WELL!
YOU'RE DATING THAT GUY?
HE'S... HE CAN BE REALLY NICE.
SO, WHAT? YOU HUNG AROUND SO YOU COULD EXPOSE MY WEAKNESSES?
AT FIRST I DID, YES...
B-BUT THEN I GOT TO KNOW YOU, AND...
I DIDN'T MEAN TO HURT YOU, WILL..!
MY HEART JUST BROKE IN MY MOUTH A LITTLE BIT.
D'WE COUNT THAT AS A KILL, SIR?

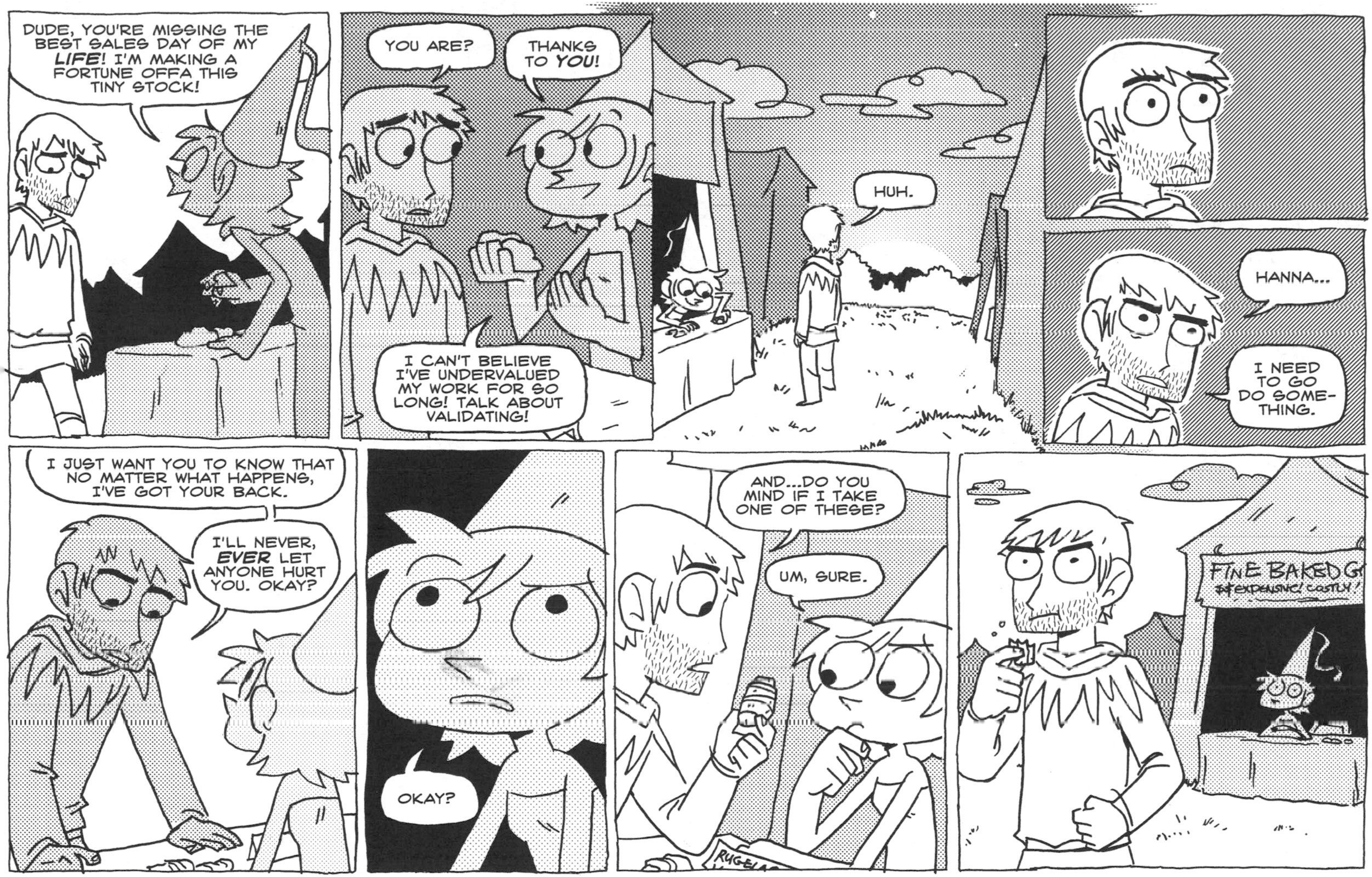

DUDE, YOU'RE MISSING THE BEST SALES DAY OF MY *LIFE*! I'M MAKING A FORTUNE OFFA THIS TINY STOCK!
YOU ARE?
THANKS TO *YOU*!
I CAN'T BELIEVE I'VE UNDERVALUED MY WORK FOR SO LONG! TALK ABOUT VALIDATING!
HUH.
HANNA...
I NEED TO GO DO SOME-THING.
I JUST WANT YOU TO KNOW THAT NO MATTER WHAT HAPPENS, I'VE GOT YOUR BACK.
I'LL NEVER, *EVER* LET ANYONE HURT YOU. OKAY?
OKAY?
AND...DO YOU MIND IF I TAKE ONE OF THESE?
UM, SURE.
FINE BAKED

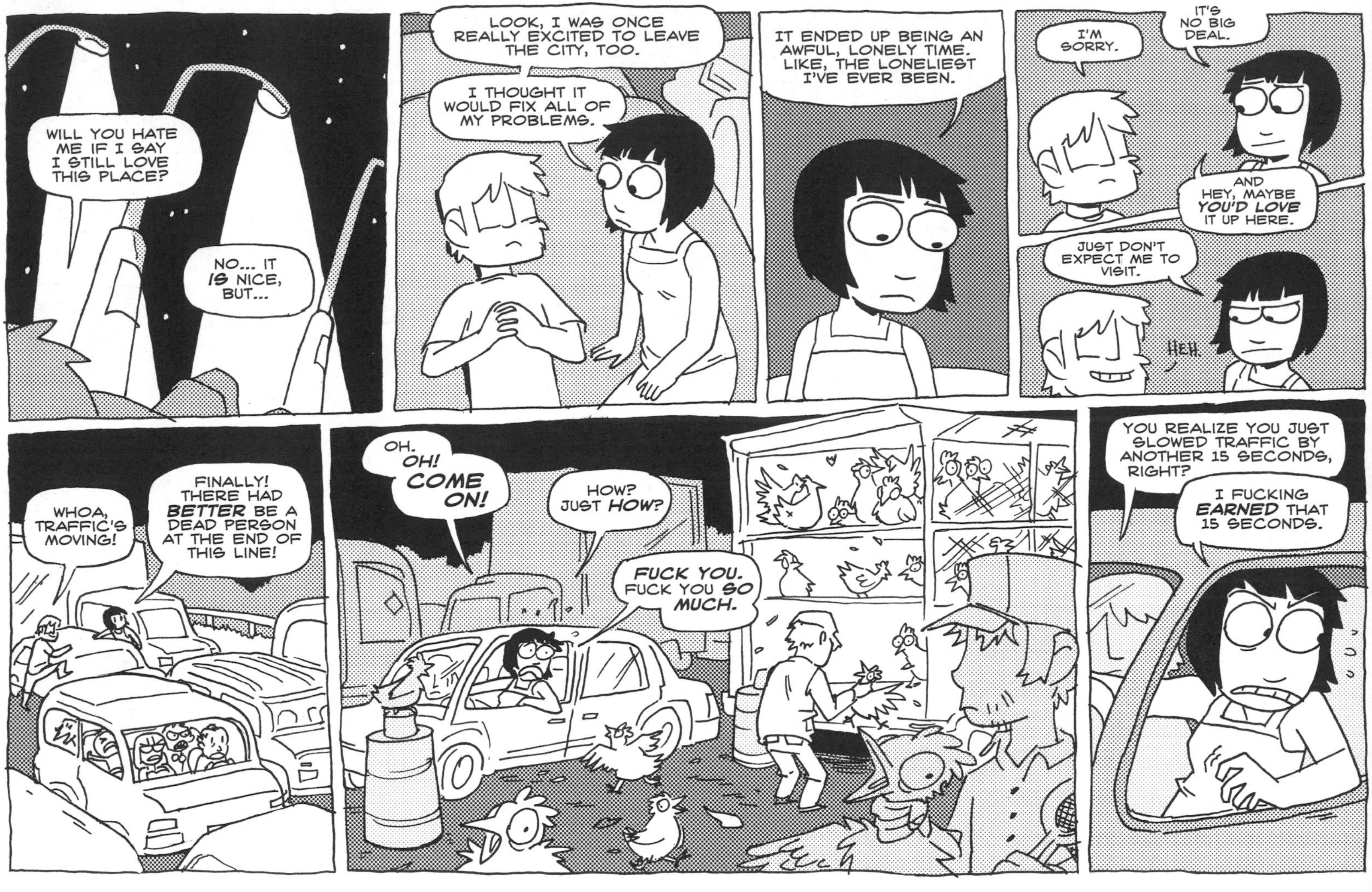

WILL YOU HATE ME IF I SAY I STILL LOVE THIS PLACE?
NO... IT *IS* NICE, BUT...
LOOK, I WAS ONCE REALLY EXCITED TO LEAVE THE CITY, TOO.
I THOUGHT IT WOULD FIX ALL OF MY PROBLEMS.
IT ENDED UP BEING AN AWFUL, LONELY TIME. LIKE, THE LONELIEST I'VE EVER BEEN.
I'M SORRY.
IT'S NO BIG DEAL.
AND HEY, MAYBE *YOU'D LOVE* IT UP HERE.
JUST DON'T EXPECT ME TO VISIT.
HEH.
WHOA, TRAFFIC'S MOVING!
FINALLY! THERE HAD *BETTER* BE A DEAD PERSON AT THE END OF THIS LINE!
OH. *OH! COME ON!*
HOW? JUST *HOW*?
FUCK YOU. FUCK YOU *SO MUCH.*
YOU REALIZE YOU JUST SLOWED TRAFFIC BY ANOTHER 15 SECONDS, RIGHT?
I FUCKING *EARNED* THAT 15 SECONDS.

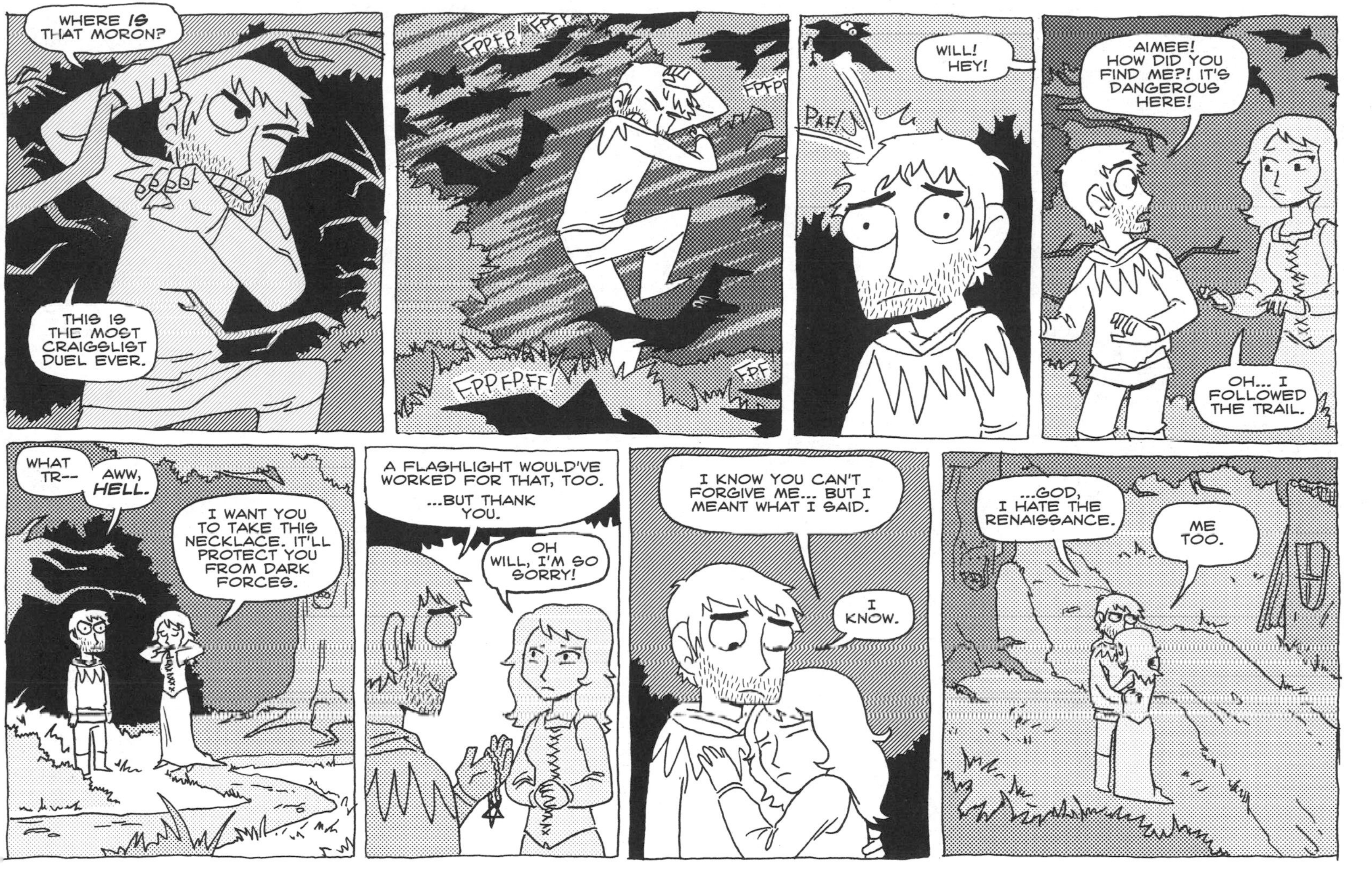
WHERE IS THAT MORON?
THIS IS THE MOST CRAIGSLIST DUEL EVER.
FPPFP! FPFF
FPFPP
FPPFPFF!
FPF!
WILL! HEY!
PAF!
AIMEE! HOW DID YOU FIND ME?! IT'S DANGEROUS HERE!
OH... I FOLLOWED THE TRAIL.
WHAT TR--
AWW, HELL.
I WANT YOU TO TAKE THIS NECKLACE. IT'LL PROTECT YOU FROM DARK FORCES.
A FLASHLIGHT WOULD'VE WORKED FOR THAT, TOO.
...BUT THANK YOU.
OH WILL, I'M SO SORRY!
I KNOW YOU CAN'T FORGIVE ME... BUT I MEANT WHAT I SAID.
I KNOW.
...GOD, I HATE THE RENAISSANCE.
ME TOO.

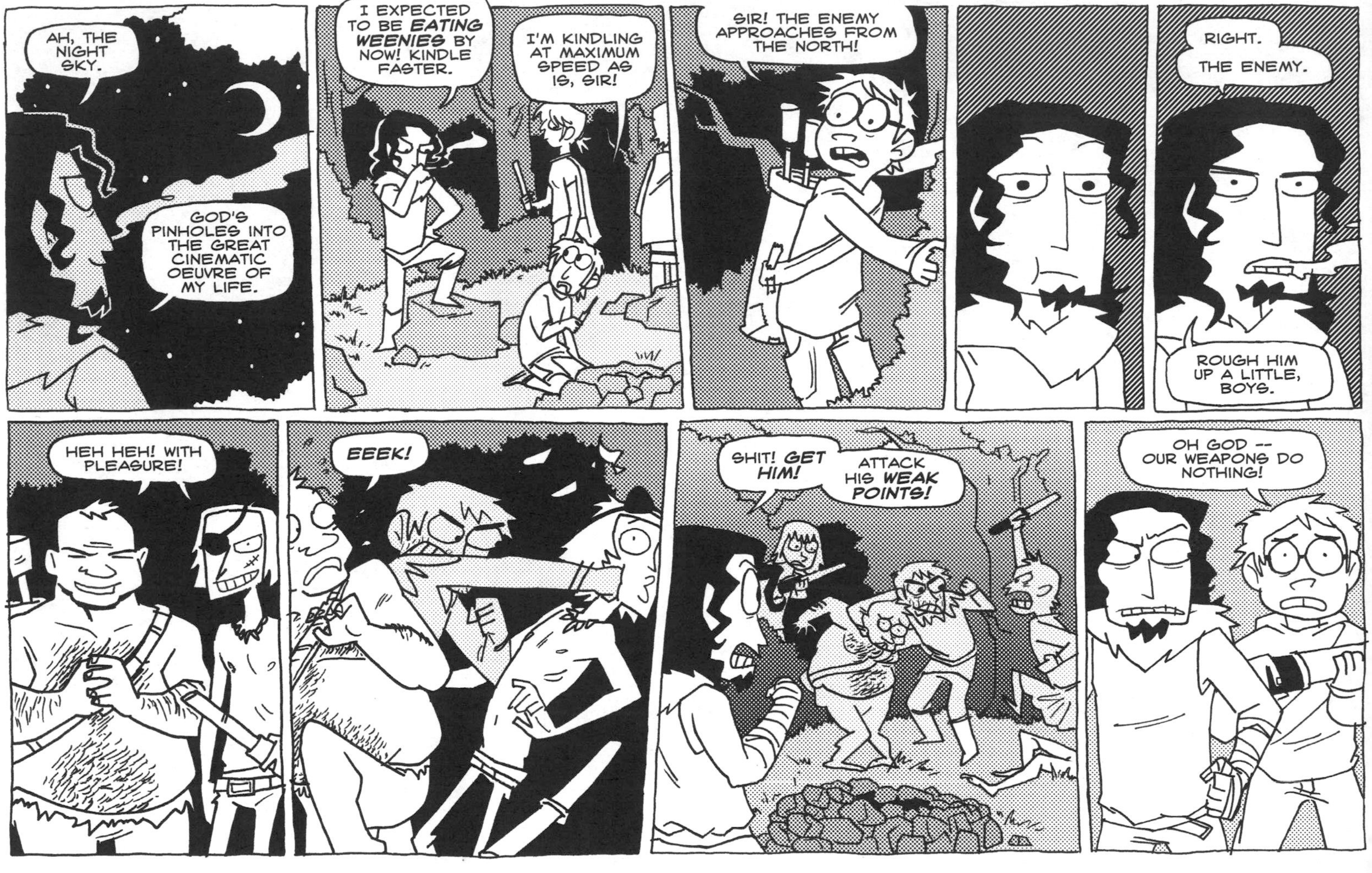
AH, THE NIGHT SKY.
GOD'S PINHOLES INTO THE GREAT CINEMATIC OEUVRE OF MY LIFE.
I EXPECTED TO BE EATING WEENIES BY NOW! KINDLE FASTER.
I'M KINDLING AT MAXIMUM SPEED AS IS, SIR!
SIR! THE ENEMY APPROACHES FROM THE NORTH!
RIGHT.
THE ENEMY.
ROUGH HIM UP A LITTLE, BOYS.
HEH HEH! WITH PLEASURE!
EEEK!
SHIT! GET HIM!
ATTACK HIS WEAK POINTS!
OH GOD -- OUR WEAPONS DO NOTHING!

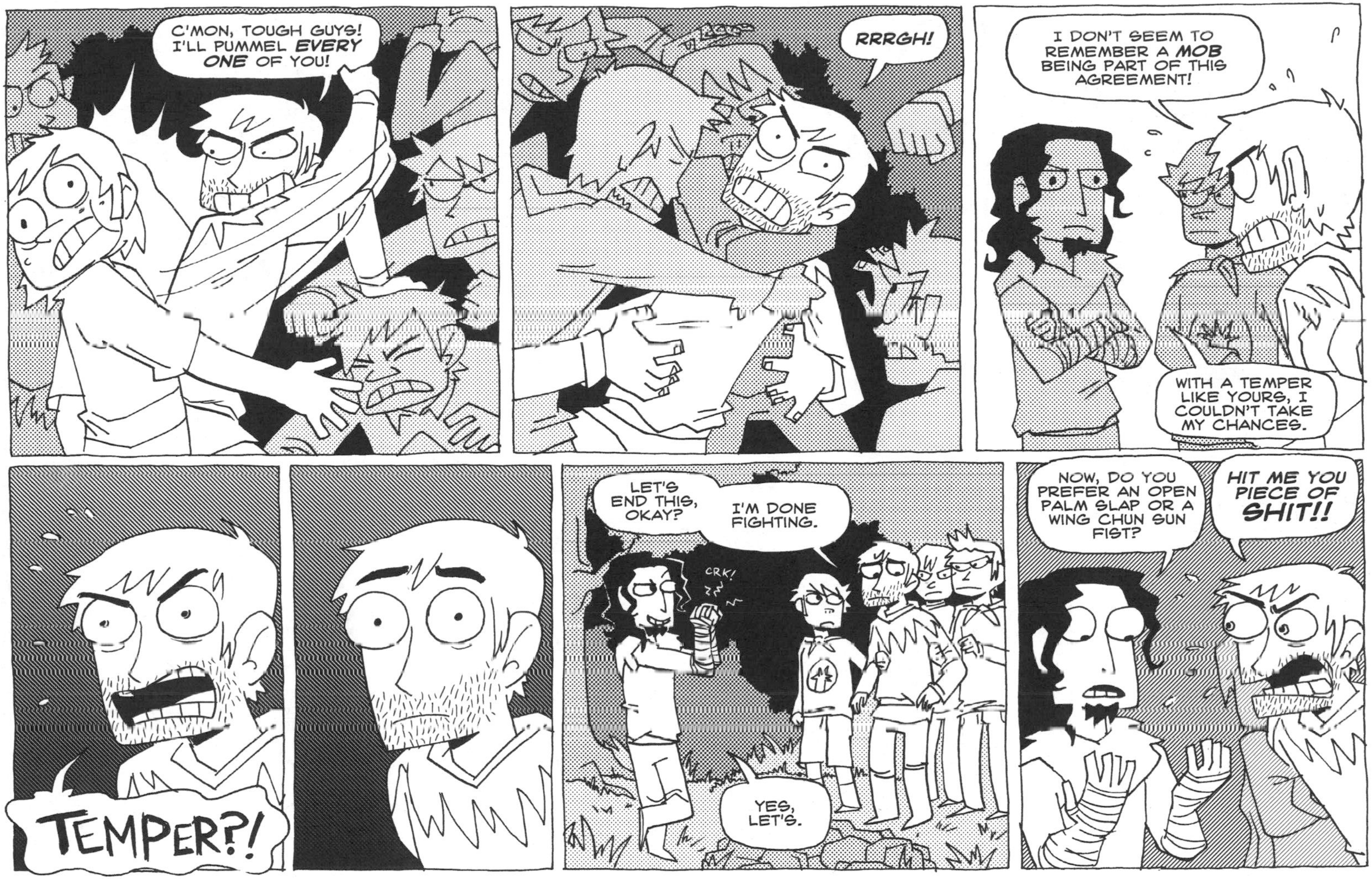
C'MON, TOUGH GUYS! I'LL PUMMEL EVERY ONE OF YOU!
RRRGH!
I DON'T SEEM TO REMEMBER A MOB BEING PART OF THIS AGREEMENT!
WITH A TEMPER LIKE YOURS, I COULDN'T TAKE MY CHANCES.
TEMPER?!
LET'S END THIS, OKAY?
I'M DONE FIGHTING.
CRK!
YES, LET'S.
NOW, DO YOU PREFER AN OPEN PALM SLAP OR A WING CHUN SUN FIST?
HIT ME YOU PIECE OF SHIT!!

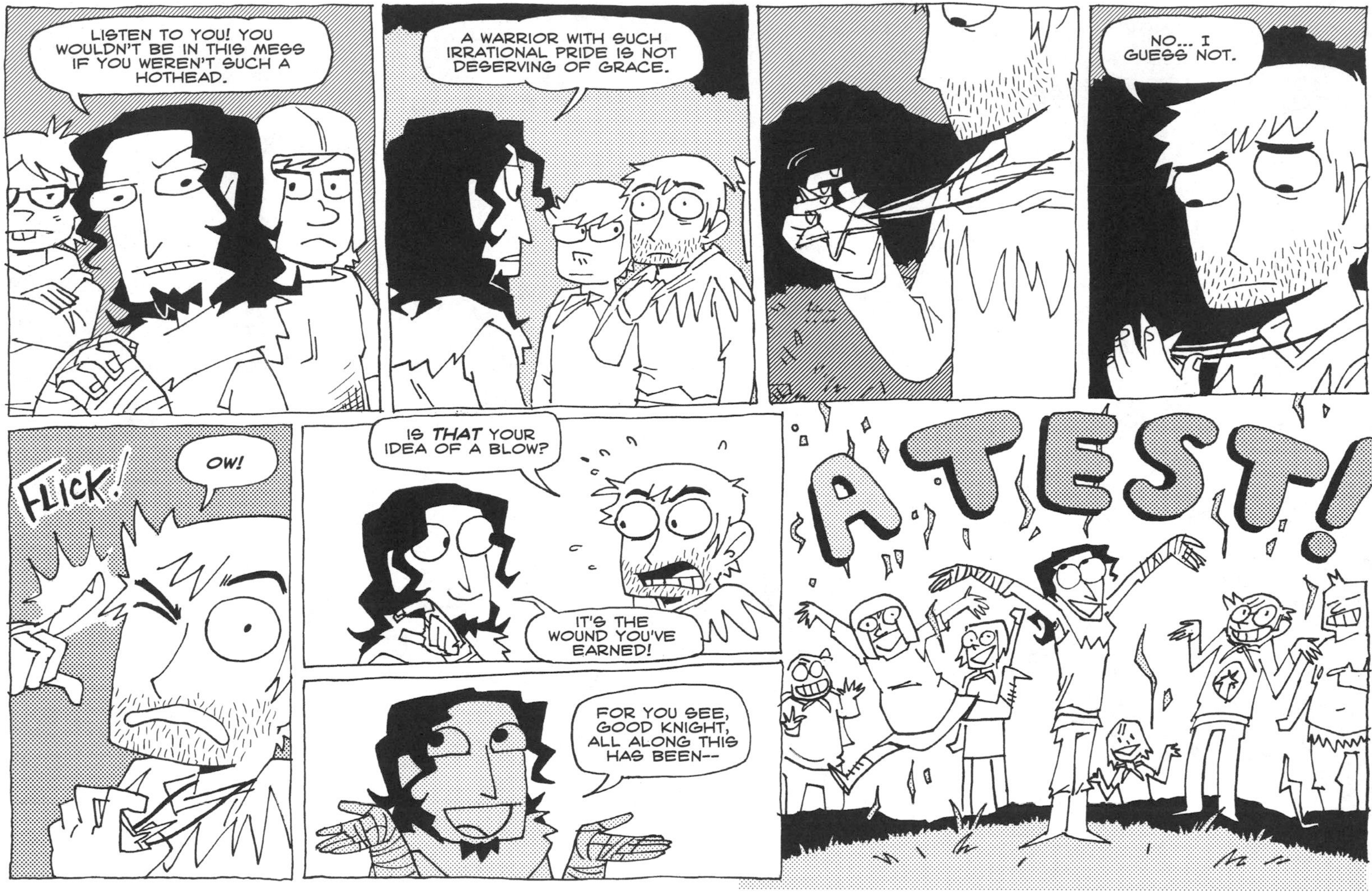

LISTEN TO YOU! YOU WOULDN'T BE IN THIS MESS IF YOU WEREN'T SUCH A HOTHEAD.
A WARRIOR WITH SUCH IRRATIONAL PRIDE IS NOT DESERVING OF GRACE.
NO... I GUESS NOT.
FLICK!
OW!
IS *THAT* YOUR IDEA OF A BLOW?
IT'S THE WOUND YOU'VE EARNED!
FOR YOU SEE, GOOD KNIGHT, ALL ALONG THIS HAS BEEN--
A TEST!

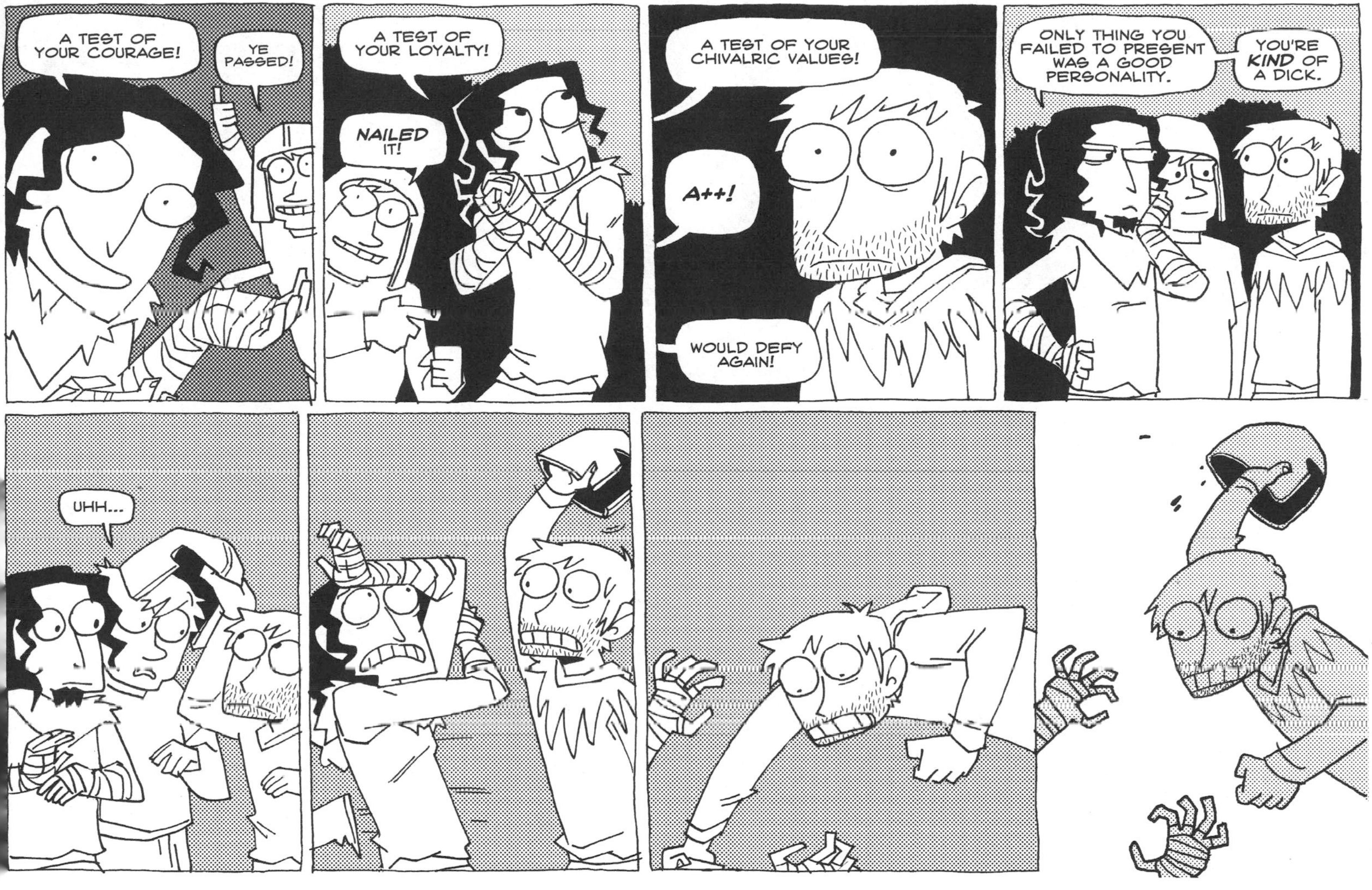
A TEST OF YOUR COURAGE!
YE PASSED!
A TEST OF YOUR LOYALTY!
NAILED IT!
A TEST OF YOUR CHIVALRIC VALUES!
A++!
WOULD DEFY AGAIN!
ONLY THING YOU FAILED TO PRESENT WAS A GOOD PERSONALITY.
YOU'RE KIND OF A DICK.
UHH...

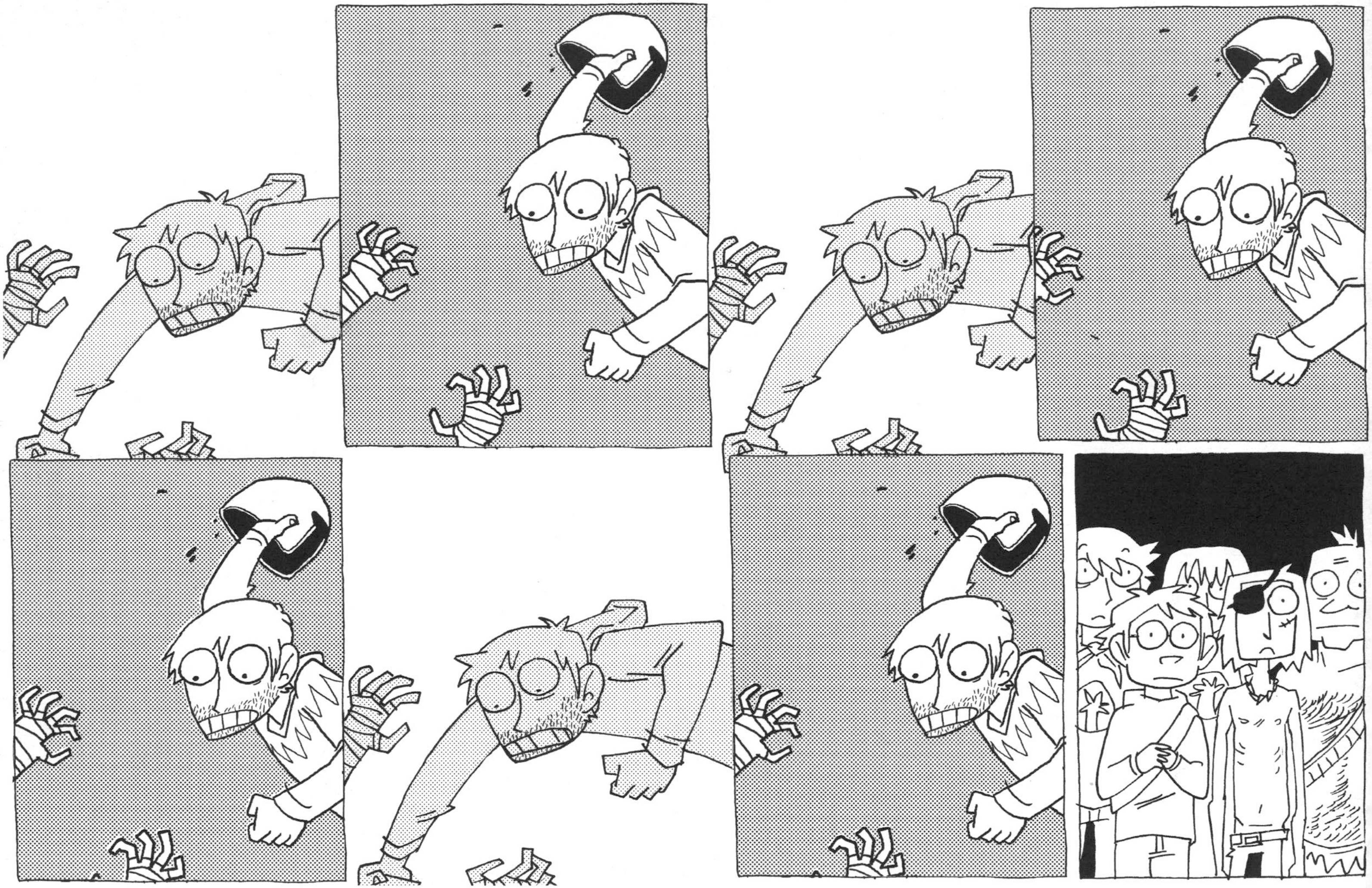

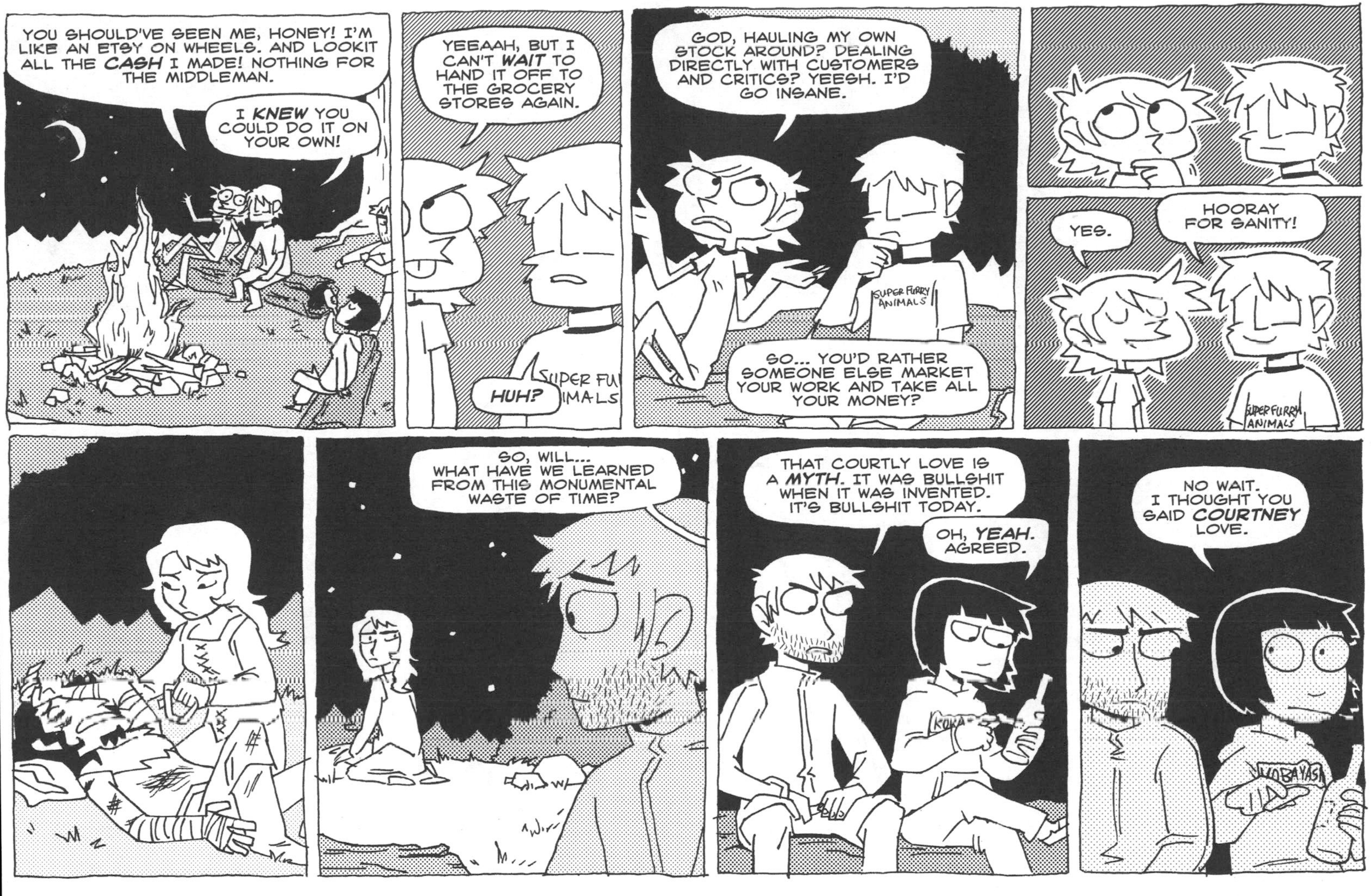
YOU SHOULD'VE SEEN ME, HONEY! I'M LIKE AN ETSY ON WHEELS. AND LOOKIT ALL THE CASH I MADE! NOTHING FOR THE MIDDLEMAN.
I KNEW YOU COULD DO IT ON YOUR OWN!
YEEAAH, BUT I CAN'T WAIT TO HAND IT OFF TO THE GROCERY STORES AGAIN.
HUH?
SUPER FU
IMALS
GOD, HAULING MY OWN STOCK AROUND? DEALING DIRECTLY WITH CUSTOMERS AND CRITICS? YEESH. I'D GO INSANE.
SUPER FURRY ANIMALS
SO... YOU'D RATHER SOMEONE ELSE MARKET YOUR WORK AND TAKE ALL YOUR MONEY?
YES.
HOORAY FOR SANITY!
SUPER FURRY ANIMALS
SO, WILL... WHAT HAVE WE LEARNED FROM THIS MONUMENTAL WASTE OF TIME?
THAT COURTLY LOVE IS A MYTH. IT WAS BULLSHIT WHEN IT WAS INVENTED. IT'S BULLSHIT TODAY.
OH, YEAH. AGREED.
NO WAIT. I THOUGHT YOU SAID COURTNEY LOVE.

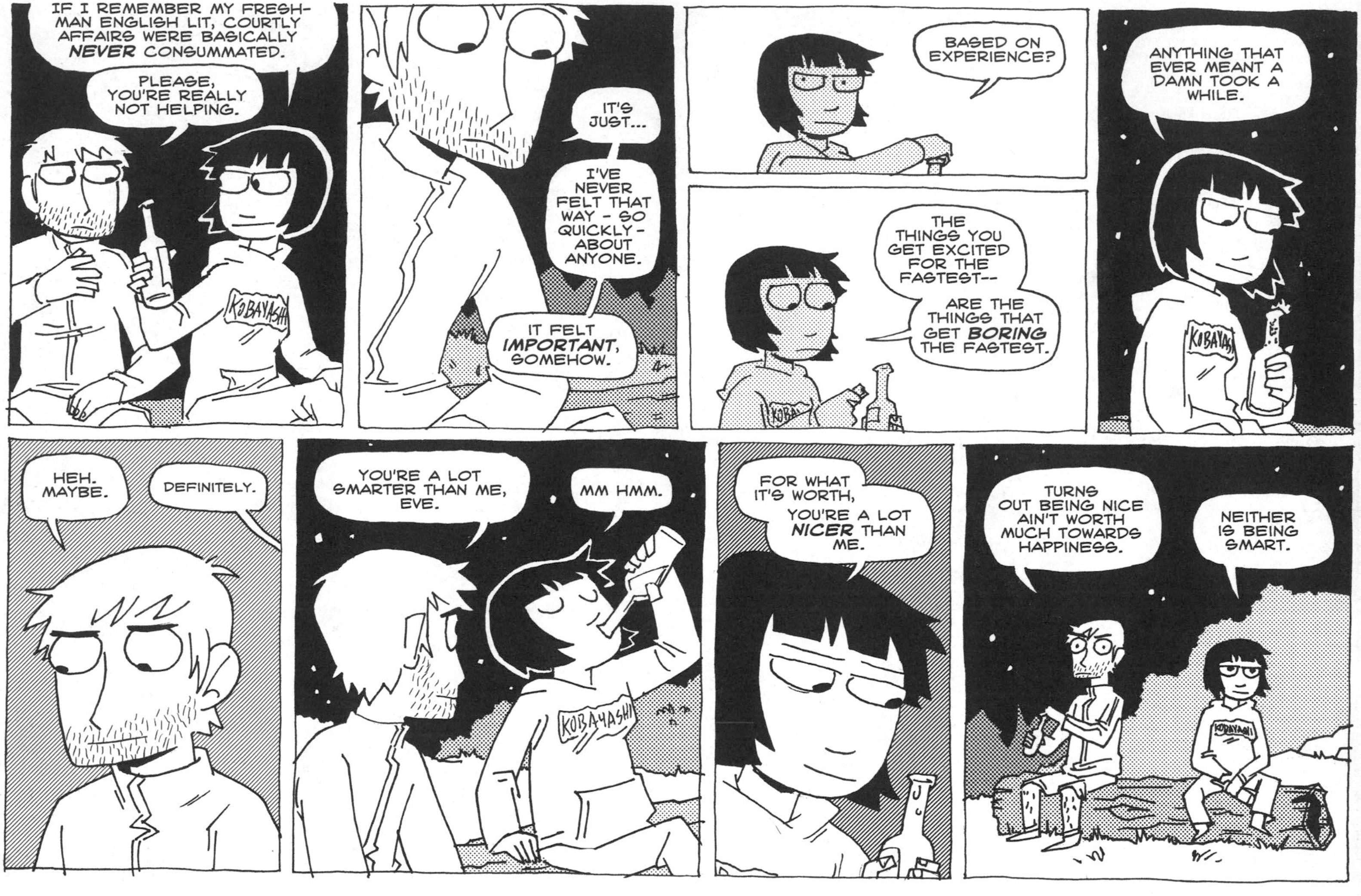
IF I REMEMBER MY FRESHMAN ENGLISH LIT, COURTLY AFFAIRS WERE BASICALLY NEVER CONSUMMATED.
PLEASE, YOU'RE REALLY NOT HELPING.
KOBAYASHI
IT'S JUST...
I'VE NEVER FELT THAT WAY - SO QUICKLY - ABOUT ANYONE.
IT FELT IMPORTANT, SOMEHOW.
BASED ON EXPERIENCE?
THE THINGS YOU GET EXCITED FOR THE FASTEST--
ARE THE THINGS THAT GET BORING THE FASTEST.
ANYTHING THAT EVER MEANT A DAMN TOOK A WHILE.
HEH. MAYBE.
DEFINITELY.
YOU'RE A LOT SMARTER THAN ME, EVE.
MM HMM.
KOBAYASHI
FOR WHAT IT'S WORTH,
YOU'RE A LOT NICER THAN ME.
TURNS OUT BEING NICE AIN'T WORTH MUCH TOWARDS HAPPINESS.
NEITHER IS BEING SMART.

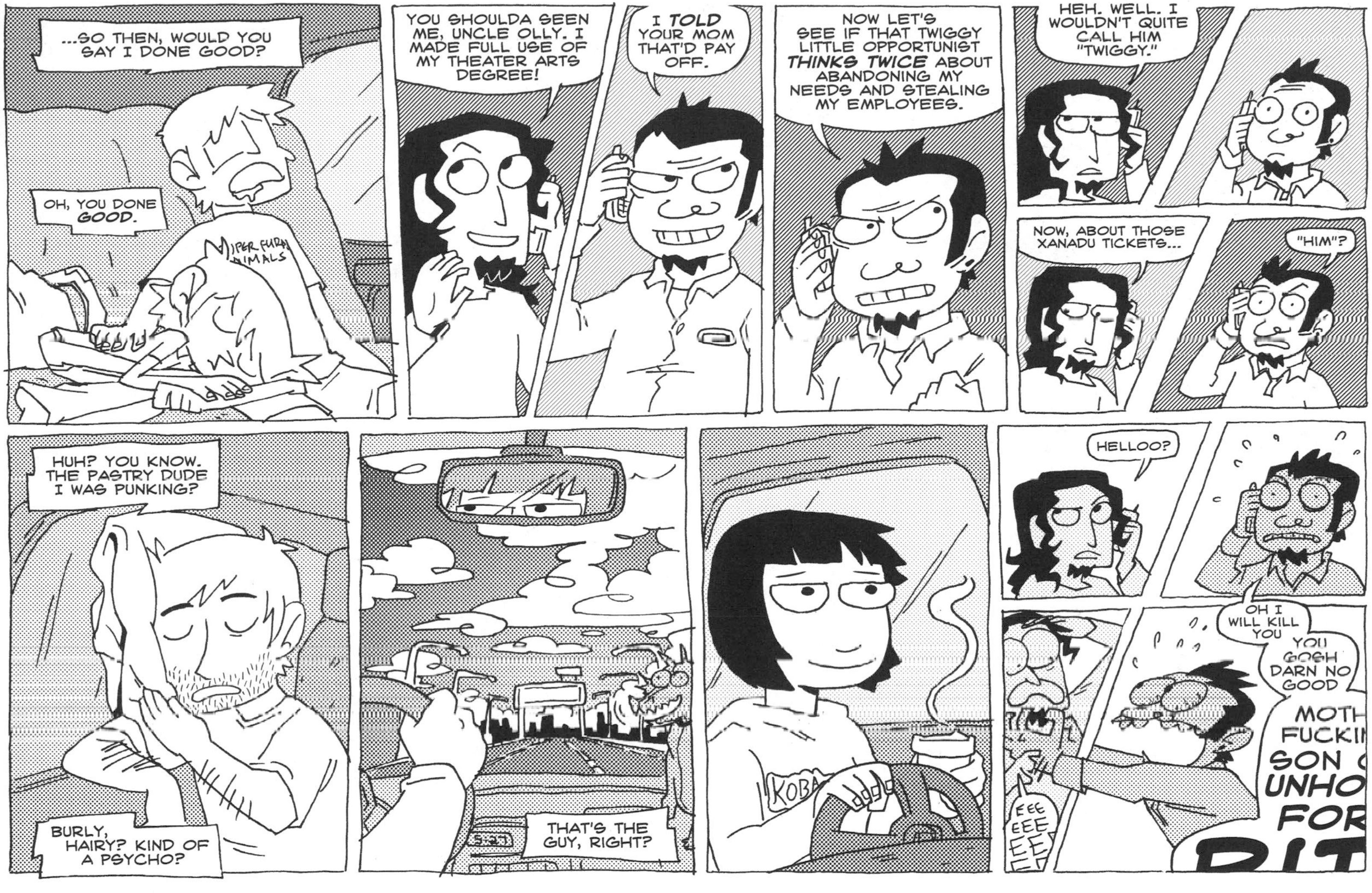
...SO THEN, WOULD YOU SAY I DONE GOOD?
OH, YOU DONE GOOD.
YOU SHOULDA SEEN ME, UNCLE OLLY. I MADE FULL USE OF MY THEATER ARTS DEGREE!
I TOLD YOUR MOM THAT'D PAY OFF.
NOW LET'S SEE IF THAT TWIGGY LITTLE OPPORTUNIST THINKS TWICE ABOUT ABANDONING MY NEEDS AND STEALING MY EMPLOYEES.
HEH. WELL. I WOULDN'T QUITE CALL HIM "TWIGGY."
NOW, ABOUT THOSE XANADU TICKETS...
"HIM"?
HUH? YOU KNOW. THE PASTRY DUDE I WAS PUNKING?
BURLY, HAIRY? KIND OF A PSYCHO?
THAT'S THE GUY, RIGHT?
HELLOO?
OH I WILL KILL YOU
YOU GOSH DARN NO GOOD
MOTH
FUCKIN
SON O
UNHO
FOR
EEE EEE EE

11

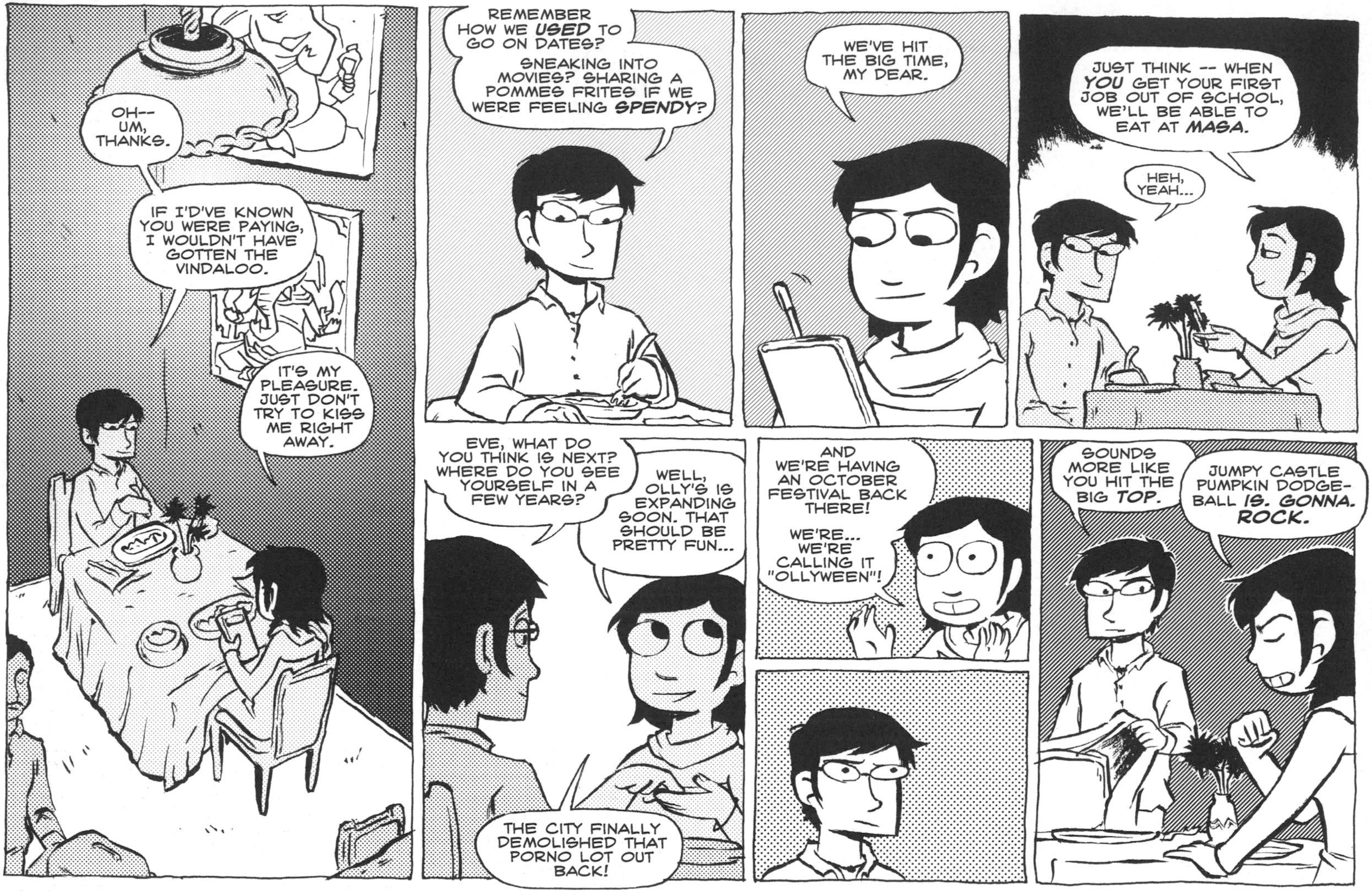
OH-- UM, THANKS.
IF I'D'VE KNOWN YOU WERE PAYING, I WOULDN'T HAVE GOTTEN THE VINDALOO.
IT'S MY PLEASURE. JUST DON'T TRY TO KISS ME RIGHT AWAY.
REMEMBER HOW WE *USED* TO GO ON DATES?
SNEAKING INTO MOVIES? SHARING A POMMES FRITES IF WE WERE FEELING *SPENDY*?
WE'VE HIT THE BIG TIME, MY DEAR.
JUST THINK -- WHEN *YOU* GET YOUR FIRST JOB OUT OF SCHOOL, WE'LL BE ABLE TO EAT AT *MASA*.
HEH, YEAH...
EVE, WHAT DO YOU THINK IS NEXT? WHERE DO YOU SEE YOURSELF IN A FEW YEARS?
WELL, OLLY'S IS EXPANDING SOON. THAT SHOULD BE PRETTY FUN...
THE CITY FINALLY DEMOLISHED THAT PORNO LOT OUT BACK!
AND WE'RE HAVING AN OCTOBER FESTIVAL BACK THERE!
WE'RE... WE'RE CALLING IT "OLLYWEEN"!
SOUNDS MORE LIKE YOU HIT THE BIG *TOP*.
JUMPY CASTLE PUMPKIN DODGE-BALL *IS. GONNA. ROCK.*

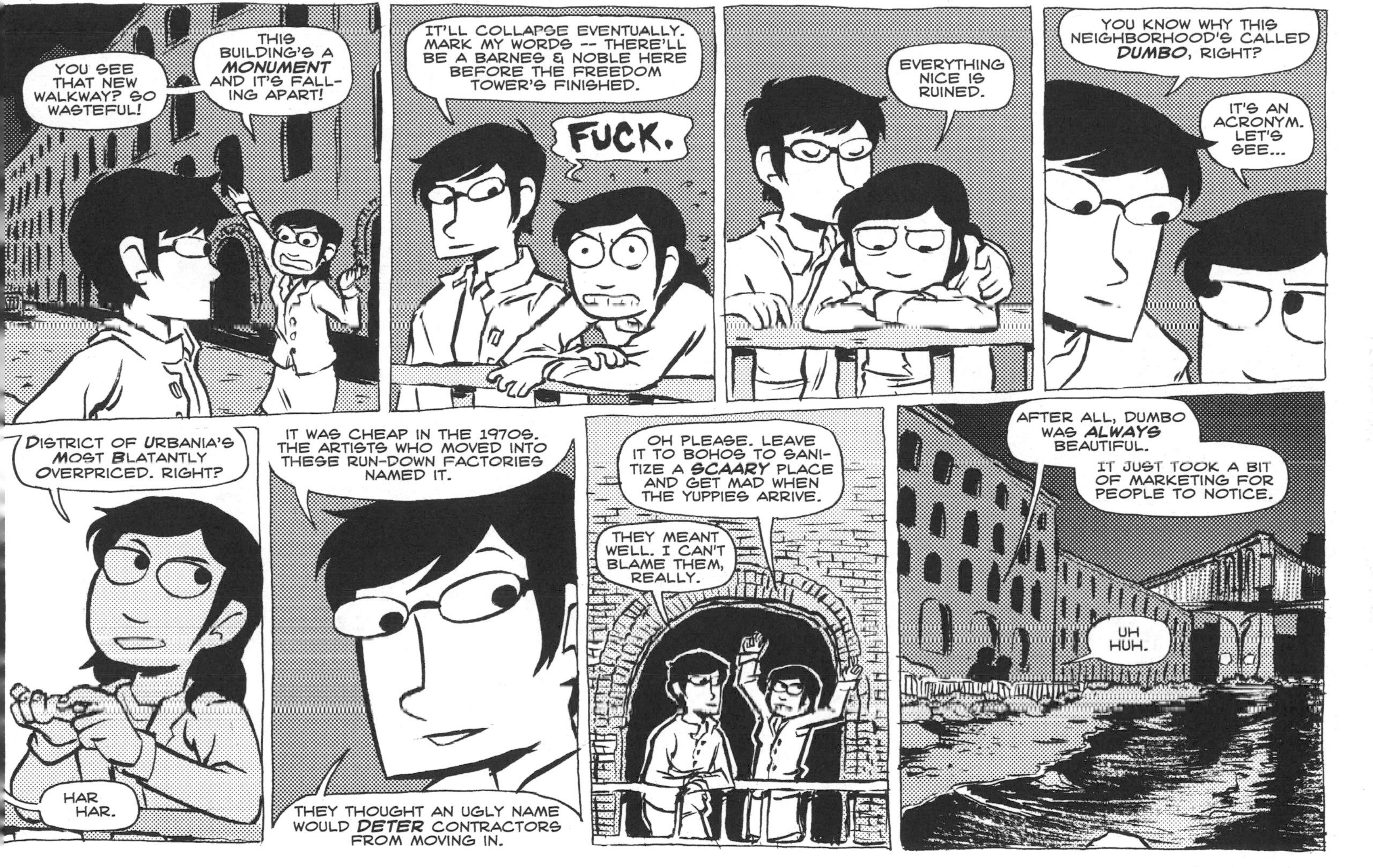

YOU SEE THAT NEW WALKWAY? SO WASTEFUL!
THIS BUILDING'S A MONUMENT AND IT'S FALLING APART!
IT'LL COLLAPSE EVENTUALLY. MARK MY WORDS -- THERE'LL BE A BARNES & NOBLE HERE BEFORE THE FREEDOM TOWER'S FINISHED.
FUCK.
EVERYTHING NICE IS RUINED.
YOU KNOW WHY THIS NEIGHBORHOOD'S CALLED DUMBO, RIGHT?
IT'S AN ACRONYM. LET'S SEE...
DISTRICT OF URBANIA'S MOST BLATANTLY OVERPRICED. RIGHT?
HAR HAR.
IT WAS CHEAP IN THE 1970S. THE ARTISTS WHO MOVED INTO THESE RUN-DOWN FACTORIES NAMED IT.
THEY THOUGHT AN UGLY NAME WOULD DETER CONTRACTORS FROM MOVING IN.
OH PLEASE. LEAVE IT TO BOHOS TO SANITIZE A SCAARY PLACE AND GET MAD WHEN THE YUPPIES ARRIVE.
THEY MEANT WELL. I CAN'T BLAME THEM, REALLY.
AFTER ALL, DUMBO WAS ALWAYS BEAUTIFUL.
IT JUST TOOK A BIT OF MARKETING FOR PEOPLE TO NOTICE.
UH HUH.

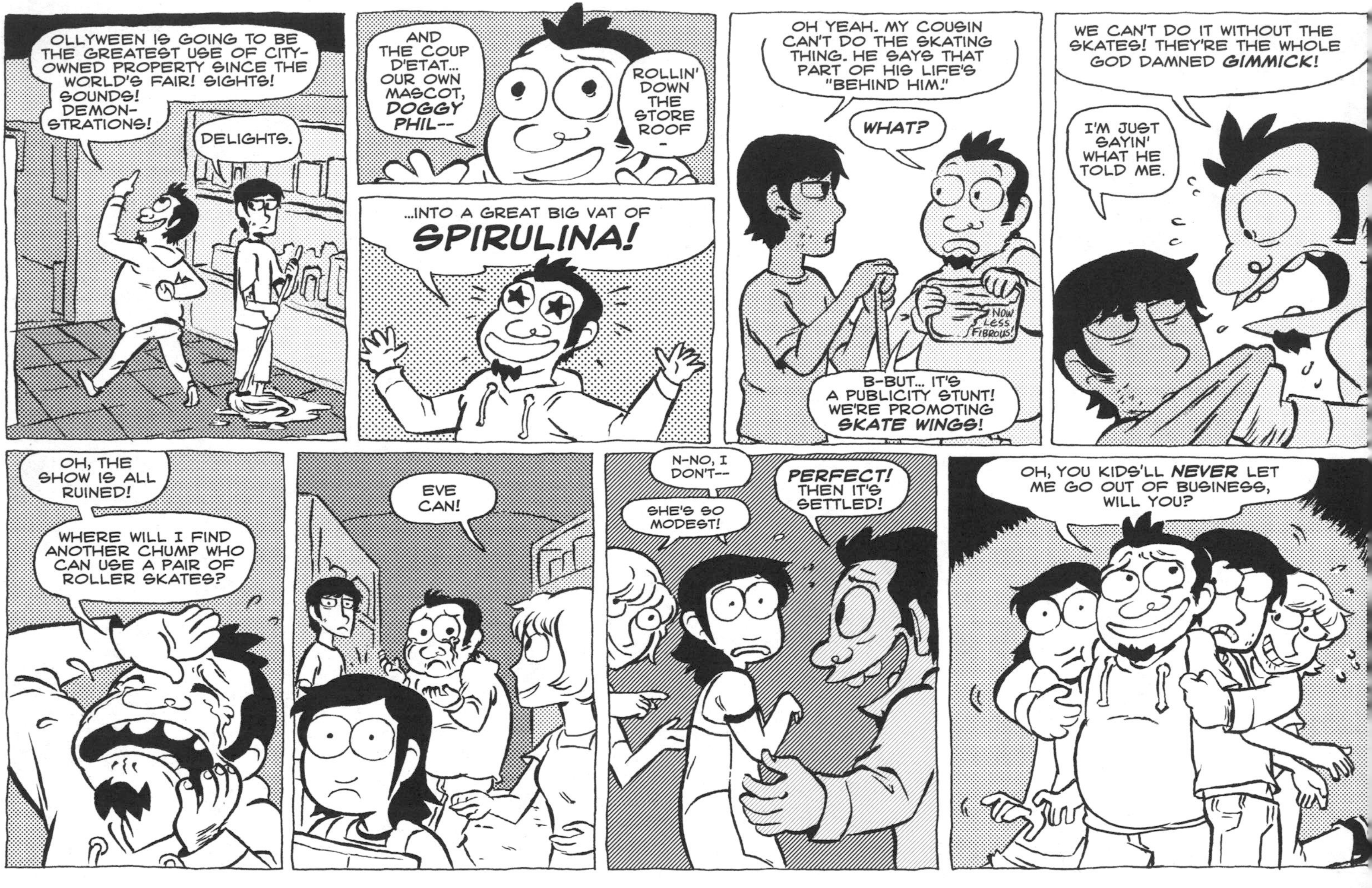

OLLYWEEN IS GOING TO BE THE GREATEST USE OF CITY-OWNED PROPERTY SINCE THE WORLD'S FAIR! SIGHTS! SOUNDS! DEMON-STRATIONS!
DELIGHTS.
AND THE COUP D'ETAT... OUR OWN MASCOT, DOGGY PHIL--
ROLLIN' DOWN THE STORE ROOF -
...INTO A GREAT BIG VAT OF SPIRULINA!
OH YEAH. MY COUSIN CAN'T DO THE SKATING THING. HE SAYS THAT PART OF HIS LIFE'S "BEHIND HIM."
WHAT?
NOW LESS FIBROUS!
B-BUT... IT'S A PUBLICITY STUNT! WE'RE PROMOTING SKATE WINGS!
WE CAN'T DO IT WITHOUT THE SKATES! THEY'RE THE WHOLE GOD DAMNED GIMMICK!
I'M JUST SAYIN' WHAT HE TOLD ME.
OH, THE SHOW IS ALL RUINED!
WHERE WILL I FIND ANOTHER CHUMP WHO CAN USE A PAIR OF ROLLER SKATES?
EVE CAN!
N-NO, I DON'T--
SHE'S SO MODEST!
PERFECT! THEN IT'S SETTLED!
OH, YOU KIDS'LL NEVER LET ME GO OUT OF BUSINESS, WILL YOU?

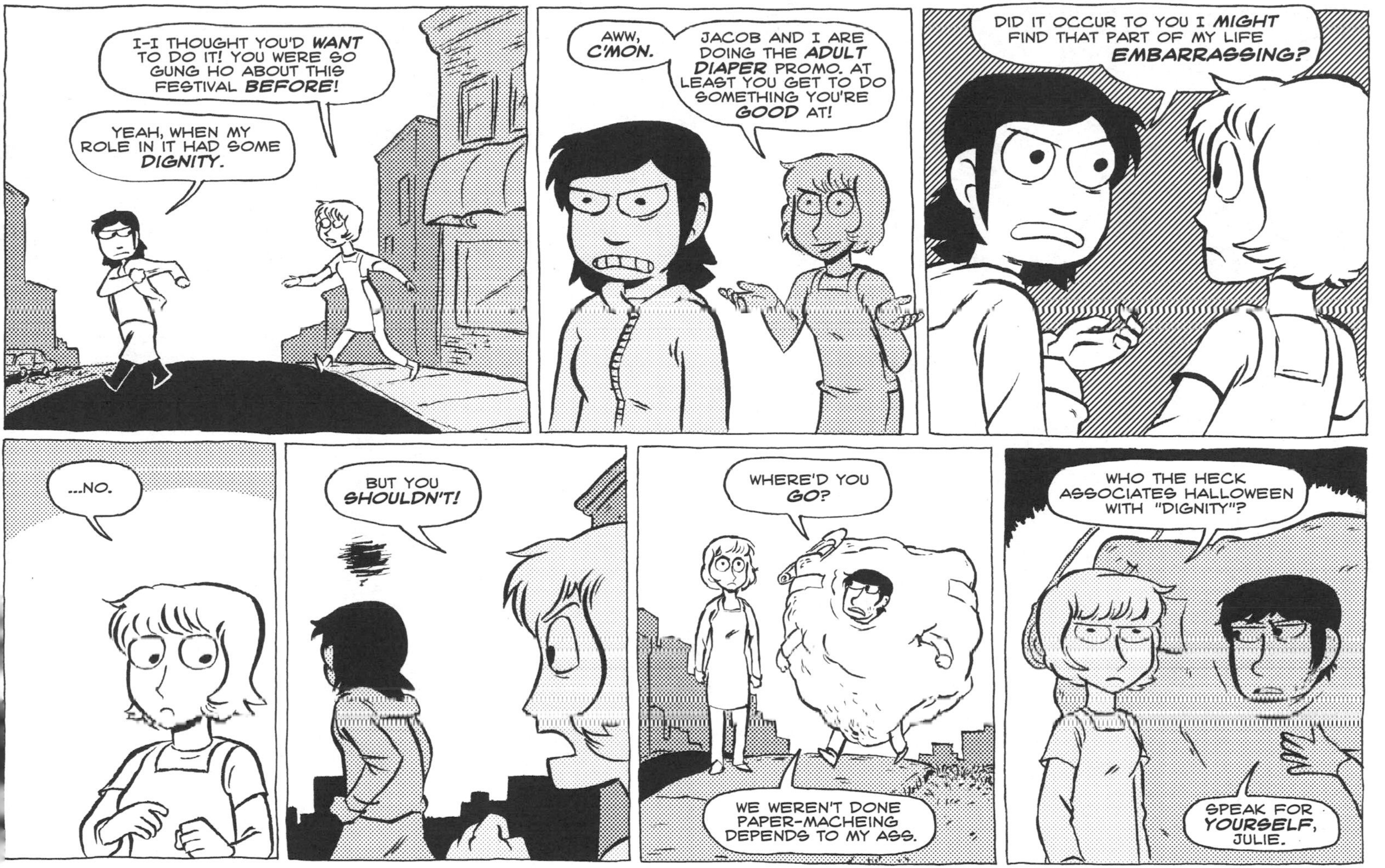
I-I THOUGHT YOU'D WANT TO DO IT! YOU WERE SO GUNG HO ABOUT THIS FESTIVAL BEFORE!
YEAH, WHEN MY ROLE IN IT HAD SOME DIGNITY.
AWW, C'MON.
JACOB AND I ARE DOING THE ADULT DIAPER PROMO. AT LEAST YOU GET TO DO SOMETHING YOU'RE GOOD AT!
DID IT OCCUR TO YOU I MIGHT FIND THAT PART OF MY LIFE EMBARRASSING?
...NO.
BUT YOU SHOULDN'T!
WHERE'D YOU GO?
WE WEREN'T DONE PAPER-MACHEING DEPENDS TO MY ASS.
WHO THE HECK ASSOCIATES HALLOWEEN WITH "DIGNITY"?
SPEAK FOR YOURSELF, JULIE.

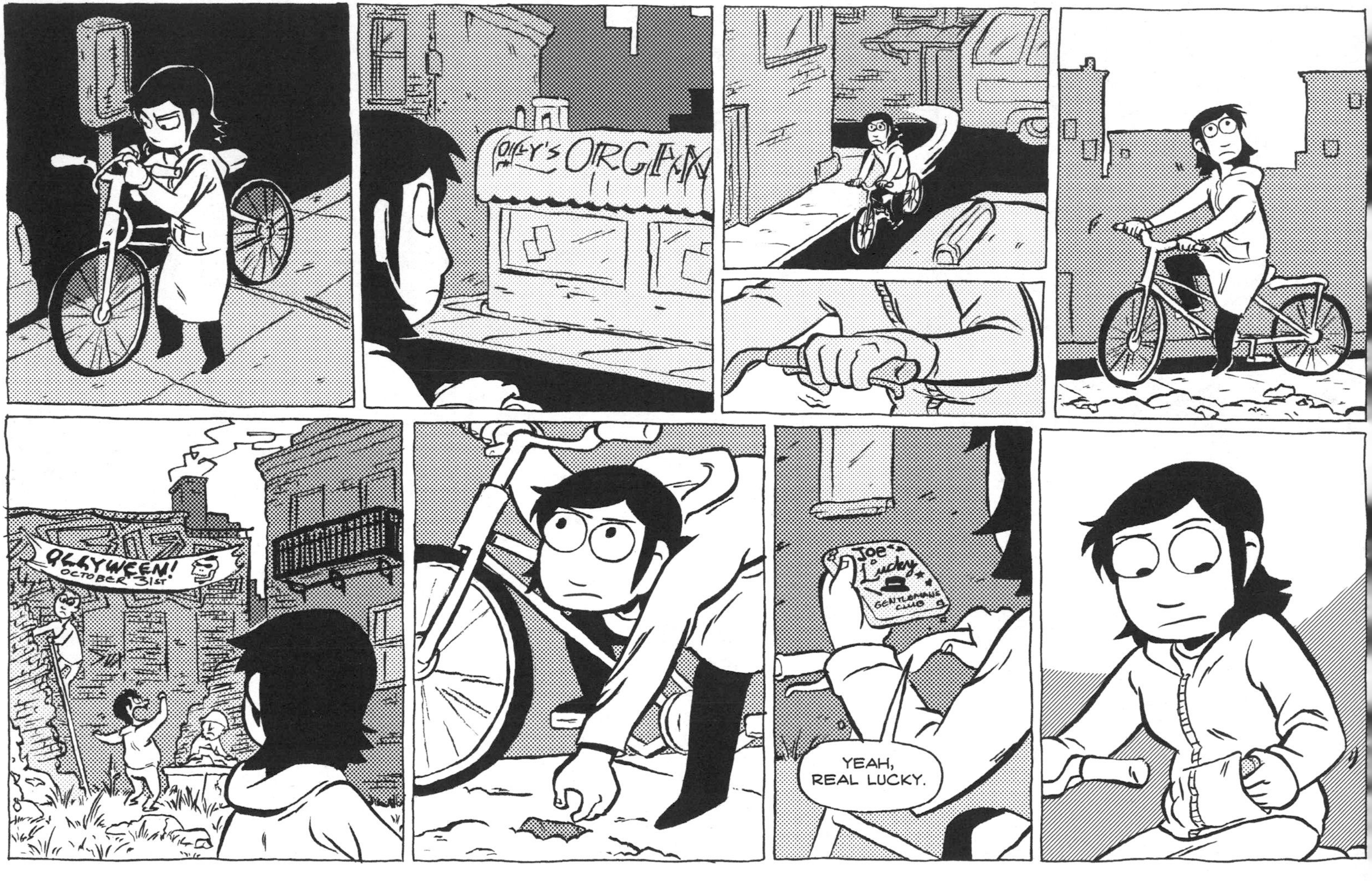
OLLYWEEN!
OCTOBER 31ST
Joe Lucky
YEAH, REAL LUCKY.

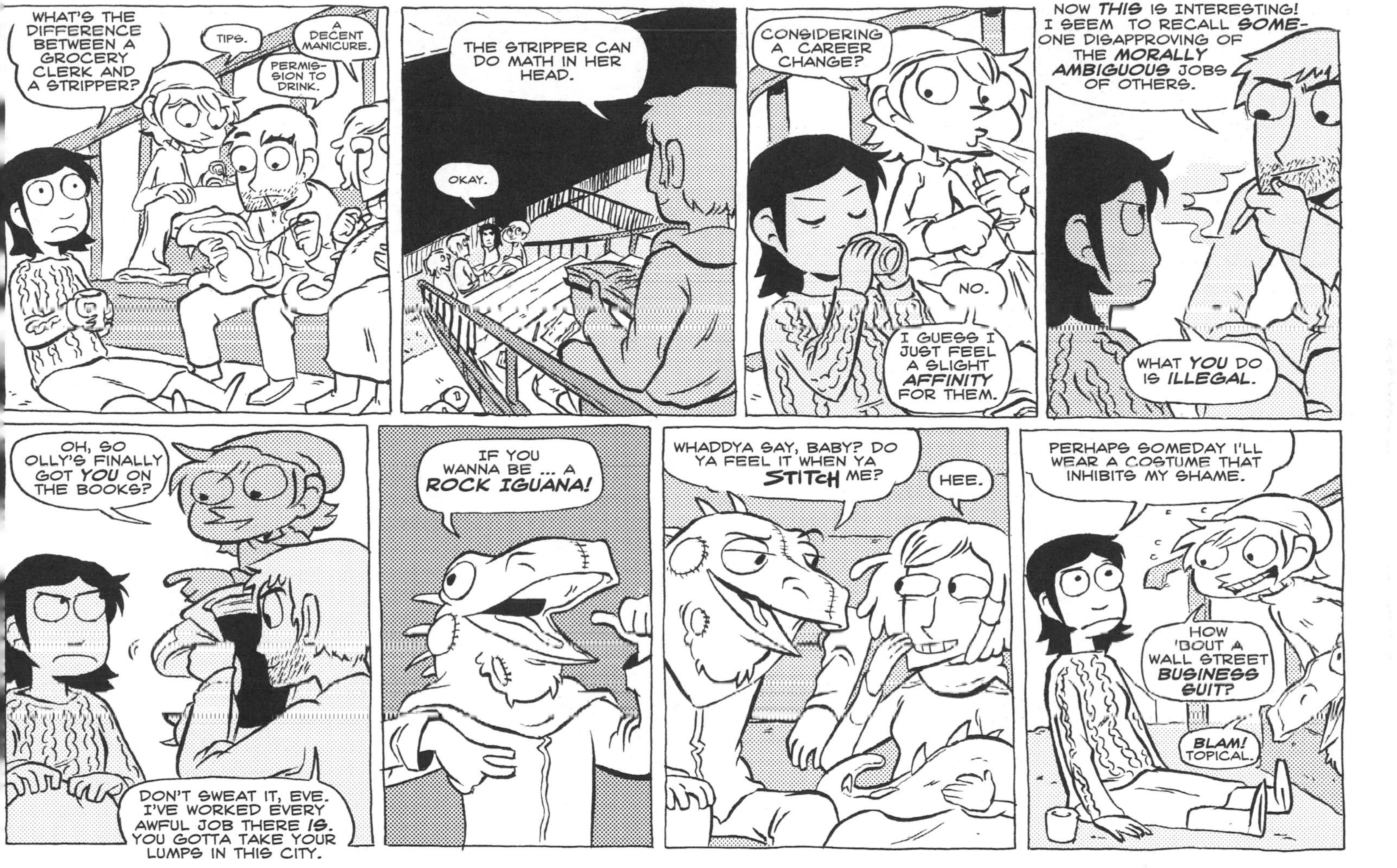
WHAT'S THE DIFFERENCE BETWEEN A GROCERY CLERK AND A STRIPPER?
TIPS.
A DECENT MANICURE.
PERMISSION TO DRINK.
THE STRIPPER CAN DO MATH IN HER HEAD.
OKAY.
CONSIDERING A CAREER CHANGE?
NO.
I GUESS I JUST FEEL A SLIGHT AFFINITY FOR THEM.
NOW THIS IS INTERESTING! I SEEM TO RECALL SOMEONE DISAPPROVING OF THE MORALLY AMBIGUOUS JOBS OF OTHERS.
WHAT YOU DO IS ILLEGAL.
OH, SO OLLY'S FINALLY GOT YOU ON THE BOOKS?
DON'T SWEAT IT, EVE. I'VE WORKED EVERY AWFUL JOB THERE IS. YOU GOTTA TAKE YOUR LUMPS IN THIS CITY.
IF YOU WANNA BE ... A ROCK IGUANA!
WHADDYA SAY, BABY? DO YA FEEL IT WHEN YA STITCH ME?
HEE.
PERHAPS SOMEDAY I'LL WEAR A COSTUME THAT INHIBITS MY SHAME.
HOW 'BOUT A WALL STREET BUSINESS SUIT?
BLAM! TOPICAL.

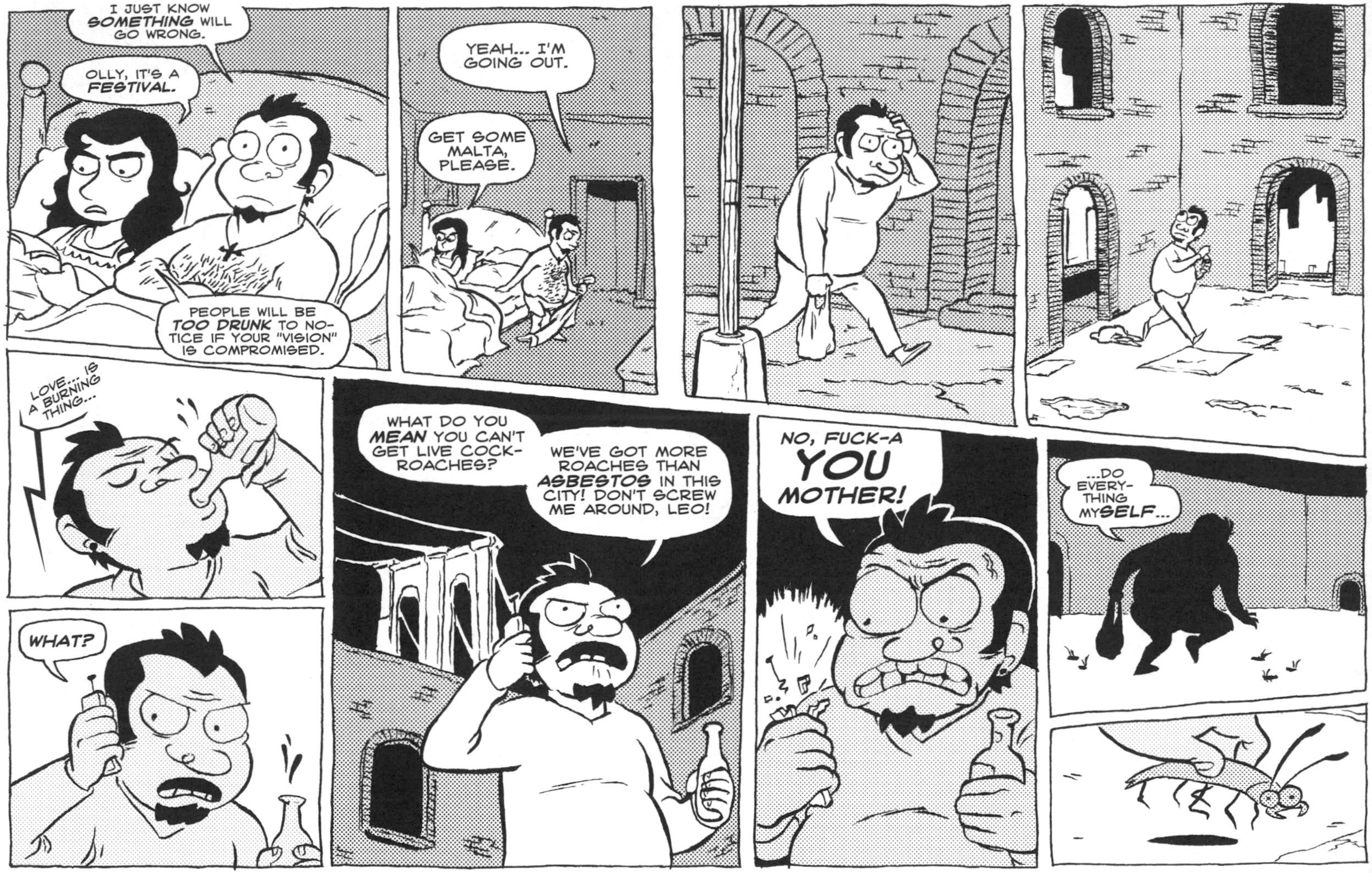
I JUST KNOW SOMETHING WILL GO WRONG.
OLLY, IT'S A FESTIVAL.
PEOPLE WILL BE TOO DRUNK TO NOTICE IF YOUR "VISION" IS COMPROMISED.
YEAH... I'M GOING OUT.
GET SOME MALTA, PLEASE.
LOVE... IS A BURNING THING...
WHAT?
WHAT DO YOU MEAN YOU CAN'T GET LIVE COCK-ROACHES?
WE'VE GOT MORE ROACHES THAN ASBESTOS IN THIS CITY! DON'T SCREW ME AROUND, LEO!
NO, FUCK-A YOU MOTHER!
...DO EVERY-THING MYSELF...

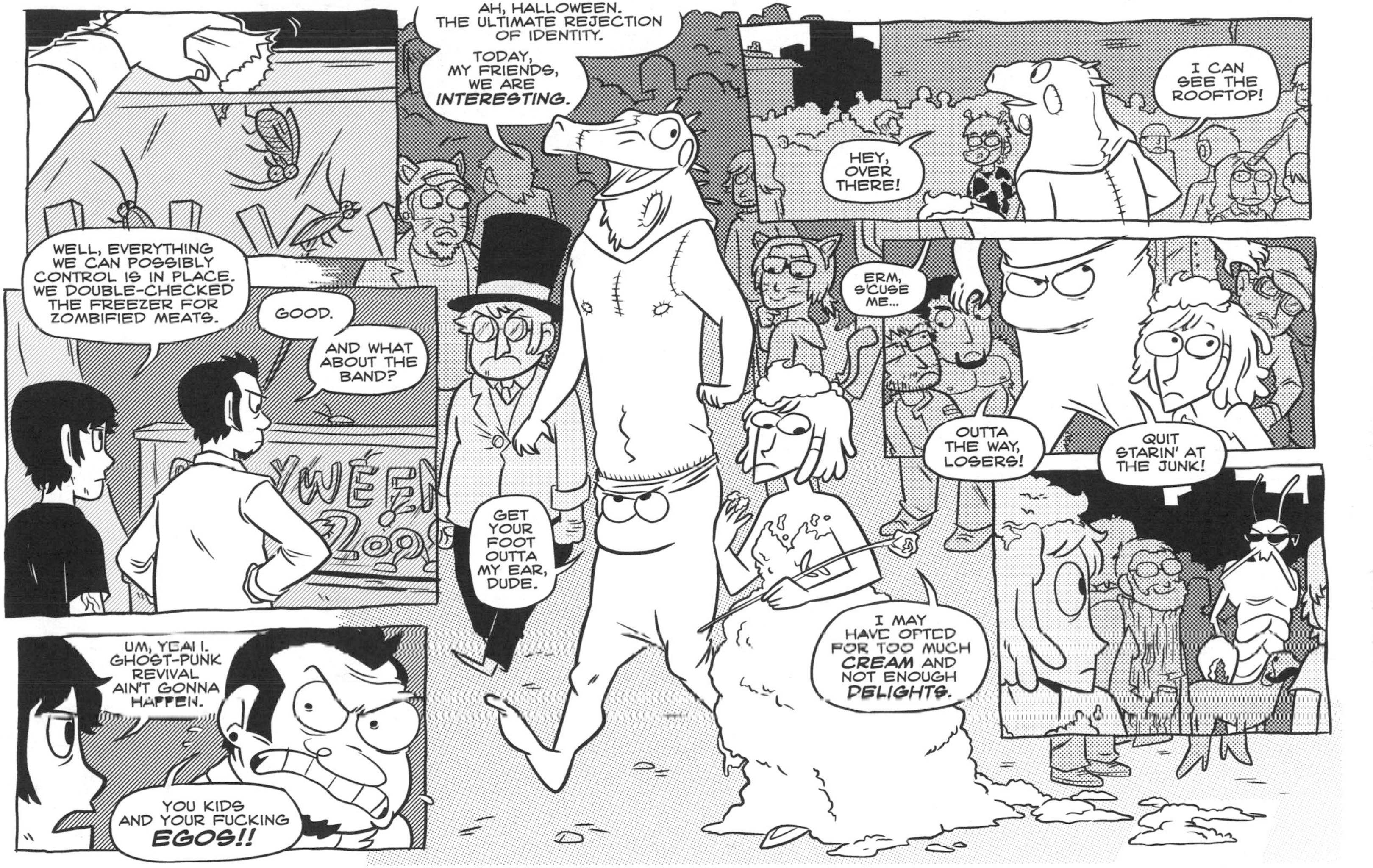
WELL, EVERYTHING WE CAN POSSIBLY CONTROL IS IN PLACE. WE DOUBLE-CHECKED THE FREEZER FOR ZOMBIFIED MEATS.
GOOD.
AND WHAT ABOUT THE BAND?
UM, YEAH. GHOST-PUNK REVIVAL AIN'T GONNA HAPPEN.
YOU KIDS AND YOUR FUCKING EGOS!!
AH, HALLOWEEN. THE ULTIMATE REJECTION OF IDENTITY.
TODAY, MY FRIENDS, WE ARE INTERESTING.
GET YOUR FOOT OUTTA MY EAR, DUDE.
I MAY HAVE OPTED FOR TOO MUCH CREAM AND NOT ENOUGH DELIGHTS.
HEY, OVER THERE!
I CAN SEE THE ROOFTOP!
ERM, S'CUSE ME...
OUTTA THE WAY, LOSERS!
QUIT STARIN' AT THE JUNK!

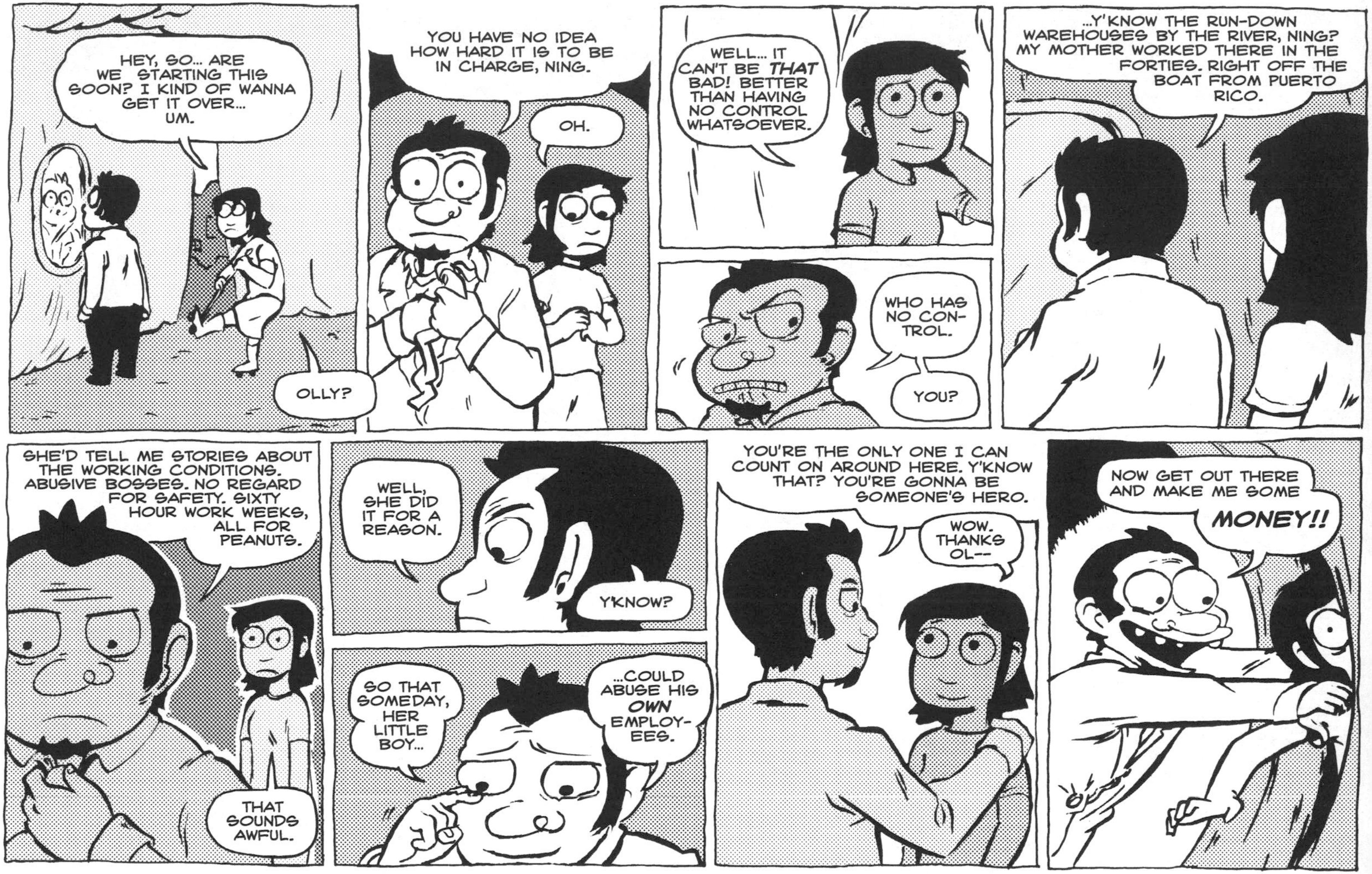
HEY, SO... ARE WE STARTING THIS SOON? I KIND OF WANNA GET IT OVER... UM.
OLLY?
YOU HAVE NO IDEA HOW HARD IT IS TO BE IN CHARGE, NING.
OH.
WELL... IT CAN'T BE *THAT* BAD! BETTER THAN HAVING NO CONTROL WHATSOEVER.
WHO HAS NO CON-TROL.
YOU?
...Y'KNOW THE RUN-DOWN WAREHOUSES BY THE RIVER, NING? MY MOTHER WORKED THERE IN THE FORTIES. RIGHT OFF THE BOAT FROM PUERTO RICO.
SHE'D TELL ME STORIES ABOUT THE WORKING CONDITIONS. ABUSIVE BOSSES. NO REGARD FOR SAFETY. SIXTY HOUR WORK WEEKS, ALL FOR PEANUTS.
THAT SOUNDS AWFUL.
WELL, SHE DID IT FOR A REASON.
Y'KNOW?
SO THAT SOMEDAY, HER LITTLE BOY...
...COULD ABUSE HIS *OWN* EMPLOY-EES.
YOU'RE THE ONLY ONE I CAN COUNT ON AROUND HERE. Y'KNOW THAT? YOU'RE GONNA BE SOMEONE'S HERO.
WOW. THANKS OL--
NOW GET OUT THERE AND MAKE ME SOME
MONEY!!

...AND MAY I REMIND YOU, **DIGNITY BRAND** ADULT DIAPERS ARE A LONG-TERM INVESTMENT. STOCK UP TODAY FOR TOMORROW'S INCONTINENCE.

NOW WITHOUT FURTHER ADO, WE'D LIKE TO WELCOME YOU TO THE FIRST-ANNUAL **OLLYWEEN FESTIVAL!** *WOOO!*

WOO.

MEH.

MEH!

HELL MEH!

UNFORTUNATELY, DJ FRAPPLE COULDN'T MAKE IT. SO ERIC'S FLORIDA ROOM WILL BE THE OPENING ACT.

AS SOON AS THEY ARRIVE.

OH, GOOD! HERE TH--

NO WAY. *ALL* OF YOU?

ALL OF *US?*

YOU SAID YOU WERE GONNA COME AS MY *MOM!*

YOU PEOPLE ARE SO *FUCKING* UNCREATIVE.

OH, THERE'S NO WAY. WE ARE *NOT* PLAYING LIKE THIS.

WHY SUCH A WHINY *BITCH,* ERIC?

GUESS WE HAVE NO BAND, THEN.

MEHHHHHH!!!

WILL, THIS IS OUR CHANCE! LET'S GET UP ON THE STAGE!

Y-YEAH? SHOULD WE DO IT?

GUYS. *WAIT!*

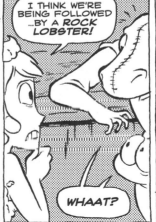

I THINK WE'RE BEING FOLLOWED ...BY A *ROCK LOBSTER!*

WHAAT?

THE ROCK IGUANA'S NATURAL ENEMY.

AND A SUPERIOR KEYTARIST TO BOOT.

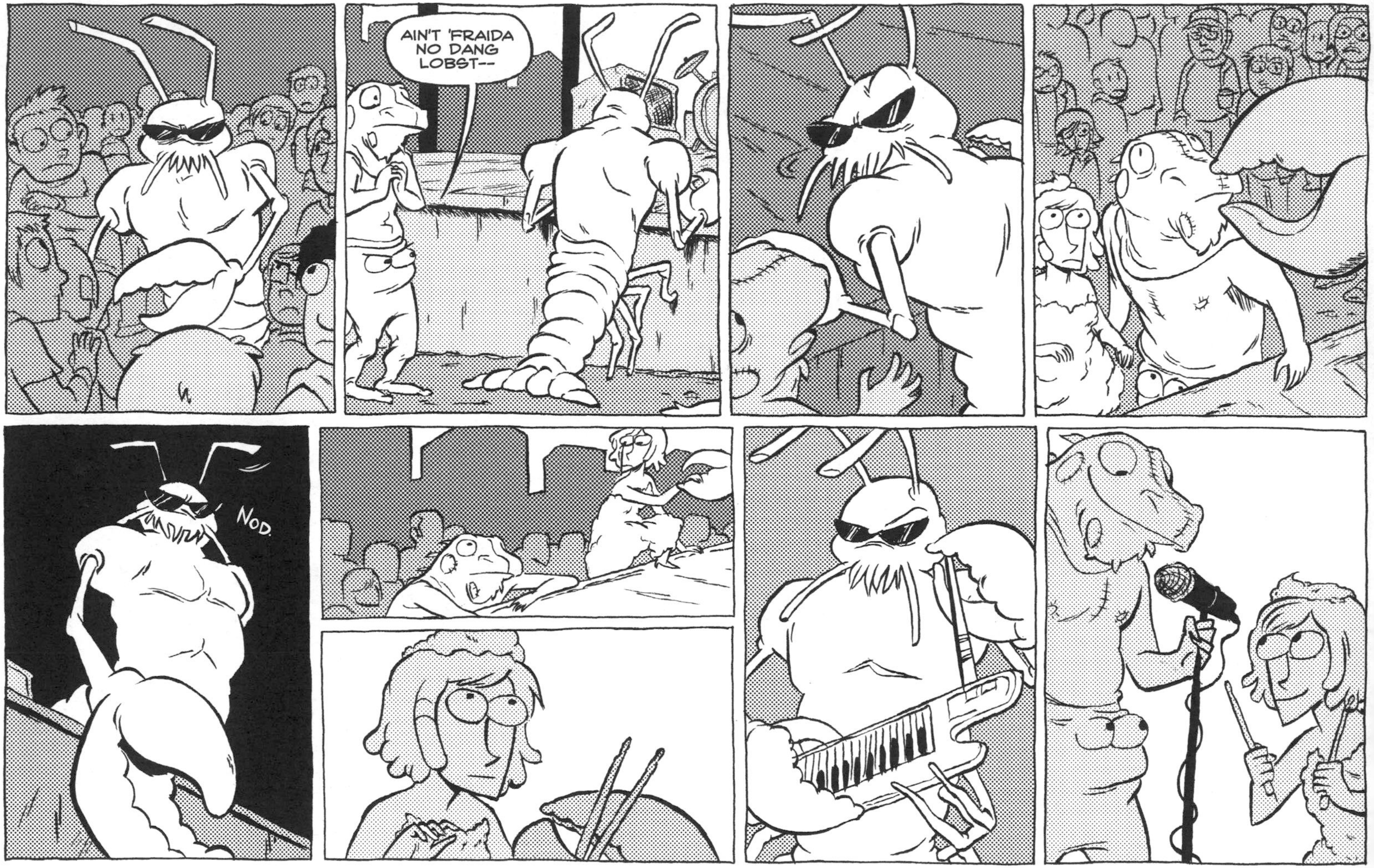

AIN'T 'FRAIDA NO DANG LOBST--
NOD.

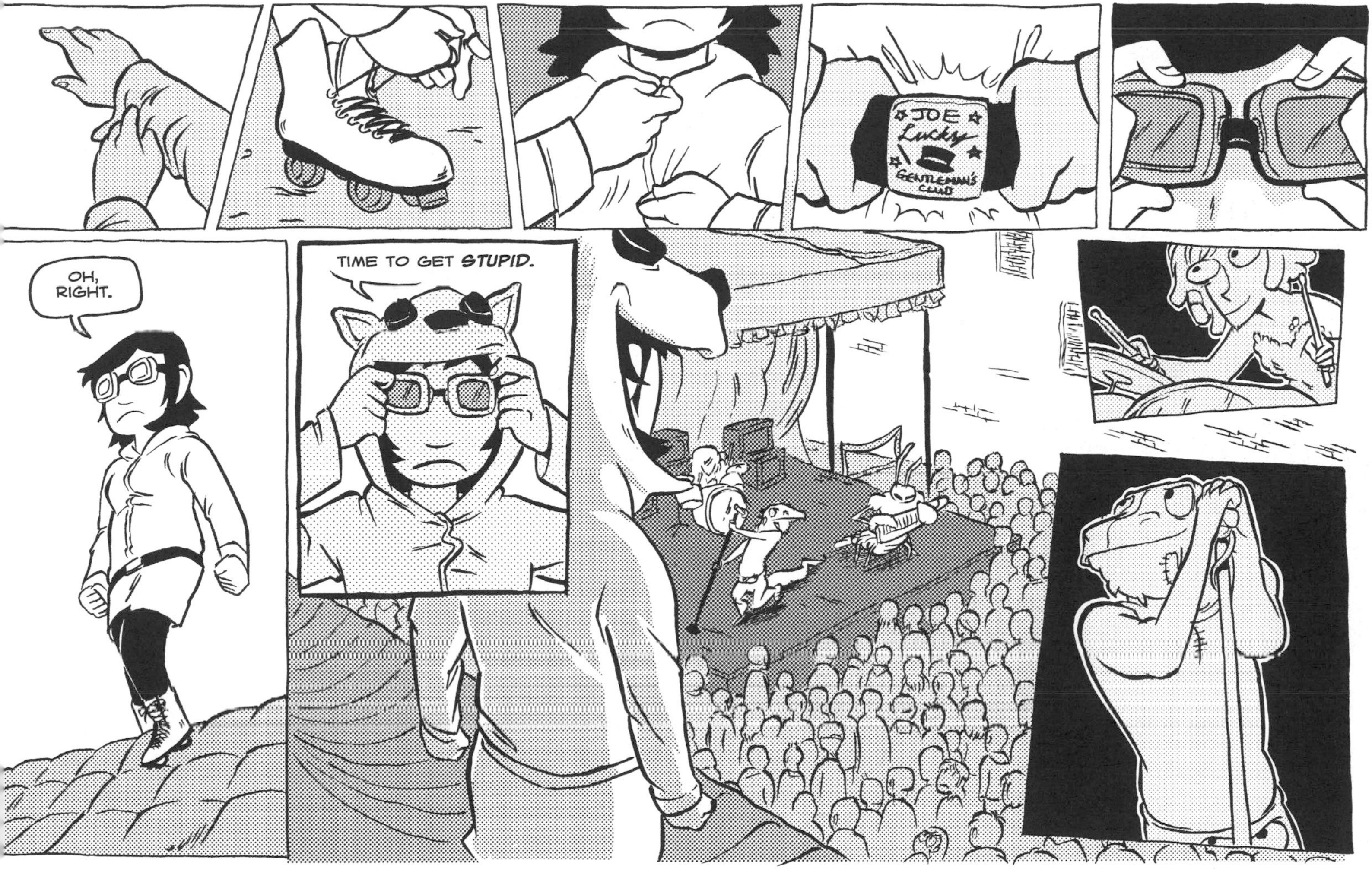
JOE Lucky GENTLEMAN'S CLUB
OH, RIGHT.
TIME TO GET STUPID.

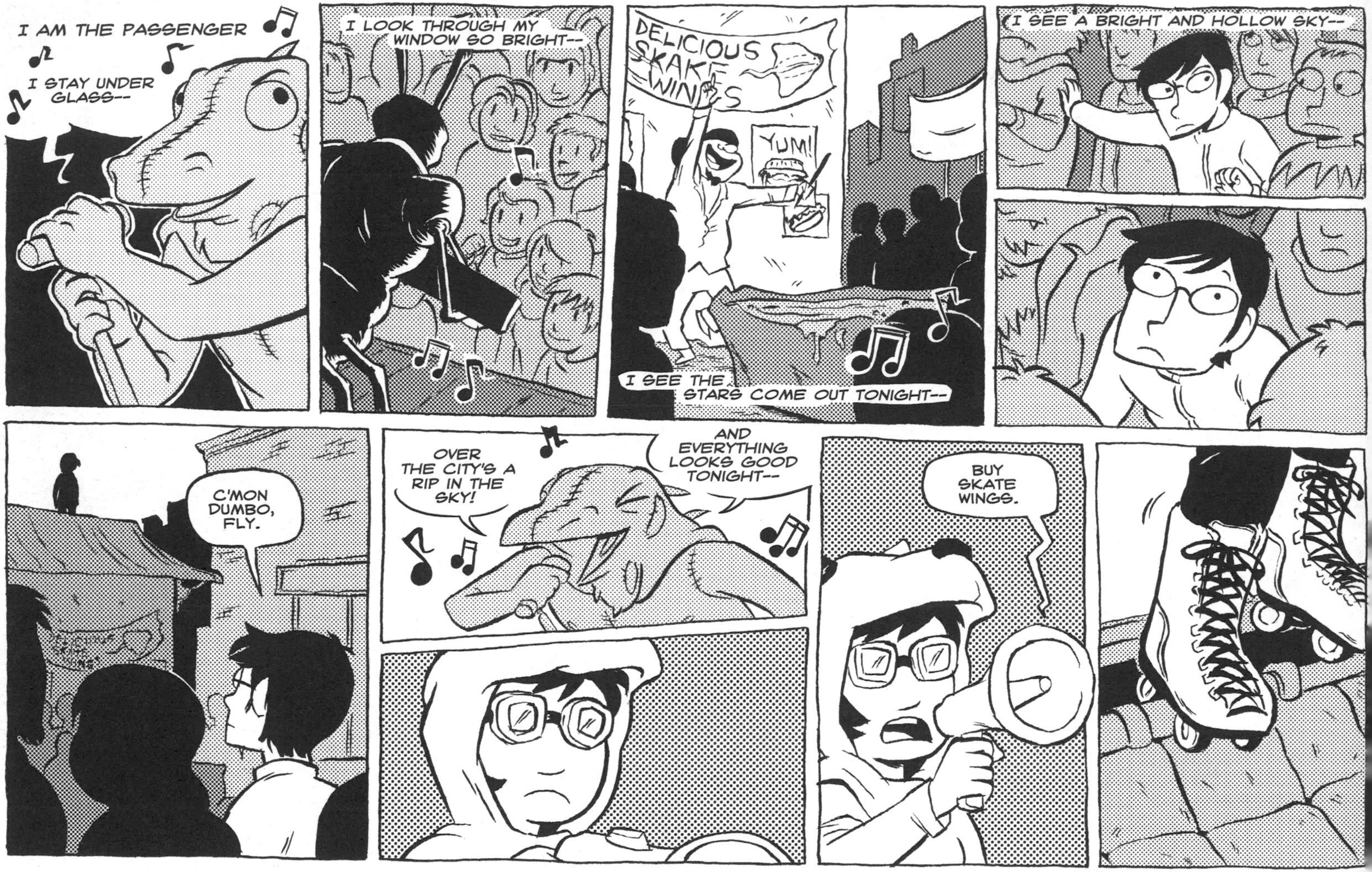
I AM THE PASSENGER
I STAY UNDER GLASS--
I LOOK THROUGH MY WINDOW SO BRIGHT--
DELICIOUS SKAKE WINGS
YUM!
I SEE THE STARS COME OUT TONIGHT--
I SEE A BRIGHT AND HOLLOW SKY--
C'MON DUMBO, FLY.
OVER THE CITY'S A RIP IN THE SKY!
AND EVERYTHING LOOKS GOOD TONIGHT--
BUY SKATE WINGS.

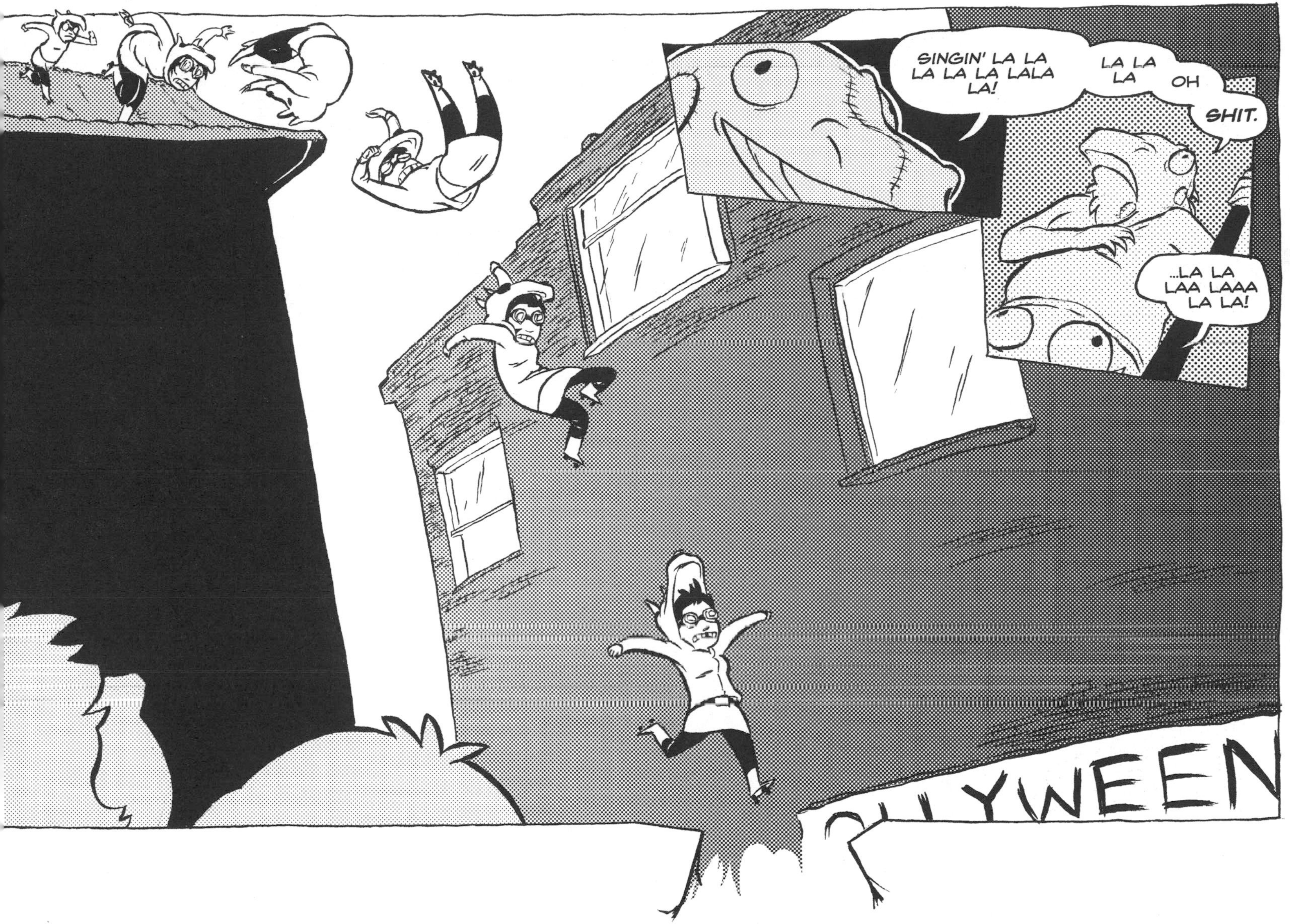
SINGIN' LA LA LA LA LA LALA LA!
LA LA LA OH
SHIT.
...LA LA LAA LAAA LA LA!

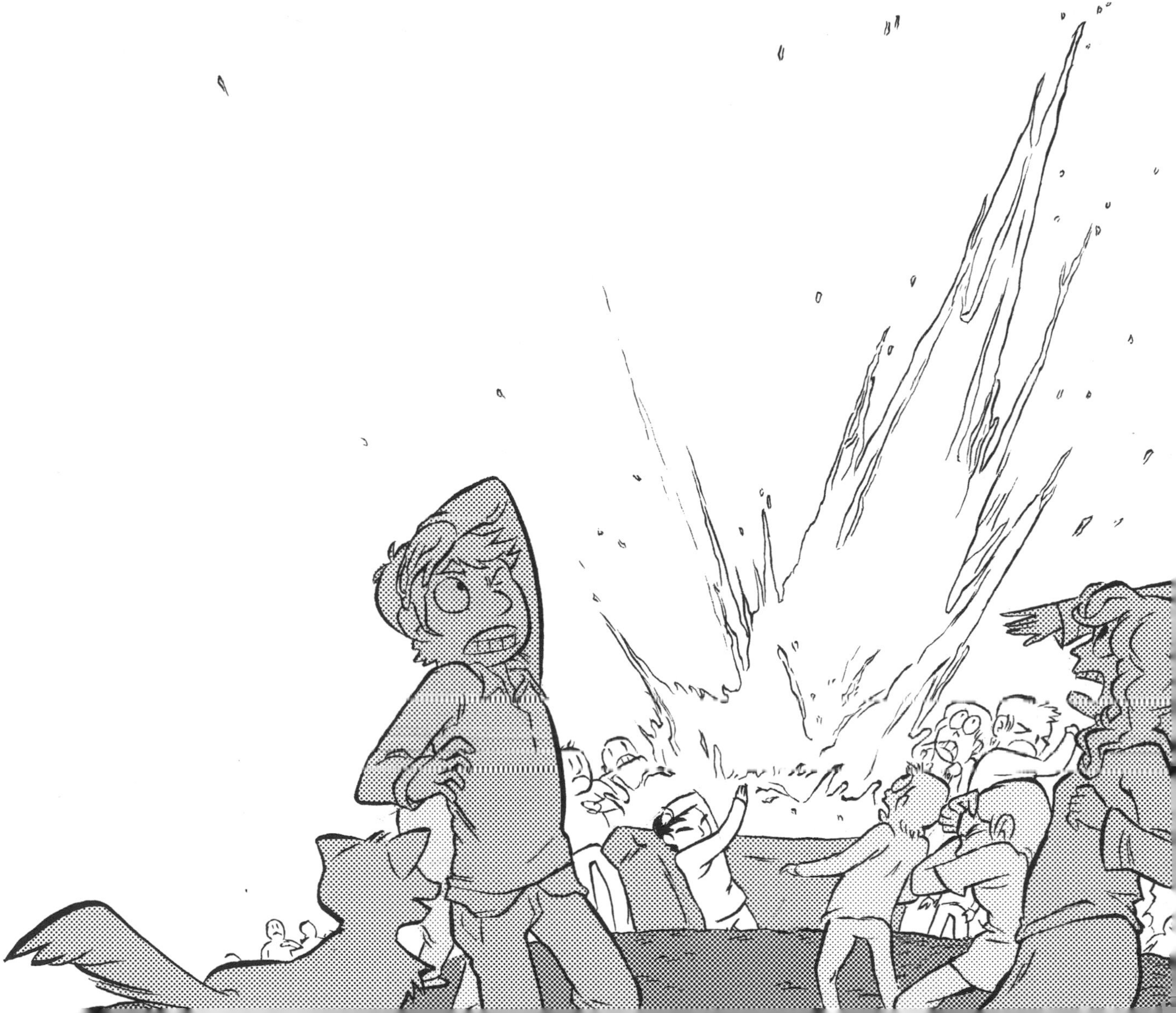

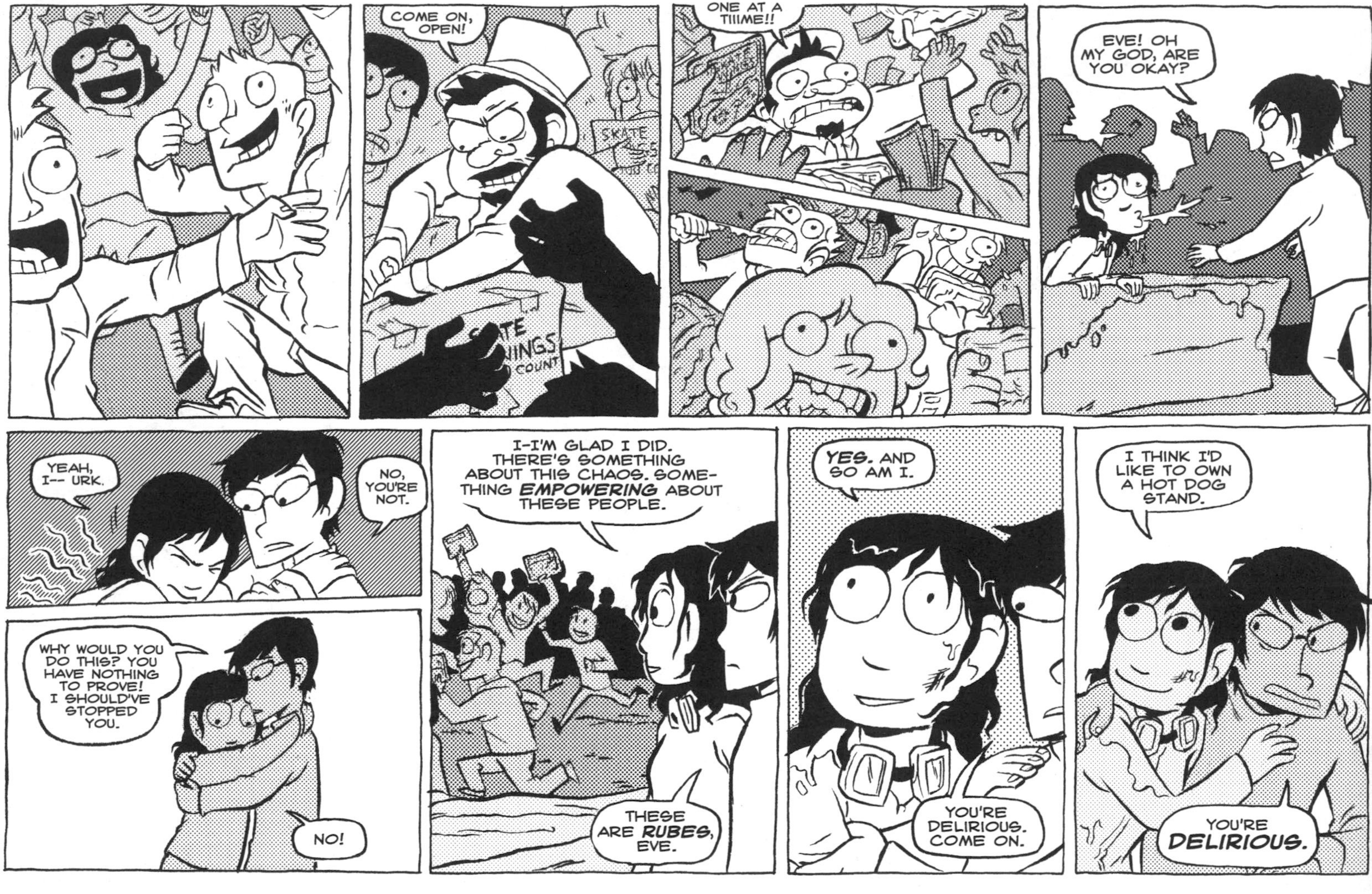
COME ON, OPEN!
ONE AT A TIIIME!!
EVE! OH MY GOD, ARE YOU OKAY?
YEAH, I-- URK.
NO, YOU'RE NOT.
WHY WOULD YOU DO THIS? YOU HAVE NOTHING TO PROVE! I SHOULD'VE STOPPED YOU.
NO!
I-I'M GLAD I DID. THERE'S SOMETHING ABOUT THIS CHAOS. SOMETHING EMPOWERING ABOUT THESE PEOPLE.
THESE ARE RUBES, EVE.
YES. AND SO AM I.
YOU'RE DELIRIOUS. COME ON.
I THINK I'D LIKE TO OWN A HOT DOG STAND.
YOU'RE DELIRIOUS.

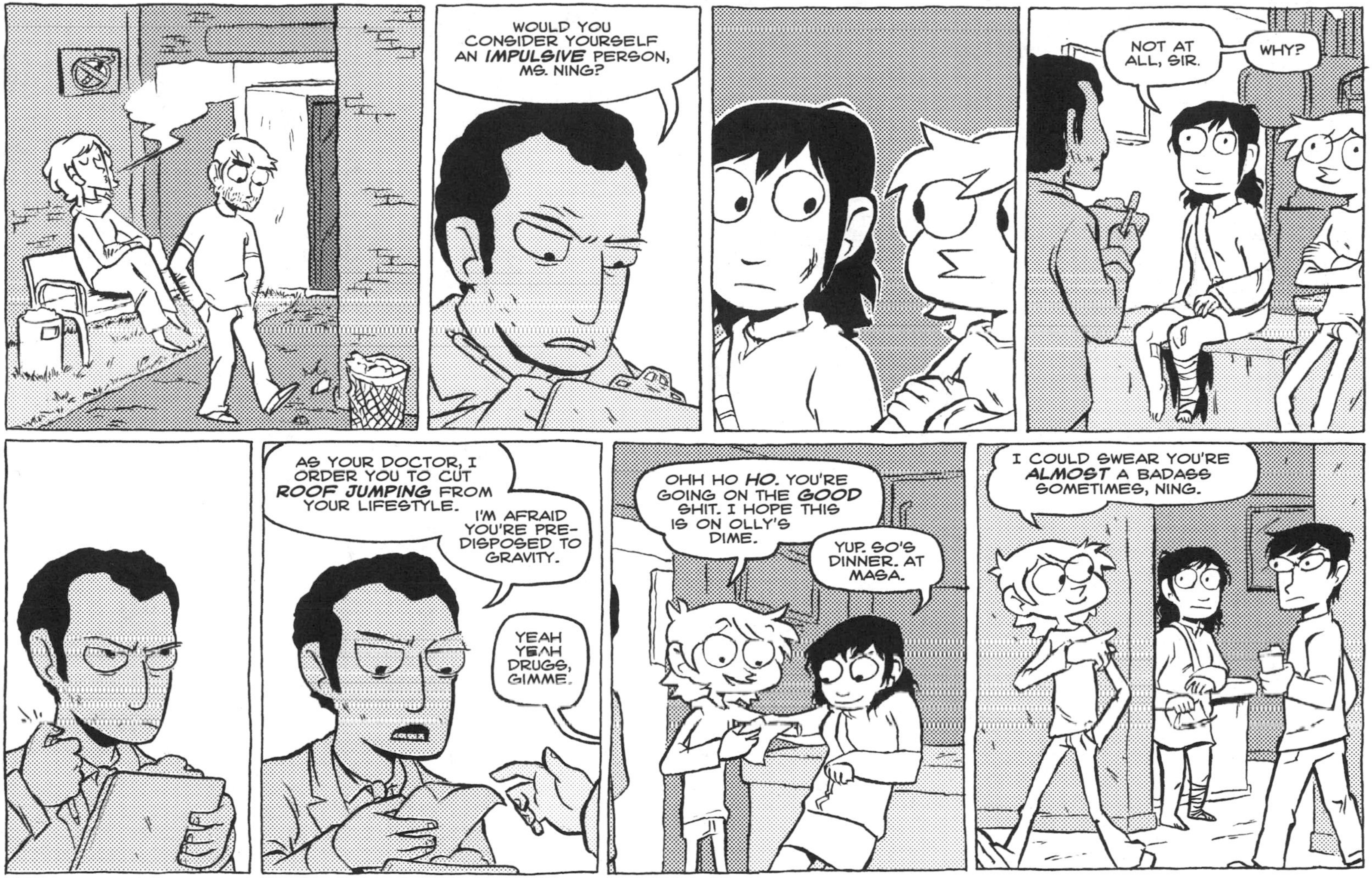
WOULD YOU CONSIDER YOURSELF AN IMPULSIVE PERSON, MS. NING?
NOT AT ALL, SIR.
WHY?
AS YOUR DOCTOR, I ORDER YOU TO CUT ROOF JUMPING FROM YOUR LIFESTYLE.
I'M AFRAID YOU'RE PRE-DISPOSED TO GRAVITY.
YEAH YEAH DRUGS, GIMME.
OHH HO HO. YOU'RE GOING ON THE GOOD SHIT. I HOPE THIS IS ON OLLY'S DIME.
YUP. SO'S DINNER. AT MASA.
I COULD SWEAR YOU'RE ALMOST A BADASS SOMETIMES, NING.

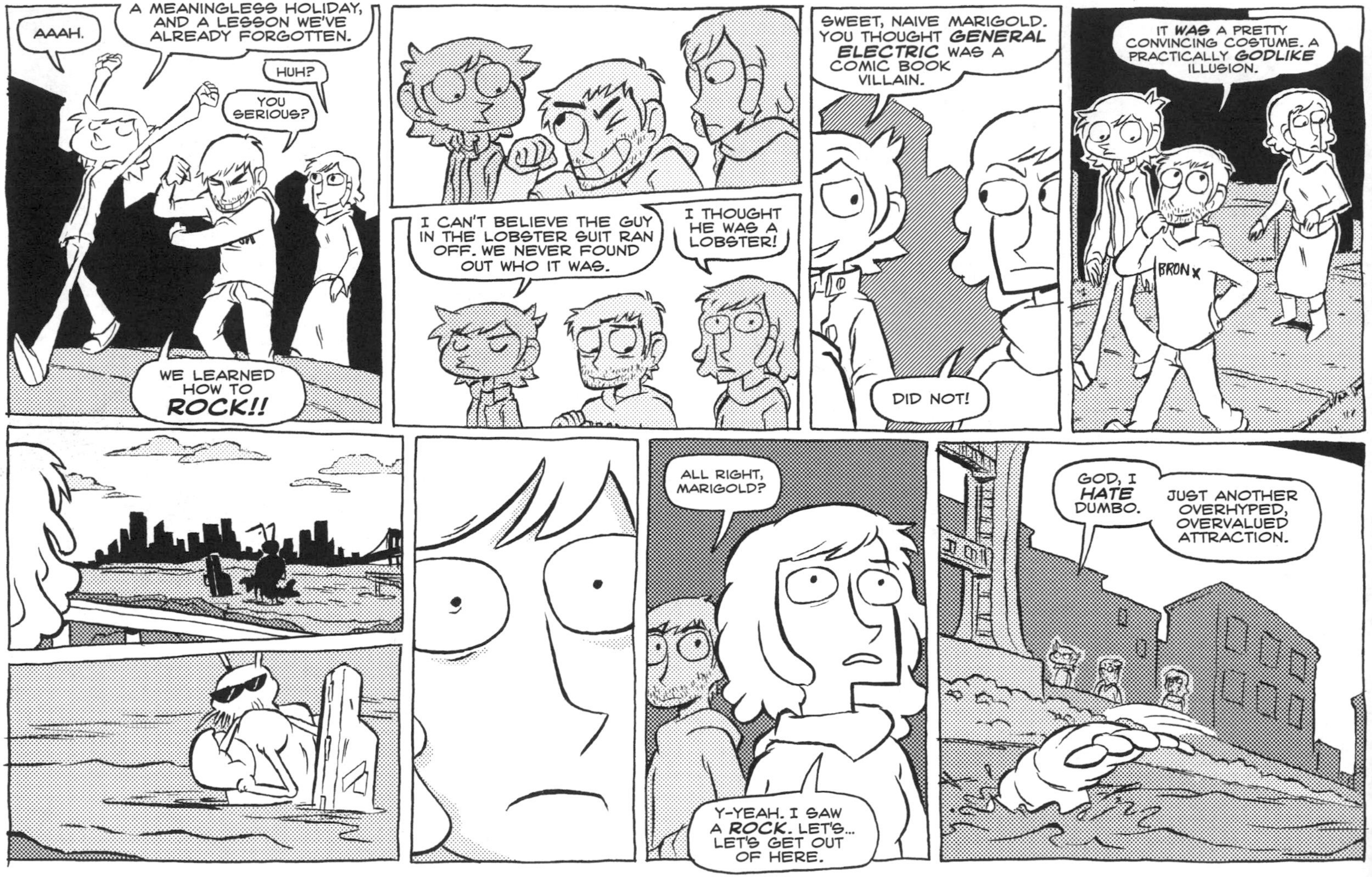
AAAH.
A MEANINGLESS HOLIDAY, AND A LESSON WE'VE ALREADY FORGOTTEN.
HUH?
YOU SERIOUS?
WE LEARNED HOW TO ROCK!!
I CAN'T BELIEVE THE GUY IN THE LOBSTER SUIT RAN OFF. WE NEVER FOUND OUT WHO IT WAS.
I THOUGHT HE WAS A LOBSTER!
SWEET, NAIVE MARIGOLD. YOU THOUGHT GENERAL ELECTRIC WAS A COMIC BOOK VILLAIN.
DID NOT!
IT WAS A PRETTY CONVINCING COSTUME. A PRACTICALLY GODLIKE ILLUSION.
BRONX
ALL RIGHT, MARIGOLD?
Y-YEAH. I SAW A ROCK. LET'S... LET'S GET OUT OF HERE.
GOD, I HATE DUMBO.
JUST ANOTHER OVERHYPED, OVERVALUED ATTRACTION.

12

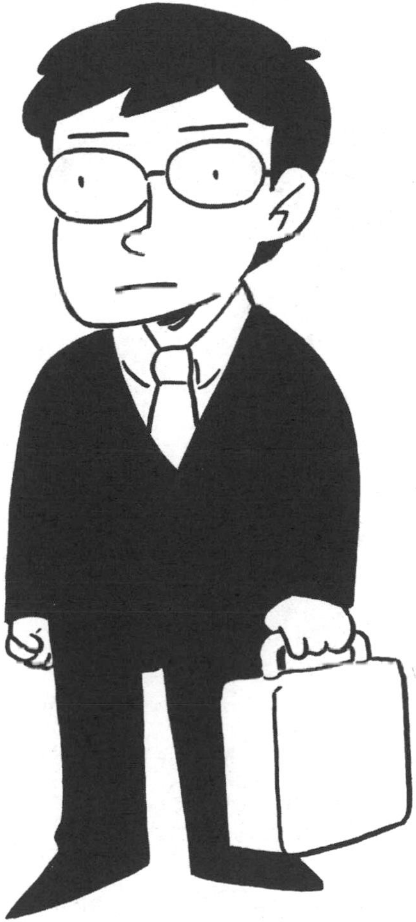

I DON'T CARE WHAT THEY SAY, DEVIN!

I KNOW IN MY *HEART* I WILL ALWAYS LOVE YOU.

EVEN IF YOU HAVE TO REMOVE IT... FOR SCIENCE!

OH, GRACE..!

ARLING! HE FOUR CORNERS ARTH FOR JUST ONE ACE IN YOUR LOVING

MORNING, GRAM.

GOOD MORNING.

PARK. DID YOU TAKE SNOWY OUTSIDE?

NOT YET. I'M WAITING FOR A FRIEND.

I WOULD DO IT MYSELF, OF COURSE.

BUT THESE LEGS...

NO, GRAM, I KNOW.

I CAN TAKE SNOWY WITH ME.

HOLD STILL, YOU BIG SLOBBERY...

SEE, HE CAN'T WAIT.

TAKE YOUR JACKET, PARK. IT'S COLD.

I TOOK IT TO THE DRY CLEANERS. SO I'D HAVE IT FOR MY INTERVIEW.

GOOD.

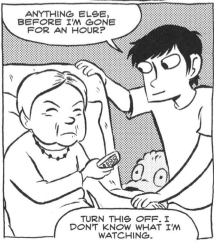

ANYTHING ELSE, BEFORE I'M GONE FOR AN HOUR?

TURN THIS OFF. I DON'T KNOW WHAT I'M WATCHING.

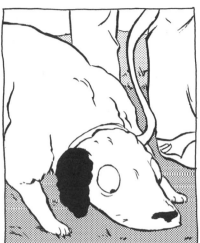

THERE YOU ARE. I WAS WAITING BY THE PAGODA FOR SOME-ONE TO BREAK OUT IN SONG.

FUNNY, I WAS AVOIDING IT FOR THE VERY SAME REASON.

DID YOU STRETCH YET?

YEAH. BUT I THINK I'M A LITTLE OUT OF SHAPE, HONESTLY.

WE'LL TAKE IT SLOW. SNOWY CAN'T GO VERY FAST.

HEY, ARE YOU WEARING CONTACTS?

IT'S FUNNY TO SEE YOU WITHOUT GLASSES.

FUNNY?

HOW IS IT FUNNY?

UH, I DON'T KNOW. I JUST DIDN'T KNOW YOU WORE THEM.

LET'S START AT THE CORNER. WE CAN LOOP BACK AFTER THE LULL-WATER BRIDGE.

YOU HEAR THAT SNOWY? YOU WANNA RUN, DON'T YOU BOY? DON'T YOU? IS YOU MY RUNNING BUDDY? YES YOU—

ROOF! ROOF ROO

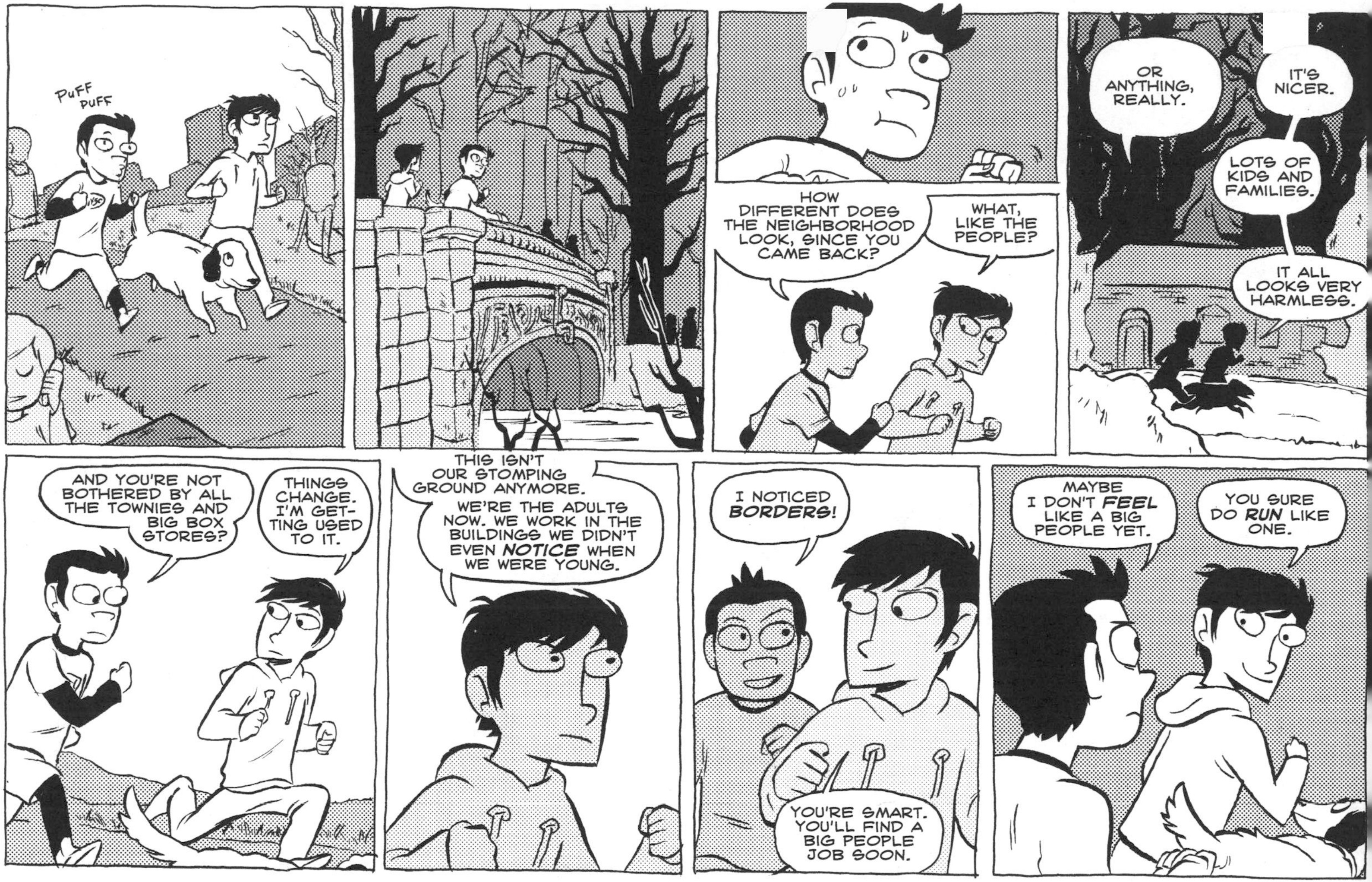

PUFF PUFF
HOW DIFFERENT DOES THE NEIGHBORHOOD LOOK, SINCE YOU CAME BACK?
WHAT, LIKE THE PEOPLE?
OR ANYTHING, REALLY.
IT'S NICER.
LOTS OF KIDS AND FAMILIES.
IT ALL LOOKS VERY HARMLESS.
AND YOU'RE NOT BOTHERED BY ALL THE TOWNIES AND BIG BOX STORES?
THINGS CHANGE. I'M GETTING USED TO IT.
THIS ISN'T OUR STOMPING GROUND ANYMORE.
WE'RE THE ADULTS NOW. WE WORK IN THE BUILDINGS WE DIDN'T EVEN *NOTICE* WHEN WE WERE YOUNG.
I NOTICED *BORDERS*!
YOU'RE SMART. YOU'LL FIND A BIG PEOPLE JOB SOON.
MAYBE I DON'T *FEEL* LIKE A BIG PEOPLE YET.
YOU SURE DO *RUN* LIKE ONE.

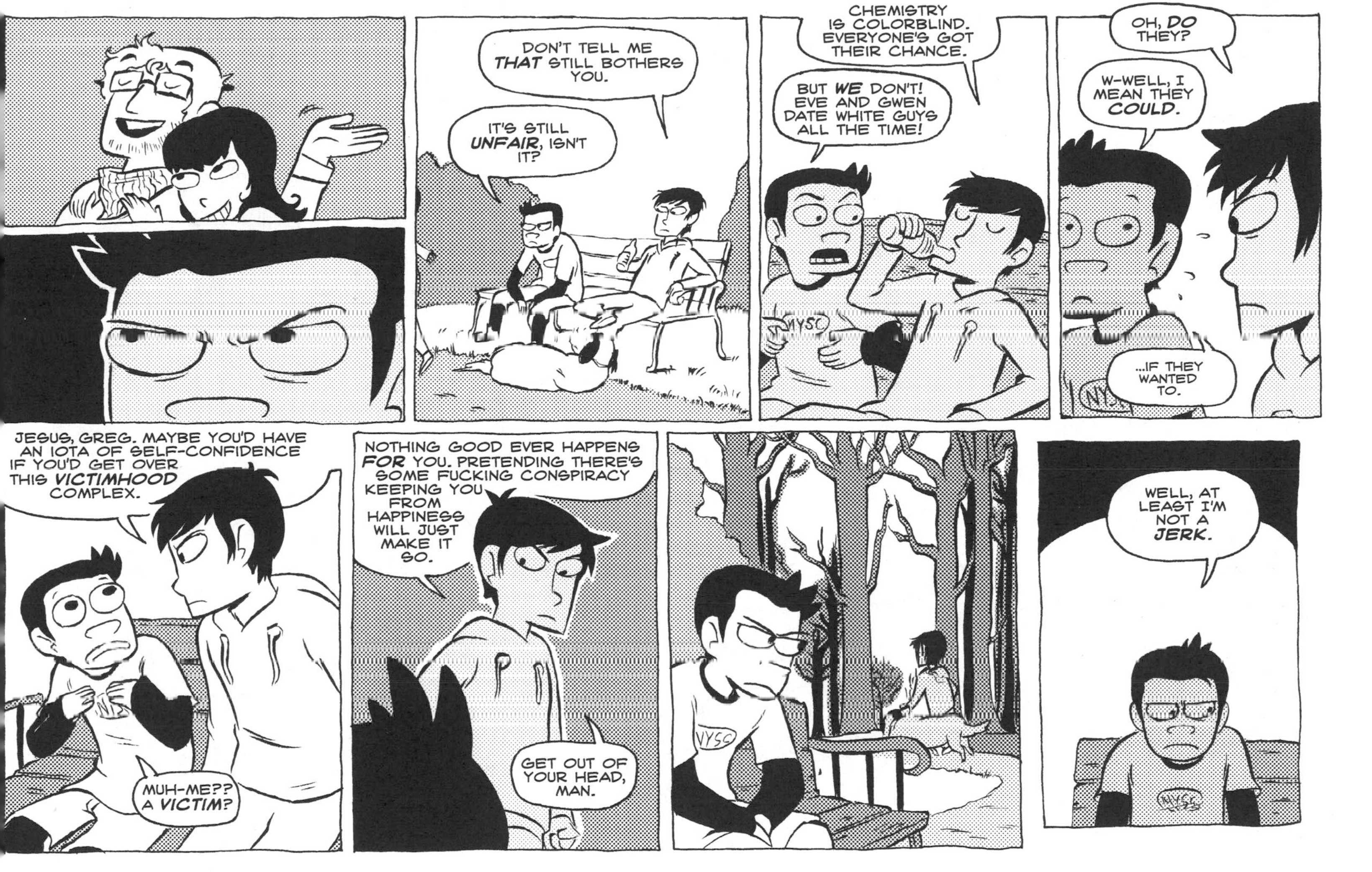
DON'T TELL ME THAT STILL BOTHERS YOU.
IT'S STILL UNFAIR, ISN'T IT?
CHEMISTRY IS COLORBLIND. EVERYONE'S GOT THEIR CHANCE.
BUT WE DON'T! EVE AND GWEN DATE WHITE GUYS ALL THE TIME!
NYSC
OH, DO THEY?
W-WELL, I MEAN THEY COULD.
...IF THEY WANTED TO.
JESUS, GREG. MAYBE YOU'D HAVE AN IOTA OF SELF-CONFIDENCE IF YOU'D GET OVER THIS VICTIMHOOD COMPLEX.
MUH-ME?? A VICTIM?
NOTHING GOOD EVER HAPPENS FOR YOU. PRETENDING THERE'S SOME FUCKING CONSPIRACY KEEPING YOU FROM HAPPINESS WILL JUST MAKE IT SO.
GET OUT OF YOUR HEAD, MAN.
NYSC
WELL, AT LEAST I'M NOT A JERK.
NYSC

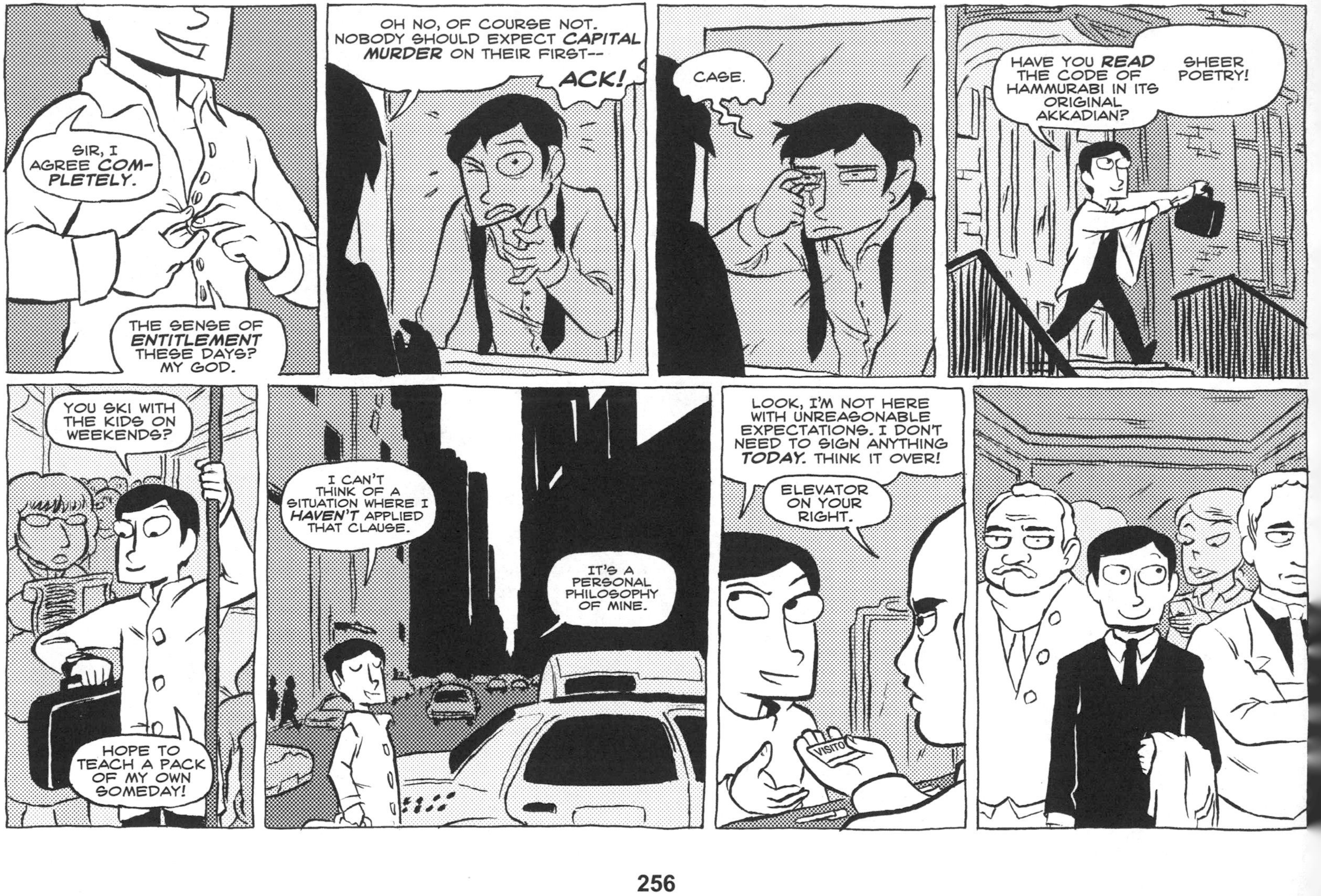
SIR, I AGREE COMPLETELY.
THE SENSE OF ENTITLEMENT THESE DAYS? MY GOD.
OH NO, OF COURSE NOT. NOBODY SHOULD EXPECT CAPITAL MURDER ON THEIR FIRST--
ACK!
CASE.
HAVE YOU READ THE CODE OF HAMMURABI IN ITS ORIGINAL AKKADIAN?
SHEER POETRY!
YOU SKI WITH THE KIDS ON WEEKENDS?
HOPE TO TEACH A PACK OF MY OWN SOMEDAY!
I CAN'T THINK OF A SITUATION WHERE I HAVEN'T APPLIED THAT CLAUSE.
IT'S A PERSONAL PHILOSOPHY OF MINE.
LOOK, I'M NOT HERE WITH UNREASONABLE EXPECTATIONS. I DON'T NEED TO SIGN ANYTHING TODAY. THINK IT OVER!
ELEVATOR ON YOUR RIGHT.
VISITO

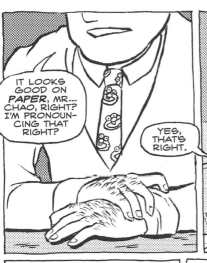

IT LOOKS GOOD ON *PAPER*, MR... CHAO, RIGHT? I'M PRONOUNCING THAT RIGHT?

YES, THAT'S RIGHT.

"PARK". HMM. IS THAT JAPANESE FOR SOMETHING?

I'M NOT SURE.

WELL, I'LL BE HONEST WITH YOU, BRO. YOU HAVE THE RESUME OF AN ACADEMIC.

NOT MUCH INCENTIVE IN HIRING SOMEONE WHO PLANS TO *LEAVE*, IS THERE?

YES, BUT-- I MEAN *NO*!

I HAVE EVERY INTENTION OF PRACTICING AT A FIRM! A-AND I'M FULLY CONFIDENT MY WORK WILL *PROVE* THAT!

CONFIDENT, HUH? WELL, WE'LL BE SURE TO CONSIDER THAT.

DO YOU HAVE ANY QUESTIONS, THEN?

NO, SIR. THANK YOU FOR--

HEY! HEY!

ONLY FIST BUMPS IN *THIS* OFFICE, CHAMP.

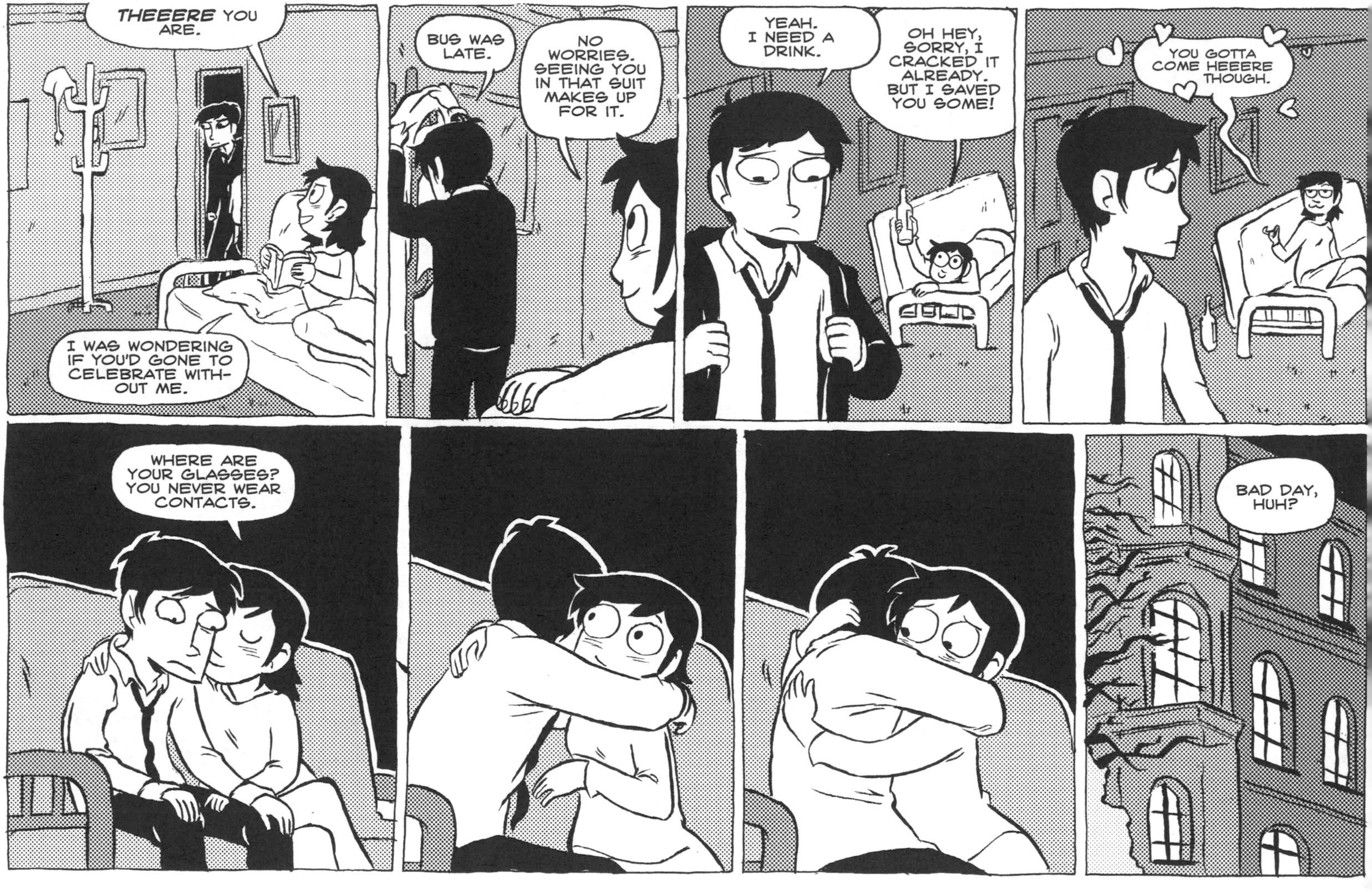
THEEERE YOU ARE.
I WAS WONDERING IF YOU'D GONE TO CELEBRATE WITH-OUT ME.
BUS WAS LATE.
NO WORRIES. SEEING YOU IN THAT SUIT MAKES UP FOR IT.
YEAH. I NEED A DRINK.
OH HEY, SORRY, I CRACKED IT ALREADY. BUT I SAVED YOU SOME!
YOU GOTTA COME HEEERE THOUGH.
WHERE ARE YOUR GLASSES? YOU NEVER WEAR CONTACTS.
BAD DAY, HUH?

13

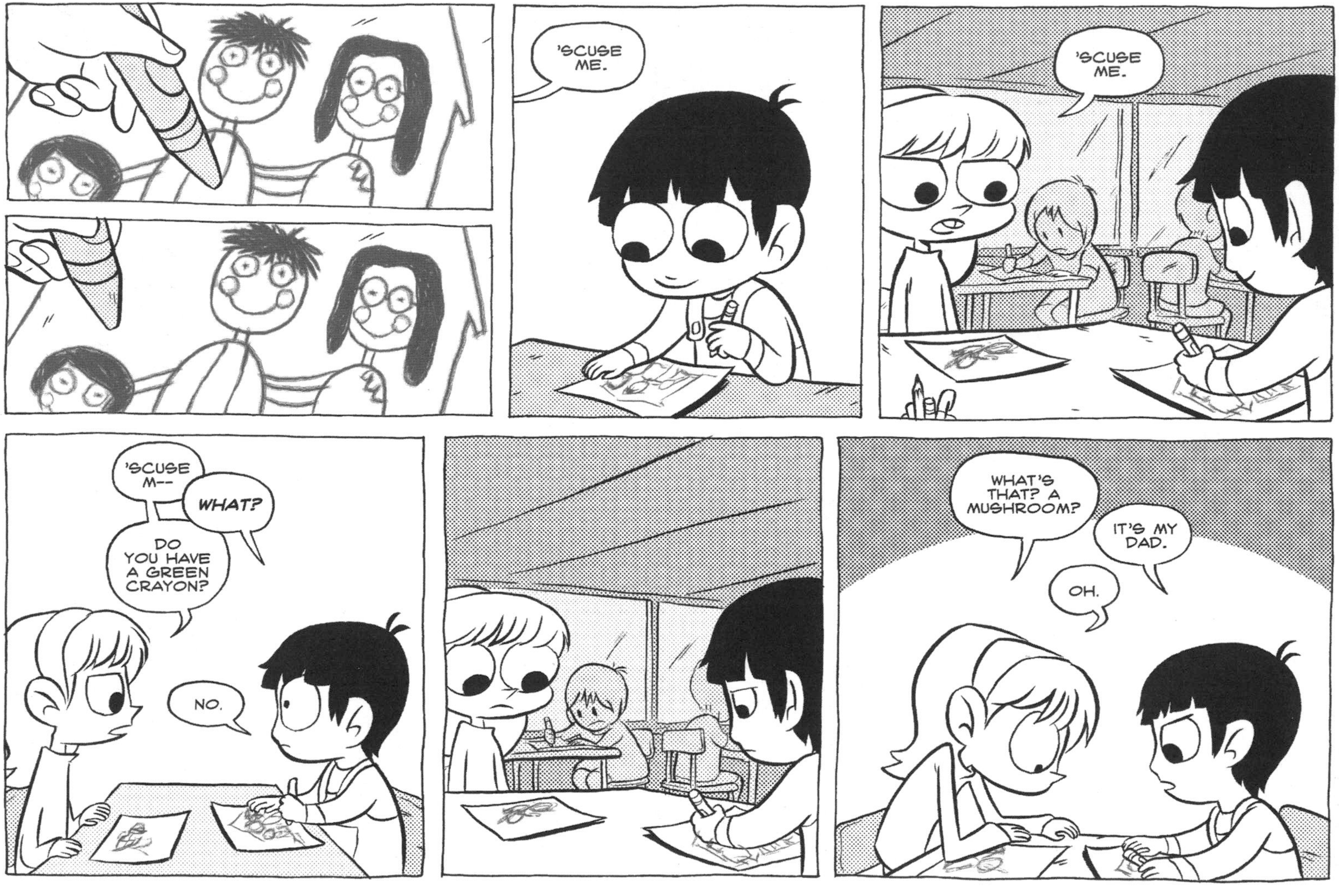
'SCUSE ME.
'SCUSE ME.
'SCUSE M--
WHAT?
DO YOU HAVE A GREEN CRAYON?
NO.
WHAT'S THAT? A MUSHROOM?
IT'S MY DAD.
OH.

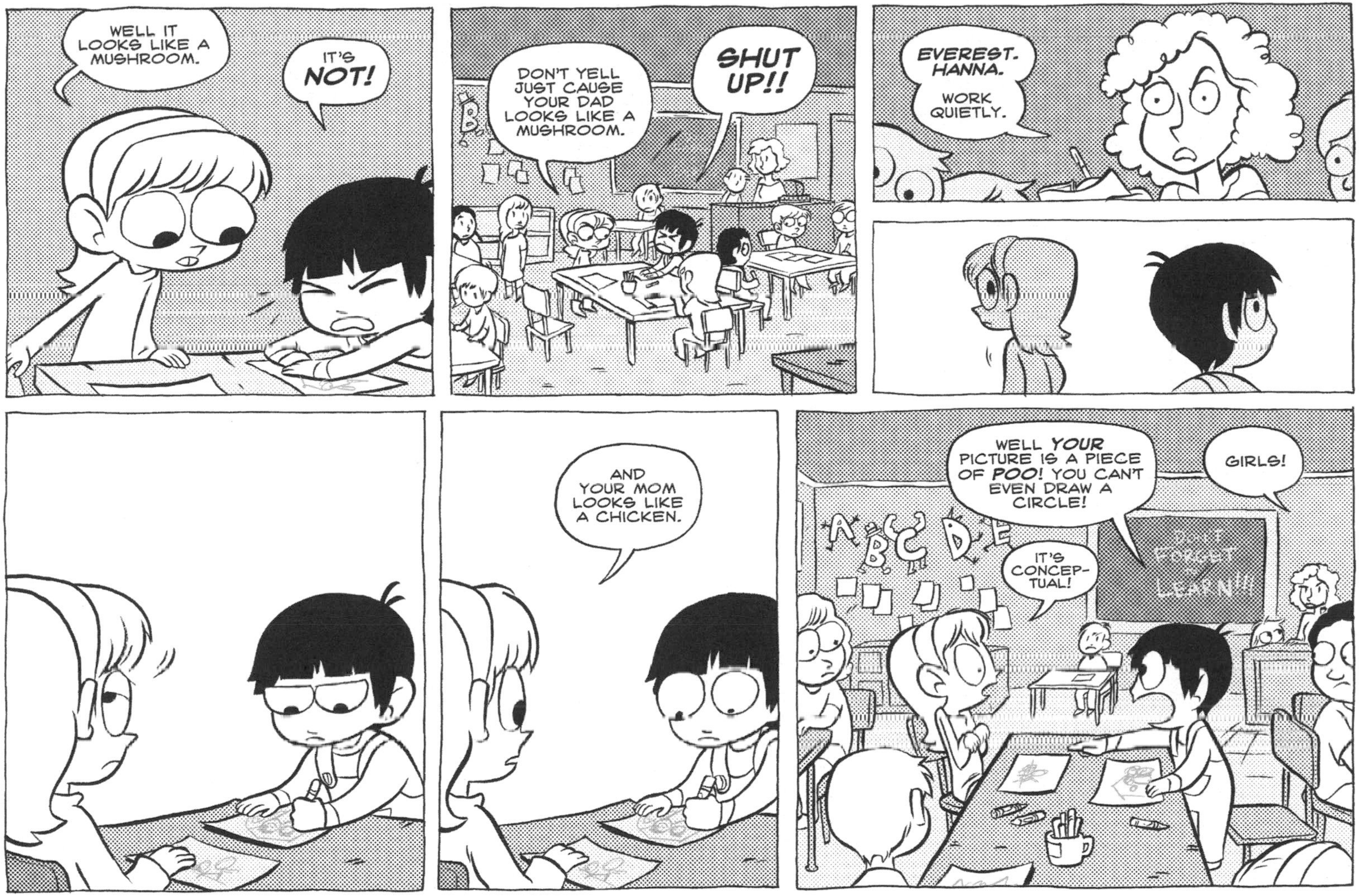
WELL IT LOOKS LIKE A MUSHROOM.
IT'S NOT!
DON'T YELL JUST CAUSE YOUR DAD LOOKS LIKE A MUSHROOM.
SHUT UP!!
EVEREST. HANNA.
WORK QUIETLY.
AND YOUR MOM LOOKS LIKE A CHICKEN.
WELL YOUR PICTURE IS A PIECE OF POO! YOU CAN'T EVEN DRAW A CIRCLE!
IT'S CONCEP-TUAL!
GIRLS!

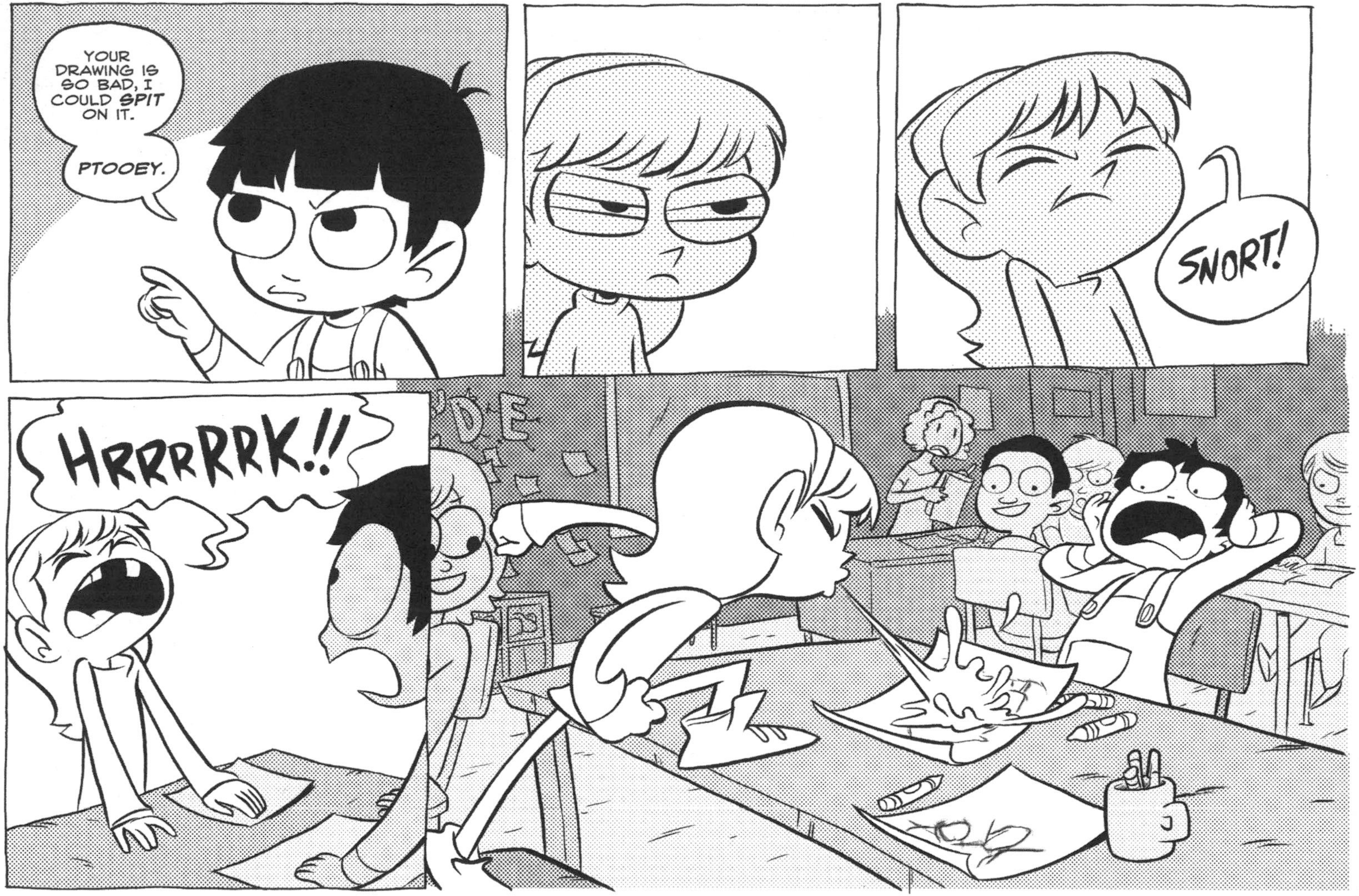
YOUR DRAWING IS SO BAD, I COULD SPIT ON IT.
PTOOEY.
SNORT!
HRRRRRK.!!

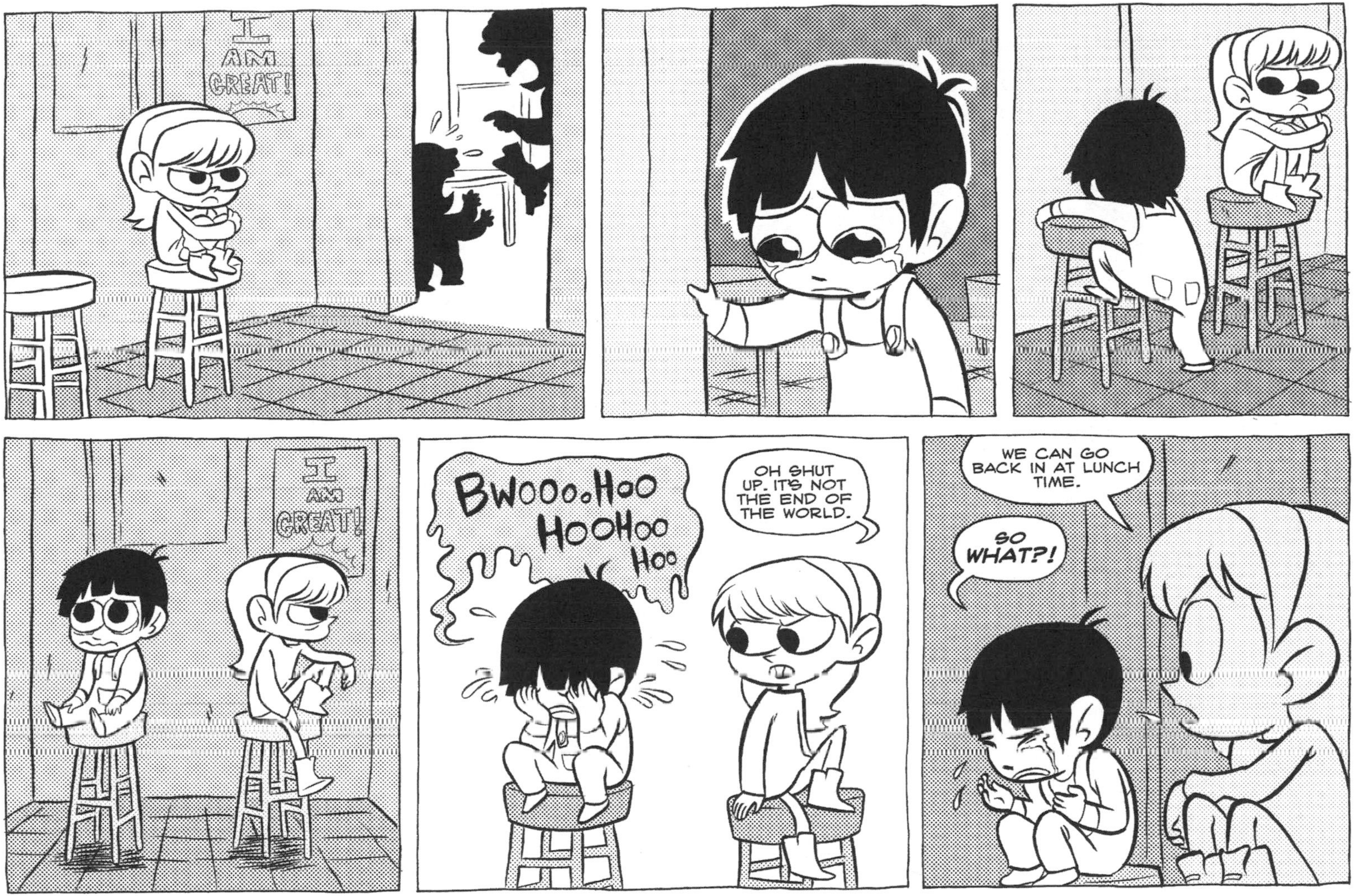
I AM GREAT!
I AM GREAT!
BWOOO.HOO HOOHOO HOO
OH SHUT UP. IT'S NOT THE END OF THE WORLD.
WE CAN GO BACK IN AT LUNCH TIME.
SO WHAT?!

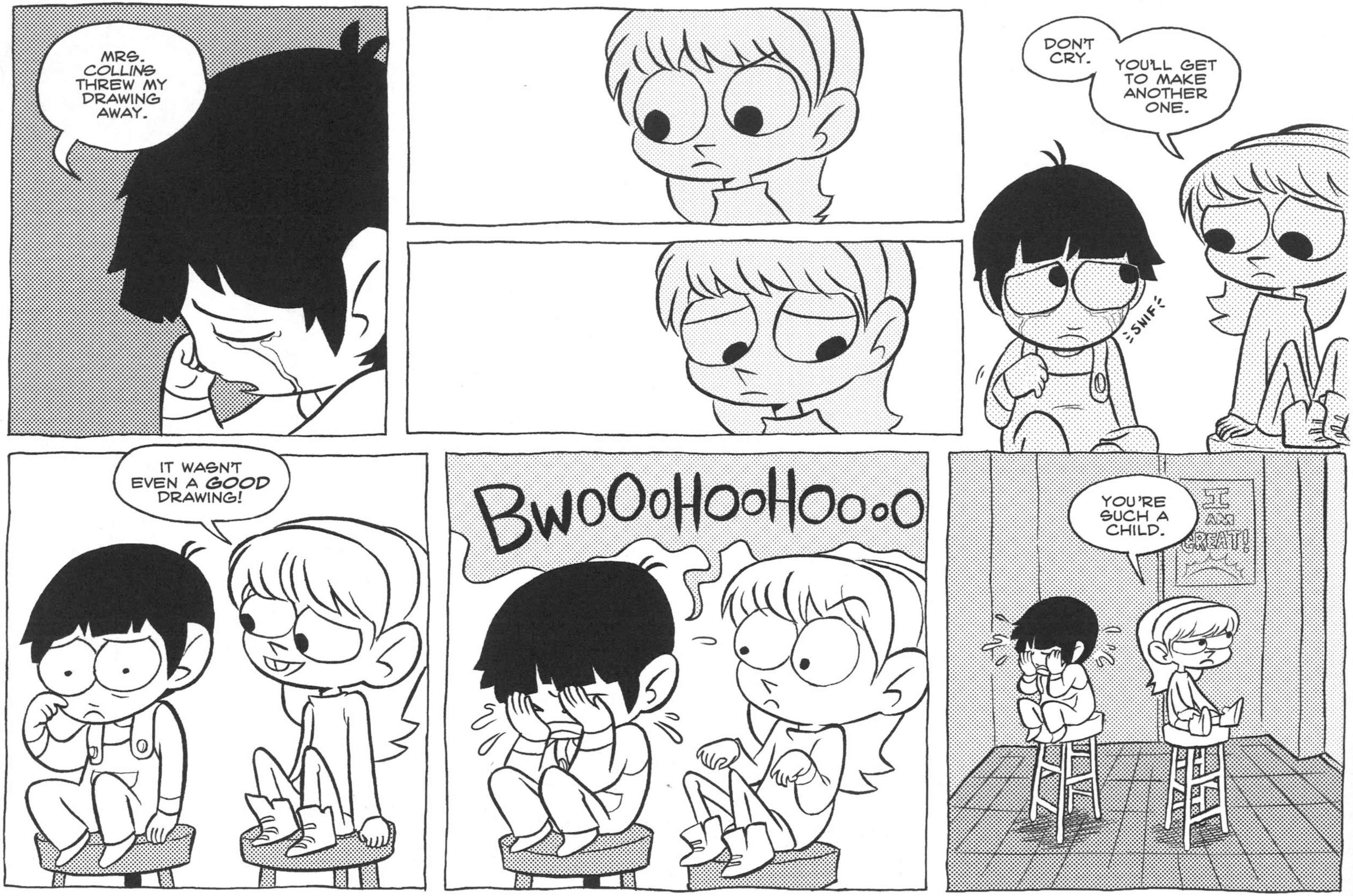
MRS. COLLINS THREW MY DRAWING AWAY.
DON'T CRY.
YOU'LL GET TO MAKE ANOTHER ONE.
SNIF
IT WASN'T EVEN A GOOD DRAWING!
BWOOOOHOOOHOOOOO
YOU'RE SUCH A CHILD.
I AM GREAT!

mongo minis

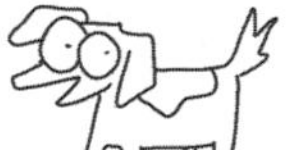

ENERGY-INEFFICIENT BULBS

No!
CRK

GOODBYE EVE

WELL, ENOUGH OF THIS.
EVE SMELLS

THIS JOKE MUST HAVE BEEN DONE ALREADY

IT'S A RACE FOR THE CURE!
IF I WAS ONLY SURE, THAT MY HEAD ON THE DOOR WAS A DREAM

DA BYGGIST BLUNT

TIME TO ROLL UP...
DA BIGGEST BLUNT!
UH, HANNA ...
LATER...
THAT WAS A PRETTY GOOD BLUNT

LOUISE C. PANTRY GETS IN TOO DEEP

LOUISE, I'M AFRAID YOU'VE CONTRACTED SYPHILIS
BUT... THAT'S ENTIRELY POSSIBLE!
ANYTHING IS IMPOSSIBLE, LOUISE...
ALL YOU HAVE TO DO IS DENY IT.
SWEET!

FRIENDS AGAINST BLANK T-SHIRTS

HUGS NOT DRUGS
HUGS N DR
HUGS
DRUGS

MAREK'S DILEMMA

DO YOU MEAN CRISPY CHICKEN PAD THAI, OR PAD THAI WITH CRISPY CHICKEN?

SPASMIC BACK QUAKES

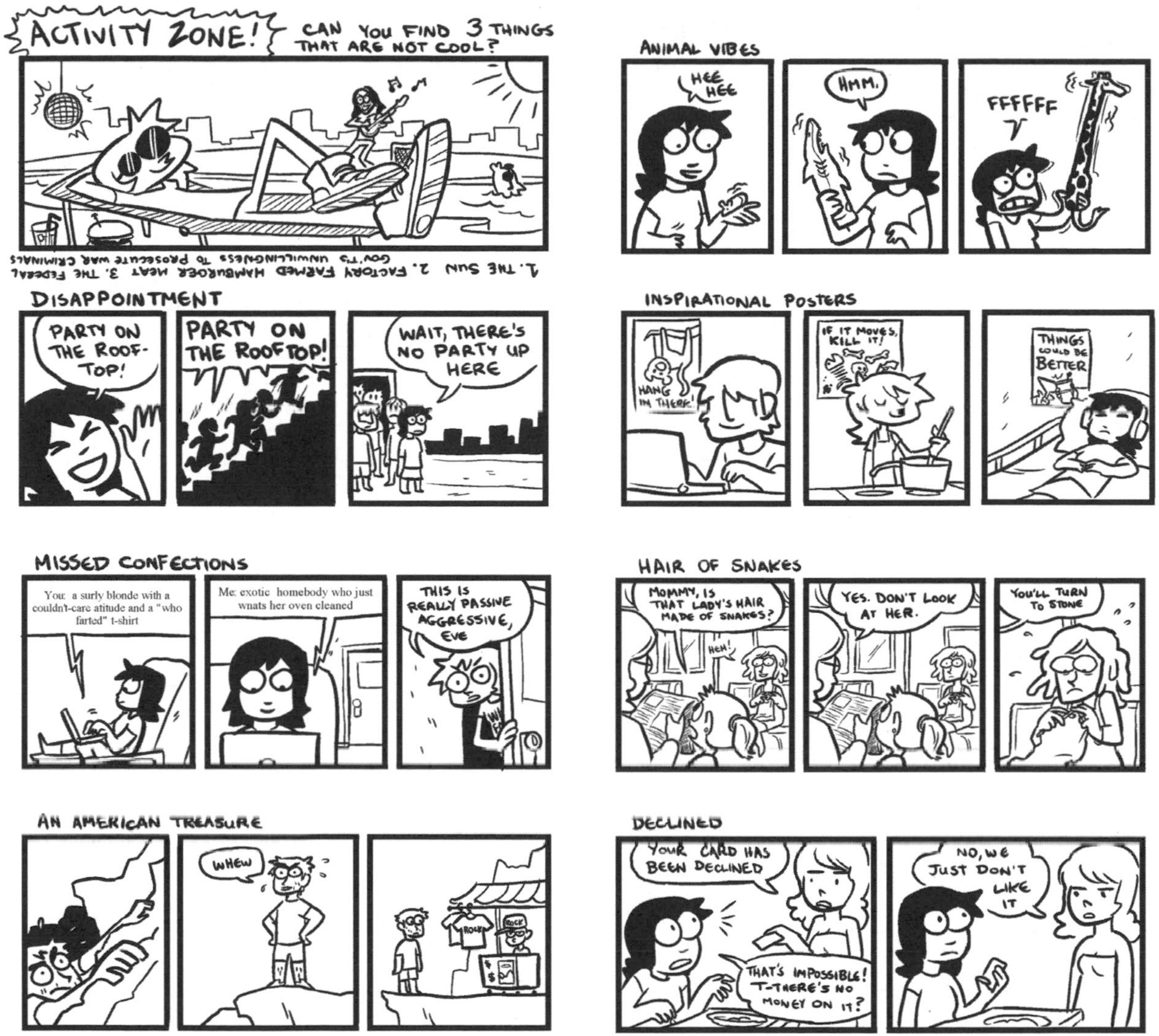
ACTIVITY ZONE!
CAN YOU FIND 3 THINGS THAT ARE NOT COOL?
1. THE SUN 2. FACTORY FARMED HAMBURGER MEAT 3. THE FEDERAL GOV'T'S UNWILLINGNESS TO PROSECUTE WAR CRIMINALS
DISAPPOINTMENT
PARTY ON THE ROOF-TOP!
PARTY ON THE ROOFTOP!
WAIT, THERE'S NO PARTY UP HERE
MISSED CONFECTIONS
You: a surly blonde with a couldn't-care atitude and a "who farted" t-shirt
Me: exotic homebody who just wnats her oven cleaned
THIS IS REALLY PASSIVE AGGRESSIVE, EVE
AN AMERICAN TREASURE
WHEW
ROCK
ROCK
$
$
ANIMAL VIBES
HEE HEE
HMM.
FFFFFF
INSPIRATIONAL POSTERS
HANG IN THERE!
IF IT MOVES, KILL IT!
THINGS COULD BE BETTER
HAIR OF SNAKES
MOMMY, IS THAT LADY'S HAIR MADE OF SNAKES?
HEH!
YES. DON'T LOOK AT HER.
YOU'LL TURN TO STONE
DECLINED
YOUR CARD HAS BEEN DECLINED
THAT'S IMPOSSIBLE! T-THERE'S NO MONEY ON IT?
NO, WE JUST DON'T LIKE IT

Meredith Gran makes comics and teaches at the School of Visual Arts. She lives in Brooklyn with her husband and her pets and all her nice things.

Read more Octopus Pie online at:
www.octopuspie.com

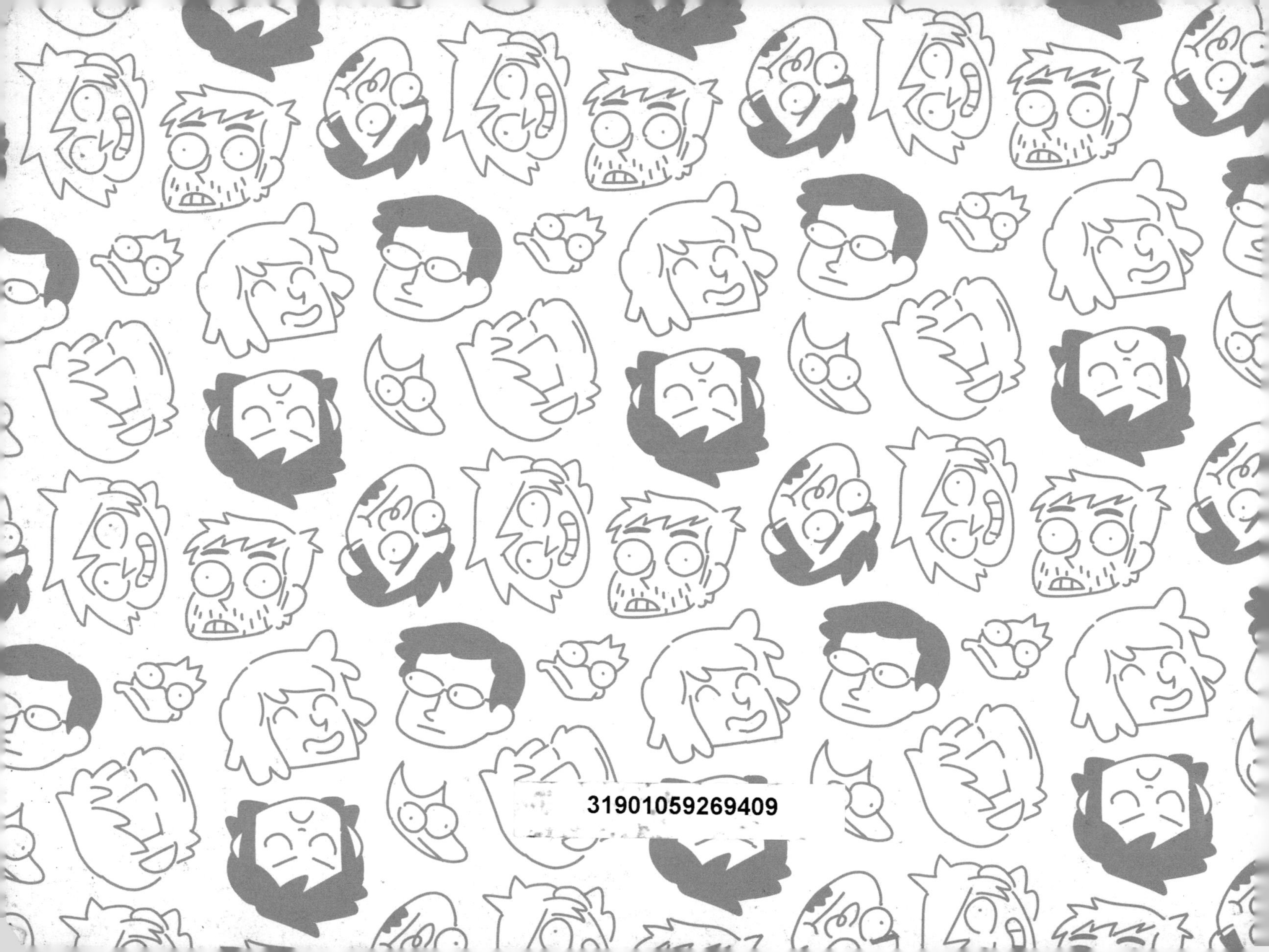